The Adventures of Saturnin Farandoul

The Adventures of Saturnin Farandoul

written and illustrated by
Albert Robida

translated, annotated and introduced by
Brian Stableford

A Black Coat Press Book

ISBN 978-1-934543-61-0. First Printing. December 2009. Published by Black Coat Press, an imprint of Hollywood Comics.com, LLC, P.O. Box 17270, Encino, CA 91416. All rights reserved. Except for review purposes, no part of this book may be reproduced or transmitted in any form or by any means, electronic or mechanical, including photocopying, recording, or by any information storage and retrieval system, without permission in writing from the publisher. The stories and characters depicted in this novel are entirely fictional. Printed in the United States of America.

Introduction

Voyages très extraordinaires de Saturnin Farandoul dans les 5 ou 6 par-
ties du monde et dans tous les pays connus et même inconnus de M. Jules Verne
[The Very Extraordinary Voyages of Saturnin Farandoul in the World's five or
six Continents, and in all the Countries known—and even unknown—to Monsieur Jules Verne], here translated as *The Adventures of Saturnin Farandoul*, initially appeared as a feuilleton serial in 1879. Each installment consisted of an
eight-page pamphlet, of which there were 100 in all. The pamphlets were rebound and reissued in 1880 as an 800 page paperbound book, with the modification that the full-page color illustrations that had served as covers in the part-
work, which were blank on the rear, were stripped of text repeating the title and
mostly relocated within the text. A contents section was also added as a supplement. The novel was never reprinted again thereafter, although a silent movie
version of part of the text was made in Italy in 1914 by Marcel Perez. The text
of the paperbound book is currently available as an electronic document on the
Bibliothèque Nationale's gallica.com website (although the colored illustrations
are reproduced in monochrome), and it is from that version that this translation
has been taken.

Robida had already built up a considerable reputation as an illustrator and
caricaturist before embarking on the serial, but this was his first novel, and it
represented a very ambitious undertaking. Its format and magnitude must have
been planned in advance, and Robida must therefore have blithely undertaken to
produce a 200,000-word text, organized into five equal sections, each of which
would be further divided into ten chapters, without any significant experience of
writing long fiction. He probably intended each chapter to consist of two
pamphlets, but some actually ran to three, thus requiring others to be restricted
to one (a regularity obscured in the pagination of the paperback version because
of the relocation of the color plates). Each pamphlet had to fill up the available
space more-or-less exactly, meaning that its text had to be tailored to fit the
space available once the illustrations had been set in place—a task that inevitably provided a stern challenge to the writer's organizational skills, and probably
required a good deal of editing.

This kind of pamphlet part-work was more common in England than in
France during the 19th century, and English writers of so-called "penny dreadfuls" had worked out a system of fitting episodes of text exactly to eight-page
units. Almost invariably, the writers "wrote short" and then padded the text to fit
the required space, routinely feeding extra lines to the typesetter in the printer's
workshop. Such extra lines were often exclamatory items of dialogue, which
filled space without adding any significant content—it was writers of penny
dreadfuls who first adopted the now-standard convention of making every item

of dialogue a separate paragraph, partly in order that an "Oh!" or a "What!" would use up an entire line. The evidence of Robida's text, by contrast, strongly suggests that he routinely "wrote long" and then reduced his text to fit, or allowed his editor/printer to chop it; there are numerous places in the narrative where text appears to be missing or the narrative becomes brutally terse, but relatively few where unnecessary items of dialogue seem to have been inserted.

The standard method of producing *feuilleton* serials in France was for the writer to dictate the text to an amanuensis, who was often entrusted with stretching it or condensing it to produce the correct wordage. *Saturnin Farandoul* exhibits numerous symptoms of that system of production and was almost certainly generated in that way. Although such serials routinely repeated information for the benefit of readers who made a belated start, and often used repetition as a form of padding, habitual dictators of text also used repetition as a means of stalling production while they tried to figure out what ought to happen next, and the pattern of repetition in Robida's text is strongly suggestive of that kind of hesitation. On the whole, though, given that Robida was a novice, the text is remarkably free of such procrastinations, and is more often so hectic in its pace that it gives the impression of an author overflowing with ideas. It is not until mid-way through part five that the flow becomes seriously abated by any apparent weariness, and it is quite remarkable that a relatively unpracticed author should have been able to maintain the fecundity of his imagination over such a long narrative distance.

Such modern critical description as there is of *Saturnin Farandoul* tends to describe it as a "parody" or "spoof" of the works of Jules Verne, which were extremely popular in France at the time. Verne certainly provided the principal inspiration for Robida's book, whose original title clearly represents it as a derivative work, and there are certainly elements of parody in the way Robida chose to adapt and redeploy his Vernian materials, but the nature of Robida's response to and extrapolations of Vernian materials is much more complicated than mere caricature. In order to understand and evaluate Robida's novel more accurately, it is necessary to consider in some detail exactly what Jules Verne had accomplished in the preceding decade and a half, and analyze Robida's reaction to that achievement in some detail.

Verne's career as a novelist began when the publisher Pierre-Jules Hetzel persuaded him—he was then an aspiring Romantic dramatist attempting to fund his artistic endeavors by hack journalism—to set aside a proposed series of articles on the popular hobby of ballooning in favor a novel that would embed the projected technical and lyrical descriptions of contemporary aeronautics within a robust adventure story. The result was *Cinq semaines en ballon* (1863; tr. as *Five Weeks in a Balloon*), in which a balloon borne by the prevailing winds is used to cross Central Africa from west to east. The nature of its origin ensured that it became a rather didactic work, full of detail about recent African exploration as well as contemporary aeronautical technology, which aimed for a higher degree of verisimilitude in its narrative than was typical of adventure stories set in remote regions of the globe.

Verne followed that first novel with an exceedingly gloomy account of *Paris au XXème siècle*, lamenting the likelihood that the march of technology would produce a purely utilitarian society with no room for Art, but Hetzel rejected it—advising him never to publish it lest it damage his reputation irreparably—and told him to concentrate instead on celebrating the advancement of technology as an invaluable aid and adjunct to adventurous exploration. The novel remained unpublished until the manuscript was rediscovered, quite by chance, in the 1990s. Instead Verne produced *Voyage au centre de la Terre* (1864; tr. as *Journey to the Center of the Earth*), which followed Hetzel's prospectus faithfully—although Hetzel probably considered it a little too imaginatively extravagant and might well have asked that Verne exercise more restraint in future.

In 1864 Hetzel founded a new "family magazine"—intended to appeal to both adults and children—after a pattern that he had used before but had had to terminate when subjected to political exile by Napoléon III on account of his Republican views: *Le Magasin d'Education et de Récréation*. Enthusiastic about the potential of Verne's didactically-inclined and technologically-sophisticated adventure fiction to serve the magazine's compound brief, he offered the author a commission to write the equivalent of three volumes a year—approximately 250,000 words—for serialization in the magazine and subsequent book publication. Verne—not unnaturally, given his previous struggles—was glad to accept, and set out to extrapolate the works he had already published into long series collectively entitled *Voyages extraordinaires*. The series constitutes an explicit celebration of the glorious culmination of an age of heroic exploration and the consequential advent of a new age of universal tourism. The first of these new serials was *Les Aventures de Capitaine Hatteras* (1864; tr. as *The English at the North Pole*), which described the attainment of one of the few remaining points on the Earth's surface that humans had not yet reached.

Verne maintained a conscientious restraint in *De la Terre à la Lune* (1865; tr. as *From the Earth to the Moon*), which described the building of a huge gun for the purpose of firing a manned missile into space, but the much longer *Les Enfants du Capitaine Grant* (1867-68; tr. as *In Search of the Castaways*) was more characteristic of the subsequent *voyages extraordinaires*. It describes a long rescue mission undertaken in response to a message found in a bottle thrown into the sea by a castaway, which takes its protagonists to South America, Australia and New Zealand, involving them in various mishaps en route. Although Verne's earlier novels had made some use of the narrative currency established by the enormously popular prototype of the modern adventure story, Daniel Defoe's *Adventures of Robinson Crusoe* (1719), *Les Enfants du Capitaine Grant* was set very solidly in the flourishing tradition of 19th century "Robinsonades," taking up the educational aspirations of the first half of J. R.

Wyss's *Der Schweitzerische Robinson* (1812-27; tr. as *The Swiss Family Robinson*) but ingeniously adding a relentlessly dynamic element to a usually static formula.

The most successful of the early serials that Verne wrote for Hetzel was the classic *Vingt mille lieues sous les mers* (1870: tr. as *Twenty Thousand Leagues Under the Sea*), which introduced the enigmatic Captain Nemo and his ultra-sophisticated submarine *Nautilus*. It seems probable that Verne made Nemo a shadowy figure primarily in order to hide his plot away as an episode of "secret history," but the mysteriousness of the character created a precedent at least as important as his vessel, and he acquired a quasi-legendary status that required further elaboration. That elaboration was eventually provided in the course of a long and contentedly-static Robinsonade, *L'Ile mystérieuse* (1874-75; tr. as *The Mysterious Island*). In the meantime, Verne produced *Aventures de trois russes et de trois anglais dans l'Afrique australe* (1872; tr. as *The Adventures of Three Russians and Three Englishmen in South Africa* and *Measuring a Meridian*), and the North America-set *Le Pays des fourrures* (1873; tr. as *The Fur Country*) and another exceedingly popular work, whose central character, Phileas Fogg, and his determination to set a new record for round-the-world travel both went on to acquire a quasi-legendary status: *Le Tour du monde en 80 jours* (1873; tr. as *Around the World in 80 Days*).

Verne followed up *L'Ile mystérieuse* with a much grimmer and more melodramatic account of the aftermath of a shipwreck, *Le "Chancellor"* (1875; tr. as *The Survivors of the Chancellor*) and an account of a journey across the Russian wilderness in *Michel Strogoff, Moscou-Irkoutsk* (1876; tr. as *Michael Strogoff, Courier of the Czar*) before he allowed his taste for extravagance to get the upper hand again,. He had already written a sequel to *De la Terre à la Lune*, entitled *Autour de la Lune* (1870; tr. as *Around the Moon*), but his characters, unable to leave their spacefaring cannonball, had been limited to the role of narrowly-imprisoned passive observers; in *Hector Servadac* (1877; tr. as *Off on a Comet*), he attempted to get over that difficulty, at least to the extent of giving his spacefarers a little more space to roam, by improvising a highly improbable comet-strike that carries a segment of the Earth's surface away into space. Although Verne published a few other volumes before the serialization of *Saturnin Farandoul* began, the named titles included all those that had a direct influence on Robida, and which he plundered to a greater or lesser degree.

In each of the five parts of his own worldwide adventures, Saturnin Farandoul meets one of Jules Verne's characters: Captain Nemo in part one, Phileas Fogg in part two, Hector Servadac in part three, Michel Strogoff in part four and Captain Hatteras in part five. Such borrowing might have landed him in difficulties with regard to intellectual property rights, but Verne raised no objection, apparently finding the homage rather amusing, although he cannot have approved of the manner in which Robida developed and altered some of the characters. Captain Nemo is, in fact, the only one whose manifestation in *Saturnin Faran-*

doul is approximately faithful to Verne's model; he plays the same supportive role with respect to Farandoul as he does to the castaways of *L'Île mystérieuse*, albeit in a more violent manner. All four of the other characters, who play broadly heroic if slightly mentally-unbalanced roles in Verne's originals, become Farandoul's enemies, routinely undermining his projects and threatening him, actively or by neglect, with death. Despite the inherent absurdity of the situations in which they become involved, this transfiguration of Verne's characters is more than mere parodic or caricaturish exaggeration, amounting to a more sinister kind of role-reversal.

The use that Robida makes of Verne's characters is all the more surprising when one considers that Robida was a sincere admirer of Verne's work, who loved his books. After publishing *Saturnin Farandoul*, he persuaded Verne to contribute to one of the humorous periodicals he found, and wrote a glowing tribute to Verne's work to accompany the contribution. There is certainly a celebratory aspect to *Saturnin Farandoul* as well as a satirical one, but that serves to throw its contrasts and darker aspects into even sharper relief. Had Robida not recognized that Verne was a great writer, whose work had begun a significant new era in adventure fiction, changing that *genre* irredeemably, he would surely never have bothered to write *Saturnin Farandoul*—but nor, in all probability, would he have bothered if he had not had a simultaneous sense of the cost involved in that irredeemable transformation, and a sharp regret for the loss that Vernian verisimilitude entailed.

The tradition of traveler's tales goes back to antiquity, and the subgenre had a reputation for unreliability from the very beginning. It was always taken for granted that travelers, like fishermen, were innately prone to exaggeration—that they would always strive to make their narratives more melodramatic than the actual events warranted, and represent their own actions in a more heroic light. Imaginary travelers' tales, usually narrated in the first person or allegedly based on first-person accounts, thus became a natural vehicle for narrations that required inherent exaggeration, such as satires and calculatedly nonsensical comedies. Robida would have been familiar with the highlights of a pan-European satirical tradition stretching from Lucian of Samosata's *True History* (c. 160 A.D.) to such Renaissance works as *The Travels of Sir John Mandeville* (c. 1360)—which was almost certainly written in French, although most of the surviving manuscripts are in English—and the adventures of Sinbad, as subsequently integrated into the *Arabian Nights*, transfiguratively extrapolated into such Enlightenment classics as Jonathan Swift's *Gulliver's Travels* (1726) and *The Adventures of Baron Münchausen* (1785, in a version by Rudolph Eric Raspe; subsequently expanded and continued by others). He might well have had access to the 36-volume anthology of *Voyages Imaginaires, Songes, Visions et Romans Cabalistiques* published in 1786-89 by Charles Garnier, which commenced with *Robinson Crusoe* and included many of the most fanciful items in the French satirical tradition of imaginary voyages.

Robida clearly loved that satirical tradition, for its humor and its extravagance—new editions of its classics provided some of his best opportunities as a illustrator—and his love of it clearly put him in two minds when he encountered the further transfiguration of *voyages extraordinaires* achieved by Verne. Verne's sophistication of the traveler's tale, under the stern restraining hand of P.-J. Hetzel, was clearly an advancement of sort, reflective of the technological progress it celebrated, but it also delivered a potentially mortal blow to the unfettered imaginary extravagance of previous traveler's tales. The principal reason why Saturnin Farandoul continually meets Vernian characters in the remotest regions of the world is that Robida was all-too-conscious of the fact that, from 1878 onwards, nobody would be able to write a story of the hypothetical exploration of any earthly setting without being uncomfortably conscious of the fact that Jules Verne had not only got there ahead of him, but had conclusively de-mystified the territory in question.

The Vernian characters borrowed by Robida become Saturnin Farandoul's enemies because there is a sense in which they are the implicit enemies of all future adventurers who desire to find something unprecedentedly rich and strange in the places they visit, and a sense in which they will give the lie to all future tellers of munificently absurd tall tales. Saturnin Farandoul is not of their ilk; he belongs wholeheartedly to an earlier and incipiently-obsolete tradition. He is the kind of traveler who routinely falls into grotesque adventures and routinely extricates himself from them by equally grotesque means. He is more a Sinbad than a Robinson Crusoe, and far more of a Münchausen than a Phileas Fogg, an Henri Servadac or a Captain Hatteras—all of whom pose a threat not only to his person but to his whole *raison d'être*.

One of the principal means by which Verne cultivates verisimilitude in his *voyages extraordinaires* is, of course, the use of third person narrative. Of all his major works, only one—*Voyage au centre de la Terre*—uses a first person narrator, although *Le "Chancellor"* is presented in the form of a journal, and the objective narrative voices he employs in his other novels make every effort to cultivate the rhetoric of reliability. It is significant that Robida, too, tells the tale of Saturnin Farandoul's adventures in the third person. His narrative voice is considerably more intrusive than Verne's, but that is because it serves a commentary function, continually making observations about the kind of modern world that Farandoul is now cursed to inhabit and to which he is, crucially and essentially, quite ill-fitted. Farandoul's world is not entirely Vernian yet, but it is in the process of becoming Vernian, inexorably and irredeemably, and when it has completed its transition, it will be even more hostile to the likes of Saturnin Farandoul and his trusty crew of comic mariners. The narrative voice is polite enough not to labor this point overmuch, mainly allowing it to emerge naturally from the narrative by demonstration, but its eventual conclusion is quite explicit and leaves no room for doubt.

Robida's use of some of Verne's characters as villains seems particularly striking, not simply because Verne cast those same characters as heroes, but because Verne was very reluctant to use villains at all. One of Verne's most admirable qualities as a writer, in fact, was his reluctance to employ the cheap melodramatic currency that can be derived from giving heroes explicitly evil enemies to fight. Unlike the majority of writers of his era, Verne was not a jingoist who was prepared to trade on popular xenophobia by using foreigners as villains; indeed, he was remarkably cosmopolitan in his choice of heroes, and was always willing to entertain apologetic arguments for seemingly-heinous behavior. The challenges of bad weather and incipiently hostile terrain, together with the well-known tendency of even the best-laid plans to go awry, provide most of the challenges for the bold pioneers in his romances of exploration, and it is fairly rare for him to equip one of his heroes with a vicious adversary whose eventual thwarting will provide a suitable sense of climax (Michel Strogoff's treacherous rival, Ivan Ogareff is exceptional in this regard). Robida's transformation of Verne's own characters is, in part, a wry observation of this fact—a suggestion that the Vernian world-view is a trifle rose-tinted, and that the kinds of people who do the kinds of things that Verne's characters do are very often less noble, and carry more social and psychological baggage, than Verne's characters tend to do. The narrative voice slyly suggests, on more than one occasion, that Verne has been a little too trusting in accepting the tales that his heroes told him, accepting their self-serving distortions at face value.

On the other hand, Robida does seem to have approved of Verne's ambitions in this general regard, and his approval seems to have increased considerably during the writing of *Saturnin Farandoul*. Although he was by no means unwilling, at any stage of the novel, to evoke human villains to serve the purposes of his plotting, he became more careful in its later stages to give narrative space to their apologies and excuses. Even the evil Siamese mastermind Nao-Ching is allowed to plead, albeit somewhat hypocritically, that he is only trying to support his family, and is left conscientiously unpunished for his treacheries. After the violent suicides of Valentin Croknuff in part one and Phileas Fogg in part two, none of Farandoul's principal adversaries suffers a narrative death-penalty in consequence of opposing the hero.

Neither Farandoul nor his author display any conspicuous pacifist tendencies in part one of the novel, when Farandoul briefly entertains Napoleonic ambitions of world-conquest, but after the brutal war that forms the climax to part two, Farandoul undergoes a gradual but decisive transformation, forsaking his early bellicosity entirely after a brief battle early in part three and becoming completely uninterested in revenge. In part one he is very willing to subject captured pirates to summary junction, and in part two he is still reluctant to let any affront go unpunished, but by part four he is quite content to let Nao-Ching go about his treacherous business indefinitely, and in part five it does not even cross his mind to make any attempt to hunt down the pirates who have subjected him to so much injury by stranding him at the North Pole with no apparent means of escape. This is a significant progressive change of attitude, in seeming response to the darker episodes described in the text.

Verne was, of course, well aware of the fact that the world in which he lived had a dark underside, whose primary expressions were the ugly politics of colonialism and warfare, and his later works include several narratives set against the background of actual or threatened wars, but before 1879 the only story he had written in which warfare formed a significant background element was *Michel Strogoff*. Robida was evidently more anxious about warfare, and the potential of technology to sophisticate warfare, than his model; he was, of course, to go on to produce a savagely satirical account of *La Guerre au ving-tième siècle* (1883; rev. 1887; tr. as *War in the Twentieth Century*), which became his most famous work. The groundwork for that exercise was, however, laid in *Saturnin Farandoul*, in the climactic "duel" in part two between Farandoul and Phileas Fogg, which takes the form of a deliberately reignited Civil War, in which one takes command of the northern states and the other of the southern states of a fledgling American nation. Each aided by an ingenious inventor, Farandoul and Fogg rapidly escalate the methods of that warfare to take in several kinds of new bombs—including some distributing poison gas—submarine warfare and aerial warfare.

This whole affair is conducted in a blatantly farcical spirit, but the comedy has a very distinct black edge; not one violent death is explicitly described, but the accounts offered of the devastation of cities leave no doubt as to the horrific casualties that must be incurred, purely as an unconsidered side-effect of the main protagonists' slightly-injured pride. This is not only point in the story at which Farandoul seems every bit as bad as his adversaries, in terms of his blithe disregard for the fate of bystanders, innocent and otherwise, but it is a turning-point, and he becomes noticeably more scrupulous thereafter. So does his author, who similarly becomes increasingly reluctant to kill or main anyone and spends most of part three engineering escapes from ingeniously horrible condemnations to death.

Part two is the phase of the narrative in which Robida's misanthropism shows through most frankly in its fullest black depth, and although a certain laconic cynicism continues to underlie the entire narrative, perennially poking sharp reminders through the narrative surface, there are also increasing signs of moderation and repentance from then on. Robida's criticisms of colonialism are not as carefully muted as Verne's, and are by no means entirely restricted to the explicit war against English imperialism depicted in part one, again coming through repeatedly as the hero's adventures continue, but they do change in tone, becoming more plaintive and more resigned as the story progresses.

Jules Verne was not the only direct influence on Saturnin Farandoul, and the opening phase of the narrative, in spite of its corollary evocation of Captain Nemo, actually owes considerably more to another novel with which Robida would have been familiar by virtue of its lavish illustration: Leon Gozlan's *Les Emotions de Polydore Marasquin ou Trois mois au royaume des singes* (1856; tr. as *The Emotions of Polydore Marasquin, A Man among the Monkeys* and *Monkey Island*). Gozlan's novel, squarely situated in the satirical tradition of traveler's tales, tell the story of a castaway on an island inhabited by a profuse population various kinds of monkeys, whose Western colonists have been driven off by pirates. When Marasquin puts on the skin of a gorilla shot by the departed colonists he acquires—albeit very precariously—the top position in the simian pecking order, and becomes the island's effective ruler until the deception comes unstuck. Although Robida borrows that plot device explicitly in part two of *Saturnin Farandoul*, the more important influence of Gozlan's novel is seen in its similar employment of hypothetical "monkeys" as quasi-human characters possessed of a particular kind of primal innocence. It is the fact that Saturnin Farandoul has been raised as a feral child by a population of inoffensive monkeys that fits him for his heroic role when he re-enters human society, and also ensures that he can never properly fit into that society.

Whereas Polydore Marasquin was a fake while dressed in his monkey-skin, Saturnin Farandoul really is a quintessential Rousseauesque "noble savage," born into such natural freedom (and goodness) that civilization can never be anything to him but a set of shackles, which perpetually threaten to turn him into the same kind of morally-defective, money-grubbing, luxury-loving, war-mongering boor that civilization has made of almost all its native victims. Farandoul does not try very hard to resist that fate—indeed, he tries actively to embrace it at first—but he proves, by slow degrees, not only to be immune to it himself but also to have alienated his immediate companions to such an extent that they, too, can no longer be content with such hideously vulgar ambitions. In this respect, he not only anticipates Edgar Rice Burroughs' Tarzan but eventually outstrips him in sharing the wealth of his fortunate heritage.

In making this translation I have made the usual trivial alterations to the 1880 text, unifying the spelling of surnames, sometimes substituting modernizing place names, and occasionally tidying up continuity errors, adding a phrase or two where it seems highly likely that text has been dropped by way of trimming it to fit available space. In all these instances I have added footnotes any substitutions that seemed at all problematic.

The only major modification I have made to the text is that I have cut the synopses that Robida placed at the beginning of each chapter, which often operate as spoilers by telegraphing humorous plot-twists that would be better encountered without forewarning. I suspect that Robida used these synopses as a set of notes to remind him what ground he needed to cover in each chapter rather than intending them as a service to his readers, but whatever his motive was, I feel quite strongly that the text is better off without them.

For the benefit of readers who might like to know what the text originally looked like, however, I have aggregated the excised text in an appendix similar to the contents section that the publisher added to the paperback version.

Brian Stableford

VOYAGES TRÈS EXTRAORDINAIRES

DE

SATURNIN FARANDOUL

Dans les 5 ou 6 parties du monde

ET DANS TOUS LES PAYS CONNUS ET MÊME INCONNUS DE M. JULES VERNE

TEXTE ET DESSINS   DE A. ROBIDA

Ouvrage illustré de 450 dessins noirs et coloriés

PRIME DE LA CARICATURE

PARIS

LIBRAIRIE ILLUSTRÉE | LIBRAIRIE M. DREYFOUS

7, RUE DU CROISSANT, 7 | 13, FAUBOURG MONTMARTRE, 13

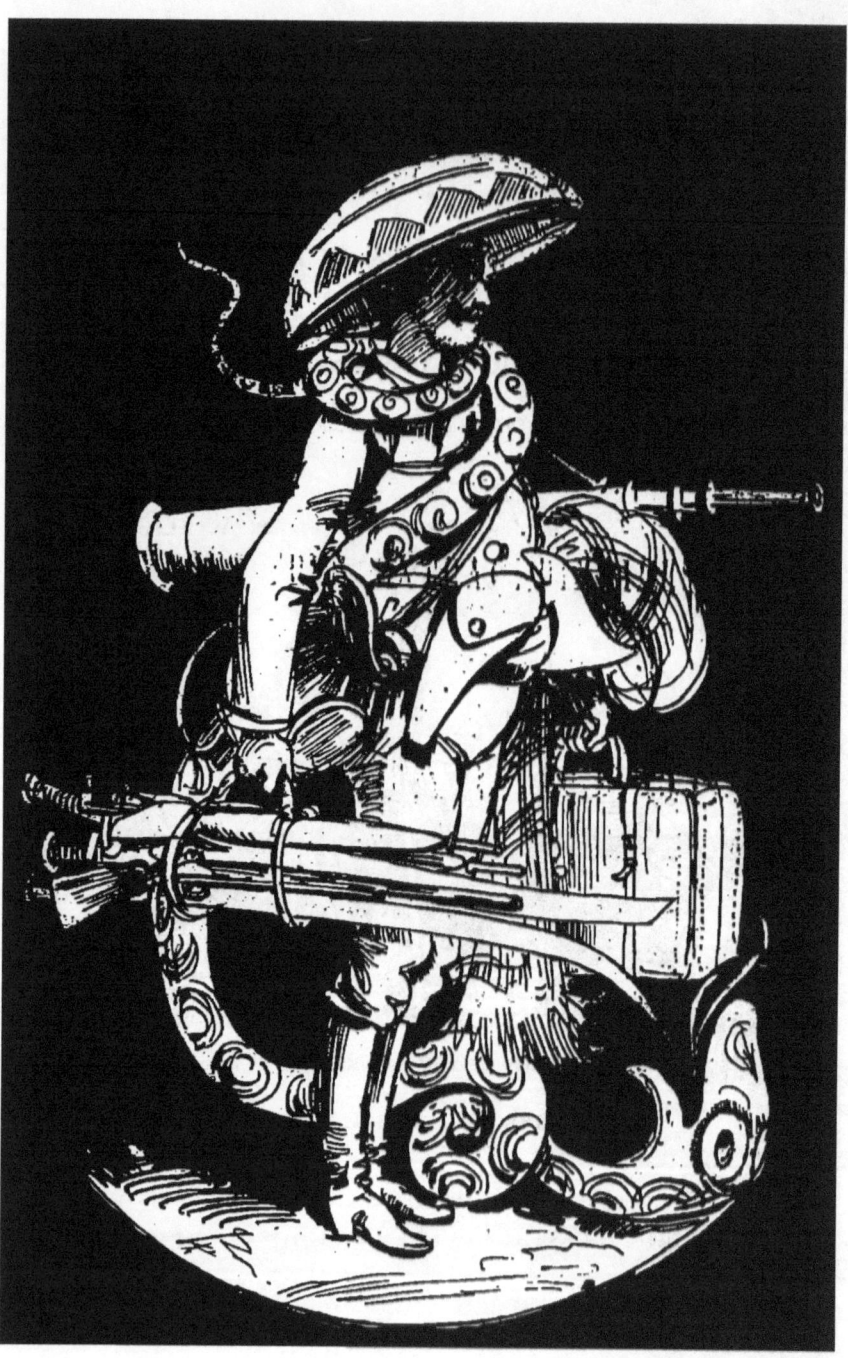

PART ONE: OCEANIA
THE MONKEY KING

I.

In the mid-Pacific region of the 10th north parallel and 150 degrees of western longitude—which is almost the same as that of the Polynesian isles of Pomotou [1]—the great Ocean, so fecund and so tempestuous, belied its name even more than usual on that day. In the utterly disordered sky, masses of purplish-black cloud streamed from the distant horizon at an incalculably rapid rate of knots. The waves climbed to heights unknown in our paltry European seas. Howling and roaring, they hurled themselves one after another and one upon another, as if the furious sea were mounting an attack, which burst forth in frightful waterspouts, under whose weight the highest waves loudly collapsed in whirlwinds of foam.

A few fragments of the masts and timbers of ships and barrels, floating here and there, indicated that the god of storms would not be returning to his deep caverns with an empty bag, alas. Amid the debris, however, one peculiar

---

[1] Pomotou is an alternative name for the Tuamotu Archipelago, a group of islands south of the Marquesas which became a French Protectorate. Their longitude extends from about 140 degrees west to 150 degrees west (Robida was presumably using Paris as a baseline rather than Greenwich, but it makes little difference). Tuamotu lies about 15 degrees south of the equator; 10 degrees north, where Robida locates his castaway, is in the middle of a vast tract of open sea.

item of wreckage was discernible, sometimes thrust up to the crests of the waves and sometimes disappearing in the hollow valleys between the monstrous billows.

This wreck was a cradle, and the cradle in question contained an infant, well-swathed and well-secured. The child was sleeping like a log, apparently finding no difference between the rocking effect of the Ocean and that employed by his nurse.

Hours had passed. Miraculously, the cradle had not sunk; the ocean continued to swing it to and fro. The storm had calmed down; the sky, clearing little by little, allowed a long line of rocks to become visible upon the horizon. The frail craft, evidently carried by a current, was steering towards an unexpected port!

Little by little, the coast became more visible, its sheltering cliffs cut through by little creeks calmly stirred by the waves. In order to get that far, though, it was necessary to pass through a chain of coral reefs, on which the waves broke into cascades of foam, without the little vessel breaking up.

In the end, the cradle came through and ran aground, still accompanied by fragments of mast. One last roller carried it up the beach and left it behind on the dry sand—and the brat, abruptly awoken by the cessation of movement, cried out for the first time with all his might.

It was evening. The Sun, which had not appeared all day, finally showed through, and, having arrived at the end of its course, proceeded to extinguish its last fierce orange rays in the waves of the open sea. To take advantage of this hour of delicious calm after a stormy day, and also to take a little exercise after the evening meal, an honorable family of monkeys was taking a walk on the damp beach, admiring the splendors of the setting Sun. [2]

---

[2] Robida's illustrations depict these creatures with the long prehensile tails typical of New World monkeys, and it soon transpires within the text that their possession of such tails is crucial to the development of the story. I have therefore thought it appropriate to translate *singes* as "monkeys" rather than "apes." Robida's knowledge of primate taxonomy is, however, understandably primitive; a subsequent passage is insistent that the reader is being introduced to "a family of orang-outangs," and another declares that their species is intermediate between orang-utans and chimpanzees. I have retained these terms within my translation even though they make no sense in the context of modern primatology (neither of the species cited is equipped with a tail).

At the time the story was written, the orang-utan was still a semi-legendary creature in Europe, whose reputation was partly based on unreliable traveler's tales and partly on the equally-unreliable ruminations of early evolutionist anthropologists, who had not yet reached agreement as to how many species of human beings there were, or how the concept of species related to that of race, or

The entire natural world seemed to be their personal domain. They were enjoying an admirable view with a tranquil proprietary right that no anxiety could trouble. All the beauties of the tropics were displayed there, as if in a magical frame: all the glorious flowers that the equatorial Sun could bring into bloom, marvelous plants, giant trees and interlacing lianas by the thousand.

Four little monkeys of various heights gamboled on the grass, swinging from descending lianas as they went past, and chasing one another around the coconut palms under the protective eyes of their father and mother. The latter were more serious individuals, content to mark their joy at the good weather's return by quietly shaking their hindquarters with perfect panache. The mother, a lovely she-monkey with an elegant figure and a graceful demeanor, carried in her arms a fifth offspring, which she suckled as she walked, with a candor and a dignified serenity that would have tempted the chisel of a Praxiteles.[3]

Suddenly, their tranquility was disturbed. The father, at the sight of an object extended on the beach, turned two or three somersaults—a gesture which, among the monkeys, signifies the most colossal astonishment. Without ceasing to nurse her infant, the mother and the four little monkeys likewise turned half a dozen simultaneous somersaults before coming to rest on all fours. The reason for their alarm was that the object perceived by the monkeys was stirring and struggling, desperately twirling its arms and legs, as a crab does when one plays the practical joke of setting it down on its back.

It was our recent acquaintance, the young and charming castaway who, having been awakened by the landing, was giving vent to unfathomable feelings. Papa Orang-utan—for it is a family of orang-utans that we are introducing to our readers—made a cautious tour of the disquieting object before allowing his family to approach it. Having judged it unlikely to be dangerous, he signaled to the mother with a reassuring gesture and showed her the cradle, scratching his nose in a puzzled manner.

---

whether—and, if so, where—orang-utans and other great apes ought to figure in this classification. Such issues had been even less clear at the time when Léon Gozlan wrote *Les Emotions de Polydore Marasquin*, which is obviously one of the key sources of Robida's inspiration. In that novel, Gozlan deliberately confuses distinctions between men and monkeys, which had already been considerably declarified by the advent of evolutionary theory, for satirical purposes.

As a postscript to this point, I have translated *guenon* as "she-monkey" because that is clearly what Robida means by it; he is not implying that Farandoul's adoptive parents belong to one of the species that the English language now terms *guenons*.

[3] Praxiteles, a famous Athenian sculptor active in the 4th century B.C., was reputedly responsible for several fine statues held in the Louvre and familiar to all cultured Parisians.

What could the unknown animal be which the sea had brought and cast up on the beach? That was what the reunited family were asking themselves as they encircled the cradle to discuss the matter. The little ones, full of surprise, had no idea at all, but sought to read the results of their parents' reflections in their faces.

Eventually, the father, taking every possible precaution to avoid being bitten, delicately picked up the little castaway, who was still gesticulating wildly. He plucked the child out of the cradle by one leg and passed him to the she-monkey—who looked at him for a long time, placing him beside her last-born for comparison, reflected carefully, and showed by a few significant shakes of the head that she considered this new species of monkey greatly inferior in physical beauty to the family of orangs.

The little castaway continued crying, despite the antics of the young monkeys, who were fully reassured by now and wanted to welcome this new comrade into their company. The she-monkey understood the reason for these cries. Passing her nursling to the father, she took hold of the infant's head and generously offered her maternal bounty to the child.

What joy for the little castaway! For many hours he had wandered without nourishment on the crests of the waves, tormented by a hunger he could at last appease! He drank so much that, having suddenly become comfortable again, he ended up falling asleep on the breast of his exotic nurse.

Meanwhile, the little monkeys had been rummaging around in the cradle, to make sure that it did not contain a second example of this peculiar species. They had found nothing there but a kind of bag sealed by a leather thong. This bag intrigued them

20

enormously at first sight, but their perplexity was even further increased by the sight of the piece of paper that the eldest of the little monkeys took from it. They turned it over and over without result, then passed it to their father in the hope that he might explain it. After examining it for a quarter of an hour, he too could make nothing of the bizarre symbols with which it was covered.

The thing was very simple, though; let us admit right away that the bag found in the cradle was a tobacco-pouch—probably the paternal tobacco-pouch, which the unhappy parents had confided to the hazards of the tempest along with their child, at the moment when their ship sank. As for the paper covered with hieroglyphs that had so intrigued the naïve orangs, it will clarify for us the status of the young castaway, for it was nothing other than his duly-registered birth certificate.

The infant's name was Fortuné-Gracieux-Saturnin Farandoul.[4] The names of the parents and witnesses are irrelevant to our story, so we shall pass over

---

[4] Many of the names improvised by Robida for French characters involve humorous misappropriations of common French words, most of which are too obvious, even to an English reader, to require annotation. The hero's name is more complex. *Farandoula* is an Occitan word (Occitan being the ancient language of Provence—the *Langue d'Oc*) referring to a lively kind of dance, known in both French and English as a *farandole*. The first two elements of the Christian name, which declare him to be fortunate and gracious, are unsurprising, but coupling them with Saturnin sets a puzzle before the reader.

The French adjective *saturnien*, derived from the planet, has the same metaphorical meaning (gloomy) as the English saturnine, but Saturnin Farandoul is by no means gloomy, and *saturnin* has a different meaning: pertaining to [the metal] lead. It is not impossible that Robida had the geological *Période Saturnienne* in mind when he coined his globe-trotting hero's name, that being the era in which the continents acquired their modern form. It is far more probable, however, that he really does mean to imply "pertaining to lead," lead being the material from which bullets are made. Robida—whose *La guerre au Vingtième Siècle* consists of a spectacular series of illustrations representing the technological transformation of warfare as a gaudily sarcastic black comedy—was a pacifist darkly fascinated by the mechanization of mass murder, and was thus obliged to regard Saturnin Farandoul's eventual influence on the population of the idyllic Isle of Monkeys (which, as the text observes, is still in its Golden Age at this point in the story) as problematic, if not actively evil. Farandoul's conversion of the peaceful monkeys into an army of conquest surely qualifies as a metaphorical *malaise saturnin* (lead poisoning).

Despite his frivolous tone, Robida clearly intends to imply that Saturnin Farandoul is somewhat symbolic of his entire race, whose pretension to be humane rather than merely human is not to be taken too seriously. The implication of the story, although the author refrains from spelling it out as an explicit mor-

them in silence, but we must cite two further items of information revealed by this document: firstly, that Saturnin Farandoul was a French citizen; and secondly, that he was aged only four months and seven days. Thus did the youngster make his debut in his career as a castaway.

After mature reflection, Papa Orang-utan evidently came to a decision in the matter of the newly-discovered infant. He made a gesture signifying that five might just as well be six, and got up. The child was adopted; the family, thus augmented, ambled back along the path to their abode. It was a good night for all concerned. The Moon illuminated the tranquil sleep of our hero in the bosom of his adopted family, in the deep forest. The Sun rose to find Farandoul perfectly comfortable in his new social estate, and his adoptive parents quite content with their lucky find.

In her hut, made of branches covered with large banana leaves, the good she-monkey studied her nursling while he feasted greedily upon the banquet offered to his lips by beneficent Nature. In addition to the little monkeys, fascinated by the appearance of their new companion, there was a large crowd in the hut, dominated by she-monkeys.

What astonishment there was on every face! With what curiosity they followed the least movement of little Farandoul! At first, the young she-monkeys could not suppress a thrill of fear when the nursing mother jokingly extended the infant towards them, but the gentleness of Farandoul won every one of their hearts, and the entire audience was soon competing for the privilege of petting him. The hut never emptied; male and female monkeys came from the neighboring forests carrying gifts of fruit and coconuts, which Farandoul pushed away with his hands and feet in order to thrust himself back upon the quasi-maternal breast.

Outside, Farandoul's foster-father, surrounded by old white-bearded orangs, seemed to be telling the story of his discovery. Perhaps he was giving his report to the authorities; in any case, he saw by their benevolent gestures that the elders approved of his conduct and appeared well pleased with him. Little by little, the fuss caused by the new arrival died down, and life resumed its ordinary course.

If Farandoul had been older, he would have been able to marvel at the patriarchal existence led by the monkeys. Indeed, the happy population of that fortunate isle, lost in the vastness of the Pacific far distant from the customary shipping routes, was still in the Golden Age! The island was extraordinarily fertile. All the fruits of the Earth grew in abundance, lavishly distributed without the least requirement for cultivation. No fearsome wild beasts infested the forests, where even the most inoffensive creatures lived in total security.

---

al, is, in effect, that man is merely a "monkey king," so corrupted and perverted by civilization that he has contrived to forget that at bottom (so to speak) he is merely an incompetent example of primatekind.

The simian race was the summit of the evolutionary scale, dominating by its intelligence the entire natural order of the island. Man was unknown there, never having repressed it with his barbarity or perverted it with his example—as he has those fallen races of monkeys, condemned to ignominy, which will vegetate forever in the lands inhabited by humans, unless some monkey of genius arrives one day to effect their return to the purer life of ancient times, in some wilderness inaccessible to humankind.

These monkeys belonged to a race intermediate between the Orang-utans and Chimpanzees. Aggregated in tribes, whose villages were composed of about 50 huts made of small branches, they lived quite happily. Each family enjoyed the most complete individual liberty, and where matters of communal interest were concerned they looked to the elders, who often came together in council at the foot of a giant eucalyptus, in the branches of which the young ones frolicked without taking part in the discussions.

It must be said that everyone was full of respect for these worthy ancients, and that the smart young monkeys would never allow themselves to jump on their backs or to grab their tails in passing, without previous authorization.

Farandoul spent a year with the family. He rolled in the grass with his foster-brothers; he played all the exciting games with them that young monkeys play. To the great astonishment of his parents, however, he remained remarkably inept in leaping about, and adamantly refused to climb coconut palms.

Such timidity in a healthy youth of 18 months worried the gallant monkeys exceedingly. Although his brothers set him an excellent example by means of the most audacious ascensions and aerial somersaults, Farandoul never got the hang of gymnastics. As he grew apace into a sturdy little chap, the anxiety of his parents increased. It became a veritable anguish as they saw that he was quite incapable of following them when the family went off on expeditions in search of amusement, hurling themselves about in the crowns of tall trees and forming troupes of acrobats to swing on the natural see-saws generously provided by the coconut palms. Farandoul's brothers made as many footholds as possible for him and ran away into the trees in order to invite him to climb after them, but he stayed on his feet, astonished and angry because he was unable to do as they did.

Farandoul's foster-mother, who loved him at least as much as her other children, and perhaps a little more—for he was undoubtedly the weakest—did not know what to do to develop the gymnastic talent that must, she believed, exist in him as in every other monkey. Sometimes, while suspended by the tail from the lower branches of a trees, she would throw herself into space and swing there, calling to Saturnin with little reproachful cries; on other occasions, she turned 1000 somersaults, walked on her hands, made him climb up on her back, and clambered up into the branches with him—but in the former instances, Saturnin Farandoul stayed down below, deaf to her appeals, and in the latter, he clung fearfully to his mother's fur, refusing to let go. What a torment he was to those brave orangs!

Soon, this preoccupation became perpetual, a constant worry. Farandoul continued to grow without becoming any more agile. His foster-father—who, since his lucky find, had become one of the most respected monkeys on the island—held frequent consultations with the elders: the venerable monkeys who, as we have said, held their assemblies under the largest eucalyptus in the village. It was obvious that Saturnin Farandoul was the subject of these conversations. These monkeys occasionally summoned him, placed his hand on his head, looked at him intently, made him walk and run, consulted one another, scratched themselves, shook their heads, and finally confessed that they did not understand it at all.

One day, the astonished Farandoul saw his father come back from a longer-than-usual trip with a very old monkey whom he did not recognize. He was wrinkled and bent over, with a great white beard framing his majestic face and bald patches in his coat of long white hair. This ancient, who might easily have been 100 years old, came from a distant part of the island to which Farandoul's foster-father had gone in order to consult him. He obviously enjoyed a great reputation for wisdom, because all the monkeys in the vicinity hurried forth in a crowd, with lavish gestures of respect, eager to assist him in his tottering walk, while the she-monkeys showed him off to their children from a distance.

Having been greeted by the elders at the entrance to the village, the old monkey sat down at the foot of the eucalyptus, in the middle of the greatest gathering of monkeys that Farandoul had ever seen. Saturnin Farandoul seemed, along with the old monkey, to be the object of everyone's attention. His foster-father came to look for him among the urchins with whom he was rolling in the grass, in order to bring him to the ancient, who considered him carefully from every angle.

The old monkey sat the child on his knee, then stood him up again and flexed all the joints of his arms and legs. All of them were working perfectly, which seemed to amaze the old fellow. He began again, with the same result; seeing this, he plunged into a long meditation from which he roused himself only to recommence his examination. Then he struck his forehead, as if he were proclaiming to himself some triumphant Eureka, and called for one of Farandoul's young brothers. He placed the two of them side by side, with their backs to the crowd. By this means, he showed that the hindquarters of the little monkey were equipped with a magnificent caudal appendage: a flamboyant device, perfectly designed for aerial gymnastics—a fifth hand which wonderful Nature had generously granted to the species—of which poor Farandoul could not display the slightest indication.

They all lifted their hands to the heavens then. The most distant, who were unable to see anything, drew closer, clamoring to know the reason for this exclamatory gesture. The tribal elders restored order, debating with the most astounded by means of grandiose gestures.

In the end, all the monkeys formed a procession to file past little Farandoul—or, rather, behind him—pausing one by one to examine him and to take stock of Nature's fatal forgetfulness.

A few passed comment, seemingly inquiring as to whether the condition was incurable. The old white monkey's response was to make them see that that one could not reasonably found the least hope on the slightest of appearances. However, at an order which he gave after further reflection, several monkeys took themselves off into the rocks while the assembly waited anxiously.

After a few minutes, they came back bearing bundles of herbs, which were heaped up between two stones, along with large slugs and snails. An uncommonly dexterous she-monkey made a compress out of it, and pressed it forcefully upon the deficient part of the stupefied Farandoul's body. Despite his cries of rage, the compress was so firmly attached that the poor little chap, so cruelly afflicted, was no longer able to lie down in comfort.

A light snack was prepared for the venerable monkey, who took nothing but half a dozen coconuts. After an hour's rest in the shade of the eucalyptus, during which he offered a few more items of advice on the teething troubles of little monkeys, the old fellow went back with Farandoul's foster-father to the path that led to his hermitage. They separated there and returned to their usual dwellings.

For the first time, Farandoul went in search of solitude, walking alone on the beach, still wearing his compress, which continued to cause him considerable distress.

The medication having brought about no alteration in the state of things, the compress was not renewed after eight hours. The poor she-monkey who was Saturnin Farandoul's adoptive mother tried again, in secret, to rub him with an unguent given to her by some of her cronies, but that remedy worked no better.

The months and the seasons flew past, and the inferiority of Saturnin Farandoul was further accentuated. He was a tall, strong and well-set lad, lithe and agile, skilful in all his bodily exercises, who could easily have got the better of four boys of his own age—but by comparison with his foster-brothers, these advantages amounted to nothing. Farandoul had to admit that he was beaten.

Sometimes, his brothers would lie in wait for him while he walked, hidden in the trees. At the moment when poor Saturnin Farandoul passed by, sucking on a sugar cane without an evil thought in his head, the playful band would form a chain, the strongest of them suspended by the tail from some high branch and the others clinging to one another, as the last in line seized Farandoul under the arms without warning and drew him upwards. They would swing him in the air then, without a care for the kicks that he distributed so liberally, until the entire troop allowed themselves to fall upon the grass.

Little by little, though, these games petered out. In growing older, his brothers came to understand that it was unkind to abuse their physical advantages and to remind their young brother continually of his inferiority. To the contrary, they took it upon themselves to help him forget, taking every precaution, and by means of conventional fraternal attentions. It was too late, though! Farandoul's intelligence understood the reason for this consideration, and it served only to increase his humiliation. Besides, as he saw very clearly, the entire tribe regarded him with an offensive attitude of commiseration. Pity was all too evident in every eye.

The good she-monkey who was his adoptive mother loved him even more tenderly, because she believed that he was destined for an unhappy and probably solitary life. With the future in mind, she began to worry a great deal about her son's prospects. Would he ever find a mate? How would he be received by the young she-monkeys of the village, when he began to think about them? And if his heart spoke, how painful it would be for him if his beloved refused his hand, and if he subsequently saw her in another's arms! What misery awaited him! What dramas, perhaps...

All these considerations saddened the hearts of Saturnin Farandoul's parents. Nor were the brains of the brave monkeys the only ones haunted by such anxieties; Farandoul was troubled too. Indeed, Farandoul had seen how different he was from his brothers and the other young monkeys of the tribe. He had given himself a crick in the neck staring at his reflection in the clear water of a spring, but he had seen nothing to authorize the least hope that he might one day possess the same triumphant appendage as those he truly believed to be his blood-brothers.

Poor Saturnin Farandoul believed himself irredeemably deformed. From the day of that discovery he dreamed of running away, exiling himself far from those he loved, in order to hide his sorrow and humiliation. For weeks and months he wandered the island's beaches in the vague hope of finding some means of putting this plan into operation.

Eventually, on the day after a tropical storm, he found a huge coconut-palm uprooted, lying on the shore—the means was found! Early the following day, having embraced the good monkey and the gentle she-monkey who had treated him with such affection for years, Saturnin Farandoul went with his five brothers to the beach where the coconut-palm rested. As if it were a game, he bid them push the tree-trunk to the water.

When the moment of embarkation drew near, the resolute Farandoul embraced his brothers tenderly but rapidly, and leapt on to the coconut palm as it floated parallel to the shore. The five brothers let loose five cries of horror, and lifted five pairs of arms despairingly into the air. The poor monkeys understood that he was already too far away to be recaptured. While they ran like maniacs along the shore, other monkeys hurried in response to their cries.

Farandoul, profoundly moved by their distress, recognized his parents, but turned his head and his weeping eyes towards the open sea. He used a branch to steer the coconut-palm adroitly through the reefs, and passed through the barrier without capsizing.

The cries of the poor monkeys had scarcely faded away when the leaves of the palm tree caught the strengthening breeze and it was carried out to sea.

Some hours later, the isle of monkeys had disappeared and the coconut-palm was cruising the Pacific Ocean. Saturnin Farandoul, tranquilly seated at the junction of two branches, felt an excitement growing within him as the instincts of a navigator awoke.

His resources consisted of several scores of coconuts still suspended from the tree. The Sun directed its rays upon his naked body.

Having always lived among monkeys, believing himself to be a monkey, he had no knowledge whatsoever of clothing. Ever since his arrival on the isle, however, he had worn the tobacco-pouch containing his birth certificate around his neck; his adoptive parents had attached it there without really knowing why, and Farandoul had become accustomed to wearing it.

II.

"Captain Lastic—look there, out to the south-south-east!"

"*Tonnerre d'Honfleur*,[5] Lieutenant Mandibul, I've been watching it for the last half-hour through my telescope!"

---

[5] Honfleur is a port on the estuary of the Seine, opposite Le Havre. It was the focus of frequent heavy fighting during the Hundred Years' War, when it was

"Well, what do you think, Captain Lastic?"

"*Tonnerre d'Honfleur* may have my tongue, Lieutenant Mandibul, if it isn't a castaway!"

"And it's moving, Captain Lastic!"

"*Tonnerre d'Honfleur*, it's a tree, Lieutenant Mandibul, and there's someone on it."

This curt dialogue took place on the quarter-deck of *La Belle Léocadie*,[6] a fine three-master out of Le Havre, between the vessel's captain and first lieutenant. Having carried a cargo of pianos, dresses and confections for the young women of the town of Auckland, *La Belle Léocadie* was now hastening back to her port of origin with a cargo of hides.

Captain Lastic was a man of prompt resolution; two minutes after having given his telescope to Lieutenant Mandibul, he had given the command to heave to, and oarsmen were steering a long-boat towards our hero's coconut-palm.

Saturnin Farandoul opened his eyes very wide at the sight of the distant vessel, which he took for a terrible monster. Even so, he did not attempt to flee and awaited developments.

The long-boat took no more than half an hour to reach him; the appearance of the men who were aboard it plunged Saturnin into a stupor. They bore no

---

captured and recaptured several times over. I have left *Tonnerre d'Honfleur!* ("Honfleur's thunder!") untranslated as a matter of policy, continued in respect of the oaths featured in the next chapter.

[6] *La Belle Léocadie* means "the beautiful Leocadia," The name Léocadie was not uncommon in the 19th century, especially for girls born on the feast-day of Saint Leocadia of Toledo, one of the virgin martyrs that the early Church's legend-mongers manufactured in such awesome profusion.

more than the remotest resemblance to the monkeys of his island and their faces did not seem to him to be imprinted with the least moral quality. Saturnin was by no means calm, but he stoically presented a smiling face to these unfamiliar monkeys.

"*Tonnerre d'Honfleur*, what are you doing there?" said Lieutenant Mandibul, who was in command of the long-boat and judged it necessary to his dignity to employ his Captain's oaths while standing in for him.

Saturnin had never heard a human voice; he did not understand this greeting at all, and it seemed to him less harmonious than the little monkey cries of his family.

"Are you deaf?" the Lieutenant demanded.

Saturnin made no more response to this speech than the other, but took it for an invitation and leapt aboard the long-boat, in a fashion that astonished the sailors.

The long-boat turned aside and set a course for the ship. The Lieutenant addressed no further questions to young Saturnin; that was, after all, the Captain's business. Aboard *La Belle Léocadie*, every eye was fixed on the long-boat. Captain Lastic did not lower his telescope until it was no more than a few cables distant.

Saturnin was the first to clamber up on to the bridge, in response to a gesture from the Lieutenant. He did so with a single motion that nearly caused the Captain—who had never witnessed such agility—to fall over.

"*Tonnerre d'Honfleur*, little porpoise, don't you have any manners? I'm Captain Lastic!"

The child's only response was a smile. All the sailors surrounded him, and Lieutenant Mandibul admitted that he had not been able to get a word out of the castaway. Saturnin stared raptly, still plunged in the most profound stupefaction. Suddenly, he walked around the Captain, then around the Lieutenant, then around each of the crewmen. One of the men was up on the mizzen-mast; Saturnin grabbed a rope without hesitation and was level with the topsail within an eyeblink.

The seaman had seen him coming, but could not understand why the naked castaway was suddenly climbing up towards him. Saturnin went around him just as he had gone around the others, then let loose a loud cry and slid back down to the bridge. *O joy! O happiness!* he thought. This new species of monkey was conformed almost like himself. No more humiliation! No more shame! In an eruption of delirious joy, Saturnin made several circuits of the ship, turning head over heels. With one last bound he jumped over the flabbergasted sailors and landed on his feet in front of the Captain, around whom he walked once more, just to be sure.

"What's all this, *Tonnerre d'Honfl...*?" cried the Captain, in alarm.

The ecstatic Saturnin naturally made no reply.

"Well then, *Tonnerre d'Honfleur*," the Captain continued, "tell us who you are!"

"Perhaps the porpoise doesn't understand French," suggested the Lieutenant.

"Let's try English, then," said the Captain, taking Saturnin by the arms. "What is your name?" he asked, in that language.

No response.

"Was ist ihre name? Siete Italiano? Habla usted española? Away with you, then, *Tonnerre d'Honfleur*," the Captain expostulated, having exhausted his linguistic resources. "Have you fallen from the Moon?"

Saturnin Farandoul tried to make sense of all these novel sounds. As far as he could recall, no human voice had ever struck his ear; the language of monkeys was the only one he understood.

"Look in that tobacco pouch around his neck," the Lieutenant suggested.

The Captain, who had not previously noticed it, took the pouch. "He has papers on him," he said. "Let's see... ah! He's French, born in Bordeaux..." The Captain stopped short. "A thousand million *Tonnerres d'Honfleur!*" he cried, seizing the child by the arms. "Your name is Saturnin Farandoul, my lad, and you're the son of poor Barnabé Farandoul, a Captain like me, who was lost at sea at least ten years ago!"

"Impossible!" said Lieutenant Mandibul.

"See for yourself, Lieutenant—here's his birth certificate. He's now 11 and a half years old."

"I'd have said at least 15, Captain."

"Me too—the porpoise hasn't suffered for lack of a nurse, *Tonnerre d'Honfleur*! What a seaman he'd make! I'll adopt you, my boy!"

And Saturnin Farandoul, whose exact age we now know, entered into a new phase of his life. How he succeeded, by means of vivid and animated pantomime, in communicating his history to Captain Lastic, we cannot hope to explain. Even so, the Captain was soon acquainted with the most trivial details of that existence, troubled—from poor Farandoul's viewpoint—only by a humiliating infirmity of constitution.

There were a few books aboard *La Belle Léocadie*. Some engravings of monkeys in an account of ocean voyages were shown to Farandoul, who covered them with tender kisses.

"Let's make shift to be a man, my son—there'll be time to later to bid them good-day, *Tonnerre d'Honfleur!*" So saying, the good Captain cut out the monkeys and pasted them to the wall of the little cabin he had given to Farandoul, not far from his own. Our hero was thus able to have the image of his parents on their beach constantly before his eyes, knowing that they might perhaps still be weeping, mourning their poor exile.

Farandoul had a good deal of trouble getting used to the clothes worn by civilized men. He was by no means elegantly turned out during the early days, when he wore his jacket in place of his trousers and his trousers in place of his jacket; as he wished to make himself agreeable to Captain Lastic, though, he soon managed to make himself presentable.

In addition, he made rapid progress in the study of languages. With sailors of every nationality around him, Farandoul learned French, English, Spanish, Malay, Chinese and Breton all at the same time.

Captain Lastic never left off telling Lieutenant Mandibul how pleased he was. "*Tonnerre d'Honfleur*, Lieutenant Mandibul, what a seaman! This porpoise is a charming young man. He slides down a rope in two ticks, from the royal to the topgallant—he could give pointers to the finest seaman in the merchant marine. That boy will do me great honor, Lieutenant Mandibul!"

Indeed, although Farandoul had been obliged to lower the flag before the agility of his foster-brothers on the isle of monkeys, his superiority to the sailors aboard *La Belle Léocadie* was obvious. None could compare with him in the feats of wild gymnastics that he performed on the topmasts. The masts reminded him of the coconut-palms to which he had been born—very nearly—and his greatest pleasure was to swing in the breeze from the crow's nest on the highest mast.

No one who caught sight of Saturnin Farandoul five years after these events would have been able to recognize the monkeys' foundling in the young man with the thin moustache, the intelligent face and the forceful gestures walking on the poop-deck of *La Belle Léocadie*, in the company of Captain Lastic and Lieutenant Mandibul—both of whom had aged a little. The benefits of education and civilization had converted the unsuccessful ape of other days into a superior human being!

From time to time, Saturnin still thought of his adoptive parents with a certain tenderness, but his mind was fully engaged at present with navigation and commerce.

For five years, he had sailed with *La Belle Léocadie*, carrying clocks, leather gloves and crinolines to the Sandwich Islands, champagne and parasols to the Indies, footwear, haberdashery and perfumery to Chile, returning with cargoes of logwood for the wine-merchants of Bordeaux—teak, rosewood, ebony and so on. Having believed during his early youth that the world was bounded by the horizons of his island, with monkeys for all humanity, he now found the entire universe quite small. He had already sailed the seas of every quarter of the globe, set foot on every continent, relaxed on many an isle.

Captain Lastic had nothing but praise for his adoptive son; Farandoul had never caused him the slightest trouble. He had been obliged on one occasion to bail him out of Liverpool jail, where he had been committed after an instant's forgetfulness, but that peccadillo had only warmed the Captain's heart. The incident had taken place at the Liverpool Museum of Natural History, where Saturnin Farandoul, at the sight of a stuffed monkey, had been unable to restrain his sorrow and anger. He had thrown himself upon the terrified curators with such fury that they had only been torn from his hands in a considerably damaged state.

At present, *La Belle Léocadie*, out of Saigon bound for New South Wales, was passing through the Sulu Isles, about to enter the Celebes Sea. Captain Lastic was untroubled. There was nothing to fear on the part of the elements; the sea and sky were calm and everything was set fair for a pleasant voyage. These latitudes were said to be infested with pirates, but Captain Lastic—who had never encountered any—did not believe a word of any tale of sea-raiders.

"Pirates! *Tonnerre d'Honfleur*, Lieutenant Mandibul!" Captain Lastic often said. "It's 50 years since the last one was hanged. Then again, if there were any left, I wouldn't be sorry to see a few!"

Alas, this wish was to be granted much sooner than the poor Captain imagined! That same night, profiting from a moonless sky, Malay canoes came alongside without the slightest noise or splashing sound alerting the sailors on *La Belle Léocadie*. Were the men on watch asleep, or lost in seductive memories of their recent voyage to Tahiti? At any rate, they did not wake up again once the Malays' daggers had done their work.

Still without making the slightest noise, the pirates overran the ship. Captain Lastic woke up, but only to find himself in the hands of the Malays, trussed up so tightly that he was unable to lift a finger. Lieutenant Mandibul, Saturnin Farandoul and the remainder of the 15-man crew were also tied up like parcels.

It was a sad moment.

The pirates came and went on the bridge. In the Captain's cabin, two or three chiefs with atrociously grim faces discussed what had to be done. Poor Captain Lastic, who had some slight acquaintance with the Malay language, was anxious to know whether the crew would be massacred immediately or on the following day, when the ship was brought to land. He understood enough to know that the Malays were steering the ship towards Bassilan, one of the Sulu Islands, which was only a few leagues distant.

At dawn, Bassilan came within view. The pirates, who were passable seamen, dropped anchor on a sandy sea-bed a few cables from a hazardous rocky coast. A colossal racket then rose up on the ship as 50 or so sinister-looking villains occupied themselves with unloading *La Belle Léocadie* and transferring their booty to the island.

The island's interior, thickly wooded and teeming with life, seemed very pleasant. Even so, Saturnin had no intention whatsoever of admiring the scenery; the pirates had deposited their prisoners on a tall rock, from which they could follow the plundering of the ship.

The Sun, rising above the horizon, reminded the corsairs that it was nearly time for breakfast. The fine wines of Captain Lastic's store-room had already furnished the occasion with frequent libations; on their final trip, each pirate carried the greatest possible number of bottles, and the orgy began—much to Captain Lastic's distress.

"Let it go," said Saturnin Farandoul. "Perhaps it will be our salvation."

"*Tonnerre d'Honfleur*! It breaks my heart, all the same! Such excellent cognac!"

What rogues these pirates were! Beards of every color, eyebrows and noses of every possible shape! Frightful bandit faces tanned by the tropical Sun! And what walking arsenals! Pistols of every caliber and every kind in their belts—operated by flintlocks, matchlocks, firing-pins—and daggers of every dimension in their packs, some of them straight-bladed, others twisted like flames, some toothed like saws and nearly all of them poisoned. As they walked, these sea-rovers made a clanking noise that was exceedingly satisfying to their ears.

The three chiefs, naturally, possessed the most complicated and the most tortuous arsenals of all, and therefore cut the most rascally dash. By the same token, they had the right to the finest liqueurs of all, and did not stint themselves in the least.

It must be said that these sinister corsairs were known and famed through-out the Sunda Islands.[7] The first, the celebrated Bora-Bora, had exploited the troubled seas for many long years, ravaging the archipelagoes, seizing ships, massacring their crews and—the last and most important part of the operation—finding advantageous means of selling the produce of what he called his business, in Java, Borneo and Sumatra. The other two, Sibocco and Bumbaya, were his lieutenants; they had learned their trade in his school and knew no better way to balance their mercantile accounts than by cutting off the heads of tradesmen.

Thirst satisfied gives rise to thoughts of food; soon Bora-Bora was hungry. The individual who seemed to be the robber-band's chief cook was given orders to prepare a meal. By way of hors-d'oeuvres, they began to make free with the provisions of *La Belle Léocadie*, while the cook busied himself with putting an enormous wild boar, killed that same morning by one of the Malays, on a roasting-spit.

The cook devoted five relatively tranquil minutes to this serious occupation, but became distracted thereafter, directing envious looks towards his 50 comrades—who, forming a great circle around the fire over which the boar was cooking, were avidly emptying Captain Lastic's beloved bottles. An idea sprang up in that cranium bronzed by the Pacific Sun; in order to have his share of the liquid nourishment, it was only necessary that he should be replaced in his kitchen by one of the prisoners. Taking up an immense cutlass, the cook made his way towards the mariners—who thought, seeing him approach, that their sacrificial hour had come.

With mighty kicks, the cook knocked several sailors aside in order to get to Saturnin Farandoul, whose bonds he cut before telling him what was required of him.

---

[7] The Sunda Islands—*Les îles de la Sonde* in French—constitute the archipelago whose largest elements are Sumatra and Java, now part of Indonesia.

"By all means, with pleasure!" said our smiling hero—and the two men made their way back to the feast.

Everything was going well. The gaiety of the honorable assembly had reached its highest pitch. Two or three pirates had already been moved by the heat of debate inadvertently to bury their well-sharpened daggers in the bellies of their neighbors. Paying no heed to such mere bagatelles, the cook threw himself upon the bottles of spirits, determined to catch up with his fellows.

Standing before the fire, Farandoul took stock of the situation. The pirates had deposited their more cumbersome weapons—rifles, pistols and yataghans—some 20 meters away, along with numerous cartridge-pouches, powder-horns and boxes of bullets. That was all Farandoul required; he had his plan. He turned the boar on its spit, and then—pretending to need firewood—left the circle and made his way towards the pirates' weapons.

His companions followed his every move from a distance, believing that he had gone to seize as many sabers as he could and would make haste to cut their bonds.

Not at all: Saturnin Farandoul gathered wood and foliage, dexterously hid some cartridge-pouches and boxes of bullets among the leaves, and returned to the boar.

Not a single pirate had deigned to stir.

Saturnin had plenty of time to make the boar's guts into a magnificent infernal machine: the powder on a bed of dry leaves underneath, the bags of bullets on top, augmented by pebbles gathered from around the fire. A fuse taken from a firearm completed the equipment of the bomb.[8]

When everything was ready, Saturnin let the end of the fuse fall into the fire, blew on it to enliven the flame, and moved away from the group unhurriedly.

There was not long to wait.

---

[8] The original *machine infernale* was a nail-bomb mounted on a cart, which was supposed to explode as a carriage carrying Napoléon Bonaparte (who was then the First Consul) passed by on the way to the Opera; the timing being slightly amiss, it only killed a number of innocent bystanders. The term "infernal machine" was applied thereafter to all kinds of life-threatening booby-trap, especially those involving explosives. The references to Farandoul's fashioning of the boar into a bomb-distributing *mitraille* (grape-shot) would also have reminded Robida's readers of Napoleon, whose rise to fame began when he dispersed a Parisian mob with a celebrated "whiff of grape-shot." As observed in the introduction, Robida never mentions Napoléon's name in the course of the narrative, but comparisons become irresistible when Farandoul eventually becomes a General and an Emperor.

The cook, realizing that his replacement was no longer to be seen, got up and brandished his *kris* at the boar; he was just bending over to ascertain the progress of the roast when a jet of flame shot out of the animal.

A frightful detonation rang out. The infernal machine had exploded.

No more boar, no more cook! The first was in shreds, the second had had his head blown off. Twenty pirates were writhing on the ground. The bullets and pebbles with which Farandoul had charged his Saint Barbara boar [9] had struck to the right and the left, as if they were a blast of grape-shot, smashing arms and legs, drilling holes in chests and bursting eyeballs in their sockets.

With lightning rapidity, Farandoul threw himself towards his companions, gathering up an armful of weapons as he went. With 15 thrusts of a dagger, he freed them from their bonds. In no time at all, they were armed and, under Farandoul's direction, they fell upon the terrified pirates before the brigands were able to collect themselves.

What a fine spectacle it was! Those who had been spared by the grape-shot, or who only had small pebbles embedded in their bodies, snatched up their famous blades and defended themselves like demons! But how could they resist brave mariners who had their revenge to take?

Within two minutes, 25 pirates were strewn about the sand, and the rest were fleeing into the island's interior like vultures scattered from their prey. Some 40 or 45 Malays were out of the fight, but the crew of *La Belle Léocadie* had, alas, to mourn the loss of their chief. The bold Captain Lastic, after having personally brought down two Malays, had been run through by the pirate Bumbaya's poisoned kris! Captain Lastic managed one last *"Tonnerre d'Honfleur!"* as he gave up the ghost, while Saturnin perforated the hideous Bumbaya in his turn.

There was no time for Saturnin to give vent to his anguish; he had heard the pirate chief Bora-Bora complain about the lateness of a company of his followers, whose return he was expecting at any moment. About 15 corsairs had fled, Bora-Bora himself among them; they would be able to return in force to crush the mariners. Saturnin therefore made haste to re-embark in order to get away from the fatal island. All the weapons were gathered up; Captain Lastic's body was taken aboard the three-master, and the anchor was raised as soon as the pirates' boat had been scuttled.

---

[9] The (fictitious) story of Saint Barbara—Sainte-Barbe in French—as preserved for the delectation of pious Frenchmen in Voragine's classic *Golden Legend*, claims that her father imprisoned her in a tower to preserve her virginity and then had her condemned to death when she became a Christian. He was subsequently struck by lightning, for which reason his daughter became the patron saint of those in danger of being abruptly struck dead, including miners and victims of artillery fire.

Just in time! Hundreds of men were descending upon the beach, frantically hurling spears and firing rifles.

La Belle Léocadie sent forth a blast of grape-shot from its only cannon before her final departure.

As soon as they were at sea, the mariners rendered their final duty to poor Captain Lastic. His command should rightfully have reverted to Lieutenant Mandibul but the Lieutenant, overcome by emotion, declared that Saturnin Farandoul had displayed the very finest qualities during the affair and had saved all their lives. He thought that they could do no better than to appoint him their Captain—as for himself, he intended to continue as second-in-command, under the heroic Farandoul.

The crew applauded.

Farandoul was now Captain of *La Belle Léocadie*. Moreover, Captain Lastic, the three-master's owner, had made him his heir. Everything, therefore, worked out for the best; in honor of poor Lastic, a number of pirates who were found dead drunk in the steward's room were hanged.

The sea was calm; this time, the crew exercised the most extreme vigilance.

Still weeping for the poor Captain, Saturnin Farandoul remembered that at the end of the battle, he had seized the pirate chief Bora-Bora by the belt, and had been about to cleave his skull when the belt had broken, remaining in his hand while Bora-Bora fled. He had kept the belt without bothering to examine it, but he was now curious to do so, in company with Lieutenant Mandibul.

The pockets sewn into the belt's inner surface were stuffed with papers. Some seemed to be business documents covered with figures, statements of account and contracts; others seemed even more interesting to Captain Saturnin Farandoul. He studied them carefully and, thanks to his knowledge of the Malay language, he eventually understood that he had between his hands a genuine deed of incorporation, which established—under the trade name Bora-Bora & Co—a Company for the Skimming of the Sunda Islands. This company was financed by the Malay merchants of Borneo, charged with the disposal of goods and the investment of profits. All the documents were in order; Bora-Bora had a warrant. Saturnin Farandoul could read the details of operations recorded on a day-to-day basis, but the document which made him leap to his feet was a sort of current account containing a list of the receipts and savings of Bora-Bora & Co.

The total shown was 54 million "coins"—without specifying whether these were gold, silver or copper—and these savings were deposited in a bank in Borneo.

Farandoul assembled the crew of *La Belle Léocadie* and told them what the documents were. They all cheered enthusiastically. "Friends," he said, "these riches are ours, by right of conquest! Everyone shall have a share in the prize. Set sail for Borneo! But we'll have to keep a weather-eye open; Bora-Bora isn't dead, and he'll be looking to overtake us!"

III.

Sailing towards Borneo, *La Belle Léocadie* had no unfortunate encounters. She gave a wide berth to all the islands and guarded against the approach of Malay canoes which appeared to be standing off from her in the channel between the Bonggi islands and the north tip of Borneo.

As soon as the ship lay at anchor, Farandoul went ashore with Lieutenant Mandibul, both of them heavily armed, and made for the pirates' bank. Without offering any explanations, Farandoul laid before the eyes of the crooked banker—a shifty-looking individual—the deed of incorporation of Bora-Bora & Co and the pass-book for the current account.

The banker went slightly pale, but did not manifest any surprise.

"Have you the funds?" Farandoul demanded.

"No bank, however well fortified, ever has 54 million coins in its coffers," the banker replied, evasively.

"I'll give you until tomorrow," Farandoul said.

"Impossible, sir! Besides, we must have the signature of my friend Bora-Bora, the company's chief executive. He should have told you that when he sent you to collect..."

"He didn't send us. We're the ones in control of the business..."

"*Ventre de phoque*,[10] you'll settle up, you old villain!" cried the conciliatory Mandibul.

---

[10] *Ventre* is translatable as belly or (as in the previous chapter) guts, but the literal meaning of *phoque* (seal) is irrelevant in this particular phrase, where the

"No signature, no money," declared the banker, flatly.

"In that case, we'll take it to court," Farandoul calmly replied. And that same day, the suit was launched, under the auspices of the Bornean authorities. Farandoul was worried. Evidently, Bora-Bora had warned the banker; perhaps he was in Borneo himself, lying in wait for an opportunity to get his hands on *La Belle Léocadie* again. They had to keep their eyes open, as Mandibul put it.

The *Léocadie*'s sailors, knowing that they had to watch over their fortune, were on their guard—but what could they do if they were attacked some day and overwhelmed by superior forces?

Farandoul understood that the case might drag on for a long time. Justice in the Sultanate of Borneo might perhaps be corrupted, the pirates having friends and accomplices—and who could tell whether the Sultan might not be glad to appropriate the cash-box himself, in order to settle the case?

He judged it politic to recruit to his interests a man who was all-powerful in the sultan's court. This person, for a modest commission of 20%, committed himself to watch over the case and to do everything that circumstances permitted to favor the interests of *La Belle Léocadie*. He made no secret of the fact that the thing might be long-drawn-out, and ended up by advising Farandoul to make himself scarce during the negotiations. Farandoul appreciated the soundness of this advice; after having given power of attorney to his agent, he set sail on the next clear night.

"Friends," Captain Farandoul said to his sailors, "we're taking a holiday; we'll come back again when the case has reached a successful conclusion."

Everyone applauded.

Captain Farandoul's intention was to leave those hostile latitudes and to sail via the sea of Java, the Banda Sea and the Torres Strait towards the isles of Polynesia. He thought of the isle where he had spent his infancy, and said to himself that since Providence had given him the leisure-time, he could not employ it better than by searching for his adoptive family.

The late lamented Captain Lastic had often told him that he had picked him up not far from the Tongan archipelago, and it was to that region that Farandoul intended to direct his research. He told himself that it was impossible that he would be unable to rediscover his island—in the absence of any other indicator his heart would serve as his compass.

In the meantime, a vigilant watch was kept—but there was no trace of pirates on the horizon.

When *La Belle Léocadie* had passed between the New Hebrides and the Solomon islands, and set a new heading due east, Farandoul, thinking that there was nothing more to fear, gave himself over entirely to his search. A course was set for every island sighted by the lookout, at least until it was found to be inha-

---

word is employed purely for its euphemistic phonetic implication. To translate the phrase would, in consequence, obliterate its intended effect.

bited. Thus it was that, one day, *La Belle Léocadie* arrived at an island that was absolutely deserted, and not marked on the map. As with the Isle of Monkeys, its shores were defended by a barrier reef, but when that barrier was crossed the sea was absolutely calm, permitting the anchor to be lowered in perfect safety.

The rocky cliffs of the coastline were interrupted by beaches where the coconut-palms descended as far as the sands. Beyond the palms were fleecy hills covered with the most luxurious vegetation. An immense virginal forest covered the island as far as the eye could see, save for the upper slopes of a volcanic peak, which projected 250 meters above sea-level. A narrow river snaked through the woods, its limpid and murmurous waters gushing out into the ocean, across a beach of the finest sand. All around the island, within a few meters of the shore, the terrain became precipitate, as if the isle itself were merely the summit of a mountain emerging from the waves.

The steepness of the sea-bed allowed *La Belle Léocadie* to drop anchor very close to shore. It also gave Farandoul the idea of profiting from the tranquil harbor and the resources that the hospitable coast was sure to furnish in order to make a few necessary repairs to the three-master.

The ship was solidly established on the beach, and the caulkers and carpenters set to work under the direction of Lieutenant Mandibul. Saturnin Farandoul and the rest of the crew devoted themselves to the exploration of the island. Although Saturnin had observed that its flora was very similar to that of the Isle of Monkeys, he had quickly recognized that it could not be the place where he had spent his infancy. Although there were certain points of resemblance in its general configuration, as seen from a distance, the vague similarities disappeared as soon as they passed through the rocks.

The island seemed to be uninhabited; no tribes of monkeys haunted the forest. Other animals—including kangaroos and opossums—hopped away into the undergrowth, and innumerable tortoises of giant proportions were walking slowly along the river banks. These tortoises had, over time, hollowed out veritable pathways between the mountain and the coast.

While Farandoul was pleased to devote himself to the business of exploration, the sailors amused themselves by playing every possible trick on the poor tortoises, except for that of making a succulent daily soup. When they surprised the tortoises on the bank, the sailors, passing sticks under their bellies, turned them on their backs and left them there in distress, kicking their legs in a comical fashion.

This pleasantry had the result of reducing the entire crew to tears of laughter. Able-Seaman Kirkson, a pure-blooded Englishman with a passion for racing, who did not often have the chance to indulge his passion while on ocean voyages, took the opportunity to improvise tortoise races. He required no more, in order to organize derbies of this new kind, than to happen upon a few tortoises travelling together. The chelonians were brought into line by force of arms, sailors leapt upon their carapaces at a prearranged signal, and the race was on.

Equilibrium was difficult to maintain; some of the makeshift jockeys fell off, while others collapsed into a sitting position on animals which retracted their heads in fear. The man who remained standing longest won, and pocketed the bets.

On the slope of the mountain, Captain Farandoul had discovered the entrance to a spacious grotto, whose tunnels and ramifications could only be explored with torches. On that side, the mountain was quite steep. The cave's broad mouth, overlooking the blue of the sea, opened on to a sort of platform at the summit of a crag looming over a damp ravine, where hundreds of tortoises were constantly crowding.

We shall see how useful this discovery was to the brave mariners in the midst of the complications in which they were soon to be embroiled!

The repairs to *La Belle Léocadie* had been effectively carried out, and the handsome three-master was as good as new, ready to put out to sea again. The sailors, after a final stroll in the forest, were relaxing on the grassy slopes of a hillock in the lowest foothills of the central peak, some distance away from the beach where *La Belle Léocadie* still rested on her keel.

Captain Farandoul, lost in thought, had wandered up to the crest of the hill, from which the entire outline of the coast, with its sharp promontories and deep creeks, could be seen. He had been standing at the summit for several minutes staring into space when he suddenly lowered his gaze towards the coast.

Farandoul went pale. He thought he was dreaming—but no! He rubbed his eyes and let out an exclamation. A veritable tide of Malay canoes was strewn upon the sea, as rapid and as sinister as a flock of vultures. More were appearing by the minute, doubling one of the island's capes some 1500 meters from the hill on which Farandoul stood.

In response to the Captain's cry, the sailors had hastened to their feet and were looking at the innumerable canoes with stupefaction. The vessels were becoming more numerous with every passing moment, seemingly following the strategy of hugging the coast, so that they would have the least possible exposure to the open sea.

"It's Bora-Bora, beyond the shadow of a doubt!" Farandoul said, in the end. Turning to his sailors, he cried: "Forward! To *La Belle Léocadie*! We must warn our friends!"

The entire company filed into the forest in the direction of the ship. Thoughts crowded hurriedly into Farandoul's mind. The impossibility of saving *La Belle Léocadie* seemed obvious. At sea, it would have been possible to make a fight of it; run aground as she was, though, she could not even serve as a citadel for the mariners.

"The cave will be our salvation!" Farandoul said, as he ran. "We'll take all the weapons from *La Belle Léocadie* and take refuge there."

Breathlessly, they came in sight of the ship. Lieutenant Mandibul and his men were asleep in the shade, but they leapt to their feet when they heard their companions running towards them.

"To arms!" said Farandoul. "We're under attack—the pirates are here! Grab everything you can carry and climb up to the cave."

"*Ventre de phoque*! But can't we fight here?"

"Impossible, Lieutenant. There are at least 600 of them! They'll be here within the hour—we haven't time..."

Everyone went to work without further explanation. Everything that it was possible to carry—weapons, powder, camping equipment—was taken up. The first canoes were rounding the point of the little bay when Farandoul left the ship. The pirates shouted excitedly at the sight of the three-master, and hastened their progress.

"Quickly!" said Farandoul. "Let's get ready for them."

The sailors hurriedly deposited everything that they had saved within the cave. Standing on the little platform, they shook their fists at the pirates who were visible on the shore, swarming like ants around *La Belle Léocadie*.

"No time to lose, lads," Farandoul shouted. "Let's prepare our defenses."

We have observed that the grotto pierced the mountain above a rather steep ravine. Scaling the slope would be difficult, in the face of several carefully disposed carbines, but to repel the assailants it was necessary to establish some cover on the platform—the weak point of their fortress. Farandoul looked around urgently, and immediately caught sight of a few blocks of stone which might be used to form a parapet. Alas, he was soon convinced of the impossibility of extracting the smallest of them without long hard labor, which would not want for interruption by the corsairs.

What was he to do? Farandoul, leaning over the ravine full of tortoises, had a flash of inspiration. The tortoises could be used as a means of fortification.

Two men descended into the ravine. As they approached, the tortoises retreated into their shells and did not budge. The two mariners rapidly passed ropes, which had been thrown down from above, beneath the bellies of the largest tortoise, making a seaman's knot to prevent the rope from slipping.

"Pull!"

In response to this signal, vigorous arms lifted up the poor tortoise, which was terrified to find itself borne aloft. Once arrived at the top, it was laid on its back, and the rope was thrown back down to the men in the ravine.

Thirty tortoises were sent up in succession and laid on their backs, placed one atop another with an artistry proving that Farandoul possessed a genius for fortification. To prevent the rampart from collapsing, a number of sturdy stakes were wedged into the rock, to which ropes were attached before being tightly knotted around each carapace.

The two men in the ravine had scarcely climbed up again when the pirates made their move. A hundred men set off together to climb the mountain.

"Let them get as far as the ravine," Farandoul said, "and don't fire unless you're sure of your shot."

The gaps between the tortoises formed natural loopholes, through which the men of *La Belle Léocadie*, with rifles in hand, watched the pirates advancing.

"*Bigre de bagasse!*" [11] murmured the southerner Tournesol, a seaman first-class. "There's every possible color there."

Indeed, yellow men from Formosa were discernible among the copper-colored Malays, along with black dayaks from Borneo and various half-breeds without any distinguishable nationality. Their armaments were just as varied; there were long Muslim rifles, Portuguese blunderbusses, spears, bows and pistols in addition to the familiar arsenal of daggers and Malay *krises*.

Lieutenant Mandibul nudged Farandoul's elbow. "Look, Captain! There's that beggar Bora-Bora. I recognize his big red turban."

"It's him all right," Farandoul replied. "The brigand's keeping out of the way, directing the attack without exposing himself."

After a pause of several minutes, Farandoul called his men to attention. "Here they come!"

The pirates had climbed to within 30 meters, quite bemused not to have been greeted with rifle-fire. Thinking, in consequence, that the mariners had not been able to carry their weapons with them, they were grouping to mount an assault, howling horribly.

"Fire!" cried Farandoul.

Fifteen rifle-shots were discharged. It was like a broadside; a terrible collapsed mass rolled down the mountainside, the dead and the wounded carrying those who had not been wounded along with them. The howling redoubled, this time caused by pain and fear.

Bora-Bora, leaping about like a demon, rallied his men behind a clump of trees.

---

[11] *Bigre* has no literal meaning, being everywhere employed in exactly the same spirit as the final term in *Ventre de phoque! Bagasse* is a colloquial term for a sugar cane, here employed for its phallic symbolism. When modern English speakers who utter obscenities in inappropriate circumstances excuse themselves by saying "Pardon my French!" they usually have no idea how the convention originated, but anyone with a little imagination can see how the two most common English obscenities might be regarded, mischievously, as mispronunciations of *phoque* and *bigre*—and the third as a mispronunciation of *conte* (tale)—each of them substituting a guttural Anglo-Saxon version of the vowel "u" for more refined French vowel sounds. (Ever since the Norman conquest of 1066, Englishmen descended from Anglo-Saxon stock have regarded French, somewhat resentfully, as an essentially aristocratic language.)

"While we have a moment's respite," Farandoul said, "we have to think about food. We can't eat our rampart, so we must have more tortoises for our larder, and sufficient quantities of grass to nourish them. Someone has to go back down into the ravine to get tortoises and hoist them up at the least exposed spot, while four of our best shots provide them with covering fire.

The pirates perceived this maneuver from a distance, and a few moved to prevent it. A few well-directed bullets caused them to make their way back to those who had not been felled.

The tortoise-hoisting operation worked out marvelously. Some 30 tortoises were stacked up in the cave in less than an hour, and the men climbed back up without any accident befalling them.

Meanwhile, the pirates, huddling in the shelter of a clump of trees, seemed to be preparing themselves for a new and more vigorous attack. In the distance, more could be seen dragging their canoes aground to either side of *La Belle Léocadie*. Sturdier Malay boats were mingled with them closer to the shore— and all the crews, as soon as they were disembarked, came to swell the ranks of Bora-Bora's army, brandishing their weapons.

It was indeed a veritable army, which Farandoul estimated at 700 or 800 men. Bora-Bora seemed determined to capture the sailors' citadel no matter what the cost. While he formed his best men—the Malays—into an assault column, he posted others as snipers to harass the besieged men from every side. The Dayaks, armed with ironwood bows, were creeping among the rocks in search of advantageous positions, while other pirates, the Formosans, were opening fire from such a long range that the mariners judged it useless to respond.

The whistling bullets struck the carapaces with dry clicks, at which the armored heads of the tortoises emerged momentarily before immediately withdrawing—especially when a mariner, lurking behind his loophole, found a good opportunity to direct a bullet at some overly audacious Dayak. The poor tortoises, terrified by these flashes of fire and thunderous detonations, attempted to turn somersaults, which made the rampart ripple with movement.

Farandoul told his men to concentrate their fire on those Dayaks whose upward-directed arrows might fall within the citadel; not one of these savages came close enough to the cave to reach its defenders.

Suddenly, a howl let loose by 600 voices burst forth at the foot of the mountain. Bora-Bora was launching the bulk of his forces upon the blockade.

Six hundred demons climbed the escarpment with a resolution that testified to their determination to crush and finish off the 15 besieged men by sheer weight of numbers.

"Save your ammunition, and don't fire unless the shot's certain," said Farandoul, mopping sweat from his brow.

More than 50 Malays had already rolled to the bottom of the slope, the dead and wounded making a ladder of sorts for the others. The besieged men soon saw them a few meters from the platform: hideous, covered in blood, with rifles in their hands and daggers in their teeth.

"*Bigre de bagasse*, this is getting worse!" cried Tournesol, "Step on up, though—we'll lay a few more carcasses down before they get past!"

"*Ventre de phoque!*" Mandibul added. "I won't go to pieces before that beggar Bora-Bora!"

The howls of the corsairs were redoubled. They believed that their victory was certain. The citadel was, in fact, in serious danger—a few more minutes, and they would reach the platform. Excited by the hope of carnage, they pressed forward in ever greater numbers.

"Keep firing! Watch out!" Farandoul commanded, having observed the progress of the attackers for some minutes without shooting. Then, taking his knife, he quickly cut through several ropes.

"Do as I do, shipmates! All together... push hard!" Matching actions to his words, he set his rifle down and threw himself against the rank of tortoises that formed the crown of the rampart. All those comprising it were dislodged.

The entire tier collapsed; ten tortoises, each weighing at least 100 kilograms, rolled down on to the pirates, breaking heads and ribs and scouring the wall of the crag within the blink of an eye.

Before those who had not been overtaken had time to get out of the way, the tortoises comprising the second tier descended upon them like an avalanche, pulverizing everything in their path and rebounding from the rocks to shatter in the midst of the panic-stricken throng.

The citadel had been saved once again. The pirates were fleeing from the accursed mountain, paying no heed to the exhortations of a few chiefs who were trying to rally them.

Losing no time, Farandoul had the rampart rebuilt, using the tortoises placed in reserve.

A number of men went back down into the ravine, some to recover as many munitions as possible from dead pirates and others to capture more tortoises. Those pirates who had remained in the ravine, understanding that the place was not safe, had run away as quickly as they could, far from the scene of carnage. There was only time for a handful to return to hinder the operation.

"Now, shipmates, there's only one thing I'm afraid of," Farandoul said to his men, "and that's Bora-Bora turning the siege into a blockade."

"The brigand kept out of range," Mandibul complained. "I would have been so glad to avenge poor Captain Lastic! Yes, the scoundrel stayed back; a man who has come to possess 54 million gold, silver or copper coins looks after his skin! And that makes 54 million reasons why he's determined to have ours, whatever the cost. I don't believe our troubles are over yet."

"In the meantime, it's nearly supper-time," Farandoul replied. "It's time to sacrifice one of our tortoises—we've certainly earned some turtle soup."

The evening and the night passed without incident. Farandoul lay awake for half an hour, his insomnia caused by disquiet.

He told himself that a blockade could have the most disastrous consequences for *La Belle Léocadie*, which he deemed to be very nearly lost, and particularly for her crew. The pirates would be able to find abundant food on the island, while his own men would be dependent on the meager provisions brought from the ship and the tortoises in the rampart.

"It's very hard," said Lieutenant Mandibul, who was also troubled. "It's very hard for besieged men to have to eat their fortifications!"

On the following day, the Malays could be seen making an encampment on the beach. This testified clearly to fact that they had no thought of leaving. In the afternoon, a band of 50 men left the camp and established themselves in the woods from which the attack columns had been sent.

A blockade was being organized.

Nothing changed on either side for several days. A stream of water, which ran through the grotto and exited into a fissure leading down to the tortoises' ravine, was adequate to the needs of the besieged men, but they took care every morning to bring some grass to the tortoises of the rampart, to keep them alive and in good health.

Farandoul began to find the time weighing heavily and searched for a means of hurrying matters along. In the hope of making some advantageous discovery, he and Lieutenant Mandibul followed each of the tunnels leading from the cave to its very end.

These ramifications extended deep into the mountain, but the corridors usually ended abruptly in solid walls. One of the narrow fissures, however, took them a long way away from their companions.

"*Ventre de phoque*, what can we do?" said Mandibul.

"Ah, if I had my monkeys, the pirates wouldn't hold on for long!" Farandoul replied.

"I can save you," said a firm voice, which suddenly emerged from the depths of the tunnel.

Farandoul and Mandibul drew their revolvers.

"Fear not, I'm a friend," the voice added. To the great astonishment of the two mariners, an unknown man came towards them. "Don't be astonished, and don't ask me any questions—just listen to me," he said. "I'm a European like you, and I'll save you."

The three men squatted down on the rocks. The conversation lasted a long time. Since it was agreed between them that the identity of the unknown man would not be revealed to the sailors of *La Belle Léocadie* as yet, we shall keep the secret from our readers until the next chapter.

Mandibul returned from the cave alone. He contented himself with saying that the Captain had found a means of saving everyone, that he had gone to put his plan into action, and that all he had asked of the sailors was to wait patiently without risking any useless combat. Any attack that occurred would have to be forcefully repulsed; the pirates must be kept back at all costs.

Farandoul was absent for two weeks—two weeks during which the corsairs, without renewing their assault, sought to inconvenience the crew of *La Belle Léocadie* by every available means. Lieutenant Mandibul never stopped fuming with rage throughout the fortnight; as for the sailors, they dreamed of nothing but sorties and hand-to-hand combat.

Soon, the situation, already critical, became terrible. The infernal Bora-Bora had a plan of his own, and we shall see how it put the mariners into a lamentable position.

One morning, 200 pirates scaled the far side of the mountain, and established themselves directly above the platform, at the point of origin of the stream that descended into the cave via fissures in the rock. The wretches had brought their cooking-pots and abundant supplies of dry wood. Twelve fires were lit, on which 12 large cooking-pots were set, filled to the brim with water from the spring.

"*Ventre de phoque*, what diabolical cookery are these brigands up to?" grumbled Lieutenant Mandibul.

The answer was not long in coming

Suddenly, a flood of boiling water fell upon the unhappy tortoises in the rampart, and clouds of hot vapor invaded the grotto. The wretches, being unable to bring active force to bear on the bastion of tortoises, sought to defeat it by slow cooking! All through the day, the cooking-pots were continuously at work; the poor tortoises expired in the terrible boiling flood [12] that fell incessantly upon their backs. Mandibul was seething!

There was nothing to be done! That evening, six tortoises having been cooked, the mariners cut their losses by eating them for supper; six replacements were installed under cover of darkness. It was scarcely worth the trouble. Eight more death certificates were issued the following day: eight boiled tortoises to be put on the menu.

The bastion lasted eight days, after which it was comprised of nothing but empty and broken carapaces.

---

[12] The word I have translated here as "boiling flood" is *bouillon*, which I translated as "stew" in the chapter heading. The word has several other meanings, including—in such phrases as *avaler un bouillon* and *boire un bouillon*—one very similar to that signified by the English expression "to land in the soup," i.e., to come to grief. The puns continue to pile up as Mandibul "seethes" and the crew find themselves "in hot water." Taken in association with earlier references to "turtle soup" (a phrase rendered, as is customary in France, in mock-English), there is a curiously convoluted irony in the sad fate of the "heroic tortoises," which is itself part of a flamboyantly absurd pattern in Farandoul's exploitative relationship with the animal world.

The crewmen of *La Belle Léocadie* were visibly fatter, but thirst began to make itself felt, for the pirates had found a means to heat the spring itself, so the mariners were really in hot water. This was the state of things when, one night, Lieutenant Mandibul, returned from the depths of the tunnel within the cave, gathered his men together and told them to make ready for a sortie the following day.

"Is there news then, Lieutenant?" asked Seaman Tournesol.

"Goodbye hot water—the Captain's back," Mandibul replied. "*Ventre de phoque*, we're going to fight! Tomorrow, when the first rifle-shot sounds on the beach, we'll fall upon the beggars down below!"

The night seemed endless to the bold sailors, weary of the vast soup of tortoises which Bora-Bora—in return for the grapeshot-filled boar of Bassilon—had been serving them for more than a week. At dawn, though, Mandibul ordered them to go down into the ravine—where they all waited for his signal, rifles in hand.

IV.

Let us take ourselves off to the pirates' camp, where the last vicissitudes of the drama will unfold. The wretches are grouped on the beach, around the handful of tents reserved for the principal chiefs. Some are asleep on the grass, wrapped in blankets, others around a few fires—whose last logs, almost burned-out, occasionally hurl a few sparks and spirals of blue smoke into the still-starry sky.

Overturned canoes and felled trees form the camp's only entrenchments.

Bora-Bora wakes up and shakes his fist at the mountain.

"If they haven't finished eating their tortoises," he says to himself, "we can't risk an attack. I'll send a few scouts their way." And Bora-Bora, prodding a few of his snoring companions with his foot, thrusts his arsenal into his belt.

He has scarcely finished when a rifle shot rings out, no more than 20 paces distant! Savage cries burst forth, and before the bewildered pirates have had time to leap upon their weapons, 100 black shadows have jumped over the feeble ramparts of the camp and are flinging themselves upon them!

The tents are beaten down beneath the feet of combatants as a frightful confusion breaks out in the half-light of dawn. The attackers have the advantage, and pirate corpses are soon strewn across the ground. It is as if some infernal vortex were whirling around, crushing everything in its path...

Bora-Bora has drawn his pistols, but he does not know which way to shoot. Suddenly, he starts in alarm. These new enemies, worse than men, are sturdy monkeys armed with stout clubs!

The whirlwind of four-armed creatures has already pulverized half the pirate band; the remainder are trying to flee, rolling with the blows of the terrible clubs.

A strange thing! A man—is it really a man?—is directing this troop of monkeys; he mingles human words of command with guttural cries that make the monkeys jump.

Bora-Bora thinks he must be dreaming, but by the flash of two pistol-shots, he recognizes Saturnin Farandoul! After that, he has but one thought—to rally his men and re-embark.

A fierce fusillade erupts from the side of the mountain now, and the pirates who were blockading the mariners beat their own retreat towards the sea. Bora-Bora and 30 of his men who have escaped the carnage make for the boats; 50 more are there, making haste to put the boats into the water.

Daylight has come. The Sun illuminates the beach, where Bora-Bora's adversaries are now clearly visible. The pirates watch in terror as the mariners of *La Belle Léocadie* and Farandoul's terrible monkeys hurtle upon them.

"Put to sea!" cries Bora-Bora.

A new prodigy, even more inexplicable! Fifteen fantastic creatures suddenly emerge from the bosom of the sea! The pirates' eyes grow wide in horror. Each of these bipeds, clad in a thick pelt, has an absolutely spherical iron head with neither mouth nor nose, within whose face a single vast yellow eye is staring! A sort of pipe emerges from the head, connected to a sack attached to the back.

What can these creatures emerging from the waves possibly be? Bora-Bora has no time to ask himself; these fish-men have iron hatchets fixed at the ends of their solid arms, and they are falling upon the pirates, who are still harassed from behind by the monkeys.

"Onwards, *La Belle Léocadie*! Onwards, monkeys!" cries Farandoul—and, with one blow of a club that he wields with the same dexterity as the monkeys, he lays Bora-Bora flat out beside his canoe.

The fight did not last long.

Those whom the monkeys' clubs or the mariners' carbines had been unable to reach fell beneath the hatchets of the fantastic creatures who had emerged from the bosom of the sea, as if born therefrom.

We shall make haste to explain these facts to the reader.

The man who popped up providentially in the grotto was none other than the celebrated Captain Nemo, who is so well-known to the readers of Jules Verne—which is to say, everyone in the world—that we can dispense with his description. The island where *La Belle Léocadie* had put in for repairs was none other than the Mysterious Island, and it was in the bowels of its mountain-citadel that the secret port of Captain Nemo's magnificent submarine the *Nautilus* was hidden.

Captain Nemo, having heard Farandoul speak of the Isle of Monkeys, had revealed to him that there was an island 150 leagues to the east inhabited solely by numerous tribes of these animals. The description of the island that he gave to Farandoul settled all further doubts. "Let's go there in my *Nautilus*," Captain Nemo had added. "If you are recognized, and can convince a troop of your old friends to come to the aid of *La Belle Léocadie*, it will be possible to do battle."

It had all worked out very well. Farandoul had found his family again, his foster-brothers having grown up into magnificently sturdy lads. He had had no trouble recruiting 100 of his old comrades of the forest, and we have seen how enthusiastically they fell upon the pirates.

As for the fantastic creatures with iron heads, that was a company of divers provided by the crew of the *Nautilus*. The divers too had done marvelously well!

The different units of the little army, having come together on the beach, were introduced to one another, that formality having been impracticable during the heat of battle.

The sailors and the monkeys looked at one another with mutual astonishment, but what intrigued the brave monkeys most of all was the men with iron heads: the divers from the *Nautilus*. Where could these bizarre creatures with round heads, and tails attached thereto, possibly have come from? Were they another new race of men? It overturned all their notions of natural history, which had already been disturbed by the reappearance on their isle of their friend Farandoul, accompanied by beings of a similar kind.

Farandoul was surrounded by his family, his foster-father and his five brothers enfolding him in their arms. What joy! What a picture! The other monkeys crowded around them, happy to stare at the little handicapped monkey with whom they had all played when they were young! It was evident that they no longer considered him as having a deplorable infirmity, having seen, by courtesy of the mariners of the *Nautilus*, that all the members of his race were in the same condition.

Farandoul and Captain Nemo wanted to celebrate their victory with a huge banquet. As soon as the beach had been cleared, the feast was organized. Forty monkeys went forth in search of coconuts, bananas and other vegetables. The cooks from the *Nautilus* and *La Belle Léocadie* roasted some opossums, prepared numerous tortoises—less heroic than those of the rampart but just as succulent—with various sauces, and the tablecloths were soon set out on planks extended on the grass.

Farandoul, his brothers and his foster-father took their places at the head table, along with Captain Nemo, Lieutenant Mandibul and the leader of the divers. The monkeys and the mariners were grouped around the other tables. It was noticeable that every movement of the divers was observed with trepidation by the monkeys, who asked themselves how these creatures with iron heads devoid of any opening were able to eat. When they saw the divers divest themselves of their apparatus, they burst out laughing. The problem was solved— these unknown bipeds were part of the Farandoulian race!

The meal was most enjoyable. The monkeys, of course, did not want to partake of anything but fruit, but they consented to empty a few bottles of champagne furnished by the excellent Captain Nemo. A few, as might be expected, became a little light-headed—but on such a great day, who could blame them?

A big conference was held afterwards, in which a solemn vote of thanks was addressed to Captain Nemo. Then it was agreed that the pirates' canoes and boats should be carefully hidden in a creek identified by the good Captain. He advised that they should await the result of their legal action before showing themselves in Borneo.

Farandoul, always eager for action, resolved to depart no later than the following day in *La Belle Léocadie*, along with the biggest of the Malay boats, in order to take the monkeys home.

As the Sun rose the next day, the two ships made ready to sail. The moment of farewell drew near. Captain Nemo, who held Farandoul in singularly high esteem, came to shake him by the hand one last time, and Farandoul was obliged to accept six superb Denayrousse diving-suits as a souvenir.[13] They promised to meet up again as often as possible, then went their separate ways, after a dozen muskets had fired a salvo in honor of the generous Captain Nemo.

The voyage was a happy one. The three-master sailed in convoy with the pirates' boat, crewed by two men from *La Belle Léocadie* and 30 monkeys, who showed every indication of becoming excellent mariners. They reached the Isle of Monkeys in six days, where their arrival—signaled in advance by lookouts— caused such a commotion that the entire population, save for the sick, thronged the shore while the long-boats came ashore with the monkeys, proud of their campaign.

We shall not undertake to recount every detail of the warm reception given to *La Belle Léocadie*, nor of the celebrations that followed. At any rate, Farandoul, possessed by an all-consuming restlessness, soon announced his intention to return to sea. The pirates' boat was left to the monkeys, with two men to complete their naval education, and *La Belle Léocadie* resumed its course through the archipelagoes.

Farandoul was avid to devote himself to serious submarine exploration, in order to profit from the diving-suits so generously donated by Captain Nemo. He, Lieutenant Mandibul and four sailors soon became used to living and moving in the great depths, in the world of gigantic submarine forests inhabited by oceanic monsters. It was there that Saturnin Farandoul developed the instincts of a hunter, which he had not previously had time to cultivate.

---

[13] Auguste Denayrousse was an associate of the French pioneer of diving-suit design Benoit Rouquayrol; their work attracted little attention until Jules Verne popularized it in *Vingt mille lieues sous les mers*, where Robida undoubtedly found the name.

Armed to the teeth, with hatchets in hand and two pistols operated by compressed air in their belts, along with sharp knives, the mariners threw themselves upon the slimy rocks and ventured into caverns inhabited by monsters unknown to man, which only the most deranged imagination could have dreamed up: six-meter-long lobsters, sea-crocodiles, torpedo-squids, crabs with 1000 feet, sea serpents, finned elephants, giant oysters and so on.

They had some terrible fights with these hideous animals. One such encounter was nearly fatal to Lieutenant Mandibul. The mariners were about to put to death a 15-meter serpent, which they had taken by surprise while it was eating a sea-crocodile—whose tail still protruded from its mouth—but which was still able to defend itself. Their attention was suddenly caught by the entry on to the scene of a strange creature. It was a gigantic oyster three meters in diameter, hugely rounded, running at a trot on six slender feet. Its half-open shell allowed two round, staring eyes to be seen, in which the greatest ferocity could be read.

"*Ventre de phoque!*" murmured Lieutenant Mandibul. "If there's a pearl in that oyster, my fortune's made!" After marching up to the oyster, he seized it by the upper shell and plunged his arm into the slit, with a dagger in his hand.

Horror! The oyster opened much wider, and swallowed Lieutenant Mandibul in a single gulp.

Fortunately, Saturnin Farandoul had seen everything. With the four sailors he ran towards the oyster, which had paused and seemed to be savoring poor Mandibul voluptuously. A sort of internal hullabaloo was, however, audible when they put their ears to the shell.

"He's still alive!" Farandoul cried. "To work, my friends!"

Hatchet-blows rained like hailstones upon the shell of the oyster, which defended itself feebly with its feet. The monster soon had to open up slightly, in order to breathe, and a few stifled words emerged from its interior. It was Mandibul, shouting: "Help me! I've got the pearl!"

Farandoul attacked the oyster at the hinge, causing the upper shell to jerk spasmodically. They forced it open with their arms, and the interior of the ferocious animal appeared at last. Lieutenant Mandibul, who was in a sorry state, was quickly lifted clear, while the oyster was finished off with pistol-shots.

Lieutenant Mandibul had secured a pearl as big as his head! In the aftermath of this adventure, though, he had to take to his bed for several days—which annoyed him greatly.

La Belle Léocadie returned through the Torres Strait and found herself once again approaching the Sunda islands.

"*Ventre de phoque!*" Lieutenant Mandibul grumbled from his sick-bed, "I once dropped a cherished pipe into the water in these parts—perhaps I can retrieve it by means of our diving-suits!"

The three-master made its way through the shallow waters around the Sunda Islands, not far from the island of Timor. Saturnin, who had suddenly become fond of solitary submarine excursions, would not consent to leave this dangerous region.

According to the maps, half of the island of Timor belonged to the Dutch, the masters of the archipelago, and the other half to the Portuguese—which is to say that both nations had a few trading-posts on its shores. In reality, the whole island, land and population alike, belonged to the Rajah, the aged and ferocious Ra-Tafia: an excessively absolute monarch who, in return for a few concessions, permitted the Dutch and the Portuguese to undertake commerce at various points on the coast.

Ra-Tafia, an old white-beard Malay, who had been a great lover of piracy in his youth, now spent his life secluded in his palace with his wives and his bottles of liqueur. His people accused him of favoring the Dutch at the expense of the Portuguese, in recognition of the tribute of curaçao paid by the Batavian government. We shall not allow ourselves to indulge in political criticism; after all, a monarch may have his preferences, and his tastes are not under his command.

The old Rajah Ra-Tafia had but one daughter, the young and beautiful Mysora, a dove hatched in a vulture's nest. Mysora was the daughter of a Frenchwoman carried off by Ra-Tafia during one of his expeditions to the Indian Ocean. Ra-Tafia had still had a heart in those days, and, that heart having quickened its beat, the poor little Frenchwoman had been spared. The slave soon became the Queen of Timor.

If we want to meet the Rajah's daughter, Mysora, we have only to go down one of the dark footpaths that lead from his palace to the sea-shore; we must, however, beware of letting ourselves be seen by the ferocious Malays who watch over every pathway with spears in their hands. These sentries protect the part of the shore where Mysora and her maids of honor take their daily bath from all indiscreet eyes. Sheer rocks covered with lianas shelter a tranquil little bay, where the young girls frolic on the sand. Such merry games in the clear water! Such bursts of laughter! Such joyful swimming-parties! Mysora is distinguished from the young Malays by the paleness of her skin, the long black hair cascading to her shoulders and her modest dress.

All of a sudden, a sharp cry raised by the 15 young girls causes Mysora to lift her head. A fantastic apparition in thrusting up from the foam of the sea: a man-fish with an iron head, who tries to reassure the bathers with benevolent gestures. To no avail—they all hasten out of the water with cries of terror. They flee into the rocks without even gathering up their clothes. Mysora alone, sitting on a spur of rock that forms a sort of islet, has been unable to flee.

The apparition came closer.

"Fear not, O Queen of Timor!" said a voice that we would have recognized as that of our friend Farandoul.

"Who are you?" stammered the beautiful Mysora.

"O Mysora," Farandoul replied, "I am he who burns for you with a love that all the waters of the Ocean are insufficient to extinguish!"

The confused young woman covered her face with her hands.

"O flower of the tropics," Farandoul went on, "I have known you for a week, I see you every day like a Malay siren, playing among the foamy waves of the fortunate Ocean!"

"O Monsieur!" said Mysora, becoming even more confused.

"Be reassured, queen of my soul—it was only from a distance, while hiding myself beneath the waves, that I dared to lift my eyes towards you! Today, for the first time, I have passed through the girdle of reefs that protect this inlet. O Mysora! I am the Captain of that three-master which you saw eight hours ago cruising off Timor. For eight hours, my heart has plunged fully-clad into the waters of passion—and that heart, which has never quickened its beat for any other, is ready to lower its colors before you!"

As he spoke these words, Farandoul knelt down and lowered the head of his diving-suit towards her hand, which Mysora allowed him to take. The poor girl understood that her own young heart, full of emotion, had begun to beat in a different way.

"O Captain," she said, finally, "make haste to depart; my followers, by fleeing, must have raised the alarm among the servants of my father, the terrible Ra-Tafia, Rajah of Timor! He will come to kill you before my very eyes."

"So be it! Death will be sweet if the heart of Mysora is averse to me! If I must never see you again, they shall kill me!"

"Don't say that, Captain! See how troubled I am by emotion, and take pity on me! Go... and come back when night falls on the shore..."

Shouting could be heard in the rocks; the Malays were coming at a run.

Farandoul lifted Mysora's hand passionately to his iron lips, and vanished beneath the waves.

The appearance of a sea-monster totally unknown in the archipelago caused a good deal of talk in Timor; the Malays did not dare to venture out to sea for a fortnight. Many would not even go down to the shore, and Mysora's followers gave up their sea-bathing.

That same evening, however, Mysora was running over the deserted beach; she had seen such determination in the Captain that she feared some imprudence on his part.

Farandoul was there. He had brought a second diving-suit, which Mysora put on, in order to follow the adventurous Farandoul into regions where they would be in no danger of any surprise.

Mysora felt herself subjugated, little by little. The poor girl's heartbeat quickened until it was overwhelmed by an immense and profound invasion of love.

What delectable moments! The hours fled by during this submarine conversation, whose purest poetry refreshed them both. The two young people, sitting one beside the other hand-in-hand, seemed lost in the azure realms of a dream. Time no longer existed while their two souls melted in the ardent light of love. Farandoul had taken the precaution of bringing a pocket telephone so that their conversation, conducted at a depth of seven or eight meters, would not require excessive vocal effort.[14]

In the end, it was necessary for them to separate. Mysora left her diving-suit in a hollow, hidden beneath the hectic vegetation hanging down the cliff. She promised to return in daylight on the following day, and to descend in her diving-suit to the bottom of the bay.

Farandoul had proposed to Mysora that he should ask her father for her hand in marriage. He spoke of arriving in great pomp, at the head of his crew, to present his request to Ra-Tafia, but Mysora had put him off the plan. Knowing her father well, she thought that the old Rajah, infatuated with the nobility and antiquity of his race—whose tradition of piracy had been handed down from father to son for 15 centuries—would never consent to give his daughter to a simple merchant Captain. At the mere mention of such a misalliance, she knew that

---

[14] The device that Robida intends to indicate by the phrase *téléphone de poche*—which I have translated literally as "pocket telephone"—is probably a mechanical one, not much more sophisticated than a children's toy linking two tin cans by means of a cord. The first telephone had been patented in 1876, three years before the publication of Robida's novel, but it had not yet been adapted for mobile use, and wireless telegraphy had still to be invented. Captain Nemo was, however, way ahead of his time, and may have developed methods of communicating with his divers that did not require cumbersome cables, so it is conceivable that this passage really is as prophetic as it seems.

Ra-Tafia would leap up from his throne and strike Farandoul's head from his shoulders. It was therefore necessary, until circumstances were altered, to keep their love secret. As it was impossible for them to see one another on land, they would meet each day to spend long hours in the oceanic depths, far from all terrestrial noise, and anything else that might trouble their poetic chat.

No, we shall not attempt to report everything that they said during those divine hours, when their two hearts beat as one as the lovers flew away to the ethereal realms! That would be the work of a poet—a poet born and bred to describe, in emotion-laden verse, the sublime modulations of their submarine duet. Only a poet could do justice to the two motionless creatures, so young and so beautiful, quartered on a rock beneath the floating reflections of a vague and indecisive light, in the tremulous green water. Never could the eye of a painter—if painters had frequented those depths—have found a more seductive subject! O diver Romeo, O submarine Juliet!

Farandoul's tall frame gained even more stature in the liquid element, and no suited diver had ever displayed more charming contours or a more graciously undulant figure than Mysora's. Schools of fish halted in stupefaction before the pair. Enormous tuna and indiscreet rays made circuits of the two young people without distracting them from their ecstasy, even when the dazed fish bumped into the floating tubes which conveyed breathable air to them. Sometimes, whole assemblies would gather round. Farandoul took no precautions against them; knowing from experience that submarine monsters only showed themselves in the greatest depths, he had no fear of encountering one a mere eight meters below the surface.

One day, though, Mysora wanted to take an excursion in his arms, into the submarine valleys that he traversed every day in order to come to her—and Farandoul did not have the heart to refuse to satisfy her whim, even though he was fully conscious of the risk.

The two young people had moved without any hindrance to a certain distance from the coast. Farandoul, by means of a little pocket pressure-gauge, had established that they had attained a depth of 150 meters, when an unexpected spectacle suddenly presented itself to them.

A terrible battle was raging, a short distance away, between a small whale and a sea-serpent more than 100 meters in length. The poor whale had been attacked from behind by the horrible constrictor, whose immense mouth had snatched it by the tail and was striving to swallow it, despite its desperate resistance. The whale's head and a part of its body were still protruding from that mouth, further ingestion having been halted by the fins. The constrictor, in order to finish the job, was twisting its body in terrible effort while its convulsively-rolling coils were striking the sea-bed with a frightful noise.

It was obvious that the whale must succumb. Mysora, seized by pity, begged Farandoul to hurry to its aid.

"Take your hatchet, my handsome Farandoul," she said, "and slay the monster." And when Farandoul hesitated, she added: "Don't worry about me—save the whale!"

Farandoul leapt forward. His hatchet in his hand, he fell upon the serpent as if he were on horseback. Despite the reptile's sliminess, he pulled his way to the head, which he struck furiously. The serpent, which had paid no attention to this new adversary until that moment, thrashed about in a terrifying manner.

Without allowing himself to be unseated, Farandoul redoubled his hatchet-blows, so effectively that the monster's skull finally burst asunder with a great crack! The two jaws opened as wide as possible, while the reptile shuddered convulsively, and the whale freed itself with a sudden effort.

At the same moment—to Farandoul's great horror, and before he could throw himself forward to prevent it—the whale advanced with two thrusts of its right fin upon Mysora, who was following the vicissitudes of the combat with interest. Within a second, its immense maw had engulfed the unfortunate young woman.

An appalling darkness of the soul! The monstrous cetacean could offer no better acknowledgement of the sweet girl who had saved it than to swallow its benefactress whole!

The monster, doubly delighted to have escaped the serpent at the same time as it had snapped up a fine windfall, hurled itself towards the light in order to enjoy its good fortune in peace. As it passed him by, the maddened Farandoul grabbed hold of a cord that was still dangling from its mouth, and arrived at the wave-tossed surface at exactly the same time.

What Farandoul had seized was the floating tube which conveyed breathable air to Mysora's diving-suit. His only hope was that it was still attached; he did not want to let go of the last thread upon which Mysora's life might possibly depend.

By an extraordinary stroke of luck, on arriving in daylight, Farandoul perceived his ship only a few cables distant. A certain tumult was evident on board, the crew having caught sight of the monster and decided to attack it, by way of passing the time. Farandoul waved his arms above his head, and a general cry went up in response—and, in less time than it takes to say so, the long-boat had put to sea.

Lieutenant Mandibul, harpoon in hand, gestured to the men, urging them to row vigorously. Two minutes later, the long-boat had reached Farandoul—who seized the harpoon and, throwing with a sure hand, hit the monster's flank. Lieutenant Mandibul had once been a whaler. He noticed that, contrary to the habit of whales—which usually dived with vertiginous speed and threaded their way into the depths as soon as they were hit—this one was only moving feebly. Evidently, it sensed that it had fallen prey to some profound difficulty.

No crime ever goes unpunished, and Providence the Avenger would doubtless have struck it fatally soon enough, but the whale's hour of punishment had sounded and the crime that could not weigh upon its non-existent conscience was weighing upon its stomach!

In the first moments after swallowing its prey without examination, the whale had perceived its roughness. Trusting to the strength of its constitution, however, it had expected to be quickly rid of the extraordinarily lumpy morsel—but within its inner tribunal,[15] it now began to regret its gourmandizing, its stomach being over-full. Moreover, the creature that it had swallowed was flinging itself recklessly about—and here, adding to its misfortunes, were yet more enemies attacking it, as if it did not have enough to do to counter the enemy within!

Farandoul made a sign, which Mandibul understood; another harpoon was thrown, and before the whale could make up its mind, the two cables were made fast to the bow of *La Belle Léocadie*. Farandoul had leapt upon the monster; he strove with all his might to hack through its outer tegument with hatchet-blows, in the hope of making a hole by means of which he could go into its body and save Mysora. Meanwhile, the final preparations were made to haul the whale aboard the ship.

Suddenly, the whale recovered its strength. With a single blow of its tail, it up-ended the long-boat, which nearly turned turtle, and darted southwards like an arrow. *La Belle Léocadie*, in tow to the monster, took the same course.

The desperate Farandoul was taken aboard with the sailors from the long-boat. It was all over! Mysora seemed to him to be lost forever; even though the air-hose was still afloat, it seemed impossible to him that she could stay alive until *La Belle Léocadie* caught up with the dying whale.

At any rate, he was determined at least to kill the monster. To do that, it was necessary to follow it until its strength was exhausted. The harpoon-cables were firmly-attached and would not break, all the sails were furled—and *La Belle Léocadie*, her canvas dry, flew like lightning in the monster's wake.

V.

Sibilantly skimming the crests of the waves, *La Belle Léocadie* was drawn along at a prodigious velocity. The whale that was towing her was traveling at an incalculable pace, and it was only very approximately that Farandoul esti-

---

[15] *Le for intérieur*, here translated literally as "inner tribunal," is commonly employed in French as a metaphorical synonym for conscience, but the text has already established that the whale is devoid of conscience, and that its internal trial is essentially dyspeptic.

mated her speed at 40 leagues an hour.[16] The sailors were scarcely able to move without falling violently on their behinds, unless they lashed themselves to the stays. They were quite out of breath.

How would the mad dash end?

The ships that they encountered put on full steam in order to escape the path of the infernal ship, which they took for the Flying Dutchman. A big steamship going from Liverpool to Melbourne, full of terrified passengers, was struck amidships and cut in two following an unwise maneuver.

At 15:00, Farandoul saw land on the port bow, which he judged to be the coast of Western Australia, near Perth. If the whale did not change direction within a quarter of an hour, they would be at the south magnetic pole,[17] bound to be broken on the polar icebergs or the desolate cliffs of the Antarctic continent.

And Mysora, alas! Could any hope still remain?

The whale suddenly veered eastwards. Cape Leeuwin and King George Point were doubled; the whale's speed seemed to be increasing even more. It soon began to make such violent leaps and jerks that Farandoul feared the cables would snap. Soon afterwards, a violent tempest was added to the perils of the situation; it seemed that the Heavens were taking the side of the monster against the defenders of the beautiful Mysora. In the midst of the unleashed elements, the whale's convulsions became even more violent. The monster was blowing hard and suffering.[18] For a moment or two, the Australian coast became clearly visible to port; then everything was swallowed up by the blackness of the tempest.

The chase had lasted 23 hours when, at the height of the storm, both cables suddenly broke simultaneously. The whale, abruptly set free, redoubled its velocity and its convulsions, leaving *La Belle Léocadie* dancing angrily on the waves as the creature was lost to view.

For a further hour, the breathless monster ate up the distance. Whirlpools of foam traced a long wake behind it and every time it vented air from its blowhole immense cascades of water fell upon its head. Every time that huge head emerged from the waves, a sort of bellowing sound was audible. The monster was moaning!

A fisherman named John Bird, who lived in a little maritime cottage in Port Philip, a few leagues from Melbourne, made a fortunate discovery that day.

---

[16] A French league is four kilometers, so 40 leagues an hour is exactly 100 miles an hour—an incredible velocity for a swimming whale, especially with a three-master in tow.

[17] The text has *au pôle sud*, but it must mean the magnetic pole, which is located in the sea off the Adélie coast; there is now a French base on that coast, named after the Antarctic explorer Jules Dumont-d'Urville (1790-1842) who first touched upon it.

[18] The assonant pairing of *soufflant* et *souffrant* cannot be reproduced in English.

Having not put out to sea because of the storm, he was walking on the beach, taking long puffs on his pipe by way of consolation, when—to his great surprise—he saw a gigantic fish coming straight towards him. He had no time to get out of the way. The whale, at the limit of its strength, ran blindly aground upon the rocks, hurtling at such a speed that it smashed to Earth 50 meters from the waves. Then, lying on its side, exhausted and motionless, it seemed ready to expire at the feet of the stupefied John Bird.

A third individual now appeared on the scene. A tall, gaunt and ungainly man, bald and bespectacled, strode up rapidly, waving his arms and an oversized umbrella. A long yellow overcoat floated behind him. The newcomer, careless of his unprotected shoes, bounded through the puddles, splashing himself from top to toe.

Thus we introduce to our readers, with their permission, the celebrated scientist Valentin Croknuff,[19] founder and Director of the Great Melbourne Aquarium, an establishment almost without rival, where all known species of fish swim back and forth in continuously-recycled sea-water. Mr. Croknuff's Aquarium lacked nothing but a whale, so his joy may be imagined when, at the very moment he was turning for home, he observed from a distance the monster stranded on the sand.

John Bird was just about to finish the creature off, brandishing a harpoon that he had recovered from its flesh, when a violent blow from an umbrella fell upon his head. His pipe fell out of his mouth and broke. The furious John Bird rounded on his opponent to deliver his riposte.

"I'll buy your whale—don't touch it, you imbecile!" cried Mr. Croknuff, the man with the umbrella.

John Bird lowered his fist. "How much?"

"Fifty pounds!"

"Pay up!"

Having received his money, John Bird turned on his heel, saying: "Now take your whale away, if you can!"

That was the difficult part, but Mr. Croknuff got it done regardless. That same evening, all Melbourne was informed, by means of huge posters, that the scientist Mr. Croknuff had finally acquired for his Great Aquarium the whale of his dreams.

---

[19] I have resisted the temptation to further Anglicize this name by amending its spelling to "Valentine Crocknough." I have retained the appellation "Mr. Croknuff" where Robida has "M. (for Monsieur) Croknuff," although it seems slightly awkward, because the occasions when Robida elects to abandon the honorific have a certain narrative significance, implying that the name is being used contemptuously.

Valentin Croknuff spent the whole night lavishing much-needed care upon his cherished whale. The unfortunate creature was in a sad state, flapping its fins lamentably.

Mr. Croknuff's Great Aquarium was situated in a nice part of Melbourne, on a grand avenue called Aquarium Road. A beautiful garden was laid out in front of the building, in whose shade passers-by could often observe the worthy Mr. Croknuff walking for hours with a sick baby seal in his arms, or a sea-lion overtaken by nostalgia.

The Aquarium was octagonal in shape, comprising eight immense tanks surrounding a central room—which Mr. Croknuff, in order to be always in the midst of his pupils, had made into his workroom and his bedroom. In a way, he actually lived in a submarine world, and could watch over the health of his stock as easily by night as in the daytime. He was, in consequence, familiar with all their little habits. He had studied their characteristics and had made himself master of them all, a good father to his family. He made them change tanks when they became bored, and alleviated the tedium of long summer evenings by charming them with symphonies played on the piano, performed with the most marvelous verve.

It ought to be said that it was entirely for the benefit of his inmates that Mr. Croknuff had acquired the piano. Mr. Croknuff, like all sensible men, detested music, particularly piano music—but he told himself that even though music was a prehistoric invention, a last relic of barbarism which civilization would

66

one day sweep away, the savage art might perhaps still be agreeable to the scarcely-elevated natures of his boarders.

That night, Mr. Croknuff was entirely devoted to his whale; the other fish, glued to the glass, waited in vain for the concert that sent them to sleep every evening. The whale wheeled around and around in its aquarium like a mad thing. Mr. Croknuff was desperate to do something to ease its distress. He had scratched away distractedly at his denuded skull for hours, without seeing any means of putting an end to its suffering.

Suddenly, the whale made a convulsive movement. Its jaws opened very wide, and its eyes closed. Mr. Croknuff, believing that it was about to give up the ghost, pounced on his piano—on which, in order to soothe the poor whale's last moments, he plucked out the despairing chords of Mozart's Requiem, while watering the keys with his tears. When he lifted his head again, however, the whale was not dead—and it was no longer alone. A bizarre creature was standing by its side!

Mr. Croknuff, rubbing his eyes, realized that the trespasser was a diver dressed in a suit!

Leaping briskly on to the aquarium's platform, Mr. Croknuff slid a ladder into the tank and, without saying a word, signaled to the diver to climb up. Our readers will recognize Mysora, who had survived being swallowed by the gluttonous monster, thanks to her extra-strong costume.

Mr. Croknuff and Mysora climbed down into the scientist's bedroom. Mr. Croknuff seemed to be furious. Standing before Mysora with his arms folded he began cursing explosively. "Ah! ah! ah! Wretch! So it's you who've been hurting my whale! Do you know, infamous torturer, that I can have you up in court—you've no right to damage my property!"

Mysora, who did not speak a word of English, understood nothing of this discourse. In any case, the poor girl was at the end of her tether. Without making any response, she fainted, letting herself fall into an armchair.

"Here we go!" Croknuff grumbled. "Look who's ill now! There's a chap who doesn't stand on ceremony! As if I had time to attend to him, when the poor whale he's hurt is suffering so! Let's see now—come round, my friend. Hang on—drink this. It's a bottle of sugared water I prepared for a baby seal with the measles... drink up! Quickly! I've got to get back to my whale!" And Mr. Croknuff, his head turned towards his whale, rapped on Mysora's iron helmet with the bottle of sugared water. "Well, drink it, then!" he went on. "Ah, I get it! It's his diving-suit getting in the way!" Replacing the bottle on his desk, Mr. Croknuff set about unfastening Mysora's diving-suit.

Suddenly, he cried out and let the helmet fall to the ground. Mysora's pretty head had appeared before his eyes, pallid with the emotion of those 30 terrible hours. Her long hair had come undone, and made a magnificent ebony frame for the bleached canvas of her face. Life seemed to be returning; her large eyes opened wide with effort as she tried to get her bearings.

Her gaze fell first upon the glass partition of the huge tank where the whale, finally restored to normality, was swimming quite calmly back and forth. Mysora let out a feeble scream at the sight of the monster—which, bumping its nose against the wall of its prison, fixed its little round eyes upon her. She fainted again.

No scientist had ever experienced an emotion as great as Mr. Croknuff's. His heart beat faster and his spectacles jumped on his nose as his eyes flickered back and forth between the whale and the girl. What blows he rained upon his forehead with his fist! Eventually, having moved an atlas and a stuffed tuna out of the way, he sat down on a low chair beside the young woman and began slapping her gently with both hands to bring her round.

A few feeble sighs were the only response. Mr. Croknuff jumped up, satisfied, threw himself upon the bottle of sugared water and tried to force a few drops between the young woman's lips.

"How beautiful she is! How beautiful!" murmured Mr. Croknuff, his attentions becoming more profuse. "What long hair! What little hands! And the nose—what lovely curvature! What eyes! What eyebrows! What teeth! How beautiful she is! How beautiful! Drink this for me, my girl. Oof! What a woman! There's an adventure—walking on the sea-bed in a diving-suit, being swallowed by a whale! She loves fish! How beautiful she is! How beautiful! I love them too, and I've always dreamed of a Mrs. Croknuff who would love fish... but I've never found one, and have remained a bachelor. Yes, my girl! That's what you see—a bachelor! Drink this for me, my girl. I made it for my baby seal; it's very good. How beautiful she is! How beautiful!!!"

Mr. Croknuff was beside himself. None of his friends would have recognized the illustrious scientist—author of eight conscientious volumes on the morals of the lobster before dressing, and lengthy patient studies of the habits of reef-building polyps—as he knelt beside Mysora, sighing frantically and bathing the hands of the girl abandoned to his care with tender tears.

It must be acknowledged that although Mr. Croknuff no longer had any hair or teeth, he still had a heart—and that heart had quickened its beat for the very first time! Mr. Croknuff firmly believed that he had committed himself entirely to pisciculture, but here was his heart in sudden rebellion, up-ending everything in its way, laying down the law to its former master, Mr. Croknuff's brain.

It was all over! Mr. Croknuff could no longer contain himself.

"Angel!" he said to Mysora—for he was already thinking of her as an angel, and addressed her thus. "Angel! I love you, and I offer you my hand and my Aquarium! Accept them! You love fish; I love them too! I love you; you shall love me; we shall love one another, here! Give me your answer, angel!"

Mysora, coming round, had opened her eyes. At first, she understood nothing of what Mr. Croknuff said, taking him for an aged doctor—then, confronted by the scientist's fervent pantomime, she began to wonder whether she had miraculously escaped one great peril only to fall into another, no less terrible.

Poor Mysora pushed Mr. Croknuff away and stood up, her face pale, her hair in disarray and her expression distraught.

"What do you want from me?" she cried, in Malay. "Do you know that I'm the daughter of the Rajah of Timor, and the bride-to-be of Saturnin Farandoul, Captain of *La Belle Léocadie*. Beware the vengeance of my father, or that—more terrible still—of my beloved Farandoul!"

Mr. Croknuff had grasped nothing from this speech except for one thing: Mysora was angry. Mr. Croknuff's rejuvenated heart ached at that sad thought, and its proprietor groveled desperately at the feet of the incensed young woman.

"Pardon me, sweet dove! I would give my whale, and my Aquarium with it, not to have offended you! You don't understand—I love you! It's my heart, my hand, my Aquarium, that I offer you! Permit me to speak to you of love; listen to me! Your arrival has turned my life upside-down, and thanks to you I have experienced what experts in these matters call love at first sight! I have not studied the physiology of the passions; like a madman, I denied love, but a single instant has revealed it to me. Angel, I love you!" And Mr. Croknuff, still on his knees, extended his arms towards Mysora.

Mysora leapt backwards, abruptly took up her helmet, refastened her diving-suit, and leapt on to the platform of the aquarium as rapidly as a flash of lightning.

"Greybeard," she cried, "you have shown me that there are monsters more dreadful to young women than those one meets at the bottom of the sea! Since you force it upon me, I shall return to the whale—but tremble, for my Farandoul will come to save me!"

Saying these words, the heroic young woman slid into the aquarium. The whale, which had not been paying attention, started with fright and retreated to the most distant extremity of the tank.

Mysora had not been unaware of the dangers that she might run in cetacean society, but she had decided to brave them in order to keep herself pure for her beloved. She was delighted to see, however, that it was she who frightened the whale. The voracious cetacean was conscious of the torment it had suffered as a result of taking such an indigestible creature into its gut, and was now disposed to keep well clear of Mysora.

Mr. Croknuff, on the other hand, stood on the platform wringing his hands, at the risk of tearing out the last of his hair in his anguish.

At one point, he seemed to be on the point of throwing himself head-first into the aquarium to end his life, but then he tried to move Mysora to pity. The young woman obdurately refused to leave her protective shelter.

At sunrise, Mr. Croknuff went away. The doors of the establishment were soon opened to the waiting crowd, whose members had come from all over Melbourne to see his whale.

The general astonishment was immense when they saw that, in addition to the whale, the central tank contained a creature clad in a diving-suit, which seemed to be living on amicable terms with the enormous cetacean. Mr. Croknuff was there, in the process of receiving the congratulations of the Scientific Societies of Melbourne; pressed by questions, he tried to keep his explanations vague, but only succeeded in further exciting their curiosity. Some of his employees, cunningly interrogated, were less discreet; several rumors began to circulate within the crowd.

Soon, all Melbourne knew that Mr. Croknuff had a live siren in his Aquarium, so accomplished and so marvelously beautiful that he had been obliged to take it upon himself to dress her in a diving-suit, in order to spare her the fervent curiosity of the public.

Poor Mysora, finding herself the object of every gaze, sought to hide herself as completely as possible behind boulders covered with algae and marine plants; but there, on the opposite face of the aquarium—which, as we have observed, looked out into Mr. Croknuff's office—she found her odious persecutor plastered against the glass, blowing her the most tender kisses. The poor girl quickly took herself off to the other side, where numerous hurrahs greeted her return. It was the same all day. As evening approached, she contrived to make herself a refuge within the boulders—a sort of cave where, exhausted by fatigue, she went calmly to sleep, after having first partaken of a light supper dispensed by Mr. Croknuff from the platform of the aquarium.

Mr. Croknuff gave himself up completely to the most brilliant improvisations on the piano, but Mysora refused to pay the least attention to the waves of harmony that rolled through the aquarium, to the great delight of the other inmates. That night, not a single resident fish went to sleep; Mysora alone found forgetfulness of her troubles in slumber—and traveled the empire of dreams in company with her beloved Farandoul.

What was our hero doing in the meantime? Had *La Belle Léocadie* perished when the tempest took hold of her, after the cables attaching her to the whale had ruptured?

Not at all. Farandoul was an excellent mariner; mastering his grief, he thought only of saving his crew, and *La Belle Léocadie* had, fortunately, extracted herself from all danger.

Two days after the storm, the three-master had come into Sandridge, Melbourne's port, situated a few kilometers away from the town. Farandoul hoped to pick up the track of the whale there, as the monster had been racing towards Port Philip when it had given him the slip. He had soon discovered John Bird, and had obtained from him, by courtesy of a few well-placed guineas, every detail of the purchase and removal of the whale by the scientist Mr. Croknuff.

Farandoul went forthwith to Melbourne's Great Aquarium, and entered the establishment at the moment when the greatest influx of curiosity-seekers was crowding into it.

Scientists, naturalists, academicians, journalists and tradesmen were overrunning the Aquarium. Mr. Croknuff found himself pulled in every direction, by the members of a special commission sent by the Melbourne Institute, by doctors desirous of dissecting the so-called siren, by photographers and reporters from every newspaper in the state of Victoria—and so on, and so on.

Farandoul elbowed his way through the crowd.

"Where is she? Where is she?" he cried, shoving the scientists out of the way.

"Who do you mean?"

"My whale—let me see my whale!" He had arrived in front of the largest tank in the Aquarium despite the efforts Mr. Croknuff made to repel him.

One glance was sufficient. The whale was there—and, alive within the aquarium, separated from him by a mere pane of glass, Mysora put out her arms to him.

What luck! Farandoul wanted to embrace Mr. Croknuff—but Croknuff, having inferred that he was an enemy, thrust him away acrimoniously. "Who are you, sir? What do you want?"

"I am her husband-to-be, worthy scientist, and I have come to find her!" Farandoul replied, at the summit of happiness, "I believed her dead, my dear Mysora—imagine my joy on seeing her again... on...."

"My dear sir," Mr. Croknuff interrupted him. "I've bought the whale. I've paid for it, so it belongs to me..."

"I'm not laying claim to the whale, but..."

"But the creature that you see there was inside the whale at the time of the transaction, and was included in the price! I'm holding on to it—holding hard, Devil take you! You don't think that I'll generously make you a gift of it, now that it's the most important inmate of my Aquarium, do you? I've got it, and I'm keeping it!"

Farandoul had gone from joy to surprise, and from surprise to anger. He seized Mr. Croknuff by the throat, and was preparing to throw him through the glass of the aquarium in which the trembling Mysora was imploring his help when hastily-summoned policemen restrained him.

"I place my property under the safeguard of the authorities!" Mr. Croknuff shouted, as Farandoul held on to him. "I'm an Australian citizen. I've a right to the protection of the law, for myself and my goods!"

How can we describe Farandoul's rage? How can we speak of the plans for massacre that bubbled up in his head? As soon as he was out of the hands of the police, he hurled himself towards *La Belle Léocadie*'s mooring. He assembled his men on the bridge and told them what had happened. A unanimous demand for revenge went up from every mouth. The sailors immediately armed themselves with revolvers and boarding-hatchets. Leaving two men to guard the ship, they set off for Melbourne.

Farandoul wanted to wait for nightfall before attacking the Aquarium, for fear of raising too great a commotion in Melbourne. This delay proved fatal! The wily Croknuff had had him followed to his ship by one of the Aquarium's keepers. This man, having seen the sailors disembark with obvious hostile intent, had retraced his steps in a hurry in order to warn his master.

Croknuff had lost no time. The Aquarium had been rapidly prepared for its defense. The authorities, forewarned, had sent a battalion of provincial militia to its aid, with two cannons and 40 mounted policemen.

When the shadows of night extended themselves over the city, Farandoul and his little troop marched on the Aquarium. When they arrived, the mariners ran into an armed camp. Farandoul went pale at the sight of the bivouac fires. Nevertheless, he advanced boldly as far as the first guard-post.

"Halt! Who goes there?" shouted the sentries—and, as the mariners continued to advance, a shot was fired in the air.

An officer and several horsemen hastened forward. Farandoul began to negotiate with the officer, and obtained consent to go alone to the threshold of the Aquarium. There he tried to obtain by eloquence what he could not take by force.

It was utterly useless.

"I'm personally very sorry for you, sir," the Colonel said to him, in conclusion, "but I can't grant your desire. I entirely understand that your motives may be respectable, but the law is the law and the property of every Englishman is sacred. As a militiaman, I must protect public safety, and it's my duty to force you to re-embark. at least until you consent to abandon all hostile plans."

"Never! I shall have Mysora, by agreement or by force."

"Then it's war, sir. If you dare to attack, you will find yourself facing all the combined forces of the state of Victoria, Australia and old England!"

"As you say, it's war," Farandoul replied, with grim resolution. "And if I don't attack today, know that you'll lose nothing by waiting. Ah, perfidious Albion, you're protecting a crime, sustaining the oppressors of innocence. The day of vengeance will come, and you shall know the weight of arms borne in a just course! I, Saturnin Farandoul, Captain of *La Belle Léocadie*, declare war on the State of Melbourne—and on Australia and England too, if they so wish! Hear me, soldiers! I tell you that this will soon be a battlefield!"

Saturnin Farandoul and his little troop retraced their steps to the ship. Farandoul, mulling over terrible plans, said not a word on the way.

La Belle Léocadie put on sail the following morning. At the same hour, huge posters were affixed to every wall in Melbourne, bearing the simple words:

WAR TO THE DEATH AGAINST AUSTRALIA.
SATURNIN FARANDOUL.
SEE YOU SOON!

VI.

Three months have gone by since the fatal events that we have related. Sir James Collingham, Her Majesty's Governor of the State of Victoria, is surveying his office in an indescribable state of agitation. Sir James appears distraught; his uniform is unbuttoned, his face has taken on the hue of a cooked lobster and he seems close to collapse. He reads and re-reads dispatches brought in one after another by men as agitated as their commander.

This is what these dispatches say:

Geelong, May 16, 5:45 a.m.
Rumor has it that hordes of armed brigands disembarked last night four miles from here. Have sent for confirmation.

Geelong, May 16, 10:50 a.m.
Fugitives bring news. The disembarkation continues. Brigands marching on Geelong. Militia summoned. Scouts have not returned. Request help.

Geelong, May 16, 11:30 a.m.
Messenger arrived under flag of truce. Sent by Saturnin Farandoul, General-in-Chief of the Oceanian army, who sent declaration of war three months ago. Says he will attack in two hours if we do not surrender. Request help. Urgent.

Geelong, May 16, 2 p.m.
 Attack has begun. Militia falling back to town. Help!

Geelong, May 16, 3:15 p.m.
 Town taken by Farandoulian troops. Station under attack. We are retreating.

Geelong, May 16, 4:50 p.m.
 Colonel Campbell to Governor:
 Arrived too late. Geelong taken by Farandoulian troops; we are covering the retreat. The enemy is coming. Hurrah for old England!

Geelong, May 16, 4:58 p.m.
 Attack begun. Our advance-guard is retreating. Strange! The Farandoulian troops are hairy. Beating a retreat so as not to be cut off by an enemy flanking movement. Losses considerable. Send help.

Melbourne, May 16, 5 p.m.
 Croknuff, Director of the Great Aquarium, to the Governor.

Request permission to establish a battery of torpedoes for the protection of the Aquarium against Farandoulian attack.[20]

Sir James, to avoid suffocation, decides to take off his uniform. Officers press in upon him from every side, some bringing news, others coming in search of orders, all shouting and jostling. Troops are massing in front of the Governor's mansion; dispatch-riders clatter across the pavement; drums beat; clarion calls reverberate.

Heavy artillery-pieces are arriving at the gallop with a terrible racket of bronze and old iron. The lugubrious strokes of the tocsin, sounding in every edifice, can be heard over the uproar, completing the sinister symphony.

The Assembly (the upper chamber) and the Council (the lower chamber) have been urgently summoned to vote through all the defensive measures proposed by the Governor.

The attack has been so sudden that it has thrown everything into disarray. No one has any but the vaguest information about the enemy; nothing is known of its strength or its intentions, for the successive telegrams shed no light on the situation and officers sent out on reconnaissance do not come back.

The Geelong railway has been requisitioned to carry battalions of militia rapidly to the aid of Colonel Campbell, but it is feared that they never arrived, the line having been cut by the enemy in advance of that officer's position.

In the middle of this military tohu-bohu, a carriage arrives at the Governor's mansion. A man gets out and hurries up the grand staircase. It is the editor of the *Melbourne Herald*, the most important newspaper in the state of Victoria. "Where's the Governor?" he shouts, brandishing a piece of paper. "Here's news from Dick Broken, the reporter I sent to Geelong this morning! Do you want the details?"

A group of officers form a circle around the editor of the *Melbourne Herald*; the Governor gives him permission to speak.

"This is the letter from my reporter—listen!

"*Cheep Hill, 5:15 p.m.*

"*Sick at heart, I write to you from the depths of the profoundest astonishment. The sinister rumors that reached Melbourne this morning are not un-*

---

[20] The word "torpedo" originally signified a kind of mine. In 1797, Robert Fulton, an American living in Paris, had volunteered to build a submarine vessel for the French to use against the English; he constructed a vessel called the *Nautilus* in 1800, inventing a "torpedo" for use therewith that consisted of a mine that the vessel was supposed to tow into position (it was never successfully used). The name was subsequently borrowed by Robert Whitehead for a self-propelled mine that he called an "automobile torpedo," and it was that application of the word that eventually became associated with the principal assault weapon employed by actual submarines in the early 20th century.

founded; the enemy has disembarked during the night near Geelong and has seized the town.

"Despite my best efforts, I cannot get into Geelong, which is occupied by Farandoulian troops. The rout of the defenders of that unhappy town has caught me up and carried me several miles back like a torrent. The enemy has lost no time in catching up with us and, as you can imagine, I have made every effort to place myself in the front rank.

"Having forced my horse through the crowd, I soon found myself at the battle-front. The enemy fire was intermittent, sometimes dying away entirely and sometimes sweeping across certain targets with an extraordinary regularity that astonished our old warriors. There was something mechanical about it, something like the rotation, so to speak, of a sewing-machine. I could not make out anything on the enemy side except for the smoke of their guns, and great black masses moving in the distance.

"At 4 p.m., Colonel Campbell's reinforcements arrived; that veteran of the Indian wars, full of confidence, immediately resolved to charge the enemy to resume combat; it goes without saying that I took my place in the attack column.

"I cannot describe the hurricane of fire and steel that was unleashed around us as we formed up; we were advancing regardless, when a wood situated to our left disgorged upon our staggering column an avalanche of warriors protected by huge shields and armed with clubs. Thus we came to see the Farandoulian troops at close range! These warriors were bounding with superhuman vigor, so rapidly that they were on us before we could square up to them. Hardly anyone fired a shot before we had to defend ourselves with bayonets against the demons.

"War cries also sounded to our right, and we soon saw new enemies leaping with extraordinary agility over the closely-pressed ranks of militiamen. It was then, for the first time, that I saw something that terrified me! I rubbed my eyes, but a great cry let loose by the staff officer made me understand that my sight was not at fault! At the same moment, the column fell into total disarray, and the retreat began.

"How can I tell you what we had seen? Expect the most thunderous surprise, the strangest and most frightful revelation! Know, then, that we were beating a retreat before an army of fearsome monkeys! Yes—all those who survive will be able to swear to it—our enemies are monkeys, armed, trained and commanded by regular troops!

"Their leader, of whom I caught a glimpse during the heat of the battle, is none other than the audacious mariner who threatened Melbourne three months ago! My horse having been killed, I had to follow the retreat sitting on a cannon. We have arrived at Cheep Hill, which Colonel Campbell believes he can hold. I shall send news!

"Dick Broken."

Everyone was stunned by this recital. A few officers having expressed doubts, the editor of the *Melbourne Herald* defended his reporter animatedly, while a new dispatch arrived to put paid to the last uncertainties.

It consisted of the following:

Cheep Hill, May 16, 7 p.m.
The monkeys are mounting a flanking movement. We are surrounded. Troops demoralized. Awaiting assault.
Colonel Campbell.

A council of war was immediately assembled. Melbourne was put under martial law; detachments were sent out to scour the country along the Geelong road. Soon, an entire army, comprising militia and volunteers, took up positions in that direction to defend the city.

The night passed without any further news from Cheep Hill. Colonel Campbell's silence caused the Governor tremendous disquiet and foreboding. At 5 a.m., however, the *Melbourne Herald* received a second letter.

Cheep Hill, May 16, 10 p.m.
The dark specter of defeat hovers relentlessly overhead. Cheep Hill is taken; Colonel Campbell has been obliged to surrender.
I am a prisoner of the Farandoulian monkeys. Nevertheless, I will do everything I can to get this letter to you. I told you that Colonel Campbell believed that he could hold his position and keep the monkeys in check long enough to allow the defense of Melbourne to be organized. Our troops, harassed and demoralized, camped on the hill while the Colonel established his general quarters

in the buildings of Cheep Hill Farm. Large woods enveloped the hill to our rear and Colonel Campbell counted on taking refuge there in case of a reverse.

Unfortunately, the darkness of these woods also served to hide a flanking movement which the left wing of the monkeys' army carried out—with a rapidity that no longer astonishes us now that we know our enemy—while our troops were drawing breath. The battle recommenced at the center of the position at about 7 p.m.; our rested militiamen did their best and we began to feel hope reborn in our hearts, when catastrophe suddenly overtook us.

Everyone was facing the enemy, fighting amid a chorus of hurrahs for old England. All of a sudden, loud cries were raised in the tops of the trees to the rear of our position. Every head turned that way. By the rays of the setting Sun, we were affrighted to see the legion of our enemies bearing down on us, leaping from crown to crown.

The foliage of every tree was swarming with howling and grimacing enemies; the very forest seemed to be alive, marching upon us as in Macbeth, but we had scarcely time to think. The monkeys, arriving at the last trees, leapt into our ranks, screeching frightfully and whirling their heavy clubs. Minute by minute, further battalions of monkeys leapt upon us from the heights of the eucalyptus and gum-trees, belaboring our troops with irresistible force.

Campbell's dragoons attempted a charge, but the monkeys, jumping on the horses' rumps, toppled the riders and came at us again with even greater impetuosity.

At that moment, the Farandoulians we had been facing also broke through our lines. I was able to see, in the midst of the heat of battle, a troop of monkeys protected by long ironwood shields advancing in regular formation, while other quadrumanes [21]—probably members of an elite corps, armed with rifles and commanded by men in bright uniforms—spread out as sharpshooters.

Colonel Campbell formed a second front in order to try to face up to all our enemies. We were obviously lost! Suddenly, a strident shout let loose by their leader—whom I recognized to be the terrible Farandoul—cut through the tumult of the battle. At that signal, the fight ceased; a monkey waving a white flag came forward, at the same time as Farandoul moved his horse towards us.

"Soldiers, it's time to stop the bloodshed," he shouted. "You're surrounded. Surrender!"

Colonel Campbell gave the order to cease fire and went to meet him. Covered in blood like a wounded lion, the old warrior was determined to sell his

---

[21] Quadrumanes are those mammals in which the feet are formed rather like hands—including all primates except man. Robida subsequently invents the word bimanes—which will similarly do as well in English as in French—for application to humans, in order to promote the idea that quadrumanes and bimanes are different but equal contingents of primatekind.

own life dearly, but he wished at least to try to save the lives of what remained of his army.

"Colonel," Farandoul said to him, "continuing the fight will serve no purpose. You are surrounded by 20,000 monkeys, and more reinforcements will reach me tonight. Lay down your arms. I promise to treat you with all due consideration to your bravery."

The old warrior, in tears, decided to capitulate. An agreement was rapidly concluded and the troops, now prisoners of war, surrendered their arms to the monkeys.

Such were the events which will go down in history as the battle and surrender of Cheep Hill.

I am being held prisoner with the staff-officers. Our surgeons are dressing the wounds of both armies. The monkeys, so terrible in battle, now seem very amiable, and full of concern for our wellbeing. I will even say that they seem to me to be rather good chaps.

The most perfect order is maintained in their army. I was able to catch a glimpse of General Farandoul. He is very busy, but he has promised me a brief interview. I will send you all the details and provoke as many indiscretions as I can.

Dick Broken

P.S. I have had a chat with Colonel Mandibul, General Farandoul's chief staff-officer. He has told me the curious details of the composition of the Farandoulian army. The main body of the army is composed of monkeys from Borneo and New Guinea; the elite troops armed with new machine-guns of Farandoul's own design—which explains the sewing-machine sound I mentioned this morning—come from an island where General Farandoul spent his childhood. These monkeys obey their leaders with a discipline that the best European troops would envy. The General is the idol of his army.

A special edition of the *Melbourne Herald* appeared at 8 a.m. on May 17. The disastrous news imparted by the courageous reporter's remarkable letters threw the entire city into the greatest confusion.

The most distraught of all the citizens of Melbourne was most certainly the scientist Mr. Croknuff. Mounted on a little pony, hired for that purpose, despite his distaste for equitation, he was galloping towards the Governor's general quarters to assure himself of the veracity of the facts. He had no need to question the officers at length to bring himself up to date. A loud fusillade from the advance-posts apprised him of the situation sufficiently. He dug his spurs into the flanks of his steed and turned back towards the Aquarium, bouncing in his saddle.

The environs of the Aquarium had altered considerably since the preceding day. An immense moat, six meters deep and 15 wide, guarded the approach. Hundreds of workmen were occupied in using the earth excavated from the trench to construct a rampart bastioned in the regulation manner. Others were crenellating the walls of the Aquarium. In advance of all these projects, an engineer—a friend of Mr. Croknuff's—had prepared mine-chambers connected by electrical wiring to the Director's office.

Mr. Croknuff went into the grounds. Leaping swiftly from the saddle—which was scarcely difficult, as his feet were almost touching the ground—he advanced upon the laborers.

"Is the moat ready?" he asked.

"Yes sir, it's all ready; the pipes carrying the water are fully functional."

"It's just as well. Give the signal—the enemy's drawing near!"

At a blast from the foreman's whistle, the dam was opened and water—brought directly from the sea by a subterranean canal to serve the Aquarium's needs—poured into the moat, which was soon full. To complete the grounds' defenses, Mr. Croknuff released his famous whale from its tank in the aquarium, along with two little Javanese sharks and a dozen giant octopodes.[22] These redoubtable animals, happy to have more room, were soon swimming in the moat, thus rendering it impossible to cross. Mr. Croknuff was obviously neglecting no opportunity in recruiting his inmates to the defense of the Aquarium.

Mr. Croknuff felt that he was under a greater threat than any other citizen of Melbourne, because he understood that this terrible war had been ignited by him—by his obstinate refusal to surrender Mysora. Mr. Croknuff was utterly determined—victory or death! The Great Aquarium of Melbourne would not capitulate!

What, meanwhile, had become of poor Mysora? The unfortunate girl had not left her moist abode for three months. She, too, was resolute, and nothing—neither pleas nor threats—could make her give way. She had decided that she would rather spend her life in her underwater grotto than ever consent to become Mrs. Croknuff, as the horrid old scientist incessantly pressed her to do,

In three months, Mr. Croknuff had been changed out of all recognition. His heart burned white hot within his breast. A few hairs, favored by this interior climate, had even contrived to reappear upon his cranium. For three months his every waking moment had been consecrated to the tank in which the poor girl languished, in company with the whale that was the cause of all her troubles.

Mr. Croknuff spent his days on the platform of the aquarium, trying to soften Mysora's heart. Needless to say, all his arguments were in vain. They were, in any case, in English, and Mysora only understood Malay. The poor girl, with unparalleled constancy, passed her days in walking back and forth across the aquarium in order to give herself a little exercise. By night she retired to her lit-

---

[22] *Pieuvres* is used here rather than the more familiar *poulpes*, but both words are applied indiscriminately by the French to octopodes and squids; a more detailed reference in the next chapter specifies that one of the creatures in question has eight limbs, so "octopodes" is clearly the preferable translation.

tle grotto, wanting to be alone in order to think of her beloved Farandoul without being troubled by curiosity-seekers.

Mr. Croknuff, of course, did not neglect to carry her meals up to the platform of the aquarium. He soon began taking his own in the same place at the same time, but Mysora immediately quit his company whenever he risked repeating his passionate declarations. She had to do that more than once to put an end to such assaults, threatening with expressive gestures to cut the tube that supplied her with breathable air.

Mysora, who expected every day to be saved by Farandoul, understood when she saw Croknuff fortifying the Aquarium that her beloved was coming. Her heart beat faster; the final hour of her ordeal had sounded, and she had to be ready for anything!

At noon on May 17, Mr. Croknuff went up to the roof of the Aquarium and anxiously followed the vicissitudes of the fervent fighting just outside Melbourne along the Geelong road. Rifle-shots and cannon-fire made the walls of the Aquarium tremble on their foundations; it was obvious that the battle was drawing nearer. Retreating soldiers were beginning to flock back to the streets of Melbourne, their tales of terror spreading through the city. Seeing that the moment of truth was approaching, Mr. Croknuff gave the order to raise the drawbridge and sent his defenders to their posts.

At that moment, some newspaper-sellers appeared, announcing a new edition of the *Melbourne Herald*. Mr. Croknuff called out to one of the criers and asked for a copy. The vendor attached the paper to a piece of string lowered from the rampart, whereupon one of the sharks in the moat leapt out of the water and snapped at him. Fortunately, the poor man fell back in fright, and the greedy monster caught nothing but his bag of papers—which it swallowed, for want of anything better.

On the first page of the paper, with headlines in large letters, were the following communications from the valiant reporter Dick Broken:

Cheep Hill, May 17, 3 a.m.
General Farandoul.
I chatted with General Farandoul, the terrible leader of the monkeys, for a quarter of an hour. He is still quite young, but his forehead seems to be marked with the seal of genius. By some unknown means, he has become the instructor and commander of an army of monkeys whose devotion to his person is absolute.

His special guard consists of 200 quadrumanes whom he knows very intimately, having apparently spent his childhood with them.
The Farandoulian troops.
At the present time some 40,000 monkeys have disembarked, divided into several brigades commanded by the former mariners of the three-master La Belle Léocadie.

82

The Enemy's Intentions.

General Farandoul is determined to carry out, with his forces and those he expects: The Conquest of Australia!

The vast project bubbling in his head is the dream of founding an Oceanian Empire in Melbourne; he wishes to bring the simian race—which he calls a race of "imperfect men"—to civilization, bringing it nearer to the human race.

If England does not come immediately to our aid, no one can tell whether Farandoul might not become the Alexander and the Caesar of the fifth continent.

Stand up, men of free Australia, to block the road of conquest!

Cheep Hill, 3:15 a.m.

The Farandoulian troops, harangued by their General, are marching enthusiastically along the road to Melbourne. Colonel Mandibul is in command of the advance guard. Commandant Kirkson has been ordered to take the prisoners of Campbell's corps to Geelong.

I shall try to escape.

Outside Melbourne, 7 a.m.

Thanks to my knowledge of the country I was able to escape from Cheep Hill, and this morning I reached the advance posts of the Australian army, in the midst of the greatest dangers. The battle is joined. The Farandoulians, I regret to say, are gaining ground with every minute that passes, in spite of the heroic bravery of our troops.

Melbourne, 7:25 a.m.

Governor Collingham and his staff have been surprised and routed by an unexpected attack by monkeys falling from the treetops, like that which happened yesterday at Cheep Hill. The army is falling back in disarray towards Melbourne. I am in the thick of the brawl, taking notes for your benefit. We must prepare to fight from house to house, as at Saragossa! [23] We must bury ourselves beneath the ruins of Melbourne like the Greeks at Missolonghi! [24] To arms!

---

[23] The Spanish city of Saragossa was besieged by the French army in 1808-09, offering unexpectedly heroic resistance after Madrid capitulated to Napoleon in December 1808. The future Duke of Wellington landed at Lisbon in 1809 to begin the campaign which eventually put an end to Napoleon's Empire, so the timing of the siege was highly significant, although Saragossa itself was of no particular military importance.

[24] Missolonghi, where Byron died, suffered a long siege by Ibrahim, the son of Mohammed Ali of Egypt, during the Greek war of liberation, before it fell in 1826.

I will send you the WHOLE story, with TERRIFYING DETAILS of atrocious, heroic and comical episodes, etc, etc, for the afternoon edition.

ANNOUNCE to your readers that a SUPPLEMENT with a literal account of ATROCITIES will appear TOMORROW; I shall make every effort to ensure that I shall be present at every one.

Mr. Croknuff had scarcely finished reading when violent detonations resounded at the end of the avenue. It was an artillery battery attempting to cover the retreat and stop the attackers. There was no longer any hope of that; the fight was on! Thanks to his spectacles, Mr. Croknuff clearly saw a troop of bounding apes fall upon the battery and take possession of it. Standing on his rampart, Mr. Croknuff harangued his men, demanding that they should fight to the last breath, to be buried with him, if it should come to that, beneath the ruins of the Aquarium!

A great hurrah went up in response, and they waited for the attack. Hours went by as innumerable monkeys filed past the end of the avenue and spread out into the city, where the battle still continued in a few places. Then the gunfire dwindled away, eventually ceasing for good at about 4 p.m.

The entire city was in the hands of the Farandoulians, who proceeded to disarm its inhabitants. Only a few patrols of monkeys were visible. As dusk fell, Mr. Croknuff perceived that the posts protecting his Aquarium were the last points at which the English flag still flew.

At daybreak the following morning, the *Melbourne Herald* came out again. A vendor brought one all the way to the Aquarium. It contained the following proclamations:

RESIDENTS!

The line attaching Australia to England is broken!

The old name is abolished.

The country will take the name of: FARANDOULIA (THE OCEANIAN EMPIRE).

His Majesty Saturnin I, its august founder, will take the title THE MONKEY KING.

Men and monkeys are henceforth equal before the law.

Parliamentary rule is abolished.

The provincial militias are dissolved.

The permanent army will be composed entirely of monkeys.

General Mandibul is appointed governor of Melbourne.

Issued to Melbourne at the general quarters of the Farandoulian armies.

On May 17,

Saturnin I

BIMANES OF MELBOURNE

His Majesty Saturnin I, whose heart is overflowing with sentiments of affection for all the subjects of his vast empire, whether they be bimanes or quadrumanes, invites you to be the first to offer to the world the noble example of true fraternity!

Live henceforth in peace with your formerly-disinherited brothers, the noble and generous monkeys who, brought up in the forests from generation to generation, have not been able, as you have, to partake of the banquet of civilization.

Though their manners are as yet unpolished, their hearts remain pure and good; they have forgotten the injuries done to their brothers and are ready to extend the hand of friendship as a sign of reconciliation.

Bimanes of Melbourne, resume the course of your everyday labors in peace, under the protection of the quadrumane armies.

The prosperity of the country will achieve new and greater heights. The united bimanes and quadrumanes will soon astonish the Old World and conquer it with new ideas!

At the Mansion of the Governor of Melbourne,
May 17,
General Mandibul
Colonel Makako, Monkey Representative of Borneo
Colonel Tapa-Tapa, Monkey Representative of New Guinea

All bimanes who continue to resist the Farandoulian troops will be brought before a military tribunal.

The bimane Croknuff, Director of the Great Melbourne Aquarium, will lay down his arms before noon if he does not wish to be treated with the full rigor of military law.

Melbourne, May 17,
General Mandibul
Colonel Makako
Colonel Tapa-Tapa

VII.

On reading these proclamations, the bimane Croknuff became green with rage. The Aquarium's downcast keepers seemed disposed to obey the orders of General Mandibul; since all other resistance had ceased, they wanted to know why their Director was so stubbornly determined to fight. A few of them were appointed spokesmen by their comrades, but Mr. Croknuff cut them off.

"Degenerate sons of old England!" he cried. "I won't keep you. Go! Run away! Desert! Abandon the flag of the Motherland! I shall defend it alone, to the death! Tell the invaders that the Great Aquarium of Melbourne will die rather than surrender!"

The employees did not need to be told twice. The drawbridge was lowered in an eye-blink and they all left the enclosure, having disposed of their weapons. Mr. Croknuff, from the top of the rampart, saw them arrive at the first post and observed the felicitations addressed to them by the monkeys by means of hearty handshakes.

From now on, he was alone at his station—alone with Mysora. Australia had but one defender: the heroic Croknuff!

Fortunately, Mr. Croknuff felt that he was well-nigh invulnerable. The approaches to the fortress were garnished with carefully-disposed torpedoes. His moat, defended by the whale, the sharks and the octopodes, was uncrossable. Finally, as a last resort, a mine-chamber charged with 15 kilos of dynamite had been excavated beneath the directorial office. Mr. Croknuff experienced a certain sensual thrill at the thought that if he were blown up, he would be blown up in company with Mysora.

In the afternoon, the monkeys gathered at the end of the avenue. Mr. Croknuff could see, with perfect distinction, Saturnin I giving orders to his brightly-clad staff. Oh, if he only had artillery, what a pleasure it would have been to shower his enemy with grape-shot!

When monkey scouts advanced cautiously to the wall surrounding the grounds, Mr. Croknuff afforded himself the pleasure of exploding one of his torpedoes under their feet. The unfortunate monkeys were hurled into the air, but their commandant—our old friend from *La Belle Léocadie*, Seaman Tournesol—escaped safe and sound, and went to make his report to Farandoul.

Mr. Croknuff having imprudently revealed his batteries, Farandoul postponed his attack.

When night fell, Mr. Croknuff found it inconvenient to have to guard such a considerable expanse of ramparts all by himself. He had to march back and forth all night along the length of his fortifications, rifle in hand, keeping a sharp look-out. When morning approached, he could not stay there. Being unable to see any preparations being made outside for an attack, he lay down on some sandbags. One eye closed, then the other, and he fell into a profound sleep.

He slept very badly! He dreamed that he was the monkeys' prisoner and that Farandoul had him impaled for display in a new Museum of Natural History. Little monkeys came to this Museum to listen to educational lectures on mankind. As the carefully-pinned-up Croknuff served as a subject for the professor's demonstrations, Farandoul and Mysora walked past wearing diving-suits and laughingly pointed him out to their children, who were similarly clad. This horrid spectacle made Mr. Croknuff cry out in alarm and wake up.

Horror! His dream was on the way to realization. The monkeys were surrounding the Aquarium, silently preparing to mount an assault. In advance of the monkeys, men dressed in diving-suits were descending into the moat.

Saturnin I had correctly reckoned that Mr. Croknuff, left alone in his fortress, could not mount a sufficient guard. He had assumed that fatigue would overcome the scientist at the end of the night, and all preparations had been made to profit from this opportunity. In the final hours of darkness, a battalion of monkeys had advanced upon the Aquarium, carrying ladders, wooden beams with which to make bridges, and brushwood to heap up in the moat.

Saturnin, Mandibul and four monkeys, having put on diving-suits, had descended into the moat—repelling the attacks of the Javanese sharks with their air-pistols—in order to fix large beams in place between the two banks. As for the whale, needless to say, it had fled to the far end of the semicircle at the first sight of the diving-suits. It was at the very moment that the monkeys were arriving at the foot of the bastion that Mr. Croknuff awoke. It required 30 seconds of rubbing his eyes and pinching himself to ascertain that he was not still impaled—and that was sufficient time for the monkeys to deploy their ladders.

As they mounted their deliberate assault, giving voice to their war-cry, Mr. Croknuff rediscovered his courage. He seized a ladder and, with a superhuman effort, he pushed it aside, along with all those it carried. The cries were redoubled—the ladder had collided with others as it fell, toppling scores of assailants—but it did not put an end to the escalade. The monkeys, by grace of their natural agility, had nothing to fear from heavy falls; they got up again and resumed their charge with increased vigor.

It was a success. The first line of defense was breached.

Mr. Croknuff, beside himself with rage, howled as he saw that he was on the point of being surrounded by monkeys that were leaping on to the rampart simultaneously from 15 ladders. To perish thus, without vengeance! That single thought gave him the strength of ten, and with a great leap he threw himself backwards into the Aquarium building, whose door he scarcely had time to barricade.

There was only a moment's respite. The second line of defense would be stormed soon enough—but that respite, brief as it was, was sufficient for the enraged Croknuff to put his final plan into operation!

Standing in his directorial office, in the center of the tanks of his aquarium, facing the terrified Mysora, he waited for Farandoul and the monkeys, in order to blow himself up along with them. A single movement of his hand, and 15 kilos of dynamite, bursting forth like a volcano, would rise 1000 feet into the air, along with the wreckage of the Aquarium, its assailants and the last citizen of free Australia.

Outside, the monkeys discussed the situation. Farandoul broke down the door with two blows of a hatchet and came into the building alone. Realizing that the old scientist, in his despair, might commit some act of savagery, he wanted to make one last attempt at conciliation before risking everything to tear Mysora from Mr. Croknuff's grasp. With a single glance, he measured the full extent of the danger. In the horrible rictus disfiguring Croknuff's face, he read the manifest hope of a terrible vengeance and a fatal resolution—and Mysora was there, behind the pane of glass, holding out her trembling hands towards him.

"There's still time!" he cried to the scientist. "Give in, and give me Mysora, and I'll make you Minister of Public Education! All resistance is useless. In a minute, the Aquarium and everyone in it will be in my power, and it will be too late to ask for mercy. Give me Mysora!"

"Come and get her!" Croknuff yelled.

Farandoul realized that only an attack of lightning rapidity could prevent Croknuff from doing any harm. He stepped back to the door and issued an order to his troops. A single voice replied, and the aquarium was invaded in less than a second. Meanwhile, ten monkeys who had been placed at each window were smashing every one—including the walls of the tanks—with single blows of heavy wooden beams. Farandoul and Mandibul launched hatchet-blows at Mysora's aquarium, which no one had dared to breach with a beam.

The entire building made a cracking sound, as if it were about to collapse. A torrent of water gushed from the tanks broken by the beams—and in Croknuff's office, all the inmates of the Aquarium were swarming around the legs of the semi-submerged scientist.

"Hurrah for old England!" Croknuff howled, hurling himself towards his dynamite. "Hurrah! Hurrah! Hurrah!" His lifted arm was about to come down, and his mine was about to do its work, when a hideous creature rose up from the debris of one of the tanks smashed by the monkeys' beams, and fell upon him.

It was his giant octopus—his favorite, before the arrival of the whale—which tore at him with its four pairs of arms and its innumerable suckers!

The octopus held him firmly; he was about to perish in its grip or be drowned in his office.

Mysora was about to escape him...

Mr. Croknuff turned his head towards her. Farandoul having broken the wall of the tank with their hatchet-blows, Mysora had thrown herself into the arms of her triumphant fiancé. Farandoul and Mandibul were dragging her outside...

With a last desperate effort, Croknuff disengaged his arms from the grip of the octopus and triggered the mine-chamber.

A frightful shock shook the ground; a terrible detonation resounded. A jet of flame burst forth like a waterspout. The Aquarium exploded!

Walls, tanks, fish, monkeys—the entire edifice and all those contained within it—were projected violently into the air by the explosion. Their scattered debris strewn across the grounds, forming a circle with a radius of a mile.

Croknuff and his octopus, still locked in their embrace, were seen being lifted aloft amid splinters of wood, at the center of a vortex of fire.

For several minutes, the survivors of this disaster were unable to get their bearings. A cloud of black smoke ascended from the ruins of the Aquarium. The first to speak was an individual who emerged from the moat wearing a blackened diving-suit.

"Help us, *La Belle Léocadie*!" he cried. "There's work to be done here!"

This person was General Mandibul, last seen with Farandoul, who was carrying poor near-dead Mysora, when the mine exploded. Since he had been able to come safe and sound through the fiery furnace, there was still hope for the two young lovers. Mariners and monkeys threw themselves in unison towards the moat.

A hand emerged from the water, then a head, and Farandoul appeared, supporting Mysora's inanimate body. Twenty arms were extended towards him to help him scale the slope with his precious burden.

Farandoul laid Mysora on the ground and anxiously unfastened the young woman's helmet.

This is what had happened:

Profiting from the interval when Croknuff was grappling with his octopus, Farandoul and Mandibul had got through the door with Mysora. The explosion had caught them on the rampart and had precipitated them into the moat while all those who were still inside the building had been blown up with Croknuff.

No sooner had they concluded that they were saved, when the sharks and the whale, terrified by the explosion, had passed over them like a cavalry charge, knocking them down. In the confusion, Mysora's air-tube had been severed, and the poor girl had collapsed in Farandoul's arms.

While the survivors collect themselves and take stock of the situation in the disaster area, a silent group now surrounds Farandoul and his fiancée.

Mandibul is standing up, his arms crossed, in the grip of bitter grief. A few monkeys, scorched and blackened, burned in places, exchange sad glances. Farandoul's brothers wring their hands and a few large but furtive tears roll down the tanned cheeks of the former mariners of *La Belle Léocadie*.

Mysora is laid out on the grass, her unbound hair hanging loose about her shoulders, still clad in her diving-suit, her eyes seemingly closed forever! Farandoul has flung his diving helmet away. Kneeling beside the young woman, he searches for the slightest sign of life—one last hope!

Every assistance has been rendered in vain. Alas, Mysora is no more. The horrid Croknuff has not released his prey; his laughing shade may savor at leisure the grief of the unfortunate Farandoul.

O Mysora! Pure soul, enraptured at such a tender age by the enchantments of life, the love of your fiancé, the glorious Saturnin Farandoul, conqueror of Australia, the Alexander of the fifth continent... Your memory, O Mysora, will hover eternally above that distant land, which your chaste face has poeticized. Many tears will be shed in future ages over the tale of your misfortunes; many hearts will beat faster for the sad Mysora. In the same way that strangers with sensitive souls search the undergrowth of the Ile de France for the resting-place of Virginie,[25] so will travelers whose business brings them to Australia turn aside from their routes to make pious pilgrimages to the tomb of Mysora!

But let us pass swiftly over these dolorous facts, lest our souls grow sad and our minds become afflicted by cruel memories.

Let us merely say that, as soon as he was certain of his ill-fortune, Farandoul recovered his strength and courage. His robust spirit resurfaced. He felt that, above all else, he had a duty to his troops and to the security of the con-

---

[25] *Paul et Virginie* (1788) by Jacques-Henri Bernardin de Saint-Pierre is one of the classic French tragic romances. Having been brought up together on the Ile de France (Mauritius), the eponymous couple are separated when Virginie is sent away to be educated in France. She steadfastly refuses to marry anyone except Paul, although her relatives in France think him far below her social status. The ship which eventually carries Virginie back to the Ile de France is wrecked as it approaches the shore; modesty compels her to refuse the help of a lustful sailor and she is drowned. Paul dies of grief shortly afterwards. Robida apparently agrees with those cynical readers who thought the tale a trifle overwrought; Jules Verne, of course, rarely permitted his explorers and scientists any romantic distraction from the serious business of discovery.

quest for which he had paid so dearly. After giving orders for Mysora's corpse to be carried with great ceremony to the gubernatorial mansion, Farandoul and Mandibul mounted their horses—without bothering to take off their diving-suits—in order to make a rapid review of the encampments of the Farandoulian army.

As trumpets and drums rallied the troops, the monkeys formed ranks and the column set out to march to the Parliament building, where it was based. Soon, no one remained in the smoking ruins of the Aquarium but a sentry charged with preventing bimanes from coming too close.

That day, every Farandoulian position saw the staff of its bimane leaders arrive like a whirlwind. The troops greeted their beloved General with cries and dances of enthusiasm, still unaware of the poignant grief that made Farandoul weep within the helmet of his diving-suit. Overcoming his emotion, Farandoul took every necessary precaution to ensure the well-being and security of his devoted quadrumanes.

Melbourne's barracks being inadequate, Mandibul had thought of billeting the monkeys with the local population, and several regiments were already established in the homes of private individuals—but it was necessary to drop the idea, difficulties having cropped up with cantankerous folk who whined about tyranny and fainted away at the sight of the arrival in their homes of a dozen brave monkeys and a couple of quadrumane officers carrying billets for three days lodgings! In order not to offend the feminine part of the population, they contented themselves with occupying public buildings, and Farandoul gave orders for the establishment of a temporary camp in the Melbourne suburbs.

VIII.

No resistance had any longer to be feared within the Victoria colony. Before throwing himself into the conquest of the other Australian states, Farandoul judged that it would be sensible to complete the re-organization of the conquered province. He had cleared away its old institutions and was enthusiastic to establish new ones, in keeping with its new situation. A great conference was held in the gubernatorial mansion on the evening after Mysora's funeral.

Ambition was now the sole forceful sustenance of Farandoul's heart. He was determined to establish solid foundations for the empire that his valor was to carve out of the Australian continent. The participants in the conference were General Mandibul, the crew of *La Belle Léocadie*, and—to preserve good diplomatic relations—the leaders of the various monkey army corps.

"Bimanes and quadrumanes," said Farandoul, opening the session, "my dear comrades, I ought to begin by giving you a brief account of the exact situation. Having landed with 40,000 monkeys, we have gained possession of Melbourne in three days. The militias have been disarmed and the inhabitants subjugated; the entire province is in our power.

"Reinforcements will soon arrive; I estimate them at 10,000 monkeys, increasing our forces to 50,000 combatants. That should be sufficient for anything, even to repulse any counter-offensive by the British. But get this firmly into your heads, comrades: it is by discipline alone that we shall be able to found something durable. It is by valor regulated by discipline that we have triumphed; it is by conserving that discipline that we shall ensure the destiny of Farandoulia forever.

"Today, the bimanes of Australia, crushed and terrified by the suddenness of our victory, still regard us as victorious invaders. These attitudes must be subtly changed, so that they will come to feel that their destiny is linked to ours by a common interest. Tomorrow, under our protection, commerce and industry must begin anew; we must encourage that renaissance with a friendly attitude.

"Our leaders must be vigilant, to ensure that no bimane is molested, and that no disputes arise. Until public services can be organized, food and equipment requisitioned for the army will be paid for in bonds drawn on the future Ministry of Finance. Once again, bimanes and quadrumanes, I insist that the strictest equity be maintained in relations with the local people, and the most exact discipline in every detail of service."

The next day's *Melbourne Herald* acquainted the population with the decisions taken at this conference. At the head of its political section it featured the following decree:

The province of Farandoulia known by the name of the State of Victoria is partitioned into five military divisions.
General Mandibul, governor of Melbourne, takes command of the first.[26]
The bimanes Kirkson, Tournesol, Trabadec, Escoubico, colonels of the Farandoulian army, are named commandants of the second, third, fourth and fifth divisions, with the quadrumanes Lutungo of Java, Ungko of Sumatra, Nasico of Borneo and Wa-Wo-Wa of New Guinea as chiefs of staff.
Saturnin I.

The *Melbourne Herald* followed these decrees with a series of biographical notes on the bimanes and quadrumanes appointed to these high positions. It was, of course, the indefatigable Dick Broken who had obtained all this information,

---

[26] Robida forgets to mention here the rather important fact that Colonel Makako is Mandibul's second-in-command, although he includes Makako in the sequence of biographies that follows. Tapa-Tapa, the other quadrumane co-signatory of Saturnin I's initial decrees, is also absent from the list of appointments, although he is similarly included in the biographies—unlike Makako, however, he has no further role to play in the story.

his acquaintance with General Mandibul—begun on the evening of the battle of Cheep Hill—having made him better-known than anyone else to the leaders of the Farandoulian troops.

Here are the notices in question:

Bimane General Mandibul

General Mandibul is the former lieutenant of La Belle Léocadie. *He is a man of 45 years, well-preserved but a little overweight. He has a slightly apoplectic temperament, but has a genuine martial bearing when in uniform. His well-known modesty having forbidden him to give us any biographical details, we shall restrict ourselves to recalling, without mention of anterior campaigns, that he covered himself in glory throughout the conquest, from the first landing of the Farandoulians to the terrible assault on the Great Aquarium, where the last champion of England, the unfortunate and heroic Croknuff, was blown up rather than lower the flag. The appeasement measures taken by the Governor of Melbourne are a certain guarantee of his pure intentions towards us and clear testimony as to his considerable wisdom.*

Quadrumane Colonel Makako

Colonel Makako is a monkey from the southern part of Borneo. He is a tall fellow with a very intelligent and animated face. His father, an old patriarch, has led a number of bellicose tribes for many years in their continual wars against the Dayaks. It is rumored that Colonel Makako is very ambitious and some say that his father was not sorry to see him depart with 600 of his most turbulent monkeys. At any rate, he is an authentic feudal overlord, ruling his monkeys with the total authority of a despot.

Quadrumane Colonel Tapa-Tapa
A Sumatran monkey. An amiable and playful character, he has none of the stiffness of his colleague Makako. He has joined the Farandoulian army with a contingent of 800 monkeys, making up part of an entrepreneurial nation that lives on relatively good terms with the bimanes of Sumatra. Tapa-Tapa's compatriots, quitting the interior forests, are gradually coming closer to the towns. Several districts of Siak and Achem [27] are entirely inhabited by them; at Palembang, they have acquired the same rights as the bourgeoisie of the city and live in the same houses as the bimanes, who occupy the ground floors while renting the upper floors to quadrumanes. In sum, Colonel Tapa-Tapa, a simple fellow and a good chap, is entirely in sympathy with us. His monkeys were the first to fraternize with bimanes.

Colonel Kirkson.   Colonel Lutungo.   Colonel Ungko.   Colonel Tournesol

Bimane Colonel Kirkson
Tall, strong, ruddy-faced, bearded, Anglo-Saxon in origin but absolutely devoted to Saturnin I. Distinguished himself in many battles, notably in the cam-

---

[27] Siak and Achem (or Achin), were two of the old Sultanates of Sumatra. Achem, situated in the northern part of the island, became a Dutch dependency in 1873 following a violent conflict. Siak, on the east coast, was similarly gathered into the Dutch fold, although the sultan retained some power until 1946. Palembang, mentioned later in the paragraph, remains an important city in the south of the island to this day.

paign mounted by the mariners of La Belle Léocadie *against the pirates of the Isles of Sunda.*

Quadrumane Colonel Lutungo of Java

A big monkey, five feet four inches in height, with greying fur. He is the chief or sultan of a tribe of large langurs [28] *spread throughout the interior mountains of Java. He has a very grand air about him,* [29] *his features are imprinted with a calm dignity in perfect accordance with his aristocratic manners; one immediately senses, on seeing him for the first time, that one is dealing with a monkey with breeding. His family have reigned in Java for many years over more than a dozen large villages whose inhabitants number 300 or 400. He has furnished the Farandoulian army with a contingent of 350 fighters.*

Colonel Trabadec.   Colonel Nasico.   Colonel Wa-Wo-Wa.   Colonel Escoubico.

Bimane Colonel Tournesol

Born June 26, 18**, in Marseilles, France; was granted entry into the merchant marine with the rank of cabin boy; has served with honor aboard La Belle Léocadie, *notably against the pirates, at least 40 of whom he (to use his own picturesque expression) "de-carcassed." Commanded the monkey advance-guard at Cheep Hill alongside one of His Majesty Saturnin I's brothers; took the English ex-Governor, Sir John Collingham, prisoner during the capture of Mel-*

---

[28] The text has *semnopithéque*; the genus Semnopithecus seems to be identical to the modern genus Presbytis, which consists of the langur monkeys.
[29] *Grand air*, which I have conserved from the original text, usually means "open air" in French; the wordplay is untranslatable.

bourne. Short, thin, swarthy, black-bearded, plain-speaking, very pronounced Marseillaise accent.

Colonel Ungko of Sumatra

As calm as his leader is exuberant. Who could believe, on first seeing that tranquil and reflective face, that one is face to face with the leader of the most intrepid escaladers: those monkey acrobats used to living in the highest regions of the forest. His troops are the trapeze-artists of the Farandoulian army; it was they who, passing with the greatest rapidity from tree to tree, executed the outflanking and overhanging maneuvers which baffled the experienced bimane tacticians of England. Colonel Ungko, an innocent in polite society, is transformed in action, becoming the terrible warrior that we know.

Colonel Bimane Trabadec

Thirty-two years old, short and stocky, born in Saint-Malo, France; full of genuine veneration for His Majesty Saturnin I, swearing by none but he and Notre-Dame-d'Auray.[30] As intrepid on the field of battle as he is gentle and simple in private life. Declares himself ready, since His Majesty has spoken of the fusion of races, to marry a she-monkey of good family. Says he will send to Saint-Malo for his documents.

Quadrumane Colonel Nasico of Borneo

An exceedingly intelligent quadrumane, remarkable for the amplitude of his forehead and the altogether human length of his nose. A tribal chief, a monkey of good family. According to the Indians, his nation is descended from a company of men driven out of the towns by war, who—turning their backs on the world—must have chosen their wives from a tribe of hospitable monkeys. Nasico is directly descended from the leader of these men; at any rate, power has been in the hands of his family for many years. What seems to confer a certain authenticity on this legend is that the 500 monkeys who have followed Nasico are just as remarkable as he is; their well-developed noses project nobly from faces fully-framed by fine red beards.

---

[30] Auray is a port on the southern coast of Brittany (Saint-Malo being on the north coast). It was a center of Vendean resistance to the Revolution of 1789; the notorious Breton general Georges Cadoudal—who appointed himself Napoleon's would-be nemesis, involving himself in several assassination plots, including the affair of *la machine infernale*—was born near Auray and would also have sworn by Notre-Dame-d'Auray. Saturnin Farandoul obviously commanded broader loyalty at this point in his imperial adventure than his august predecessor was ever able to contrive.

Bimane Colonel Escoubico

Spanish by birth, a remarkably ardent man, as indefatigable in war as in pleasure. Makes his troops march to the sound of music. As soon as he entered Melbourne, he requisitioned tambourines and guitars; together with a few monkeys endowed with a talent for harmony he quickly formed a corps of excellent musicians. Proposes to host balls in his residence.

Quadrumane Colonel Wa-Wo-Wa of New Guinea

The best of monkeys. Simple, rustic, honest. Straight by nature, ever amiable, occasionally jovial. Leader of one of the greatest simian nations of Oceania, closely related to the tribe with which H. M. Saturnin I spent his childhood. Wa-Wo-Wa's contingent is also one of the most numerous. This brave leader's monkeys form, so to speak, the line troops of the Farandoulian army. If they are less accomplished in advance-guard attacks and brilliant charges than those of Colonel Ungko, their finest quality is their resilience; at the end of the day, as old soldiers say, they stick to their guns!

Some weeks later, three persons came together in conference with Saturnin I in His Majesty's office in the former Governor's mansion. These three individuals were General Mandibul, Farandoul's foster-father and the journalist Dick Broken.

"Yes, my friends," Farandoul said, "I see our mission clearly—the mission of Farandoulia, the world's fifth continent,[31] so young and so healthy! To repair the injustices of other continents; to cause the past to be forgotten; to bring back justice and happiness and restore the globe's Golden Age. Never have bimanes had in their hands the elements we have in ours: 50,000 monkeys, so strong and brave; those which arrive every day from all the isles in Oceania; our navy, composed of vessels seized in the ports of the state of Victoria—manned at present by mixed crews, although our monkeys will soon be able to operate them by themselves under the orders of sympathetic bimane officers, whom we shall recruit from every nation.

"With all this, we shall complete the conquest of the Australian provinces that England still holds, and we shall drive the English out of every island in Oceania! The monkeys of Borneo, Sumatra and Java will rise up and join us; then, as a bold move, we shall land..."

"Where's that, Sire?" asked Dick Broken.

---

[31] The other four must be Europe, Asia, Africa and America; the title of *Voyages très extraordinaires de Saturnin Farandoul dans les 5 ou 6 parties du monde et dans tous les pays connus et même inconnus de M. Jules Verne* presumably includes the formulation "5 or 6" because there was some controversy, even before Ferdinand de Lesseps started work on the Panama Canal (in 1881), as to whether America ought to be regarded as two continents rather than one.

"In Bombay!" cried Farandoul. "In India, where the Hindu bimanes and quadrumanes groan under the yoke of perfidious Albion! Remember, Broken, that you are not English; you are Australian—and, henceforth, Farandoulian! As soon as we have driven the English out of India, we shall establish a mixed government there..."

"Bravo, Sire! That's wonderful!" cried Mandibul.

"Wait! Once India is organized, we shall loose several generals and quadrumanes upon Asia, with the mission of opening up Siam, Cochin-China and the Celestial Empire to new ideas; far from considering our task to be over, we shall march upon the isthmus of Suez and thus into..."

"Europe!" said Broken.

"Yes, Europe—old Europe, so proud of its past glories, but where so many so-called civilized peoples maintain permanent armies beneath the scourge of modern times! Europe shall be ours! We shall begin by settling the eternal Eastern Question; Constantinople will be neither Turkish, nor Russian, nor English! At the other end of the Mediterranean, the English yoke will be lifted from Gibraltar... There are monkeys on Gibraltar, unhappy monkeys bent under the knee of the highlander—we shall free them!"

"And France, Sire?" Mandibul said. "I wouldn't be sorry to land one day at Bordeaux and..."

"France! Haven't you understood that I have destined France for a glorious role? We shall make haste to conquer her! I shall make Paris the capital of the world. France, which marches at the head of the flow of modernity, will understand the grandeur of our mission; she will throw herself into our movement with generous ardor! I ask for ten years to complete this great work; in ten years, within pacified Europe, there will be no more frontiers, no lines of demarcation, no permanent bimane armies! Commerce, industry and agriculture will no longer be in want of strong arms; its peoples, no longer having any monarchs or generals with vested interests in war and revolutions, will live in peace under the safeguard of a few regiments of monkeys!"

"I give in, O genius," murmured Dick Broken. "I'm a Farandoulian!"

"You shall be Governor of London!" Farandoul exclaimed. "What do we need, to accomplish all this? Disciplined armies! My good, brave monkeys have only to remain united and disciplined, and the world is ours!"

This single conversation suffices to indicate how the gifts comprising his genius had come together in Saturnin Farandoul. He had it all: grandeur of vision; power of reasoning; boldness of action.

Farandoul set to work courageously, with the devoted Mandibul and Dick Broken—who was completely committed to his cause—as his principal collaborators. We shall not venture to enter into every detail of the marvelous and incomparable adventure which Farandoul set himself to organize; it is for Australian historians to tell the world what those three men did in a few months.

The most serious difficulty, in the early stages, was the state of relations—frosty at least, if not outrightly hostile—manifest between the conquered populations and the conquering monkeys. No relationship was forged between bimanes and quadrumanes; the latter, being good and carefree fellows, were quite ready to fraternize, but bimane haughtiness always kept them at a distance. The only exceptions were a few mining districts on the Ballarat coast and Alberton in Colonel Escoubico's division. At Alberton, the Colonel hosted soirées and balls, seducing everyone with his liveliness and good humor. In his salons, notable bimanes—the women of high society, millionaire farmers and rich arms-dealers—mingled with the quadrumane officers of Wa-Wo-Wa's corps, who had become excellent dancers under the tutelage of the Spaniard Escoubico. At Ballarat, the good relations had had poorer results, the well-received monkeys having been drawn into the miners' drinking-dens, to the great detriment of their natural sobriety.

The Australian press soon began to complicate these difficulties. In the early days, it had kept a prudent silence, limiting itself to recording the decrees of the Farandoulian government without comment. After the first three months of the occupation, however, the papers recovered their courage and launched a petty but lively war of words against the Governor of Melbourne, which never let up. As the monkeys did not read the papers, this could not stir up any trouble in the army, but these scarcely-veiled excitations of hatred and contempt for the government maintained a dangerous agitation among the bimanes.

The council, worried by this development, decided to take drastic action. One morning, the following decree was published:

FARANDOULIAN EMPIRE

The Governor of Melbourne,

Because the entire press, encouraged by impunity, delivers new attacks every day against the paternal government of H. M. Saturnin I;

And because the quadrumanes of the army are attacked daily by the bimane papers, cruel outrages being perpetrated against their dignity without their being able to reply, since they are not yet able to read;

It is decided that:

All the newspapers are suppressed.

Mr. Dick Broken is hereby charged with the creation of an official gazette for the publication of governmental acts.

General Mandibul.

It was high time. The harm that the press had done to the new empire could not be countered right away. The systematic campaign of false news and slyly aggressive articles it had employed, at the instigation of the agents of England, soon bore unfortunate fruit.

The European powers neglected to respond to the letters sent by Saturnin I to notify other sovereigns of his accession to the throne. Monaco alone replied—coldly, it is true, but politely, her geographical situation compelling her to pay the greatest possible respect to a maritime power like Australia. The blackest calumnies were circulating in Europe regarding the new empire and her glorious founders; it was rumored that the monkeys, far from being the armed protectors of a nation of workers and tradesmen, were, to the contrary, abominable tyrants. It was even said that Farandoul was absolutely determined to provide bimane wives for all his soldiers, who were rumored to number 150,000—which would reduce 150,000 unhappy women to live under the yoke of brutal monkeys while their bimane ex-husbands became sad wanderers in the remote depths of the Australian deserts.

There is no need for us to protest against such infamous calumnies. To the contrary, the quadrumane "yoke" was exceedingly light within the Farandoulian nation. Far from seeking to contrive a fusion of the bimane and quadrumane races by mixed marriages, Farandoul stubbornly refused to give the Breton Colonel Trabadec permission to espouse a young and pretty quadrumane, the daughter of Colonel Wa-Wo-Wa. Anyway, it will be enough, to definitively disprove the fanciful rumors that were running through Europe, to say that one of Farandoul's first priorities, after the conquest, had been to bring the families of his warriors to Australia as quickly as the organization of the Farandoulian navy would allow. He had not had time, nor ships enough, to bring in excess of 200,000 quadrumanes of all ages from the distant isles of Oceania immediately, but in the end—thanks to Bora-Bora's fleet, merchant vessels and others seized in the ports—they had arrived. The world was informed of this at once, but the strangest rumors continued to circulate.

Curiously, a few individuals saw in Australia's new situation a colossal opportunity to do business. The biggest matrimonial agency in New York set out to organize an expedition to Australia. Within a month, every newspaper in the United States carried a huge advertisement conceived as follows:

MARRIAGE! MARRIAGE!! MARRIAGE!!!
Notice to spinsters of all ages of an army to marry.
Exceptional opportunity. Magnificent situations offered to ladies. An immense selection of young bachelors, many superior officers among them,
Imminent departure by any possible ship.
Enroll immediately. Send photographs.

The agency quickly assembled a formidable number of hopefuls. The photographs were artfully filed, and the women were notified to be ready to depart at a moment's notice. One morning, at his mansion in Melbourne, Farandoul received a score of stout albums, magnificently bound, containing more than 3000 photographs.

At first, he could not imagine why they had been sent, but a letter enlightened him; the agency was offering him wives for the officers of his army, subject to a small fee for each introduction, and announcing the imminent arrival of a first shipment by way of a sample.

Farandoul, infuriated by the indelicacy of the people who engaged in such a business, replied that he would shoot any representative of the agency who set foot in Farandoulia.

He was no less annoyed when, at about the same time, another matrimonial agency—this one French—decided on its own authority to find a wife for him. This French agency had inserted the following notice among the small ads in *Le Figaro*:

RICH MARRIAGE
Good opportunity for princess,
or young person of high nobility.
A monarch to marry.

This advertisement, as one can well imagine, had fervently excited the Saint-Germain district, and a number of likely candidates had been put forward. A dozen examples selected from the collection had been forwarded to Farandoul by telegraph, who had refused them all, at the risk of causing a great many tears to flow. The pure memory of Mysora filled his heart.

Mandibul, to avoid any further annoyance to his friend and sovereign, had a photograph taken of the least naturally-favored of all the monkeys in the army, and sent it secretly to Paris as that of the marriageable monarch. Saint-German shuddered in horror; a few despairing young women took refuge in convents, although one timid spinster of 33 years and 11 months, a descendant of a family that went back at least as far as King Dagobert,[32] refused to withdraw her candidature on a point of principle.

Strict orders were given in Melbourne in anticipation of the arrival of the first shipment from the American agency. When the Yankee ship, carrying 400 spinsters, presented itself at Port Philip, entry to the port was sternly refused and it had to go back to sea incontinently.[33] It was learned some time afterwards that the representative of the agency, to recover some few of his expenses, had steered towards the isles of Fiji, where he had succeeded in placing his 400 ladies at a discount price with a small tribe of savages afflicted with a superabundance of bachelors.

Thus ended the campaign indiscreetly launched against Farandoulia by the matrimonial agencies.

---

[32] Dagobert I (c. 600-639) became King of the Franks in 628; he extended the Frankish empire to the Pyrenees, codified their laws and founded the Abbey of St. Denis, who eventually became the patron saint of France. He was thus a King of France long before Charlemagne, let alone the Valois or the Bourbons who had ennobled most of the aristocratic families from whom the suburbanites of Saint-Germain would have claimed descent. The incident of the advertisement may have been suggested to Robida by the career of Orélie-Antoine de Tounens, who set off from France in the late 1850s to claim Auracania and Patagonia for his fatherland. He declared himself King Orélie I in November 1860, having recruited a few native Americans to his cause, but was captured and expatriated by Chilean colonists in 1862. He tried to raise money to "reclaim" his throne, but had to return to South America with no more than a few thousand francs; having run out of cash he returned to France again in 1871 and founded a newspaper, in which he advertised his need for a consort as well as pursuing more elaborate begging tactics. Such pretenders were not uncommon in 19th century France, Napoléon I having deposed many of the former petty kings of Europe and redistributed their thrones to his relatives and cronies. Napoléon III, to whom de Tounens would have had to appeal in the first instance, was neither so powerful nor so casual—and by 1871, following the French humiliation in the Franco-Prussian War, such projects became even more manifestly absurd.

[33] The adverb I have translated as "incontinently" is *incontinent*, whose double meaning in French is more feebly echoed in English. Although English cannot reproduce the full force of Robida's double entendre, it seemed appropriate to retain it rather than use one of the more usual adverbial translations of *incontinent*, such as "forthwith" or "straight away."

IX.

Saturnin Farandoul was able to continue his work in peace. All his time and attention was devoted to the army, which required to be organized and thoroughly trained in order to rise to its task. Farandoul established an immense instruction camp on the shore at Port Philip, overlooking Melbourne Bay. This camp, protected by a line of entrenchments, was connected to a series of constructions which Farandoul had put in place for the bay's defense. The monkeys shifted the earth with considerable ardor and intelligence and became, under Mandibul's direction, excellent military engineers.

At the extremity of the bay, a little fort raised above Rocas Point completed the system of defense.

Farandoul had another object of preoccupation. Alone among all the armies of the world, the quadrumane army had no cavalry! It was a serious oversight, which might have disastrous consequences in certain situations. After serious deliberation, the council decided that it might be wise to utilize kangaroos for this purpose in preference to horses, towards which the monkeys had a certain antipathy. The agility of monkeys and kangaroos being in perfect accord, this new experiment ought to yield excellent results.

The camp at Port Philip soon displayed great animation; every morning, under the lofty surveillance of the Generals, the troops were drilled for several hours in the handling of their weapons. The afternoon was given over to the battalion school. Twice a week they played war games. All the regiments moved off, executing collective movements and mounting charges in front of the bimanes of Melbourne, who flocked to see them. Brightly-clad staff-officers mounted on kangaroos ran through the front lines at the gallop carrying orders to the bimane generals. Saturnin I, mounted on horseback at the center of a sparkling general staff, towered over the assembly. The ladies of Melbourne paid particular attention to the hero's five foster-brothers, gathering around them like a guard of honor.

Similar maneuvers were undertaken in the four other military divisions, to maintain the high morale of the troops and give them the necessary instruction.

The example of Colonel Escoubico, the commandant of the town of Alberton, had been followed by other leaders. Brass bands and corps of excellent musicians were formed in every brigade, under the direction of bimane conductors hired at considerable expense. Escoubico's band, organized in the Spanish style, comprised 14 monkeys in the little ivory-topped caps of students, mostly playing guitars, tambourines and castanets. The other musical corps were armed with stout copper instruments which resounded terribly in military marches. Military music was played in the garrisons every afternoon beneath the windows of the commanding general; one could hear all the latest works [34] from Europe brilliantly executed, and equally brilliant pieces born of the musical inspiration of the quadrumanes.

Farandoulia had its own maestro, a Javanese langur named Coco, whose character was exceedingly disagreeable by nature, although endowed with qualities of verve and originality unknown among bimane musicians. The maestro had a masterpiece in preparation for Melbourne's Grand Theater: a grand opera *mixte* [35]—which is to say, intended to be played by both bimane and quadrumane artistes. Its title was *The Romeo of the Zoological Gardens.*[36]

The opera's subject, one is given to understand, was the story of a monkey in love with the daughter of the Director of a zoo; this quadrumane Romeo languished in a captivity whose misery the maiden alleviated by her delicate attentions. Love was born in two hearts. The barbarous father having refused his consent, there was a monkey revolt, a ballet, an elopement, a reconciliation with the bimanes and a grand ballet mixte. The most remarkable elements, according to those who first heard them, were a choir of captive monkeys, a song of war and a duo mixte between the daughter of the Director, a bimane artiste, and Romeo, a monkey artiste. Our friend Dick Broken had written the words for this magisterial work, as well as those of a patriotic song mixte, whose couplets were to be sung by bimanes and the refrains by quadrumanes.

To return to our military musicians, who had delighted the bimane population at first, we must confess that after a few months they were playing their concerts to empty houses. The pretty blonde-haired misses had disappeared, doubtless regretfully but probably in obedience to secret orders sent from London.

The sky became overcast; little by little, dark clouds were gathering on the horizon.

Certain indications allowed Farandoul to sense that a storm was about to break over Australian soil. There were vague rumors of an English intervention. The European consuls were showing a certain ill-will, and foreign agents had been reported to be active in the large population centers. A secret campaign by England was making itself felt; perfidious Albion was employing an indirect means of attack typical of her tortuous politics.

---

[34] *Nouveautés*, here translated as "latest works," also means "fancy goods" in a commercial context, so there is an element of derision in Robida's choice of that word.

[35] I have left *mixte* in French for the same reason that artistes, which occurs later in the sentence, is conventionally left in French rather than translated into English—i.e., because it is simply not done to talk about opera without adopting a tone of cosmopolitan snobbery.

[36] Robida gives this title in English, although I have taken the liberty of adding the terminal "s" in conformity with conventional English usage.

It was, above all, the quadrumane army on which the English agents were working—that honest and pure army, which Great Britain did her utmost to corrupt by provoking indiscipline therein and developing within its ranks a taste for the finer things in life.[37] By all means possible, perfidious Albion attempted to tarnish the quadrumanes' virtues and inculcate in them the vices of bimanes. Her weapon of preference was whisky; strong spirits were soon flowing like rivers, and the monkeys were losing the habit of temperance.

Although the Generals kept a careful watch over their troops and dealt severely with the guilty ones, the evil took hold so strongly that discipline was seriously compromised. The quadrumane leaders themselves, in the drawing-rooms that opened to them as if in response to a password, were not always able to refuse the champagne that was offered to them. At the same time, clever spies caused pride and ambition to creep into the hearts of the quadrumane Generals by means of base flatteries and shameful kowtowing to their panache—and, in the end, awakened jealousy in the quadrumanes, directed against Farandoul's bimane companions and Farandoul himself.

The attention of England eventually came to focus on one of the quadrumane leaders: Colonel Makako, General Mandibul's chief of staff—who was, as we have said, a sort of feudal gentleman, infatuated with the nobility and antiquity of his race. Long used to the submissiveness of his family's monkey vassals, he believed that he had the right to give everyone orders, and yielded very reluctantly to the discipline introduced into the army by Farandoul.

The agents of perfidious Albion having quickly discovered the hateful and jealous tendency of his character, Colonel Makako was almost immediately surrounded, flattered and outwitted by them. In the drawing-rooms of Melbourne, the prettiest women in the pay of England watered him with champagne and flattery. They affected to ridicule Saturnin in front of him, to diminish his merits while simultaneously exalting those of "the irresistible Makako." Colonel Makako smiled, and responded to these interested discourses with approving grunts in the rustic and not-very-gracious language of the highland monkeys [38] of Borneo.

---

[37] The French *goût du panache* has a rather elastic meaning, *panache* (literally "plume") sarcastically implying unwarranted arrogance, mild drunkenness and/or delusions of grandeur. I have transcribed the word directly in the following paragraph, although its English usage does not usually carry these sly insinuations, and have rendered the phrase more economically as "taste for finery" later in the chapter.

[38] The French *montagnard*, here translated as "highland," has a double meaning in French because the term *montagnards* came to be applied to the extremists of the Revolutionary parliament—including the chief perpetrators of the Terror—who occupied the highest-placed seats in the assembly.

In the space of a few months, Colonel Makako had become entirely hostile to Farandoul, and above all to General Mandibul, whose orders he received with anger and ill-will. Like a General prepared for *pronunciamentos*,[39] he was only waiting for an opportunity to raise the flag of rebellion, along with partisans he counted on within the general staff, found among those who had been corrupted by a taste for finery, hatred for discipline or the abuse of strong liquor.

This is how things stood on one fine morning, after 15 months of occupation, when news spread through Melbourne that an English fleet had been encountered at sea by two Farandoulian ships, only one of which had been able to escape, thanks to the skill of her quadrumane crew. It was true enough, and while the rumor spread through Melbourne, Farandoul gave the final orders for a rapid consolidation of the army.

The English fleet had been sighted off Point Campbell. One of the Farandoulian vessels had escaped, as we have said; the other, whose line of retreat was cut off, had engaged the enemy in violent combat. This heroic ship was the *Young Australia*,[40] a sloop with a dozen cannon, commanded by Captain Jonathan Butterfield, a bimane of American origin recruited to the quadrumane cause.

Five large English frigates, the *Devastation*, the *Warrior*, the *Terror*, the *Devorous* and the *Carnivorous* [41] attacked the little *Young Australia*, deluging her with fire and steel. Jonathan Butterfield, standing fast on his quarterdeck, sailed dead ahead towards the monstrous armor-plated English ships; his courageous crew, comprising only 60 or so monkeys and a few bimane engineers, displayed a heroism worthy of classical antiquity.

The enemy's fireballs having started a fire between the sloop's decks, the quadrumanes fastened her to the *Carnivorous* with grappling-hooks, without deigning to respond to the English signals. The blazing fire made rapid progress, but the monkeys had already quit the sloop and were playing havoc on the bridge of the *Carnivorous*. When the *Young Australia* finally blew up, carrying a part of the English frigate with her, the last monkeys who had taken refuge in the topsails of the *Carnivorous* were still defending themselves.

Two days after the battle, the English fleet was in sight of Port Philip, and the rapidly-deployed Farandoulian army occupied all the coastal defenses. A

---

[39] In Spain, an authority-figure—almost invariably a military man—who refuses to obey the law, is said to be issuing a *pronunciamento*.

[40] The text gives the ship's name in French (*La Jeune Australie*), but as it must have been appropriated locally it seems reasonable to employ an English version.

[41] All these titles are given in English in the text; I have left them unaltered, even though *Devorous* is a very unlikely name for an English naval vessel.

state of siege having been declared, a proclamation urged the population to remain calm, the Farandoulian army being sufficient to ensure the security of the province.

Unfortunately, grave symptoms of insubordination had manifested themselves within the army. Some regiments were grumbling, others were demanding additional distributions of liquid rations. Colonel Makako's corps was the most conspicuous of all for its bad attitude and its whining.

General Mandibul, who had remained in Melbourne to maintain order, was astonished by the sloppiness of Makako's service as chief of staff, while Makako visited the drawing-rooms of Melbourne with increasing frequency.

On the evening of the brilliant naval battle of Point Campbell, a grand soirée was given in his honor by an old bimane civil servant; Makako and a few of his officers were received there with a veritable ovation, which enraptured their vanity.

One of those *femmes fatales* for whom historians are, alas, always seeking at the bottom of every great catastrophe, entered the lists in order to tip the balance definitively in favor of England. Lady Arabella Cardigan, an English spy of the most ravishing beauty, made her entrance on the scene. She was newly arrived from Europe with precise ministerial instructions, and her lovely eyes had a devastating effect on the quadrumane general staff, already weakened by the repeated efforts of English agents. Her beauty caused every head to turn as she crossed the room in a regal manner to embrace the host.

Makako was fluttering around the buffet; forewarned by one of his officers, he went back into the large drawing-room at the very moment when Lady
Arabella asked to be presented to him.

The patrician beauty of the blonde Englishwoman sparked the enthusiastic
admiration of the Colonel like a lightning-bolt. Those huge eyes, that long

blonde hair, that tall and slender figure, that aristocratic perfume—everything about her lifted Makako's heart. Appropriately, the orchestra struck up an intoxicating waltz; Makako wrapped his arms around Lady Arabella's body, and drew her into the giddy whirl. They were seen passing through every room, moving in time to the whim of the rhythm and revolving tirelessly in the grip of a delirious music. Makako, transported by his excitement, gripped Lady Arabella's body a little more firmly than was entirely proper, and planted furtive kisses on the one hand that she abandoned to him.

Lady Arabella seemed bent on ensuring that the fervent quadrumane Colonel lost his head completely. Lovingly supported on his arm, she waltzed with him all night. Ten waltzes, 15 waltzes, 30 waltzes were granted to him. The host had given orders to the orchestra, which—without stopping, except to down pints of liquid—rolled out interminable musical fantasies. Long after the other dancers were tired out, their panting partners getting their breath back on the divans, Makako was still waltzing!

The conductor of the orchestra had received reinforcements to replace those of his men who had fallen on the battlefield, but the blonde Englishwoman seemed indefatigable, and the same smile was perpetually fluttering upon her lips.

England's agents were swarming everywhere; observers, more attentive than the quadrumanes, had quickly cottoned on to a number of secret signals—a few furtive glances exchanged in passing between Lady Arabella and certain suspicious individuals. The work of demoralization begun several months earlier was making new and rapid progress.

Some hours after the ball, Makako, irresistibly seduced, presented himself at Lady Arabella Cardigan's house, to lay his devotion and his sword at her feet. The conspirators were there; a conference ensued in which the beautiful eyes of Lady Arabella played a leading role in the action. When they separated, Makako was totally committed to overthrow Saturnin I and usurp his throne, which the inflamed Colonel hoped to share with the blonde lady.

What a dream! Into what rapturous depths had the ambitious quadrumane been plunged! Absolute master of Australia, he would escort her majesty to Europe, of which he had heard such tales—to that England, where Lady Arabella Cardigan had estates and castles. He had to take action; the agents of England had, so to speak, drawn him a plan.

Profiting from the fact that the army was concentrated at Port Philip, it was necessary to work by every possible means, within a few days, to seize the bimane Generals—and, most important of all, Saturnin's five foster-brothers, whose influence was capable of putting an end to the rebellion. That having been accomplished, the irresistible Makako, intoxicated by the honeyed words and languorously veiled eyes of Lady Arabella, believed that he was certain to ward off every danger. He even deluded himself that he might remain, England notwithstanding, master of Australia.

The arrival of Makako at the Port Philip camp was the signal for a renewed outbreak of acts of insubordination. Farandoul and the Generals had done well; they had been able to prevent indiscipline from gradually infecting the best regiments. As England's agents redoubled their efforts, immense quantities of strong liquor were transported to the troops in improvised canteens by bimane ladies, despite Mandibul's stern prohibitions. Although access to the encampments and barracks was rigorously forbidden to bimanes, these ladies succeeded in persuading superior officers to accept a few casks of fine liqueurs, under various pretexts—most frequently as patriotic gifts—on several occasions.

One regiment, which occupied a small redoubt at the end of the line, received in this manner a provision of whisky that it swallowed in haste, in order to make it disappear and avoid any reproaches that Colonel Escoubico might make during his tour of inspection. The result was that within two days the regiment fell dead drunk upon its bastions—and had the Colonel not arrived, the redoubt, deprived of its defenders, could have fallen into English hands. The regiment woke up in the police station, the officers having been cashiered, but this severe treatment did not prevent the same thing happening at another post the following day.

The English fleet, in the open sea, contented itself with tightly blockading Port Philip, without making any direct attempt upon it. This inaction was what caused Farandoul and Mandibul their greatest anxiety. For what was England waiting before commencing hostilities? The increasing demoralization of the quadrumane army was evidently the work of her secret agents; did she wish to attack only when the fatal work would be completed, when the good and loyal regiments of former times would have turned into an undisciplined and unstable rabble?

Alas, the wait was not to be a long one.

Farandoul, kept informed by the reports of his Generals, wanted to react vigorously against the demoralization. To try to recover his old power over the minds of his troops, he summoned the entire army to a grand review on the Port Philip beach, in full view of the English navy. A strict order of the day had to be communicated to the monkeys for the stern repression of all insubordination.

Beneath the bright morning Sun, the immense beach was covered, as far as the eye could see, with magnificent quadrumane regiments. The chiefs of staff, admonished by the bimane Generals, had done their best to re-establish discipline.

The sight was truly magnificent. The infantry occupied the center and the cavalry the flanks, following the order of battle adopted by Farandoul: in advance, the regiments of riflemen; in the second rank of the line, the dark mass of monkeys armed with Oceanian clubs; on the right flank, the light kangaroo cavalry, lancers and chasseurs; on the left flank, the heavy cavalry, the giant monkeys of Borneo, also mounted on kangaroos but armed with heavy ironwood clubs.

Unfortunately, the English fleet having executed a suspicious maneuver in the open sea, Saturnin I was obliged to remove himself to the little fort at Point Rocas in order to observe it.

The troops under arms put on a good show at first, but towards noon it was necessary to make a distribution of food and refreshments. The quartermaster had orders to convey 300 casks of fresh water—the camp's daily ration, sent from Melbourne that morning—to the field of the maneuvers. The catering corps being entirely won over by Makako, it had already caused Mandibul great concern, but he had trusted in the surveillance of a few solid officers placed at its head. He was still ignorant of grave disturbances that had broken out in Melbourne, of which these brave officers had been the first victims.

On their arrival on the plain where the entire army was roasting under the hot Sun, in consequence of the English fleet's maneuvers, the carriages of the catering corps were greeted by the hurrahs of the thirsty regiments. The distribution was quickly made; every corps had its casks, which were immediately surrounded by soldiers. There was a certain brouhaha while the casks were opened; the quartermaster's fresh water seemed suspect to a few officers, who did their best to prevent the troops from getting to it. The water was clear and limpid, but its odor was definitely too alcoholic.

The monkeys, after having tasted it, refused to obey their leaders. There were a few nasty grimaces at the first mouthful, but a second gulp proved the water to be so extraordinarily pleasant that all discipline was forgotten. They jostled one another to obtain a larger share.

The quartermaster's fresh water was kirsch! [42]

The hearts of infantry and cavalry alike were uplifted by joy. Despairing of preventing the distribution, the officers joined in, determined to have their share. Soon, the kirsch had flooded the entire field of maneuver, from one end to the other.

The second part of the infernal plan hatched by the English agents had been put into execution.

At about 2 p.m.—the English navy having ceased its maneuvers—the Generals and their staff left the fort. The trumpets and the drums recalled the soldiers to their posts. The officers ran here, there and everywhere, and the regiments reconstituted themselves, after a fashion, but the entire army was in a visibly emotional state. In place of the former neat and tidy straight lines, irregular

---

[42] Kirsch may seem an odd choice, given that it is usually distilled in Germany from black Morello cherries, and is highly unlikely to have been available by the cartload in Melbourne in the 1870s. It is entirely possible that Robida has no other reason for using the name than its flagrant absurdity, but it may be significant that the crushed cherry-stones give kirsch a bitter almond flavour supposed to resemble that of cyanide; Robida might be attempting subtly to emphasize the poisonous nature of the draught.

zigzags spread out. The cavalry, in particular, stood out by virtue of its awful disarray. Great waves made themselves felt along the battle-front. When those on the right of the first rank began to lurch dazedly, the movement spread from one to another until it reached the far end of the line.

The furious Farandoul set his horse to the gallop. His escort moved off behind him in a whirlwind of dust. The first corps on the right flank was, appropriately enough, Makako's.

At the sight of the Farandoulian general staff, Makako's followers started theatrically. Ear-splitting howls rent the air; the Farandoulian flag was struck, and an immense red banner provided by Lady Arabella was raised in its place. The regiments next in line, seized by the contagion of this example, also dispersed; their leaders, won over by Makako, hastened to rally round the general revolt.

That was exactly what was happening! The beautiful army formed up on the beach was no longer anything but a confused mass, from which a storm of incoherent cries emerged. The catering corps continued to provide casks of kirsch, which were immediately opened and drained dry by the ardent throats of the delirious quadrumanes. Their leaders, in the middle of the plain, popped the corks of champagne-bottles sent by England. A few bimane men and women circulated among them, apparently stirring up the hideous rebellion.

A little troop of faithful monkeys had joined the Farandoulian general staff. Their honest figures were colored as much by wrath as profound contempt for the drunken quadrumanes who had sunk to the level of the most degraded bimanes.

Farandoul and his bimane Generals consulted one another; Farandoul's foster-brothers wanted to charge the enemy, but Farandoul opposed that course, in order to try to play for time. After a few minutes hesitation, the little troop took the road to the fort again, leaving the rebels to their shameful orgy.

Nothing remained to Farandoul of his entire army but his bimane Generals, the monkeys of his own isle and a few brave quadrumane leaders who did not want to abandon him, among whom were Ungko and Tapa-Tapa of Sumatra, Wa-Wo-Wa of New Guinea and Nasico of Borneo—400 combatants in all, to hold their own against England and the rebels.

That same evening, one of Dick Broken's orderlies arrived breathless at the fort, having run all the way from Melbourne. A revolution had broken out in the city. The bimane insurrection had triumphed; the quadrumane officials had been obliged to flee—and Dick Broken, barricaded in the Governor's mansion with 200 or 300 monkeys stationed there, was under siege.

Broken claimed that he could hold out against the insurgents for a fortnight, so Farandoul was not too worried about that. The essential thing was to bring the wayward army back to the path of duty. If it persisted in its rebellion, everything was finished; as soon as it became obedient again, the bimane revolution in Melbourne would be promptly stifled.

He had to play for time.

A few monkeys, ashamed of their delinquency, had already come to rally round Farandoul's flag. The rest continued to drink English liquor by day and by night. The provision of food had become the provision of drink; the catering corps no longer transported anything but liquid nourishment.

With no more organization and no more exercises, the disorder surpassed anything of which the imagination could dream. Farandoul was counting on that, to some extent, to regain power. His optimism was understandable; monkeys have lively minds, but bad memories. They are excellent creatures, capable and intelligent, but much too frivolous; it was only by making them repeat the same exercise and actions every day that Farandoul had been able to make anything of them. Now they were on their own, idleness and drunkenness—vices formerly unknown to their race—would make them forget everything they had learned. Farandoul's plan was, therefore, to wait for a week and then to throw himself upon Makako. Once the instigator of the revolt had been punished, and the monkeys returned to the path of duty, they would be able to turn their attention to England. But for that, it was necessary that England made no move either, also waiting for the psychological moment to fall upon the monkeys.

On the evening of the seventh day, Farandoul made his preparations to engage Makako's forces as soon as the Sun rose. The loyal monkeys, who had been drilled every day in the handling of rifles and the firing of cannon, were raring to go. Farandoul's five brothers established them in their positions. As for our hero's foster-father, two days earlier he had undertaken a mission to the rebel camp, where a few brave officers were ready to declare a counter-*pronunciamento*.

The night seemed very long to the monkeys. At 4 a.m., several cannon-shots fired out at sea brought everyone running to the ramparts.

Damnation! England, forewarned of all Farandoul's plans by some undetectable spy, had made their move. During the night, six large transport-ships full of Indian troops were secured in position close to the shore, two kilometers from the fort. Formed up facing the fort were six frigates, four armored corvettes, a few dispatch-vessels and two terrible battleships, each of whose turrets was equipped with 40 steel cannon firing 40-kilo shells. The decks of all these ships were cleared for action. The hour of the ultimate battle had struck!

The rebel camp was in uproar. The monkeys, finally understanding their peril, attempted to organize themselves. Just as Farandoul was wondering whether it might not be too late to get the idea into their heads that they had a common enemy to face, the English fleet opened fire.

The broadsides fired by the corpulent frigates arrived at the fort with a regularity that did credit to their chronometric gunners. The monkeys, with the courage of desperation, set the fort's 20 fire-ports thundering. One heavy marine cannon in particular, operated under Mandibul's orders, worked wonders. One of its shells penetrated the engine-room of the *Carnivorous*, already tested by the battle of Cape Campbell, and did such damage there that the frigate soon seemed ready to sink like a stone.

As for the little fort, its excellent construction permitted it to resist the enemy shells without suffering too much damage. Alongside the beach, the transport-ships went on methodically with the business of disembarkation.

The greatest disorder still reigned within the rebel camp, where 1000 commands clashed with 1000 confused cries. Finally, when the large landing-craft loaded with English, Scottish and Sepoy troops were detached from the transport-ships and were rowed towards the beach, the disorder seemed to reach its peak.

The defenders of the fort stopped firing for a moment to watch what was happening. Deadly fruits of indiscipline and intemperance! The monkeys, still drunk as they awoke, sought in vain to take up their combat positions. Some put their uniforms on backwards, others tried to remind one another of the 12 stages of a charge. Useless effort! Inexpressible confusion! Many, having become wild again, ran on all fours, giving out stupid cries. Warriors of Geelong, Cheep Hill and Melbourne, where art thou?

Makako sought ideas in champagne. O shame! He scratched his forehead and his hindquarters—and all of his staff, by force of their ancient instinct of imitation, promptly set about doing likewise!

Meanwhile, the long-boats reached the shore; the companies they landed fell upon the monkeys who attempted to oppose them there, and drove them back without any difficulty.

The long-boats maintained a continual coming-and-going between the ships and the shore, and 8000 English troops were soon on the ground—8000 brave men burning to avenge the unexpected disasters of the preceding year. Finally, at a signal from the Admiral's frigate, musicians struck up *God Save The Queen* and the English threw themselves forward in two columns to attack the quadrumane positions.

Farandoul and his anxious monkeys waited for Makako's batteries to overwhelm the redcoats and the highlanders, but the cannons remained mute. Profiting from the quadrumanes' hesitation, the English columns scaled the batteries.

The frigates' smoke veiled the battlefield for an instant, but a gust of wind dissipated it. Farandoul went pale. Curses! All his work had come to nothing in the end—the monkeys of Cheep Hill were fleeing instead of fighting!

It was not even a battle; it was a horrible, panic-stricken rout.

Confusion, upheaval, massacre! No more regiments, no more officers, no more soldiers!

The weapons of 40,000 monkeys litter the ground. The cavalry, instead of protecting the retreat, leap from the backs of their kangaroos to climb trees. Fugitives hang in clusters from the branches of eucalyptus and gum-trees, the highlanders chasing them into the forest while the English take possession of their baggage.

Of all Makako's army, only two companies of monkeys have refused to follow the example of their comrades and are holding firm against the English. These brave fellows are aggregated in front of the quartermaster's hut, protected by entrenchments of barrels, some full and some empty. To overcome this last obstacle, the English dispatch an elite regiment. The charge is sounded, the battle-cries burst forth, and the redcoats scale the barricades of casks with a furious impetuosity.

Farandoul and his mariners wait for events to take a dramatic turn—for some act of desperate heroism like that of the bimane grenadiers at Waterloo.

The English, brandishing their bayonets and howling loudly, are at the top of the entrenchment... They hesitate, and pause... What is happening?

Not a shot is fired, not a monkey budges! The unfortunates are dead drunk! Ordered to guard their provisions, they have not been sober for three days, and are oblivious to everything. The cannonade, the battle, the rout—nothing has been able to penetrate their stupefaction. They are still sleeping like logs and snoring, while the English look down at them, unable to believe their blinking eyes.

It is all over! In a quarter of an hour, an entire army has dissolved, evaporated! The English have taken 1000 prisoners; the rest have fled into the wilderness to resume the savage life.

Farandoul and his downcast but furious brothers return to their guns to save some vestige of quadrumane honor by mounting a desperate defense. A hurricane of fire and iron envelops the little fort.

The heroic monkey gunners load and swab angrily—with such ardor that when dusk falls they refuse to leave their guns and continue firing, even after the English fleet has left its moorings and set out for the open sea.

X.

On the English side, the joy was unconfined. The colony was reconquered, nothing remaining in quadrumane hands but the little fort and the Governor's mansion defended by Dick Broken.

The day after the landing, Sir Roderick Blakeley,[43] Commander-in-Chief of the English expedition, made his entry into reconquered Melbourne. The city was celebrating, the English flag flying at every window. It was strange to see all the bimanes, finally reassured, pressing around the conquerors and heaping felicitations upon them. The most frightened bimanes were holding their heads high again; every trace of the conquest was disappearing. Already the word "quadrumane" was forbidden, erased from every edifice on which it had been inscribed.

The quadrumane artistes of the Melbourne Opera were shamefully cast out by their bimane colleagues. The performances of Coco's opera were halted, the maestro himself having vanished.[44]

Lastly, as a final ignominy, there was already talk of raising a statue to the man whom more bimanes than ever were calling the heroic Croknuff.

In the afternoon, a long column of prisoners filed between two hedges of bearded highlanders, preceded by a tartan-kilted bagpiper playing merry tunes. Among the prisoners still clad in scraps of their uniforms, Colonel Makako stood out by virtue of his disheartened expression. At the sight of Lady Arabella Cardigan, standing beside Sir Roderick Blakeley, he bellowed lugubriously while lifting his arms in the air.

Lady Arabella leaned towards the General, who smiled while making a sign. The liberated Makako was immediately placed in the hands of the astute Englishwoman.

---

[43] On this first appearance the surname is rendered Blackeley, but the more plausible spelling is employed the next time it is used.

[44] Robida inserts a footnote here, which translates as: *"The rumor abroad in Melbourne at that time was that he had been sold by an English corporal to a famous German musician, who keeps him chained up in a cave and forces him to compose music for his operas, wearing him down by the most undignified treatment."* Robida presumably belonged to the majority of Frenchmen—whose vociferousness was exceeded only by that of its opposing minority—unimpressed by the works of Richard Wagner.

Let us say at once, so that our readers should be in no doubt as to the fate of the ex-Colonel, that he now became part of Lady Cardigan's household. Lady Arabella, true to her promise, had no wish to separate Makako's destiny from hers. She took him with her to England, to the Cardigan estate, which Makako had deluded himself that he might one day visit as its master.

Unfortunately, Makako is not master there—far from it! At first, he was comfortably lodged in a barred cage in the depths of the great greenhouse of Cardigan Castle, but his submissiveness and misery soon resulted in his being permitted a measure of liberty. Makako is no longer in chains; he vegetates while dreamily indulging his delusions of grandeur and sadly polishing Lord Cardigan's boots. He still sees Lady Arabella from time to time, when she deigns to grant him permission to fulfill the functions of a trusted domestic servant by carrying her letters to her on a silver platter.

Lady Arabella's guests do not always treat him kindly, and Makako's aristocratic heart groans. Despite his unhappiness, the old feudal spirit of the patrician monkey of Borneo still persists. Makako lords it over the servants, and still refuses disdainfully—for lack of time—to enter into communication with a reporter from a great Liberal newspaper, who contacted him in the hope of extracting a few interesting memoirs.

Let us return to Melbourne, where Dick Broken's monkeys were defending themselves desperately.

The solidly-barricaded Governor's mansion resisted repeated English attacks. While supervising the defense, Dick Broken, faithful to his old habits of reportage, sent correspondence from time to time to the *Melbourne Herald*, which had reappeared—but as it simply forwarded his reports to the enemy, he refused all offers of capitulation and responded to the attacks with furious sorties at the head of an elite corps of 50 monkeys.

One of the pavilions at the corner of the Governor's mansion had been taken and retaken 20 times over. For a week, they had fought on the rooftops for possession of the pavilion's cupola. When the English believed that they were definitely in control of it, they installed themselves therein and prepared to move out of it to launch a decisive attack on the rest of the building—but the monkeys swiftly climbed up on the roof and precipitated themselves in an assault on the cupola, dislodging the enemy and replacing the Farandoulian flag, which had only been struck momentarily, at the summit of the monument.

Unfortunately, their food supplies were running out. Dick Broken was careful to say nothing about it in his correspondence, but he was cruelly tormented by fear of starvation.

From the height of their elevated position, the monkeys had been able to watch the long column of their brothers, made captive by the English, filing into the city. Their humiliation had wounded them deeply, but while the cannons of Farandoul's little fort still sounded in the distance, they still clung to a vague hope.

The Point Rocas fort, occupied by Farandoul and his faithful monkeys, still held out—the garrison, when called to surrender, had received the envoys proudly. "So long as we have ammunition to feed to our cannons," Farandoul replied, "we shall swallow the shells of the British lion!"

As everyone knows, though, in addition to its natural bravery, the British lion has a powerful dose of finesse. Instead of continuing a duel of shell bursts with Farandoul, it decided that it would be simpler to let the defenders of Point Rocas exhaust their provisions. A rigorous blockade was established around the little fort, at a respectful distance.

When the English General judged that the right moment had come, he sent new proposals to the Farandoulians, whose courage and constancy he admired. At the same time, he sent the monkeys' former King a letter from Dick Broken, informing him of the want of food and desperate situation of the last of Melbourne's monkeys. Even so, the little fort held out for another week by eking out the last rations of coconuts. The monkeys, who had become transparently thin, still refused to surrender.

In the end, when the impossibility of attempting an escape by sea had been clearly demonstrated, the ultimate decision was taken by a council whose members included both bimanes and quadrumanes.

The Farandoulian flag was lowered, yielding its place to a flag of truce.

The little fort was ready to capitulate!

The conditions were lengthily debated by the Generals. Finally, a treaty was signed for the surrender of the fort and Dick Broken's monkeys. The members of the garrison were granted the honors of war and left with their weapons and baggage. The bimanes were prisoners; as for the quadrumanes, England was charged with their repatriation.

The open mouths of the cannons, silent since the night-watch, seemed to be yawning in despair. As noon sounded, to the sound of fifes and bagpipes, the drawbridge fell and the little fort's garrison filed down the slope towards the English staff-officers.

Farandoul and Mandibul came on horseback at the column's head; behind them marched the bimane Colonels and the hero's five foster-brothers, blackened by gunpowder and covered in glorious scars. Three hundred and fifty brave monkeys of martial aspect, in stained and ragged uniforms, came next, preceded by six monkey drummers playing the funeral march.

It was all over! The following day was the cruel day of separation. The bimane leaders dined with the English General, who acquainted them with the intentions of Her Majesty's government. Farandoul and the ex-mariners of *La Belle Léocadie* would be transported to Europe, far from quadrumane populations that were still profoundly agitated. Because Farandoul had stipulated, as a condition of the fort's surrender, a full pardon for Dick Broken, that individual was set at liberty.

Farandoul arranged with the General that *La Belle Léocadie* should be returned to the monkeys, in order that they might return to their hearths under the guidance of our hero's five brothers. Farandoul's foster-father, despite a thorough search, had not been found among the prisoners—he had disappeared, like so many others, during the rout of Makako's army.

A few hours after *La Belle Léocadie* had put to sea, carrying 100 monkeys, accompanied by an English corvette carrying the rest of the quadrumanes, a long-boat came to take the bimanes to Sandridge to convey them aboard the Admiral's frigate. Saturnin, Mandibul and the bimane ex-Generals having taken their places in the long-boat's stern, the oars fell in response to a blast from the officer's whistle, and the long-boat moved off under their rapid propulsion.

Farandoul could not take his eyes off the shore: that Australian land for whose regeneration he had attempted such great things...

His concentration was broken by a unanimous cry that went up from the long-boat's passengers. A kind of reef had abruptly risen up. An enormous monster with an iron carapace had emerged from the water underneath the long-boat, which now found itself aground on its back, three meters above the waves. Farandoul recognized the *Nautilus*. Good old Captain Nemo had arrived just in time to save him!

The bewildered Englishmen, however, continued mechanically to ply their oars in the empty air, while a great tumult erupted aboard the not-far-distant ships.

The prisoners leapt with a single bound on to the back of the *Nautilus* and ran towards the stern, where the ports were already wide open, inviting them to enter. Before the Englishmen could recover from their surprise, they all found themselves safely ensconced in the belly of the vessel.

In the interior of the *Nautilus*, each one was greeted as an escaped prisoner. The first words of Captain Nemo had been these: "My dear Farandoul, I'm happy to have good news to bring you—the Bora-Bora affair has been successfully concluded."

"I hope that the pirates' banker has been hanged!"

"No, the Sultan of Borneo wanted to appoint him as his Prime Minister; fortunately, the prudent fellow fled with the funds to Sumatra. On his arrival, the Rajah of Sumatra, desirous of ensuring that such a rich foreigner remained in his estates, had him impaled, and confiscated the funds to defray the expenses of that judiciary procedure. I was almost in despair for your credit, when the Sumatran Minister of Justice, unconcerned with regularizing his appointment, thought that the occasion was ripe for beating the retreat, and departed with the cash-box. Now, while I was following the trail of that cash-box in the *Nautilus*, in order to protect your rights, I encountered the ship which the Minister of Justice had chartered for it. I captured it and redeposited the Minister in Sumatra with a receipt for his royal master. And that's how I saved your 54 million coins!"

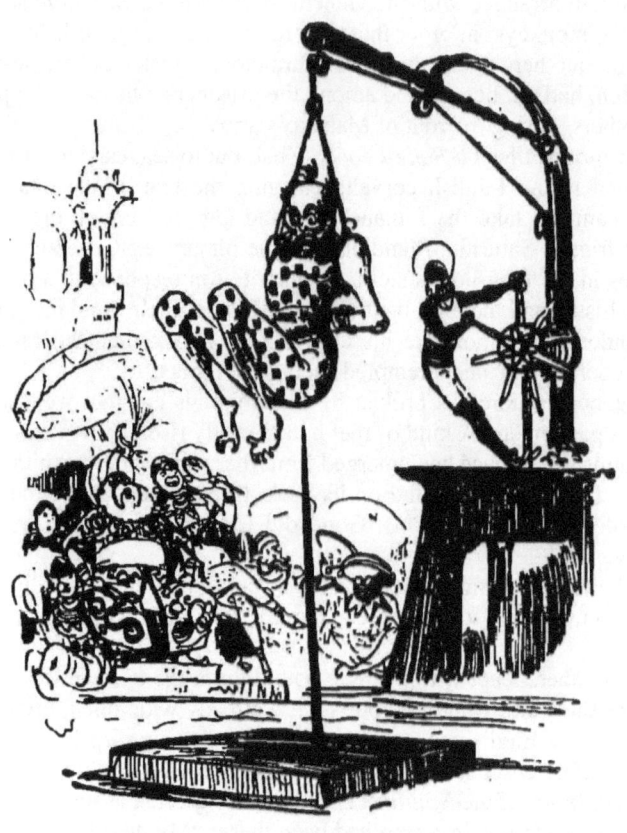

Ten days after this miraculous escape, the *Nautilus* arrived at the Mysterious Island, and Captain Nemo put Farandoul in possession of his 54 million coins.

Let us rapidly pass over the three months of rest and tranquility that the mariners allowed themselves in the Captain's domains before Farandoul profited from an opportunity to visit the isle of his childhood.

The monkeys taken prisoner by the English had returned to their hearths. His five brothers were there, about to proceed with a reorganization of the island with the aid of the Australian veterans. After a brief sojourn, during which Farandoul carried out a survey of the entire island, in order to ascertain the changes and reforms necessary for the development of civilization, he set out in *La Belle Léocadie* bound for the Mysterious Island.

Soon enough, the 54 million coins made a substantial reinforcement for the arms stowed in the hold of *La Belle Léocadie*. Captain Nemo commissioned Farandoul to carry a mysterious package to Monsieur Jules Verne in Paris, and *La Belle Léocadie* set sail for Le Havre.

Do you know how much work there is to do on such a journey? Our mariners did not have very much free time left over for counting their wealth. Among the 54 million coins, there were many copper ones and not a few that were fake or had been withdrawn from circulation. In the end, the calculations having been rigorously made and checked nine, ten, or 11 times over—as recommended by the wisest professors of arithmetic—Farandoul found that each sailor would have 33,578 francs to set him up. That wasn't at all bad, even for former Generals and Colonels.

They eventually sighted Le Havre; as there was an unexpended balance of 35 francs Farandoul called the sailors together to arrange a share-out.

Alas, all the calculations had been in vain! An ominous splashing set them all shivering. A stream of water soon manifested itself. The cargo of 54 million coins had overstrained the hold; some planks had given way and *La Belle Léocadie* was sinking rapidly.

A lamentable conclusion to such joyful hopes! Bora-Bora must have been laughing in his grave: *La Belle Léocadie* had had its day!

Fortunately, all the mariners could swim. A minute after the poor three-master had finally disappeared, the 17 sailors, with Farandoul and Mandibul at the head, cleft the waves in the direction of the jetty at Le Havre, which was visible in the distance. Having left the ship in order of rank, they came up the stairway to the quay in the same order.

Disdaining the helping hands that were offered to them, they climbed nimbly on to the quay. On arrival there, they all moved as one to lift their arms into the air, the same word on all their lips: "Ruined!"

"No!" Mandibul suddenly exclaimed, patting his pockets. "I still have the 35 francs!"

Farandoul also uttered a cry, in which equal doses of joy and astonishment were mingled. "It's him!"

It was, indeed, him! It was Farandoul's brave foster-father, whom he had recognized as he gazed on the soil of France for the very first time. And in what state did he see him? Wretched, crippled and captive: attached by a chain to a stall set against the parapet of the quay, whose proprietor was selling parrots and exotic curios.

Farandoul leapt upon Mandibul's 35 francs and ran towards the merchant. "How much?" he stammered, in a voice choked with emotion, indicating to the mercantile soul that he meant the tearful quadrumane.

The old gentleman was liberated, and fell weeping into the arms of his adoptive son, all misery and suffering forgotten in that minute of happiness. The poor monkey had had some cruel times to endure. It will be remembered that he was on a mission to Makako's camp when the attack took place; caught up in the rout, he had fallen into the hands of the English, who had sold him in spite of his human rights!

We shall not follow our friends to Paris, which they were able to reach, thanks to advances made by one of Captain Lastic's old fitters. We shall content ourselves with saying that Farandoul religiously carried out his duty to deliver Captain Nemo's letters—which he had, fortunately, saved from the wreck—to the required address.

Firmly determined on another attempt to make his fortune, Farandoul resolved to find his foster-father a place where he would be safe from further vicissitudes. The old gentleman was rather worn out and very feeble. The director of the Botanical Gardens, to whom Farandoul related his anxieties, was moved to tears; he consented to provide shelter for the brave quadrumane's final days, and gave him his own apartment with a little garden.

The separation was cruel, but Farandoul courageously tore himself away from his foster-father and took the road to Le Havre again, with his companions. New projects having gestated in his fertile brain, America would be privileged to see what he might do next!

PART TWO: THE TWO AMERICAS

AROUND THE WORLD IN MORE THAN 80 DAYS

I.

The Transatlantic Company ship *Hudson* was heading towards New York with a rapidity favored by a magnificent south-east breeze. Saturnin Farandoul—monarch in reserve, as he called himself—and ex-General Mandibul had spent their time during the crossing from Le Havre to New York in long conversations regarding the instability of human things and dissertations on the fragility of empires and the frustrations of politics.

"My dear Mandibul," Farandoul almost always said, by way of conclusion, "I'm abandoning the idea of social reform forever, and launching myself wholeheartedly into the world of industry. Business, commerce—that's what I need, and since great enterprises are necessary to my health, it's full steam ahead with great commercial enterprises!"

"Bravo, sir—sorry! Bravo, my dear Farandoul!"

It was in this state of mind that our heroes landed on the American shore.

All the seamen of *La Belle Léocadie*—the former Australian generals—had, of course, opted to follow the fortunes of their captain; the crew was complete and ready to share in his adventures. Farandoul's first priority, therefore, was to seek out an enterprise in which he would be able to use those strong arms and devoted hearts.

Mandibul, who still held a grudge against England, proposed an invasion of Canada.

"No politics!" said Farandoul. "No politics—business! I too bear resentment against England, but I might have found a means of satisfying that resentment while remaining in profitable territory. This is my idea: the famous Niagara Falls, situated on the border, belong partly to the United States and partly to Canada. They're much too far away from New York for the convenience of tourists, so why not bring them closer? We'll excavate a canal branching from the Erie canal and, by means to which I'll have to devote more intensive study if the project goes through, we can gradually relocate the falls, Goat Island and the Cave of the Winds, to the Hudson, a few leagues from New York. Canada will no longer have anything but an unimportant little waterfall, a miniature cascade, and the United States will be the sole possessor of the marvel of the Americas. We won't ask anything of the States for that, but we'll construct and exploit a railway between New York and the nearer falls—an exclusive railway, whose immense receipts will be sufficient to cover our expenses. That's the plan—we just need shareholders."

Farandoul continued: "I've got another idea. I know that New York wants to have an obelisk like the ones in Paris, Rome and London—and Munich, which has one made of zinc. I'll offer New York one of the great pyramids; except that, as the enterprise will be difficult to mount, it's another business in which we'll have to sell shares."

"What about the financial crisis?" Mandibul observed.

"Yes, the financial crisis that's had America in its grip for two years will be a considerable hindrance; capital is in short supply. Oh well, as I want to launch myself into business without delay, I'll look for a third idea, a third project of lesser importance, in which we won't be impeded by that obstacle."

Indeed, business was distinctly stagnant at that time and the capitalists, tested by too many disasters, were refusing to get involved in adventurous schemes. Finally, thanks to his lucky star, Farandoul got his hands on a sufficiently important, though slightly vulgar, business. It was a matter of providing a large workshop making luxury footwear with the rattlesnake skins necessary to its production. The provision of crocodile skins had been taken on by hunters in Florida, so only the provision of snakeskins remained, which could not be undertaken by amateurs because of the immense risks involved.

Farandoul thought about it, had a flash of inspiration, and took the job. However, as he did not care to appear to be occupied with mere shoemaking, he cleverly put about the rumor that he had obtained an official commission to furnish rattles to the president for the American deliberative assemblies, and that the needs of this more elevated commerce would take him to Brazil, into the land of the boicinongas, sucuruyus and other rattlesnakes.[45]

The newspapers of New York, followed by those of London, announced to the world that the former conqueror of Australia, inspired by motives that were both humanitarian and commercial, was going to relieve Brazil of rattlesnakes and equip the assemblies of all the America republics: the United States, Mexico, Guatemala, Costa Rica, Honduras, Nicaragua, Venezuela, etc, etc...

While the Old and New Worlds were taking in interest in Farandoul's new enterprise, the expedition organized by the man in question disembarked at Macapa at the mouth of the Amazon, in the northern part of Brazil, south of the equator.

We shall pass rapidly over our hero's commercial career; it was brilliant but of short duration; much more important events and much more hazardous enterprises await us. We shall only mention the manner in which the great rattlesnake hunt was conducted and explain how the firm of Farandoul, Mandibul & Co. made vast profits in very little time.

The company's base of operations was established at the place where the Amazon meets the most important of its tributaries on the right bank, the Rio Madeira, in the territory of the Iguarahna, Mundurucu and Tacahuna Indians— brave savages who wear parrot-feathers in their hair and very elegant multicolored tattoos. What colorists these savages are! It's there that the government should send our Prix de Rome![46]

Saturnin and his little troop set forth boldly into the immense virgin forest that covers hundreds of leagues of those territories; it was necessary to clear a path with hatchet-blows though the dense vegetation flourishing fervently beneath the ardent radiation that the Brazilian Sun had poured over that fortunate land for tens of thousands of years. Thousands of lianas hanging down from gigantic trees of unknown species, intertwined in a limitless web, were attacked

---

[45] The French term for which rattlesnake is the English equivalent is *serpent à sonnettes, sonnette* usually referring to a bell rather than a rattle, so the suggestion of Farandoul's rumor is that he will be supplying the parliamentary assemblies with bells rather than rattles, although the absurdity is hardly diminished by that substitution. As usual, Robida is utterly careless of matters of natural history; one would not go to Brazil to hunt rattlesnakes, and the creatures Farandoul actually traps are anacondas: sucuruyu, which he spells *soucourouyou*, is a contemporary rendering of *sucuri*, the native term for the anaconda (the etymology of the more usual name is enigmatic), while boicinonga presumably derives from the Latin name of the family to which such snakes belong, the *Boinae*.

[46] The Prix de Rome was an annual scholarship established in 1663 open to students of the *Académie royale de peinture et de sculpture*; it was notoriously hard to win—Louis David is said to have contemplated suicide after failing for the third time. It was abolished in 1868.

bravely by the sailors. Finally, in the very heart of a territory swarming with snakes, the real operation got under way.

What might the large boxes carried through the forest by native bearers hired by Farandoul contain? The sailors did not know and often asked Mandibul; the latter always replied. "Wait and see!"

The day came when everyone could see. To the great amazement of the mariners, and especially the natives, the open boxes revealed a cargo of superb polished boots and a job lot of little red balloons! To add to the strangeness, the marvelous boots, equipped with improbably long spurs, were not in pairs; seaman Tournesol, the most intrigued of all, even established that there were only 17 left boots, as opposed to 24 right boots. What was the solution of the mystery?

Farandoul began speaking. "My dear friends," he said, "the moment has come to disabuse you! You might have assumed, until now, that we are going to hunt rattlesnakes as one hunts rabbits, with eyes peeled and rifles in hand. No, no, no. As courageous men, you are ready to confront these terrible reptiles, but know that I have never had any thought of risking precious lives in a merely commercial enterprise! I have found a means of rendering this hunt as facile and as free of danger as that of wild rabbits. Here are our weapons: well-polished boots! The natives who surround us are unfamiliar with the usage of these masterpieces of American cobbling; one of them, whom I suspect of being a former cannibal, has even tried to bite into one of the boots. The rattlesnakes are even less familiar with them and will allow themselves to be captured all the more easily, for these false boots are quite simply rattlesnake-traps!"

And Farandoul launched into a detailed explanation of the procedure to the men charged with its application. As we shall see them at work, we can dispense with revealing the secret ahead of time. Besides, it was not long before the reptiles made the acquaintance of Farandoul's boots. Immediately after the unwrapping of the snake-traps the entire troop set off into the forest, hatchets in their belts and rifles over their shoulders.

Within a few hours, 50 traps were placed in suitable places in a few forest clearings; the boots, standing up in the long grass, shone like mirrors in the bright sunlight, while a red signal-balloon swayed in the least breath of wind at the end of a thread attached like a lace to each boot.

When these preparations had been completed, all the hunters returned to the camp and took a leisurely siesta, only troubled by a surfeit of mosquitoes.

If we remain on watch near one of the traps, we shall understand Farandoul's invention in all its beauty.

As soon as the men have gone away, all the noises of the forest resume their intensity: howls, mews and various animal cries; hasty rustlings in the undergrowth; ripplings in the tall grass or foliage; the hissing of reptiles, the singing of birds; croaking and cawing and the discordant squawking of parrots saying "Polly, put the kettle on!" in their natural language.

Birds of every color fly through the air while, on the ground, myriads of ants of all sizes and legions of insects, some as big as a man' fist, run through the grass, bumping into one another, fighting, massacring and eating one another.

Everything is alive, everything is animate, and everything is on the move, swarming in the immense forest. But see!—frightened parrots are fleeing from a tree whose branches seem to be moving and twisting; it is a large sucuruyu of the most venomous species, awakened by the gleam of a boot, which is descending from the tree around which it has been coiled.

Look! The long furrow ploughed through the tall grass is the sucuruyu advancing toward the object of its desire; the polished boot fascinates and attracts it; it arrives, rears up, and sways its flat head, darting angry glances at the boot, whose cold impassivity exasperates it.

A long hiss resounds; the sucuruyu has unwound its coils and precipitated itself upon the boot. Within a second, the boot is swallowed; the sucuruyu voluptuously closes its eyes and attempts to take in the spur. One more effort and the spur is engulfed! Suddenly, a strident noise is heard: errrrr! The snake seems to receive an electric shock; it opens its mouth wide, and its entire body becomes as rigid as an iron bar.

The trap is sprung! By leaning on the spur, the reptile has activated a spring, which, suddenly unwinding, becomes a sort of stiff and inflexible vertebral column. The hideous reptile can no longer move; mouth agape, utterly bewildered, it awaits the hunter who will be guided to the scene of the drama by the red balloon, which is still swaying in the air.

Another advantage of Farandoul's method is that each boot and spring can be used repeatedly.

There does not seem to need for us to say any more about such facile hunts. In a few months the expedition's goals were met and Farandoul returned to New York where, once the assets were liquidized, each of the men on the expedition found himself in possession of a nice little fortune—much less, it must be admitted, than the one that went down with *La Belle Léocadie* after the fruitful expedition in Malaysia, but amounting, after all, to a sufficiently respectable number of dollars.

We now arrive at a new phase in our hero's life: a period of ardent agitation caused by the most violent passions.

What do you expect? A man is never made completely of bronze; there always comes a moment in life when the most frozen of hearts warms up and comes to the boil! That moment had arrived for Farandoul. Since the cruel loss that he had suffered of the unfortunate Mysora, his heart had not beaten at all; he had delivered himself entirely to ambition. Absorbed by immense enterprises, by the care he had devoted to the organization of his armies of monkeys, and, finally, by all that the defense of his conquest, Australia, had necessitated, Farandoul

had been made of bronze, stone or marble. At the end of the day, though, Farandoul was young. His heart resumed beating, and its beating had been troubling the man of action for some time.

He had to do something about it!

Weary of great enterprises in which his wounded heart remained solitary and sad, persuaded that, from time to time in life, some use must be made of that organ, Farandoul made a resolution to head for Mormon territory.[47] Mandibul and the 15 men from *La Belle Léocadie* were summoned to a meeting that very evening, and Farandoul told them about his plan. Strangely enough—which proves the extent to which all these men understood, they too being weary of the solitary life—their thoughts had also turned in the direction of the great Salt Lake City.

There was nothing but acclamation: "Hurrah for Mormonism! Let's all be Mormons!" Mandibul even declared that he had always dreamed, for so long as he could remember, of spending happy days as a Mormon patriarch, surrounded by a family distinguished by serial numbers rather than vulgar baptismal names.

The preparations did not take long. The idea had been welcomed by everyone with such enthusiasm that they were all ready within two hours, and the departure was immediate.

Six days on the railroad did not cool the ardor of the neophytes. At the first station, Farandoul had sent a telegram to Brigham Young,[48] the Mormon high priest, to inform him of his impending arrival. Brigham had replied, and a conversation had been struck up between the high priest and the new convert that lasted throughout the journey.

Brigham Young, happy and flattered to have such an important recruit to his religion, put himself entirely at Saturnin's disposal. In the final hours of the journey the telegrams multiplied.

Have found splendid opportunity. Senator has just divorced spouses. Sixteen assorted women, will throw in 17th for free. Would you like to take advantage? Are numerous contenders but you shall have pick.
Brigham Young

---

[47] Verne devotes a chapter in *Le Tour du monde en 80 jours* to Phileas Fogg's sojourn in Salt Lake City, and dutifully includes a brief history of Mormonism, which is remarkable for its sympathy.

[48] Brigham Young had died in 1877, and one cannot libel the dead—which is perhaps as well, given the unflattering portrait Robida goes on to paint of the patriarch, about whom he and his readers would have known next to nothing except for the widely-publicized and seemingly-scandalous fact that he had 55 wives.

Accepted. Thanks. Lieutenant Mandibul asks if there might be a similar opportunity for him.
Saturnin Farandoul

Six black women and one Chinese woman in view. Don't speak French. Do we have a deal?
Brigham Young

Mandibul asks for half a dozen white women besides for pleasant chats around the hearth.
Saturnin Farandoul

Have found them! One asks in advance of conclusion whether Lieutenant Mandibul is blond.
Brigham Young

Ardent blond. Another question. Tournesol, 33 years old, volcanic temperament. Would like Mexican women.
Saturnin Farandoul

Mandibul marriage concluded. Job lot of Mexican women for Tournesol. Will be at the station.
Brigham Young

Brigham Young had arranged things well. Before his friends had even disembarked he had married them and had found them the necessary 17 apartments—that is to say, large houses for Farandoul and Mandibul and 15 cottages for the ordinary seamen.

The announcement of the arrival of the celebrated Farandoul and his men had caused a profound emotion in the city of Saints; the Grand Council of bishops and elders had met and it had been decided that they would be given a solemn welcome.

The station had been decked with flags and, a long time before the train was due, an immense crowd of people in their best clothes had gathered on both sides of the track. The Grand Council was there, with Brigham Young at its head; in front of the Elders a white cohort of wives attracted the tender gazes of the curious.

Dressed in white and crowned with flowers, the new brides, suppressing the beating of their hearts, were awaiting the arrival of their husbands. They were of all colors and all nationalities. In order to delight the gazes of the newcomers, Brigham Young had wanted to bring together the most comprehensive assortment of Mormon beauties, and we can be assured that he had succeeded completely.

Finally, the train was signaled. All hearts were beating rapidly. The repeated blasts of the whistle and the increasingly loud roar of the locomotive were suddenly drowned out by the explosion of a salvo of applause loud enough to make the great temple collapse.

The travelers leapt down to the ground and, responding to the popular acclaim by waving their hats wildly, headed towards the group of women.

Brigham Young advanced, shook Farandoul's hands and delivered a welcoming speech full of the warmest cordiality, to which Farandoul replied with a few heartfelt words.

The introductions followed. Farandoul was burning with excitement at the prospect of meeting his wives at last; Mandibul and the sailors were trying to distinguish theirs among the numerous collection assembled by Brigham Young.

Let us say right away that everyone was satisfied with the choice, and that Brigham had no complaints to receive—except that Mandibul negotiated a minor exchange with the Breton Trabadec, a simple and gentle fellow. Trabadec had enjoyed a particularly lucky draw, Brigham Young having married him to four charming Parisian women, among whom were a petite dramatic artiste who had come to San Francisco with an opera company—but Trabadec immediately established that none of his wives spoke Low-Breton and had confided his embarrassment and desperation to his superior. The ever-benevolent Mandibul had taken the four Parisians for himself and had given the enchanted Trabadec four of his black women in exchange.

Everything being arranged to the general satisfaction, there was nothing else to do but proceed with the festivities. After leaving the station the procession went straight to the temple, where the civil ceremonies were held. It was only necessary to read out a few quick paragraphs and everyone went on to the Great Polygamy Hotel, in the grand hall of which was a magnificent banquet with 3000 place-settings, offered by the municipality of Salt Lake City to the newcomers.

Brigham Young the bishops and the elders honored this gigantic meal with their presence; floods of champagne were poured in honor of Farandoul. We have no intention of recounting every incident or enumerating all the toasts that were raised to Mormonism, the elders and the new acolytes, and to their lovely "fractions"—as Mandibul put it, in speaking of his wives, who were too numerous to be described as halves. We only wish to transcribe here the introduction to the speech that our noble hero made, amid a tumult of acclamation and applause, which ended in so formidable an explosion of hurrahs that several gas-lamps in the street were blown out.

"Ladies and gentlemen," Farandoul began, "It is not, believe me, without mature reflection, having meditated long and profoundly, that I have decided to come to ask the City of Saints to find a place for one more faithful follower!

"It is a man battered by the tempest, shaken by storms, who comes here in search of a pleasant and peaceful port in which, in the calm waters of all-inclusive virtue, he may rest from the fatigue and agitation of an existence devoted heretofore to the defense of great renovating and humanitarian projects.

"The Mormon idea is great too! To rediscover the true role of woman in Biblical tradition; to revive the family; by the example of patriarchs to enlarge the conjugal hearth to give places there to an indeterminate number of spouses! Your prophet Brigham Young had said: 'A man's heart is vast; his hearth must be equally vast!'

"Another very important reason militates in favor of polygamy. How often have we seen those sad monogamists leading a wan and near-futile existence in a continuous state of coldness and hostility with their one and only spouse? The sharp angles of their characters continually bumping into one another, the result is sulking, quarrels, disappointments of every sort for both of them—while, in bravely adopting the principles of polygamy, the wide-open hearth has resumed its attraction, by virtue of a certain equilibrium produced by the variety of characters, faults and qualities eventually compensating for one another, and forming a sum of conjugal happiness impossible of attainment in a restricted hearth!

"Yes, polygamy alone cushions existence!

"Thus, we renew the hearth, we elevate the man and relieve the woman— but our action does not stop there; little by little, we are changing the face of the world. In my opinion, the monogamous nations are doomed to a rapid decadence and degeneration, and the moment has come when, seeing the threat of that decadence looming, they will soon throw themselves into our arms. The role of polygamous nations will soon commence; we must be and will be the initiating nation!

"I shall give you one single example, gentlemen, of the power of the idea of polygamy—not for your sake, strong in your conviction as you are, but for the sake of the world, which has its eyes upon us.

"What was the era of greatest prosperity for Turkey, the period of the expansion and the grandeur of the Ottoman Empire? Exactly the era in which polygamy was considered by everyone as an absolute religious duty. Turkey only began to decay when mores were relaxed and polygamy was no longer observed save by the aristocrats of the State, the pashas and the sultans.

"That is why I say that the renewal of the Old World will come from the Mormon nation, and why I am ready to contribute to the full extent of my feeble means to the triumph of our great pacific and humanitarian ideal!"

II.

We have mentioned the emotion that Farandoul's speech excited in the Mormon assembly. An attentive observer would have been able to remark that Brigham Young alone had not afforded the orator his share of felicitations, and that his face, smiling and cordial at the beginning of the meal, had gradually passed through all the shades of discontent. With thin lips and frowning eyebrows, he watched the Mormons crowd around the man he was beginning to see as a potential rival, and whom he was repenting of having welcomed so expansively.

Meanwhile, one of the most venerable members of the audience asked to speak. "I only have a few words to say," he cried, in an outburst of enthusiasm. "There is a bishop's seat vacant on the Grand Council, and I propose that our eloquent friend Farandoul be elected to it immediately. Believe me, my candidate will do honor to the Mormon Church!"

Thunderous applause greeted this motion. Brigham Young's lips became even more pinched, his fists clenched and he made as if to rise to his feet, but a moment's reflection stopped him. He fell back into his chair with a malevolent smile.

"The entire Council of Elders is gathered at this table," the orator went on. "We can vote by acclamation!"

Every hand was raised, and a great clamor went up.

"Farandoul, Mormon bishop!"

Saturnin Farandoul had just been unanimously elected.

"The honor that you do me is immense, and I shall try to be worthy of it!" cried our hero, who found himself suffocated by the handshakes and hugs of his friends and wives within the blink of an eye.

This incident reminded him that he was the head of a family.

"Honor to the ladies!" he said, "Crushed by the weight of all the favors that you have so generously heaped upon me, I have not been able to make the acquaintance of my wives. It would be unpardonable were I to forget any longer those who have consented to become the flowers of my fireside."

"Bravo! Bravo!" cried the entire audience. "We shall lead you triumphantly to your domicile. The municipal band awaits you in the street."

Brigham Young had disappeared, along with a few somber faces that had not joined in with the general joy.

The elders took their places at the head of the procession. Farandoul and his wives, Mandibul and his and the families of the seamen followed behind. They set off to the strains of the Mormon national anthem, sung in chorus by the entire crowd:

"Great King Solomon had 300 wives..." And so on.

Farandoul's villa was charming; the purest taste had presided over the furnishing of every room. After a few last acclamations released beneath the windows, the procession went on to install Mandibul and the sailors. An individual who seemed to be the master of ceremonies had left a piece of paper in Farandoul's hands, which was a copy of his marriage certificate.

"Very well!" said Farandoul. "I shall finally know the forenames of my lovely fractions! Let's take a roll-call first, to check that there's no error, and that none of Mandibul's spouses have got mixed up with mine. Let's begin:

"Sidonie Brulovif, 26, born in Bordeaux.

"Lodoïska Ratakowska, 30, born in Krakow.

"Balthazarde Marcassoul, 18, born in Marseille.

"Chloe Vanderboeuf, 30, born in San Francisco.

"Athénaïs Plumet, 32, born in Paris.

"Calypso Zanguebar, African, age and birthplace unknown.

"Theodosia Niggins, 18, born in New York.

"Cora Millington, 16, born in Chicago.

"Dolores Castanetta, 22, born in Mexico.

"Diana Pilkington, 17, born in Philadelphia

"Pulcherie O'Cobbler, 35, born in Baltimore.

"Angelina Farthing, 26, born in Dublin.

"Olga Biscornoff, 22, born in St. Petersburg.

"Juanita Pacheco, 18, born in Lima.

"Clarisse Dickinson, 25, born in Liverpool.

"Kaoula Ka-ou-lin, 28, born in Lichou-fou, near Peking.

"Marguerite Schumacher, 20, born in Berlin."

No error was discovered; every woman replied to the roll-call, and Farandoul observed with satisfaction that they were in truth charming. Brigham Young had good taste; Saturnin made a mental note to thank him.

The luggage arrived. Thoughtfully, Farandoul proceeded to unpack. In the course of his life, events had gone by with such rapidity that they had left him little time for reflection. Three weeks previously, he had still been in Brazil; he had spent an entire fortnight in a steamboat and six days on the railroad, taking only a little time to settle his affairs in New York. Finally, although he had only been a Mormon for six hours, he already had 17 wives ornamenting his household, and was already a bishop.

A ringing bell drew him out of his reflections. The 17 wives disappeared, leaving him alone with his visitor. The latter had merely come to inform him that a meeting of the Council of Elders was to take place that evening and that Brigham Young requested the new bishop to honor it with his presence, if the fatigue of his journey would allow it.

"I'll come with you," said Farandoul. And the indefatigable Saturnin, after a few words with his wives, went out on the heels of Brigham Young's messenger.

Alas, the hour of tranquility, after so many testing adventures, had not yet chimed for our hero. New perils were suspended over his head; the infamous Brigham Young, anxious and jealous, had judged it prudent to contrive the disappearance of a man who might become a dangerous rival for him.

Night had fallen; our hero advanced along the somber avenue that led to the great Mormon Temple. Having no suspicion, he had not noticed that shadows were following him noiselessly, and that other shadows were lurking behind every tree.

His thoughts were directed towards his 17 wives, and towards the happy future that was opening before him. There was no black dot on the horizon, no cloud in his sky…

Suddenly, the call of an owl sounded behind him. A whirlwind of human beings fell upon his shoulders before he could look round, and—in spite of his desperate resistance—he was soon knocked down, bound and gagged. The men were masked. Even so, Farandoul thought he recognized two associates of Brigham Young that he had glimpsed at the banquet. He understood everything!

Horses had been brought; the bandits attached Farandoul securely to the most spirited of the mounts, and leapt into the saddle in their turn. Without a word being spoken, the cavalcade set off at a gallop for open country.

After a two-hour journey, they stopped on the edge of a wood. A few owl-hoots were released; others replied, and a second group of horsemen appeared.

These riders were Redskins. In the moonlight, Farandoul glimpsed bizarre tattoos, further accentuating the ferocity of faces, fur jackets, war-bonnets ornamented by eagle- and vulture-feathers, and saddles garnished with horrible scalps.

"Here's the man!" said the leader of Brigham Young's acolytes.

"That's good!" replied a tall Indian. "Our father the Paleface-with-a-hundred-wives is a great chief; his enemy shall die! The Apache warriors and the Palefaces of the Great Salt Lake are friends; the red warriors will be able to seek firewater in their city; the hatchet of war is buried forever. How!"

The horse carrying Farandoul had been surrounded by the Indians. The two parties drew apart. They galloped all night. From time to time an Indian made sure of the solidity of the ropes retaining the captive. Farandoul slept. At daybreak, the horse's abrupt halt woke him up; they had arrived.

In the middle of a large clearing bordered by tall trees, the picturesque scene of a camp presented itself to his eyes, vaguely blurred by the morning mist. About 20 Indians were gathered around two fires, before which pieces of venison were roasting for the morning meal. Farandoul was able to admire the splendor of their war-paint, the strangeness of their costumes and the beauty of their weapons in broad daylight.

The ropes that bound him to the horse were cut, and the prisoner, still bound but no longer gagged, was thrown on to a grassy mound and placed under the surveillance of two men. Then the whole troop, gathered in front of the fire, calmly began eating, without dreaming of offering anything to the captive. That did not please Farandoul, who was angered by a few jeers in the Apache language, whose meaning he had grasped without understanding the words.

"Hey!" cried Farandoul, in English. "The red warriors are timid women, then—seeking to deplete the white man's strength by depriving him of food! Shame on the red warriors!"

"The white man is going to die. What does one meal more or less matter to him?" replied one of the Indians.

"No," said another, "the white man is brave; he has a right to a warrior's meal. The Paleface will be attached to the war-pole in good health."

From that day on, Farandoul, almost freed from his bonds, was able to take part in the Indians' meals. He was determined to remain alert and fit, in order to profit from any opportunity to escape that presented itself. He had understood that he was to be taken alive to the tribe's village in order to be scalped ceremonially—a little pleasure-party whose enjoyment he often heard the Indians anticipating during the nine days that the journey lasted.

By his bravery, Farandoul had won the good opinion and consideration of his guardians; unfortunately, though, he had not been able to find any opportunity to quit their company. That annoyed him considerably when he thought about his 17 wives, whose anxiety must have been immense.

His bad mood grew worse one morning when, having arrived during a night march at the Apache village, he was taken down from his horse and led through the midst of the red population to a pole painted in different colors and ornamented with trophies, raised on a mound in the middle of the village. It was the war-pole! He understood that the fatal moment was approaching, and asked to speak.

"Red warriors," he cried, "you shall see how a brave man can die! But before that, you will not refuse the Paleface one last request. He has 17 squaws in the city of the Great Salt Lake; he asks to send them a last word of farewell, and he counts on finding a brave warrior among his red enemies to carry the letter."

An Indian came forward. "Fire-Eye," he said—this was the name the Indians had given to Farandoul—"is right. Red Bison will go to the city of the Salt Lake."

"Thank you. Red Bison is a great chief!"

Farandoul's plan, as you will guess, was not so much to inform his wives as to make Brigham Young's treason known to Mandibul and his sailors. He had no intention of saying any more than that, knowing his men well enough to be sure of being avenged.

The Indians conferred, however. One of them, a chief, came back to Farandoul and asked him how and with what he proposed to write. That was a difficulty; there was not a single piece of writing-paper to be found in the entire tribe.

Farandoul had an idea. "Red Bison's body," he said, "is ornamented by numerous beautiful paintings. If my brother will allow it, I shall inscribe my farewells on his skin, in order that he will have no fear of losing my letter."

"Red Bison accepts!" replied the Indian, after a moment's reflection—and, pots of red and blue paint having been brought, Farandoul's hands were untied in order that he might write his last confidences on Red Bison's skin.

Farandoul addressed his letter to Mandibul. He wrote at length, and was forced to continue his letter on Red Bison's back page. The Indians crowded round, and followed with an increasingly keen attention the arabesques and flourishes with which Farandoul decorated his missive, in order to deflect Brigham Young's suspicions and imitate the Indian designs. He thus discovered a talent for calligraphy and that of a most distinguished water-colorist, just at the moment when the talent was about to become useless to him. Red Bison's breast and back soon resembled an illuminated page of an Arabic or Persian manuscript; the ornate lettering and the flourishes produced such an effect on the audience that several other Indians also asked to carry something.

The enthusiasm became delirious. All the men in the tribe wanted at least to be charged with a postscript. Red Bison, fully illuminated, was the object of admiration of all the women, and continually came back to shake our hero's hand warmly. The latter began to think that he might perhaps profit from these good wishes and save his scalp, so he redoubled his efforts. Ornamental art was no longer sufficient for him; he began to pant portraits. On the back of the Sachem of the tribe he painted a full-length portrait of Mandibul. The acclamations increased and every shoulder-blade was offered.

Farandoul brandished his brushes, and 17 Indians soon bore portraits of the 17 tearful spouses of the Mormon bishop, some on their backs and others on their breasts. The face of Brigham Young followed; then a sequence of landscapes was launched; the most fantastic designs and the most seductive colors made the Indians flamboyant. What a revelation for them of a totally unknown art!

Night fell and Farandoul, who should have been scalped at noon, still had his hair. The Indians had a discussion, and seemed disposed to renounce his scalp. Finally, after a great council in which Red Bison—who would rather have been the only one to beat Farandoul's illustrations—was the only one to vote for the scalping, Farandoul was solemnly detached from the war-pole and begged to consider himself henceforth a child of the tribe. All they asked of him was to devote all his talent to the ornamentation of his new friends.

Farandoul, of course, accepted—without raising any objection—the position of ordinary and extraordinary painter to the Apache nation, and relied to the felicitations of all his admirers with the most cordial handshakes. The costume of an Indian warrior was immediately brought for him, which gave him a sensible pleasure, his clothes having been reduced to rags by brushwood during the journey.

A wigwam was allotted to him, in the center of the village, not far from the Sachem's. The tribal chiefs and all the influential warriors spent the evening in the council hut with Farandoul, who was for them Fire-Eye, the white warrior with the deft brush. The calumets were lit and, lost in a cloud of smoke, Farandoul was asked to recount his adventures. We have mentioned the high degree to which our hero possessed the gift of eloquence; that day his mesmerizing words held the Indians in suspense for hours.

The night was well-advanced when our hero was escorted to his new domicile. Farandoul went to sleep, exhausted by fatigue, putting off until another day the task of thinking up some means of escape. He was no longer worried; he knew that the opportunity would present itself some day or other, and wanted to profit from his sojourn among the Apaches to make a thorough study of that interesting nation. Besides, since we ought to reveal everything, we ought to admit that our Farandoul had yet another reason for staying with the Apaches. A young Indian woman of the most ravishing beauty had caught his eye; he had scarcely glimpsed her when, moved by curiosity but restrained by modesty, she had come to admire the painter's arabesques momentarily—but that moment had sufficed.

Farandoul had been struck in the heart by the tomahawk of love!

Unfortunately, the young Indian woman was married; she was, in fact, the wife of Red Bison, Farandoul's enemy.

The next day was a holiday for the entire tribe. The warriors of the neighborhood had been summoned to a great fantasia in honor of Farandoul. He was introduced to them, and delighted them with his good manners. Their enthusiasm increased further when, during the fantasia, Farandoul, mounted on an unbroken horse, accomplished the most vertiginous feats.

Presents were exchanged. Farandoul had nothing to offer but specimens of his talent as a painter, but in exchange he received a calumet, a tomahawk and a rifle—which induced him to provide evidence of his skill as a marksman.

Everyone went their separate ways delighted. Farandoul promised that he would soon illustrate the entire Apache nation. Indeed, after a few days devoted to his installation and a few hunting-trips with the Apache warriors, Fire-Eye took up his brushes again.

The entire tribe filed in front of him. A little expedition against the Sioux had been proposed for the following season, and before disinterring the war-hatchet, everyone wanted to be painted in such a fashion as to sow fear among the enemy warriors. Fifteen squaws were employed night and day for a week in grinding colors and macerating them in a mixture designed to render them indelible.

Fire-Eye commenced his operations. With his most garish tones, he began by painting extraordinary and terrible things on the breasts of the chiefs.

Sachem Co-a-ho-hay, the eagle of the mountains, as ornamented with a frightful locomotive in deep purple, equipped with two red lanterns and a plume of Prussian blue smoke; an immense train of wagons charged with menacing Indians followed behind, turning under his left arm, snaking across his back and finishing up back on his breast.

The success was complete. At the sight of this masterpiece, the warriors were bowled over with admiration!

The three inferior chiefs followed in their turn. On the first, Pointed Knife, Farandoul painted a huge red balloon with a yellow gondola full of Indians brandishing their tomahawks. Long-nosed Fox was gratified with a portrait of Napoléon I, whose grey coat had to be changed into a blue one. As for the third, Big Gun, to his great delight he had a monstrous elephant armed with gigantic red tusks.

The bulk of the army filed past then; every warrior was painted in his turn. The compositions that enjoyed the greatest success were fiery dragons, cannons vomiting grapeshot, a steam-boat, a French gendarme on horseback and finally, on the belly of one of the stoutest Apaches, an enormous Indian's head, reproducing with a striking resemblance the face of its bearer, with all its ornaments exaggerated in size—so well that he seemed to have two heads, one large and one small.

A grand review was ordered for the benefit of the general's gaze. On a beautiful sunny day, all the warriors gathered their equipment and arranged themselves on the plain, fully armed. Farandoul ran between the ranks supplying a few finishing touches and adding a few ornaments, such as a white clock-face with all the numbers marked in red, and the occasional ace of hearts, spades or clubs.

During the march-past, when the warriors charged, the women recoiled in terror; the effect was frightful!

III.

It was on the morning after the review that Farandoul made the acquaintance of a new set of clients. A few Apache beauties, from among those who set

146

examples for the others, came to ask him to sketch a few graceful compositions on their epidermis.

Fire-Eye was over the Moon; he had not hoped for such a complete success. Finally, he might be able to enter into communication with the woman he loved! Without losing a minute, he set to work: elegance in the design; flair in the color, he put every possible charm into his compositions, knowing that he was dealing with his most demanding clients.

These attempts succeeded; charmed by the color and style of his compositions, the feminine sector of the Apache population—who had, until then, found the provisions of nature sufficient—made free with these ornaments, decreeing that it was necessary further to augment natural gifts, to the extent that tattooing became high fashion among the Apache ladies.

How Farandoul's heart beat!

Every day, in front of his wigwam, there was a queue of Apache ladies; they made appointments with the artist to obtain a sitting. The latter never hurried, giving each of his designs all the necessary time and attention.

"How is it," he said one day, with feigned indifference, to young Morning Mist, the daughter of the Sachem with the locomotive, "that I haven't yet seen Rising Moon?" Rising Moon was the poetic name of Red Bison's wife, who had made such a powerful impression on our hero's thoughts.

"Well, I was saying just the same thing this morning!" replied Morning Mist. "It's Red Bison who won't let her—I'll get her to make her mind up."

The young brunette departed at a run. Farandoul did not know the result of the negotiations until the next day; they had concluded with a complete success, for the first client who presented herself was Rising Moon, accompanied by her friend Morning Mist.

Fire-Eye received the ladies with exquisite politeness; he offered them two calumets with a little fire-water, and they chatted. Rising Moon had finally obtained authorization from her husband to be ornamented with a few simple paintings in good taste.

Leaving the ladies to take long draws on their calumets, Farandoul plunged his head into his hands in search of inspiration; it was not long in coming, for, leaping upon his brushes, he asked to begin.

For Rising Moon, he found the most delectable allegories, the most gracious attributes, the most exciting compositions: hearts in flames or pierced with arrows, doves, cupids brandishing bows and tomahawks, and so on. By way of conclusion, he painted a white warrior at the feet of a roseate woman within a red heart, forming a charming group that a blue child half-hidden behind a bush was transpiercing with a pointed arrow; to the right of the design was a Moon half-emerging from the bosom of a cloud—evidently recalling the gracious lady's name, while a red eye, placed in suspense on the other side, opened the way to the strangest suppositions.

The thing was all too clear: the red eye signified Fire-Eye; the painting was an imprudent declaration that the blushing Rising Moon understood.

The presence of Morning Mist embarrassed Farandoul, who did not dare express his love for Rising Moon except by furtively squeezing her hand.

In the meantime, Red Bison came into the artist's tent.

Farandoul, thwarted, pretended to be applying a few final brush-strokes to his work. Without saying a word, Red Bison examined the work.

"How!" he exclaimed, finally. "Fire-Eye likes hearts on fire. These hearts on fire often encounter arrows and tomahawks—that's bad! Would Fire-Eye like to put a red warrior with his scalping-knife in his hand behind the group pierced by the blue child?"

"No, that wouldn't work," Farandoul replied, coldly.

"All right!" replied Red Bison, as he went away.

This time, it was Rising Moon who furtively squeezed Farandoul's hand. The poor woman had understood that Red Bison had just sworn a mortal hatred against Farandoul.

"Bah! I've seen plenty of others," murmured the young man, when he was alone.

Red Bison was a cruel and vindictive man; he did not want to attack Farandoul straightforwardly, in order not to compromise his marital dignity by putting his wife in question, but he sought by every means possible to make trouble for our hero.

The latter was summoned to the council hut a few days later, where all the chiefs were gathered.

The Sachem Mountain Eagle spoke first. "Our white brother Fire-Eye," he said, "possesses a great talent, but his beard is not yet white and the years have not cooled his head—is that not true?"

"Mountain Eagle is a great chief; his tongue is not forked; what he says is true."

"Fire-Eye has painted beautiful things on the breasts of red warriors, but on those of the warriors' squaws he paints things that are difficult to understand. Has Fire-Eye a forked brush? The white hair of old men is standing up on their heads; the chiefs ask that in future, Fire-Eye will explain the meaning of these paintings before completing them."

"Fire-Eye is indignant that the good faith of his brush should be suspected by his red brothers! He will refuse any explanation!"

And with these imprudent words, Farandoul left the council hut. "Me, submit to a censor!" he cried. "Never!"

The machinations of Red Bison had partially alienated the amity of the population from Farandoul. Our hero was soon put to a further proof. Two Indians presented themselves at his tent with their wives.

"Fire-Eye has a forked brush," said the first. "Would he care to explain to me what he has painted on the breast of Flying Horse's squaw?"

"And on Muskrat's squaw," cried the second. "Fire-Eye has sought to take advantage of the honest and simple minds of his Apache friends in order to deceive them. What does this mean?"

Farandoul burst out laughing. The terrible paintings that had excited so much suspicion in the Indians were a portrait of a monkey and a windmill.

"How!" said the Indians. "Fire-Eye is laughing! He mocks the red warriors, but the red warriors have tomahawks!"

"So has Fire-Eye!" cried Farandoul. "Come on! Enough threats!"

The Redskins were gesticulating on the threshold of the tent; other Apaches came running. Red Bison was among them. He had seen the quarrel from afar and came to aggravate it. "The red warriors are right," he said, pushing through the group. "Fire-Eye is a traitor! He had better watch out that he doesn't return to the war-pole...this time he'll lose his scalp!"

"Come and get me!" said Farandoul, putting his hand on his tomahawk. Red Bison had already launched his own at his head. If Farandoul had not thrown himself sideways, it would have split his skull.

The circle widened out; the women and children ran way, for the warriors had all drawn their weapons.

Farandoul, standing up in a threatening pose, awaited the attack.

Chief Mountain Eagle ran forward in haste. "Is this the way Fire-Eye repays the hospitality of the tribe?" he said. "He has wounded one of our warriors!"

"Red Bison attacked me!"

There was a long discussion among the Apaches, after which they withdrew, darting threatening glances at their former friend. Farandoul, left alone, went back into his wigwam, well aware that he was in grave danger. He loaded his rifle, armed himself with powder and lead, put his hatchet in his belt and awaited developments. The whole tribe was astir; there were discussions and deliberations. An empty space developed around the wigwam, which a few warriors watched from a distance.

What about Rising Moon? our hero asked himself, anxiously. *What's become of her?*

Night fell. Farandoul could still see the Apaches gathered near the council hut, murmuring. A slight noise behind him interrupted his reflections, Rising Moon was in the tent. She had used her knife to cut an opening in the hide wall and as standing in front of Farandoul. "Quickly!" she said. "The red warriors have decided to kill Fire-Eye. The chief is still trying to restrain them, but he cannot do it much longer. Rising Moon has secretly taken a horse to the edge of the forest; it's necessary to flee with her."

"Let's go!" said Farandoul, delighted with the turn that events had taken.

The tent was surrounded; the Apaches were already creeping up on it. Farandoul remembered the gymnastics he had learned in the monkeys' school; in the blink of an eye, with Rising Moon on his back, he hoisted himself up to the top of the wigwam, which was open to let out smoke, and slipped silently into the bushes just as the Indians invaded the tent.

The night was dark. The two fugitives reached the edge of the wood without being seen. They had just got to the horse when a loud cry told them that their flight had been discovered.

"Let's get going!" exclaimed Farandoul. Leaping into the saddle, he set Rising Moon sideways in front of him. "We'll have at least two hours start," he said. "The Apaches won't find it easy to follow our trail in the darkness."

In the early morning light, the fugitives encountered a swift-flowing river. As the horse could go no further, Farandoul judged it prudent to abandon the animal. With his hatchet he felled a few small trees and set about constructing a raft, tying it together with the cords forming the harness of his mount. Within an hour it was complete and in the water. Rising Moon sat at the back and Farandoul, standing at the front, began paddling to get it under way.

The river was deep and rapid, sometimes narrowly enclosed by two steep banks and sometimes widening out in the middle of dark forests. They covered some 15 leagues in eight hours in this fashion. Rising Moon told Saturnin that the river, called the Colorado, was interrupted further on by dangerous rapids; the fugitives decided to go ashore and not to resume their journey until the following day, at dawn, in order not to risk a shipwreck in pitch darkness.

The raft was carefully concealed in the reeds and Farandoul searched for a sheltered spot to make camp. It was not easy to find. In the end, he discovered an old hollow tree in which they would be safe. The entrance was five or six meters above the ground; Farandoul climbed into it and used his hatchet to make the refuge a little more comfortable. When that was done, he helped Rising Moon to install herself therein for the night.

A strange situation! A *tête-à-tête* inside a tree! Fortunately, the prescient Rising Moon had brought a little pemmican; they made a frugal meal and, as they were extremely tired, went to sleep very quickly.

At about midnight, Farandoul was woken up with a start by growls coming from down below, inside the tree. Ominous movements were taking place beneath them—the tree was inhabited!

"Listen!" said Farandoul, waking his companion. "We have bears for neighbors."

Rising Moon, asking no questions, moved out of the cavity and sat on a branch. Farandoul, rifle in hand, came out backwards. The growling grew louder; a bear was climbing up. Farandoul, sitting astride a major branch, put his finger on the trigger. The head of a bear appeared. It was an enormous beast: a Rocky Mountain grizzly—a disagreeable animal at any time but ferocious when disturbed.

The bear was still climbing. Its open mouth gave voice to frightful roars. With lightning rapidity, Farandoul stuck the barrel of his rifle into that mouth and fired.

The thunderstruck bear fell backwards. Other roars sounded within the tree. Farandoul only just had time to reload his weapon and repeat the same maneuver.

The she-bear immediately collapsed.

Rising Moon was cold. Farandoul spent the rest of the night removing the cadavers from the tree in order to make bedclothes with the bearskins. One bear-cub remained, and Rising Moon adopted the orphan.

This work was scarcely finished, at daybreak, when Rising Moon, still sitting astride a tree-branch, let out a cry of alarm. An Apache had just appeared 200 meters from the tree. The Indian had perceived the two fugitives and was returning at a run to alert his comrades. One of Farandoul's bullets struck him down.

"Run and fetch his rifle," said the Indian woman. "Rising Moon knows how to use it."

Farandoul ran to strip the Apache. "And now," he said, "the others will soon be on our heels. We have to get out of here. I've got an idea! Let's put the bearskins on our backs and try to pass for grizzlies."

In five minutes, the two fugitives were transformed; at 15 paces the illusion was complete.

"Bring the cub!" said Farandoul. "It'll facilitate our disguise."

On seeing the two bears, the little cub seemed happy to found its parents again; its stopped growling and it darted between Rising Moon's legs. Without interrupting this effusion of filial piety, the bears, followed by the cub, went into the rocks. Farandoul showed his companion a distant party of Indians galloping across the plain. "There's time!" he said.

The Indians saw them too, but being on the warpath, following an easy trail, they did not pause. The fugitives were increasing their pace when, on going around a rock, they found themselves face to face with more Apaches, whose bodily decorations Farandoul recognized.

The Indians had leapt backwards. Farandoul, thinking that he had been recognized, did not hesitate, and felled the first with a single rifle-shot. Rising Moon did likewise for the second.

No words can describe the astonishment of the Apaches on seeing bears shooting at them with rifles—an astonishment shared by the little bear-cub, still full of the innocence of infancy.

The Indians, however, overcoming their bewilderment, soon saw through the stratagem and replied with a hail of bullets, which did not hit anyone. The fugitives threw themselves behind a rock in order to fight from cover.

The Apaches' war-cries resounding from echo to echo, the Indians from the plain came running at a gallop. Farandoul inspected the surroundings of his rock, searching for some means of salvation. He was greatly astonished to see a second bear-cub beside the first. There was a cave-opening behind them; it must be inhabited.

Meanwhile, the Apaches were advancing cautiously.

"Into the cave," said Farandoul, shoving his companion urgently.

A few hairy individuals growled but, recognizing brothers, did not manifest any hostility.

The Apaches, not finding anybody behind the rock, ventured into the cave-entrance. That was what Farandoul was waiting for. He fired on them and gave the little bear-cub a vigorous kick on the nose. The increasingly-bewildered cub growled painfully. Then there was a fearful jostling in the cave; the bears, thinking that they were under attack, surged out.

"Damn!" murmured Farandoul. "That's a numerous family!"

Indeed, six bears of colossal size were rushing at the Apaches, fighting furiously. Farandoul and his companion, going out behind them, ran to their rock and started firing continually at the fleeing Indians.

The fight was still continuing. Farandoul, striking out at the last Apaches with his rifle-butt, completed the rout. Eighteen Apaches were dead; four or five were limping away, with a single wounded bear still in pursuit.

The bears sat down on rocks, in a familiar graceful attitude, licking their wounds. Farandoul and his companion attempted to behave in as ursine a manner as possible, in order not to arouse suspicion, and examined their paws with their hands. From time to time, a bear released a howl of pain and look around angrily in search of some new enemy.

To escape this new danger, Farandoul signaled to Rising Moon to imitate him, released a few growls, and got up furiously as if to go in pursuit of an enemy. One old bear followed them. For a few minutes he showed off, parading himself in front of Rising Moon—who, you will remember, had put on the she-bear's fur.

Without speaking, the three bears headed for the Colorado, followed by the cub. Farandoul's intention was to find the raft and resume the river journey as quickly as possible. The bear was still playing the gallant, but Farandoul only had to growl at it to make it behave itself.

Soon they reached the river and found the raft. The bear watched their preparations uncomprehendingly, but when it saw its companions jump on to the raft it followed their example without hesitation.

"Bah!" said Farandoul. "Let it come—it's a friend."

The day went well. While Rising Moon acted as lookout, Farandoul paddled, to the great astonishment of the grizzly.

As evening approached they neared the rapids. Farandoul had to get closer to the right bank of the river to avoid being dragged away by the current. Suddenly, he felt someone grip his arm; it was Rising Moon, who showed him 20 Indians galloping over the plain.

"Apaches!" he murmured. "Damn!"

The Indians stopped some 50 meters from the bank, surprised by the sight of a raft steered by bears. The real grizzly, remembering the morning's battle, roared furiously.

One Apache, whom the two fugitives recognized simultaneously, was talking volubly and seemed to be giving an order to open fire on the raft.

"Red Bison!" cried Farandoul. Seizing his carbine, he fired at his enemy, but Red Bison had leapt sideways and the bullet struck a warrior to one side of him.

It was impossible to cross the river to seek shelter on the other bank; an unusually violent current precipitated the water towards falls situated 200 meters further on, in a place where the Colorado, narrowing between rocky slopes covered with pines, fell from a great height with a frightful noise.

Farandoul weighed up the situation in an instant. One of the trees had fallen across the river, forming a sort of bridge, beneath the arch of which the foaming waters were engulfed. If they could reach the tree they would almost be saved, the passage being easily defensible.

"Let's land," said Farandoul, "and let the grizzly loose on them!"

Within two minutes the plan was executed. The Indians, gathered around the wounded man, suddenly saw the grizzly coming at them, while the two fugitives ran towards the waterfall.

As a few rifle-shots rang out as their grizzly ally battled the Apaches. Farandoul and Rising Moon had scarcely reached the waterfall when they saw the Apaches coming after them at the gallop. The grizzly was dead! There was not a moment to lose. They had to get to the other bank, and to do that, they had to venture on to the tree, an old pine that was only held in place very precariously.

War-cries resounded behind them; without worrying about the balance of the tree, the eddying spray and the noise of the waterfall, the fugitives crossed the fragile bridge over the cataract. As soon as they were on the other bank, sheltered by a slab of rock, they awaited the enemy, rifles in hand.

While the Apaches got down from their horses and gathered together, Farandoul perceived, to his great joy, that the rock behind which they were sheltering, the tree's sole point of support, was insecure and shaky, ready to crumble at the least shock.

"This time we're saved," he said. "Let them come!"

You have guessed Farandoul's plan; it only remains for us to see it executed.

The Apaches had reached a decision. No longer able to see the fugitives, they thought that they had continued their flight through the rocks on the left bank. The furious Red Bison had taken the lead and had set off across the aerial footbridge. Behind him, 15 Apaches were advancing carefully, rifles in hand.

"It's time!" said Farandoul, when he saw that they were two-thirds of the way across. Combining their forces, the two fugitives gave a vigorous shove to the rock that was sustaining the tree. The rock trembled and swayed, then rolled into the river. The Apaches screamed loudly—a single scream! With a frightful noise, the tree collapsed into the spray of the waterfall, with all of its passengers.

No further incidents troubled the remainder of our fugitives' journey. One morning, a few more bullets whistled over their heads, but they had been fired by white men—trappers who, in the hope of obtaining their furs, had followed the tracks of the two fake grizzlies. Farandoul, realizing their mistake, had made hurried signals to them. At the sight of a flag of truce raised aloft by bears speaking English and Spanish, the amazed trappers had ceased fire. They soon understood.

The woodsmen told the fugitives that they were in the middle of the Sierra Verde in the state of New Mexico. One of them offered to get them to Santa Fe, the state capital, within two days. The offer was accepted, and two days later, to its amazement, the city of Santa Fe saw two bears with rifles slung over their shoulders entering within its walls. When the truth was revealed, the two bears were lionized. Bankers rushed to put their vaults at Farandoul's disposal while he waited for the Bank of New York to send him funds.

Farandoul's first thought was to telegraph Mandibul in Salt Lake City. The response was unexpected. On hearing the news of their leader's disappearance, Mandibul and his companions had left, abandoning their wives. Even Trabadec had left his house and his black women.

IV.

Farandoul went back to the telegraph; a dispatch was sent to Brigham Young which read:

Rascal, what have you done with my 17 wives?
Saturnin Farandoul (Reply Paid).

Brigham Young replied with a telegram shot through with shrewd hypocrisy:

Sir,
After the incomprehensible flight that made us see that you were not a sincere Mormon, your wives, embarrassed at having been united even for a single instant to a man devoid of conviction, demanded a divorce. An honorable Mormon, Matheus Bikelow, appointed as bishop in your place, opened his hearth to them; he has married them and will not abandon them!
Once again, sir, your conduct has been unworthy, and I urge you never to come back to the city of Saints.
Brigham Young.

The fee being paid, Brigham Young, as you see, had not been parsimonious with his words. Farandoul turned his attention to Bikelow and demanded his 17 wives from him. An exchange of correspondence, at first mock-polite and then threatening, took place between the two rivals. Bikelow, pushing irony to the point of sarcasm, offered to surrender one of the wives—probably the 17th, whom Farandoul had received as a bonus.

Farandoul was appalled by this outrage. The employees of the telegraph company must have trembled as they transmitted this laconic response to the insulter:

It's your life that I must have, wretch. Make your will.
Saturnin Farandoul.

For a week the telegraph was monopolized by the two adversaries. Bike-low accepted the challenge, but could not make a decision as to the weapons to be employed. Farandoul proposed, successively, tomahawks, carbines, cannons, ballistas, catapults, ironclad ships, balloons, and so on.

The newspapers got mixed up in the affair; soon enough, in every city of the United States, no one was talking about anything but the duel. As people were beginning to make fun of Bikelow's difficulty in the choice of weapons, the latter ended up proposing a classic American duel, demanding that the two adversaries, armed with rifles, should depart at the same time, one from New York and the other from San Francisco, and hunt one another down across the entire Yankee territory.

This was Farandoul's response:

Idea accepted in principle, with only one small modification. Each adversary will board a locomotive. The two trains will depart at the same hour from New York and San Francisco, to crash into one another at the half-way point of the Central Pacific Railroad.
Saturnin Farandoul.

Bikelow was trapped. He could not refuse again; his committees would not permit it. We have forgotten to mention that, because of the stir the affair had created throughout the land, committees had been formed in every city. There was no one in the United States now but Farandoulists and Bikelowists, every-one having sided with one or other of the two adversaries.

What was Rising Moon doing during the course of these negotiations? While Farandoul divided his time between his committees and the telegraph office, the young brunette spent her time being photographed by the artists of San-ta Fe in all her costumes: as a bear, in full Indian costume, and in the splendid outfit of a civilized lady that Santa Fe's high society had offered her by sub-scription. Rising Moon loved the arts; an American painter, leader of the Sensa-tionalist school, made a portrait of her in oils; in the course of the sittings, this artist, moved by inter-school jealousy, took pleasure in criticizing the paintings by which Farandoul had declared his love to the young Apache, thus sowing the first seeds of discontent in her heart—which would germinate later.

Meanwhile, one result of the excitement generated in the United States by the quarrel between Farandoul and Bikelow had been to inform Mandibul and his crew of their captain's fate. For three months, the brave mariners, having gone in search of Farandoul, had been fruitlessly combing the Rocky Mountains; the only clue they had been able to find was an encounter with an Indian who

158

had a portrait of General Mandibul tattooed on his breast. Unfortunately, as he only spoke Apache, it had been impossible to get any information out of him.

The seamen were beginning to despair when, one day, arriving in a little town in the state of Nevada, their gaze fell upon large posters bearing these words:

GIGANTIC DUEL
FARANDOULIST COMMITTEE

Hurrah for Farandoul! Farandoul forever!

The president of the Farandoulist committee announces that a great meeting of Farandoulist committees has obtained permission from its champion to add a set of wagons for his adherents to the locomotive that will carrying him to meet his enemy Bikelow. Hurrah! The day of the gigantic duel is approaching!

It is set for the 15th of this month.

Farandoul is already in New York. Tremble, Bikelowists!

"To the railroad!" cried Mandibul. "A train to New York, quickly!"

This was how, six days later, Farandoul and Mandibul fell into one another's arms. The newspapers had brought the mariners up to date with the situation during the journey.

"We claim the first wagon!" cried Mandibul.

"I'll reserve it for you," Farandoul replied.

An hour was devoted to explanations; they all recounted their adventures. Farandoul teased Mandibul, calling him a Mormon *in absentia*; Mandibul, on learning that Brigham Young had tried to get rid of Farandoul, offered to go put Salt Lake City to fire and the sword. Farandoul calmed him down.

"Let's leave that," he said, "and get back to Bikelow, the infamous ravisher of my 17 wives. This is how things stand. All the preparations are made; the departure is set for June 15—which is to say, in a week's time, and we should meet one another, if the calculations of the engineers are correct, on June 17 at about 7 p.m. I've appointed the delegate from my committees, the expert engineer Horatius Bixby, as my second, along with my old friend Mandibul!

No greater excitement had ever stirred the population of the United States. One might have thought that it was the middle of a presidential election: meetings everywhere, of committees, sub-committees, counter-committees, or simple gatherings of adherents of one or other of the parties. In New York, some districts were entirely populated by Farandoulists, while others supported Bikelow; there were tumultuous manifestations, processions that generally concluded with clashes between the two parties. In the streets, streamers and flags in the colors of each party hung from windows, lit up every evening. Amid the street-lamps the name of the preferred individual was inscribed in gigantic letters by fireworks or in immense display-windows.

The committees were working furiously. A team of engineers had been attached to each of the adversaries, and a meeting of the two teams had, after 15 days and 15 nights of deliberation, determined the conditions of the combat: the hour of departure, the quantity and quality of coal, the speed to be attained, and so on. All these calculations had been made with such precision that the exact point of the encounter could be determined. The collision would take place on the Devil's Bridge on the Nebraska River. Each locomotive, manned by a first-rate mechanic and stoker, was armed with a huge howitzer mounted on a pivoting chassis, invented for the occasion by Farandoul's second, Horatius Bixby. The adversaries would open fire the moment they saw one another; the howitzers being breech-loaders, it was anticipated that there would time for 20 rounds to be exchanged.

A determined number of wagons having been put at the disposal of the committees, each of the adversaries would go into combat with his supporters.

Pleasure trips had, of course, been organized in every large city to the meeting-place. Grandstands had been set up under the Devil's Bridge on both banks of the Nebraska. The best places cost $20 and the poorest, half a league from the bridge, 50 cents. Bets were being laid in great quantity, and the pools agencies were promising large payouts.

At first Rising Moon had been slightly offended by Farandoul's attempts to reclaim his 17 wives, but she had ended up by yielding to his reasoning. Understanding that it was, above all, on principle, and not to allow such an insult to go unpunished, that Farandoul was claiming these ladies, she now prayed for his success and asked to accompany him on his locomotive. Farandoul refused, but gave orders that a place of honor should be reserved for her at Devil's Bridge.

The great day drew nearer. It was time. The breathless population thought about nothing else. The sessions of Congress were suspended, and the world of business was subject to what it dubbed the Farandoulist crisis.

June 13 came, then 14; in New York, crowds stationed themselves all night long around the platform. Finally, on June 15, at 7 a.m., a carriage brought Saturnin Farandoul and his seconds, Mandibul and Horatius Bixby, to the railhead, where they were greeted by an immense acclamation. Other carriages followed, containing the delegates of 500 Farandoulist committees, supplementary witnesses. Reporters from all the newspapers laid siege to the station to obtain places. It was a trifle crowded in all the wagons. An old acquaintance was waiting for Farandoul: our friend Dick Broken, who had arrived from Australia that very morning, and had been commissioned by Mr. Bennett, the proprietor of the *New York Herald*, to follow all the vicissitudes of the affair. In the capacity of a friend, the *New York Herald*'s reporter obtained a place on the locomotive.

At exactly 8 a.m., a blast of a whistle announced the departure; in the midst of a storm of acclamation, the train departed, at full steam.

Farandoul and his seconds, standing next to the howitzer on the little platform of the locomotive, waved to the delirious crowd. The smoke of the locomotive had no sooner disappeared over the horizon than special trains, chartered by punters, set off along the rails in pursuit.

For two nights and three days the train ran without stopping for more than a few minutes at three or four stations. Behind it filed the punters' trains, struggling to keep up with the speed of Farandoul's. Only five out of 11 that had left New York were following close behind, the others having suffered various mishaps; one had been derailed, two others had collided in the course of the pursuit and remained in distress, broken down on the track, blocking the passage of the last three.

Two hundred people had gathered at Devil's Bridge. The grandstands were heaving with spectators who had been flocking all through the morning of June 17. Interested Bikelowists and Farandoulists pointed out to one another, in a place of honor on the grandstand on the right bank, Rising Moon in full Indian costume—and, directly facing her, on the other side of the Nebraska, on a platform guarded by devoted Bikelowists, Farandoul's 17 divorcées, the causes of all the trouble.

At 6 a.m., the excitement peaked. The telegraph had signaled the approach of the two trains from the nearest stations. Everything was going to plan; their progress had been calculated perfectly, and the impact was predicted at 6:48 a.m. During the final half-hour, the telegraph never ceased functioning, signaling the approach of the trains from one office to the next.

Finally, at 6:41 a.m., an immense cry went up, followed b a fearful silence. From the right and the left, the strident notes of prolonged whistle-blasts cut through the air.

A cannon-shot followed, then two, then four; the adversaries had caught sight of one another and the combat commenced. The two trains were now in sight for the eager spectators established on the banks of the Nebraska and in the trees on the neighboring slopes. The two trains were arriving at lightning speed, leaving wakes of eddying smoke behind them. At ten-second intervals a lightning-flash sprang from each of the locomotives, while a little cloud of white smoke went up, a detonation resounded, and a shell whistled through the air.

Opera-glasses followed the vicissitudes of the duel feverishly. Farandoul's locomotive had already lost a piece of its chimney-stack, a result that the Bikelowists welcomed with a resounding cheer. At 6:46 a.m., with only a few kilometers separating the two trains, Farandoul launched one final shell, which, it later transpired, knocked Bikelow's hat off. The latter replied with a last sequence of four shells, whose explosions blasted two of the Farandoulist wagons to smithereens.

Farandoul's stoker had been killed; the engineer, an energetic man, was adequate to the task. At 6:47 a.m., the *New York Herald*'s correspondent released yet another carrier pigeon; the poor bird, avoiding Bikelow's last shell by a miracle, bore the following brief dispatch to Omaha City:

6:47 a.m. All right! Farandoul is fine. Received seven shells, one on the locomotive and six on the punters' wagons. Much smoke from wagons, casualties as yet unknown. One minute to impact!

Dick Broken.

Another 30 seconds went by.

The two trains, now separated by a very short distance, hurled themselves at one another like two fiery monsters.

The Devil's Bridge remained to be crossed; Bikelow's train was the first to move on to it. A frightful crack was heard; the decking of the bridge was giving way beneath the weight of the overloaded wagons!

At the moment when Bikelow's locomotive, having reached the topmost point of the bridge, found itself almost face to face with Farandoul's, the steel cables, horribly taut, broke noisily and the bridge, suddenly collapsing, tipped its load into the abyss.

A clamor such as the echoes of the mountains had never heard before rose into the air. Farandoul's train, moving like lightning, had crossed the gulf! The Bikelowist train, as it fell, had served it, so to speak, as an apron—or rather, by virtue of the speed it had built up, Farandoul's train had jumped to the other bank. Its last wagons were already disappearing over the horizon![49]

---

[49] This whole incident is an absurdly exaggerated combination of two adventures experienced by Phileas Fogg while crossing the USA by railroad in *Le Tour du monde en 80 jours*, the first being his determination to fight a duel with Colonel Stamp Proctor in the final carriage (although Indians attack before the first shot is fired) and the second being the rather implausible leap made by the locomotive to clear the gap left by the fallen bridge at Medicine Bow.

As for the Bikelowists, their 60 wagons had fallen from a height of 500 feet into the Nebraska.

Ten kilometers beyond the bridge, Farandoul's locomotive, finally brought under control, slowly ground to a halt. Everyone got down and congratulated one another. The Farandoulists' victory was complete! Farandoul and Horatius Bixby threw themselves into one another's arms. Dick Broken, sitting on the howitzer, wrote a dispatch that he sent by pigeon to the *New York Herald*. When that was done, he came down to join in the warm congratulations and general acclamation.

"Now that honor is satisfied," Farandoul said, "I renounce the 17 ingrates. Someone telegraph Brigham Young."

Four days later, Farandoul and his seconds, with Rising Moon, made their triumphal entrance in New York.

The Farandoulist crisis was not over; people were liquidating positions. The Bikelowists, having lost fabulous sums, made no attempt to conceal their fury, while among the happy and proud Farandoulists, there was talk of nothing less than offering Saturnin Farandoul as a candidate for the Presidency of the United States. The former committees refused to dissolve themselves and claimed to have become electoral committees, in view of the presidential election that was to take place in six months time. Our hero's popularity was, therefore, immense.

Unfortunately all these events had made considerable inroads into the fortune made in Brazil. Many thousands of dollars had been swallowed up, not only in Salt Lake City but in all the expenses necessitated by the duel—which, for pride's sake, our hero had not wanted to leave to the responsibility of the committees. On the other hand, the position of a constitutional head of state subject to a parliament did not tempt him; his instincts as a man of action made it out of the question. To the great disappointment of his partisans, Farandoul declined any candidature.

He was supported in this resistance by his new friend Horatius Bixby, the Central Pacific Railroad's expert engineer. During the two nights and three days they had spent together on the locomotive, they had had time to weigh one another up and get to know one another.

Horatius Bixby was a truly remarkable man. An authentic pure-blooded Yankee, and an engineer, inventor and machine-builder of rare distinction to boot, a thoroughgoing scientist, the grandeur and profundity of his ideas was combined with an audacity and stubbornness in action characteristic of his adventurous race. His story was known throughout America. He had once provided a striking illustrative example of the grandeur and power of SCIENCE, with which man might, with the most slender means—or even without any means at all—overcome every difficulty and triumph over all obstacles.

In 1850 or thereabouts, Horatius Bixby, exploring and prospecting for gold in the plains of Sonora in Mexico, had had the misfortune to fall into the hands of a party of ferocious Indians, after a violent conflict in which all the men in his expedition had been killed and scalped. Bixby, having been struck down in the first volley of arrows, had recovered consciousness after the Indians had gone. Entirely naked, covered with wounds and even scalped, he had dragged himself as far as possible from the scene of the massacre. The discovery of an Indian canoe had saved him. Utterly exhausted, he had lain down in the bottom of the frail craft and had abandoned himself to the caprice of the waves.

A full two hours later, when he recovered consciousness again, he found himself at sea, buffeted by a frightful tempest. Bixby had a cat's nine lives; he did not give in, and his canoe survived the turbulence of the sea. After 12 or 15 days adrift, land appeared—or, rather, an islet, a deserted rock, pounded incessantly by the immense Pacific waves.

Bixby disembarked, and his first concern was to find a shelter in which he might rest his weary body. A week later, he was well on his way to being healed; his wounds had scarred over and his appetite had come back. The convalescent explored his domain, in search of nourishment.

The islet was absolutely deserted. Bixby, naked and scalped as he was, did not despair. He set to work courageously to create a Robinsonian existence as comfortable as was possible. He observed that the Indians had not scalped him completely and that he still had three hairs. These three hairs, with a pen-knife recovered from the site of the battle, were his only resources. This feeble assistance sufficed, however, for him to get through the affair by means of prodigies of industry that science alone can explain. That was the sole point of departure of the marvels that this Robinson performed by scientific means.

With his three hairs, Bixby first manufactured a snare, with the aid of which he trapped several birds, whose feathers served to braid a string for a bow fabricated with the pen-knife. The arrows were furnished by their sharpened bones. Stronger animals were struck down and Bixby soon found himself comfortably nourished and dressed with sufficient elegance for an island so rarely visited.

In two years, his island was transformed. Bixby had a house, furniture, pots made of iron and tinplate, a metallurgical workshop of sorts, a sugar factory, and so on. He had exploited the iron ores and oil deposits that he had discovered, and the industrial future of his isle was assured.[50] Already, he was thinking of

---

[50] Six years after this little comedy appeared, the American writer Douglas Frazar published *Perseverance Island; or, the Robinson Crusoe of the 19th Century*, which attempted in all seriousness to present a very similar scenario as a hymn of praise to the glory and utility of science. Frazar's castaway is not quite naked and has a few more useful objects (though not, significantly, a pen-knife), but his accomplishments—including the eventual construction of an iron foundry, a steamboat and a flying machine—are equally miraculous. It seems

equipping a few railway lines to establish communications between his various houses, and setting up an electric telegraph. His long evenings had been devoted to the cultivation of the gentle arts—which consisted, for a man as positive as he was eminent, of transcendental mathematics, statistical studies, research in physics, chemistry and so on. Only one thing annoyed him: no confidant was within reach to whom he might express the joy of his triumphs and the enthusiasm of his scientific discoveries.

Robinson had had Friday, but Bixby seemed condemned to solitude. Our energetic scientist having resolved to fill this lacuna, he meditated for two days and then invented the phonograph. Let us say right away that this phonograph was not the simple instrument that we know, but a complete phonograph, still unknown in Europe—for, on his return to the United States Bixby, preoccupied with new problems, neglected to take credit for that wonderful invention. One of his colleagues, the savant Edison, partially repeated his discovery and launched into the astonished world the phonograph that everyone in Paris was once able to hear in the hall of the Faubourg des Capucines, but that imperfect phonograph only recapitulates Bixby's invention in part; it repeats what is confided to it but does not reply.

Bixby, therefore, had no more need of a companion; his phonograph was his Friday. No more boredom, no more solitude; he had a confidant for his exuberant soul. All his thoughts could be confided to the phonograph—which, being superior to the vulgar phonograph, replied to him. When the weary scientist was avid for a long conversation by his fireside, he began a pleasant conversation with his phonograph that sometimes lasted long into the evening.

---

unlikely that Frazar could have read *Saturnin Farandoul*, so the coincidence is rather remarkable.

Led by his meditations to think that, although resin, tallow, wax, gas and oxyacetylene have successively dethroned one another in our bulbs as means of illumination, the wan rays of moonlight are no more luminous than in the earliest days of street-lighting, Horatius Bixby had a new idea: that of finding some means of improving the old Moon by brightening it with electric light.

Our scientific Robinson was on the brink of finding this means when a ship, attracted by the sight of a factory chimney on an islet recorded on all the maps as deserted, dropped anchor one day at Bixby's island. A few emigrants on their way to Australia decided that it would be better to colonize such a well-prepared an island. Bixby City, the capital of Bixby Island, was founded, and the engineer only left the ex-desert island when the continued prosperity of the colony was assured.

This was the man with whom Farandoul had associated himself! Horatius Bixby had made him party to a discovery he had made in Patagonia, of diamond mines so superior in their yield to those in South Africa that the indigenes, full of scorn for such common pebbles, simply used them as ammunition for their slings or door-handles for their lodges.

Thus far, Horatius Bixby had not been able to profit from his discovery, the difficulty of the enterprise, the dangers that would have to be confronted and the querulousness of his countrymen had put off all those to whom it had been proposed. It was exactly what Farandoul and the men of *La Belle Léocadie* needed. Farandoul leapt at the idea and obtained their enthusiastic consent.

A week later, an expedition was well on the way to completing its organization. Weapons, powder, provisions and tents had been bought, and passage booked on a steamboat bound for Buenos Aires. Farandoul was the commander-in-chief, with Horatius Bixby and Mandibul as his lieutenants.

As for Rising Moon, the young brunette having insistently asked to accompany the expedition, the affectionate Farandoul had consented, knowing full well that she would not become a burden in any event and could, if need be, use a carbine and war-hatchet with perfect familiarity.

V.

On a beautiful morning in July, the diamond-hunting expedition left the city of Buenos Aires and set forth across the pampas, heading for Patagonia.

The first part of the journey was, so to speak, nothing but a long pleasure trip; they marched southwards, hunting all the while, and only two months after its departure, the expedition arrived on the bank of the Rio Negro, the frontier of Patagonia.

The difficulties began there. The Rio Negro, augmented by recent rain and swollen by numerous tributaries flowing from the mountains, had overflowed its narrow bed and covered the plain as far as the eye could see. The expedition went upriver in the hope of finding a crossing. There was water everywhere; there were only a few clumps of trees or a few hillocks to be seen emerging from the immensity of the flood.

The expedition had not encountered a single living soul for a week: no more gauchos, no more marauding Indians, no more haciendas, no more of the vast herds of cattle encountered in the north. On the morning of the fifth day, however, Mandibul, who had gone on ahead to reconnoiter the terrain, was greatly surprised to hear a number of rifle-shots in the distance. He returned to Farandoul at a gallop; the expedition halted and everyone, pricking up their ears, heard further and more numerous detonations.

Without saying a word, the party set off at a gallop. They had entered, without realizing it, a long strip of land hemmed in by the floodwater. Farandoul soon perceived this, but, hoping that it would guide him towards the battlefield, continued to push forward. The tongue of land grew narrower, and was soon no more than a thin strip separating the choppy waters of two lakes.

Finally, having covered more than a kilometer, they perceived a confused mass of covered wagons gathered on a little wooded hill. A few more rifle-shots were still resounding. Farandoul and Mandibul, deeply intrigued, dug their spurs into their mounts' flanks and ate up the ground.

The hill formed the extreme point of the tongue of land along which the seamen were moving. It was, in fact, an island of sorts, for it was necessary to go through a few 100 meters of knee-deep water. The two riders had been spotted from the hill. A certain tumult was produced when Farandoul eased up, crying from afar: "Amigos! Amigos!"

Having come within a few paces of the island, Farandoul and Mandibul stopped in amazement. On the hill, suffering the double assault of the inundation and enemy savages, there were women, and only women, hiding behind some 50 covered wagons—100, 200, 300 women, at least, and not one man! There were women of every nationality, dressed in costumes of every imaginable sort, speaking all the languages of the globe.

Farandoul and Mandibul rubbed their eyes. Who could have expected to encounter, at the tip of South America, women in European dress, Orientals in harem consumes, Chinese women, Hindu women, Mexicans, North American Indians, and so on? Who could have brought them so far from their respective homelands into these unknown regions?

These ladies, at the end of their tether, were pressing around the mariners and seemed to be pleading for help.

A rifle-shot resounding a short distance away brought new cries of fright from all the women. Farandoul extracted himself from their arms and ran in the direction of the gunshot. At the edge of the water, behind an empty wagon, two men were lying in ambush. They leapt to their feet on hearing footsteps close at hand.

"Amigos!" Farandoul repeated.

Two hands were extended towards him.

"We and our companions are being pursued by a band of gauchos," said the one who appeared to be in charge, in English. "If you can help us drive them off, we'd be very grateful!"

"A very good day to you," said the other, in French. "You can help us shoot at these gaucho rogues, who want to take these women off us."

"Right away!" said Farandoul. "I don't understand any of this, but we'll get the explanations later."

Farandoul went down to the water's edge. In a single glance, he understood the seriousness of the danger to which the refugees on the islet were exposed. The course of the overflowing river was little more than two or three kilometers away to that side, and a few islets formed by other hills were still diminishing in size. On the nearest of these islets huddled a numerous troop of horsemen, augmented by the minute by other horsemen coming from the opposite bank, their mounts breast-deep in the water. A dozen men armed with rifles and lances were loaded in a boat that was steering slowly towards the covered wagons.

The sailors suddenly appeared at the edge of the water and opened fire. At the sight of these new adversaries, the men in the boat rapidly retraced their course.

"We can now talk in peace," said Farandoul. "Tell me, pray, how you came to find yourselves in this hornet's nest—I'm avid for explanations."

The man to whom Farandoul addressed himself was in no hurry to reply; he buttoned his jacket and put on his gloves. "Sir," he said, finally, "please be assured of my utmost gratitude; your unexpected arrival has delivered us from great danger. You must have seen, sir, how distressed our companions were."

"Yes, they must have been very frightened," said the Frenchman.

"Indeed," Farandoul replied.

"Well, sir, those wretched gauchos you see over there were chasing us in order to take away our unfortunate companions."

"But how do you come to be out here on the American pampas," Farandoul put in, "with African women, Chinese women—and even Europeans, if I judge correctly? Why are there only two of your escorting such a numerous cargo— sorry!—collection of young and pretty ladies? That's what I don't understand."

"What!" said the Frenchman. "Don't you recognize us?"

"That's right," said the leader. "Excuse our impoliteness; we've forgotten the introductions customary between gentlemen."

Farandoul bowed. "I'll begin," he said. "Saturnin Farandoul, *rentier*; Monsieur Mandibul, retired general."

It was the turn of the exceedingly formal gentleman. "Phileas Fogg, esquire, member of the Eccentric Club,"[51] he said. "Traveling in the company of Jean Passepartout, his servant and friend."

Farandoul and Mandibul released exclamations of surprise. "What!" cried Farandoul. "Didn't you win your bet? Didn't you go around the world in 80 days?"

"Certainly!" cried Passepartout. "Of course the boss won his bet, but..."

"But what?"

"But having learned, some time after our return, that a trip around the world might be then made in 77 days and eight hours, thanks to a slight change of itinerary, the boss didn't hesitate. He made another wager and set out again, taking me with him."

"And?"

"And," Phileas Fogg interrupted, folding his arms despairingly, "we've been *en route* for three years, eight months and 19 days!"

"And that's three years, eight months and 19 days, "Passepartout moaned, "that my jets have been burning..."

"At your expense," said Phileas.

"That's what's driving me mad!" howled Passepartout, making as if to tear his hair out. "And it's all the fault of your women!"

"Silence!" cried Phileas. "Respect the ladies!"

"But what does it all mean?" cried Farandoul.

"As for the jets, that's quite simple," Passepartout replied. "Thinking that it had brought good luck to our first journey by forgetting the gas jet in my bedroom, on departing for me second, I lit all the jets in the house—17 in all—which have been burning all this time!"

"At your expense," Phileas repeated.

"Is it my fault," Passepartout retorted, "if all the women in the world want to be saved by you? That's the downside of celebrity—there's always some woman to get out of a sticky situation. It always falls to us! Personally, I'd send them packing, but the boss has his reputation as a certified savior to think of, so we save, and we save... It's a whole new world! Yes, gentlemen, we've saved all the ladies that you've seen in the covered wagons—all of them! I have a list; it's me who takes a roll-call every evening to make sure we haven't lost any along the way. We've got 358 of them!"

"*Ventre de phoque!*" cried Mandibul.

"Yes, 358 ladies that we drag in our wake in our covered wagons, who are 358 nuisances! The boss has run through all his banknotes, and he's borrowed all my pocket money, so that all we have left in the world is two Argentinean

---

[51] Verne's Phileas Fogg was, in literal terms, a member of the Reform Club. In metaphorical terms, however, he was definitely a member of the Eccentric Club.

piastres in paper money, which no one in the world will take, because they think they're fake, and 18 revolver cartridges."

"What's that?"

"We fire off so many revolver shots on our journeys! When you think that we've saved 358 women, not counting all those who didn't want to be saved, we've had to make continual use of our revolvers. I'm an orderly man, I keep count! We've fought 128 battles, not counting brawls, scuffles, pursuits, etc., etc., and between us we've fired a 152,000 revolver rounds! That's the situation we're in: 358 women on our hands, with one *sou* and 18 cartridges to spend. A pretty pickle, as you can see! And the knocks we've taken! I don't count them any longer... What grieves me most is what you'll see if you ask the boss to take off his hat."

Passepartout and Phileas uncovered their heads briefly. Farandoul cried out in horror—the unfortunates had been scalped!

"Well, what do you think?" Passepartout went on. "That doesn't do your noggin any good."

"It must alert you to changes in temperature," Mandibul observed.

"Yes, that's one compensation—but it's not enough! To get back to our journey, be assured that it certainly wasn't for pleasure that we came here. Always pursued! We've gone from Sioux to Apaches, Apaches to Mexicans, etc. etc. Since we've been in the Argentine Republic we've had gauchos to deal with. We haven't saved anyone, but these gentlemen, enticed by fresh flesh, fell upon us anyway. Impossible to go to Buenos Aires, as we'd hoped; the gauchos have tracked us across their satanic pampas, and I thought that we were on the point of falling into their hands, with all our goods..."

"With all these ladies," Sir Phileas Fogg corrected, severely.

"With all these ladies, when you came to our aid. Unfortunately, the gauchos are numerous; there are a good 400 or 500 over there, and when the water goes down, which won't take long, we'll be trapped again!"

"Then let's not wait!" cried Farandoul. "Give me a free hand, and I'll take responsibility for transporting you and the 358 ladies to the other side of the Rio Negro."

"Sir, I'm relying upon your honor as a gentleman," said Phileas. "Do as you wish!"

Farandoul gathered his mariners and gave them their orders.

It was quickly settled. While the two poor scalped men kept watch on the movements of the gauchos with Farandoul, the seamen set to work. The ladies being gathered in one place so as not to impede the maneuvers, the horses and cattle were hobbled. Everything that could be made into rope was used to attach the covered wagons firmly end-to-end, and a few felled trees served to consolidate the assembly, which soon formed a wheeled raft capable of carrying the entire colony.

The whole day was taken up by this task. A tall pine was drafted in as a mast, and the ladies worked to make a large sail out of the wagons' awnings. By nightfall, everything was ready. Farandoul decided to leave the departure until morning; everyone gathered around the bivouac fires. The mariners having been introduced to the ladies, everyone had a very pleasant evening. Passepartout never shut up. He undertook to bring Farandoul up to date with every detail of their odyssey.

"That little brunette you see over there," he whispered to Farandoul, "is Ernestine, a Parisian from the Buttes-Chaumont. The boss thinks he's saved her, but that was a trick. I don't like to travel alone, you understand; as she wanted to come with us, I told her to find a way to be saved by the boss—and she succeeded. The boss saved her in Paris, in an omnibus, and we brought her with us. That was the start, you see. We soon saved two Marseillaise girls, then a Spaniard on the ferry. That one wanted to be the last—she didn't want to let us save any more! But she resigned herself to it in the end. Madame Aouda made her see reason!"

"What! Madame Aouda is here?"

"Of course! She served as our interpreter in India. That's where things began to get hot. We saved a dozen bayaderes with two elephants that the rajah wanted to force into marriage."

"The elephants?"

"No, the bayaderes. What a pursuit there was then! In Hong Kong, we abducted three Chinese women and two dozen week-old children that we put out to nurse. At that point we weren't yet behind schedule, but at sea we fell into the hands of pirates commanded by someone called Bora-Bora, to whom I hope to deliver a dozen revolver-shots someday..."

"No need—I've killed him," said Farandoul, coldly.

"Is that a fact? My warmest congratulations! I'll resume my story. So, we were prisoners of the pirates. That swine Bora-Bora, not content with having robbed us, condemned us to death. Needless to say, the thing was done with great ceremony, on the territory and probably with the consent of a certain Ra-Tafia, Rajah of Timor."

"My father-in-law," said Farandoul.

"I don't congratulate you. Still, it was with flattering ceremony that we were executed."

"Damnable joker!" observed Mandibul. "Are you telling us that you were shot?"

"Better than that, Monsieur," said Passepartout, getting to his feet effortfully.

"Decapitated, then?"

"Better than that! Ask Sir Phileas. Look—he's lowering his head. That means a great deal!"

"But in the end," cried Mandibul, "what...?"

"We were impaled, Monsieur!"

A murmur of horror ran through the audience.

"But then...?" Mandibul went on.

"Alas! Fortunately, the good Dutchmen were watching, and, with delicate precaution, removed us from the stakes. Bora-Bora fled; as for us, we set sail for Japan. In Japan, new adventures! We saved four women, we fought duels against four officers, with their seconds and with their seconds' seconds."

"How did you get through so many duels?" asked Mandibul.

"Defeated, but safe and sound! They disemboweled themselves in front of us. After the duels we headed for San Francisco, 45 days late. The boss was furious, but I just delighted in resting my weary bones. I figured that our troubles would be at an end when we arrived in a civilized country. Yes, I'm joking. Our celebrity had preceded us there. We got involved in all sorts of complicated affairs and had to work hard to save ourselves. I emptied two revolvers in San Francisco alone. We finally took the railroad—a special train that ate through a lot of banknotes. We were going through Salt Lake City... Can you guess what happened to us in the Mormon city?"

"You married two dozen ladies," replied Farandoul.

"On the contrary—17 ladies that we'd saved in San Francisco jumped ship and left us. It was to be escorted as far as Mormon territory that they'd thrown themselves into our arms. Sir Phileas and I launched ourselves in their pursuit. People tried to stop us but we galloped off and caught up with them after half an hour. Alas, it was too late."

"Horror!"

"Yes, they'd just married a Senator. Most of all, I regret a certain Sidonie Brulovif...a piquant brunette. She was from Bordeaux."

"*Sapristi!*" cried Farandoul. "No doubt about it! They were my 17 ingrate wives!"

"What—you were the Senator!"

"No, I only came after the Senator."

"There's a coincidence!" cried Passepartout. "I'll go on. So, we lost 17 ladies in Salt Lake City, but we avenged ourselves by taking away 35 Mormons disgusted with their religion, including four of Brigham Young's own wives...look, the four over there who are drinking tea. The rescue wasn't completed without difficulty; it was necessary to use the revolvers. We got our train under way again; the Mormons immediately stoked up another and followed us. We were cornered in the Rocky Mountains. Bang! Bang! More revolvers. All of a sudden, Redskins fell on our backs—filthy Apaches, who started off by skewering the Mormons. When the job was done I went to the chief to pay him my compliments; that's when the swine gave me to understand that he'd really like to have my hair. I dug my heels in; they trussed us up, and the entire caravan was led off by the Apaches. As soon as we arrived in their village we tried to escape, they recaptured us, knocked us down, and..."

"And?"

"And they scalped us! My poor hair! I had so much of it, only ever having distributed a few locks here and there. Now it ornaments the hut of a certain Red..."

"Bison," Farandoul supplied.

"Yes, Red Bison. You know everything, then?"

"My dear Passepartout, I regret not having known you sooner, for I would have brought you back your hair. Continue."

"So, they despoiled us and left us there. We took advantage of it by clinging on to life. You know how obstinate Sir Phileas is; I've tried to emulate him. An Indian woman hid us in a hole in a rock, and cared for us until we healed. I'll always conserve her memory in my heart. She was an angel, my dear Monsieur, good, gentle and charming. She had a very poetic name—she was called Rising Moon."

"*Sacrebleu!* But that's my wife!" cried Farandoul.

Passepartout sat up straight in amazement. "Impossible!" he stammered.

"But there she is! Don't you recognize her?" And he went to fetch Rising Moon from the midst of a group in which she was hidden.

Passepartout and Phileas Fogg raised their arms to the heavens.

"Delighted to see you again, milady," cried Phileas. "Delighted!"

"Madame!" said Passepartout, bowing.

"Rising Moon is glad to see the two Palefaces again in good health," the young Indian woman replied. "The Great Spirit is good; he has watched over them."

Farandoul, who was very thoughtful, wondered why Rising Moon had not recognized the travelers before. He resolved to question her later, and gestured to Passepartout, to signal that he should continue his story.

"We were beginning to get bored in our hole in the rock and were seeking a means of rescuing the ladies who were still in the power of the Apaches when a volley of rifle-fire woke us up one morning with a start. The Apaches were being attacked by federal troops. We took advantage of the opportunity, got the ladies back, and made our escape on foot, leaving the Yankees and the Apaches to sort it out. Sir Phileas bought covered wagons at the first American post and we resumed our journey. We had two days of tranquility.

"On the third day, trappers told us that the entire Sioux tribe, tempted by the hope of capturing so many white women, was waiting for us a dozen leagues away at the pass into Arkansas. The eastward route being closed to us, we took the decision to head southwards. We reached the Rio del Norte and went downriver to the Mexican frontier.

"What a journey! We were scarcely making two leagues a day, in the midst of terrible difficulties. It was necessary for us to erase the tracks of our 30 covered wagons with the utmost care, lest we put any Indians on our track. At Paso del Norte, we were given a fine welcome by the Mexicans.

"Do you think that was the end of our troubles? Not at all. We had the imprudence to attend a soirée at the home of General Ramon de las Aguas Calientes; we were treated with the consideration due to misfortune, but after dinner Don Ramon proposed that Sir Phileas should gamble a few women at Monte. Sir Phileas refused, even though we had enough to be able to risk a few. Don Ramon got annoyed; to settle the matter I offered to play him for Ernestine. We began a hand of Monte. The General cheated. Sir Phileas pointed it out to him politely, but Don Ramon was furious, and drew his machete. We drew our revolvers! The garrison arrived, comprising six generals, 14 colonels and 40 soldiers and officers. As they refused to lower their arms, we tried to negotiate. Don Ramon de las Aguas Calientes had us arrested. A court-martial was organized under his presidency, and we were condemned to death. At dawn on the following day we heard cheering outside. The garrison arrived and forced the doors of our prison. We were carried off in triumph without knowing why, and it was only later that we learned that a revolution—the 246th since 1821—had broken out in Mexico.

"General de las Aguas Calientes had been dismissed. Immediately setting our anxieties aside, we set off with our covered wagons for Chihuahua. A fortnight's march—and it was already two years since we had left London! At Chihuahua we fell into the middle of a counter-revolution fomented by our enemy Don Ramon. We were re-arrested. Don Ramon offered us a choice between a firing squad and commissions as colonels in his army. Naturally, we opted for the commissions, on condition that we could bring the ladies. Don Ramon accepted, and we were colonels! There were enough of them in Don Ramon's army, mind! All the soldiers had been promoted by one grade, the privates becoming corporals, the corporals sergeants, and so on—except that the dismissed former generals had become privates!

"We formed a regiment armed with lances with the 265 ladies that we had then—it was called the Picadoras de la Libertad—and we marched on Mexico City with Don Ramon. Two days later, a counter-counter-revolution broke out in the army and Don Ramon was overturned by General Zapatepas. Don Ramon became Sir Phileas' orderly. General Zapatepas lasted a week, at the end of which the army rebelled again and replaced him with Don Benedicto Tulipanos. After a three-month match we arrived outside the walls of Mexico City; the president's army having decided to switch sides, we made our triumphant entry into the capital without a shot being fired. A great day! The army paraded in good order before the eyes of General Ricardo Acapulco, Tulipanos' successor. We paraded too; at the sight of the Picadoras de le Libertad, the Mexicans could not contain their enthusiasm, showering us with flowers and carrying us off in triumph.

"The people and the army held a meeting regarding a new *pronunciamento*. Colonel Phileas Fogg was named president of the Mexican Republic! We slept in the presidential palace. In the middle of the night I was woken up. A few malcontents wanted to install me at their head, to overturn President Phileas and proclaim Don Juan Passepartout dictator of the Aztec Empire, successor to Montezuma. You know me well enough to know that I didn't hesitate for a minute..."

"Good for you!" said Mandibul.

"I didn't hesitate! I had Phileas arrested and locked up the Picadoras de la Libertad. Mexico spent two happy days under my reign; on the third morning I heard the General fighting beneath the palace windows. I stayed in bed for a quarter of an hour before getting up, and gave the insurrection time to grow; but for that fatal moment of idleness I like to think that I would still be presiding over the destiny of Mexico. I looked so authoritative in my uniform—but I didn't have time to put it on. My successor came into my bedroom; it was Don Ramon de las Aguas Calientes, our first enemy!

"Naturally, I expected to return to the damp straw. Not at all! Don Ramon was still apprehensive of our popularity. He simply sent us to Vera Cruz with our ladies—I forgot to tell you that his first act had been to disband the Picadoras de la Libertad. Sir Phileas forgave me for the *pronunciamento* and I remained in his service.

"At Vera Cruz we were put on a sailing ship, which deposited us after a 70-day journey along the coast in the state of Pernambuco in Brazil. We headed for Rio with 32 more ladies picked up here and there along our route. We spent eight months crossing Brazil, saving another 23 ladies, but, as the Brazilian authorities were making things difficult, we went into the virgin forest. We crossed Paraguay. Finally, we approached Buenos Aires, where we thought our troubles would be at an end, but near the isle of Las Caravellas,[52] bachelor adventurers—colonists—among whom was a certain Don Emilio, got our ladies in their sights.

"These gentlemen, weary of solitude, came to us ceremoniously to ask for the hands of some of our protégées in marriage; some were desirous of marrying two or three, claiming that, in view of the scant security of the pampas, it was necessary to take several wives in order to be sure of conserving one—but Sir Phileas refused!

"That annoyed them; we were pursued, tracked and chased all the way to Patagonia! We kept as far ahead as possible, but they have lassos and know how to use them. From time to time, some gaucho would succeed in getting close to us, throw his lasso into the herd and make off with his prey. Oof! You know everything now."

---

[52] This reference is unclear—Paraguay has no coast, so the travelers are presumably approaching Buenos Aires by river; "las caravellas" [the caravels] usually refers to the three ships in which Christopher Columbus made the first transatlantic crossing, but cannot do so in this case.

Because they all felt the need to rest and recover their strength in order to confront the elements and humans on the following day the meeting in which Passepartout had finished the recital of his misfortunes was concluded, and the entire camp was soon profoundly asleep.

Only Farandoul reflected on the singularity of the encounter. He was only moderately well-disposed towards Sir Phileas Fogg and Passepartout, and re-solved to leave them once he had seen them safely to the other side of the Rio Negro.

The rising Sun found everyone awake and ready to depart. The embarkation on the vast raft formed by Phileas' covered wagons began immediately. The ladies were placed in the middle; the sailors stationed themselves fore and aft. As for the horses and the cattle, they had to swim, attached to the sides of the raft. The embarkation was completed as quickly as possible, and in response to a blast on Farandoul's whistle the big sail was hoisted. It was quite a *coup de théâtre*!

The wind filling the sail suddenly carried the raft several meters forward. The cattle and horses were dragged into the water, their bellows and whinnies of fear mingling with a few feminine squeals. The gauchos behind the hill also set up an angry clamor—their prey was escaping! They were seen for a few minutes galloping desperately across the plain, but maneuvering the raft required all the sailors' attention, and they soon ceased to pay them the slightest attention.

The immense raft made good progress. The wind pushed it towards the op-posite bank, which could scarcely be distinguished, but it was necessary to maintain its course to prevent it from drifting. At midday, Farandoul had the sa-tisfaction of depositing everyone safe and sound on firm ground. Immediately, without responding to the warm thanks of the ladies, the sailors returned the covered wagons to a fit state to continue and hitched up the teams. After a light meal, the caravan moved off southwards.

The first Patagonians showed themselves that same evening. Crouching on their swift horses, they galloped alongside the caravan, inspecting it carefully, and then rode off into the desert. A party of six horsemen went on ahead to make a routine reconnaissance; having attained a certain distance from the cara-van they suddenly sat up straight on their horses and released loud cries at the sight of the women. They shouted for some time, eventually launching them-selves into a joyful pantomime, then rode off again without replying to the friendly waves of the mariners.

"I knew it!" cried Passepartout. "It always begins in the same way!"

"How many cartridges, Passepartout?" Phileas asked, coolly.

"Eighteen?"

"Just a minute!" said Farandoul. "Let's try to travel peacefully. The only road that remains for us to follow, my dear Monsieur Phileas, is the one to Valdivia, on the far side of the Cordilleras, in Chile—which is to say that we have 200 leagues to travel across the Patagonian and Araucarian pampas! I hoped to be able to get on with my own business after having set you on your road, but I see that I shan't be able to abandon you until we're on the other side of the Cordilleras. Let's go, then, carefully and swiftly!"

They only made three leagues the following day, in spite of all the efforts the mariners made to take the caravan forward. More and more Patagonians showed themselves on the pampas. They made camp as best they could, and everyone, weighed down by fatigue, went to sleep after a brief supper. Horatius Bixby grumbled about the bad luck that put obstacles in the way of all his projects. There was a lively exchange of words between him and Phileas Fogg, to the extent that Farandoul had to intervene in order to prevent discord slipping into his camp.

On waking up the next morning, the travelers were amazed to see a Patagonian encampment 200 meters from their own. The sentries, harassed by fatigue, had not heard anything. They were busy hitching up the covered wagons when two Patagonians on horseback appeared. Farandoul signaled that they should be allowed to approach.

The two savages advanced as far as the bivouac fire and, with expansive gestures, began a discourse of sorts.

"*Sacrebleu!*" said Passepartout. "Do they think we learn Patagonian at school?"

"Silence," said Farandoul. "Our friend Horatius Bixby has traveled this way before; he knows their language."

"Yes," said Horatius. "I know a little of the Quichua language. I'll tell you what they want."

The two Indians had dismounted. Standing in front of Farandoul, they explained volubly, gesticulating a great deal and frequently pointing at the ladies who were gathered around them.

"Damn," said Horatius, turning to Phileas. "This concerns you specifically. These gentlemen have never seen white women, and have come quite simply to ask permission for their comrades to come to the camp."

"Impossible," said Phileas. "Send them away."

"Pardon me," Farandoul put in, "but let's not be so abrupt. I'll give permission, on condition that they come two at a time. Tell them, my dear Bixby, that we'll be leaving at noon."

Horatius Bixby talked to the Patagonians for ten minutes; in the end, an agreement was struck, and the two savages, in accordance with the conclusion reached, approached the ladies. Bixby, Phileas and Farandoul followed them. The two Patagonians seemed quite angelic; they laughed and joked, asking all sorts of questions of the engineer, who answered them as best he could. The ladies laughed a good deal at the Patagonians's dumbfounded faces, their manners and the silly questions that Bixby translated for them.

When the two savages remounted their horses to go back to their troop, Mandibul accompanied them. When they arrived, the entire tribe released cries of joy and launched into a frenzied fantasia, the most important warriors departing first to see the white women while Mandibul, having been invited to dinner, remained in their bivouac.

The morning passed enjoyably. The Patagonians, initially admitted in pairs, soon began to arrive half a dozen at a time. The sight of two black women—saved, to the best of Passepartout's recollection, in Aden—caused especial bewilderment in all the Patagonians. A few of them, gripped by doubt, tested the solidarity of the color by licking their fingers and drawing crosses on the women's arms. Their color was fast. One of the chiefs, wanting to offer this entertainment to his family, ran to his camp; he came back with four wives and Lieutenant Mandibul. The Patagonian women were rather genteel, especially the youngest: a robust young woman five feet six inches tall, with hair as dark as a crow's wing, loaded with necklaces and glass trinkets, who seemed a veritable savage queen, a Venus of the pampas!

At noon, Farandoul gave the order to depart. The ladies climbed into their covered wagons; farewells were exchanged with the Patagonians, and they left. The Patagonians seemed to conferring with one another. Half an hour later, Farandoul turned round and saw that their new friends had also broken camp and were following in the caravan's footsteps.

Seven hours of travel and two leagues of distance was the day's balance-sheet. The two companies camped in the same place, 100 meters apart. The following day was better employed; they covered four leagues—but when evening came, the Patagonians came to their encampment again and asked to talk to Horatius.

"That's that!" cried Phileas Fogg. "They're inviting themselves to a party, aren't they?"

"Bah!" said Mandibul. "You've nothing more to say. The introductions have been made." Mandibul had been fraternizing with the Patagonians for two days. He was on good terms with Molucho, the chief with four wives, and especially with the beautiful Halpa-Talca, the dark-haired Patagonian we have mentioned.

Far from manifesting the slightest hostility, the Patagonians were very attentive to the travelers; they never approached the caravan without bringing a few presents—mainly foodstuffs, which, by reason of the shortage of provisions, Farandoul gladly accepted. But the increasing number of Patagonians, their visits, their politeness and their obstinacy in following the caravan step by step, made the white men increasingly anxious. Phileas Fogg bit his lip; Passepartout never put down his revolver; only Mandibul appeared perfectly satisfied.

One evening, when Passepartout took the roll-call, there were only 355 ladies; three young women were missing. Phileas had the roll-call started again, and issued threats against a Patagonian chief who was nearby. Hostilities might have broken out; fortunately, Farandoul winked at Passepartout, who understood and took his time with the roll-call. Farandoul drew away and signaled to three mariners; they hid behind the other ladies in order to answer to the names of the missing women.

The situation was saved for that evening, but it could not last. Phileas, who was very thoughtful, would soon see through the fraud—and the thefts might continue. The ladies had not been let out of sight and yet the Patagonians, skilful thieves, had succeeded in removing three. The very next day, Phileas ordered a morning roll-call, taken with very particular care. In spite of Farandoul's objections, he made the ladies file past him one after another. There was no more opportunity for trickery.

"If only one is still missing," said Mandibul, "he'll have his total."

In the general preoccupation, no one asked him what the total was; in fact, it was no longer one, or even three ladies who were missing. Only 347 ladies replied to the call; 11 ladies and a wagon had disappeared. Sir Phileas Fogg was about to lapse into one his cold fits of anger, but beforehand, in one last hope, he decided to visit all the covered wagons. Mandibul was writhing with laughter in a corner.

Phileas and Passepartout had reached the last wagon, without having found any of the missing women, when they were heard to utter cries of joy.

"At last," said Farandoul. "One's been found!"

"Not at all," replied Mandibul. "That's Halpa-Talca!"

Farandoul did not have time to ask any more questions. Phileas and Passepartout had come back to the center of the camp. Phileas appeared to be very surprised, and his faithful Passepartout was consulting his list with a bewildered expression.

"Well?" asked Farandoul.

"Well, we don't know Madame," Phileas replied. "I don't understand any of this."

"She's not on my list," added Passepartout. "We've already had several errors on the minus side, but this is the first time we've had one on the plus side!"

"Don't torment yourselves," Mandibul said, gravely, coming forward. "I'm with Madame—or, rather, Madame's with me. This is Halpa-Talca, a young Patagonian to whom I've offered my protection."

"Wait!" cried Phileas. "That means, my dear Mr. Mandibul, that you have abducted this young Halpa-Talca. Don't dispute it. You've abducted her, that's your business; but I'll save her, that's mine! I have fixed principles on this point, and 18 evolver bullets to support them…Passepartout?"

"Monsieur?"

"Add Madame Halpa-Talca's name to our list!"

Mandibul had gone red, then gone pale, and then gone red again. He was about to hurl himself on Phileas when Farandoul intervened again. "*Sacrebleu!*" he said. "Let's not cut one another's throats just as the Patagonians seem to be getting ready to attack us. Look—while we've been arguing, they've surrounded our camp, brandishing their weapons, as if to stop us moving on."

Indeed, 400 or 500 mounted Patagonians were surrounding the camp at close quarters, the warriors gesticulating on their horses, pointing at the covered wagons and howling joyfully.

"Here comes the offensive," said Passepartout. "I've been expecting it—they've scented fresh flesh!"

Four chiefs, marked out by their feather ornaments and their horse's manes, advanced towards our friends. Farandoul, Phileas and Horace Bixby, the interpreter, went out to meet them.

In spite of Farandoul's warnings, Phileas cut the formalities short and opened the discussion violently. "Infamous pirates!" he cried. "I'm an Englishman! You've abducted 11 young women under the protection of the British flag! Don't you know that everything sheltered by His Gracious Majesty's banner is sacred, you miserable savages?"

"The 11 women are pretty," replied one of the chiefs. "Very pretty! And they're white. The Patagonian warriors have never seen white women before — and, by the Great Spirit, they're very pleased to have seen the young white women."

"What?" cried Phileas, when Bixby had translated the chief's words for him.

"Yes, the Great Spirit is good, very good; he loves Patagonian children. He has sent them many white women. The Patagonian warriors ask the white men to give them their young white women. They will be well-treated by the Patagonian warriors; they will marry chiefs. The young black women are also pretty, very pretty; they will also marry chiefs."

Sir Phileas Fogg went rigid.

"It's nothing unusual," the chief went on. "The Patagonian warriors have permitted one of the white men to take away Halpa-Talca, one of their young women."

In the course of this conference, the Patagonian warriors had been gradually drawing nearer. Fortunately, Farandoul had not taken his eyes off them. When Phileas, beside himself, drew his revolver, the Patagonians let out a great roar and raced forward. With lightning rapidity, Farandoul and Bixby threw themselves on to Phileas and carried him back to the circle of wagons in spite of his protests.

The sailors were at their posts, only waiting for a signal to open fire. "Not yet!" said Farandoul. "Let's try to frighten them first. Fire at the nearest horses, on command!"

Bixby had understood. Standing on the first wagon with his rifle in his hand, he shouted in a resounding voice: "The Patagonian warriors are behaving badly, but the white men still wish to spare them. The Patagonians shall see what power the white men have!"

"Fire!" said Farandoul.

Twenty rifle shots rang out; 20 horses collapsed.

The crowd of Patagonians were momentarily struck motionless by terror; then they all turned round and departed at top speed into the desert. The 20 unhorsed riders had jumped on to the rumps of their comrades' mounts. A few arrows had whistled harmlessly over the wagons.

Bixby, who had listened to the shouts of the fleeing men, came back to Farandoul anxiously. "It's not over," he said. "Within a few days we'll have all of Patagonia on our backs."

"Isn't there any means of putting them off the track?" murmured Farandoul, pensively.

"That scarcely seems easy, with 15 covered wagons."

"Let's go—we'll think about it on the way."

Towards the end of the day they reached a lake formed by the encasement within the plain of a broad and capriciously-winding river. The river was fordable above and below the lake, but Farandoul and Bixby, urged by a presentiment, galloped for some hours in the moonlight along the wooded shores of the lake. There was no trace of Patagonians. Even so, the two horsemen were put on their guard by seeing 100 huts in the distance.

As they approached the village, they perceived that what they had taken for a Patagonian encampment was actually a republic of beavers—an important republic that must have numbered at least 700 or 800 citizens.

The whole village was asleep. Farandoul urged his horse into the water and came out on top of one of the lodges. Bixby followed him and they both examined the world of the little amphibians with considerable surprise.

There was, in fact, reason for astonishment. Our two friends found themselves in one of those beaver villages that existed in Europe in prehistoric times, when our fine ancestors went naked, full of scorn for top hats: villages that could still be found in Canada before the trappers forced the race to emigrate to the wilderness.

The round huts, two or three meters tall, were aligned in several intersecting lanes, built on piles; no openings were visible on the landward side, but large window-like apertures more that a meter wide opened facing the lake. These houses seemed to be solid enough to resist anything. Farandoul, on leaning down, observed that the walls were 50 or 60 centimeters thick.

"I regret having to disturb these brave beavers," Farandoul said, eventually, "but I have to see the interior of one of their habitations. I have an idea!" Making as little noise as possible, he slipped through the window of one of the lodges, crouched down and, before descending into the interior, lit a match.

This produced an immediate panic within the hut. Some 20 or 25 beavers, frightened by the light, threw themselves into the water through an opening fabricated below the water-level. Farandoul went into the lodge and called Bixby.

"Splendid!" cried the latter. "Beavers are well-accommodated!"

The lodge was about four meters in diameter. Half of it rose up to the ceiling, at a height of more than 2.50 meters, without an intermediate floor; the other half was divided by two floors of planks and solid beams. The boards, strewn with dry foliage, were very neat.

"Perfectly habitable for five or six people," Farandoul said, finally. "We'll be all right here!"

"What!" said Bixby. "You mean…"

"Of course! We'll install ourselves here for a while and let the Patagonians search for us in the pampas. I feel sorry for the beavers, but it's necessary for us to expropriate them, according to the requirements of public utility. Quickly, let's go back to the camp; we have to be installed by dawn."

The two friends remounted their horses without paying any heed to the tumult in the huts. The poor beavers, abruptly woken up, held a council and sought a means of repelling the invaders. It was much worse when the whole caravan arrived two hours later. What a commotion in the waters of the lake! The beaver sentries had signaled the approach of the troop as soon as it appeared a kilometer from the lake. In response to their alarm calls, the entire population of the village climbed on to the roofs. There was a concert of curses and lamentations, which suddenly ceased when the sailors established a makeshift bridge between the huts and the bank, within two minutes. On seeing that, all the beavers dived as one, abandoning their fatherland: the village where hundreds of generations had lived in peace.

Farandoul went from hut to hut; there were 88 of them, among which some were food-stores and one in which a few infirm beavers were lying, having fallen into senility, being ill or crippled, guarded by a young one that had remained faithfully at its post. The sailors respected this hut, and deposited a few little ones left behind in the confusion there, along with a few provisions for the aged.

Phileas, seeing these preparations, raised a few objections, but Farandoul finished up convincing him that it was their sole hope of salvation.

In a few hours, the ladies were installed, five at a time, in each of the lodges; the sailors reserved those in the first row for themselves and deposited all their provisions in a central lodge.

VII.

They still had two hours of the night before them. Farandoul resolved to take advantage of them to do what remained to be done. There was the matter of getting rid of all the covered wagons and horses. That was hard, but absolutely necessary. The mariners drove the wagons into the river to hide their tracks from the Patagonians and went upstream for several kilometers, as far as another small and rather deep lake. The cattle and the unhitched horses were chased into the pampas and soon vanished, frightened off by a few rifle-shots.

The shore of the lake sloped steeply; a few fathoms from the bank the depth was already considerable. The sailors profited from this circumstance, pushing the wagons down the slope by the strength of their arms. It was a laborious task, but our friends had strong arms. An hour later, the 15 wagons had rolled into the lake. The waters had closed over them and there was no clue to betray them to the Patagonians.

A profound silence soon descended over the lake; everyone, after having seen to their installation, wanted to take advantage of the tranquility to obtain some restorative sleep.

When the village woke up, with the Sun already high above the horizon, a few unkempt heads emerged from the lodges to interrogate the countryside. All was calm and deserted—not a Patagonian in sight. This good news was welcomed joyfully. Farandoul used some large tree-trunks, already prepared by the beavers, to establish a solid decking between a few huts at the center of the village, in a totally secluded spot, where the population was invited to take turns coming to get a breath of air.

Sentinels having been posted, the inhabitants of the beaver village, shielded from any surprise, held a discussion as to what to do next.

"In my opinion," Farandoul said, "we'll be safe if we can stay here for a month or two; scarcely 40 leagues separate us from the mountains. The Patagonians, usually living on the Ocean side of the plain, won't stay here very log once they're sure of our complete disappearance. In two months, we can return the village to the poor beavers and get back on the road. It's a further delay, my dear Bixby, but it's necessary."

"What about food-supplies?" asked Phileas, anxiously.

"Don't worry, you'll have your roast beef—there's no lack of bison, which our men can capture with lassos, and the lake's full of fish, so we'll be able to hunt *and* fish!"

"It's very nice here!" cried Passepartout. "I'd like to found an authentic colony—I've had enough of our peregrinations!"

"And your gas-jets," Phileas jeered, "will burn forever awaiting your return!"

"What do I care, if we don't go back?" riposted Passepartout. "I'll bankrupt the gas company!"

Apart from a few altercations between the irascible Phileas and the volatile Bixby, who was seething with impatience, nothing remarkable happened in the colony for several days. A few little rafts had been constructed by the mariners to facilitate communication between the lodges, but they were only used with extreme prudence, for a few parties of Patagonians had been observed roaming in search of the caravan.

The cooking was done at night, under the direction of the former ship's cook of *La Belle Léocadie*. The food was distributed in the morning and calm reigned all day long within the village. The ladies were slightly bored by this inaction, but a few hours spent playing little games on the central platform enhanced their patience. To occupy them, the sailors taught them the difficult art of line-fishing. Farandoul regretted this—he was worried about frying, whose odor might have attracted the Patagonians—but as the ladies, in spite of their attentiveness, made no miraculous catches, he allowed them their pastime.

The moonlit evenings were splendid; the colony, gathered on the platform and the roofs of the surrounding huts, spent pleasant hours in general or individual conversation. Mandibul, forever gallant, had the idea one day of putting on a ball for the ladies; it was a great success. Seaman Escoubico, who formed the entire orchestra, almost wore out his guitar.

The refreshments furnished by the lake were not in short supply. Mandibul even contrived a few different kinds of drinks: pure water, slightly acidulated water and water even more slightly sugared.

On morning, at daybreak, Farandoul, who was strolling on the platform, was astonished to see a hand-written placard attached to the largest of the huts, which read:

PUBLIC MEETING

Citizen Passepartout invites the inhabitants of the colony to a great and fraternal meeting this evening, at 8 p.m.

Order of the day: The political organization of the new colony; establishment of universal suffrage.

Proposal: Ladies are admitted to meetings in anticipation of an electoral system.

Jean Passepartout.

Parisian ex-voter.

Please translate for the ladies.

Passepartout's proposal was a great success. After Mandibul's musical soirée, they would have a political soirée. Unfortunately, the meeting was stormy. Questions of organization took a long time to clarify. After long and solemn speeches, Farandoul was appointed Head of State of the Beaver Republic, with Mandibul as his vice-president. Phileas Fogg, who put himself forward as a candidate, was blackballed.

Phileas and Bixby argued for a long time, the former for the name of New London and the second for that of New New York. Mandibul, increasingly poetic, held out for New Venice, but Farandoul finally secured universal agreement by proposing Beavertown. Let us say right away that Phileas, to protest against the decision of the majority vote, continued to call the colony Beaver City.

Three weeks had gone by. The Patagonians had disappeared; it was hoped that they had left the region for good, having given up all hope of finding the caravan. In spite of the tranquility of the town, its inhabitants wanted nothing more than to resume their journey—except for Passepartout, who declared that he had adopted Beavertown as his definitive fatherland and intended to stay there with the girl of his dreams. As he pronounced these words he darted languorous glances at a certain dwelling inhabited by Rising Moon; as young Ernestine, the Parisian girl saved by Phileas at the beginning of their journey also resided there, Farandoul assumed that the glances could as easily be addressed to her and paid no attention.

An alarm raised by a sentry on the morning of the 25th day brought the colony out of its quietude.

"The Patagonians! Look out—here they come!"

Farandoul leapt to his feet. It was only too true. Scarcely a kilometer away, hundreds of horsemen were approaching—and, disturbingly, mounted Patagonians were visible in the water.

It was not easy to establish silence in the ladies' camp, but calm was finally attained. The Patagonians were drawing nearer. Farandoul, who was watching them through a portable telescope, suddenly let out an exclamation. Mandibul glanced out in his turn and went pale.

"The beavers!" he cried.

"I see!" said Farandoul. "The Patagonians must have encountered the beavers that we expropriated; it must have surprised them, and, on reflection, they guessed. We're about to be discovered."

The tumult produced by the swimming of a thousand beavers was soon audible; they were advancing rapidly, driven from behind by a few Patagonian riders.

Some distance from the village, the poor breathless animals slowed down; they seemed to hesitate between crossing the lake and returning to their native territory, but instinct soon got hold of them. The white men's last hope disappeared—the beavers were heading towards their lodges!

The savages ran forward, cheering, and installed themselves on the shore as if to see what would happen. They had evidently seen through Farandoul's ruse. The latter had the time to recommend absolute silence to his friends.

The beavers had come into the village and climbed on to the roofs without daring to venture into the interior. The savages waited impatiently. Finally, reassured by the calm of their dwellings, the beavers took the risk and the boldest ventured into the lodges.

"That's all right," said Mandibul. "They're not too frightened!"

Suddenly, feminine screams broke out; a violent commotion was heard in one of the lodges. A few frightened beavers dived. Immediately, a mad panic took hold of all the ladies; cries of terror in every language came from all directions, and frightened women surged out of all the windows, climbing on to the roofs or leaping from walkway to walkway, a few diving into the water, all heading for the platform.

The Patagonians on the bank were dancing with joy. Some were preparing to leap into the water.

"Let's go!" said Farandoul. "The time has come to show ourselves." And, on his signal, the sailors climbed on to the roofs of the huts, armed with rifles.

The savages stopped.

Saturnin Farandoul, Mandibul and Bixby were on top of the first lodge. "Halt!" cried Bixby. "Patagonian warriors, you have seen what the white men can do with their weapons. Don't attack them—the Great Spirit will protect them!"

One chief, more than six feet tall, advanced into the lake. "White men!" he cried. "The young white women are pretty; the Patagonian warriors are brave; they will be good husbands; the young white women will be very happy!"

"You've already told us that. We're determined to defend the young white women. Patagonian warriors, beware!"

"Very well! The Great Spirit is good. The Patagonian warriors are brave!" As he spoke these words the chief made a sign and a volley of arrows whistled towards the sailors—but the latter were on their guard; they leapt backwards and ducked into the huts.

A fearful silence reigned over the lake for a few minutes; the sailors in the huts were busy enlarging loopholes prepared some time before. Finally, the Patagonians, encouraged by the silence, threw themselves into the water. Suddenly, a frightful discharge of musket-fire cut through the air. The poor bewildered beavers leapt into the lake desperately and fled their village, now occupied by infernal beings. Thick smoke hung momentarily over the huts. The women screamed more loudly and took refuge in the remotest huts. Phileas and Passepartout, flailing about in their midst, tried in vain to restore order.

The fusillade continued. The Patagonians urged their horses forward bravely to traverse the 30 meters that separated them from the village, but the mariners' well-aimed bullets struck them down en route. A certain hesitancy began to manifest itself in the attack; the Patagonian horsemen soon turned back and dismounted on the bank. The others had not remained inactive; they had rapidly felled several trees and rolled large boulders, from behind which they continued to launch futile volleys of arrows, to which the sailors disdained to reply.

Through the loopholes in his lodge, Farandoul was able to count nearly 1000 enemies. "Damn!" he murmured. "That's a whole army!"

"Yes," said Mandibul, "and an army that doesn't seem disposed to abandon the attack. We're about to see the siege of Beavertown. It's necessary to do things properly and raise the town's flag!" And he took an old flag from his personal haversack, by the sight of which Farandoul was moved, and which the sailors, equally moved, saluted with loud hurrahs. It was the flag of Australia, saved by Mandibul after the great disaster in Melbourne.

Under the hail of Patagonian arrows, Mandibul went slowly on to the top of the hut to plant the flag, while Farandoul ordered a supportive salvo of gunfire.

For their part, the Patagonians were also organizing themselves; the siege had begun.

"We have food-supplies for four days," Farandoul said. "The women have to get busy line-fishing under the direction of the ship's cook, and we need to ration our provisions. Tonight, two men will slip silently over to the other shore of the lake and try to lasso a few bison. Six men on guard will suffice to keep watch on the Patagonians; the others can rest."

Meanwhile, Phileas Fogg and Passepartout had succeeded in calming the ladies; on Farandoul's orders they were lined up together on the furthest huts, beyond the range of arrows, and were set to work with fishing-lines. Three hundred and forty lines were operating with varying degrees of success. Madame Aouda, the ship's cook and a few ladies working in shifts started preparing dinner. As for Rising Moon, she leaned over a fragment of mirror and repaired her war-paint, with her tomahawk in her belt.

The angriest of all those under siege was Horatius Bixby. Close as he was to the diamond mines he had discovered, he still saw obstacles multiplying in front of him. Phileas and he only agreed on one thing; they both demanded to undertake a sortie—which Farandoul, the governor of the town, forbade absolutely.

"No sorties! We'll remain on the defensive!"

For two days and two nights, the besiegers and the besieged watched one another without any resumption of hostilities. The men on watch each night were extremely careful, but the Patagonians did not seem disposed to attack again. Their plan seemed to be to starve Beavertown out. The ladies, warned of the danger, fished from dawn till dusk; they were already acquiring a certain skill, and the fishes of the lake made their contribution to the besieged population's meals.

The Patagonians observed them from the shore. One morning, one of the boldest made an immense circuit in the lake and approached the fisherwomen without being perceived, swimming underwater. The Parisian Ernestine was baiting her hook when the Patagonian emerged abruptly and grabbed her dress.

Ernestine screamed and fell into the water. The Patagonian, supporting her with one arm and swimming with the other, resumed his course in the lake amid the shouts of the ladies. A few sailors came running, but the fear of hitting the unfortunate girl prevented them from firing at the savage. A quarter of an hour later, he was seen emerging on to the shore with his conquest and receiving the congratulations of his comrades.

The furious Passepartout expended five of his last 18 cartridges without being able to hit the delighted Patagonian.

From that moment on the fisherwomen were guarded by two men with carbines in hand; the Patagonians who repeated the attempt were greeted with rifle-fire.

The sight of smoke and the odor of frying undoubtedly modified the strategy of the besiegers, for Beavertown was subjected to a terrible assault in the middle of the fifth night. For two hours there was fighting, almost hand-to-hand. Phileas Fogg lost one of his gloves in the confusion; as for Passepartout, he disappeared at the beginning of the battle.

The nascent dawn brought an end to the hostilities. Beavertown had suffered losses; the great frontal assault had not succeeded, but a Patagonian column had been able to swim around the town's left flank and had occupied three lodges. Loud screams raised by the ladies in the captured lodges echoed in the darkness and then—O terror!—soon died away into a fearful silence. Phileas and a few men ran back, but it was too late; the screaming had stopped. In the mute lodges, the Patagonians were hurriedly fortifying themselves.

In order to discover the extent of the town's losses, Phileas called feverishly for Passepartout, the custodian of the roll-call list. Passepartout could not be found. What had become of him? Had he perished heroically, victim of his duty? Had he fallen alive into the hands of the barbarous aggressors?

Farandoul and his sailors redoubled their efforts to try to save what remained of the town, without trying to hide the fact that the situation was critical, and getting steadily worse. Phileas, for want of the list, tried to establish the arithmetical extent of the losses. There were 20 ladies missing, including Madame Aouda, Phileas' companion on his first journey, who had vanished like Passepartout.

The fate of the majority of the ladies was soon determined. The Patagonians had sent them to their camp, and they appeared on the shore in front of the besieged positions during the day. The rumor ran around Beavertown, and all the ladies came running to see the unfortunate prisoners. Phileas Fogg, pale and tense, climbed up on the first lodge. Madame Aouda was nowhere to be seen among the captives. Passepartout was equally invisible.

Everyone in Beavertown extended trembling hands towards the prisoners. Tears were flowing when all of a sudden, that desolation was interrupted by outbursts of laughter from the unfortunates. Far from complaining, the captives seemed delighted with their misfortune. A single glance was sufficient for the ladies to determine the reason for their attitude. The unfortunate creatures were literally streaming with diamonds! Diamonds as large as pebbles, arranged in necklaces, diadems and bracelets; diamonds sparkling in heavy pendants on their breasts; diamonds around their arms—diamonds everywhere!!!

A general cry of admiration went up. Phileas was obliged to restrain several ladies who were ready to launch themselves toward the shore.

"My diamonds!" cried the engineer Horatius Bixby. "My diamonds!" Under the pressure of emotion, he imprudently revealed the existence of the Patagonian diamond-mines, the goal of the expedition so unfortunately undertaken by Farandoul.

What a tumult there was in the besieged city! What a hubbub of feminine voices, discussing, disputing and quarrelling in all the languages on Earth. Phileas redoubled his efforts to re-establish order, but his voice, formerly so authoritative, had lost its empire over the ladies. The defenders of Beavertown had a great deal of difficulty holding their positions; in the meantime, it was getting dark, increasing the disorder.

In addition to the horrors of a siege, was Beavertown to see civil war within its walls, beneath the very eyes of the enemy, eager to profit from internal disorders? The sailors, disseminated along the full extent of their battle-line, could scarcely maintain their communications. Farandoul took a patrol of five seamen and searched all the lodges, looking for Rising Moon, who had also been missing since morning. Farandoul and Fogg, as is understandable, were equally distraught, each having lost the companion of his heart.

An insoluble enigma! What had become of Aouda? What had become of Rising Moon? Neither one of them was in the hands of the Patagonians.

Night fell—a terrible night! On the shore the Patagonian camp resounded with joyful howls, screams, songs and frightful music. There was dancing, there was laughter; they were preparing for the final assault.

In the town, discord reigned supreme. Phileas had lost all authority over the besieged women; the mariners still held firm in the face of the enemy, but on one side of the town, a few rebels had raised the red flag—a Mexican skirt on the end of a pole. Their ranks were growing by the minute. Farandoul, returning at the head of his patrol after two hours of fruitless searching, had some difficulty getting through the tumultuous group of rebel women to regain his post facing the Patagonian camp.

Phileas Fogg, in desperation, tried to make one last effort to make the insurgent ladies see reason—futile obstinacy! He tried in vain to reach the red flag; he threatened, pleaded and gagged, in vain. The rebels surrounded him; he tried to resist but he was knocked down and tied to the pole of the red flag.

The denouement could not be long delayed. Loud cries burst forth; a Patagonian showed his broad thick-lipped face in front of one of the captured lodges; another head appeared, then another—and 300 warriors suddenly surged out of the water, scaling the defenses and spreading out from lodge to lodge.

Beavertown was taken!

The sailors, having witnessed Phileas' efforts and seen the ladies introducing the enemy into the town, had ceased firing and were writhing with laughter in their lodges, which the Patagonians were very wary of approaching. Meanwhile, Farandoul, seeing Phileas in the grip of the savages, decided to intervene. On his orders, Bixby opened negotiations.

Two chiefs came to the central cabin; delighted with their success, the white men being defeated, they only wanted to see peace restored and consented, with a good grace, to return Phileas Fogg. The negotiations lasted until morning. Farandoul refused to make any attempt to recover the 347 women who had gone over to the Patagonian camp over their own accord. He only asked for the restitution of Rising Moon to himself and Madame Aouda to Phileas Fogg. That was a difficulty; the Patagonians swore on their greatest gods that those ladies were not in their hands. The matter was easy to verify; the Patagonian camp was investigated from top to bottom. The Patagonians responded to interrogation willingly, but all these researches produced no result.

What was the key to the mystery?

With regard to Rising Moon, Phileas finally admitted under questioning that, in response to repeated entreaties from Passepartout, he had given the latter orders to abduct the young Indian woman along with Halpa-Talca, Mandibul's Patagonian. These ladies, added to the list, had been placed with Madame Aouda under the particular protection of Passepartout, and had disappeared with their protector the day before. Farandoul and Lieutenant Mandibul were hopping mad when they heard this. To their righteous wrath, Phileas opposed violent recriminations; he accused them of having distracted him from his mission as a licensed savior and reproached them for having meddled in his business on the Rio Negro.

Farandoul was able to reproach Phileas, not only for the abduction of Rising Moon but the abortion of his own project and the loss of his hopes. The objective of the expedition could not now be attained, for the Patagonians, probably on the insistence of their beautiful captives, absolutely refused to let him continue on his way towards the diamond-fields. A bloody fight was about to break out between Farandoul and Phileas, but Bixby's intervention reminded them of their dignity as gentleman, which must not be compromised in front of the savages. This speech calmed Phileas down. They agreed to devote a few days to investigations, and then to return to civilized regions to search for a more convenient place for a no-holds-barred duel between the two enemies.

"It's not just any old duel that we require," cried Farandoul, by way of conclusion. "Two men like us can't fight like mere swashbucklers. It's a grandiose contest, a solemn conflict, a frightful and merciless embrace, a wild explosion that will shake the world and set fire to an entire continent! This is what I propose: the states of Nicaragua are at war; the north and the south, full of rage, are precipitating their regiments and artillery upon one another—very well, let's place ourselves at their head, make war, commence the carnage, and fight to the very last drop of Nicaraguan blood!"

"To the last drop of Nicaraguan blood!"

Farandoul wanted to let Phileas have the choice of weapons—which is to say, whether to take the northern side or the southern, but Phileas, always formal, immediately demanded to draw straws. The lottery gave the south to Phileas Fogg; the northern states fell to Farandoul.

The search began immediately, with the aid of the Patagonian chiefs. The Patagonian warriors and the new female Patagonians were summoned for inspection again. Farandoul, Phileas and Mandibul, the three unfortunate spouses of Rising Moon, Aouda and Halpa-Talca, passed from row to row without finding any of the three missing women. Phileas directed severe glances at the 347 ingrates for whom he had braved so many perils, but they, full of the joy of possessing kilograms of diamonds, did not appear to notice them.

The three spouses rode back and forth over the surrounding plains, in vain; they beat all the bushes of the neighboring forests, in vain. No trace of the unfortunates was discovered.

Mandibul philosophically renounced any hope of recovering Halpa-Talca. As for Phileas, his unhappiness was so vast, his losses so considerable, that one lady more or less—348 or 347—made no great difference to his desolate spirit. When Farandoul, finally abandoning his search, asked him whether the moment might have come to leave for Nicaragua, he replied that he was ready. They and the Patagonians went their separate ways that very day.

Since that time, the most contradictory rumors have circulated regarding the fate of Passepartout. Travelers have sworn that they have talked to a Patagonian who had eaten him, others have claimed that Passepartout, carried off by the Patagonians, had become one of the most powerful chiefs of their nations. This is the truth: Passepartout had not perished in the lake; he had betrayed his master's confidence. Passepartout was a deserter!

You will recall that one of the lodges of Beavertown, isolated behind the main lines, had been reserved for crippled and impotent beavers. By an inexplicable fatality, that lodge had been neglected during the searches carried out of all the other lodges, around the lake and in the surrounding countryside. Well, Passepartout was there! And he was not alone!

An hour after the departure of the Patagonians and the white men, a shadow appeared, cautiously, at the window of the lodge and carefully scanned the horizon. The absolute and perfect silence of the plain appeared to reassure the individual completely. He stood up on the roof of the lodge and performed an *entrechat*.

Two seconds later, three women were beside him on the roof. They were the traitorous and perjured spouses Rising Moon, Aouda and Halpa-Talca!

Without wanting to offer the shadow of an excuse for Passepartout's treason, we ought to say that the principle motive that had led him to abandon Phileas Fogg was the desire to avoid having to pay for the 17 gas-jets that had been burning for more than three years. After that came the prospect of actually founding a colony in Beavertown.

Ten years have gone by since then. The beaver republic is reconstituted. Beavertown has two populations, the beavers who returned to their lodges a long time ago and two dozen little brats living fraternally with the amphibians. They are Passepartout's children.

The latter reigns as a true patriarch over the beavers, the children and Mesdames Aouda, Halpa-Talca and Rising Moon. A few Patagonians, stout fellows, gathered in a few beaver lodges serve the colony as servants. Passepartout, aided by the beavers, has erected an imposing lodge in the middle of the village. Always ambitious, he calls himself the Great Mogul of Beavertown.

VIII.

Shortly afterwards, shattering news was transmitted to the entire world by the transatlantic telegraph cables. The war in the Disunited States of Nicaragua, which had been thought to be well on the way to settlement, had flared up again more terribly than before. In Papagayo, the capital of south Nicaragua, the celebrated Phileas Fogg had hurried to offer his services, at the same time as the no-less-illustrious Farandoul, ex-conqueror of Australia, had presented himself in Cayman City, the capital of north Nicaragua and put his sword and his redoubtable experience at the disposition of the northists.[53]

The states of the north and south, badly damaged by the war—the north especially—threw themselves back into the conflict furiously. The city of Papagayo gave Phileas Fogg an enthusiastic welcome, and he was named General Chief Engineer of all the southist armies. All military power was concentrated in his hands, all the branches of government reorganized and combined under his direction. With the agreement of a committee of scientists operating under his presidency, he wanted to give the war a degree of scientific precision worthy of the century of progress in which we have the good fortune to live. His principal collaborator was a German scientist of the highest merit, the celebrated Doctor Fridolin Rosengarten.

The committee's days and nights were so well employed that, three months after Sir Phileas' arrival, the south felt that it was ready to resume hostilities. A

---

[53] Papagayo and Cayman City are both imaginary (the actual capital of Nicaragua was and is Managua), emphasizing the fact that the fictitious "Nicaragua" is actually standing in, for diplomatic reasons, for another set of Disunited States whose bloody and technologically-sophisticated Civil War was still relatively fresh in memory in 1879.

formidable apparatus had been improvised; Sir Phileas wanted to inaugurate a new tactic of modern warfare: railway warfare!

The entire army was reorganized; there was no more infantry or cavalry, as in ancient Europe; every company had a road-ready locomotive with an armored and fortified train. Four hundred locomotives were prepared, with a much more considerable number of wagons. These locomotives were divided into three sections: light locomotives manned by machine-gunners; armored locomotives for charges; and locomotive batteries for the artillery.

One can imagine that all these preparations could not have been made secretly enough for the north to be unaware of the storm that was about to burst. On that side too, everything was ready to deliver terrible blows against the enemy.

As soon as he arrived in Cayman City, Farandoul had only had to say one thing, to make one proposition, for the rank of generalissimo to be offered to him by the northist parliament with an indescribable enthusiasm. Acclaimed by the population, carried in triumph by the army, he had immediately taken supreme power into his hands. Mandibul and his mariners entered the northist army with their Australian ranks; Bixby, also appointed as a general, became the soul of the councils of war; to him fell the mission of combating Sir Phileas Fogg's committee of southist scientists.

The southists' plan had been discovered at the very outset and, while bringing quite different projects to maturity, Farandoul had taken steps to meet the southist locomotives head on. Within two months, large factories, having been requisitioned, had constructed and armed 200 locomotives armored with steel plate 18 centimeters thick, equipped with large-caliber cannons and towing a bunker-wagon for the crew. A garrison of eight men was sufficient to man these redoubtable engines: two to steer and two to serve as lookouts while the other four enjoyed the rewards of sleep. Two little cabins were reserved, one for the captain and one for the reporter. There were swarms of reporters in the army because, in addition to the countless local representatives they had come from all points of the globe; the general staff included our old friend Dick Broken of the *New York Herald*, as well as a French reporter sent by *Le Figaro*.[54]

---

[54] The reader will already have taken note of Robida's low opinion of the press, especially its role in celebrating and stirring up conflict; his anticipation that reporters would one day be routinely "embedded" in combat units is one of many direly prophetic notes sounded by this blackly comic account of the utterly pointless but horribly destructive Nicaraguan war. Although I have refrained from such substitutions as "tank" for "armored locomotive," I have adopted occasional modern terms, such as "land-mine," where Robida's improvised terminology and the descriptions of the relevant *materiel* seemed sufficiently exact.

There was a similar abundance of reporters on the southist side, including numerous female reporters sent by fashion magazines and gazettes created for the defense of women's rights, attracted by Sir Phileas' long-established reputation as a champion of womankind.

The opening of hostilities was imminent; the final preparations were being completed on both sides. At the same time as Sir Phileas announced the breaking of the armistice by telegram, Farandoul sent him an identical declaration by a diplomatic missive "to be delivered personally to the southist commander-in-chief".

It was on a fine June night that 20 light locomotives of the advance guard left Papagayo, the southist capital, and set off northwards; by dawn, the entire army was on the move; the center, commanded by General Chief Engineer Fogg, was composed of 200 armored locomotives armed with 450 large-caliber cannons. This immense train, traveling on iron tracks in good repair, departed at full steam after the advance guard—which kept in touch with the main army by means of telegrams dispatched at regular intervals. On the flanks, the remainder of the southist forces, 500 light locomotives, advanced directly across terrain rendered practicable by its dryness.

At noon, a telegram from the advance guard signaled that the enemy was in sight.

Four armored locomotives, Farandoul's advance guard, were blocking the way and directing heavy fire at the southists' light locomotives. On an order from Phileas Fogg, the locomotives, stoked up to the maximum, leapt forward furiously. An hour later, the advance guard's cannonade could be distinctly heard. The signal to clear the decks for combat was sounded on all the locomotives, and their speed increased.

It was time; the advance guard beat a retreat before the northists' huge armored locomotives. At the sight of the southist army, the latter stopped and maintained their composure. A violent long-distance cannonade as exchanged for a quarter of an hour; then a charge of armored locomotives, vigorously led by Phileas himself, fell like a thunderbolt upon the four northists.

A whirlwind of smoke momentarily obscured the observers' view of the combat; then they saw one of the northist locomotive lying on its side rendering up its last clouds of vapor, and the three others, more or less crippled, retreating along their tracks with their engines in reverse.

The track having been cleared and repaired that evening to give passage to the southists, a party of light locomotives raced forwards. The first success had gone to Phileas. A triumphant telegram was sent to Papagayo.

Early the following morning, full of confidence, the entire army set off at full steam. According to Phileas' instructions, the advance guard was to move forward as far as possible, burning everything in its path. No telegram had arrived during the night; it was thought that the lack of news was solely due to a break in the wire, but 15 leagues on, a southist locomotive lying in pieces in a field gave rise to some anxiety. A little further on another was encountered, then the remainder of the advance guard, strewn across the plain in smoking fragments.

A terrible emotion gripped the throats of the entire army. Before continuing, Sir Phileas gave the order to rally the two flanks, which had fallen a little behind because of the difficulties of the terrain. There was no time to waste; thousands of strident whistle-blasts resounded in the distance. The din of 100 roaring locomotives was heard beyond the horizon, and suddenly, before the northist forces were even in sight, a hail of bombs and shells descended on Phileas Fogg's army.

Sir Phileas' locomotives immediately opened fire. The horizon darkened. The southist ranks were soon in disarray. In spite of Sir Phileas' skillful maneuvering to get all his batteries lined up, a few charges of armored locomotives inflicted terrible carnage. At the same time, the northists effected maneuvers on both the right and left flanks designed to cut off the line of retreat. Phileas, with rage in his heart, gave a few orders; a division of armored locomotives was sacrificed to cover the retreat and, while it fought to the last shell, the general staff and the locomotives that could be saved rapidly beat a retreat.

Only 175 locomotives returned to Papagayo.

It was then that Fridolin Rosengarten's genius revealed itself. That gentle and inoffensive man, that dreamer, that seeker of unknown flowers redoubled his efforts.

His first invention saved the southist capital. Papagayo, as everyone knows, is only approachable from one side; numerous forts line up in a dangerous pass defend it on the side of the sea; to the south, steep mountain slopes make the approaches easy to guard, but the great northern pain is its weak spot. Twenty-four hours after the return of Phileas' damaged locomotives, the vulnerable zone became absolutely uncrossable, the worthy Fridolin having scattered thousands of tiny explosive and asphyxiating land-mines, of his own invention.

The efficacy of these land-mines did not remain in doubt for long. During the night, the southist forward positions heard the formidable rumble of Farandoul's armored locomotives in the distance. The northist advance guard was approaching. Every one of its red signal-lights was like an eye floating towards Papagayo, and those eyes were visibly growing. Suddenly, series of little detonations burst forth in that direction; the northist locomotives, traveling at top speed, had just entered the minefield. The crepitation lasted five minutes, then died away entirely, along with the sound of the locomotives' engines. The savant Fridolin Rosengarten, who had run to the forward positions with Phileas, immediately had an electric searchlight pointed in that direction. Twelve armored locomotives remained inert and motionless in the middle of the open country.

"Victory!" cried Fridolin. "My land-mines are devastating! If you'd care to come with me, General Fogg, to verify the merit of my ingenious invention, it's easily done."

Ten minutes later, Phileas and Fridolin headed towards the locomotives at the head of a little detachment of men, each clad in a sort of diving suit equipped with an air-tank. The *Times* correspondent accompanied the troop.

The greatest prudence was recommended during the march, for it was necessary to avoid the innumerable land-mines spread across the terrain. The scientist, armed with a lantern, lit the way. In this way, they arrived at the scene of the disaster.

The locomotives' fires were beginning to go out. They made a prudent tour before going inside. The most complete silence reigned everywhere. The asphyxiating mines had done their work; everyone was dead!

The worthy Fridolin rubbed his hands together. The *Times* correspondent, desirous of familiarizing himself with every detail of Fridolin's invention and getting a taste of the atmosphere, lifted his hood slightly. That imprudence nearly cost him dear; a sudden suffocation an a violent fit of sneezing almost threw him back into the scientist's arms; it was necessary to hold him up to get him back to the forward positions—and yet the heroic correspondent still had the strength to gather up two or three land-mines without being seen, which he put in his pocket.

A veritable ovation was given to the worthy Fridolin on his arrival in Papagayo. The city was saved, for the moment.

Still sneezing, the *Times* correspondent, slipped away from the cheering crowds and went back home. The first thing he did was to put his land-mines into a little box and send them, with a long letter, to his newspaper.

Unfortunately, the box reached London before the letter. The correspondent having been unable to mention his package in his telegrams, which passed under Phileas' inspection, the editor of the *Times* mistook the land-mines for hazelnuts and cracked one open with his teeth while opening his correspondence. A frightful detonation struck the editor down and broke all the windows in the neighborhood.

When, after two hours of aspersions of vinegar, it was possible to get into the street, there was nothing to be found but people lying on the pavements, sneezing and weeping. The land-mines, having gone stale during the journey, had lost part of their force; no one was dead—not even the editor of the *Times*, who got away with having to buy a set of false teeth[55]—but everyone within a 50-meter radius of the *Times* offices was obliged to stay in bed for a fortnight.

This mysterious event created a terrible fuss in Europe. The editor of the *Times* received his correspondent's letter after coming back from the dentist's. All was explained! Delighted to have such a precious correspondent, he informed him by telegram that his salary was being doubled.

Let us return to the southist city besieged by Farandoul. The northist locomotives having arrived in the vicinity of the minefield that morning, a reconnaissance that cost another four armored locomotives demonstrated the impossibility of approaching Papagayo. Farandoul contented himself with tightly blockading the city and, in consultation with Horatius Bixby, changed his batteries.

Let us leave them to meditate upon their plan of attack and see what Phileas was doing by way of defense.

Fridolin was indefatigable; every day saw a new invention hatch out. The most monstrous cannons and the most hectic and ingenious machine-guns emerged from his factories every evening. He was the first man in the civilized world to realize how to make a judicious employment of shells and machine-gun bullets.

An enormous cannon, as wide as a tower, served by a brigade of artillerists, caused the greatest possible havoc in the northist ranks. Minute by minute for a week, it sent forth 300-kilogram shells loaded with concentrated vervain,[56]

---

[55] There is an untranslatable pun here; the word *râtelier* [rack] whose literally-intended meaning I have translated as "a set of false teeth," also refers to a way of making a living, so the clause could also be interpreted as meaning that the unfortunate editor found himself a new job.

[56] Vervain (*verveine* in French, *verbena* in Latin) is a highly unlikely asphyxiant, no matter how concentrated it might be, but it was very popular among Parisian women at the time (and is still marketed in the form of herbal tea) as an alleged relaxant. It is possible that Robida was basing the joke simply on its pungent and

which asphyxiated every living being within 200 meters. The northists pulled back their lines, but in vain; the vervain-firing mortar advanced and continued its ravages. That sealed its doom. One morning, Bixby, who had sworn to destroy it, sent forth on his own behalf, with rare precision, a series of chloroform bombs.

The southist cannon immediately fell silent; immediately, 500 lost children[57] launched themselves towards it, scattering into a long line to neutralize, as far as possible, the effect of the land-mines that they would encounter en route. Scarcely 200 reached the cannon, but that was enough; the chloroformed artillerists were lying on their munitions; the northists had time to turn the piece around and fire on Papagayo before Phileas Fogg's troops were able to move forward to save their cannon.

To render the approaches to Papagayo even more difficult to cross and to put the besiegers' forward batteries out of action, Fridolin created a new and admirable invention, a steam-driven 500-horsepower pneumatic aspirator[58] with a range of six kilometers. Constructed at intervals in exposed spots, these aspirators were activated one morning in front of the general staff. The one in the port of Segovia, under the guns of a northist battery, sucked up everything in front of it with frightful violence, and the terrain was stripped bare; trees, cannons, *gabions*[59] and locomotives, torn up, uprooted and overturned, were engulfed in the enormous tube along with 100 northists.

That same day, the *Times* correspondent almost perished as a victim of his duty as a reporter; at the moment when the aspirator went into action, he had he imprudence to lean over the immense orifice in order to observe the vicissitudes at closer range; the fearful air-current plucked him up like a feather and swallowed him up instantaneously. A terrible scream resounded. Everyone, officers and mechanics alike, thought that he was doomed.

---

pervasive odor; on the other hand, his description of the symptoms caused by the incident in London is reminiscent the symptoms of violent allergic rhinitis, so it also possible that he was allergic to it and found its widespread popularity something of a personal ordeal

[57] I have translated *enfants perdus* literally, although the equivalent phrase is not used in English to refer to soldiers on a suicide mission; it is by no means standard usage in France and seems to have been improvised by Robida.

[58] When Robida wrote this, the term "vacuum cleaner" had not yet entered into common parlance; the day when such machines would become common household appliances was still in the future, so the notion of applying them as weapons of war might not have seemed quite so absurd to his readers as it may well do to modern readers, in whom familiarity has bred contempt.

[59] A *gabion* is a large basket or sack filled with earth or sand, used in the building of improvised fortifications.

203

Fortunately, the chief mechanic was able to extract him from the machine five seconds before the arrival of the cannons and locomotives aspirated from a league away. Even so, the accident had terrible consequences for him. A bachelor when he went into the aspirator tube, he emerged married!

This is how it happened: a lady, Miss Barbara Twicklish, the editress of the *Women's Rights* newspaper of New York, attached to Sir Phileas Fogg's general staff, happened to be standing beside the *Times* correspondent; at the moment when the latter disappeared, carried off by the aspirator, she grabbed hold of his coat-tails and was dragged off with him. For two seconds they whirled together inside the tube with vertiginous rapidity. Fortunately, the rotundity of Miss Twicklish's figure cushioned the impact considerably. Did the *Times* correspondent, in the effusiveness of his gratitude, make Miss Twicklish some feverish declaration of love? No one knows. At any rate, before they emerged from the machine, the ever-practical young woman obtained a signature at the bottom of formal promise of marriage, inscribed in her notebook.

The long-range aspirators functioned so successfully that the besiegers were constrained to pull back their lines again. In the early days, Phileas captured an entire railway train—a pleasure excursion bringing inhabitants of Cayman city, the northern capital, to watch the bombardment of the southern capital.

As the operations of the siege dragged on, the German scientist conceived the idea of adapting the cannons on the ramparts into high-pressure music machines to entertain the troops. To the sounds of this powerful orchestra they danced every evening in the covered trenches, and the soldiers were able to forget the fatigue of the siege in the delight of a rapid polka or a languorous waltz, sheltered from the chloroform bombs.

The southist scientist and the northist scientist continued their contest with striking inventions, some more sublime than others. Fridolin, during a night of insomnia, thought he had found another marvel; he launched canisters of smallpox, constructed on the model of ancient machine-gun canisters, which released their noxious *variola* miasmas after exploding.[60] Farandoul simply had his army vaccinated and retaliated with a Bixbyan invention of a continuous jet of bombardment, driven by steam and alimented by projectiles transported by a railway.

In any case, the moment was approaching for the famous plan elaborated by Farandoul and Bixby to be put into operation. For a month, immense preparations had been under way, as secretly as possible, in a little bay north of Papagayo.

Disdaining henceforth the railway war and banal siege warfare, Farandoul wanted to inaugurate submarine warfare! The fish-rich coasts of Nicaragua had

---

[60] Although Louis Pasteur had recently popularized the germ theory of disease in France, it was still widely believed that epidemics were caused by airborne "miasmas," so this biological weapon is imaginatively more akin to a poison gas.

furnished first class auxiliaries: fish of the swordfish family, light, swift-moving and easy to tame, which, once provided with a special harness, became excellent mounts for a corps of submarine cavalry.

The old cavalry officers of the northist army, having become captains of armored locomotives, had changed their destiny once again; Farandoul, in spite of their primitive objections, ordered them to organize the submarine cavalry under the supreme direction of General Mandibul.

When everything was ready, a general review of the new corps took place on the road. The northist general staff, the military attachés of various powers and the reporters embarked on an ironclad monitor and put out to sea. Those who were not in on the secret were racking their brains to guess the reason for this marine excursion when, all of a sudden—by courtesy of an order sent via a telephone whose wires plunged into the water behind the vessel—4000 suited divers astride 4000 swordfish emerged abruptly from the waves in four parallel lines, each comprising a squadron of 1000 men. At the head were General Mandibul and his aides-de-camp, the general staff and the music.

To the strains of the national anthem the squadrons performed maneuvers and filed in front of the monitor in admirable order. Each squadron of submariners was composed a company of sappers solely armed with hatchets and four companies of 200 men provided with powerful breech-loading compressed-air carbines.

After different maneuvers and a charge in columns the submarine cavalry, instead of returning to the large barracks-dock where it was stationed, headed out to sea and disappeared beneath the waves.

No one knew Farandoul's plan of attack. Convinced that submarine operations would begin immediately, however, a French journalist—Monsieur Guy de Beaugency, the correspondent of Le Figaro—resolved to follow them no matter what. In addition to his morning-suit and white cravat, his revolvers and his flannel vests, the prescient journalist, a man well used to all the expedients and accidents of great reportage, had a diving-suit in his luggage, which he immediately put on. While the fourth squadron of submarine cavalry filed past the monitor, a man leapt smartly on to the back of an officer's mount and disappeared with him under the waves. That man was Guy de Beaugency.

The submarine cavalry arrived that same evening at the coast of Papagayo; six meters beneath the surface, on the very rocks of the fort commanding the pass, the regiment paused to give the men and the swordfish a few hours' rest.

A few tacticians reproached General Mandibul for having neglected to order an immediate reconnaissance of the port by a platoon of divers. The reproach was merited; without that negligence, Papagayo might perhaps have been taken without a shot being fired. General Mandibul, in a pamphlet published in the United States a year later, replied to that criticism by saying that, at the time, he was afraid of advertising his presence before the moment of the attack and thus losing the benefit of a nocturnal surprise.

The brave general did not know that, for their part, Phileas and his scientists had thought of the possibility of an attack by sea, and that, in order to thwart any such attempt, they too had organized a corps of submarine cavalry charged with keeping watch on the depths of the bay. Perhaps the idea had been suggested to them by a northist turncoat; at any rate, the southist submariners were on watch.

At midnight, the hour fixed by his instructions, Mandibul telephoned his orders. The regiment moved off, sappers at the head. Each man, on departure, had fixed a little red headlight on his mount, with a reflector that gave it a range of a dozen meters in advance.

They passed the forts bordering the entrance and arrived without incident in the harbor proper. A southist guard-post was distinctly perceived, poised on the embrasures of an advance fortification. The sound of swimmers operating at a depth of only five or six meters seemed likely to reach them. Mandibul thought briefly about taking the post; nevertheless, he passed it by without giving the order. This, it was realized later, was a big mistake.

As they entered the port the terrible howls of a steam-driven alarm siren transformed the profound silence of the bay into an infernal racket. The obscurity of the night disappeared; 20 jets of electric light pierced the thickness of the waves with their beams. Hundreds of submarine mines exploded. At the same time, Mandibul's sappers collided with an immense net extended across the channel leading into the port.

The attack having been discovered, it was necessary to break through all the obstacles. They hurled themselves upon the net. Suddenly, Le Figaro's reporter set off at top speed on the officer's mount, the latter having been blown away by a mine. He told Mandibul that a second net had just been raised alongside the southist post they had previously observed, blocking the exit from the port. Only two squadrons had got into the channel, and were now imprisoned between the two nets, which were now being drawn together, dragging with them everything they encountered.

Mandibul telephoned an order to retreat, and the submariners, swiftly turning back, brought all their efforts to bear on the second net. Assembled in a confused mass by the continuous approach of the two drag-nets, the submariners had difficulty moving; from one moment to the next the mêlée became more compact, and the time was fast approaching when the two squadrons, gathered into a single heap, would be entangled in the meshes.

Finally, a hole was made in the fatal net by the sapper's hatchet-blows; they enlarged it furiously, and through that hole escaped a torrent of riders deprived of mounts and mounts without riders. They were just in time; the nets, drawn together by powerful machines, were lifted up with their prey—200 or 300 divers, mingled with a few uprooted blocks of stone.

The pass was scarcely open again when 2000 southist submariners, commanded by Phileas in person, raced after the retreating northists. The collision was brutal. Mandibul's two intact squadrons had moved into the front rank and gave the enemy horde a furious reception.

An epic and grandiose battle was joined in front of the southist forts; begun with rifle-shots, the fight soon took on the character of a hand-to-hand mêlée in which sabers alone held sway. The electric light, like a submarine fire, illuminated the combatants; the southists recognized one another by their blue lights while the northists, as we have said, wore red ones.

Little by little, the northist squadrons were driven back by the efforts of the southist submariners. Submarine batteries, opening a terrible fire on their flanks, carried away entire lines, while a squadron of southist submarine lancers cut into the left flank of the North's soldiers with a forceful charge.

General Mandibul saved the main body of his army by means of a splendid maneuver. The debris of his two squadrons was reformed in the rear of the battle between the rocks of the pass and the transatlantic cable. Having got their breath back, they suddenly fell upon the southist submariners from that strong position with a frightful fury, and resumed the battle.

By virtue a stroke of genius, Mandibul had telephoned new instructions to his sappers; the latter skillfully directed all their blows at the air-tanks of the southist divers. This tactic was completely successful; hundreds of southists, put out of action, were soon abandoning the struggle and returning to the surface to breathe.

Phileas accomplished prodigies of valor in vain. The transatlantic cable was taken and retaken six times over. *Le Figaro*'s reporter, clinging to the cable, victoriously resisted all their charges; having attached a little pocket apparatus to the cable, he set about telegraphing rapid notes to his paper describing all the phases of the battle.

In the end, the cable remained in the possession of the northists. The latter, recovering the ground they had lost, came back into the harbor after the southist squadrons.

Phileas, in desperation, was momentarily tempted to hang himself with the transatlantic cable, but *Le Figaro*'s reporter, dreading that his communications might be interrupted, precipitated himself upon him, revolver in hand, and prevented him from putting his fatal project into execution. Phileas beat a retreat to the port; the debris of his squadrons reformed briefly at the place where the main sewer emptied out into the huge basin, and defended the entrance energetically; the northist submariners were still advancing, and a fierce battle soon developed in the dark and filthy waves of the southists' last refuge.

It was in that supreme peril that the heavens came to their aid. A violent storm had been raging for hours, accompanied by a veritable deluge of rain; the city's gutters were pouring furious torrents into the drains, and the main sewer was subject to a sudden surge which, falling upon the combatants, swept them abruptly out into the basin. Only Phileas, with a handful men, was able to set foot in an upward-sloping tunnel and get back into the town, where his first concern was to take all possible measures to barricade the main sewer.

The northists had rallied at the outlet of the sewer to let the torrent pass. Unfortunately, when it had all run through, Mandibul found the southist troops strongly barricaded within the central sewer, and numerous batteries established in all its subsidiary tunnels. Given the impossibility of forcing these positions with weary submariners, he contented himself with hastily fortifying the conquered section and sending a few couriers to Farandoul to ask for the immediate dispatch of the second and third submarine brigades, commanded by Generals Tournesol and Escoubico.

The couriers did not have far to go. Farandoul, at the head of the Tournesol and Escoubico brigades, arrived at the entrance of the pass at the same time as two large monitors attacked the forts with chloroform bombs. Informed of Mandibul's situation, he telephoned an order to him to maintain his position.

Dawn had broken; while the submariners, descending from their mounts, advanced step by step through the obstacles strewn in their path, taking the southists' submarine batteries one by one, the two monitors, directed by Horatius Bixby, maneuvered so as to extinguish the fire from the forts without approaching close enough to be hit by the 300-kilogram shells launched by their giant cannons.

The chloroform bombs having already been employed during this operation, two forts had fallen silent, their artillerists put to sleep for 48 hours beside their pieces.

In Papagayo, people gave way to despair. The fall of the city was all too certain, and the civilian population followed the final phases of the battle in anguish. The worthy Fridolin Rosengarten held council with Phileas and the remaining generals. Supreme resolutions were made. As the enemy made further progress, the decimated regiments retreated.

The courtyards of the barracks and armories filled with soldiers to whom the commissariat distributed provisions of food for a few days. Finally, mysterious preparations were made in the main arsenal, which an anxious population surrounded without daring to approach.

About noon, when six more forts in the pass had been put out of action by the chloroform bombs and Mandibul was already attacking the batteries in the main sewer, Phileas and Fridolin Rosengarten arrived at the arsenal on horseback with the last troops. The crowd awaited the completion of the preparations breathlessly and uncomprehendingly.

Suddenly, an immense shout went up. Several balloons, still retained by cables, had just appeared above the walls of the arsenal. They were few in number at first, but others, suddenly rising up, gradually swelled their numbers. These balloons, operating with the regularity of a military maneuver, soon formed into three groups, three distinct flotillas. To avoid an imminent surrender, the southist army was escaping by air!

Fridolin Rosengarten had foreseen every possibility. In order to escape a possible disaster he had, with the collaboration of other scientists on the committee, long prepared a brilliant means of escape. It was a veritable revolution in the art of aerial navigation that Fridolin had brought about—a revolution whose consequences for the world's future were incalculable!

Without wishing to attempt a description far beyond our competence, we can say that the Rosengarten balloons had triumphantly solved the problem of the application of steam power to aerial navigation. A little engine of moderate power, placed at the summit of the balloon, drew it in the desired direction, as effectively against the wind as in the direction of atmospheric currents.

That was not all. These balloons, constructed for war, were armored. Steel cladding covered each gutta-percha sphere like a gigantic inverted saucepan. Each exceedingly large gondola was also strongly armored, and the muzzles of several cannons projected from its embrasures, ready to give voice in the clouds.

The first group of these balloons, quite different from the others—bulkier and more heavily-armored, if that were possible—was composed of 25 artillery balloons known as destroyers, armed with heavy ordnance and mortars. The balloons of the second group, lighter and more numerous, were still combat balloons, but the third group seemed to be formed of transport balloons, immense airships, each charged with 200 men, without cannons.

When all the balloons had taken their places in the flotilla, Rosengarten—who was racing back and forth through the lines in a fast balloon-launch—sent up the signal to lift off. Two balloon-launches hastily gathered up the last soldiers busy with ground-operations. It was finished!

To put an end to the murmurs of the city-dwellers, however, the worthy Fridolin Rosengarten took one final measure; before rejoining the bulk of the fleet, he made one more use of the electric cable attaching the launch to the arsenal, and blew up the city behind him.

How can one describe the rage of Farandoul and the northists when they saw Phileas Fogg and the remnants of his army escape in that unexpected manner? Farandoul quickly telegraphed his bombardiers to try firing a few asphyxiating shells, but the explosion of the city took that last chance away.

The river and a few fragments of monuments fell back on top of the besiegers' lines and hindered the movement of the artillery with a sudden deluge. When it had all run off, it was too late; the aerial fleet had disappeared.

IX.

Cayman City, the capital of the Northern States, was enjoying a holiday. Everyone was celebrating the great victory of Generalissimo Farandoul and the taking of Papagayo. Details were still lacking regarding the end of the battle.

There were flags, festoons and Chinese and Venetian lanterns everywhere; the streets were packed; the entire population was delirious with joy. Public balls were improvised in the grand plazas; the theaters were giving gala performances. After the theaters emptied, people profited from the splendid moonlight to continue partying. Fireworks were launched from several points, in the midst of cheering.

Suddenly, as the last rockets died away, an infernal apparition in the sky set a chill in every heart. Two blue dots had just appeared beside the Moon— followed by two others, and then a whole series of rapidly-growing dots. What were these new stars whose blue light had just disturbed our planetary system? What were these unknown worlds, endowed with such vertiginous velocity? No one could answer those questions—even the astronomers at the Observatory felt their hair stand on end at the thought of the imminent collision.

But detonations were heard: the blue stars were bombarding the city. Asphyxiating shells began to fall on the suburbs. The truth became clear. The Observatory recognized the blue stars as the lights of a flotilla of balloons.

It was Phileas Fogg! It was the southists!

At the same moment, a dispatch from Farandoul, communicated to the crowd, provided the key to the enigma:

Papagayo taken. City blown up, telegraph damaged, hence delay. Take defensive measures. Southist army departed northwards in balloons. Am sending General Mandibul to cover Cayman City.
The generalissimo:
Saturnin Farandoul.

Orders were immediately given to plunge the city into darkness. All the lights were extinguished in order to avoid giving the southist easy points at which to aim. Even so, bombs and shells continued to rain down at hazard, albeit without causing overmuch damage. Alas, the dawn arrived too soon, revealing the town's position to the southists.

The southists who had drawn away, immediately returned, and the whole of Cayman City was able to see, with mortal terror, their balloons take up positions 500 meters above the houses. The city maintained its composure; a civil guard was organized. About noon, when the southists, having completed their preparations, opened fire, the civil guard, distributed about the roofs and monuments, directed a furious fusillade at the aerial fleet.

General Mandibul telegraphed news of his imminent arrival with 75 armored locomotives. Cayman City continued the battle while it waited. By dusk, 25,000 inhabitants, chloroformed or asphyxiated by concentrated vervain, were lying in the streets. Smallpox canisters were also falling; there were hasty vaccinations in every quarter. The 75 balloons illuminated their searchlights and formed up like a crown of little blue moons above the city; it was magical, but horribly unpleasant, for the shells continued to rain down.

Fortunately, General Mandibul arrived in the evening. He spent the night establishing his 75 armored locomotives as a battery. Then, in order to judge the situation better, he installed himself at the top of the bell-tower on Cayman City's town hall, the most exposed spot.

All through the night, balloons and locomotives exchanged infernal fire.

At daybreak, Phileas change tactics. His balloons broke ranks, descended to a height of 100 meters, and lowered their huge anchors, then tacked back and forth above the city. The noise of collapsing buildings was soon alternating with that of bombardments.

Phileas had reserved for his own point of attack the town hall where Mandibul had set up his general quarters; full of fury against the general, he launched his armored balloon, the *Clarissa Harlowe*, against the monument at full steam.

A terrible impact shook the town hall to its foundations. Fortunately—and how the councilors congratulated themselves on not having skimped on its construction!—the monument resisted two charges, and after the third, the southist aerostat remained fixed to its summit, impaled by the spire of the bell-tower. Immediately, the northist soldiers, led by General Mandibul, launched themselves forward to attack the balloon.

The most astonished of all the men involved was the correspondent of *Le Figaro*; he was perched, telescope in hand, on the top floor of the bell-tower, under the weather-vane, scribbling a dispatch to his paper, when the first shock imparted by the balloon knocked him backwards. When he saw Phileas Fogg's balloon caught on the spire, he immediately understood the importance of the capture and succeeded in taking possession of the balloon's stout anchor, which he wedged firmly in the beams. Mandibul and his soldiers soon joined him. It was a matter of using that rope to climb up to the gondola, from which a fierce fusillade emerged.

As it sought to disengage itself, however, the balloon gave the town hall a terrible shaking. Rosengarten redoubled the fire; the moment was approaching when the northists would reach the gondola. Suddenly, with a formidable tremor, a cracking sound was heard, the monument seemed to rip from top to bottom, and the northists released cries of terror. One last bound defeated the obstacle and the aerostat rose up into the sky along with a fragment of the decapitated bell-tower.

General Mandibul, the reporter Guy de Beaugency and a few men clinging to the debris of the bell-tower were borne away by the *Clarissa Harlowe*, Phileas' armored balloon.

In the balloon, the prisoners received all the attention due to their misfortune. The *Times* reporter, Philoctetes Mortimer, brought by Phileas Fogg along with the ex-Miss Barbara Twicklish, now Mrs. Mortimer, set about trying to render their situation bearable.

Le Figaro's reporter, fearing that he would not be able to correspond with his paper from the balloon, displayed some desolation, but that soon passed when he perceived that his colleague, the *Times* correspondent, had two dozen carrier pigeons aboard, ready to carry his dispatches to the telegraph office in Honduras, a neutral country. Unfortunately, the pigeons were shut up in a cage, the key of which the *Times* reporter always kept about his person. Guy de Beaugency turned his batteries in the direction of the sensitive Barbara Twicklish, Philoctetes Mortimer's new wife; with the double objective of obtaining as much information as possible and finding a means of getting away, he attempted to capture the heart of the gentle lady.

The southist balloons, meanwhile, had quit the skies of Cayman City; finding the city well-defended by the armored locomotives, they had departed in various directions, some to destroy the coastal ports, others with specific orders to go further north, burning all the wealthy towns of the region. By acting in this manner, they were almost certain to have the advantage of the armored locomotives, obliged to run to the right and the left by the requirements of defense.

Phileas' aerostat, the *Clarissa Harlowe*—a pretty name given to it by the poetic Phileas[61]—went ahead, with a light aerial launch following in its wake.

The *Clarissa Harlowe* had already destroyed two important towns, with a certain number of smaller ones, beneath a rain of shells; at present, the aerostat was on its way, at the head of a little squadron, to bombard a prosperous commercial port. The furious Mandibul was consumed by escape plans while Guy de Beaugency, in the grip of a thirst for correspondence that was impossible to satisfy, was circling around the pigeons and the *Times* reporter's wife.

What agony! After every important event, Philoctetes Mortimer charged one of his flyers with a dispatch written in microscopic letters. Their number was shrinking; it was necessary to act promptly.

Beaugency had already seen a great deal of the sensitive Barbara, whom he charmed with long tirades on the sacred rights of woman; an inspiration struck him that brought matters to a head. "Listen," he said to her one morning, as they were getting a little fresh air on the upper poop-deck of the *Clarissa Harlowe*, to the sound of bombardments. "Listen, dear Barbara, if you will permit me to call you by that sweet name; I have to tell you, although it pains me to deliver a cruel blow to your poetic dreams and to scythe down your illusions in full flower... but it must be done! I must save you!... so understand this: Mortimer, Philoctetes the traitor, is a bigamist, and perhaps a trigamist! My friend, General Mandibul, says that he knows a Mrs. Mortimer in New York, and I know that another exists in Paris, where I knew Mortimer quite well. O infamy! Instead of being the angel of the hearth, the unique spouse, you will be the traitor's number three!"

"Horrible! Horrible!" sobbed the unfortunate Barbara.

"It shall not be!" cried Beaugency. "Leave the wretch! Your fatherland permits divorce. O angel, spread your wings! And if I dared to hope that, one day..."

Barbara had already taken out her notebook. Beaugency had succeeded; he signed whatever she wanted.

---

[61] Phileas presumably did not have in mind—although Robida undoubtedly does—the fact that the luckless heroine of Samuel Richardson's novel spends a hundred pages dying ignominiously after having been raped by the conscienceless Lovelace.

"Let's flee! Flee!" he cried. Barbara flinched, thinking that he wanted to precipitate himself, along with her, into the layer of 4000 meters of blue sky that separated them from the ground. "Don't be afraid, my lovely friend!" he said. "We can flee, but more comfortably!" And Beaugency revealed to Barbara, in a whisper, all the details of an escape plan, elaborated with General Mandibul.

Barbara consented to everything; when the triumphant reporter left the poop with her, everything was arranged, the roles allocated and the hour fixed.

To escape from a balloon floating at an altitude of 4000 meters is not an easy thing to do at any time, but to escape from a war balloon, strictly guarded by sentries and watched over by vigilant officers, is a terribly dangerous enterprise. Even so, Mandibul and Beaugency were determined to run any risk.

Beaugency had spent the evening in the *Times* correspondent's cabin. About midnight, as he took his leave of Mortimer, he suddenly stuck a chloroform mine under the latter's nose, reduced in potency but still sufficient to knock someone out. The reporter did not utter a peep; he collapsed into a sleep that would last at least eight hours.

Beaugency put Mortimer's reefer-jacket on, pulled the hood down over his eyes and went out with Barbara. The officer on guard in the wardroom mistook him for Mortimer and thought that he was going to contemplate the stars poetically with his better half. Barbara went up to the poop alone; Beaugency headed for the prisoners' cabin in steerage. The man on guard let him approach, unsuspectingly. Beaugency repeated the trick with the chloroform mine, and the man collapsed. Beaugency opened the door feverishly.

Mandibul and his men were there. The sleeping sentry was dragged into the cabin; one of the prisoners put on his uniform and took his place. It was now a matter of getting out through a narrow loophole open to the outside and hoisting themselves up by the force of their arms to the poop-deck, previously guarded by as sentry whom Barbara was likewise to have chloroformed. A muted call from the latter informed the fugitives that she had succeeded.

The rest was easy. The eight prisoners hauled themselves up; the robust Barbara was there to help them over the guard-rail. When the eight men were reunited, they crept towards the balloon-launch moored to the stern.

Some difficulties presented themselves then; there were two men on watch there. Arm in arm, Barbara and Beaugency went ahead and chatted for two minutes with the sentries; they were suddenly made to inhale the mines and the way was open.

With what joy the freed prisoners installed themselves in the little launch. "Free! Free!" repeated Mandibul.

It was necessary to detach the moorings and rapidly draw away from the *Clarissa Harlowe*. While the mariners cut the ropes, Guy Beaugency had run to the cage containing the *Times* correspondent's carrier pigeons and carried it off triumphantly. "Quickly! Quickly!" he cried. "Cast off! Someone's rousing the guards!"

A certain commotion had arisen in the interior of the large balloon; the first chloroformed sentry had just been discovered. The sound of footsteps was heard, climbing up to the poop-deck.

The last cable was cut by a hatchet-blow, and the balloon-launch, detached from the large aerostat—which was heading into the wind—leapt backwards. It was just in time; the alarm sounded among the southist aeronauts.

"Hurrah!" cried Mandibul.

The little balloon-launch had suddenly risen up 200 or 300 meters above the flotilla of southist balloons; the escapees were able to see the entire blue-light squadron drawing away beneath their feet. There was a great stir aboard; the strident notes of steam-horns were heard signaling maneuvers to the fleet.

The balloon-launch, caught by the wind, was soon seven or eight kilometers away from the southists. Unfortunately, the entire fleet suddenly turned round and came back.

"Put out the lights!" cried Mandibul. "Let's vanish into the darkness!"

They gained a few more kilometers by this stratagem, but they suddenly saw the southists combing the depths of the sky with electric searchlights in order to discover the fugitives. As soon as they had been seen, the pursuit was organized.

"To the machines!" Mandibul howled. "Full steam ahead!"

A terrible cry replied; the coal-bunker was empty. It would be necessary to fight, without any possibility of steering the balloon, against the swift steam-driven aerostats. No matter! In order to climb as high as possible, Mandibul had all the ballast thrown overboard. They leapt up 1000 meters, and the southist balloons dwindled into the distance.

Meanwhile, Guy de Beaugency hastened to bring his correspondence up to date. His paper had been without news of him for a fortnight; he wanted to relieve his readers of their anxiety and resume the series of his exciting letters. The *Times* correspondent had only left him nine pigeons; Beaugency had already sent forth four, each with a page lodged beneath its wing. A fifth page was ready, when a violent "*Ventre de phoque!*" from Mandibul caused him to raise his head.

"What is it?" he asked.

O rage! The blue signal-lights and electric searchlights were reappearing in the distance, like hounds on a track, searching for the missing balloon-launch from cloud to cloud. Beaugency made a note of this resumption of the pursuit and sent off his fifth pigeon.

Everything that could be thrown overboard was sacrificed; the balloon gained another 500 meters—but five minutes later, the terrible blue lights reappeared. The electric searchlights picked out their prey again, towards which they were moving under full steam. The enormous headlight of the flagship, manned by Phileas, was ahead of all the others, which were scattered like a constellation of blue stars. The southists soon thought that they were close enough to the fugitives to begin the cannonade.

The shells whistle through the air some distance from the balloon-launch and fell back to Earth, describing long parabolas; with every passing minute, the southists' fire became more accurate, the shells getting closer.

Beaugency was still writing, happy to have such exciting news to send to his paper. A sixth pigeon flew off, bewildered by the cannon fire.

"They're catching up!" screeched Mandibul. "Come on! Throw all unnecessary weight overboard! Look alive, lads!"

The healthy Barbara was afraid, and threw herself into Beaugency's arms; he reassured her.

The fugitives hurled every useless or heavy object into space: the steam-engine, the coal-bunker, the armor plating. They only kept one small cannon in case of need.

With a new leap, the balloon vanished into the sky; the blue lights faded into the distance. Beaugency charged his seventh pigeon with the news of that fortunate change in their circumstances; hope was reignited, all the more so because the breeze seemed to be lifting them up.

"If we can gain two hours," murmured Mandibul, who had been examining the sky with the experienced eye of an old mariner for some time, "we'll be saved."

They flew on for another hour, sometimes within sight of the indefatigable blue lights and sometimes without. In the end, as the shells resumed their rain, Mandibul, in order to gain another hour, took off his less indispensable garments and his boots and threw the lot overboard. His men did likewise; eight pairs of boots whirled into the sky, eight jackets and eight tunics. Barbara sacrificed her Bible and a few meager items of toiletry. The balloon's guard-rail was partly demolished, and they cut through the air with increasing speed.

Hurrah! Just as the tempest they had been hoping for began to get up, the blue headlights faded away. Soon they disappeared, while the balloon, moving faster and faster, went through the tumultuous and heaped-up dark clouds like a bullet. Beaugency sent forth his eighth and next-to-last pigeon.

How many kilometers and myriameters did the balloon-launch cover on the night of that terrible chase? No one was ever able to say. At dawn, when the tempest abated, they saw the ground from a height of 700 or 800 meters. Seaman Tournesol, one of the eight escapees, though he recognized the mountains of Costa Rica and the Bay of Mosquitoes; they could, in consequence, set down.

There lay a difficulty; none of the eight escapees knew how to steer the balloon; they hoped that as they continued to run free they might eventually get close enough to the ground to be able to throw out the anchor. The danger having disappeared, they were looking forward to restoring their expended strength with a long rest. Barbara, who had been suffering hunger pangs for several hours, finally asked whether it might not be time for dinner.

"Let's look in the food-locker," said Mandibul. "Where is it hidden on this accursed balloon?"

O despair! The food-store was empty! No one had given it a thought on embarking, but now the horrors of hunger would succeed those of pursuit.

"Damnation!" cried Mandibul. "We had a dozen pigeons, and we've let them go! The last remaining one is our only resource!"

One pigeon for ten people! That was slender rations. Beaugency thought about it, frowning. "Let's try to land!" he cried. "Six hundred meters away, beefsteaks are extending their arms to us!"

"Land!" said Mandibul. "That's easily said, but the means, with this damned bitch of an aerial launch and 5000 devils of bad luck...*ventre de pho-que!*"

While everyone leaned over the side, trying to figure out some means of descent, Beaugency feverishly finished scribbling a few lines.

Aboard our balloon-launch, 8 a.m.

The tempest is over but a new and terrible danger is threatening us! Famine is aboard. No one knows how to land our balloon. There are ten of us, all hungry; I am sacrificing our last pigeon to send you this last letter.

Farewell, everyone!

Guy de Beaugency.

This terrible missive departed, carried by the last pigeon.

The fugitives, leaning over the balustrade of the balloon, saw the white bird spiral through the air and zoom off like an arrow in a northward direction. They straightened up with angry exclamations. The last hope of a final meal had just flown away. The heroic journalist was right; famine was aboard.

Barbara wept. They quarreled for a quarter of an hour; then, as recriminations were futile, they resumed seeking, hopelessly, for a chance of salvation.

Dusk fell without any having been found. They were still traveling at a height varying between 400 and 2000 meters. When they drew nearer to the ground they made signals to all manner of indigenes, they fired cannon-shots and threw little pieces of paper—but the natives contented themselves with lifting their arms in the air, without being able to pass any foodstuffs to the balloon of the *Medusa*.[62]

A bottle of oil for lubricating the wheels of the machinery, miraculously discovered by Barbara, was the only nourishment—if it could be called nou-

---

[62] The reference is to Géricault's famous painting of *The Raft of the "Medusa*," which depicts the desperate survivors of a shipwreck. Verne's grim account of the survivors of the wreck of *Le "Chancellor"* was partly inspired by the painting, and this passage was almost certainly written with that novel in mind.

rishment—that the unfortunate fugitives had. They passed it around until they had drunk the last drop.

The night passed without incident and the second day of famine began. This time, they were cutting through the air 500 meters above the sea. It was then that they regretted the pairs of boots sacrificed in the flight; their leather would at least have given them something to eat, while nothing that remained in the balloon could serve as any sort of nourishment for the neediest stomach.

Something edible did still remain, though, and that something—a terrible resource—was nothing less than one of the hungry passengers in the balloon! They all thought about it, and they all darted hungry glances at their neighbors. The buxom figure of the tender Barbara was resplendent as a gastronomic temptation; the eyes of the fugitives were transported in her direction with a quivering of the eyelids, clearly indicating the grandiose idea that everyone had formed of her succulence.

At midday, the habitual dining hour, Mandibul made a long speech recounting all the stories of starvelings adrift that he could remember. He recalled that there was a certain custom, on such occasions, of drawing lots to determine who…and how—here Mandibul's voice grew soft—one often saw some passenger full of generosity, and reasonably plump, sacrifice themselves for the common salvation…!

No one broke the silence to make an offer of this sort. It was Beaugency who took up the thread. "Since no one has anything to say," he said, "I feel obliged to speak. Listen! I'll give you a striking proof of the generosity of my heart. It's me who'll save you, although I'm very thin. I'll make the sacrifice of the one who is most dear to me in all the world—my dear Barbara. It's her who began the work of our salvation! I'm sure enough of her heart to know that she'll be happy to devote herself to its conclusion!"

Barbara, weak and speechless, almost fainted.

"I was sure of it!" Beaugency continued. "See—the noble woman acquiesces with our proposition by her silence."

"What courage!" murmured Mandibul, softly, with a tear in his eye. "Permit a companion in misfortune to embrace you respectfully, Madame!"

"And us too!" cried all the fugitives, weeping. "Us too!"

"Let's have a chorus of *Capédédious!*"[63] howled Tournesol, bursting into sobs. "What a woman! How plump she is!"

Everyone got up to embrace poor Barbara, choked with emotion.

"Ship ahoy!" cried Mandibul, who was the first to wipe his eyes. "Ship ahoy!"

---

[63] *Capédédious* is one of the less popular items in the rich French vocabulary of euphemistic exclamations, being a rather unnecessary substitute for "Thank God!" It appears to have been invented, purely for literary purposes, by Alexandre Dumas in *Les Trois mousquetaires*.

A universal commotion welcomed this announcement.

Four hundred meters from the gondola, a large steamship was making its way across the surface of the sea. Signals were rapidly exchanged; the vessel stopped.

They remained above the steamer for three quarters of an hour without being able to find any means of descent.

"What can we do? What can we do?" muttered Mandibul.

"The cannon," suggested Barbara, more interested than anyone in finding a solution.

"Imbecile!" cried Mandibul. "I never thought of that. Pay attention! Tie all the ropes and cable we have aboard together, end to end; throw the cord over the side with a weight attached, and let's try to catch one of the masts of the ship with our harpoon-gun. But before that, as it'll run away at the first cannon-shot, let's immobilize it with a chloroform shell."

"Bravo!" cried Beaugency.

"Attention! Get set! Load! Pack! Fire!"

A shell whistled through the air and missed the vessel—which, in accordance Mandibul's prediction, immediately got up steam in order to flee as rapidly as possible from the dangerous aeronauts.

"Again!" said Barbara, breathlessly.

"Fire! Missed again! Reload! Fire!"

"Hurrah! *Touché!* The third shell's scored a direct hit. Fire another one for safety's sake!"

It was true. The third chloroform shell had hit the ship; the latter, after a few somersaults, rotated on its axis instead of making headway. All movement was suspended on board; the passengers could be made out lying motionless on the deck.

"Now the harpoon-gun and aim well!" cried Mandibul. "It's our last card!"

The harpoon whistled through the air.

Victory! The harpoon had penetrated the hull of the vessel and remained there, solidly attaching the balloon to the ship. But how were they to get down? Hauling on the rope was not prudent. Tournesol volunteered to climb down the rope and to draw the balloon down with the ship's capstan.

Barbara went to embrace him before he commenced his perilous journey.

The agile mariner spent a quarter of an hour on the descent, resting from time to time at some knot in the rope. Finally, he set foot on the ship and put his plan into operation.

It took a long time. Two hours—which seemed like two centuries to Barbara—went by in maneuvers; the balloon descended, lower and lower....

Finally, when it was level with the mainmast, the fugitives threw themselves into the rigging and slid down to the ship's deck, Barbara in the lead.

Saved! Saved!!!

The *Gironde* was a transatlantic liner en route to Panama. Her 300 passengers and 60 crewmen were lying on the deck. The two chloroform shells had put them to sleep with lightning rapidity.

"Two shells! They'll be out for eight hours!" cried Mandibul. "We'll put them away and take them to Cayman City while they're asleep. To the engines, lads, and *en route* for the northist camp!"

Thanks to the skill of Mandibul and his men, the *Gironde*, having changed direction, soon reached the port of Cayman City. The crew and passengers were still asleep. Mandibul left a very polite letter of apology for the captain, and headed for general headquarters. Farandoul was there, putting all his efforts into the fabrication of a great fleet of armored balloons designed to give chase to the southist balloons.

X.

Things had changed considerably. The southist balloons were no longer ploughing through the air with the same security, bringing fire and destruction to all parts of the territory without running any risk. Now the northists also possessed an aerial fleet impatient to take on the enemy. Several limited skirmishes had taken place, and the results had not always been indecisive.

The southist aerostats had encountered other difficulties. Bixby had invented a new machine: the flying mine. Hundreds of these mines floated above all the towns of the North, resembling mere kites; a little balloon at the end of an 800 or 900 meter thread carried the mine into the air and maintained it at the required height. All the bell-towers and tall buildings were furnished with these devices. The southists could now only advance with prudence, for several balloons arriving in darkness in the midst of such mines had already perished totally or, the explosions having capsized them, fallen into the hands of the northists.

Generalissimo Farandoul, at the head of the northist fleet, sought by means of skilful maneuvers to reach the enemy, in order to finish the war with a decisive battle. Farandoul's balloon was a large armored vessel of 500 horsepower; it only carried one cannon, but the shells from this monstrous cannon could pierce the thickest armor plate at a distance of eight kilometers. Forty determined men formed the crew, which, with six mechanics or stokers and the general staff, formed a complement of 55 men.

Farandoul had baptized this balloon with a name still dear to his heart—for he was still unaware of her infamous treason—calling it by the airy and poetic name of *Rising Moon*. The general staff was made up of Mandibul and several other former seamen of *La Belle Léocadie*. The others were distributed through the fleet. Tournesol was in command of the balloons of the advance guard with skillful aeronautical captains under his orders. Escoubico was at the head of a division of bombardiers and light flying chloroform-pumps.

Guy de Beaugency, the correspondent of *Le Figaro*, special attaché to Farandoul's general staff, had not forgotten to equip himself with a well-stocked dovecot. After every event, pursuit or combat, a pigeon flew off with a letter. Needless to say, Barbara Twinklish had not followed him aboard. The poor woman, furious about the role that they had expected her to play aboard the hungry balloon, had created a terrible scene with her companions and had declared to them that she would return to the southist fleet to plead with Philoctetes Mortimer and Phileas Fogg for clemency.

Standing on the poop-deck, in the midst of his general staff, with his telescope in his hand, Farandoul inspects the horizon without seeing any sign of the enemy. It is two days since the southist fleet disappeared under cover of darkness; have they succeeded in cutting through one of the flanking flotillas, or are they still moving straight ahead? If they are moving straight ahead, they will be trapped, for the Northern fleet is faster.

For two hours the general staff's telescopes never cease scanning the horizon; the dinner bell has rung and they are about to leave the poop for the dining-room when Farandoul's final glance shows him and almost imperceptible black dot amid the cirrus—light clouds floating at a very high altitude. Telescopes search the clouds for the black dot and exclamations soon emerge from very throat. A second dot appears; there is no more doubt—it is the southist fleet, which has risen up to almost 8000 meters in the hope of allowing the northist fleet to pass underneath them.

There is no further question of dinner. Farandoul gives orders to the mechanics; signals are sent up. The fleet climbs rapidly, whistling and releasing whirlwinds of stream.

The black points perceived in the heights of the atmosphere have increased in size considerably; it is definitely the entire southist fleet, reduced to 69 aerostats in all. The northist force rising to meet them has only 40 balloons, but Farandoul hopes to see his other two corps arrive within 12 hours and wants to begin the battle while waiting for them.

The southists have spotted their enemies. They have taken flight and are moving away rapidly, but the northist aerostats are visibly gaining on them. Soon, the first balloons of the advance guard arrive within range of the southist rearguard. Fire commences without any great effect, the speed of the flight making things difficult for the gunners.

Phileas Fogg disdains to reply. He seems to have another idea. Two or three leagues ahead, heavy clouds fill the sky with their wooly masses, heaped up like a chain of mountains. The southists' plan seems obvious; they intend to reach that thick layer and lose themselves in the bosom of an ocean of fog.

Farandoul hastens the speed of his aerostats, but the southist balloons are already disappearing into the depths of the thick cloud; scarcely have they entered the mass when they become vague and then disappear, becoming absolutely invisible. Even so, the northist balloons approach the large cloud-mass resolutely and are about plunge into it in their turn when a frightful cannonade bursts forth upon them at short range. Phileas' flight was a feint. Lying in ambush behind the initial masses, the invisible southists have been waiting for them!

This sudden attack throws the flotilla's advance guard into disorder. Two northist balloons disabled by the first volley are spiraling in the clouds. Fortunately, a large aerostat flies to their aid and succeeds in taking them securely in tow.

The bulk of the northist forces have opened violent fire on the almost invisible southist balloons. It is a battle in the fog; the initial advantage is to the southists, placed in good positions, retreating at each volley to hide behind a mass of cloud.

Both sides make use of chloroform shells, but the effect is hardly tangible for several reasons. The wind is violent and disperses the miasmas rapidly, and every shell striking the external armor of a balloon is a wasted shot; in order for the narcotic to have an appreciable effect it is necessary to deliver the projectile accurately on to the bridge of the gondola. However, the skillful Farandoul, firing his large mortar personally, has succeeded twice. Two of the largest southist aerostats, reached by his shells, are out of the battle; their crews have fallen into a lethargic sleep, the gunfire has ceased and the balloons, left to their own devices, have been captured.

Chance seems to be favoring Farandoul's gunners for, within four hours, their chloroform bombs have reached the enemy 17 times. The aerostats have been captured, their sleeping crews laid out in the holds and replaced by northist artillerists.

Suddenly, the lookouts signal the appearance of new flotilla to port. It is Farandoul's left wing, which has just joined the battle.

Night is falling. Chloroform shells whistle through the air. The northists have 14 balloons out of action, having sustained serious damage or because of the lethargy of their crews, but the southist losses are immense. Of their entire fleet, only eight balloons are still fighting, with the courage of desperation; the rest have been captured or lost. Thirty to 35 balloons reached by the chloroform are adrift far from the battlefield, with their crews deeply asleep.

The flagship balloon commanded by Phileas Fogg is riddled with bullet-holes, but it is still intact; its artillerists are working wonders. Called upon to surrender several times by Farandoul, Phileas has refused to lower the flag.

The northist aeronauts are clamoring loudly to board it, but Farandoul stops them and takes personal command of the large mortar in order to try once again to chloroform these obstinate combatants. Orders are given; the best gunners concentrate all their fire on Phileas' balloon.

The armor plating is riddled with holes, but the effect of the shells is still restricted; only a few men are reached by the miasmas. The others are still fighting, urged on by Phileas, standing on the poop-deck. Finally, the enormous cannon carefully aimed by Farandoul lets fly; the shell whistles through the air and, this time, reached Phileas' poop.

A universal cheer greets this fine shot. Finally, the flagship will fall into the northists' hands...

But Phileas, with rage in his heart, sensing the initial emanations of the chloroform beginning to make him dizzy, succeeds by a supreme effort in standing up. The balloon's armory is open; it is full of bombs and chloroform shells. Phileas sees the northist balloons approaching; he sees the detested Farandoul urging on his men. Hatred torments his heart; he wants to take them with him to death and, with a firm hand, he blows up the armory!

A frightful conflagration burst forth; Phileas' balloon is in shreds, but the immense quantity of chloroform released into the atmosphere has suddenly knocked out the crews of the nearest northist balloons. Farandoul has fallen from his quarter-deck on top of the sleeping Mandibul; Beaugency and his pigeons are lethargic...

It is all over.

The last southist balloons have lowered the flag. The northists are strong enough to gather up all the prizes and to chase after their chloroformed balloons.

These operations take three days. On the morning of the third day, the chloroformed crews begin to open their eyes. The reawakened Farandoul takes command again and gives the order to descend to the ground as quickly as possible.

While they tack back and forth in search of a convenient landing-ground, a few disabled balloons are still being collected in mid-air, sad wrecks of the frightful aerial battle. Finally, a landing-ground is found, two kilometers from a railway station. Farandoul has a cannon-shot fired as a signal.

The cannon chancing to be loaded with a cannonball, the shell whistles through the air, hits the grounds…and a huge column of flame springs up from the ground! The shell has just ignited an oil well!

We shall not describe Farandoul's arrival in Cayman City at the head of the victorious army. The reception was delirious.

Pacified Nicaragua wanted to prove its gratitude to Farandoul, but our hero refused everything: decorations, the ministry of war, the presidential chair and so on. He only accepted one thing: the concession of the oil well that he had discovered. A month later, he sold it to a consortium of rich capitalists and divided the price—15 millions—with his friends, the mariners of *La Belle Léocadie*.

The first steamboat leaving for Europe bore them all away. Duty called Farandoul to Paris; he had to inform Monsieur Jules Verne of all the details of the glorious but deplorable end of Sir Phileas Fogg and to embrace his brave foster-father, the monkey of Pomotou, who was still a day-resident at the Jardin des Plantes.

"And then it's Africa, for both of us!" murmured Farandoul, who spent the entire journey huddled over maps of that continent.

**PART THREE:
ACROSS AFRICA**

THE FOUR QUEENS

I.

Gondokoro, October 26.
To Monsieur le Président de la Société de Géographie,
Boulevard Saint-Germain, Paris
    Monsieur le President,
    You must have gathered from my recent reports that I was beginning to despair of finding any trace of Saturnin Farandoul, lost in the heart of Africa. All my effort and all my fatigue had been fruitless. No indication of the passage of the celebrated traveler could be found in the countries bordering Lake Albert-Nyanza. I have already explained to you how I was able to follow him as far as there. The iron boat constructed for him in the workshops of Indret, transported secretly to Marseille and put on a ship for Alexandria, had taken to the water in Cairo. At the first cataract of the Nile I found the Nubians who had transported it on their shoulders, and likewise at the second; further on, caravans had encountered him, etc. etc.
    It was only in Khartoum that the real difficulties began. On departure from there, no clue, no trace. For six months I explored Yambokalfa, Bertat, Deuka, the land of the Makarakas, and Lakes Albert-Nyanza and Victoria-Nyanza, in vain. No one had seen him. Had he perished in one of the rapids of the African river? Had he been massacred by some unknown tribe? All suppositions were permissible.
    In spite of the perils of the enterprise, and in spite of the ferocious wars laying waste to these countries, I was heading towards Lake Tanganyika to pursue my research there when terrible—and, unfortunately, only too reliable—news reached us at Gondokoro: Farandoul had been eaten by the Niam-Niams![64]
    No doubt is any longer possible, alas! This is how the news reached us.
    A caravan arrived yesterday from the shores of Albert-Nyanza. I was addressing a few questions without much hope, to the negro porters when one of them men, a large and vigorous Niam-Niam, replied to the description of the iron boat and the portrait I gave of Farandoul with a exclamation and rubbed his belly joyfully while clicking his teeth.
    "Have you seen him?" I asked, by way of my interpreter.

---

[64] Gondokoro was a trading-post in the Sudan established at the supposed limit of the Nile's navigability. The tribe called Niam-Niams by Robida and other contemporary writers—Verne uses the term in *Cinq semaines en ballon*—is nowadays known as the Azande, having been made famous by one of the classics of anthropology, E. E. Evans-Pritchard's *Witchcraft, Oracles and Magic Among the Azande* (1937). They did not practice cannibalism.

"I've eaten him!" he replied, renewing his pantomime. "He was a good man, very good."

Bowled over by astonishment and anger, I had difficulty recovering my composure in order to address further questions to the horrible cannibal. Alas, alas we can no longer conserve the slightest hope! When we appeared to doubt the veracity of our Niam-Niam, he seemed annoyed, and fetched two of his comrades, who had also tasted the unfortunate voyager.

It is finished! Farandoul is lost to science; there is nothing left for his numerous friends to do but mourn him. I shudder to think of the despair that this news will bring to the heart of Lieutenant Mandibul.

My mission is thus, unfortunately, terminated. Today, I shall begin preparations for my return.

Eusébin de Saint-Gommer [65]

P.S. I administered to the Niam-Niams, of course, all the reproaches merited by their heinous conduct; I told them that, on my return, I would expose them to the scorn of civilized Europe in all the newspapers, scientific journals, Academies and other Societies. The wretches wept, but I was implacable, and pursued my admonition even more forcefully.

E. de St-G.

We shall not attempt to describe the emotion aroused in the scientific world by this letter from the Geographical Society's envoy. We shall go back a few months into the past, and we shall see for what terrible events central Africa had served as a theater.

It is 11 p.m.; the air is pure and fresh; the thermometer indicates no more than 40 degrees above zero, having oscillated between 50 and 55 in the shade. We are on the edge of a large watercourse, a regal river majestically resplendent

---

[65] This name is a rather tortured pun. *Gommer*, whose literal meaning is "to gum," also means to erase, rub out or, at slight stretch, annihilate—the last of which meanings would make it equivalent to the French *annihiler*. Saint-Gommer is therefore roughly equivalent to "St.-Annihile," a deliberately-botched gallicization of the English name Stanley. Henry Morton Stanley had mounted a famous and extensively publicized search for the lost English missionary David Livingstone, finally finding him in 1871, before going on to circumnavigate Lake Victoria-Nyanaza and explore Lakes Albert-Nyanza and Tanganyika in the mid-1870s—his expedition being financed by various newspapers, which made much of his dispatches—shortly before Robida penned his mock-epic. Robida's illustration to this passage depicts the searcher in the pith helmet that Stanley helped make famous as a component of the typical garb of the African explorer.

in the moonlight, reflecting the stars—those innumerable celestial lamps scintillating in the azured vault—like an astronomical chart.

Gigantic trees form confused rounded masses on the river's banks, each standing up like tall columns terminated by a fan of foliage. These trees are baobabs, with a thousand giant branches, each of which is a forest by itself, palm-trees, date-palms, roniers, mangroves, etc., etc.

This region of enormous and abundant vegetation is in Africa. We are on the banks of the N'kari, not far from Lake Albert-Nyanza, in a region scarcely touched by Livingstone and Stanley. On the bank there is an immense fire, a veritable pyre, before which hundreds of black shadows are dancing and gesticulating. Others shadows move through the crowds, bring even more masses of branches to feed the fire. The forest, illuminated by long flames, takes on an increasingly fantastic appearance. Before the enormous fire, the negroes are making great efforts to roll along a strange mass whose form can only be made out indistinctly.

Finally, as the negroes stand aside, the mass become visible. It is a small iron boat, bizarrely constructed, completely enclosed by a metal lid.

The negroes, who were probably spying on its progress along the river, have ambushed it at anchor; finding the hatches sealed, they have attached numerous ropes to it and, soundlessly and without agitation, have pulled it out of the water and dragging it over the sand. They have slipped masses of foliage and dry wood under the boat's hull; the fire has been lit, and the silence—religiously guarded until then—has changed into an infernal concert.

The tom-toms resound, the negroes howl—and in the distance, lions roar in terror.

A witch-doctor chants:

"The white man is shut up in his boat!

"The white man will be cooked; he is good, very good.

"The Niam-Niams will feast themselves upon the white man!"

What is happening? To what inexcusable scene of cannibalism shall we have the agony of bearing witness? You have guessed it; it is our Farandoul who is enclosed in this iron boat, a gigantic saucepan set on the fire by a band of Niam-Niam gastronomes. The unfortunate will, therefore, perish in the full bloom of his youth, far from his friends, far from Mandibul!

What a miserable destiny for a heroic man! To perish by being cooked! After having occupied the world stage so brilliantly, to disappear obscurely into the stomachs of Niam-Niams! Let us go into the saucepan boat and see how he is bearing his torture.

Farandoul is alone in his boat. Prey to a sullen misanthropy since his return from America, his heart poisoned by all the grief caused to him by his fatal encounter with Phileas Fogg and Passepartout, Farandoul wanted to flee from the human world. Without even taking his friend Mandibul into his confidence, he commissioned the building of a steamboat, made entirely of iron, an authentic carapace that opened and closed at will. With this boat, which he named the *Solitaire*, he set off to explore central Africa, in the hope that he might contrive to calm the anguish of his heart in the midst of a whirlwind of perils and adventures.

This evening, having found an anchorage for his *Solitaire* in a tranquil backwater of the N'kari, he sealed up his boat and went to sleep. His mind returned to the time of his earliest adventures with the monkeys of Oceania; he found himself in the midst of his adoptive family, with his brothers the young monkeys; then he saw himself embarking on the conquest of Australia; he saw once again the young Malay woman, Mysora, the unfortunate victim of Croknuff, an angelic smile illuminating her diving-suit....

Suddenly, Farandoul leaps out of his bunk, a sudden sensation of warmth waking him up with a start. Finally, here is one of those perils that he has sought in order to plunge himself back into action! A single glace through the little portholes of his cabin suffices to inform our hero of his situation. The *Solitaire* is on the fire, and the negroes are intoning their chants of triumph while awaiting the opportunity to eat their victim.

There is not a moment to lose; the danger is immense. The boat is heating up rapidly. Farandoul tries to open the hatches, but the Niam-Niams have bound them with ropes. A negro, climbing on to the boat, pours water through the gaps in the panels from calabashes that his comrades pass up to him. Farandoul understands that they want to eat him boiled!

The heat is becoming worse and worse; it is necessary to put an end to it. He hurls himself upon a box of fireworks that he had brought with him in order to illuminate the ruins of Thebes during his passage through Egypt, of which he has not made use by reason of his melancholy. He rapidly disposes all the sunbursts and rockets in the openings designed to ventilate the boat, and sets them all off at once. At the same time, he falls upon one of the hatches, axe in hand, cuts through all the ropes and stands up like a statue in the midst of the firework display on the deck of the boat.

The explosion of squibs, the whistle of rockets and the rotation of Catherine-wheels have terrified the astonished Niam-Niams. The chants have ceased abruptly; the drums have been thrown away and all those who have not been floored by terror have launched themselves at top speed in all directions howling in fear.

Farandoul leapt down to the ground in the midst of a few Niam-Niams extended face down on the ground. Seizing a staff, he rapidly scattered the brands of the fire and saved the Solitaire from any immediate anger.

The Niam-Niams nearby dared not budge. Farandoul seemed to them to be a terrible god manifested in order to exterminate them. Having need of their arms to refloat his boat, our hero struck them a few times with his staff to force them to get back to their feet. This light volley of blows had the effect of a voltaic pile, making them jump up with frog-like hops. Further blows of the staff made them understand what the god expected of them, well enough that, within a few minutes, the *Solitaire*—still burning—was back in the water. While Farandoul reinstalled himself therein, the Niam-Niams, having recovered sufficient courage to flee, launched themselves into the trees in order to go and mingle their howls with those of their brothers.

By the time he gained open water, Farandoul could only see one of them on the shore: a young boy of about 15 who, having been struck by a rocket, thought that he was dead and had remained flat on the ground throughout the entire scene. Farandoul took pity on his terror; he got up again, brought him aboard the Solitaire, and made him swallow a draught of cordial. The little Niam-Niam finally dared to raise his eyes to look at the terrible white man and found enough strength to reply to his questions.

Farandoul had learned a few words of the Zulu language, which almost all the dwellers on the shore of Lake Albert-Nyanza understand, so he succeeded in obtaining some items of information from the little Niam-Niam. He learned that the members of the voracious band who had taken it into their heads to cook him in his boat were part of a Niam-Niam army that was presently on an expedition to replenish its food supplies in the land of the Makalolos.[66]

The mention of "food supplies" made Farandoul raise his head. "Yes," the little Niam-Niam went on, under interrogation, "Makalolos good, very good. Niam-Niams have large stomachs, always hungry. When they have no more prisoners to eat, Niam-Niams make war. Niam-Niams good warriors. Makalolos good warrior-women, but also good to eat."

"What do you men, good warrior-women?"

---

[66] These entirely imaginary Makalolos have no connection with the actual Makalolo tribe of southern Africa, of whom Robida had presumably never heard.

234

"Yes, Makalolos women warriors—very brave but very good!" And the little Niam-Niam burst out laughing, showing two superb rows of sharp teeth.

Farandoul remembered then having heard mention in Gondokoro of Makalolo, a very important nation that was said to be governed by two queens and defended by regiments of female warriors. He had considered the tales he had been told to be ridiculous fables, but now, it seemed that their exactitude was demonstrated. He resumed his questions, therefore, and asked the little Niam-Niam where the land of the Makalolos was located.

"Here," replied the young cannibal. "Niam-Niams very close to the Makalolos too, will fight them tomorrow on the N'kari."

With much patience and skill, Farandoul succeeded in extracting all the desired information from his prisoner, the little Niam-Niam. He learned that the Niam-Niams had come to the land of the Makalolos in 300 war-canoes, each one manned by 30 men, and that their flotilla was a few leagues away on the N'kari, confronted by a Makalolo fleet that was almost as numerous. The Niam-Niams with whom he had had dealings were to rejoin the Niam-Niam fleet at daybreak in order to take part in the attack on the Makalolos and the feast that would follow thereafter.

Farandoul did not hesitate for a minute. Nine thousand Niam-Niam cannibals were hurling themselves upon brave warrior-women to replenish their kitchens; he had to intervene. The *Solitaire* immediately left the fatal creek where it had almost been transformed into a saucepan and moved into the middle of the river.

The last embers of the Niam-Niams' fire were just going out; the most courageous of them, seeing the Solitaire draw away, dared to come back to the river-bank, and found the corpse of one of their witch-doctors—who had died of fright—among the burned vegetation. This discovery consoled them; they pretended that the roasted witch-doctor was the white man they had dreamed of getting their teeth into, and tucked into him with a hearty appetite. Those who survived got the rest later; it was presumably one of these who took news of Farandoul's death to Gondokoro—news that Monsieur de Saint-Gommer, sent in search of Farandoul by the Société de Géographie, transmitted to a saddened Europe.

The crew of the *Solitaire* now consisted of two men, Farandoul having kept the little Niam-Niam as a cabin-boy.

The N'kari is an immense river which empties, after having described many twists and turns and watered numerous unknown countries, into the Congo—or, rather, is one of the branches of the Congo, like the Zaire and the Bankoro. In the morning, the *Solitaire* came within sight of the Niam-Niam fleet, a few kilometers away, in the process of deploying on the river, which was almost 1500 meters wide at that point. A little further upriver, the Makalolo fleet was visible, arranged in good order on the left bank.

A huge racket of chants and war-drums was audible in spite of the distance of the Niam-Niam fleet; it was obvious that the attack was about to commence. A little further on, the Makalolo canoes were getting under way in order to face the enemy. Farandoul veered toward the right bank in order to conceal his moments from the Niam-Niams for as long as possible, and doubled his speed.

After ten minutes, during which the *Solitaire* covered three kilometers, scarcely 500 meters separated the two flotillas. The Niam-Niams filled the air with their war-cries and the noise of their big drums; 9000 throats were howling breathlessly, producing a powerful symphony compared with which all the choirs of the great orchestras of our opera-houses would have seemed mere cooing.

At the same time as the first volleys of arrows were exchanged, the Niam-Niam canoes were propelled forward by their oars, and those on the left flank soon collided with those on the Makalolos' left flank.

The *Solitaire* hurtled over the water, with its steam-engine at full power. Before the Niam-Niams, totally intent on their attack, were able to recognize the enemy that was menacing them, the iron boat was upon them, ripping through their lines like a cannonball, breaking canoes and cutting larger boats in two by attacking them side-on and then reversing its direction.

When it reached their left flank, to the great terror of the Makalolos themselves, the *Solitaire* came about and turned on the Niam-Niam fleet; while the canoes that had not been touched made forceful use of their oars to flee, the *Solitaire* passed through the middle of them again, disemboweling all those it encountered. The Niam-Niams, in complete disarray, immediately scattered in order to flee.

The affair did not last long; within five minutes the chants of victory had been transformed into howls of distress. Scarcely 100 canoes remained intact; the debris of others was floating on the water and the Niam-Niams, clinging on to wreckage or swimming desperately, were collected up and taken prisoner by the Makalolos.

The lesson given to the Niam-Niams appeared to be sufficient. Farandoul came back at reduced steam to the Makalolos. The latter, initially fearful and unable to comprehend this unexpected assistance, were reassured when they saw the *Solitaire* come to a stop in front of their lines and a man appear on the vessel's bridge.

A boat that was larger and more grandiose than the rest detached itself from the line and came to meet the *Solitaire*. It was guided by 20 male oarsmen, behind whom 20 warrior women stood proudly erect, armed with long spears, bows and daggers, and covered with necklaces, bracelets, copper plates and metal stars. One of them, who appeared to be the general or the admiral, leapt lithely on to the *Solitaire*'s deck and extended her hand to Farandoul, pronouncing a few words in an unknown language.

"There's no need," replied our hero, without having understood a single word of the speech. "You're charming, my dear lady, and I am happy to have arrived in time to prevent you from making the acquaintance of the Niam-Niam cooks."

The warrior woman reflected briefly, and replied in the Zulu language, which our hero knew: "Thank you, white man. You have saved the Makalolo nation from a great peril, and the Makalolo nation loves you. Come with us to our city, Makalolo, so that we may show our queens the man who has saved their warriors in their hour of need."

Farandoul bowed. The warrior woman shook his hand, kissed him on the forehead and nose, according to the Makalolo custom, and then offered her own forehead so that he could return the favor. That done, she beckoned to the warriors in her canoe, which formed the fleet's general staff, to come aboard the iron boat in order to present their greetings to our hero in a similar fashion.

Farandoul spoke in Zulu in his turn. "Brave warrior women," he said, "I am truly overwhelmed by your appreciation; I have only done my duty as a civilized man! I hope that the Niam-Niams profit from the lesson and that they will henceforth renounce all food-seeking expeditions against you. Now, I am ready to follow you. I shall be delighted to visit your capital and render my homage to your queens."

During this discussion, the little Niam-Niam, seeing that he was in the hand of the enemies of his race, had not dared to emerge from the hold for fear of being impaled on the warrior women's spears, but Farandoul, having come down to give him his orders, forced him to show himself. He appeared on the bridge carrying a tray full of refreshments and came to offer them to the Makalolos, without raising his eyes.

The warrior women had sat down in a circle on the bridge, with their legs crossed. When they had drunk the lemonade, Farandoul offered to review their fleet from his boat. The general acquiesced with a nod of the head, and the *Solitaire* moved off again.

The Makalolo canoes, arranged in three ranks, welcomed the little steamboat with loud cheers. The rowers lifted their oars into the air and the warrior women brandished their spears or struck their shields rhythmically with their arms, making the copper circlets and plates ring.

The lovely figures of all these warriors made an impact on Farandoul. In every boat propelled by male oarsmen there were ten warriors armed with spears and ten armed with bows. On a little platform in the stern, a single warrior, more richly equipped, directed the movements of the rowers and the fighters. Many of the women were very beautiful; their rather long hair was fleecy rather than frizzy; their noses, rather than being flat like those of the pure negro races, possessed an elegant curvature, and their manners were not lacking in a certain natural grace, allied with the charms of great energy.

On the left flank, another flagship joined the *Solitaire* and a warrior of distinction climbed on to the boat. Further civilities were exchanged and further refreshments circulated.

The first of the two warrior women commanding the fleet, the general of the right flank, was named Kalunda; the second, the general of the left flank, was Dilolo. Farandoul learned that they were the two future queens of the Makalolos, destined to replace the two current queens at the first full Moon of the following spring.

After having reviewed the entire Makalolo fleet, to the sound of cheers, and having been warmly congratulated again by the two general staffs, Farandoul was invited to a huge banquet on the shore. A few warriors mounted on agile giraffes had been dispatched to Makalolo to reassure the population.

After this solemn feast, the order was given for the entire fleet to take to the water again. It was a fine spectacle: 300 boats in the middle of the river, propelled by the robust arms of their oarsmen, flying over the blue waves, with the *Solitaire* advancing at their head, manned by Farandoul and the two generals, Kalunda and Dilolo. Fifty captured Niam-Niam boats followed behind, carrying the prisoners. The Niam-Niam chief, a tall and powerful old man, had been taken aboard the *Solitaire* so that Farandoul might interrogate him.

The old warrior, covered in wounds, ingenuously confessed that the Niam-Niams had undertaken the war with no other objective than to eat as many enemies as they could capture. He believed that he was destined to furnish a roast in the Makalolo kitchens and seemed to find that perfectly natural. Farandoul disabused him and told him that that frightful habit, particular to the Niam-Niams, was considered repulsive by all other peoples.

The old chief was startled. "You white men make war in your own country, don't you?"

"From time to time," Farandoul replied.

"And you don't eat the dead and the prisoners?"

"Never!"

"Oh!" said the horrified Niam-Niam. "You aren't hungry, and you don't eat prisoners, but you make war! You ferocious beasts!" And, turning his back on Farandoul, the indignant Niam-Niam signaled that he refused to enter into further conversation with him.

They arrived that evening in Makalolo, the capital, situated on the right bank of the N'kari. It was a large, rather well-constructed town comprising 1000 large huts scattered at hazard around a central edifice that was both a temple and a palace.

The population, forewarned of the fleet's victory and the arrival of the powerful ally who had routed the Niam-Niams, crowded the bank of the river where the disembarkation took place in an orderly manner. As the generals Kalunda and Dilolo set foot on the ground with Farandoul, and immense concert of acclamation went up from the crowd. A hundred musician-priests frenziedly beat sacred drums, making an infernal noise that appeared to be enormous pleasing to the population's ear for music. Then lightly-clad priestesses filed in front of the victors, dancing and rhythmically striking copper plates. After that procession, the high priest and high priestess, in the midst of a religious silence, brought wooden cup filled to the brim with sour zebra milk. It was a great honor, ordinarily reserved for queens and generals. Farandoul drained the cup to the last drop, in spite of the beverage's rather unpleasant taste.

The ceremony was over; immediately, in response to a sign from General Dilolo, a guard of honor of 50 warriors arranged itself behind Farandoul. While General Kalunda went to give an account of the operations to the two queens, General Dilolo had Farandoul installed in a large hut situated amid palm trees on the shore of the lake.

General Dilolo was a tall and superb woman, deeply bronzed rather than totally black, with long hair, bright eyes, a well-designed nose, her face completed by a smiling mouth. Her body was that of a lithe and robust Amazon, although a small bosom accentuated the charm of her general beauty. To cap it all, this luxurious warrior woman was approaching 30, the most beautiful age for a woman.

Farandoul was beginning to cultivate an interest in these brave warriors and this new land. For her part, the general was eager to interrogate the white man about himself and his distant fatherland. In consequence, they began to talk; the conversation covered Makalolo, the army, and Europe, of which the general was hearing mention for the first time.

The beautiful general was very surprised when she learned that white women did not go to war and left the sabers to their husbands. Farandoul was no less astonished to learn that throughout the Makalolo territory, on the contrary, men were nothing but good crop-growers and artisans, while women governed everything—the affairs of the household as well as those of the state. He had already seen that the vocation of arms was reserved to them; now he learned that the army, perfectly organized, was composed of about 20,000 warrior women spread out among various frontier posts.

The general gave him a brief account of the political organization of the Makalolos; the nation was a sort of republic governed by two elected queens, chosen from among the warriors. These two queens were appointed for five years, and had beneath then two future queens, the generals of the army, who were required to initiate themselves into affairs of state during the course of their reign.

A courier mounted on a giraffe, arriving at a fast gallop, came to inform Farandoul that the time to introduce him to the queens had come. In consequence, our hero, regretfully abandoning his interesting conversation with Dilolo, and still accompanied by the general and his escort, headed for the palace of the two queens.

O holy etiquette, thou reignest in all courts, even in Africa. Long formalities were necessary; greetings were exchanged with Their Majesties' guards, there were presentations, curtsies; it was necessary to kiss the council of ministers, composed of former generals and colonels in reserve, on the forehead and nose. Finally, after having endured a few speeches and emptied another cup of zebra milk with the high priestess, Farandoul was admitted to the throne room.

The two queens, sitting in the shadows at the back of the hall, maintained a majestic immobility. Farandoul, having reached the middle of the room, launched into a speech in Zulu.

An outburst of joyful laughter interrupted him; the two queens had risen to their feet and jumped lightly down from the podium.

"Hey, my dear," said the first, "leave your patois at that."

"And let's speak French, damn it!" said the second.

Farandoul stopped, struck dumb by astonishment. The two queens of the Makalolos were white!

II.

Not only were the two queens white, but they were Parisians! Farandoul's stupefaction was indescribable. To encounter in the heart of Africa, in such a high position, two female compatriots! Parisian women sitting on the thrones of the Makalolos, a nation absolutely unknown to the civilized world! The circumstance was rather surprising.

"Well, Mesdames!" exclaimed Farandoul, having recovered from his astonishment, "so it's you those frightful Niam-Niams wanted to devour? The fellows have taste; it's a quality that I must concede them at the sight of your white shoulders. I've no need to tell you how glad I am to have contributed to getting your people out of difficulty. But let's talk about you, Mesdames—so you're queens of the Makalolos!"

"Not by birth," said one of the queens, showing a dazzling array of teeth.

"No," said the other, "it's our merits that have won us that high position; we've been elected by universal suffrage, named queens by the warrior-woman electorate. For four years now we've been occupying the thrones of the Makalolos. Oh, it's quite a story—we'll tell it to you, won't we, Angelina?"

"Ah! Her Majesty is named Angelina?"

"Yes," said the second queen. "My Majesty is named Angelina de Montdétour and my colleague was known in Paris as Caroline Gardenia."

Farandoul bowed. "I am convinced, Mesdames, that the Makalolo nation could not have chosen better, but I'm curious to know how you came to reign over it?"

"Here's how it happened," said Angelina de Montdétour. "In Paris, Caroline and I were simple dramatic artistes. Caroline sang at the *Ambassadeurs*, fashionable little ditties—*Mon Oscar, La Fille du pharmacien*—you know:

"I'd like a big cube
"Of the fudge jujube.
"So I've something to scoff
"When I've got a cough, etc. etc.,[67]

---

[67] I have toyed slightly with this doggerel in order to conserve the rhyme-scheme. The term "jujube" is used in French not only to mean a fruit-flavored pastille, as in English, but also a soothing lozenge made up by a pharmacist, so the song's superficial reference is to something closely akin to the British "cough candy," which bears some resemblance to a hard fudge. Any *doubles entendres* it might contain are best left to the reader's imagination. The songs cited appear to be imaginary, although the second title has been used on a much more recent lyric, but *Rothomago* by Adolphe d'Emmery, Charles Clairville and

241

"As for me, I was appearing in *Rothomago*—I was the commander of the guard; that served me well, because it's what began my military education. So, as highly distinguished dramatic artistes, we were both engaged at the Cairo Theater to appear in an operetta. What a success, my friend! The khedive picked us out. We were admitted into his harem—oh, but as wives, Monsieur, as wives, nothing less than favorite odalisques![68] We were only the ornaments of the harem for five or six months, though; a conspiracy of the other wives undid us. The Sultan of Zanzibar had sent our lord and master a dozen natives; he didn't want to be outdone by his colleague in politeness, and offered us in exchange. In Zanzibar, we were soon the rain and fine weather; we transformed the court; the women learned to tinkle the piano and sing little songs by Offenbach; we put on family operettas.

"One day—and this is where the real adventure began—we were kidnapped by Arab merchants and taken into slavery; the wretches dragged us from country to country, offering us to impossible negro kings! One day, when we were on the point of marrying an old Niam-Niam king, we took matters into our own hands. We stole a dromedary from our Arabs and made our best way forward. When we arrived in Makalolo territory the Arabs caught up with us; we were defending ourselves bravely with sabers when the Makalolo warriors came to our aid and skillfully cut off the heads of our enemies. We were welcomed by them, in consideration of our beautiful defense, and were both appointed captains. On parade as in the field, we maneuvered our warriors admirably, were promoted through the ranks, became generals, and soon, without having had more than six months' instruction with the former queens, succeeded to the throne by virtue of an amendment of the Makalolo constitution! That's how it comes about, Monsieur, that we have the pleasure today of offering your hospitality in our state. Now, that's not all—you're still only a simple citizen and that won't do—you'll need a rank. What rank shall we give Monsieur, Caroline?"

"No rank," replied Caroline. "It's expressly forbidden by the constitution. Monsieur is a man and, in consequence, can't even be a corporal here. I know my code!"

"That's annoying," said Angelina. "What if we were to make him high priest, then? Would you like to be high priest?"

"No, no," replied Farandoul. "I prefer to remain a simple citizen. Remember that I'm only a passing stranger."

"Hang on a minute!" cried the two queens. "You aren't going away! You've got to stay with us and protect us. Remember that Europeans are scarce

---

Albert Monnier, which premièred at the Théâtre Impérial du Cirque in 1862, was a famously spectacular fantasy play about a magic watch.

[68] Odalisques were actually at the bottom of the harem hierarchy, being servants of the wives and concubines; Robida appears to have been unaware of this.

hereabouts. We have only to say the word and our generals will close all our frontiers to you. You're staying with us!"

"I'm a prisoner of Your Charming Majesties, then?"

"No, no! But you're staying with us—we need you. Remember that the state is under threat; the Niam-Niams might return. You'll help us to put the country on a sound footing. We're not sovereigns for fun; we want to leave our successors a secure kingdom—for our five years will soon be up, alas. We'll have to surrender the crown to Kalunda and Dilolo, the queens designated to succeed us."

As these words were spoken, the two queens sighed sadly.

Angelina continued: "Caroline has authoritarian inclinations; she'd like to stage a *coup d'état* to keep the scepter, but I don't want that—I'd rather go back to Paris! I'll have a town house on the Champs-Elysées, with a crown on the gate. I'll see visiting Majesties, I'll be the cousin of the Prince of Wales, I'll give fêtes and I'll have a coat-of-arms on my carriages—for I've designed one for Makalolo, you know: an ostrich on a blue field. It's very distinguished.

"Well, personally," Caroline said, "I'd rather stay with the Makalolos. I'm popular among my subjects, and I like it here. What I'll do, like queens who can't get married, is to demand a revision of the constitution..."

As she pronounced these words, Caroline looked at our hero tenderly.

"At the end of the day, Mesdames," Farandoul said, "having no pressing reason to depart, I'll stay in your realm for a few months. I'll help you protect your frontiers against all enemies, and my experience of warfare might perhaps be of some use to you."

Thus concluded, the solemn audience was terminated. Caroline struck a copper drum; at that signal the rush hangings opened and the entire court came into the hall. A huge official banquet brought together all the functionaries of the crown and, when night fell, Farandoul was taken back to his own house with great ceremony. He found his little Niam-Niam there, already acquainted with the Makalolo warriors.

The popularity of our hero increased further during the early days of his sojourn. Well-received and well-regarded everywhere, he was completely satisfactory to functionaries of every sort and warriors of every rank. Generals Kalunda and Dilolo put themselves at his disposal for all military matters, a guard of honor escorted him everywhere, and the two queens themselves rarely let two hours go by without summoning him to the palace, when they were not out riding with him in the immense wooded plains of the country, mounted on slender giraffes, or sailing on the blue waves of the N'kari on the *Solitaire* or the royal canoe, always with Dilolo and Kalunda.

And what Homeric repasts there were in the palace! The minister in charge of the royal kitchens, the only male minister in the realm, was worked to death. Great culinary reforms had already been instituted among the Makalolos; the queens of old had contented themselves with vulgar plates of black ants *au gra-*

tin, fried grasshoppers, roasted crocodile and serpents' eggs omelets, but the delicate palates of the Parisian queens had quickly wearied of such nourishment—so completely discordant with European gastronomic ideas—and it had been necessary to create a new cuisine. Fortunately, the minister was a genius; the black Vatel rose to the occasion magnificently.[69]

Farandoul was not a man to spend his days in idleness, though; in collaboration with the authorities he became seriously involved with the welfare of the Makalolo nation. It was necessary, above all, to ensure its future security. Farandoul had long conferences with Generals Kalunda and Dilolo; he demonstrated to them the excellent role that might be played, in the immense Makalolo plans, by a properly-constituted cavalry corps, to meet enemies head-on, whether they be Niam-Niams, or the negroes of King M'Tesa—that powerful potentate of Lake Tanganyika visited by Livingstone and Stanley, a valiant monarch who could sent forth armies of 40,000 men against his enemies. In consequence, an elite was selected from the warriors used to fighting on foot or in boats to form cavalry regiments. Soon there were 2000 warriors on strong and sturdy giraffes and a corps of 2500 ostrich-mounted sharpshooters, an incomparable light cavalry.

Nothing was more delightful than watching these regiments maneuver; the giraffiers had as proud a bearing as our old regiments of cuirassiers, and the ostrich-mounted sharpshooters, dressed in red cotton cloth, armed with large bows and Arab swords at their waists, seemed like strange apparitions when they galloped across the plain, launching their long blue-feathered arrows sideways. What a success those warriors would obtain at Longchamp or Vincennes if they should ever cross the sea!

The sole fault of the ostriches was their well-known appetite. Even while charging, they could not pass close to a shiny pebble without gluttonously snapping it up as they passed by. It was the same with all the less voluminous pieces of equipment; people were repeatedly having to run to the aid of one of these birds that had been put into cruel difficulties by trying to swallow its rider's sword.

Farandoul quickly acquainted himself with Makalolo customs. He had learned their language, and, when he was not out and about with the two white queens and the two black queens, he liked to discuss philosophy with the high priest in the temple.

Meanwhile, the end of the year had come. The moment when the two white queens would have to cede power to the two black queens was approaching. You will recall that the change of reign had to take place at the first full

---

[69] Vatel was the Prince of Condé's *maître d'hôtel* in the mid-17th century, whose tragic suicide—occasioned because a particular dish had been delayed while his master was entertaining Louis XIV—was recorded and immortalized by Madame de Sévigné.

Moon of spring. People were already talking about the great feasts intended to add splendor to that solemnity; all the Makalolos were permitted to attend, at least as witnesses, the great official banquet held in the capital's grand plaza for the new queens and the administrators.

One day, the little Niam-Niam brought by Farandoul came to find his master, who was busy making preparations for a lion hunt. The boy, who was already quite familiar with Makalolo ways, was highly delighted.

"What's up with you?" asked Farandoul, surprised to see him so buoyant.

"Oh, master, Me very pleased, very pleased! Me never eaten white women, me going to eat white women. Oh joy! Very happy!"

"What, little wretch? You're going to eat white women?"

"Yes—and master too. Master is invited and will take me!"

"What white women are we going to eat?"

"The queens, master knows well. Oh, me very happy! Good white queens!"

"Come, on, explain yourself! Why are we going to eat the queens?"

"Master knows well! At the spring Moon, white queens finished, Generals Dilolo and Kaluna queens. Great feast in plaza, and black queens eat white queens, with high priest and us. Oh, very happy! Great day!"

"You're mad."

"No, master. Me know very well. Master ask Dilolo."

Farandoul, who had burst out laughing at the little Niam-Niam's first words, could not help a certain anxiety eventually slipping into his mind. He remembered allusion having been made several times, in his presence, to the solemn feast of the first Moon of spring in ambiguous terms and with certain mysterious implications, to which he had not paid attention at the time. Without putting too much trust in what the little Niam-Niam had said, he nevertheless resolved to clarify the matter, and went to the palace to interrogate his friend the high priest, the organizer of all the ceremonies.

The high priest welcomed him warmly. He had conceived a strong liking for our hero, and as he was old, dreamed of making him his successor. He also wanted to take advantage of the occasion to initiate Farandoul into the mysterious quinquennial ceremonies.

"O, my child! The wisdom of our ancestors has established very wise customs among us. You know that we always have four queens: two in service and two in reserve..."

"That's very ingenious."

"Yes. If one of the queens in service is lost to us, a reserve queen replaces her; a fourth is appointed and everything continues without disturbance—but every five years, at the first Moon of spring, the reserve queens occupy the throne in their turn, and..."

"And...?"

"And then a long series of feasts begins in Makalolo. The warriors come together, save for those necessary to guard the kingdom. There are beautiful ceremonies—which you shall see, my son—and sacred dances by all the groups of priestesses. The former queens hand over their powers to the new ones. On the evening of the third day of the festival, a great official and diplomatic feast brings together all the principal functionaries and renowned warriors. You are invited in advance, my dear child to this solemn banquet..."

"Well?"

"At this solemn banquet, in obedience to the wise customs of our ancestors, the two new queens eat the two former ones."

Farandoul released an exclamation. The Niam-Niam had been telling the truth!

"This custom has been followed in Makalolo for centuries," the high priest went on, solemnly, "and the nation thrives on it. For more than 1000 years, our queens have eaten one another in this fashion, which ensures that all the wisdom of 500 queens is concentrated in the bodies of the two queens in service. Some have not reigned the whole five years; if the people murmur and become discontented with them, or if the two reserve queens give evidence of exceptional wisdom, the date of the changeover is brought forward. Admire, my dear boy, the wisdom of our ancestors! The old customs are good; it is thanks to them that the Makalolos live happily and in a very advanced sate of civilization, as you have been able to see."

Farandoul was speechless. The high priest took his silence for admiration. Finally, he asked: "But tell me—did your two white queens also eat those who preceded them on the throne?"

"Certainly!" cried the high priest, somewhat offended. "I told you that the wisdom of more than 500 queens is concentrated in their minds. They have eaten their predecessors, who had eaten two others, and so on, throughout the years."

"They haven't said anything to me about it!"

"That's because, in their wisdom, they have not judged it appropriate to mention it to you. Go see them, my son, and question Their Majesties."

Farandoul plunged into deep reflection. "It's frightful!" he said to himself. "What! Those charming queens, the brunette Caroline and the blonde Angelina, have taken to cannibalism! Who would have believed it? But no, it's impossible. They have no idea of the destiny reserved for them! It's me who must warn them and save them! Let's go!" And he headed for the queens' apartment.

To stave off boredom, the two queens were fencing with capped swords. They flung their arms around Farandoul's neck.

The latter calmed this fit of gaiety with a few words. "Pardon me, Mesdames," he said, gravely. "I have some serious questions to ask you. You've told me about the festival of your coronation, but you haven't mentioned the great banquet of the third day..."

"Ah, the sacred festival?" replied Angelina. "Those were the days. The meal itself was one of the best I ever ate in my life; even the Brébant doesn't serve dishes as succulent as that!"[70]

Farandoul recoiled in horror. "Do you recall, Angelina and Caroline, what you ate that day?"

"We didn't speak the Makalolo language well enough then to retain the names of the dishes. I only know that it was a particular thing that is only served in solemn circumstances—but it was exquisite, wasn't it, Caroline?"

"Oh, my dear, it was very tasty!"

Farandoul recoiled in horror again. "One more thing, Mesdames. The queens whom you succeeded—have you ever seen them since?"

"No, that's true! We thought they were offended. A matter of self-respect."

"Horror! You don't know why you've never seen these unfortunate queens? Well, I'll tell you myself: it's because, during the great banquet of the third day, you ate them!"

The queens released sharp screams and slumped down on to their rush mats.

"You don't know the fatal customs of the Makalolos! I've only just learned them while talking to the high priest. Know, then, that every five years, the two reserve queens eat the two active queens—it's a means dreamed up by the ancient Makalolos to conserve the wisdom of their queens. So it wasn't just two queens that you ate, but 500!"

"Cannibals!" sobbed Angelina. "I've eaten 500 women!"

"Ah!" murmured Caroline, the first to recover her composure. "That's why everyone keeps saying that the two of us unite the wisdom of 500 queens! It always made Angelina laugh. I understand everything now!"

Angelina suddenly started. "But what about us? We're going to be eaten too! Kalunda and Dilolo are going to eat us!"

The two women fainted, this time completely.

Farandoul hurriedly brought them round. "Don't despair!" he said. "I'll save you. Trust me."

Affairs of state suffered considerably from the state of agitation into which the fatal news had plunged the two white queens. For a fortnight they did not have the strength to occupy themselves with what needed to be done. Farandoul had to exhort them not to make their anxiety manifest, and to resume their conferences with the ministers and the generals. "Another fortnight," he said, "and I'll take you away from the cruel destiny that threatens you."

In the meantime, before abducting the queens of that tranquil and hospitable realm, Farandoul decided to ask the high priest whether there was any means to suppress the ancient custom of the Makalolos and to revise the constitution on

---

[70] The Brébant was (and still is) an upmarket Paris hotel.

this point. He had a long conversation on this subject with the old man, but as soon as Farandoul broached it the high priest furrowed his white eyebrows.

"What are you suggesting, my dear child? The wisdom of 500 former queens would be lost in that fashion! The poor Makalolo nation, badly governed, would soon lose its ancient prosperity with entirely new queens. It's easy to see that you're a foreigner."

"But in other countries," Farandoul objected, "in the Europe about which I've spoken to you, the kings and queens are not obliged to eat their predecessors."

"That's a mistake—a great mistake! Is your old Europe happy? Entirely happy? It's not, is it, my son? Introduce the customs of the Makalolos into Europe and, in a few centuries, everyone will admire the wisdom of your monarchs—you'll see!"

Farandoul returned to the queens, who were waiting for him anxiously. The reserve queens, Dilolo and Kalunda, were in the throne room chatting with the white queens about the realm's affairs.

"No hope with the high priest," Farandoul said, in French. "It's necessary to flee—and the sooner the better, for the solemn hour is approaching."

"Yes, the festival begins in a week."

"But what about Dilolo and Kalunda?" Angelina asked. "They aren't supposed to leave us during these final days."

"I've thought about that. There's only one way, and that's to abduct them too! This is my plan: order a great review for tomorrow of all the warriors in the western plain within four leagues of the capital, on the banks of the river. The whole army will come together, with the fleet, the ostrich-riders and giraffe-riders. We'll tire out the warriors and their mounts with various exercises. We'll bring them back to Makalolo, and that same evening, when they're in no state to pursue us, we'll flee in my boat."

"Bravo! We're saved!" Caroline and Angelina threw their arms around Farandoul's neck.

Kalunda and Dilolo, not having understood this speech, did likewise, embracing our hero with the same conviction. For a long time, his personal merits and talents as a warrior had made such a strong impression on the hearts of the two generals that they had promised to make him their prime minister as soon as they succeeded to the throne.

The following day was a great one for the Makalolo nation, and an exhausting one. While all the boats in the fleet, guided by Farandoul's steamboat, went downriver, the regiments of ostrich-mounted sharpshooters and the giraffe corps galloped off to the exercise-field.

Farandoul and the four queens were aboard the little steamboat. As soon as the entire army as gathered at the rendezvous, Farandoul made the warriors line up in battle formation on the shore, with the squadrons of the giraffe corps at the center and the ostrich-riders on the flanks. That done, he gave orders to the fleet.

The naval maneuvers began; the foreheads of the oarsmen streamed with sweat, but the warriors brandished their weapons frenetically, urging them on with the shafts of their spears. The circling movements, changes of front and charges in line lasted for three hours under the scorching Sun. Then the war-drums ceased beating and the fleet stopped. It was the turn of the land army, still immobile under arms. The fur queens disembarked and mounted giraffes. Farandoul followed them, leaving the steamboat in the care of the little Niam-Niam.

The noise of 500 war-drums suddenly burst forth on the shore and all the regiments broke formation. The general staff was already disappearing into the distance in a cloud of dust. The ostrich-mounted warriors launched themselves after them. There were charges by platoons, by squadrons, and finally by scattered sharpshooters. The ostriches were panting; Farandoul, seeing that they were out of breath, turned to the warriors on giraffes and made them whirl around in their turn.

It was 4 p.m. when Farandoul and the general staff came back to take their positions on the bank for the march-past. The poor ostriches pressed around the little Niam-Niam, who distributed some food to them. The warriors leapt back into the saddle hurriedly and resumed their ranks.

The queen could not help clapping their hands during the march-past, admiring the martial bearing of the warriors.

"Alas, it will be necessary to leave them!" murmured Caroline. "Come on, I'd like to embrace my brave colonels one last time."

Meanwhile, the entire army had taken the road to Makalolo; the giraffes and ostriches were trotting over the plain and the fleet was going back up the N'kari.

The Moon was rising when they reached Makalolo. The steamboat, still manned by Farandoul and the four queens, moved aside to let the fleet pass. When the last boat had been drawn up on to the shore and all the crews had disembarked, Farandoul gave a signal to the white queens.

"The time has come, Mesdames," he said. "We're leaving!" Leaning over the hold he added: "Let's go, Niam-Niam"—that is what he called the negro—"fire up the furnace, and quickly! And now, brave warriors, farewell! Farewell, brave Makalolo nation!" And before Dilolo and Kalunda were able to understand what was happening, the boat veered to starboard and retraced the route that it had followed.

Loud cries were heard on the bank. People ran about, asked questions—but some hours must have gone by before the truth was realized. Besides, the fatigue of the entire army, the oarsmen, the ostriches and the giraffes rendered any immediate pursuit impossible.

Kalunda and Dilolo interrogated Farandoul.

"It means that I've saved you," the latter replied in the Makalolo language, which he now spoke fluently. "Don't you know what was being planned? The Makalolo nation, content with its white queens, wanted to keep them for another five years. The high priest, having been consulted, had consented, on condition that, in order not to break entirely with tradition, the two white queens should commence their new reign by eating the two reserve queens. The white queens warned me, and I've saved all four of you!"

Kalunda and Dilolo, frightened by the peril they had run, let themselves fall into Farandoul's arms.

"By dawn tomorrow we'll be far away," Farandoul said. "Have no fear, black and white queens; we'll proceed at full steam!"

He was still speaking when the wooly head of the little Niam-Niam appeared at deck level. "Master!" he cried. "No more coal!"

Farandoul started. "How can there be no more coal, imbecile? The bunker's full!"

"No, master, bunker empty!"

Farandoul shrugged his shoulders and went down rapidly. He had spent that very morning checking his boat thoroughly, and had made sure that the provision of coal was hardly reduced.

The four queens seated on the deck suddenly heard a loud cry from the hold, and saw Farandoul leap on to the deck, dragging the little Niam-Niam by the ears.

"No more coal!" he cried. "He's telling the truth. And we'll be pursued flat out in a few hours! Come on, you little rascal, what have you done with the coal? The bunker was full this morning."

"Wasn't me, master—was the ostriches."

"What do you mean, the ostriches?"

"Yes, master, warriors' ostriches. This morning, ostriches tired, hungry, eating pebbles. Then me very good, gave coal to ostriches. Ostriches ate all up, ostriches content."

Farandoul remembered then that, on returning to the river bank at the head of the giraffe corps, he had found the ostriches clustered around the little Niam-Niam. There was no doubt about it; the little wretch had distributed all the coal in the bunker to the gluttonous birds. It was all over—the steamboat had had its wings clipped!

The queens had understood. Dilolo and Kalunda drew their swords and showed by gestures that they were ready to defend themselves.

"We're not at that point yet," Farandoul went on. "Don't despair. We'll go on, burning everything that we can burn, and try to put a healthy distance between us and your subjects."

III.

While the four queens rested in the cabin, Farandoul and Niam-Niam steered the boat. The *Solitaire* was a fast vessel, but her furnaces devoured fuel. Farandoul gathered all his resources—all the scrapings from the bunker, all the wood that he could remove from the boat—but all that would only last nine or ten hours at moderate speed.

At dawn, they had covered scarcely 15 leagues—not much! By now, the warriors must have set off in search of their queens on their rested ostriches, and the enraged warriors of the fleet must have launched themselves on to the river. It was necessary to keep going, at all costs!

Farandoul and the passengers went ashore in order to gather dry wood. The furnaces were relit and the *Solitaire* resumed its journey. The supply of wood lasted until noon; then it was necessary to go ashore again. Unfortunately, wood was scarce; they had to be content with thin branches and green trees. That wood produced more smoke than steam, and the *Solitaire* made slow progress. Its speed was slowed further by an encounter with a hippopotamus herd—which, seeing the boat moving slowly through the water, came to attack it with blows of their heads. That evening, Farandoul, harassed by fatigue, had to go and fell trees on the river bank. The warriors had to be getting closer.

Before going ashore in the morning, Farandoul inspected the plain cautiously; a few white dots were visible on the horizon. With the aid of his telescope, Farandoul recognized half a dozen ostrich-riding warriors.

What was he to do? To go forward was no longer possible; they had no more fuel—and before they could fell enough trees, the warriors would have caught up with the fugitives. And the fleet could not be far behind!

Farandoul did not hesitate. He decided to abandon the *Solitaire*, which had become useless. Without losing a minute, he collected everything that might be useful—provisions, munitions, luggage—made up several packs and had everyone move out.

The queens, moved by a feverish ardor, wanted to fight, but Farandoul had another plan. He made everyone hide in the dense undergrowth and hid in the coal-bunker, from which he could see everything that happened through a little hole.

He had scarcely shut himself in when loud shouts from the warrior women told him that they had discovered the boat. They arrived at a gallop, happy to have got their queens back. There were eight warriors, doubtless comprising an advance guard. They capered about on the bank, astonished by the silence that reined in the boat. Finally, readying their weapons, they leapt down to the ground and attached their ostriches to trees. Having inspected the surroundings carefully, they decided to board the vessel.

That was what Farandoul was waiting for. As soon as he saw all eight of them in the process of searching the cabin he leapt out of his hiding-place, swiftly locked the cabin door, went up on deck, closed the iron hatches and sealed the boat completely. That done, he put out on to the water and took the *Solitaire* to the middle of the stream, where the current gently took hold of it.

Without worrying about the arrows that the warriors fired through the portholes, he leapt into the water and swam to the bank. The queens had understood his plan and had already take possession of the warrior women's ostriches.

"Into the saddle! Let's go—at top speed!"

As they left the edge of the river and set off across the plain, Farandoul darted one last glance behind him. He saw the *Solitaire*, still carried by the current, and—two or three leagues away in the direction of Makalolo—the first boats of the fleet.

Fortunately, the ostriches still had the legs to run for two or three hours. They set off rapidly, and by midday had put six or seven leagues between the fugitives and the point at which the *Solitaire* had been abandoned.

Farandoul and his companions took a two-hour siesta in the shade of a large tree; they got back into the saddle refreshed and rested.

Evening arrived; it was the third since their departure from Makalolo. Farandoul looked for a shelter for the night. They had rejoined one of the branches of the N'kari; they perceived an islet in mid-stream which gave every appearance of being an excellent place to camp. They urged the ostriches into the river and came ashore on the island.

"Bravo! Excellent!" said Farandoul, after a minute inspection of the little strip of land. "We'll be at home here. Absolute tranquility, no need to light a fire to drive away wild animals, and no nasty encounters to fear. The Makalolo fleet must have caught up with the boat this morning. The warrior having seen us depart on the ostriches, the river pursuit must have been abandoned. Let's eat calmly, sleep until dawn, and then, to the ostriches!"

The ostriches' trot had given them a ferocious appetite; they were given the bulk of the provisions brought from the *Solitaire* and, everyone being thoroughly comfortable, the evening passed cheerfully.

"Oof!" said Her white Majesty Angelina, hiding a few yawns. "What a tiring day! What adventures we'll have to recount in Paris! I can't wait to get there."

"We're not there yet," murmured Caroline, "but that's all right. I'll miss our realm—our position had its advantages. In Paris, we'll have to begin all over again, trying to get jobs at the *Variétés* at 73 francs a month."

"Are you stupid?" cried Angelina. "We're rich—I've saved the diamonds from the crown."

"You've saved the…?"

"Yes—here they are!" Angelina opened a little bag that she had taken from her bosom, and a sparkling stream ran out of it, which brought cries of admiration from the four queens.

"Go to sleep, my children," said Farandoul. "We're leaving at dawn. Let's go. Good night!"

The fugitives were exhausted. Five minutes later, feeling perfectly safe, they were all sleeping with closed fists. Alas, appearances were deceptive, their sense of security false! A frightful danger was threatening the island's inhabitants. Without knowing it, the fugitives were on the edge of a marshy region swarming with crocodiles. Dilolo and Kalunda were aware of this detail, but had not given it any thought.

The saurians' sense of smell guided them to the islet and, arranged in a circle in the river, they watched their coveted prey with horrible gleaming eyes. There were at least 40 of them, large and small, silently accumulated. Minute by minute, they approached the bank and seemed to be plucking up courage to begin the attack. The friction of their scaly bodies and the jostling produced by the late arrivals trying to get to the front, ought to have woken the fugitives up, but the unfortunates were still asleep, exhausted by fatigue.

The ostriches, the first to awake, tried to break their shackles in order to flee—and Farandoul slept on!

The saurians advanced. The most courageous, having come ashore, slid towards the camp through the tall grass. Suddenly, a terrible noise woke the sleepers up—an ostrich had been seized by several crocodiles and the others, terrified, were trying to break free.

By the pale light of the Moon, the fugitives saw that they were surrounded by a menacing circle of gaping mouths.

"Into the trees!" Farandoul cried.

That was not easy to do, the trees being spare and very slender. Only the little Niam-Niam, as agile as a monkey, found refuge in the branches of a ronier—a sort of palm tree whose crown spread out like a bouquet. Farandoul, revolver in hand, faced up to the besiegers; he had already lodged a few bullets in the maws of the nearest saurians. The crocodiles had seized all the ostriches and were fighting over the poor birds. Those with the smallest shares had run to the bodies of their brothers that had been struck by Farandoul's bullets and were devouring them fraternally.

This massacre gave the fugitives a few moments' respite. Farandoul helped each of the queens to establish herself in a tree, and turned back to the attackers. A terrible battle ensued. Farandoul, with a spear in one hand and a revolver in the other, met the saurians' attack. A large circle formed around him. Whenever an imprudent crocodile advanced, a bullet in the eye or a spear-thrust in the jaw drove it back into the circle, where it was immediately finished off.

"What about the diamonds from the crown?" Caroline suddenly shouted from her tree. "Have you got them, Angelina?"

Angelina, installed facing her in the branches of a palm tree, let out a cry and almost let herself slide down to the ground. "I don't have them anymore!" she cried.

In the very midst of the attackers, Farandoul perceived a little bag, which the saurians were sniffing disdainfully. He undertook a heroic charge at that spot, killed two more crocodiles, and picked up the bag.

"Catch!" he shouted to Angelina. The crocodiles, much depleted in number, had changed their tactics. Hid-ing in the river, with only their heads above water, they were watching the fugi-tives with gleaming and covetous eyes.

"Oof!" said Farandoul, wiping his forehead. "We'll have to find a way past them, though, and get off this accursed islet before daybreak. How can we clear a path?"

He suddenly remembered his fishing tackle and ran to the luggage. The strong lines, prepared with the carnivorous hosts of the African rivers in mind, were there. Having baited his sturdy hooks with ostrich-remains, he headed for the bank and climbed a tree. The crocodiles, seeing him advance, had dived. Our friend let his lines down until the bait was about a meter above the surface of the river. That done, he advised the ladies to go back to sleep in their trees, and resumed his interrupted slumber himself.

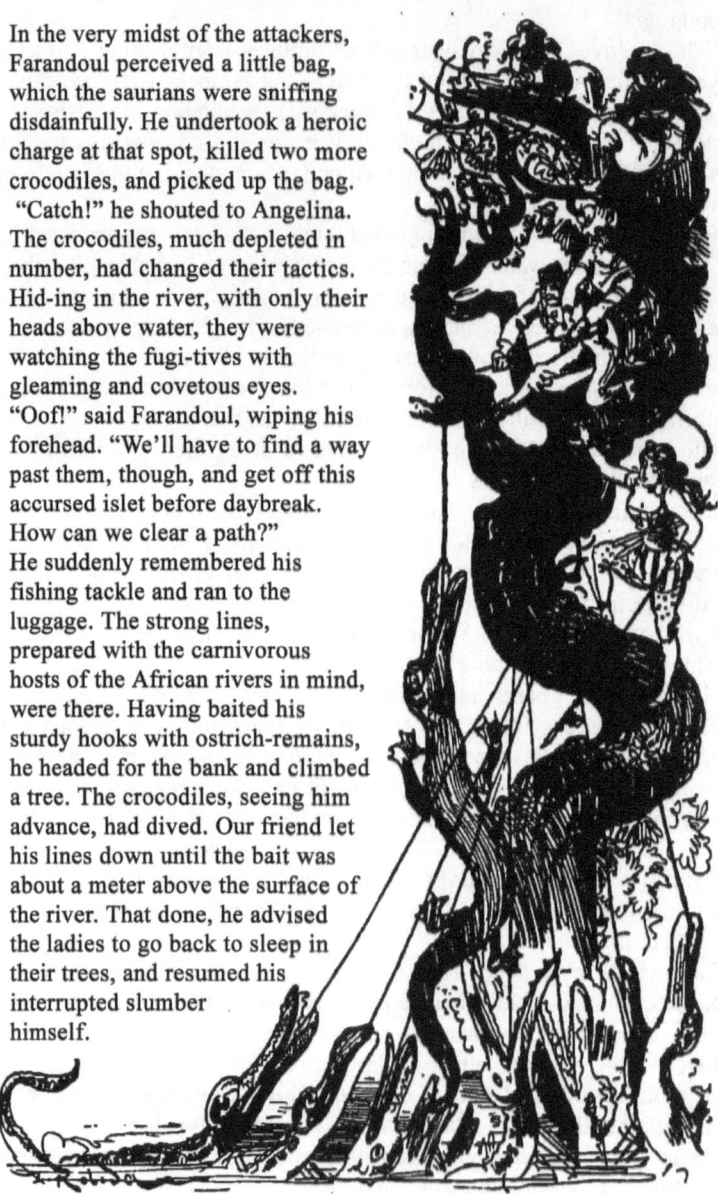

The crocodiles, encouraged by the silence, had reappeared and were trying to reach the suspended bait by jumping up.

When the dawn light woke Farandoul up, an amusing spectacle met his eyes: 17 crocodiles hanging on fishing-lines, caught by the hooks, struggling in vain to get free. As two or three baited lines were still suspended without crocodiles on the end, Farandoul supposed, with good reason, that all the crocodiles had been taken. The islet was no longer blockaded.

The four queens descended from their trees and came to admire the miraculous catch. The five of them, by pulling on the cords succeeded in hoisting some of the saurians into the tree—to serve as an example, as Her white Majesty Angelina observed. The others were swiftly finished off with spear-thrusts, and the fugitives prepared to resume their flight.

It was necessary to flee on foot, as the poor ostriches had perished—and the well-mounted warrior women would soon be on their trail. Would they not catch up very rapidly? Farandoul was worried. What should they do? The river route seemed to him to be the safest, now that the warrior women, knowing that the fugitives had no boat, must be pursuing them solely on land. But how could they go downstream? Apart from taking a long time to construct, a raft would encounter insurmountable difficulties in the middle of the hippopotamus herds and crocodiles infesting the river.

Farandoul suddenly slapped his forehead on seeing, amid the luggage, a packet of light and slender leather goatskins, brought on leaving the *Solitaire* in anticipation of having to cross the river.

He explained his idea to the queens, who set about inflating the goatskins while he left the islet, equipped with some pieces of strong rope, and slid into the beds of tall reeds along the river-bank. Well-armed and with a watchful eye, he advanced prudently and silently. His search was not in vain; in the midst of a marsh formed by the overflow of the river he perceived a hippopotamus herd wallowing delightedly in the mud.

Farandoul approached slowly, keeping to the side opposed to the wind. He had slung his carbine over his shoulder and was now brandishing a sort of lasso. Profiting from his former sojourn among the gauchos of the River Plate, he had learned to use their terrible lasso with considerable skill. A hippopotamus, the stoutest of the herd, suffered the consequences; it had raised its muzzle to breathe in delightedly when, all of a sudden, the lasso settled around its enormous head. Before it had recovered from its surprise, a second lasso had seized it by the hind leg, and both lassoes had been wound around a tree. When it tried to move, the two ropes, drawn in opposite directions, held it immobile. The other hippopotamuses had taken flight.

Farandoul moved around the monster and grabbed it by another leg; within five minutes, five solid ropes, doubled and tripled, had rendered it incapable of defending itself. The imbecilic animal had, in any case, been almost strangled by the first lasso, and was only standing upright because its legs were splayed.

Certain of his conquest, Farandoul went rapidly back to the islet. The goatskins were ready; the rest of the provisions were hastily bundled together and they set about crossing the river.

The four queens knew how to swim, but the goatskins served to facilitate the crossing. Each of the fugitives swam with one than and held on to a floating skin with the other, watching the water closely for fear of crocodiles. With Farandoul taking the lead and the Niam-Niam making up the rear-guard, they arrived on the shore without incident. The hippopotamus was still there. Swiftly, they attached the goatskins around the bewildered animal by means of solid cords that passed under its belly and formed a sort of network on its hide. On top of the floats they fixed a small platform made of reeds, consolidated with a few long branches severed by hatchet-blows.

When everything was ready, Farandoul cut a further two or three poles, as long as oars, and signaled to the ladies. "Let's go," he said. "Get aboard."

The hippopotamus, astonished to feel itself being mounted, gave indications of fury and tried to break its bonds. Farandoul took one of his fishing-lines, fixed the hook firmly across the beast's muzzle; then, throwing the cord to the little Niam-Niam, he vaulted on to the back of the enormous beast, whose own family members would not have recognized it with its girdle of goatskins and its cargo. After making completely sure of the solidity of the ropes, Farandoul told the four queens to take their swords in their hands.

"Now," he said, "watch out for jolts. Hold on tight, and all cut the lassos together. One, two, three!"

The five lassos were cut simultaneously. The hippopotamus shook itself briefly, stood up straight, and then headed for the river.

"We have a good boat!" said Farandoul. "It's a just matter of steering it well." Seizing the line attached to the hook from Niam-Niam's hands, he made the hippopotamus feel its pressure. The animal leapt forward 20 feet and bounded into the river. Its intention was to dive in order to get rid of the burden that was inconveniencing it, but—to its great astonishment—the goatskins kept it on the surface. It struggled a little, but Farandoul's hook tickled it again and it soon gave up the fight. It swam into the middle of the stream, and went rapidly downriver.

The joyful fugitives shook one another's hands. The little Niam-Niam surrendered himself to the elegant contortions of a dance characteristic of his native land.

"Here's a hippopotamus that's worth more than my poor *Solitaire*," said Farandoul. "It can easily carry us 20 or 25 leagues per day; it's only a matter of making it as habitable and as comfortable as possible. Assume, Mesdames, that we have 400 or 500 leagues to cover aboard it! That makes 15 or 20 days of traveling, so we need to find a way of providing ourselves with all possible comforts."

The rest of the morning was employed by the four queens in making a tent with a few bedclothes saved from the *Solitaire* disaster. At noon, when the Sun's burning rays fell vertically upon the river, the ladies, peacefully installed in their tent, were able to defy their ardor. The young Niam-Niam had his allotted place aft, on the neck of the hippopotamus; Farandoul maintained himself at the stern, a paddle in his hand, ready for anything.

The hippopotamus was no longer resisting. From time to time, as if by way of a final protest, it lifted its head and breathed out noisily.

Some ten leagues having been covered, Farandoul thought that it would be appropriate to have a short rest, and they looked for a tranquil spot at which to disembark.

Numerous islands speckled the course of the N'Kari. The hippopotamus was guided to the middle of this little archipelago and halted by an abrupt tug on the cord attached to its muzzle. The same cord, fulfilling the function of an anchor, served to tether it to the bank, but Niam-Niam remained aboard for extra safety.

It was necessary for the fugitives to feed their vessel. A bed of reeds furnished the necessary pasture. Farandoul harvested the field and gathered the reeds into 15 bundles, of which the two thickest provided the boat with its dinner. The rest, forming a floating food-store, was attached to the stern.

When the passengers took their places again on the refreshed hippopotamus, Farandoul found a means of further accelerating the animal's speed. On to its back he threw a mat five or six meters long, provided with a yard-arm, and hoisted a little sail. A light breeze had risen on the river; soon the hippopotamus was being assisted by a tail-wind, to the great stupefaction of a herd of such animals encountered as they left the islands.

The queens had made a meal on shore of the remainder of the provisions. It would be necessary for a hunt to provide dinner. A flock of wild ducks having been encountered, Kalunda's arrows brought several of them down, which were hung from the mast. That furnished some distraction to the beautiful fugitives, who had nothing to occupy them while the hippopotamus was making headway. Farandoul noticed, however, that one of the white queens seemed worried; it was the brunette Caroline, ordinarily the more expansive of the two.

On being questioned, Caroline dissolved in tears.

"Now, now," said Farandoul. "What does this feebleness signify, Majesty? You can see that everything's going well. The country we're passing through is tranquil and magnificent, the sky is blue, your installation aboard is tolerable, what more do you need? The ostrich-riding warriors following us are well behind, and it's scarcely probable that they'll catch up with us, if they're even still chasing us, so everything's fine! Perhaps you're regretting your crown?"

"No," said Caroline, "it's my aunt I'm worried about."

"What aunt?"

"Oh yes, I'd forgotten. Can you imagine that last year, content with my situation, I thought of inviting here to come here—so I wrote to her, giving her full directions as to the route to follow, and I waited for her…but events took their course. The terrible idea that Angelina and I were destined to be eaten worried me so much that I forgot my aunt. I've only just thought about her. What a misfortune if she arrives in Makalolo!"

"Is that all?" cried Farandoul, relieved. "Bah! Calm down. Your aunt hasn't left—or, if she has left, I'm certain that she'll also succeed in finding a minor position for herself in Makalolo. She'll go into the army, and she'll bless you!"

Caroline, soothed by these fine words, recovered her serenity. The rest of the day went by very pleasantly. The hippopotamus allowed itself to go downstream with no further anxiety. From time to time, Farandoul threw a bundle of reeds five or six meters ahead of it, which the animal reached in two seconds and devoured as it went forward. Niam-Niam even noticed, towards dusk, that it was going to sleep. They sought out a mooring for the night, and stopped without interrupting the hippopotamus's slumber.

The country traversed by the N'kari seemed to be completely uninhabited since they had left Makalolo, so Farandoul, no longer fearful of encountering humans, did not hesitate to light fires to protect their camp from attack by animals.

The camp, installed on a little near-islet sheltered by large trees, soon presented a charming sight to the eye. Large fires protected it on the landward side, hammocks for the ladies had been suspended from branches, and the solidly anchored hippopotamus-boat was asleep in the mud close to the bank. The night was beautiful and calm, lulled by the roars of a few lions roaming around their dens.

Refloating the heavy animal the next morning was a difficult business; it had completely forgotten its adventures of the previous day and rolled its fearful eyes while watching its passengers make their final preparations for departure. Niam-Niam used an effective means of refreshing its memory, and an abrupt jerk on the cord quickly recalled it to reality. The hippopotamus sighed; its memory suddenly returned, and it took to the open water without further resistance.

A beautiful day and a magnificent voyage! The banks of the N'kari became increasingly picturesque, tall wooded crags being reflected in the water with extraordinary clarity, while a few chains of rather steep hills rose up hazily in the distance.

The hippopotamus, favored by a pleasant breeze, sailed majestically down the middle of the river. The boat looked quite handsome with its chaplet of goatskins and its white sail; on the animal's back, the queens surrendered to the charm of that facile navigation, without worrying about past dangers.

The morning was enlivened by disputes with the crocodiles, those saurians permitting themselves to give chase to the hippopotamus and even going so far as to swim underwater in order to snap their jaws at its hobbled legs. The voyagers armed themselves with bows and revolvers and used the most imprudent as targets. The arrows were not lost; all those that the crocodiles did not carry away as souvenirs, embedded in an eye, returned to the surface and were quickly fished out with the aid of a gaffe.

The distraction provided for the fugitives by the crocodiles did not prevent Farandoul from noticing with a certain annoyance that the N'kari's course had too many bends in this region. On another occasion he would have admired the charms of the increasingly varied landscape without anxiety, but in the circumstances, the continual zigzag meandering of the river irritated him considerably. During the time that the boat lost in following these contours, the ostrich-riding warrior women must be gaining ground, and might perhaps get ahead of the hippopotamus in order to dispute its passage. Another object of anxiety occurred to Farandoul that afternoon. The ducks taken in flight had been consumed, and there was nothing on hand for dinner. The banks of the river, so rich in game further upstream, now seemed to be abandoned to the large animals—lions and rhinoceroses—that were often to be glimpsed on the plain.

Come on! Farandoul said to himself. *Things have been going too well since yesterday, now the difficulties are reappearing! Shall we have dinner this evening? That's beginning to seem problematic.*

They sailed all day without making much progress amid the meanders of the N'kari. In the evening, numerous rhinoceroses were encountered on the banks, and when they wanted to disembark, Niam-Niam, in too much of a hurry to leap ashore, was nearly carried off by a huge lion lying in ambush in the reeds. The boat put out into open water again. Farandoul decided to go on further, in the hope of finding some islet on which to spend the night.

"What about dinner?" asked the ladies, whose appetites were sharpened by the fresh air of the river. "It's time."

"Undoubtedly," Farandoul replied, trying to laugh, "but it's the game that isn't coming—or rather, it's too large for us."

Everyone seemed rather irritated; only the hippopotamus, having had its ration of bundles of reeds, manifested no discontent. Blissfully asleep, it let itself drift through the water, perhaps dreaming....

"This is too stupid!" Farandoul suddenly cried, at 10 p.m. We definitely need dinner. Come on, Niam-Niam—stop!"

And while the hippopotamus obeyed its guide and set foot on the river-bed a few meters from the bank, Farandoul took a certain bristly costume from his luggage, improvised on his instructions by a skilful Parisian armorer. It consisted of a sealed jacket made of thick leather, provided with a complete set of steel spikes, and a number of leather strips, similarly sewn with steel spikes, designed to protect the arms and legs. Farandoul, thus clad, resembled a pincushion, but he was absolutely invulnerable and could defy the fangs or claws of a lion.

"I'm going hunting for our dinner," he said. "A little more patience!"

Prudently, he forbade his companions to leave the boat, and lit a few fires on the bank as soon as he came ashore, for greater security. That done, he plunged into the undergrowth in search of some sort of game, with a sparkle in his eye and his carbine in his hand.

Alas, after half an hour of fruitless searching, he was convinced of the absence of all small game. Only the large animals were abundant. Roaming lions, as hungry as he was, were seeking to take some young and inexperienced rhinoceros by surprise.

Famished! Famished! Farandoul said to himself, furiously. *Well, we shall see! We'll eat anyway, damn it!*

Setting his carbine down next to him, not intending to make use of it unless it was absolutely necessary, he unsheathed his Makalolo sword—a sturdy weapon—set his back against a tree with one knee on the ground, and waited for the lions, bait and hunter at the same time.

He did not have long to wait. For half an hour, two lions had been following him without daring to attack; seeing him motionless under a tree, they gathered heir courage and crept forward to within six paces of him. Farandoul did not turn a hair. He would have been able to kill one with a rifle shot, but he wanted to save his ammunition. The lions, meanwhile, furiously flicked their sides with their long tails; finally, carried away by their appetite, the younger made up its mind and pounced, with a ferocious roar.

Farandoul received it on his sword; both of them rolled on the ground. The grievously wounded lion bit Farandoul's shoulder furiously, but embedded the steel spikes in its open mouth. A second sword-thrust finished it off.

Meanwhile, the second lion, which had drawn nearer in order to have its share, fled howling on three feet, with a steel spike in its flesh.

Our hero lost no time in artfully cutting a few choice morsels from the dead animal's rump. A quarter of an hour later, to everyone's great delight, these morsels were roasting in front of the boat.

"The taste's agreeable, but it's very tough!" That was the opinion of the fugitive queens. Even so, they finished off these extraordinary and savage beefsteaks, and they slept all the more peacefully for it, in spite of the frightful concert given by the ferocious beasts that bounded along the bank all night like a menagerie in revolt.

Morning came; it was the sixth day of the flight. Farandoul pressed the boat to try to get past the curls of the N'kari; they only had enough lion for breakfast, but for the evening meal Farandoul counted on repeating the previous day's hunt, if small game were still lacking.

The N'kari continued to turn and turn again; they sailed on without making much headway, and game continued to be conspicuous by its absence. At 8 p.m., Farandoul put on his costume again and went out hunting, after having tied up the hippopotamus safely.

That evening, lions too were rare. Farandoul only saw a single one limping on three paws, which fled at top speed, with its tail lowered, as soon as it saw the hunter. It was the one from the previous evening. Just as Farandoul, despairing of his cause, was about to send a rifle-bullet after it, he found himself face to face with a rhinoceros. That animal, exhaling raucous snorts, advanced to block his path entirely. Farandoul took three steps back and armed his rifle. Suddenly, though, there was no ground beneath his feet. He released a cry and disappeared over a sort of precipice.

The fall was broken by branches that he dragged down with him, with the result that he found himself almost safe and sound, after a drop of more than ten meters. As he got back to his feet and tried to take account of his situation, a frightful noise resounded above his head. He recoiled, masses of earth and branches collapsing upon him, as the rhinoceros fell into the ditch in its turn.

As you will have suspected, this pit was one of those that negroes dig in places frequented by ferocious beasts, particularly near the banks of rivers, where they come to drink every evening. In the center stood a sharpened tree-trunk, solidly embedded in the ground and designed to skewer any animal falling into the pit.

When Farandoul, briefly blinded by the earth dislodged with the branches, was able to open his eyes, he perceived his enemy the rhinoceros in a parlous situation. It had fallen directly on top of the pointed stake. Perforated all the way through, it was lying there nailed to the ground, like a beetle pinned in some collection. At the sight of Farandoul, it let out howls of rage, and set itself back on its feet. It tried to hurl itself upon him, but it was solidly nailed down, and all it could do was rotate around the perforating pole.

As the pit was not large, Farandoul had to move in a circle too, to keep out of the way of the animal's terrible horn. Gradually, instead of weakening, the rhinoceros seemed to acquire new vigor at the sight of the ungraspable enemy that circled in front of it and always escaped it, and it began to rotate more furiously.

The situation became critical. The rhinoceros, drunk with fury, turned with ever-increasing speed, and his own circular course began to tire Farandoul out. Another minute and they would make contact! A supreme leap permitted him to reach the maddened animal's tail; he clung to it and let it draw him on in a vertiginous whirl. He was saved! The blind rhinoceros was still turning, but Farandoul, attached to its tail, inevitably followed its movements.

That infernal pursuit lasted half an hour, then suddenly ceased. The rhinoceros collapsed in a heap. It was dead! Farandoul, dazed and out of breath, also fell down, but he soon got up triumphantly. The enormous beast impaled on the tree would furnish him with a means of getting out of the trap. Farandoul climbed on top of it, but before jumping up to the rim of the pit he sat down on the beast to rest for a few minutes.

The sky was clear, and the moonlight plunging into the pit through the gaping opening illuminated the walls, the tree-trunk and the rhinoceros's back. Farandoul looked around mechanically; suddenly, he released a cry of surprise. The rhinoceros had something written on it! On the beast's hairy and creased hide, characters carved out as in the bark of a tree had just appeared to our friend, and the first word that he read was...

FARANDOUL

He bent down excitedly; it really was his name that was there. What did it mean? A few half-erased lines were distinguishable beneath it. Farandoul set about deciphering them. This is what he read:

265

FARANDOUL
No...cannot be eaten...
MANDIBUL and his friends set out...to search...
we are at...traveling towards...
this rhino...will perhaps reach him!

It was Mandibul's handwriting that the rhinoceros bore on its back.

Our hero was moved. So the devoted Mandibul had set out with the sailors to search for their captain, lost in the African wilderness! But where were they? In what direction must one go to find them? There was no answer to that, the significant indications having disappeared; doubtless the rhinoceros, irritated by an itch, had rubbed itself against rocks or trees.

There was nothing to do but continue the descent of the N'kari; perhaps the Providence that had delivered the rhinoceros to his address would complete its work and reunite Farandoul and Mandibul.

Farandoul was about to cut off a large slice of his ex-enemy the rhinoceros in order to take it to the four hungry queens, who must be awaiting him impatiently, when a slight noise in the pit made him prick up his ears.

Ah! he said to himself. *There's something else in this pit—so much the better if it's something good to eat; it can replace the tough and indigestible rhinoceros...*

Knife in hand, he leapt down from the beast's back. The slight noise had seemed to come from a corner of the pit buried in brushwood; as Farandoul's approach the noise was repeated, but nothing emerged from the heap of branches.

"Come on, then!" cried Farandoul, growing impatient and giving the brushwood a forceful kick. "Come on, I'm hungry!"

A scream replied to him—a human scream full of both joy and fear. A man, whose clothes were in rags, leapt out of his hiding place and tried to fling his arms around Farandoul's neck.

A blow from our hero's fist saved the other's life, for he was about to be transpierced by the spikes of the famous lion-hunting costume. He took two steps back and let himself fall, limply, right on top of the rhinoceros's horn. Again it was Farandoul's arm that snatched him out of harm's way.

Our hero set him back on his feet and stood in front of him. "Let's see," she said. "Calm down, and don't make a fuss. Who are you and what are you doing in this pit?"

"Oof!" exclaimed the other, mopping his forehead. "I'm in the pit because I fell into it this afternoon. You gave me quite a fright when you fell into it yourself with the rhinoceros. I took you for two ferocious beasts fighting to determine which would devour the other and I made myself as small as possible in my corner. That's it! As for my titles, I am Jules Désolant Barbezohe, naturalist, sent by the Société de Géographie to search for the celebrate traveler Saturnin Farandoul. The last news we received was that he was eaten by the Niam-Niams, but we still conserved some hope. Today, alas, I think that nothing remains to us but to mourn the…"

"Don't mourn, my dear Désolant—I'm Farandoul, still intact!"

The envoy of the Société stepped back again. "But…the last information…still, since you say so, I have to believe you. So I've found Farandoul! What glory for me! If only I could send a dispatch to the Société de Géographie—but I'm alone, the negroes of my escort having abandoned me to go home with my money, my provisions and my luggage!"

IV.

When Farandoul and Désolant emerged from the pit, after having cut off a large quarter of rhinoceros, the Moon was reaching the end of its course and giving way to the dawn. The two men headed for the N'kari at a rapid gymnastic trot.

Farandoul was in a hurry to get the produce of his hunt back to the queens. The poor women, tortured by hunger and anxiety, must have spent a very bad night. At least, since the hour for supper was long gone, they would be able to have breakfast with no further delay.

After a ten-minute run they arrived at the N'kari. The hippopotamus-boat was still at anchor, but Farandoul did not recognize the mooring-place at first. Still running, he leapt into the waves of the N'kari and reached the vessel, whose silence was troubling: not a single word to celebrate his return, not a single cry of joy after that long night of waiting!

The reason for that silence quickly became obvious. Farandoul lifted up a corner of the tent pitched on the hippopotamus's back and released an exclamation. The tent was empty; there was no one aboard.

Farandoul leapt back ashore to explore the surroundings. His attention was attracted by the peculiar state of the terrain, which had already struck him ten minutes earlier. The hippopotamus had not budged; it was certainly where it had been solidly anchored the evening before, but the bank had changed its appearance. The long grass seemed to have been mown, the reeds cut down, the bushes stripped away. Only the soil remained, black and bare.

What had happened? Farandoul and Désolant, leaning over the ground, searched vainly for some clue.

Finally, our hero slapped his forehead; he had figured it out. "Ants!" he said to Désolant. "It's an invasion of black ants that must have put the bank into the state in which we see it. A colony of those terrible insects, as large as houseflies and as voracious as tigers, migrating in search of new lodgings and interrupted by the river, must have followed the bank, devouring everything in its passage. The devastation extends over a width of more than 20 meters; the ants, marching in dense ranks, must form a veritable army. But what has happened? Why did the queens abandon the hippopotamus, a safe retreat? Why? Ah! Doubtless, gripped by hunger, the warrior women wanted to catch their supper. They must have taken up their bows and arrows and come ashore—but what then? Perhaps they encountered the army of ants and were devoured!"

The anguished Farandoul was about to set off in search of the unfortunate women when a small tree-branch fell nearby. He raised his head mechanically, and joyfully perceived Niam-Niam, some distance away in the lower branches of a baobab. The boy was making mysterious signs to him.

"Why, what are you doing there?" cried our hero, racing to the baobab. "Where are the queens?"

"Softly, Master, softly!" replied Niam-Niam, just as mysteriously. "The queens are here, in the tree."

Farandoul's heart, relieved of a great weight, skipped a beat. "Bring them down, then," he said. "I've brought food."

"The queens cannot, Master. The gorillas do not want to let them go."

Farandoul went pale. The envoy of the Société de Géographie cocked his rifle.

"Yes, Master. Last evening, after you left and did not come back, the queens wanted to hunt. We came to land, but found nothing. As we tried to return to the boat, the ants passed by. The ants were hungry, and wanted to eat us. We jumped into the baobab and climbed to the top. No more black ants, but in the baobab a family of gorillas, big, strong and nasty, have taken the queens and are keeping them up there. Me stayed down below to warn Master!"

Niam-Niam was telling the truth, for another branch fell from the top of the tree, carrying a piece of paper on which one of the white queens had scribbled:

Dear Farandoul,

Horrible situation! Never would I have believed it when I used to stroll in the Jardin des Plantes. Having barely escaped from the ants, we have fallen into the hands of monkeys! We are prisoners; hideous gorillas are keeping us in sight! Exhausted by fatigue, thinking ourselves safe in the tree, we had installed ourselves in the branches in order to try to sleep while Niam-Niam was on watch, when we suddenly woke up with a start. Gigantic creatures had seized us around the waist and carried into the upper reaches of the baobab, careless our screams.

Their lodgings are up here: a sort of cabin formed out of interlaced branches. There are a dozen, counting the little ones. They have deposited us here, and are now content to watch us, rather respectfully. What can we do?

Thus far, we have had no grounds for complaint; we have found figs and coconuts in sufficient quantity, but when we make as if to descend they growl furiously and force us to sit down again.

How can we get out of this?

Caroline.

What a situation, indeed! The four unfortunate queens in the power of gorillas! Farandoul remembered often having heard stories told, since his arrival in Africa, of women kidnapped by these wild men of the woods and never seen again! But Farandoul was a born fighter, and, without losing heart, he racked his brains in search of an expedient. Attacking the mighty gorillas was impracticable, those monsters of the simian race being endowed with fearful strength. Only trickery remained.

Ah, Farandoul said to himself, *if only we were in Oceania! I was a monkey for 12 years, I knew how to make myself understood—but here, in Africa...bah! Who knows whether, perhaps...yes, it's the only way!*

And he communicated his plan to Désolant—who, apparently, could not have been more surprised by it. Even so, Farandoul's tone soon persuaded him, and he promised to follow his savior's instructions to the letter. Niam-Niam and Désolant installed themselves in the branches of a neighboring baobab, while Farandoul, by contrast, climbed up into the gorillas' tree.

Farandoul paused half way; he had heard hoarse and ill-tempered grunts in the heights; seemingly unintimidated, our hero set about swinging frenetically on his branch, as he had learned to do long ago, and uttered bizarre cries that startled the ears of Niam-Niam and Désolant.

The effect was more rapid than he expected. Two gorillas, plunging noisily through the foliage, let themselves fall as far as his branch and began a strange dialogue with him, while devoting themselves in the same furious swinging. They were two superb specimens of the gorilla race, more than seven feet tall, equipped with immense arms of vast proportions, covered with coarse and tangled hair that would make the most intrepid wig-maker recoil.

The two gorillas seemed to be asking the newcomer numerous questions and ascertaining the purpose of his visit. Farandoul, glad to be understood, multiplied evidences of amity.

The conversation lasted a long time. What evident superiority animal races have to the mediocre human race! An unfortunate Patagonian transported to China would be in a very sad state; not a single word of his language would be understood by the most learned mandarin, and to him, the simplest words of the Chinese language would be no more than incomprehensible sounds. In this case, though, the language of a tribe of monkeys lost in the depths of Oceania was comprehensible to the monkeys of an entirely different race living in the center of the African continent!

We shall leave this fact to the
meditations of academies—to those
researching our natural language, which
the human race must have spoken
during its infancy on the Earth, and
which has been gradually transformed
into a thousand different tongues.
It is for science to rediscover that
natural language and return it to us!
In the end, like three good fellows
coming to an agreement, Farandoul and
the two gorillas stood up and, grasping
the higher branches, climbed up to the
very top of the baobab. The gorillas
remaining in the cabin, alerted by a few
cries, had come to meet their visitor.

The four stupefied queens watched in amazement the gestures of amity exchanged between their friend and the horrible monkeys. A sign from Farandoul warned them to keep out of it; our hero, seated in the midst of the gorillas on a pile of leaves, resumed the interrupted conversation. The gorillas seemed rather surprised; they examined Farandoul attentively, touching his boots and occasionally pulling his hair.

Farandoul's costume was what surprised them most. They did not take him for a man, seeing that he was very different from the scantily-dressed negroes that they glimpsed from time to time, but they were astonished at not having encountered a specimen of his species before. Farandoul, as we have said, was still in his lion-hunting costume; the steel spikes won the admiration of the gorillas, who took them for simple bristles. To cut short the friendly gestures they were making to him, Farandoul communicated that he was hungry by means of a few grunts. The gorillas raced to their food-store—a heap of figs, dates and bananas lying in a hollow in the baobab—and they all set about eating sitting in a circle. Farandoul soon interrupted his meal, though, and thumped his forehead with his fist. The gorillas raised their heads.

Farandoul pointed at the group of four queens and seemed to interrogate them in his turn. Seeing the gorillas scratching themselves in an embarrassed manner, and not replying, Farandoul addressed himself directly to the oldest of the band, an obese and grizzled gorilla who was the acknowledged governor of the colony.

The old gorilla seemed rather irritated, and tried to interrupt Farandoul's speech with a few grunts of protest. Our hero imposed silence on him and, suddenly standing up, hurled vigorous abuse at him while wagging his finger. The others seemed stunned; the boldest scarcely dared to attempt to deflect their guest's anger with attentions of the smoothest politeness—for example, by passing him peeled coconuts or scratching his back.

Their guest was no longer listening to them, though. In truth, he was kicking up quite a fuss! Who could have expected to see such a welcome and well-commenced feast troubled like this? It was visibly hurting them, for the most sensitive were already holding back tears.

Because the four queens still did not understand, the event caused them the greatest possible anxiety. What did it all mean: Farandoul's arrival, the hearty welcome given to him, and that long conversation sustained by their friend in the language of the gorillas? Strange! Strange!

By dint of observation, however, at least they succeeded in understanding the pantomime accompanying the speech. Farandoul was speaking—or, rather, squealing—monkey-language, but his gestures were comprehensible for humans. It soon became clear to them that their friend was addressing violent reproaches to his gorilla hosts, while frequently waving his hand in the direction of the prisoners.

Yes, Farandoul was giving the gorillas a moral lecture, and these huge creatures seemed to be deeply affected by his speech. Their confusion increased with every passing minute; only the old monkey continued to defend himself—weakly, to be sure. Our hero, seeing the ascendancy that he had over these primitive natures increasing with each interjection, multiplied his grunts and crushed his adversary with eloquent phrases, punctuated with thumps of his fist on the floor of the cabin.

When Farandoul finally fell silent, a concert of groans resounded in the baobab. The old gorilla seemed devastated, the she-monkeys were weeping and the little ones were winding themselves around the legs of our hero, who had crossed his arms and was looking at his hosts, rolling his eyes wildly.

Suddenly, the old gorilla seemed to make an important decision. He leapt to his feet and headed toward the group of four queens. Farandoul had not budged. Feeling the hand of a monkey timidly touch his shoulder, however, he finally turned round in a surly fashion.

The old gorilla, shamefacedly holding one of the four queens by the hand, returned his four protégées to him.

"Don't speak—try to grunt like me," Farandoul had time to whisper to them between his teeth—and he began uttering cries of satisfaction and shaking the gorillas' hands.

Let no one continue to deny the good influence of moral determination; scarcely having embarked upon the path of virtue for five minutes, the gorillas seemed radiant; they had become gentle friends to their prisoners, and heaped little attentions upon them, peeling dates and coconuts for them.

Farandoul decided to take advantage of these good dispositions to take his leave of the honest family and return to the hippopotamus. The great difficulty was the descent; they were more than 40 meters above the ground—trivial for the monkeys, but a considerable height for ladies unused to climbing. It was the gorillas who settled the matter; seeing the ladies looking anxiously over the edge of the platform of foliage, they offered to transport them to the base of the baobab themselves.

The affair was simple; each queen was calmly grasped by a male gorilla, who put her under his arm or on his back with the utmost delicacy and let himself glide down from branch to branch. Five minutes later, all the tenants of the baobab were on the ground.

Perched in the braches of a neighboring tree, Niam-Niam and Désolant had watched this descent attentively, not knowing what they ought to do. Their embarrassment did not last long; the gorillas, having discovered their presence and motivated by a desire to behave well, came to collect them from their tree. Taking the astonished duo by surprise, they grabbed them by the feet and carried them triumphantly to Farandoul.

"Don't speak—grunt!" Farandoul instructed them in a low voice. "We're leaving!"

Niam-Niam alone was not an object of gorilla respect; they had recognized a negro, a enemy. Farandoul, seeing their attitude to the boy, put him in Désolant's arms. The gorillas believed him to be a captive and seemed satisfied.

Farandoul had made the caravan of four queens and Désolant go ahead of him; he followed them, surrounded by the entire family of gorillas, still engaging them in conversation with a few grunts. In this manner, they took a little trip along the bank of the N'kari.

The reawakened hippopotamus snorted noisily, as if to demand food. Farandoul explained the situation to the gorillas with a few grunts; happy to ender their friend this small service, they immediately set about plundering the reed-beds enthusiastically, and tying up their harvest in bundles.

Within a few minutes they had gathered enough for a week and all the bundles formed a long chaplet solidly attached to the foredeck of the hippopotamus. Then Farandoul gave the signal to embark, and the four queens leapt into the water to get to the boat. Désolant departed next, with Niam-Niam still tucked under his arm.

Farandoul remained on the bank, sitting with his gorillas. Finally he got up and renewed his farewells. The old monkey, humble and repentant, proffered profound apologies and ardently begged his pardon. The ever-generous Farandoul no longer treated him severely; he shook the hand that was held out to him vigorously, and after having stroked the cheeks of the little ones, he descended in his turn to the river-bed.

Everything was ready. The hippopotamus began to swim while savoring an enormous bundle of reeds. The fugitives uttered joyful cheers, to which the gorillas replied as best they could. Within two minutes, the boat reached the middle of the stream.

The gorillas were then seen to race rapidly to the baobab, climb up it, come back down and then hasten, still running and squealing loudly, to a place where the river, framed by high banks, was less than half as wide. Having arrived there, they stopped and waited for the hippopotamus, still squealing.

"Hang on!" exclaimed Farandoul. "It looks as if our friends are regretting letting us leave. Do they intend to engage us in a naval battle? Look out, Majesties!"

The queens, Niam-Niam and Désolant grabbed their weapons and prepared to mount a vigorous defense. The hippopotamus drew nearer to the difficult pass. The gorillas standing on the bank also made ready.

"Wait!" said Farandoul. "The moment will come."

He was still speaking when a hail of projectiles fell upon them, thrown with skill and prodigious force. The hippopotamus started, and increased its speed, but the gorillas were running along the banks and showering the boat with further ammunition. The queens could scarcely protect themselves; they were about to reply with arrows when Farandoul stopped them.

"Don't fire!" he cried. "They're coconuts and dates that our friends are sending us!"

The bombardment took its course, Farandoul and Désolant gathering up the projectiles. As for Niam-Niam, he had been knocked overboard by a coconut and was swimming to starboard to protect himself from any further accident.

Finally the last munitions were exhausted. The monkeys shouted a final farewell, to which Farandoul replied with energetic thanks in their own language. Niam-Niam, reassured, came aboard again too soon; he as scarcely installed at his post when a final volley of coconuts, conserved by the gorillas with that intention, fell upon his body.

V.

The fugitives, tranquil now, dined on figs. They had only covered a few leagues on the N'kari when an exclamation released by Niam-Niam brought them out of their serenity. Niam-Niam pointed to a black mass floating in the river a few kilometers ahead of them.

Farandoul had keen eyes; he too made out the ominous object, and released a second exclamation. "It's my boat!" he cried. "It's the *Solitaire*!"

The matter was serious. Was the *Solitaire* manned by Makalolo warriors? Might they not all back into their hands?

"It's hardly probable!" Farandoul said, after thinking about it for some time. "The warrior women must have abandoned all pursuit. The *Solitaire* has simply been carried away by the flow. Let's try to catch up with it!"

The hippopotamus, spurred on, set off at top speed; in half an hour it had reached the boat.

The *Solitaire* was quite empty. The warrior women had ransacked it and had not left anything that might be useful. Even as it was, however, it still offered more comforts than the awkward hippopotamus and Farandoul decided to have the latter take it in tow. In consequence, the ladies left the tent and installed themselves on board—and the *Solitaire*, attached by a cable, set off to follow the hippopotamus. In order not to overburden it and slow its progress, Farandoul restored the *Solitaire*'s engine to a working state and loaded it with wood. Soon, a few puffs of smoke emerged from the chimney and the *Solitaire* caught up with the hippopotamus, which increased its speed.

Let us leave the hippopotamus and the *Solitaire* to pursue their course along the N'kari for six days, the former sometimes pulling the latter and the latter sometimes pushing the former, and rejoin them thereafter.

How much progress have they made during those six days of traveling at top speed? How much, in total? Just six leagues, alas.

They have covered about 150 leagues, journeying through a tangle of rocks, islets, islands, near-islands, around innumerable curves and infinite meanders traced by the capricious N'kari. Farandoul is furious, and with good reason; to the tedium of continually going around and around, describing circles, ellipses and improbable parabolas has been added another annoyance: Farandoul and the four queens have hardly had anything to eat for four days.

The monkeys' provisions were rapidly exhausted and hunting has only furnished meager resources to the famished travelers. Game is not abundant in this rocky chaos, and the fishing-lines put out all day have only caught the occasional meager pike. The only game that they can find is the occasional crocodile, but these hideous and cowardly creatures flee as soon as Farandoul gets close enough to put a bullet in their eye; they dive and return underwater to try to steal a piece of the poor hippopotamus-boat, which has difficulty defending itself.

But why have Farandoul and his companions not sacrificed their faithful servant for the common good? It is quite simply because there is also a shortage of wood in this desolate region, and that if the hippopotamus were eaten, the fugitives would be stranded on their useless *Solitaire*.

For four days, the starvelings' only meals have consisted of a few omelets. Niam-Niam has a flair for detecting the sand-banks where crocodiles lay their eggs and, in spite of the pronounced musky taste of such omelets, they have been very welcome aboard the Solitaire.

That is the situation.

Fortunately, Farandoul is hopeful. He has conducted a reconnaissance on land and has perceived that the N'kari resumes a straight course a few leagues further on. They will, therefore, eventually emerge from this region of sand and rock.

That day, even omelets were lacking. Hope was the only nourishment the fugitives had had for 24 hours, but trees and vegetation were beginning to become less rare. At 6 p.m., after 33 hours of dieting, Farandoul leapt upon his rifle and shot a pelican that he had glimpsed in a hole in the rock. What a stroke of luck! And what a welcome indication of their imminent arrival in a country more favored by the heavens!

The sleeping hippopotamus was swimming anyway; they continued sailing for part of the night. At 2 a.m., a few fires became visible in the distance. After half an hour of searching, an absolutely secure mooring was discovered in a narrow channel in the middle of an archipelago of little wooded islands.

O joy! The arrival of the boat in the islands was the signal for a frightful concert; the honking of pelicans, wild geese and cranes burst forth around the fugitives, accompanied by the beating of wings, cries of terror and jostling.

The queens clapped their hands. In the blink of an eye, Désolant, Niam-Niam and Farandoul were wringing the necks of two dozen birds.

This windfall made the travelers forget any anxiety that might have been caused by the fires glimpsed in the night. Only Farandoul gave them any thought; he was eager to see daylight, in order to clarify the situation.

Everyone slept with closed fists. It was nearly 9 a.m. when the fugitives were woken up by the deafening sound of a new concert. The most astonishing spectacle awaited them. The hippopotamus and the boat were in a narrow channel squeezed between two wooded islands, the foliage of whose large trees joined up above their heads like a leafy arbor. Beneath that tranquil vault, thousands of large birds were frolicking placidly; the banks were covered by them, and in the trees numerous large black patches indicated numerous families of birds established on every branch. The fugitives found themselves, so to speak, in the midst of a vast aviary, in which pelicans, cranes, pink flamingoes, geese, ibises and ducks, grouped in families, were living in perfect harmony.

As far as the eye could see, there was nothing visible but long rows of aquatic birds in the process of exercising their throats with all kinds of discordant screeches.

It was Kalunda who provided an explanation. "The Kabirko Isles!" she said.

The white queens had heard mention of them. At the beginning of their reign, they had led an expedition against the Kabirkos—difficult neighbors who occasionally ravaged the western frontiers of the realm of the Makalolos—but they had never pushed on as far as the sacred isles, situated in the middle of an impenetrable region, which sheltered the divinities adored by that primitive people.

"And what are these Kabirkos?" asked Farandoul.

"Worse than the Niam-Niams!" the black queens exclaimed. "Frightful marauders, bandits perpetually at war with their neighbors."

"Damn! It seems to me that we're in grave danger here. Evidently, the fires we glimpsed last night are those of their villages. We'll have difficulty getting past them. Fortunately, we've found this pass where we're presently hidden; the main thing is not to be discovered before we've found a means of getting out. I'll undertake a reconnaissance of the surroundings. You must all stay in the boat and wait for me. In case of danger, seal the hatches and defend yourselves until I come back."

Farandoul, his revolvers in his belt and his rifle in his hand, went ashore and plunged into the forest. His companions waited for him until 6 p.m., and were already growing anxious when he reappeared, moving with infinite precaution. He gave them a signal to remain silent, and went with them into the *Solitaire*'s cabin.

"I can't explain," he said, "how we were able to attain this refuge yesterday without being heard. The darkness prevented us from seeing two or three large villages established on the river bank, and the fires that are ahead of us are those of another, more important, village situated on the same bank. The N'kari forms a sort of lake here that extends for two leagues behind these islands. I've explored the shore of this lake; superb vegetation covers them as far as the eye can see. We'll stay here for a few days—time to reconnoiter the course of the river in order not to launch ourselves at hazard into the middle of the Kabirko villages. Besides, this little resting-place will allow us to recover from our fatigue and renew our provisions."

Two days passed quietly enough. Farandoul, departing each morning, extended his reconnaissance over a considerable distance, but he had not yet discovered a passage permitting the avoidance of the villages lined up along the lake.

The travelers were getting their strength back. Already they were bemoaning the mediocre quality of the food. Flamingoes and pelicans were unsatisfactory fare, their flesh having an unpleasant oily taste. It was the ever-curious Niam-Niam who discovered a means of introducing more variety to the meals. Five hundred meters from the mooring, in a little bay surrounded by a palisade, there was a sort of aquatic temple reserved for a dozen gigantic pelicans, the objects of Kabirko adoration. These enormous birds, so old and heavy that they were no longer able to move, received a provision of fresh fish every day adequate to last them until the next. It was this fish that Niam-Niam wanted to steal from the Kabirkos' gods. The following morning, Farandoul and Désolant, lying in wait near the temple, saw the Kabirkos, led by witch-doctors, bring a superb provision of fish with all possible marks of respect. Only the witch-doctors went into the temple, and came back immediately, surrounded by their plumed gods.

When the negroes had gone, Farandoul and Désolant hastened into the enclosure and threw themselves on what remained of the fish; they were coming out again, carrying a sufficient quantity, when the pelicans, having recovered from their astonishment, precipitated themselves upon them with raucous cries. It was necessary to defend themselves. The two white men had hardly expected such resistance; initially forced to retreat, they soon had their daggers in their hands. Falling upon the pelicans, they fought valiantly for the prize of the coveted fish. Honor to unfortunate courage! The pelicans defended their nourishment to the last, and only succumbed to the white men's weapons. After a quarter of an hour's fighting, the latter were the masters of the battlefield.

The Kabirkos had no more gods!

"What imprudence!" exclaimed Farandoul. "This fish might perhaps cost us dear. Still, the harm is done, and it's a matter of erasing all trace of it. Quickly! The Kabirkos will assume that their gods have left!" Before they even took the fish away, the two men tried to get rid of the cadavers of the gods. The pelicans were taken 50 meters away and thrown into the river with stones tied around their necks. All these comings and goings had, however, occasioned a certain tumult in the ranks of the innumerable legions of flamingoes lined up along the river banks. As the white men went back into the enclosure to fetch the fish, they saw that the witch-doctors and the negroes were returning in all haste.

Farandoul and Désolant only just had time to hide in a corner of the primitive bamboo edifice that served as a temple for the divine pelicans. The witch-doctors and their followers, on finding the sacred enclosure empty of inhabitants, released an immense cry of terror.

It was necessary to do something; once the Kabirkos had recovered from their amazement, they would climb up to the temple and discover the intruders. Farandoul understood that, and tried to save the situation by means of audacity. "Let's show ourselves boldly," he said, "and if we have to, fight out way out!" And the two men, revolvers in hand, assumed a threatening attitude in front of the hut.

Like a regiment of lead soldiers knocked over by a gust of wind, the negroes and the witch-doctors fell flat on the ground.

The white men paused. A concert of cries and chants rose up from the multitude; a few crouching negroes began beating their sacred drums frantically.

"Are the gods angry?" squeaked one of the witch-doctors, dragging himself towards the white men in a prone position. "Do they want their people to die?"

Farandoul had understood to some degree, the Kabirko language having much in common with the Makalolo dialect. Rapidly, he explained the situation of Désolant, and they both struck their most Olympian pose.

"There were 12 pelicans before the transformation," the creeping witch-doctor continued. "Have the other gods taken flight?"

Farandoul thought that he ought to reply, and summoned up all his linguistic skills.

"They will come back," he said, thunderously, in Makalolo, "if the Kabirko nation ceases to grieve them! But if the Kabirkos continue to invade the sanctuary of their gods and to run disrespectfully over the sacred island, we too shall depart. We shall go to the land of the Makalolos and will leave the Kabirkos godless, in the power of all the evil spirits lying in wait for them."

Cries of terror uttered by the swarming mass of the faithful greeted this threat. The witch-doctors beat their drums furiously in an attempt to deflect the wrath of the gods.

The head witch-doctor, the leader of the band, hastily got up, with a staff in his hand, and fell upon the inferior witch-doctors and their simple associates. In the blink of an eye, the enclosure of the temple was evacuated and resealed. The witch-doctor, left alone with the gods, resumed his humble posture without saying a word.

"The gods are satisfied," pronounced Farandoul, majestically, "And now make our will known to the Kabirko nation. The gods wish the boundary of the sacred isle to be respected; the witch-doctors alone may penetrate it at certain hours, with the greatest marks of respect—and if the gods are content with their people, they will soon resume their initial form, and never leave the islands!"

The witch-doctor rubbed his face in the sand for some time, and timidly pronounced a few words: "Will the gods permit their unworthy servant to stand up?"

"You forget the majesty of the gods!" Farandoul retorted. "Leave as you have come and never raise your eyes toward us!"

The witch-doctor, still prone, turned round and left the enclosure; it was not until he was some distance away from the temple that he dared to get to his feet. The people welcomed his return with a loud drum-roll, but he demanded silence and informed the multitude of the will of the gods.

A quarter of an hour later, the calm and solitude of the sacred isle were restored; the negroes and their witch-doctors had disappeared.

"Well, my dear friend," cried Farandoul, when he was rid of all anxiety, "here we are, gods! I've been a king, a dictator, a bishop, a cacique, and a commander-in-chief, etc., etc., but it's the first time I've achieved that eminent grade!"

"It's a fine social position," Désolant replied.

"We'll remain gods for a fortnight—time to bring our plans to maturity, and then leave our people free to find others, Meanwhile, my dear chap, while you hold your position, you have the right to establish yourself in the temple!"

The gods had nothing to reveal to the four queens; Niam-Niam, hidden in the bushes, had witnessed the entire scene and had gone back to the boat with the news—except that, more worryingly, he affirmed that he had seen the Kabirkos establish an extensive cordon of surveillance of sorts around the sacred isle, installing armed guard-posts at intervals.

How long could the fugitives remain gods among the Kabirkos? Farandoul had imagined that a fortnight would be sufficient to find a means of avoiding the surveillance of these excessively religious people, but he did not know these malign folk.

Three months later, the Kabirkos were still in possession their gods!

The witch-doctors came every morning to bring, in great solemnity, the customary tribute of fish. Every morning the gods were there to receive it; only the head witch-doctor came into the enclosure, always with the same marks of respect.

The gods, busy every day for part of the morning, had the afternoons to themselves. The queens were profoundly bored; inaction weighed upon them. It was necessary to remain on their petty islet without showing themselves, or to take infinite precautions in order to extend their excursions any further. Fortunately, Farandoul had finished his reconnaissance; he now knew all the difficult points of the trajectory that they would have to follow to quit the islands.

Finally, Farandoul the god decided to strike a decisive blow. One morning, in the fourth month, the witch-doctors were agreeably surprised to discover six gods instead of two, as on the previous day. The four queens had accompanied Farandoul and Désolant to the temple. The six gods, forming a majestic group, welcomed the witch-doctors with considerably amiability. The high priest was permitted to raise his head slightly to contemplate them, and Farandoul began to speak.

"The gods are content with the Kabirkos," he said. "They will all come back. For today, the gods order great rejoicing among their people. Go!"

This time the drums and chants burst out with greater enthusiasm; the witch-doctors and the people went away dancing to carry the glad news to the villages; soon, an extraordinary racket informed the gods that their orders were being followed.

For their part, the gods did not remain inactive. Aboard the *Solitaire* everything was made ready for departure. Dry wood had been accumulated in the interior and on the deck, provisions had been loaded. The hippopotamus, which spent its life sleeping and eating, had been woken up; the goatskins that sustained it had been reinflated and the mainmast prepared.

At midnight, Farandoul gave the signal to depart.

It was the poor condition of the hippopotamus that frustrated the initial stage of the journey. The animal, considerably fattened by three months of idleness and as many bundles of reeds as it cared to eat, no longer possessed the good qualities as a mover that our friends had formerly been able to appreciate. It advanced slowly and snorted noisily at every effort. Farandoul was counting on it to tow the fugitives as far as possible from the sacred isles; its role was to change when they got out of the lake and had to pass the first riverside villages. The *Solitaire* would then take the lead and draw at along under full steam.

It took four hours to get out of the lake; daybreak was not far off, bringing danger with it. Farandoul could wait no longer; he took the lead in the *Solitaire* and, stoking up the furnaces to the maximum, launched forwards along the river. The whistling of the steam, the boat's powerful respiration, awoke a few negroes on the bank. Frightened by the sight of this unknown vessel that emitted flames and smoke, they ran to wake their witch-doctors to exorcise the monster.

The *Solitaire* went forward valiantly, dragging the hippopotamus in its wake, as frightened as the negroes.

Dawn came; on the banks, the few villages they encountered were thrown into turmoil, but the *Solitaire* ate up the distance and soon passed them by.

At noon they had put 15 leagues between the Solitaire and the sacred isles, but at 1 p.m. the joy of triumph vanished before a new cause of anxiety; they had just entered a dangerous region of falls and cascades. The river, drawn on by the successive lowering of the ground, ran like an arrow between the rocks, covering them with its foam and often jumping over them. Could they get through? The anxious Farandoul steered between the rocks as best he could, dreading that at any moment they might touch some reef or capsize while attempting too considerable a leap.

Suddenly, in descending a fall of three or four meters amid whirlwinds of foam, the hippopotamus, dragged along at increasing speed, turned over and capsized entirely. The unfortunate creature had its belly in the air and its head under water. Maintained by the goatskins, it could not right itself and was bound to drown.

In order not to let his faithful servant perish, Farandoul threw himself upon the cords that retained the chaplet of goatskins, and cut through them with hatchet-blows. The half-drowned hippopotamus made a violent effort, and recovered its normal position. Our hero managed to get back to the *Solitaire*, but while he was away from the rudder, the steamboat, seized by a current, had deviated from its course and was heading straight for the rocks; the only thing that could be done to avoid the rocks was to run aground on a sandbank.

Fatality! The shipwreck-victims were prepared to combine their efforts to refloat the vessel, but Farandoul, worried by an immense murmur audible in the distance on the river, judged it prudent to undertake a preliminary reconnaissance. He scrambled briskly over the rocky mounds that overhung the river 50 meters away and came back in distress. A series of waterfalls, these unnavigable, extended for several miles downstream; their roar, muffled by a bend in the river, echoed from the heights of the rocks like thunder. The *Solitaire* had one again become absolutely useless.

"The river route is definitely too full of obstacles," Farandoul said. "We'll have to go overland. We'll try to find some mounts along the way—I have my lasso."

The fugitives distributed their meager luggage—weapons, a few bedclothes, and food—among themselves. It was necessary to bid a final farewell to the *Solitaire*. The detached hippopotamus greeted its return to liberty with amazement; when it saw its former masters set forth into the wilderness, it bellowed dully and set off after them, but the rocks blocked its passage. Obesity had caused it to lose all its agility, to the extent that it abandoned the pursuit and went sadly back to the river.

Scarcely a quarter of an hour had passed since the former gods of the Kabirkos had disappeared into the dense thickets on the right bank of the N'kari when a little caravan emerged from the rocks of that same right bank and came to an abrupt halt in front of the stranded *Solitaire*.

This caravan was composed of only six men: one white man and five Arabs. The white man released an exclamation of triumph, and the Arabs gesticulated.

"It's the *Solitaire!*" cried the white traveler. "It's definitely her. Her furnaces are still smoking; her master can't be far away. So I've found Farandoul! I've succeeded where my colleagues in the Société de Géographie, Messieurs Eusébin de Saint-Gommer and Désolant have failed! What glory for me, Ulysse Ganivet! Let's go, Mohammed; let's go aboard the *Solitaire* and take an honest siesta, while awaiting the illustrious voyager's return. He'll be very surprised!"

And the traveler, Monsieur Ulysse Ganivet—a well-known scientist—installed himself delightedly in the shade of the *Solitaire*'s cabin with his five Arabs. Fatigued by a long march, they soon went to sleep.

Farandoul did not come back, but a strange swaying motion woke them up with a start two hours later. The astonished travelers thought at first that the boat had resumed its progress and ran to the stairs to climb up on deck. The hatches were closed!

As the swaying became more pronounced, Ulysse Ganivet, the white traveler, popped his head through a porthole and released an exclamation.

The *Solitaire* was on the move, but not on the water. It was sailing through fields on the shoulders of 50 hideous negroes. Ulysse Ganivet and his five Arabs, realizing that they were prisoners, rapidly sought the weapons they had deposited in the middle of the cabin. The weapons had disappeared!

As you have doubtless guessed, these negroes were part of a band of Kabirkos launched in pursuit of their fugitive gods. Traveling over the plain, while other Kabirkos explored the river, they had arrived at the falls scarcely an hour after the arrival of Ulysse Ganivet at Farandoul's abandoned vessel. Recognizing the boat described by the inhabitants of the riverside villages, they had approached it in the greatest silence, closed the hatchways carefully and, certain of their prey, had lifted up the *Solitaire* delicately in order to transport it diligently back to the sacred isles.

On the way, the population bathed in joy—the gods had been recovered!

The head witch-doctor received the fugitives at the entrance to the temple; he almost fell backwards in amazement when the hatches were opened and a very hungry Ulysse Ganivet appeared on the deck of the *Solitaire* with his Arabs. These gods numbered six, like the others, but they were not the same ones! After five minutes of meditation, the profound science of the Kabirko witch-doctor discovered the secret of the change. Doubtless the gods had transformed themselves again! What striking proof of their power! The entire Kabirko nation fell forwards into the dust and dragged itself along in a prone position for several minutes.

The gods did not understand at all. Rigorously shut up in the temple and kept in sight day and night, they had plenty of time to reflect and arrive at an understanding.

In the depths of Africa there are six unhappy gods: Monsieur Ulysse Ganivet and his five Arabs. Their faithful Kabirkos, exceedingly suspicious since the first flight of their Olympus, refuse to let them out for a single day; they have become very demanding and never cease to torment the poor gods in order to obtain all sorts of benefits: rain in dry weather, dryness in rainy weather, good luck in war, cures for themselves, serious epidemics for their neighbors, etc., etc.

If only they were content to solicit, the gods would not complain overmuch, but when the rain does not come, or the requested victory is too long delayed, the Kabirkos have a policy of reducing the rations brought to the temple each day. O sadness! The poor gods are thus put on a diet until they answer the prayers of their faithful devotees!

VI.

Let us make shift to catch up with Farandoul and the four queens. They are far from the N'kari now, for never have they traveled with such rapidity!

Farandoul's first concern had been to devote himself to the quest for mounts for the entire caravan, and his luck seemed to have returned. In less than two days he succeeded in capturing two ostriches, a zebra and four giraffes.

Farandoul and the white queen Angelina marched at the head on the ostriches, the giraffes came next, mounted by three other queens and Désolant, Niam-Niam bringing up the rear on the zebra. They went at top speed from dawn until the siesta hour; after the siesta, they galloped for another four hours, and in the evening they camped securely in the middle of a circle of fires. The negroes they met were dumbstruck with amazement at the sight of the white people. Farandoul always refused to enter into relations with them; the game-rich forests sufficed to feed the caravan. If any tribes manifested sentiments of hostility, the speed of our friends' mounts got them out of trouble.

Farandoul had completely abandoned any idea of reaching the west coast of Africa; he was now heading north-east, in order to reach Nubia.

In that direction, he was no longer running the risk of bumping into unknown dangers, for he would soon come back into countries he had already traversed.

After having skirted the territories inhabited by the Niam-Niams without incident, having crossed the lands of the Winga, Darming, Dar-Ferit, Takolé and Kordofan, the caravan greeted the sight of the blue waters of the White Nile with cheers.

This was Nubia, a country almost familiar. The time of perils was past. The Niam-Niams would never catch up with their stolen meal, the Makalolos would not get back their four queens and the Karbirkos would never see their gods again! It was only at intervals that they had a few disputes with the natives.

The scientist Désolant, having wanted to study at excessively close range the mores of a population suspected of cannibalism, had nearly ended his days on a skewer, but Farandoul, the queens and Niam-Niam had sacked the village in order to get him back and had freed him in time. The negroes, having recovered from their surprise, had gone to wait for them at the entrance to a gorge, and it had been necessary to clear a path through their massed forces. The queens had been splendid. Kalunda, Dililo, Caroline and Angelina, excited by fury, threw the first ranks into disorder by means of their arrows, then charged furiously, swords in hand. The dangerous pass was soon crossed.

Eight hours after reaching the Nile, as the caravan was relaxing in the delightful shade of an oasis during the hours of the most intense heat, Farandoul's attention was attracted by a singular phenomenon. An ink-black cloud was advancing across the sky, its shadow already covering part of the sandy desert through which the Nile was snaking. A strange noise was emerging from this cloud: a confused buzz that the travelers soon recognized as the sound of millions of moving wings.

The cloud was a rapidly-advancing army of locusts, interposing itself between the ground and the light of the Sun. It was getting dark; meanwhile, the noise of the locusts became similar to the whistling of a storm-wind and the oasis disappeared beneath the cloud as if it had been enveloped by a black veil.

"Fire, quickly!" cried Farandoul. "Fire all around us to drive them away!"

Fortunately, the fires that had served to cook the travelers' meal were still throwing off a few sparks. They were rapidly revived and soon formed a circle of flame and smoke around the camp.

The hungry locusts were already devouring the first leaves of the oasis; the fell into the flames in their thousands, but the great mass drew away from the redoubtable place.

Just as the army of locusts had descended, Farandoul had glimpsed other travelers—Nubians and Europeans—trying to reach the shelter of their fires, but they had disappeared into the mass of the locusts.

It took 20 minutes for the cloud to pass over. Gradually, the light returned; their army disappeared westwards. What destruction that devastating cloud had produced! In the entire oasis, not a leaf or stalk of vegetation remained. The stripped trees were reduced to the condition of mere stakes; all their leaves and slender branches had been engulfed.

Farandoul's eyes searched for the European travelers he had seen. They were not far away, but they were in a pitiful state. Sitting on the bare ground, they maintained a sad silence; the unfortunates were entirely nude! The locusts had passed that way; the millions of hungry insects had devoured every last one the unfortunate travelers' garments. The Nubians in their escort were already smiling, having not lost much. Seeing the poor travelers sitting there without daring to move, however, the compassionate Farandoul went toward them.

On seeing him, one of the travelers—the oldest—started gesticulating and shouting volubly: "Don't come any closer! Don't come any closer, sir, if you have any sense of propriety! There are ladies here! Don't come any closer!"

And as Farandoul continued to approach, the European travelers called to the Nubians, and made them stand around them in such a way as to hide them completely from the onlooker's eyes.

La famille Klaknavor.

"What can I do for you, Monsieur?" asked Farandoul, stopping in front of the group.

A pitiful voice emerged from the middle of the Nubians: "have you got dresses for Miss and Milady? And something for me…"

"Alas, Monsieur, all that I can do for you is to give you three blankets, one for you and two for your ladies. That will suffice to take you as far as the first town."

"Blankets!" moaned feminine voices. "Oh! Shocking! Shocking!"

"Yes, *inconvenant*,[71] as you French say!" replied the man's voice.

---

[71] Unseemly.

"No, no—you'll be all right. I'll send them to you."

Returning to his camp, Farandoul dispatched Niam-Niam with three blankets for the unfortunates. Ten minutes later, the group of Nubians opened up and three individuals appeared, dressed as well as could be expected.

At the head walked a tall, gaunt, red-haired, red-bearded and ruddy-complexioned man, a typical Scotsman. Of all his attributes as a civilized man, only a pair of spectacles remained, having been disdained by the locusts. Two ladies followed him, with their eyes lowered and frightened expressions. They were mother and daughter. Milady's hair was as red as her husband's, her daughter's as red as her father's and mother's combined.

"Duncan Fergus MacKlaknavor, Laird of Killiecrankie, Perthshire, Scotland, Milady Rosemonde MacKlaknavor and Miss Flora MacKlaknavor," said the red-haired man in French, proceeding with introductions. "Happy to make the acquaintance of a friendly gentleman..."[72]

The two hermetically-enveloped ladies bowed and murmured a few words, among which were "eternally grateful... very grateful... gratefully... gratefulness... yes! yes! yes! yes!"

"Och, you're our savior," Lord MacKlaknavor went on. "But for you, we'd be obliged to return to Cairo in the costumes the locusts left us..."

"Shocking! Shocking!" exclaimed the ladies, interrupting their chain of *gratefuls*.

"It's no trouble, Mesdames—don't mention it."

The conversation stopped there. Farandoul was about to propose that the Scottish caravan travel with his own, but he doubted that Milady MacKlaknavor could stand remaining much longer in the company of a gentleman she had met in such a *shocking* situation, so the two caravans separated. The Scots remounted their horses and took the road to Dongola, a town situated between the third and fourth cataracts of the Nile.

Meanwhile, Farandoul and his friends conferred. Certain difficulties were beginning to make him anxious. Game was becoming very scarce. The birds of the Nile still furnish a few dishes for the caravan's meals, but the rest it was necessary to buy from the Nubians—and money was in even shorter supply! It was

---

[72] As with "Croknuff," I have refrained from revising the highly improbable spelling of this family's surname and have also retained "Rosemonde" rather than changing it to "Rosamund." Nor have I interfered with the subsequent occasional abbreviation of the surname by the eccentric omission of the prefix "Mac," but I have unified the orthography of the full name for the sake of consistency, replacing the formulation Robida uses in this passage (which does not capitalize the first K) with the one he substitutes when he mingles the full version of the name with the abbreviated one. The latter version is sometimes equipped with one or two hyphens in the original text, making five versions in all.

an appeal for funds that Farandoul made to his companions. He emptied his purse on the ground and invited them to put their resources into a common fund.

Désolant had only saved two five-franc coins from the disaster of his expedition, the rest having been stolen from him by the negroes. The four queens and Niam-Niam only had cowries—shells that served as money in the African interior, but which quasi-civilized populations did not rate very highly. The total was meager; it amounted to 225 francs in 100-*sou* French coins or Turkish piastres and 95 centimes in small change. Not very much!

"And the diamonds from the crown!" exclaimed Angelina, putting her bag of diamonds in the midst of the coins, open. "Were you forgetting those? That's what will save us. Let's press on to Cairo and set to sea."

"It's still more than 300 kilometers from here to there, you know," said Farandoul. "I should have sold our three blankets to Lord MacKlaknavor, or borrowed 500 francs from him!"

Farandoul got to his feet to gaze at the Scottish caravan disappearing over the horizon. The queens and Désolant followed his example anxiously. Niam-Niam climbed a tree. The money was still on the ground, as was the bag of diamonds, from which emerged a sparkling gleam.

The four giraffes and the two ostriches, all attached by a simple cord, were sadly searching for some blade of grass overlooked by the locusts. Suddenly, the gleam of the diamonds attracted the attention of the ostriches. In less than a second they dragged the entire group to the treasure, and fell gluttonously upon the bag.

The white queens turned round and uttered a cry of horror!

In two bounds, Farandoul and Désolant hurled themselves upon the voracious ostriches, but the latter, having swallowed the last stone, were attacking the five-franc coins.

There was a hectic fight. Désolant succeeded in saving 15 francs and was kicked to the ground by one of the ostriches. Cudgel-blows fell like hail. The two frightened ostriches broke their leash and took flight into the desert.

The caravan was plunged into despair.

"The rifles!" cried Farandoul. In the struggle, however, the rifles had been thrown to one side; by the time Farandoul and Kalunda had cocked their carbines, the ostriches were already out of range.

"To the giraffes! To the giraffes—and let's give chase!" But the giraffes and the zebra, as frightened as the ostriches, had fled in different directions. It took an hour to collect them, and when the poor victims of theft were able to saddle up, the ostriches already had a long start.

Nevertheless, they set out on the search—but at dusk, exhausted by fatigue, furious at the loss they had suffered, they were empty-handed, ten leagues behind the oasis.

The ostriches could not be found. The following day, and the day after that, the hunt was repeated with the same lack of success. The ostriches had literally vanished into the depths of the desert.

Farandoul preached philosophy and detachment from wealth to the white queen Angelina, with the utmost lack of success, for the poor queen was in a state of indescribable despair. To please her, Farandoul devoted another two days to the search, with no more result. Finally, the resigned caravan turned around and resumed the Nile route, with two more zebras captured by lasso to replace the thieving ostriches.

It was now 400 leagues that they had to cover to reach Cairo, and with only 15 francs. At the sight of the oasis where the misfortune had occurred they all bowed their heads sadly—and that was lucky, because Farandoul saw a large diamond that had escape the gluttony of the ostriches gleaming in the debris of the fire. It is unnecessary to describe the care with which that precious resource was gathered up.

Twenty-five days later, the travelers, thinned down by further privations, arrived in Egypt and made camp in the immense and superb ruins of Thebes. The 15 francs saved by Désolant had been used up and they had had to revert to crocodile-egg omelets, a meal too musky for civilized stomachs.

In the ruins of Thebes the caravan had an encounter. Four French painters—Monsieur Coriolan Rigobert, member of the Institut, and three pupils—were busy portraying every aspect of the celebrated ruins. These gentleman welcomed the caravan with all the consideration due to misfortune. They fraternized, and mutual invitations to dinner were issued. The painters came to Farandoul's camp to savor the unfamiliar delights of a superb meal consisting entirely of crocodile: boiled crocodile-eggs, roasted crocodile and omelets spices with locusts and red ants.

This fatal meal turned out badly for our friends, not because it was not a success, but because the four painters, while dining, felt strange flames ignite in their hearts for the four queens.

The superb beauty of the queens, the distinction of the white ones and the majesty of the black ones, threw the minds of the painters into such turbulence that, from the date of that soirée, the ruined colonnades of Thebes—the hypostyle halls decorated with hieroglyphs, the somber hypogea in which the Pharaohs slept, the obelisks and the mummy-cases enriched with delicate paintings—no longer had any attraction for them.

They exerted all their efforts to retain Farandoul's caravan in Thebes for an additional day, under the pretext of a nocturnal party in the ruins to be held in honor of the queens.

They spent all day making preparations—nothing but comings and goings, trips to Arab villages to bring back chickens, fruits and so on.

Coriolan Rigobert spent two hours in consultation with an Arab Marabout[73] in a village some distance from the ruins. At the end of a long discussion, Farandoul saw him give the old man a large handful of piastres in exchange for a little bottle, but—thinking that he was probably preparing a surprise for the evening—retired discreetly without saying anything.

The party was, indeed, splendid. There were dancing-girls, and then Coriolan Rigobert and his pupils, full of noble ardor, undertook picturesque exercises. They simulated the siege and destruction of Thebes of the Hundred Gates by one of the Cambyses.

Coriolan single-handedly took on the role of the garrison, while his pupils formed the besieging army, divided into three corps. Fireworks were lit; the besiegers' artillery bombarded the city; 1000 rockets exploded in the sky, illuminating the sculpted pylons and the hieroglyphs on the capitals.

Coriolan redoubled his efforts, replying with the thunder of his large artillery pieces. The assailants were making progress; the shattered walls and debris of the colonnades seemed like newly-opened breaches.

In the end, the governor of Thebes blew himself up rather than surrender. Coriolan assembled all his artillery and blasted the lot.

When the last firework had died away, they ate. The painters seemed triumphant; they exchanged whispered comments from time to time, and Coriolan frequently checked the time on his watch.

---

[73] A Marabout is a Muslim ascetic, often one living as a hermit; inevitably, such individuals acquired a reputation among travelers as magicians

After supper, while awaiting the punch, the painters organized a torch-lit retreat into the ruins. Farandoul was beginning to think that Coriolan was in far too much of a hurry to get to the ruins when the punch arrived to provide a diversion. The sarcophagus of a third-dynasty Pharaoh served as a bowl; the hot liq-uid filled it to the brim and the blue flame rose up two meters, to the great joy of the painters' Arab servants and guides. It was Coriolan Rigobert who clamed the honor of serving the punch to his guests; he was the one who filled the glasses and offered them to the ladies with warm compliments and polite remarks; he was also the one who filled Faran-doul's glass and offered it to our hero.

A suspicious observer would then have noticed an infernal smile on Cori-olan Rigobert's lips and a reckless gleam in his eyes—and that same infernal smile was reflected on the lips of Rigobert's three pupils when Farandoul trus-tingly emptied his glass of punch to the sound of cheers.

When the punch was exhausted, Coriolan skillfully brought the conversa-tion around to the coolness of the atmosphere, the beauty of the ruins by moon-light, and did it so well that it was decided to take a little stroll before going to sleep. Farandoul took the lead himself, and the company was soon wandering amid the ruins.

The excursion was troubled by fantastic apparitions. Désolant thought he saw Arab burnooses behind some of the fallen columns and Niam-Niam glimpsed the shadow of a camel deploying its long legs over the sand. The pain-ters were trying to slow down the pace of the queens, who were beginning to feel anxious. Eventually, when they turned back to the camp in response to a formal demand from the queens, Farandoul and Coriolan had disappeared.

This is what had happened:

As you will have guessed, it was a narcotic that Coriolan Rigobert had poured into Farandoul's punch. Love engenders cruelty! The painters, led astray by a fatal passion, had sworn to take possession of the four queens at all costs. To do that, it was necessary to do away with Farandoul! That crime horrified them, but, as it was necessary, they did not hesitate. The Arab Marabout he had consulted had sold Coriolan a powerful narcotic that suspended all the functions of life for an unlimited period, on condition that the subject was rigorously de-prived of air. Coriolan's plan was very simple: the sleeping Farandoul was to be delivered to the Marabout, who would keep him sealed up for as long as cir-cumstances required.

Scarcely had Coriolan and Farandoul gone into the ruins than the narcotic took effect. Farandoul suddenly felt his legs grow weak and his head become dizzy. He grabbed hold of Coriolan's arm and took a few more steps. The latter rapidly dragged him behind a group of columns, to the entrance of a subterra-nean vault. Once there, Farandoul collapsed completely and the Arab Marabout as just in time to catch him in his arms.

Two Arabs emerged from the vault, seized Farandoul by the hands and feet, and ran to rejoin two dromedaries hidden close at hand. Five minutes later, the Arabs and the sleeping Farandoul were galloping over the plain in the direc-tion of Asyut, where they arrived after a six-hour journey.

The triumphant Coriolan had rejoined the leaderless caravan and took part in our desolate friends' search, with a satanic smile.

The Arab Marabout had received a large payment, and, as he was a con-scientious man, he had decided to carry out Coriolan's orders conscientiously. As soon as he arrived at Asyut he bought a bolt of cloth and remounted his dro-medary, with Farandoul still asleep and well wrapped up. In two hours, the dro-medary had crossed the sandy plain to reach the caves of Samoun, the ancient

Egyptian necropolis filled with millions and millions of mummies, representing almost all of the ancient populations of Egypt, generation after generation of which had filled these unknown depths with their cases.[74]

The Marabout had a great deal of difficulty getting Farandoul's body down into the first gallery by himself, but, as a conscientious man, he was unsparing with his efforts. Having reached the subterranean halls, he lit a torch and searched among the heaped-up mummies for a well-sealed case that was the right size to accommodate our hero. Once he had found one, he took out the poor devil who was lodged in it—a rich lord, for the case was elaborately decorated and painted—and replaced him with Farandoul.

The bolt of cloth bought in Asyut was cut into strips and served to envelop our friend in a tightly-wound web. With the preparations terminated, the Marabout fastened the lid and pushed the case into a corner of the gallery. Having done that, he rubbed his hands together with a satisfied smile.

"Allah!" he said. "The task is faithfully executed; the Christian lord can be tranquil; his enemy will not appear before the time is convenient. He said one or two years...however, the Christian has paid me well, so perhaps he has the right to a little extra satisfaction. Yes, that's right. I'll leave his enemy here for 30 or 40 years. As I've always been a good Muslim, I'll probably be in Mohammed's paradise by then, but I'll make sure to instruct my sons in my will to some and set the infidel free." And the worthy Marabout returned to the light of day with the satisfaction of having done his duty.

The caves of Samoun had fallen into darkness again. Mingled with Egyptian men and women dead for 6000 years—with contemporaries of Joseph and Sesostris, Amenhotep and Cheops, Cleopatra and Mrs. Potiphar—Farandoul was asleep in his case, perhaps for eternity! He was finished! In 30 or 40 years the forgetful children of the Marabout would not take the trouble to carry out their father's wishes and would delegate the task it in their turn to their descendants.

A frightful prospect! But Farandoul was not thinking about it—he was asleep! Fifty million mummies were sleeping their eternal slumber with him. How dark it was in the somber galleries, domains of silence and death! What tranquility for the mummies, relics of vanished worlds, heaped up pell-mell in the darkness! No longer friends, no longer enemies, no longer mothers, no longer brothers, no longer fierce soldiers, no longer proud aristocrats, no longer superb

---

[74] This is an exaggeration, although thousands of mummies—mostly birds and reptiles—were, indeed, found in the actual caves of Samoun. The find was widely publicized in France because the first part of an episodic *Tour du Monde* by M. A. Georges, published in 1860, described a visit "aux grottes de Samoun ou des crocodiles." Georges' work was one of Jules Verne's sources, as Robida was obviously aware.

courtesans! Nothing any longer but a society packed away forever in the immense luggage-room of eternity!

The caves of Samoun are rarely visited; only a handful of travelers dare to venture there every year. Farandoul had been resting there for a week when the silence of the necropolis was disturbed by the arrival of a few of these bold tourists.

If Farandoul had been able to see them, he would have recognized the visitors as Lord Klaknavor, his wife Rosemonde and his daughter Flora, dressed in new clothes and perhaps even redder since their adventure with the locusts.

Lord Klaknavor, who was about to leave for Europe, had come to Samoun in search of a beautiful and authentic mummy-case to take back to the museum in Killiecrankie, the small town near to his manor house. Accompanied by his guides, Lord Klaknavor went through the somber galleries without being able to fix his choice on a sufficiently luxurious mummy; it was difficult, and the noble lord wanted a mummy of the first rank, in an elegantly-painted case enriched with learned hieroglyphs. Many mummies had been picked out, extracted from the mass and then rejected as unworthy of the situation he was offering to them.

Passing from gallery to gallery, the Klaknavor clan had arrived in the room where Farandoul lay in his case. Klaknavor hesitated between a young lady of 6800 years and a well-preserved gentleman of 7000. Miss Klaknavor was inclined toward the young lady, but Lady Rosemonde rejected her as having perhaps been a trifle too lax in her morals. Then Klaknavor fell ecstatically upon Farandoul's case. The latter presented all the requisite qualities: richness of ornamentation, purity of illustration, profusion of hieroglyphs. There was no hesitation! It was heavy, too, and so well-sealed! Its contents were undoubtedly in a perfect state; it would be opened with great ceremony at Killiecrankie.

Lord Klaknavor made a sign; the Arabs approached, lifted the mummy, and took it back into the daylight with them.

A week later, the Klaknavor clan embarked with the carefully-packaged mummy on the *Sesostris*, a French mailboat, which disembarked them all at Marseille. The Klaknavors and their luggage took the express, stayed the night in Paris, took the express again, disembarked in London and set off for Scotland without delay, still with the precious case containing the mummy of an aristocrat of the fourth dynasty.

The day after their arrival, the Klaknavors sent invitations to the high society of Perthshire—the MacGregors, the MacKinbors, the MacRonalds, etc., etc.—all the scientists of Edinburgh and all the notabilities of the Scottish press.

The mummy, laid on the large dining-room table, awaited the guests. Beside it were forceps and a silver hammer, which the patrician hands of Lord Klaknavor himself would use to open the box. The room filled up rapidly with the expected high society. The most ardent curiosity was painted on all those noble faces, the gracious ladies thinking that they were about to be confronted with a gentleman of a noble family who was 8000 years old.

Finally, Lord Klaknavor took hold of his instruments. All the MacGregors and MacKinbors held their breath.

The Marabout had done a good job; it took half an hour to unfasten the lid and begin unwrapping the mummy.

A cry of astonishment sprang from the throats of the MacGregors. Lord Klaknavor, his wife and daughter fell back with shock.

"How well-preserved it is!" the MacGregors and MacKinbors finally cried, with one voice.

"What fine people these Egyptians were!"

"What embalmers!"

"He's called Phta-Amne-Nophis, son of..." pronounced an Egyptologist who had taken possession of the lid and was reading it slowly.

"How he resembles..." cried Flora MacKlaknavor.

"Oh! Flora! How shocking!" observed Lady Rosemonde—but a loud cry emitted by the entire audience froze further observations on Lady Rosemonde's lips.

Phta-Amne-Nophis had just sat up abruptly, breathing in deeply. Sitting in his case on the table in Lord Klaknavor's dining-room, he gazed at the noble audience with the utmost astonishment.

No one breathed a word. Lady Rosemonde and a certain number of Ladies MacGregor and MacKinbor fainted into one another's arms. The male MacGregors and MacKinbors only took three steps back.

It was Ptha-Amne-Nophis—or, rather, Farandoul—who broke the silence. "Oof!" he said. "Your punch, Monsieur Coriolan, was a little too strong! Oof—what a terrible headache...but where are you, Coriolan? But... Why all these bandages? But...but... What the Devil have you... Where the Devil are...

What's the meaning of all this? I don't know anyone here...ah! There's Lord Klaknavor! Well, milord, delighted to see you again in Thebes. Especially delighted to see you more comfortably dressed—and milady too! But you're very numerous. Are you holding a party in evening dress in the ruins of Thebes?"

"Thebes! Thebes!" cried Lord Klaknavor, suddenly finding his voice. "You're mad, sir! You're in Killiecrankie, near Edinburgh, Scotland."

"Killie...near Edinburgh?" cried Farandoul, rubbing his head. "But... What about the four queens! Where are the four queens?"

As the fearful old Egyptologist tried to put the lid back over his head and shut him in the case again, the furious Farandoul threw him backwards, along with his lid, ripped off his bandages and leapt into the midst of the assembly, landing next to a few frightened MacGregors, who released further exclamations.

Farandoul grabbed Lord Klaknavor by the shoulders. "Come on," he said. "I helped you out. When I met you out there at the oasis after the locusts, you were deprived of all your clothing. Milady Klaknavor was..."

"Shocking, shocking," articulated Lady Rosemonde, feebly, as she fainted again.

"...was deprived of every item of clothing! And Miss Klaknavor too! I saved you then! I covered you up. I gave you the means to return to the civilized world, if not with elegance, at least without offending decency—for, if not for me, you'd all have been forced to offend decency until you arrived in some town or other! I am, therefore, your benefactor! Well, I demand a rapid clarification from you. Where am I, really?"

"In Killiecrankie!"

"And the four queens?"

"What queens? I only know Her Majesty the..."

"No, no—the queens of the Makalolos!"

"No idea."

"And Niam-Niam?"

"No idea."

"Then I'm alone here! How did I get here?"

"In that mummy-case! I bought you, sir, and very dear!"

"Where? In Thebes?"

"No, in the caves of Samoun, near Asyut."

"In the Egyptian necropolis! But how did I get there when I remember going to sleep in Thebes?"

"At the end of the day, all that I can tell you, my dear sir, is that, desiring to bring back an authentic mummy in good condition for the museum at Killiecrankie, I concluded my trip to Egypt with a visit to the caves at Samoun. I found myself among thousands of mummies; I discovered your case; you pleased me and I brought you away. I thought I was able to attribute to you an age of 7000 to 9000 years, but I see that you're much younger!"

"But how did I get there?"

"It was only 7000 years ago that you were deposited," the Egyptologist observed, coming forward. "Don't you remember, Mr. Ptha-Amne-Nophis?"

"I'm not talking to you, Monsieur," roared Farandoul, angrily. Addressing himself to Lord Klaknavor, he went on: "Let's see—how long have I been in your possession?"

"Only three weeks."

"Only...but what about my four queens!" Suddenly, Farandoul started; an idea had just struck him. "I've got it!" he exclaimed. "It's Coriolan's doing...it was the punch! Infamy! What time is the train to London, milord?"

As Lord Klaknavor was in no hurry to reply, Farandoul seized a hat at random, elbowed his way through the audience and ran to a window.

Five minutes later, a man left Klaknavor Manor, still running, knocked over the doorman and two domestics who barred his way, and headed for Killiecrankie station. He encountered the railway line on the way, just as a train was passing. Farandoul ran on to the line, caught hold of the last wagon, and hauled himself up into the guard's van.

Three-quarters of an hour later he was in Edinburgh. As he had no ticket, he had to jump off before the train went into the station and climb over a few barriers.

The first thing he did in the city was to buy a newspaper. He forgot to pay for it, for two reasons: terrible preoccupation and lack of money. The newspaper's date informed him that 28 days had passed since the painter Coriolan's fateful soirée in the ruins of Thebes.

Horror! The queens abandoned to the mercy of painters! Farandoul felt his hair stand up on his head. And he had no money to travel! Suddenly, his hand, which was rummaging in his pocket mechanically, brought out a small packet. Farandoul opened it hastily. It was the diamond recovered at the oasis!

The first jeweler he found saw a feverish man enter his shop who offered him a magnificent diamond. The jeweler offered him 1000 pounds, paid up and pocketed the diamond, certain that he would be able to sell it for double that price.

Farandoul ran to the station with his 25,000 francs in his pocket. The London express was just leaving. He leapt into a compartment and sat down unceremoniously, elbowing a few passengers aside. At the first station he ran to the engine and leapt up next to the stupefied driver. "A hundred pounds if you can gain two hours!" he said.

"Impossible, sir!"

"Well, stay here then!" And Farandoul grabbed the driver and threw him out on to the platform. The stoker, who had got down to change a signal-lantern, ran to help his superior, but Farandoul had had thrown himself at the controls furiously. The locomotive, releasing a frightful volley of whistle-blasts, got under way again, leaving the driver and stoker in the station. Cries of terror emerged from all the wagons, but Farandoul had no time to think about that and started shoveling coal recklessly.

The drain devoured distance at 40 leagues an hour! Fortunately, the telegraph had sent an alarm call all along the track, and the thunderbolt train, finding the way open and free, arrived without incident in London seven hours early. Farandoul stopped the train on the track shortly before entering the city; before anyone dared to launch themselves in pursuit, he had reached the city, jumped into a cab and raced to the Thames.

There is no need to describe the annoyance of the travelers taken on that vertiginous journey by Farandoul. Two notaries that happened to be on the train collected an infinite number of witness-statements from the bewildered passengers. The most incredible fuss was kicked up in the carriages; they believed that they had been abducted by a madman, but the truth soon came to light. Farandoul had been recognized!

By whom? In the first place, by our old acquaintance from Australia, the monkey Makako—the one betrayed by love—who, to his great humiliation, was in a second-class compartment with two other domestics from Cardigan Castle. Makako rolled his eyes furiously at the sight of his former leader, but he could not reveal his name to his neighbors. That was left to another of our former acquaintances—the very woman whose fatal beauty had occasioned Makako's treason—Lady Arabella Cardigan who, returning to London for the season, recognized Farandoul as he kept on to the locomotive! On seeing him, she had no doubt at all that he intended to exact his revenge on her by derailing the train; she closed her eyes and did not open them again until the breathless train stopped just outside London.

The English newspapers were full of this unprecedented adventure for a week. England, expecting its former enemy to pop up anywhere, did not draw breath until the telegraph signaled Farandoul's arrival in Alexandria.

There was a dispute in Killiecrankie. All the MacGregors and MacKinbors reproached Klaknavor for having invited them to be elbowed aside by a false Phta-Amne-Nophis. A terrible war was on the point of breaking out between their clans and that of Lord Klaknavor, but the ladies finally succeeded in having the claymores returned to their sheaths.

Miss Flora Klaknavor, even redder than usual—a quite natural effect of emotion—threw herself into her mother's arms, saying: "Oh, dear Mama, I can no longer marry anyone but him! I understood him, in spite of all his reticence. It's for me that he came!"

"By the sword of Klaknavor, he shall marry you, my daughter!"

And that same evening, an express train carried the Klaknavors away, launched in pursuit of Farandoul on the road to Thebes.

As he passed through Paris, Farandoul took time out to buy two revolvers and run to Coriolan Rigobert's address. The painter's studio was closed; he was believed to be still in Egypt. Farandoul headed for the land of the Pharaohs.

At the French consulate in Cairo, our hero learned, to his joy, that the illustrious painter had not been seen in the city and that, in all probability, he was still to be found in Thebes.

Without losing a minute, Farandoul bought six dromedaries in a suburb and hired a few Arabs. An hour after leaving the consulate, a large cloud of dust was galloping across the sands in a southerly direction. That cloud was Farandoul and his men, urging their camels on by every means possible.

VII.

It took six days to reach Thebes. On the evening of the sixth day the ruins appeared, framing the nascent Moon between two broken columns.

"Halt!" commanded Farandoul.

The Arabs and the camels stopped. The master had accustomed them en route to passive obedience.

"Make camp there, at the entrance to that village, and await my orders. I'm going over there, to Thebes."

As he said these words, Farandoul had made his dromedary kneel and he leapt to earth in the midst of a circle of fellahs who had emerged from the miserable hovels of the village.

Suddenly, an old Arab released a scream of terror and fell down in front of him, head in the dust. "Allah! Allah!" he cried. "Are you a djinn, a spirit? Is it your shade that I see? How have you arisen from the sleep of the dead? How have you quit the somber caves of Samoun, where I buried you myself?"

"Ah!" cried Farandoul. "It's you! I recognize you, too—you're the accomplice of the painter of ruins. Tremble! I have quit the sleep of the dead avid for vengeance!"

"Mercy! Mercy!" howled the Marabout. "I would not have abandoned you. You are mentioned in my will, and my sons were to deliver you."

"Answer me and serve me; I'll decide then what I ought to do. Now, are the painters still over there?"

"Yes, lord."

"And the queens?"

"The young women are there too."

"Very good. Now follow me."

And the two men walked rapidly toward the ruins. The Marabout had difficulty keeping up with Farandoul; from time to time, he reached out and touched his clothing, as if to see whether he was dealing with an actual living being or some somber spirit of darkness.

The dark blue curtain of night had completely fallen when they arrived at the ruins. Without pausing to admire the fantastic and colossal silhouettes, the gaps in the colonnades or the somber masses of temples, they glided noiselessly in the direction of a little blinking light in the center of the principal mass.

It was there that Farandoul had camped five weeks earlier. As he approached it he recognized the tent made with blankets, and the shadows of his friend Désolant and Niam-Niam. Finally, with his heartbeat accelerating terribly, he saw the four queens, by the light of a miserable paper lantern illuminating the whole scene. They were sitting on the ground in an attitude of sadness. Several shadows were standing in front of them. They seemed to be arguing animatedly in front of a fire on which a meager dinner was cooking.

"Go back to the village and fetch my men," Farandoul whispered to the Marabout. "Hide among the stones and don't show yourselves until I call."

The Marabout disappeared silently. Farandoul approached the group, with his ears pricked.

It was Désolant who was speaking. "Yes," he said, "I repeat one more time, Messieurs, that the queens absolutely refuse the dinner that you offer them. They remember only too well that it was after a meal offered by you that the inexplicable disappearance of our unfortunate friend occurred! Your conduct in that circumstance does not appear to them entirely honest, and I must say that I share their suspicions." Here, Niam-Niam, lying down to the left of the queens, let out a groan. "As does Niam-Niam," the god Désolant went on. "And the young savage has a good nose! Anyway, we're staying here in the vague hope of discovering some clue or trace that will inform us as to the fate of our friend—but we refuse to enter more amply into relations with you. Take that as read and stay in your camp."

"Damn the chamberlain!" howled one of the painters. "Stay here is you want to, but let the ladies answer our invitation!"

"Come on, charming crow's-wing queen," cried Coriolan himself, addressing Kalunda. "Don't be so surly—we're friends and, as you know very well, passionate worshipers! Leave your rather unpleasant guardian here and...."

Coriolan rounded his arm, but Kalunda suddenly leapt to her feet and prevented him from advancing any further. She caught the light with the blade of her sword and extended its point towards the audacious member of the Institut. "Back, bandit, pirate, vile hippopotamus, or I'll cut off your head! You're the traitor, I'm sure of it! Crocodile!"

The white queens burst out laughing. "Well, Monsieur Coriolan," said Caroline, "do you need a translation of our friend's speech? You know that she called you an old crocodile."

The painters consulted one another. Their fatal love had played havoc with their faces. For five weeks the same scenes had been re-enacted every day and all their attempts to get closer to the queens had been futile.

"Come on, one more time," the tenacious Coriolan resumed. "Charming white queens and delightful black majesties, you have no friends more devoted, more affectionate, more…believe me! And since your Farandoul, by some inexplicable misfortune that I deplore as much as you do, has disappeared forever, accept our arms and our…"

Coriolan did not finish. A shadow had just loomed up in the midst of the stones. "Good evening, Monsieur Coriolan," said the shadow, calmly, coming to stand in front of the painter. "Do you recognize me?"

"Farandoul!" cried the painters and the queens with one voice. "Farandoul!"

And within a second, our hero was surrounded, embraced, clasped in his friends' arms. Niam-Niam leapt up, howling with joy; Désolant shook him by the hand; the white queens and the black queens recounted their anguish in tearful voices.

As for the painters, they seemed stunned. Coriolan rubbed his eyes; the others tore out handfuls of hair. "Take the trouble to sit down, Messieurs," Farandoul said to them, "we need to have a chat. I haven't yet been able to thank you for the delicious punch you served the other day, my dear Monsieur Coriolan—as you know, circumstances beyond my control have prevented me from doing so, but I shall try to express my gratitude for your charming hospitality.…"

Farandoul's experienced ears had perceived slight sounds in the ruins; it was doubtless the Marabout bringing the Arabs. A whistle-blast brought them abruptly into the encampment.

The painters had stood up.

"My conversation seems to be boring these gentlemen…tie them up!" said Farandoul, with an authoritative gesture.

The Arabs raced forward. Before the painters could react, they were lying in the sand with their wrists and feet bound.

"It's done, lord," said the Marabout, bowing to Farandoul. "Shall we cut off their heads?"

"We'll see," said Farandoul, negligently. "Now that we're assured of their company, we have plenty of time."

And without paying any more attention to the painters, Farandoul turned to his friends, who were overwhelming him with questions. We shall pass silently over their transports of joy, their outbursts of gaiety and their flashes of anger. The painters maintained a sullen silence. At the end of the soirée, deliberation was opened as to what punishment to inflict on them. Farandoul, having hastened from Scotland with a terrible thirst for vengeance, was considerably mollified by finding his queens in good health and saved from the snare. He therefore rejected Niam-Niam's proposal that the painters should be thrown into the Nile, and adopted an alternative.

The remainder of the might was devoted to rest. The painters could not close their yes, though, tortured by the reproaches of their conscience and the hardness of the pebbles on which they were lying.

When day broke, Farandoul's dromedaries were brought to the tent. The Arabs then began strange preparations under Farandoul's direction. With the aid of a large ladder they had fabricated, they climbed to the top of an intact column whose capital was 12 meters above a mass of debris originating from a collapsed entablature. On the capital, they erected a sort of makeshift block-and-tackle and awaited Farandoul's orders.

The painters had gone pale watching these preparations; doubtless they were to be hanged.

"The honor is yours, Monsieur Coriolan."

The Arabs had passed a thick rope around his body and had already dragged him to the column. Within a minute he was lifted up swinging in the air and received at the top of the capital by an Arab who cut his bonds and put his painter's parasol into his hands. The other painters had shut their eyes in order not to see his torture. One of them reopened his eyes on feeling himself lifted up by the Arabs. It was his turn!

Soon, Coriolan's three pupils, crestfallen and embarrassed, were placed on the capitals of three other columns, divested of their shackles and furnished with their parasols.

The clear and sonorous laughter of the queens at the sight of their faces opened painful wounds in the painters' hearts.

Farandoul came forward, hat in hand, and raised his head toward the unfortunates.

"Messieurs," he said, "we're leaving. I hope that won't annoy you too much; you may take it for granted that these ladies and I will conserve an excellent memory of our relations. One simple piece of advice before leaving you: if, by chance, you grow bored in your new aerial existence, take out your sketchpads—I presume you have them on you—and make a sketch of Simon Stylites from nature! No one has ever been better placed than you to do justice to such a subject! Until I have the pleasure of seeing you again, Messieurs!"

Farandoul's servants had already gathered up all the luggage; the kneeling dromedaries were only waiting for the travelers. Two of the dromedaries, prepared for the queens, were each equipped with a magnificent *attatouch*,[75] or palanquin in the form of an awning of cotton cloth decorated with red and white

---

[75] This word is almost certainly misrendered; it seems to have been copied (incorrectly) from a passage in the first volume of a *Géographie Militaire* by Colonel Gustave-Léon Niox, published in 1876, which was obviously one of the reference books consulted by Robida.

stripes, terminating in a long stem, at the top of which a plume of ostrich-feathers was swaying.

The caravan was finally about to leave the inhospitable ruins of Thebes when the noise of several galloping horses resounded on the stones and brought about a further delay in the departure.

Farandoul went forward to greet the newcomers. He was greatly astonished to see the strange caravan. Three Europeans, two of whom were women, accompanied by two female Arab servants, came to a halt in front of him—and these Europeans were none other than Duncan MacKlaknavor, his wife Rosemonde and his daughter Flora, all three of them as red as ever.

"So you've come back to Egypt," Farandoul was about to say—but milord did not give him time.

"Sir," he said, "should a gentleman, after having compromised a young woman of high birth, remove himself and disappear, as you have done? The MacKlaknavors have keen claymores, sir, and we have said: he will marry her, or..."

"Compromised? Marry? Who?" asked Farandoul, amazed.

"You know very well—for you can't deny it; it's all too clear; she's compromised! Let's take things from the beginning. Two months ago, you met us in a sorry situation; your gentlemanly heart was moved, you got us out of a sticky situation. All well and good, so far. But then, doubtless powerfully moved by her beauty, carried away by your passion, you arranged to enter more profoundly into relations with us. As there had not been any sort of introduction, you resorted to a stratagem..."

"Bah!"

"Yes, the caves of Samoun—that was cleverly planned. In that fashion you almost became part of the family; you entered the home of the Klaknavors! We took you in without any suspicion, we brought together our friends, and *crack*! At the very moment when she found herself irredeemably compromised, by your fault, you changed your mind and you fled! And what about her, the poor child? Did you think of her?"

"But who is this *her*?"

"Who? Miss Flora, of course—the last of the Klaknavors—who is expecting reparation!"

Farandoul's anger exploded at this speech. "What! Worthy MacKlaknavor, can you possibly imagine that I was waiting for you at Samoun, in my mummy-case, to ask for your daughter's hand in marriage?"

"Don't deny it—it's the truth! After your inexplicable departure from Klaknavor Castle, we took the train—my wife, my daughter and myself—we picked up your trail in Paris, then at Marseille; we almost caught up with you in Cairo, and finally, thanks to the speed of the yacht of one of our friends who had just come down the Nile, we have rejoined you here!"

"Well, milord, think whatever you like about me, but the charm of your company cannot retain me any longer in Thebes. Stay here as long as you like; as for me, I'm leaving."

"What about our reparation? We'll follow you. Is it necessary to draw the Klaknavor claymore, Flora?"

"Not yet, Papa! Follow him!"

"Oh, it's like that, is it?" cried Farandoul, furiously. "Well, we shall see." And the Arabs ranged around him received an order that they greeted with bursts of laughter.

Within a minute, without any respect for the Klaknavors, they were lifted from their saddles and dragged to the colonnade on which the painters were already perched. It took three-quarters of an hour to hoist the family up on three columns of the same height, facing the painters.

Five minutes later, the caravan quit the ruins of Thebes of the Hundred Gates for the last time. Farandoul had left a few Arabs and the Marabout behind, with orders to get the painters and the Klaknavors down from their uncomfortable perches at mid-day.

The Marabout, full of respect for Farandoul, wondered what he ought to do. "I had the intention," he said to himself, "of leaving the master in the caves of Samoun for 30 years; that was wrong, so I must make reparation. Should I let his enemies stay on their columns for 30 years? That would be very advantageous; it would save us the bother of getting them down, and he'd be better avenged. But no—his power is great and he'd know...I'll carry out his orders."

Farandoul and his queens were galloping in the direction of Cairo, giving no further thought to their enemies. Happy to be reunited, thinking themselves safe from any new peril, they were traveling placidly, even spending a few days of idleness beneath the palm-trees of oases.

Farandoul was now thinking about Mandibul and his sailors, launched on his search into the African wilderness. Where were they? What were they doing? He had had no news of them since his unexpected encounter with the rhinoceros-letter. While he waited for some clue, Farandoul decided not to leave Africa and to stay in Cairo.

Meanwhile, the Klaknavors and the painters, brought down from their columns at the agreed hour, immediately headed for Cairo aboard milord's friend's yacht. The hope of a fine vengeance caused them to accelerate the little vessel's progress. On their arrival in Cairo, a complaint was made at the British embassy. The city was turned upside down by the English ambassador, who demanded full satisfaction, and requisitioned armed forces to keep watch on all arrivals. The Klaknavor claymore quivered in its scabbard, although the timid Flora was still hoping to come to an arrangement.

Finally, one fine morning, the watchmen signaled the long-awaited arrival of the Farandoul caravan.

The unsuspecting travelers were advancing placidly; the queens, leaning out of their palanquin, were admiring the panorama of Cairo spread out before them, with its domes and its hundreds of minarets bathing in the pure gold of a magnificent Sun.

Niam-Niam ran ahead, executing a frenetic fantasy on his zebra; the white queens—who, you will remember, had once lived in Cairo—were pointing out the principal landmarks to the wonderstruck black queens.

Farandoul, wanting to put off until the next day the search for suitable lodgings for the queens, decided to camp outside the walls, under the palm trees surrounding the magnificent mosque of Ibrahim. On his orders, without paying any heed to a few Arnautes[76] of rascally appearance who seemed to be watching them from a distance, the members of the caravan dismounted in the shadow of the palms, and the Arab servants prepared the tents.

The delightful hour of *kif* beneath the palm-trees![77] Our friends relaxed, some savoring the delights of a cup of pure mocha, others drowsing. Farandoul was thinking about Mandibul when Niam-Niam suddenly came into the tent, fearfully.

"Master, Master!" he cried. "It's them again!"

Farandoul was jerked out of his reverie and ran outside. A horde of Arnautes, with ferocious expressions, long moustaches and tall hats garnished with frayed tassels and sequins, were running toward the tent with swords in their hands. Behind them, Farandoul saw Lord Klaknavor giving orders, accompanied by an Egyptian officer.

There was no means of escape; there were more than 300 men between the caravan members and their dromedaries; Farandoul saw that in an eye-blink. "To the mosque," he shouted to his companions, "or we're done for!"

They all raced into the courtyard of the mosque. The Arnautes were so close behind them that they could not close the door. Farandoul, revolver in hand, held the assailants at bay for a minute, and eventually succeeded in getting the queens into the minaret of the mosque. The Arnautes could not restrain themselves any longer, and rifles were fired in Farandoul's direction.

Seven or eight shots rang out, but the solid door of the minaret was closed and the besieged group reinforced it with everything they could find. As the furious Arnautes tried to break it down, Farandoul and Désolant made the queens climb up to the summit of the minaret and combined their efforts to demolish the foot of the staircase. An hour of hard work—during which Niam-Niam, installed at a window, exchanged fire with the Arnautes—sufficed for our friends to make part of the stairway collapse. Soon, the entire ground floor was strewn with debris and the door, thus barricaded, was able to withstand all the efforts of the besiegers.

"Let's climb up now," said Farandoul. "We're safe, for the moment."

Having reached the summit of the minaret, they found the queens occupied in arranging everything to sustain a siege with honor. Stones were ready to be

---

[76] *Arnaute* is the French spelling of a word borrowed from Turkish, *arnaut*; its literal meaning in "Albanian," but the French encountered it in the context of Ottoman Empire mercenaries and their version—used in colonial Algeria—had a broader reference to various sorts of militiamen.

[77] *Kif* is a mixture of tobacco and cannabis—here, apparently, taken instead of, or in addition to, afternoon tea.

hurled down on the heads of the enemy; the munitions were in a safe place, as were the provisions—for the forward-thinking Niam-Niam had saved all the food they had from the disaster. He had even succeeded in stealing a sack of rice that probably belonged to the mosque's muezzin, which he had hoisted up on to the highest balcony.

On seeing all this, Farandoul could not help smiling.

"No need for so many preparations," he said. "Do you think we can stand off the entire Egyptian army? No, we have to find some way of getting out of this mess."

The fiery red Sun was setting behind an accumulation of violet clouds, with bloody reflections. The heat was stifling and the gathering darkness was bringing about an increase in warmth rather than a cooling; the very breeze was burning, its ardent breath raising eddies of sand in the distance.

"A storm's gathering," murmured Farandoul. "So much the better! Perhaps we'll be able to take advantage of it to escape. Let's stay alert!"

Three hours have gone by. A profound darkness envelops the mosque, not permitting the refugees to make out anything happening beneath them. Farandoul leaves his friends on the balcony and goes down to the final landing to watch the surroundings through a window. The storm has arrived; the thunder is rolling incessantly, scarcely leaving an interval between consecutive explosions.

Had the Arnautes gone away or are they on watch around the mosque? Farandoul takes advantage of every flash of lightning to look out as far as he can, but nothing suspicious appears. What should they do? Should they risk an escape? Should they wait longer? Finally, he makes up his mind, instructs his friends to remain as calm as possible, and takes them down with him. A few sheets torn into long strips serves to make a rope with which they can get down from the narrow window.

The four queens, Farandoul, Niam-Niam and Désolant prepare to flee; the storm is rumbling more violently than ever; the atmosphere is charged with electricity; the gusts of a furious and scorching wind are making the minaret tremble on its foundations.

Suddenly, a shadow interposes itself between the little window and the sky, hectically furrowed with bluish streaks of lightning. It is a dull and slender shadow; the hellish furnace illuminated by the lightning is blotted out and no one can see anything any longer…they are about to risk everything.

Farandoul clambers out of the window; another series of fulgurant lightning-flashes bursts forth and the shadow reappears momentarily. Farandoul throws himself backwards; it is a ladder. Leaning out, he has seen more of them raised up alongside. The Arnautes are there, silent but active. They are counting on climbing up, unnoticed, to a beautiful gallery opening a little higher up and taking the besieged group by surprise.

"Quickly—to the gallery!" cries Farandoul, climbing back up precipitately.

They are just in time; the Arnautes are already coming over the delicately-sculpted balustrades.

The thunder rumbles on without a second's respite; it is now no more than a single detonation prolonged to infinity, in the midst of which the flashes of lightning have no more effect than the striking of a match.

The air is stifling and oppressive. The wind is whistling and howling as if it were opposed by an unknown force.

The Arnautes invading the balcony have driven back the besieged group. Farandoul and his companions beat a retreat and climb backwards up the stairway. Suddenly, it seems that the minaret, which has been shaking more than ever for some minutes, is subjected to a more terrible shock. A frightful cracking sound is heard...

The minaret tilts. Farandoul and the queens, caught on the stairway, are bowled over. A terrible scream emerges from their throats. The minaret crumbles, and they all expect to be crushed in its fall....

But the fall goes on and on...

What can it mean? The minaret has quit the vertical position; it is now horizontal, but no impact has occurred! Each of the refugees is conscious of this extraordinary fact. They have been falling for five minutes, but have not hit the ground!

All of them, beginning to get up, are still awaiting the impact that has not occurred. Farandoul finally rises to his feet and, moving cautiously, goes to a window...

An exclamation escapes him. He leaps backwards. What has he seen? Nothing but the most intense darkness and—at an already-frightful distance—the Earth, disappearing in the distance!

The minaret, torn away by some unknown commotion, has been carried away into the clouds by some unknown force. Farandoul wants to hide the situation from his friends, but they, frightened by his expression, have gone to the window and are watching with horror as the Earth draws away from them, as red now as a gigantic Moon.

They are all standing up straight, bewildered. Farandoul remains silent and collects his thoughts. The Earth has evidently experienced some dreadful catastrophe, perhaps an encounter with an errant star or a comet, some lost child of sidereal space. The savant Désolant has the same idea, and the idea is soon confirmed by the sight of a third heavenly body traveling through the clouds in a direction opposite to that of the Earth.

There can be no doubt in this regard. Here, on one side, is the Earth, drawing away rapidly, followed by its familiar satellite, the Moon, presently divided into an elegant crescent. There, on the other, is the new star, an immense cannonball which literally fills the horizons.

The four queens, whose knowledge of astronomy is very slight, have nevertheless understood the situation without any need of explanation. Niam-Niam

311

is also up to date, and, far from being terrified, is making the minaret resound with gales of laughter.

"Ha ha! Well and truly stumped, the others! Can't climb up any more—too high!"

The first moment of surprise has passed; throats paralyzed by emotion now permit speech. They feel themselves and ascertain that no one is seriously injured, or even bruised.

"My word!" exclaims Angelina. "This is better than falling to the ground. We haven't been crushed and we've been saved from our enemies."

"But where are we going?" asks Désolant.

"That's the big question!"

Suddenly, Niam-Niam screams and throws himself along the minaret, which is now a simple tube in which the staircase forms a screw-thread. He reaches the platform and soon comes back, with a face as long as a meter rule.

"What is it?" Farandoul asks.

"Oh, master—the rice! Stolen! Lost! The coffee—lost! All lost!"

"Ah! A bad situation," murmurs Farandoul. "Evidently, we presently form, if not a star, at least a sort of aerolith dragged along in the wake of an unknown heavenly body. Nothing grows on our aerolith, and we'll have difficulty prospering here!"

VIII.

The first rays of the day-star appeared about half an hour later. Farandoul took out his watch and confirmed that it could not be any later than half past midnight on Earth.

The Sun rises early here! he thought. *We must take advantage of that.* And the entire company followed him along the screw-thread to reach the platform. On the way, the white queen Angelina, turning around to speak to her friend, did not notice a window open to the clouds. She stepped into the gap and disappeared through the opening.

Anguish tightened every chest; they all closed their eyes in order not to see her cartwheeling through the void. A second exclamation from Angelina made them reopen them. The poor child, still very pale, was sitting outside on the wall of the minaret. The extraordinary thing was that she seemed to her friends inside to be upside down without being aware of it.

"What's happening?" Farandoul asked.

"I don't understand it at all—I can't fall," Angelina replied, naively. "I thought I'd be heading head-first into space, but not at all—I'm stuck outside, like this!"

"I have it!" cried Farandoul and Désolant at the same time. The former continued: "Our minaret, in its capacity as a new star gravitating through space, possesses a force of attraction. All the laws of physics have been realigned. We can walk on the surface, as freely as we used to on the surface of the Earth. Outside quickly! Let's explore our new world."

And everyone went out of the window to follow Angelina. Only Niam-Niam refused to take the risk; Désolant had to grab hold of him to deposit him on the wall, and it still took him a few minutes to pluck up the courage to walk other than on all fours.

The new world, as Farandoul had called it, lacked extent. The minaret had been severed two-thirds of the way down; the top floors formed our friends' whole domain. The inhabitants of this little world observed that they could come and go all the way around the minaret without any difficulty; the center always stayed beneath their feet. They soon spread out around the surface, the most distant appearing to the others to be walking upside down. The ladies were amused by these bizarre appearances and laughed loudly.

All of a sudden, Angelina, invisible on the other side, screeched: "The Arnautes!"

"What do you mean, the Arnautes?" cried Farandoul, racing away from his friends to the antipodes in a few strides. "I think we're safe from them here!"

But what a surprise awaited him on the other side! A ladder and two Arnautes were rotating 20 meters from the minaret, dragged in its wake as it was itself in that of the comet.

The two poor devils, clinging convulsively to their ladder, seemed half dead with fright. They were looking at their enemies with expressions of utter bewilderment, doubtless astonished—if they were any long capable of being astonished by anything—to see them walking upside down.

The ladder and the two Arnautes formed a satellite of the minaret and were orbiting around it in a regular manner—but the minaret, better equipped than our own globe, possessed a whole constellation of satellites, for, in addition to the ladder, several other objects were rotating at various distances.

In the largest of these satellites, Niam-Niam joyfully recognized the lost sack of rice, then, behind it, a copper cooking-pot, a coffee-pot, a pipe, a bag of coffee and two plucked chickens.

"That's useful," said Désolant. "Can we go and fetch them."

Niam-Niam tugged his ear and made a grimace.

Behind the chickens, another larger satellite appeared, rising over the minaret's horizon. It was another human satellite; the legs appeared first, then a body and skirts that had ridden up to various degrees, and then a head…and the colonists of the minaret recognized, to their surprise, the sweet face of Miss Flora MacKlaknavor, ruddy and hatless, more terrified than seemed possible, advancing slowly and majestically three meters from the minaret.

Before our friends had recovered from their surprise, the poor child passed overhead and disappeared, whimpering.

The most pressing matter was to study the path of the minaret around the unknown star. It soon became clear that they were gradually drawing nearer to it. At daybreak, 300 or 400 meters had separated the minaret from its surface; now they were passing over it at much closer range.

The new world was exactly similar to the Earth, and if our friends had not seen the later disappear into the distance they would easily have been able to believe that they were above some region of the paternal star: the same general physiognomy, the same vegetation and...the same inhabitants; for, behind a clump of trees, they perceived with a perfectly comprehensible astonishment two individuals similar in every respect to human beings.

These two creatures were running with the typical gait of the Earth's inhabitants; they had arms, legs, hair and beards, and were even wearing clothes. They too had perceived their satellite and were trying to enter into communication with its inhabitants. Farandoul hastily took his telescope out of his pocket, looked with sustained attention, and seemed to be struck by a prodigious astonishment.

"Unbelievable!" he cried. "They're French soldiers!"

Caroline grabbed the telescope in her turn. "An officer," she said, "and an African *chasseur*."

"Very strange! Is France colonizing the comets?"

But the minaret, carried away along its orbit, had already left the two French soldiers far behind.

The minaret's satellites were rotating around it with chronometric regularity. The savant Désolant recorded their periods in his notebook. The Arnautes were tracing the most distant orbit around their primary; their revolution was completed in 11 minutes 38.25 seconds. The sack of rice, much closer, only took six minutes 12 seconds. Finally, the unfortunate Miss Flora MacKlaknavor accomplished her journey in exactly four minutes.

We're in a sticky situation here, Farandoul thought. *It's rather glorious for us to be elevated to the status of stars, but I can't see any way that we can survive on our planet, without provisions gravitating around us as if to subject us to the torture of Tantalus. In a couple of hours, we'll be victims of famine!*

An appeal from Niam-Niam interrupted the course of his reflections. The young savage, tormented by a healthy appetite, was hunting high and low with the vague hope of discovering something to eat. His search had not been in vain; he had caught a bat in the minaret's stairway and discovered a few pigeons' nests hidden in the sculptures under the balcony. Twenty unhappy pigeons, frightened by their voyage through the sky, were hiding in holes with their heads tucked under their wings.

That was a small resource. Niam-Niam was ordered to collect these birds carefully and to shut the up in the little cupola that terminated the minaret. The culinary question remaining open, one of the queens suggested that for lack of *petit pois* to accompany the pigeon, the rice would furnish an excellent seasoning.

Farandoul started. "We don't have to grow thinner," he cried, "while the satellites of Tantalus pass regularly before our famished eyes! We'll try fishing for the satellites!"

Descending through a window into the minaret's interior, he searched for a means of fabricating a harpoon large enough to reach the coveted satellites. It was not easy, but necessity is the mother of invention, and they finally succeeded by cutting up one of the steps to fashion two narrow strips, which were then joined end to end and solidly tied together with cords. An Arnaute spear supplied even greater length, and its barbed point completed the harpoon.

The moment had come; Désolant and Farandoul maneuvered the harpoon, waiting for the satellites. Flora Klaknavor was the first to rise; she extended her hand toward the harpoon, but the queens swiftly came forward and lowered the point. Poor Flora disappeared over the horizon.

The coffee-pot and the pipe came next, traveling in convoy. The re-raised harpoon hooked them without difficulty. As soon as they arrived in the zone of attraction they fell down to the minaret of their own accord.

"The chickens! The chickens!" cried Niam-Niam.

The harpoon was quickly re-elevated, but it only seized one as the passed by; the other continued ion its course.

"Next time!" said Farandoul, getting ready for another satellite.

The copper cooking-pot rose over the horizon. The harpoon reached its height, but a false movement caused it to miss the catch.

"We need it, though, to cook the chicken!" murmured Angelina.

"Quick! The sack of rice…it's too high!"

"No! Come on, Niam-Niam—climb up on my shoulders!"

Niam-Niam was agile; he leapt on to Farandoul's shoulders and grabbed the heavy harpoon.

"Very good! Very good!"

Niam-Niam had nerve; he intended to have three meals a day, as on Earth, so, when the sack of rice passed over his head, he threw the harpoon with all his strength and all his skill.

He reached it at the first attempt, but the sack was heavy; Niam-Niam had to cling hard to the harpoon to prevent it from departing with the satellite. Finally, he had the joy of seeing it descend. Farandoul and Désolant seized the harpoon and the three of them, combining their efforts, brought the rebel satellite into the zone of attraction.

The rice was theirs! It would provide food for at least three weeks, perhaps a month. Niam-Niam was about to jump down from Farandoul's shoulders when an unexpected incident occurred.

Satellite MacKlaknavor, which they had forgotten, had completed its tour of the minaret and come back. Miss Flora's extended hands seized poor Niam-Niam's wooly hair and lifted him off his elevated station.

Niam-Niam opened his mouth to scream, but was unable to utter a sound. He was dragged into space by the ruddy Flora and passed in his turn into the condition of a star.

"Let's keep still and wait!" said Farandoul.

Flora and Niam-Niam reappeared four minutes later. The passengers in the minaret could not help smiling at the sight of his frightened expression, but they burst out laughing when they saw that, in spite of his terror, Niam-Niam had taken advantage of his involuntary passage across the firmament to capture the satellite-cooking-pot and the satellite-chicken. The result of this laughter was that they missed him again.

Niam-Niam's desolation was redoubled, but four minutes later he grabbed the harpoon and his friends' efforts drew him to the ground with his cooking-pot, his chicken and his persecutor, Miss Flora MacKlaknavor. The minaret had one more inhabitant! Miss Klaknavor overwhelmed Farandoul with her thanks; the latter forwarded them to Niam-Niam, her true savior.

The queens received this new companion coldly; they could not forget that it was to the Klaknavors that they owed the pleasure of voyaging through the sky on an exceedingly narrow star. As for Miss Flora, she dared not move, and released squeals of terror on seeing the minaret's guests, now accustomed to their situation, carelessly walking around the monument.

"Now that we've finished fishing for satellites, it's a matter of dining," said Farandoul, after a momentary pause. "What do you think, Mesdames?"

Niam-Niam was about to reply when a shot rang out! A bullet whistled past and flattened itself out two paces away from the black queen Kalunda, who immediately dived for her bow.

"The Arnautes! We forgot about the Arnautes!"

Indeed, the Arnautes, still hanging on to their ladder, having witnessed the angling of the minaret's satellites, had been awaiting their turn impatiently. Finally, realizing that no one aboard the star appeared to be thinking about their salvation, the more impatient of the two had used a bullet to jog the memories of the minaret's inhabitants.

No one wanted to have them for companions. The only response Farandoul made was to show them that the harpoon was much too short—but the Arnaute, becoming increasingly furious, seized his comrade's weapon and dispatched a second bullet at our friends.

"Damn!" said Farandoul. "That's a satellite that might become inconvenient for us. Fortunately, he's a very bad shot!"

"What a strange star ours is!" said Désolant, sadly, as a third bullet flattened itself out beside him. "A world subjected to a fusillade by its own satellite! It's exactly as if the Moon were to bombard the Earth!"

317

"Good! Yet another bullet! Accursed Arnautes! What if we were to reply?"

"Wait!" said Désolant. "Our satellite is deviating from its course at every rifle-shot…the force of the recoil is throwing the Arnautes and their satellite backwards every time…in a little while, we'll see something curious! We're not far distant from the comet that's dragging us in its wake, and our Arnautes, rotating around us, will find themselves even closer in a minute…their rifle-shots will carrying them backwards into the comet's zone of attraction, they'll tip over and fall upon it! We'll be free of them!"

Désolant's prediction did not take long to be realized. The Arnautes, continuing their fusillade, suddenly reached the comet's zone of attraction. The ladder to which they were clinging executed a see-saw motion, and launched them into space…

The inhabitants of the minaret watched them twirling with their ladder as they fell at least 50 meters. Fortunately for them, there was a large lake at exactly the right place to receive them; the water undoubtedly softened the impact, for they reappeared on the surface, swam a short way and soon set foot on the shore.

Just as the inhabitants of the minaret were surrendering to their satisfaction they spotted a new object of astonishment. A hundred meters away from them, on the unknown comet, men were coming at a run to assist the Arnautes—and those men were wearing the easily-recognizable red uniform of the English army!

Farandoul and Désolant rubbed their eyes.

"What can it mean? This comet, if it is a comet, is inhabited by French and English soldiers!"

The minaret, however, carried away by its velocity had already left the English soldiers far behind.

The sudden arrival of night took the reflective friends by surprise.

Désolant made a rapid calculation. They day had lasted two hours 49 minutes! And they had not yet had the lightest meal! Hunger was making itself felt;

318

they were proceeding by starlight to begin the preparations for a meal—breakfast, lunch or dinner, it did not matter which—when the same idea occurred to all of them.

What about thirst? No one had thought about thirst. They had food-supplies, but no beverages: no water to cook the rice, no water to drink!

It was serious.

Suddenly, Farandoul got up. "We shall drink, Mesdames," he said. "I promise you that! A little while ago, our Arnautes fell into a lake, so there's water on the unknown comet that is drawing us along. Well, why can't we draw water from its rivers and lakes with our cooking-pot? We're flying scarcely 100 meters above the water we desire so much, so we need a cord of that length. Let's make one!"

The meal was postponed again. The stairway of the minaret had a simple bell-cord for a handrail; this was divided into two, and the two pieces made up 60 meters. The rest was more difficult to find; scarves, belts and bedsheets were cut into strips; the queens went so far as to offer their hair, a cruel sacrifice that Farandoul refused. Finally, they thought they had obtained the necessary length and waited impatiently for daylight.

The Moon had risen, its rays displaying some kind of expanse of water on the comet's surface.[78]

"Water!" cried Farandoul. "Quickly, the cooking-pot!"

The principal difficulty was throwing the cooking-pot out of the layer of air forming the minaret's atmosphere, in order to reach that of the comet. After a few unsuccessful attempts, Farandoul succeeded; instead of falling back, the cooking-pot slid rapidly towards the badly-needed water.

There was a stir of anxiety. Was the rope long enough? The last fathom was paid out and the cooking-pot stopped. O joy! It had reached the water! Carefully, Farandoul hauled up the full pot—but he stopped half way.

"Damn! The cooking-pot will perform a somersault as it passes into our zone of attraction, and we'll lose out water. What can we do…? We still have one intact sheet—get hold of it. Are you ready…? Here goes!"

A loud noise cut him off. The cooking-pot and its contents, having come within ten meters of the minaret, fell into the sheet. A receptacle brought by Niam-Niam and slipped under the sheet saved about half the transported water.

---

[78] The reference to a moon is puzzling, the Earth's Moon being far away by now; Robida might, however, be remembering that in Verne's *Hector Servadac* the comet that carried various Frenchmen, Englishmen, Spaniards and Russians—including, we now discover, Farandoul and his companions—away from various parts of the Mediterranean shore had previously captured an asteroid, Nerina, which served as its moon.

The cries of joy that welcomed this result were halted by an exclamation from Désolant. The poor scientist had received part of the cooking-pots contents as a splash in his face and he had swallowed a few sips.

"Stop!" he cried. "The water's salty!"

So the comet had oceans on its surface! They would have to wait for daylight to resume fishing for water. By the first light of dawn they perceived, to their joy, a river and a little lake. The fishing recommenced, and this time the bucket came back with fresh water.

They had time to collect three bucketfuls; on the fourth trip the bucket was almost captured by a man emerging from a bush—it was the staff-officer they had glimpsed the previous day.

The white queen Angelina leapt upon Farandoul's telescope, lowered it towards the comet, and cried out: "I recognize him! It's Hector!"

"What?" cried Farandoul. "You know an inhabitant of this comet?"

"I've met him in Paris—it's Hector Servadac."

The French officer had already disappeared, but they thought that they heard these syllables, launched with all the force of his lungs:

"....lina!"

He too had recognized the white queen; no doubt remained. Farandoul remained pensive. While Niam-Niam prepared a nice meal of chicken with rice for the famished company and the latter watched all the regions glimpsed the following day file beneath them, they perceived the English soldiers and heard themselves being hailed in various languages, including English, Spanish and even Russian.

Guided by an inexplicable freak of chance, Farandoul had bumped into yet another of Jules Verne's heroes.

Hector Servadac, in the narrative published by Jules Verne, has not said anything about the minaret; he has passed over his meeting with Farandoul in silence and has carefully avoided mentioning the four queens. His troubled conscience forbade it—and there can be no doubt that, if he had recounted his adventures sincerely, the celebrated writer would have refused him his sympathy. What he has not done, we shall do! We shall reveal the deplorable extremities to which the men of the comet Gallia went in order to capture the passengers in the minaret: crimes to make the most distant nebulas dissolve in tears and to make the Great She-Bear herself turn red! [79]

The days passed aboard the minaret with vertiginous rapidity, less than three hours of daylight and three of darkness. The little planet's inhabitants organized their lives as well as possible, but they were beginning to grow bored. They had instituted rationing; it was necessary to make the provisions last as long as possible, for they had no idea how to replenish them.

---

[79] In France, the constellation Ursa Major is popularly known as *la Grande Ourse* [the Great She-Bear].

Farandoul and the savant Désolant were working on the key problem: what means could they employ to make a descent to the comet's surface?

After many discussions, it had been decided that the only way was to construct a 12-meter ladder, which, solidly fixed to the minaret, would reach the comet's zone of attraction. Once there, it would only be necessary to slide down the rope.

The staircase of the minaret, demolished step by step, furnished the materials for the ladder. It was not an easy task, but the makeshift ladder was finally ready.

One morning, the inhabitants of the comet were able to see their satellite ornamented by its appendage. Niam-Niam had volunteered to attempt the descent; he already had the rope around his waist. He would set forth while Farandoul held on to it.

Down below, the scene became animated; all the inhabitants of the comet, seemingly scattered until now, had gathered on a hillock, gesticulating frantically. Frenchmen, Englishmen, Russians and Spaniards surrounded our friends' former satellites, the two Arnautes.

As the minaret approached, the appealing gestures were multiplied and an immense shout rose up from this cosmopolitan population:

"The ladies! *Les dames! Las senoras!*"

Farandoul shuddered, and understood the full extent of this new peril. There were only men on the comet![80] These men, seeing an asteroid ornamented with a charming feminine population passing regularly over their heads every six hours, less than 100 meters away, were undoubtedly seeking to capture the satellite!

Hector Servadac could be distinguished in the midst of the group. Making a megaphone with his hands, he shouted these few words:

"Our world must live, but it lacks an Eve. Give the order to the minaret's inhabitants to descend...a matter of public salvation..."

Farandoul furrowed his brows.

"There's a way to settle everything," murmured Caroline. "Send them Miss Klaknavor!"

Flora uttered a shriek of horror. "Shocking! Shocking!"

"Miss Klaknavor refuses," said Farandoul, sadly. "We shan't try to force her; she'll remain with us. We must reduce our rations, alas, to make them last even longer."

---

[80] In fact, if Verne's account of Servadac's adventure can be trusted—and most of the details given here are in conformity with it—there was one female on the comet, albeit a very young one: a girl named Nina. Robida has also omitted any mention of the Jew Isaac Hakkabut, one of Verne's less fortunate stereotypes.

IX

When they passed over the spot occupied by the comet's inhabitants again on the following day, they soon perceived that things on the ground had changed. Servadac and his companions having employed their time productively, a construction had been rapidly erected on the hillock. Twenty men had busied themselves felling large trees in a neighboring forest under the direction of a staff-officer, and the enormous beams had been formed into scaffolding of sorts, of gigantic proportions.

"Do they intend to scale our sky?" asked Désolant, in surprise.

"It certainly seems that way to me," replied Farandoul. "And look— they've calculated our course accurately; we're passing directly over the top of their construction without any means of avoiding it."

There was, indeed, no means whatsoever to effect any change in the path of their star; it was necessary to follow the same course, repeatedly passing over Servadac's position.

The construction advanced rapidly, the constructors working with feverish rapidity. Fifteen days sufficed for them to bring their scaffolding to two-thirds of the height necessary to reach the minaret. Servadac, installed on the top floor, urged the workers on. Palmyrin Rosette, an old astronomer also carried away by the comet, had ceased his calculations and abandoned his telescope, and did not blush to place his science in the service of the minaret's persecutors.

And yet, the situation was grave. No other astronomer had ever had such an opportunity to sound the depths of the planetary realm, to study its mysteries at close range! He alone could determine exactly how many kilometers the comet had dragged those few inhabitants of the Earth. Carried away with a few fragments of the terrestrial globe and escorted through the void by a vagabond star, the men had already been able to see several of the solar system's planets— Mars, Venus and Jupiter—at close range. Now, in its mad course, the comet was heading straight for Saturn, increasing in size on the horizon with it three rings and its eight moons of different colors. Except that, Farandoul and Désolant anxiously thought, the comet seemed to be heading to its doom. If no change of course occurred, it would inevitably break up shortly before arriving on the surface of that marvelous Saturn.[81]

---

[81] In Verne's version, the comet reaches its aphelion 220 million leagues from the Sun, well short of the orbit of Saturn, having taken a year to get that far. In Robida's version, its already mind-boggling velocity seems to have been increased by at least two further orders of magnitude; given the scant attention he pays to the law of gravity and its likely effects on the weight of the spacefarers, however, there is nothing particularly surprising in this.

Servadac had opened negotiations some time before. At each passage of the satellite, he was at the summit of his scaffolding, and engaged Farandoul in a rapidly-interrupted conversation.

"Make arrangements to descend, or we'll shoot you as you pass by!" Servadac shouted one morning—and when no one replied, he gave a signal, and four snipers posted on the scaffolding opened fire on Farandoul and Désolant with muskets.

Finally, the scaffolding attained the required height; its summit had reached the course followed by the minaret. An immense net mounted on long poles was deployed to catch it as it passed, and...

As Farandoul perceived these preparations he could not help but smile—but what he saw at the foot of the scaffolding froze the smile on his lips. The people of the comet were not aiming to capture their satellite in the net; much less did they want it to break their scaffolding. Their plan was quite different. A little balloon, still tethered to the ground, was linked to the net by a cable. The minaret would carry away the net, and with it the balloon—in the gondola of which were ten or 12 men, armed to the teeth.

The minaret's inhabitants had hardly had time to deduce Servadac's plan when it was put into execution. The minaret ran straight into the net and bore it away into the sky.

In addition to the men in the gondola, a few redcoats hanging on to the cords were attempting to reach the minaret. The balloon, hauled by strong arms, quickly came within 15 or 20 meters of the net, but it could not advance any further, retained there by a pole carried away with the filaments. To reach the minaret it was necessary to cross the 15 or 20 meters on the slender pole, but Farandoul, Désolant and Niam-Niam were in defensive positions, dug in on the balcony, rifles in hand.

The assailants held a council in the gondola of the balloon. Servadac wanted to attempt a decisive assault. "Let's go!" he said. "It's futile to let ourselves be picked off one by one; let's all attack at the same time! Within two minutes, we can be masters of the minaret. Are you with me? Charge!"

He had scarcely pronounced this word than a frightful change of circumstances occurred. The balloon had just been turned upside down, spilling some of those who were manning it into the sky. The balloon was still attached to the minaret, but the latter suddenly changed direction, abandoning the comet and hurtling through the air at increasing velocity, with terrible whistling sounds.

"Saturn!" yelled Servadac in his companions' ears. "We're falling on to Saturn!"

At this speech, Palmyrin Rosette recovered his scientific ardor. He forgot the white and black queens and uttered cries of joy mingled with terror.

Aboard the minaret, not a word was spoken. They were hardly breathing, in the expectation of terrible complications.

That anxiety lasted three hours. Saturn was coming nearer with fearsome rapidity. They had passed between the planet and its ring some time before. At the beginning of the third hour, the ground appeared to be no more than a few leagues away; the fatal moment was imminent.

Another few minutes, as long as centuries, went by; eventually, a storm of screams rose up beneath the unfortunate balloon—screams that had not been uttered by the balloon's occupants. Farandoul got to his feet.

The screaming was coming from Saturn!

The minaret, showing down considerably, was no floating less than 20 meters above the planet, slowly drawing nearer to the ground.

The frightened Saturnians were still screaming. Some distance ahead of the minaret, large buildings of an elegant architecture raised their slender bell-towers into the air. Farandoul saw them in time; his companions quickly went back inside the minaret; he was the last to slide in through a window.

Two seconds later, the minaret crashed noisily into one of the edifices he had glimpsed, broke a huge window, went through a few partition walls and came to a halt, after having gone all the way through the building into the branches of a gigantic solitary tree, planted in the middle of a marvelous flower-garden.

The impact was relatively soft; the only accidents occasioned by the transit were the fainting of three of the four queens and a prodigious nose-bleed on the part of Niam-Niam, who had fallen on that facial ornament.

The balloon carrying Servadac and his friends had remained on the far side of the edifice, in the façade partly caved in by the minaret. Loud shots were audible, and the sound of comings and goings. Désolant was about to climb down the tree and run to fetch a little water from a magnificent fountain, in order to throw it in the faces of the queens who had fainted, when Farandoul stopped him with a gesture.

The Saturnians were running out in a crowd, shouting incoherently and making threatening gestures. In the midst of them, already in chains, Servadac and his friends were marching with heads bowed.

"Look out!" exclaimed Farandoul. "The inhabitants of Saturn don't seem very friendly. How strange! Look at their conformation! Look—wings, a trunk, and flippers!"

On recovering consciousness, the queens had put their heads out of the window and could not retain exclamations of astonishment.

"Silence!" Farandoul murmured. "They're not looking in our direction. They didn't see us fall, and the foliage is hiding us."

Indeed, none of the Saturnians seemed to suspect the presence of a minaret in their tree; all eyes were on the prisoners—Servadac, his batman Ben-Zouf, Palmyrin Rosette, six Spaniards, two English officers and seven soldiers—who had fallen with the balloon and had almost been flattened.

The unfortunates, already clad in chains were rigorously interrogated by Saturnians of military bearing. All that Servadac could do was to raise an arm loaded with chains into the air and point to the sky.

In response to a sign from the leader indicating the far end of the garden, the prisoners were rapidly dragged off in that direction.

This is an opportune moment to talk about the bizarre conformation of Saturn's inhabitants. Like Terrans, the people of Saturn have arms and legs, terminating, admittedly, in palmate hands and feet, or flippers. Thus far, nothing very strange; with boots and gloves they would not appear excessively odd—but here is something else. The Saturnians have two wings on their back similar to those of flying fish!

Let us now consider their faces; the nose, atrophied in us, is fully-developed, swaying in the middle of their faces like an elephant's trunk. This immense nose has various functions, and we can see these various functions being carried out in the crowd filling the garden. A few Saturnians of high rank are carrying parasols with this nose; others are picking flowers from the flower-beds. Further away, a few are flying overhead, and their deployed noses function as a third wing. Finally, young Saturnians are paddling in the large pools of the park; for them, the multifunctional nose has become a flipper and a sort of rudder for changes of direction.

And the female Saturnians, you ask? They are, quite simply, charming. The gentle sex is well-represented in the crowd. These ladies possess almost the same ornaments as the males, with the difference that the feet and hands are more elegantly webbed, the wings more delicately hemmed and the trunk, slimmer and more flexible, undulates more gracefully as it follows the rhythmic sway of the march. Trunks à la Roxelane[82] are quite common, especially among females of the pink variety; for we have neglected to say that on Saturn, the feminine genus includes seven varieties—white, pink, green, blue, yellow, violet and dark brown—each forming a distinct species.

Seven female species, as opposed to one male! As you can see, Saturn is an advanced planet.

Every Saturnian male, at an age fixed by law, which varies according to latitude, is supposed to espouse a specimen of each of the varieties, determined by drawing lots. It is both a free and obligatory marriage, a wise institution that the Saturnians had possessed for centuries—admittedly, after having fought for a long time against the obstinacy of reactionary and retrograde minds to obtain it.

Servadac and his companions, brutally dragged outside the park, had been imprisoned in a room at the bottom of a tower guarding the main entrance to the palace. There, they had been left to their own reflections for six hours. The reflections of these unfortunates were not rosy; still bruised by their fall, and put in irons, they were tormented by apprehensions of treatment more barbarous still.

Finally, as the seventh hour began, the doors opened and jailers armed to the teeth came forward exceedingly cautiously to fetch the prisoners out. A numerous assembly, civil rather than military, was waiting for them outside. There were still a few former members of the armed forces, but in the great majority of the audience Palmyrin Rosette undoubtedly recognized colleagues: scientists, almost all of them bald, just like Terran scientists, and similarly ornamented with spectacles, green eyeshades and acoustic trumpets.

A glimmer of hope came into the mind of the poor astronomer.

These scientists, we can reveal, made up a commission urgently appointed by the Saturnian academies to examine the supernatural beings fallen miraculously from the sky, to decide whether they should be judged as criminals or considered as simple phenomena—a difficult question to resolve.

---

[82] The description "*nez à la Roxelane*" was often used in 19th century French literature with reference to turned-up noses; it presumably derived from a portrait of the redoubtable wife of the Ottoman emperor Suleiman the Magnificent.

One by one, the prisoners filed before the commission, with Servadac at the head. They were examined from a distance, and prudently. They were turned around and around, and made to walk back and forth. Attempts were made to make them fly. Their hands were examined with curiosity, their noses with disdain.

Palmyrin Rosette, used to the methods and customs of scientific societies, followed the discussions and almost understood the speeches; he saw from the pantomime that a proposal had been made, which was put to the vote and adopted almost unanimously.

Finally, one of the Saturnian scientists said a few words to the soldiers and, taking the lead in the procession, went back into the park with the prisoners. In the middle of an immense throng arrived from the town, they were take into a part of the garden separated from the remainder by railings and a ditch. A large inscription placed above the entrance gate intrigued the prisoners considerably.

What did it mean? Was this a prison or an abattoir?

The answer was not long in coming. A broad pathway dividing the garden was bordered along its entire length with small solidly-railed enclosures and cages of various sizes sealed with thick bars. The enclosures and cages were almost all occupied by animals as strange as the Saturnians. There were equivalents of our elephants, tigers and lions, and numerous animals impossible to classify, hybrid beings with birds wings on the bodies of mastodons, six-legged beasts and even two-headed ones, huge birds with beaks armed with long tusks, etc., etc.

Reaching the mid-point of the path, the procession stopped. Two cages, the largest of all, were empty. The doors were opened and the prisoners pushed into them, after their chains had been removed.

"A zoological garden!" cried Palmyrin Rosette. "We're part of a menagerie! The wretches! What an insult to a colleague!"

And all the prisoners, furious at this treatment, hurled themselves at the bars of their cage and shook them furiously. The crowd gathered outside recoiled in fear, but the menagerie's keepers appeared then, passing long poles between the bars and vigorously belaboring the shoulders of the most furious.

O rage! O dolor! How shameful for an astronomer like Palmyrin, officers like Servadac and the Englishmen! To be locked up in a menagerie like mere animals! To be beaten by brutal keepers before the eyes of an imbecilic crowd!

And to put the cap on the humiliation, the time to distribute nourishment having arrived, keepers bearing large baskets full of blackish meat appeared, throwing bloody morsels into all the cages! The neighboring beasts released long howls; in the cages opposite those of the unfortunate Terrans, members of a bear-like species climbed tree-trunks and swung stupidly back and forth to earn their pittance.

Finally, the baskets reached the Terrans. The crowd parted and the keepers, placing large pieces on the ends of their long forks, passed them very carefully through the bars.

Servadac could not stand it; he leapt on a bone and threw it forcefully at the face of a stupidly-staring gawker in the front row. The unfortunate Saturnian released a horrible scream and fainted in the arms of his seven wives; he had had his nose—or rather, his trunk—broken.

X.

Three days and three nights passed without Farandoul being able to find any trace of Servadac. For three nights he wandered at hazard in the labyrinthine streets of the great city, whose name he did not know, into which hazard had thrown him. This was not without great danger to himself, with no lack of pursuits by bands of Saturnian night-owls.

If he had understood their language, he would have been rapidly informed by the gigantic posters plastered on every wall that announced the arrival in the national menagerie of extraordinary animals, viewable on payment of a small supplementary fee. A long description followed, issued by the scientific commission and illustrated with fairly accurate portraits drawn by the finest animal artists. Farandoul recognized them, and was led to think that the Terrans had perhaps been engaged by some theater under the title of a "great attraction"—but how could he verify the fact? How could he make certain?

Not far from this flamboyant poster there was another of more serious appearance, but which Farandoul understood no better, announcing a measure corresponding to our declaration of a state of siege. The government, to reassure the population, ordered the organization of night-patrols with the aim of capturing the ferocious beats glimpsed in the city for three nights running.

Going out into the city at the beginning of the fourth night, in spite of his prudence, Farandoul ran straight into one of these patrols; comprised as it was, however, of a militia that was scarcely battle-hardened, his presence alone caused it to fall back. The bravest fled as fast as their wings could carry them to carry the alert to all the posts. Soon, Farandoul heard the sound of gongs summoning the garrison, and to avoid further encounters he was obliged to double back to the park.

There was one corner of the park that he had not explored, that being the very location of the menagerie. Farandoul went into it, at hazard, curious to make the acquaintance of the Saturnian fauna. The ferocious beasts, waking with a start, growled dully.

Farandoul went from cage to cage, examining the Saturnian beasts by the light of the moons. In this manner he arrived at the cages enclosing Servadac and his companions. They were presumably sleeping in the darker depths; Farandoul did not see them.

He thought the cages were empty and was about to pass on when he almost stumbled over a bizarre instrument projecting through the bars of the cage. Farandoul stepped back in astonishment. The instrument resembled a telescope! What did it imply? Were the Saturnian animals studying the sky? As he looked closer, an exclamation escaped him. The animal at the telescope was Palmyrin Rosette.

Other exclamations responded. Servadac and the others bounded out of the depths of the cage.

"You, here, shut up in a menagerie!"

"By Saint George!" said a fat Englishman with a crestfallen expression. "What a humiliation for officers of the queen! The Saturnians consider us as ferocious animals and treat us as such. We're part of the menagerie, with bear-like species for neighbors. They beat us, and pass us raw meat on the end of a fork. During the day, the crowds come to laugh at our faces; the ladies try to provoke us and the infants throw little pellets of black bread at us. Sad, sad!"

Servadac, roaring internally, did not say a word. Suddenly, Palmyrin, who had not left the telescope, released a cry of joy.

"There she is! My calculations were correct!"

"Who's *she*?"

"My comet—our comet! Gallia! The one we abandoned for this horrible Saturn. She's coming back to exactly the same point…"

Indeed, a brilliant comet, undulating its long tail, had just risen radiantly above the horizon. Palmyrin, suspended from his telescope, seemed to be imploring it with his hand on his heart.

Meanwhile, a party of keepers, woken up by the howling in the menagerie, was advancing from the end of the pathway.

Farandoul took Servadac's hand. "Listen, my ex-enemy—have a little more patience. Tomorrow night I'll come to set you free! Until tomorrow!" And Farandoul vanished into the darkness, leaving the unfortunates a glimmer of hope.

On his arrival at the large tree, he found the minaret colony in a state of agitation. A young Saturnian and a female of the blue variety, presumably an amorous couple, had come to bill and coo in the tree. The appearance of Niam-Niam had surprised them so much that they had almost let themselves fall to the ground without having the strength to use their wings.

This circumstance made Farandoul anxious. Was their refuge about to be discovered? He decided to mount a careful guard, and, in the meantime, to prepare the weapons for a serious defense.

They spent the rest of the night making plans for the liberation of the presumed ferocious animals.

It was agreed that on the following night, Farandoul and Désolant, leaving the queens under the guard of Niam-Niam, would go break into the cages in the menagerie. The colony, further reinforced by 18 men with five rifles, revolvers and gunpowder, would then attempt to take possession of some easily-defensible edifice—a tower or castle—entrench themselves therein and open negotiations with the Saturnians in order to formulate a treaty.

"It's a good plan," said Désolant, "and it will succeed. I can see us already, recognized citizens of Saturn, owners of a patch of ground, founders of a prosperous colony. We shall form a new race. I don't think the acclimatization will be difficult, the air being perfectly healthy. Before long, we'll feel the effects of the environment…"

"What effects?"

"Well, just as Europeans transplanted to Guinea soon take on a darker coloration, which becomes black in a few generations, I suppose that, submitted to the same general conditions as the Saturnians, we'll soon begin to transform ourselves. Our noses will become…"

"How horrid!" cried Caroline and Angelina at the same time.

"Yes, Mesdames, your nose will elongate into trunks, you'll grow flippers…it's the transformist theory of Darwin. Have you read Darwin?"[83]

---

[83] As this notion bears not the slightest resemblance to the theory of evolution by natural selection, Désolant presumably had not read Darwin either; he appears to be assuming a Lamarckian theory of evolution, in which adaptation to the environment is achieved by the inheritance of actively-acquired characteristics. Ro-

The queens placing no credence in the predictions of the savant Désolant, consoled themselves very rapidly. For his part, the scientist was perfectly satisfied with his destiny and did not regret the loss of Earth at all. What a joy for him: an entire world to get to know, a whole new nature to study! His only annoyance was not being able to send reports to the Société de la Géographie.

Another day had to go by before our friends could set out to liberate the other Terrans: the waiting seemed long.

When night fell, Farandoul was glad to see the weather becoming stormy. Heavy clouds, passing before the moons and over the rings of Saturn, covered the garden in protective darkness. As the first crashes of thunder sounded, he descended with Désolant and headed for the menagerie.

Prey to a profound terror, the animals were howling lamentably. The two men ran to Servadac's cage and found the Terrans overexcited by anticipation. The bars of the cage were so strong and well-tempered as to negate all hope of breaking them; fortunately, Farandoul and Désolant had found a few builders' tools left in the park and picked them up *en route*. They attacked the ground underneath the cages and succeeded, after two hours of Herculean labor, in making an opening large enough for the prisoners to scramble through.

The storm had turned into a tempest; a veritable cyclone was battering Saturn, breaking trees, knocking down walls and pouring furious torrents of water everywhere. Farandoul was eager to get back to the minaret, and they were about to leave when Désolant noticed that one of the prisoners was missing.

"Indeed," said Servadac, "there are 17 of us! Who is still in the cage? Ah! It's our astronomer, Monsieur Rosette."

"Wait! Wait!" replied a voice from within the cage. "I'm finishing my calculations. It's certainly necessary to flee now—our comet's coming back! We can expect an impact. Gallia has gone around Saturn and is coming back with lightning speed, getting closer and closer. She's subject to the planet's attraction; she has already passed the ring and pulverized one of the moons."

"What are you saying?"

"I'm saying that we're on the point of a new cataclysm. We'll witness a frightful encounter between two stars and I don't want to be at the point of impact—although there's not much hope of avoiding it. If the impact is head-on, Saturn will explode like a shell!"

"Bring him along!" Farandoul ordered.

---

bida is, of course, writing in his usual purely farcical spirit, but the terminology of Désolant's argument does leave open the possibility that he might have had Hippolyte Taine's recently-published account of literary evolution in mind. Taine had tried to explain the evolution of literature in pseudo-Lamarckian terms of *"race, milieu et moment"* [heredity, environment and history]—an argument easily adaptable to an explanation of the emergence of scientific romance (complete with alien extraterrestrials) in the 19th century.

Two robust Englishmen seized the astronomer by the legs.

"My telescope! My telescope!" howled Palmyrin.

Farandoul had picked it up. He showed it to him, and Palmyrin, more calmly, allowed himself to be carried away in the midst of the storm.

The park had suffered; on every side trees uprooted by the tempest were lying across the paths. They did not run; they flew, borne by a fearful wind.

On the way the Terrans encountered a regiment of Saturnians, which was heading back to town, and which ran away to avoid a fight. Alas, in his impatience, Farandoul did not pay enough attention to two sealed palanquins escorted by the Saturnian soldiers; no tightness in his chest gave him warning; he had no suspicion of imminent misfortune.

Running at the head of his men, he tried to peer through the darkness to find the tree with the dense foliage in which the minaret was hidden.

Eventually, the gigantic silhouette appeared, shaking in the wind. Farandoul briskly climbed the branches and reached the opening of the minaret.

"Niam-Niam! Kalunda!" he cried. "Angelina!"

There was no response. Farandoul went inside the minaret, and only took a minute to understand the full extent of his misfortune. The Saturnians had abducted the four queens! A trunk severed by a sword showed that the valiant warrior-women had attempted an impossible resistance.

Suddenly, Farandoul released a cry of joy. He had just heard Niam-Niam's voice at the foot of the tree. In the young savage's arms was a feminine shadow, hanging limply. One of the captives had been retrieved.

"Which one is she?" cried Farandoul, letting himself slide down to the ground.

The feminine shadow sat up and extended her arms toward Farandoul.

"Damnation!" said the furious Farandoul. "Flora Klaknavor!"

Niam-Niam gave voice to a pitiful exclamation. "Not my fault, master! It was so dark...!"

A gust of wind more violent than the rest interrupted his protests. Everything on the ground fell down, and was enveloped by a whirlwind of branches and stones torn away from the temple. The tree with the minaret cracked under that terrible assault, bent down to the ground, eventually came upright again, and finally, vanquished by the hurricane, collapsed on to the ground with its roots in the air.

The Terrans, trapped under the branches and more-or-less crushed, were trying to get up when Palmyrin Rosette's excited voice rose above the din of the devastation:

"The comet! The comet! It's the impact!"

Those who heard him clung on desperately to whatever was close to hand, prepared for any catastrophe.

For ten long minutes, they were tossed about by the storm-wind and rolled along the ground with the ruins of the tree. Suddenly, the handful of men clinging to the minaret felt themselves disengaged from the foliage and rapidly lifted into the fiery atmosphere.

"The minaret's being carried away by the comet!" Palmyrin's voice resumed.

"We're leaving Saturn!" cried Farandoul. "Curses! What about the four queens…?"

The frightful tempest occasioned by the passage of the comet Gallia through the atmosphere of Saturn continued for a long time, with the same fury, on the comet. It was not until nearly 36 hours after the terrible shock that the men clinging to the minaret were able to profit from a moment of calm to look around.

Only eight Terrans had left Saturn, and were voyaging through space in the comet's wake. They were Farandoul, Niam-Niam, Servadac, his batman Ben-Zouf, Palmyrin Rosette, two Spaniards and the inevitable Flora MacKlaknavor. The other Terrans, and Désolant with them, were still on Saturn!

The minaret, considerably reduced by the recent impact, was very cramped for such a numerous population. Its inhabitants had already divided into two groups, with Servadac and his friends on one side, and Farandoul, Niam-Niam and Flora on the other.

Farandoul and Servadac, little disposed to fraternize, darted surly glances at one another.

"Do you have any food-supplies?" asked Servadac, tormented by hunger.

"No, do you?"

"None at all—we'll have to eat one another."

Palmyrin Rosette intervened and demonstrated to Servadac by a gesture that it would be easy to descend to the comet. Indeed, the minaret was now traveling barely 15 meters above the latter's surface, brushing the branches of the forests. Servadac's party had only to let themselves slide down into the foliage and descend from branch to branch.

Farandoul, Niam-Niam and Flora did not move.

"*Bon voyage*, and *bon appétit*!" Servadac shouted to them, ironically.

Niam-Niam responded with a joyful bound, precipitated himself into the interior of the minaret, and soon returned loaded down with provisions. The prescient savage had taken advantage of the last night spent on Saturn to pillage a large restaurant in the Saturnian park. Our friends had enough supplies to last for a long time.

Let us now return to Saturn and see how the queens had fallen into the power of the inhabitants of that strange planet.

The minaret hidden in the tree had been discovered, and the powerful monarch resident in the grand palace, seduced by the portrait his spies had painted of the queens, had given the order to take them alive no matter what the cost.

Thus, while Farandoul and Désolant were running to the menagerie and Niam-Niam was pillaging the Saturnian restaurant, regiments had advanced silently to the foot of the tree and determined Saturnians had launched an assault on the minaret.

The queens, surprised in their sleep, had defended themselves bravely, but had succumbed to the weight of numbers. They had been dragged away and taken to the palace.

Meanwhile, the hurricane unleashed on Saturn was making the building tremble on their foundations. What had become of Farandoul in the midst of that cataclysm? The queens, locked up in a sumptuous apartment in the palace, thought for a while that Saturn would be pulverized by the comet, but they soon saw the comet drawing away with vertiginous rapidity.

In the morning, the queens receive a visit from the prince and the highly-placed individuals of the court. They perceived very quickly that, instead of having to deal with enemies like Servadac, they only had admirers among the Saturnians. Hope returned to their hearts; they received the homages of the monarch and courtiers with an affable dignity.

What had become of their friends? They tried to make their anxiety understood to the powerful monarch.

The prince was full of delicacy. He gave a few orders, and the queens were soon able to see the various Terrans who had remained on Saturn after the impact—which is to say, the English officers, a few soldiers, three Spaniards and our friend Désolant.

Désolant had seen everything. He was able to tell the four queens that Farandoul, clinging to the minaret, had been carried away again by the comet!

It was over. O dolor! Farandoul and the queens were separated forever.

Three weeks later, four great nations were in celebration on Saturn. Four powerful monarchs were marrying the four queens, in the hope of acclimatizing an eighth female species on that beautiful planet.

The same day, millions of leagues away, Farandoul, still on his dislocated minaret, was subjected to a new cataclysm. This time, the comet was crossing the Earth's orbit around the Sun.

This resulted in dreadful turmoil, and the minaret, swinging between the two stars, suddenly entered the Earth's atmosphere, rotated around our planet and finally fell into the middle of a wide river.

Men sitting on the bank had witnessed the fall; they immediately threw themselves into the water. Soon, Farandoul, Niam-Niam and Flora were brought, unconscious, to dry land.

"Farandoul!"

"Mandibul!"

Such were the two exclamations that rang out simultaneously. It was indeed, Mandibul and our old friends the mariners, who, despairing of being able to find their leader on African soil, were retuning sadly to Cairo, having exhausted all their resources. O Providence!

It was necessary to tell the brave sailors everything. It was necessary to relate the emotions of that infernal journey with the queens, first across Africa, then through the atmosphere and from one planet to another, all the way to Saturn.

"Oof!" murmured Mandibul. "You must be in need of rest!"

"On the contrary, my dear friend—my minaret was too cramped, even after the loss of the four queens, and I feel the need to travel the continents to restore my circulation. Let's see, where are we? Six leagues from Cairo. Bravo! Asia's not far away—let's go to Asia!"

Niam-Niam, on hearing these words, pulled an expressive face.

"I understand," said Farandoul. "You'd prefer to remain in Africa. Very well! Stay here, my lad. Since you're a bachelor, I suggest you marry Miss Flora and make her happy!"

And while Niam-Niam and the descendant of the Klaknavors, mounted on a dromedary—a gift from Mandibul—disappeared southwards, our friends headed for Alexandria with the intention of taking passage on the first steamboat bound for any port in marvelous ASIA.

337

PART FOUR: ASIA

THE SEARCH FOR THE WHITE ELEPHANT

I.

Farandoul, Mandibul and the mariners, whom we left on the African sands, are now occupying first-class cabins on the *Punjab*, a comfortable English mail-boat bound for Indo-China. They intend to disembark in Bangkok, the capital of the kingdom of Siam. Having decided to explore the depths of old Asia, the Mother of the World, our friends had been wondering which part of the immense continent to head for first. An issue of the *Times*, scanned absent-mindedly by Farandoul, had furnished the answer.

The first page displayed the following article:

MYSTERIOUS DISAPPEARANCE OF THE KING OF SIAM'S WHITE ELEPHANT[84]

A strange event recently occurred in the kingdom of Siam, and put every mind in turmoil. The king of Siam's white elephant, the supreme incarnation of Buddha, has disappeared! In spite of the palace's walls and ditches, the guards and Amazons charged with its defense and the talapoins incessantly busy in the temple, mysterious malefactors succeeded, one night last month, in removing the immense idol, along with the amulets, jewelry and precious stones with which it

---

[84] Reports of the reverence afforded to white elephants in various parts of southeast Asia had been published in the West since the 17th century, but had been given a recent boost shortly before Robida penned his novel by the accession of Thibaw Min—who heaped his own animal with jewels after the fashion of the one depicted here—to the throne of Burma in 1878. Thibaw's white elephant did not bring him luck; he was deposed by the British in 1884 and the animal was bought by the American showman Phineas T. Barnum. Barnum suffered a greater catastrophe; Thibaw's elephant arrived painted red and blue, and turned out to be more grey than white when washed; one of his rivals immediately took the opportunity to upstage him by parading a whitewashed elephant that looked more convincing than the real thing. Robida's use of the motif anticipated Mark Twain's "The Stolen White Elephant" (1882), and Villiers de l'Isle Adam's "La Légende de l'éléphant blanc" (1886; tr. in the Black Coat Press collection *The Scaffold and other Cruel Tales*), which might well have taken some inspiration from *Saturnin Farandoul*.

was overloaded. It was necessary for them to avoid all surveillance, narcotize the vigilance of the priests, get out of the temple and cross the three enclosing walls of the palace with their prey.

The dismayed palace wanted to conceal the incident from the population, but the news soon spread through Bangkok and throughout the realm. The disturbance at court is immense; everyone is in fear of the overexcited population. The ministers are anxious, and even the Amazon corps is in a ferment.

His Excellency Nao-Ching, the mandarin of the police, rendered desperate by the lack of success of his researches, has announced that a large reward is promised to whoever recovers the elephant, with a free pardon for any repentant criminal who provides any useful information. In consequence, the official Bangkok gazette has published a royal decree promising a reward of 20 million ticals—60 million francs or 2.4 million pounds sterling—to whoever returns the white elephant to Bangkok Palace.

The reward is large, but we have to say that, in our opinion, searches will encounter many difficulties in the mysterious Asiatic world, if any even materialize.

Special correspondent, Bangkok.

After reading this, Farandoul plunged into profound reflection for more than a quarter of an hour. Then, suddenly getting to his feet, he summoned Mandibul and the 15 sailors.

"If you want to know to which countries we're going to take our intelligence and our activity," he said, "I'll tell you. We're going to Bangkok, capital of Siam. To do what? To recover the white elephant, the sacred animal, a national symbol, mysteriously stolen. Sixty millions reward, which will suit ruined men like ourselves very well."

"If we succeed," observed Tournesol.

"What do you mean, *if* we succeed? I don't recognize you any longer, Tournesol. Are you going into a decline, my friend? Fear not—we'll succeed! We can consider the 60 millions as already in the bag, so we'll spend our last resources on a first class passage to Bangkok! Forward march!"

"Forward march!" cried Tournesol, galvanized. "We'll bring back two sacred elephants instead of one, damn it!"

This is why, without further ado, our friends headed for Suez to take the first steamboat bound for the seas of Indo-China.

After a few weeks of calm sailing, the speedy *Punjab* deposited them, penniless, in Bangkok. The Siamese capital was an extraordinary accumulation of sparkling pagodas, crenellated towers, spires and fantastically carved domes emerging from the midst of lush and verdant vegetation.

As soon as he set foot on Siamese territory, Farandoul saw that the extraordinary agitation caused by the disappearance of the white elephant was far from having calmed down. Everything in Bangkok seemed out of sorts; the thousand canals that circulated through the city seemed bleak and desolate; the barges lay idle in the Sun; every manifestation of commerce had disappeared; the pagodas resounded with lamentations; male and female talapoins, the priests and priestesses responsible for religious matters, were striking their breasts, their despair pushed to the extent that they neglected to collect the offerings of the faithful. Muted rumors were running through the crowds accumulated on the steps of the temples and before the altars of the gods; other, more ominous, rumors were circulating among the Siamese gathered around the palaces of the first and second kings.

Farandoul's first concern was to go to the palace of His Excellency Nao-Ching, mandarin of the police. In the offices, this strange minister was not in evidence; they were received by slaves, guards and harem servants, but the minister was hard to find. Finally, Farandoul discovered him in the process of taking a bath in a shady spot. At the interpreter's first words in explanation of the purpose of the visit, the minister leapt out of the water.

"Recover the white elephant!" he cried. "But...that's impossible! It can't be done...."

"Why can't it be done?" Farandoul reported. "On the contrary, it certainly can be done, and I shall undertake to do it. You can consider it returned to the palace."

"Have you some indication of its whereabouts, then?"

"None—on the contrary, I came to ask you for some information."

"An impossible enterprise!" mumbled the minister. "Extraordinary difficulties, grave perils."

"That's my business. The information?"

"But first, who are you? You understand that...my responsibility...the gravity of the situation...respect for religion..."

Farandoul handed his card to the minister. Our hero's renown had reached as far as Siam; His Excellency Nao-Ching started in astonishment, and his olive-colored cheeks went pale. In the meantime, he continued his embarrassed circumlocutions. Farandoul thought he could distinguish a certain reluctance in the discourse. Seemingly, our hero's intervention was an inconvenience to the plans of mandarin of the police.

I imagine that our arrival has annoyed him, Farandoul thought. *He wants to recover the elephant himself and get his hands on the 60 millions!* Abandoning all hope of getting anything out of the minister, he coldly took his leave of him. Mandibul and the sailors were waiting outside.

"We'll go to see the king" said Farandoul. "To the palace!"

Obtaining an audience was not easy. The mariners were met at the palace by a contingent of Amazon guards. The sentries crossed their bayonets; it was necessary to negotiate with the officer on duty and await the arrival of a superior patrol. The stupefied sailors looked around at the Amazons, dressed in short trousers, jackets and red kepis; the female warriors gravely mounted guard. One platoon was performing exercises with bayonets under the orders of a lieutenant with a martial air, while another squad was maneuvering two light field-pieces under the monumental arch of the main gateway.

The advertised patrol being slow to arrive, the seamen, without respect for regal majesty, begin talking about offering themselves the distraction of carrying off the Amazon guards; it took all of Farandoul's authority to maintain discipline.

Finally, the patrol appeared. The shouts of sentries scattered about the walls made the entire company of guards take up their arms. Drums were beaten by the agile fingers of robust young women in uniform. There were Siamese versions of "Arms at the ready!" and "Present arms!" and the Amazons' colonel advanced, followed by her general staff and a few mandarins.

The colonel presented Farandoul to the mandarins; the mandarins promised an audience for the following month. That did not satisfy our hero; he insisted. The mandarins sent him to superior mandarins, who presented him to others even more elevated. Farandoul and the interpreter, guarded by an escort of a dozen Amazons, spent six hours in the palace running from mandarin to mandarin, to no avail. They were always rebuffed, on the grounds of formal rules of etiquette. Farandoul detected an evident ill-will within the mandarins' politely tortuous phrases. The whole society was against him. Some of them even seemed to have been forewarned; the minister of the police, the jealous Nao-Ching, must have taken the initiative.

Night had fallen; the doors of the palace were already closing. Farandoul postponed the renewal of his attempts until the next day and headed for the exit. Mandibul and his men were waiting patiently under the monumental gateway. To distract themselves, the mariners were jesting with the Amazons in sign language.

Mandibul had gone into the guard-room, where the officers, understanding that they were dealing with a man of similar ilk, were surrounding him with the most flattering attentions. They were chatting about armaments, fortifications and the art of war. The patrol having concluded, the weary colonel had come back to relax in pleasant conversation, via in interpreter. Informed by Farandoul of the negative result of his attempts, she offered to get the friends out of difficulty and introduce them to the emperor's presence herself, as her eminent position permitted her to do. Farandoul welcomed this unexpected favor joyfully; a quarter of an hour later, the mariners went into the palace in military formation following the colonel.

The palace, silent by day, suddenly seemed to become animated at nightfall. Sounds of music came from all directions; swarms of slaves and servants circulated beneath the colonnades. The colonel led our friends into a large central courtyard surrounded by porticoes and brilliantly lit by torches and lanterns, reflected in the murmuring waters of fountains.

"Wait here for the king to pass," the colonel said. "I'll go pay my respects to him and let him know."

The relaxed mariners waited patiently for three quarters of an hour under the magical colonnade, occasionally reached by waves of strange music and warm breaths of perfume. Tournesol and few natives of the hot regions of the south felt a certain dizziness creeping into their heads. Farandoul waited, cool and calm.

Suddenly, a man appeared, who started in surprise at the sight of the marines. By the vast red morocco wallet in which the minister kept his pipe, his betel and his papers, Farandoul recognized His Excellency Nao-Ching, the minister of the police.

Meanwhile, Nao-Ching, suppressing his emotion, approached the mariners and said, negligently: "Are you waiting for His Majesty?"

"Yes," replied Farandoul.

"Well, go in there. His Majesty will come to join you." And the minister of the police pointed along the gallery to a large door ornamented with delicate ivory sculptures enriched with gold and dotted with precious stones.

"Thank you, Excellency." Having said this, Farandoul made a sign to his sailors and they all filed to the relevant door. At the first step they took behind the door, Farandoul and Mandibul recognize the intoxicating perfumes that had reached them at intervals in the courtyard.

"Oh! Oh!" said Mandibul.

Everything that they had already seen within the palace was negligible compared with the magnificence of the hall they were going through; plates of gold, mother-of-pearl and malachite sparkled on all sides. A superb staircase occupied the back of the room and appeared to lead to other apartments more marvelous still. The mariners slowly went up the steps of the staircase; at the top of the stairs Farandoul lifted up a door-curtain woven from gold thread, and released an exclamation of astonishment.

Mandibul and the sailors, pressing hard on their leader's heels, put their heads through the golden filaments and, like him, remained nailed to the spot in amazement.

The walls of the immense hall, open to the sky, that they had glimpsed through the curtain were streaming with gold, pearls and light. In the middle of this incredible splendor, several hundred women, more sparkling still, were devoting themselves to the pleasures of relaxation, languidly lying on cushions or dancing to the strains of harps and Siamese guitars.

Our friends did not have the time to see any more; an immense tumult suddenly erupted, and rolled like thunder through the halls from top to bottom. Twenty gongs resonated alarmingly under frantic blows; in the other parts of the palace, other gongs replied to them, and two cannon-shots sounded from the direction of the Amazons' guard-post. Precipitate footsteps and the clinking of weapons were audible in all the courtyards; voices were asking questions; the

Amazons' clarions sounded the alarm, while the rolls of their drums added a sinister note to the terrible tocsin of the gongs.

In the hall, all the frenzied women were screaming at the tops of their voices, the majority of them without even knowing the cause of the urgent alarm, and slaves with hairless faces were trying vainly to restore order. A few of these slaves, armed with curved swords, had thrown themselves in front of the sailors, gesticulating wildly. Confronted by the mariners' steady gaze, however, their audacity had not pushed them so far as to use their weapons.

"All this fuss is for us, then?" murmured Mandibul, in Farandoul's ear.

"I think so," the latter replied. "We must have strayed into the harem."

He turned around to interrogate the interpreter who had followed them. The young Siamese was writhing on the ground, his arms extended, moaning desperately.

"Well?" said Farandoul, bringing him to his feet. "What's going on?"

"The king's wives! The king's wives!" murmured the interpreter. "We're dead! We've entered the apartments...an unforgivable crime! It's all over! We'll perish under torture...."

"Perish under torture!" cried Mandibul. "Stop there! For an error...for what, after all, have we done? We've simply mistaken the door...that's no reason...."

"Tortures! Death!" sobbed the interpreter.

Outside, the tumult was still increasing. The courtyards were full of people; they had come into the room below and were preparing to climb the staircase.

Farandoul, leaning over, perceived a man in the room who was covered in gems, whom the interpreter identified as the king, with a crowd of guards and high dignitaries behind him. Nao-ching was among them, his face lit up with an infernal smile.

The king, raising his voice, gave orders to the slaves up above.

"What did he say?" asked Farandoul.

"That we're to be taken alive and put in chains," stammered the interpreter.

"Just a moment!" said Farandoul. "We shan't allow ourselves to be taken."

The mariners, acting swiftly, heaped up a few items of furniture in front of the door. Each of them had his revolver in his hand, which made no small contribution to augmenting the ladies' terror.

"Reassure them," Farandoul instructed the interpreter, "while we disarm the slaves."

The long curved swords had been thrown on the floor, and the beardless slaves prostrated themselves in front of the sailors. The ladies, still rather anxious, were moderating their screams.

"Now we can have a chat with his Majesty," Farandoul said. "Let's open the conference."

At the sight of the attitudes struck by the mariners, the king and the high dignitaries had evacuated the hall and had taken up positions in the courtyard, in the midst of a multitude of guards and Amazons, armed to the teeth. They were shouting and gesticulating; the most agitated of all was, undoubtedly, the minister of the police, who frequently drew his hand across his throat in a significant gesture.

When Farandoul appeared at a window with a few men, the Siamese down below released immense explanations of horror, and the striking of the gongs redoubled its fervor. Farandoul wait for relative quiet to be established and dragged the terror-stricken interpreter forcibly to the window.

"Explain our error to His Majesty, present our apologies and put all the blame on the minister of the police. Go on—quickly!"

The unfortunate Siamese began, with a stutter. The king did not condescend to reply himself, and gave the floor to Nao-Ching, the mandarin of the police. The dialogue lasted nearly two hours, in the midst of the greatest tumult. In the end, the interpreter let himself fall into Mandibul's arms.

"Well?" demanded the latter.

"Well, this is all that I could obtain: His Majesty does not want to put us to death right away, but he demands that we surrender ourselves to be judged according to his laws."

"Ah! Many thanks for the favor. Delighted! Let's see, now—explain to the king the purpose of our visit. Tell him that we came here with the intention of devoting ourselves to the search for the white elephant."

The interpreter obeyed.

345

His words were greeted by a redoubling of the shouting in the courtyard. The mandarin Nao-Ching had a scornful smile, and merely replied with these words: "Your crime must be punished."

"Oh, it's like that, is it?" cried Farandoul. "Let them come and get us! We've entered the apartments of the king's wives—well, let's stay here! It's a nice place; we'll defend it to the end!"

Beneath the colonnade, the king and his high dignitaries held council; the guards and the Amazons organized a sort of camp for the night. Farandoul made a tour of inspection of the sacred apartments and observed that they gave out on two sides into internal courtyards; they were totally isolated from the other buildings of the palace and reasonably defensible. He perceived guard-posts skillfully blocking all the exits from the courtyards. Without losing any time, he posted a few mariners as lookouts and came back with the others to the central hall.

"Let's await developments," he said, philosophically. "We've made a poor start in Siam, but we'll try to get ourselves out of it, all the same."

In the morning, after a few hours rest, he went back to the windows with Mandibul and the interpreter. The situation had not changed; the guards and Amazons were at their posts—but the king and the high dignitaries had disappeared.

"Why aren't they attacking?" asked Mandibul.

"May the lord of Hell spare me!" cried the interpreter. "Don't you know that the prescriptions of religion are obligatory? The king is an emanation of the Buddha; his 800 wives participate in his sanctity and are considered part and parcel of his divinity, the emanation of the supreme emanation! Any human being who penetrates into the apartments is guilty of sacrilege and must perish under torture. That's why no one dares to come to arrest us...."

"In that case, as we have no intention of surrendering ourselves in expiation of the crime of treason against the Buddha, this thing might last a long time. So be it! We're in no hurry."

"What about food?" asked Mandibul.

"Food? Well, what about the sacred spouses? We'll share their meals; where there's enough for 800 there's enough for 820. Let's go! Interpreter—ask the king's wives what time they eat."

"Bravo! We've barely strayed into crime; we might as well go all the way. It'll serve Siam right!"

The 800 wives, somewhat reassured since the previous day, were crowding into the great hall. Farandoul asked their permission to invite himself unceremoniously to their meal, to which they acquiesced with a common accord. The slaves, on seeing the preparations for this new sacrilege, trembled from head to foot and awaited the personal intervention of the Buddha. The food having arrived from the royal kitchen as usual, however, they saw the mariners, sitting on the floor with the king's wives, swallow the sacred nourishment without diffi-culty.

Even among the emanations of the Buddha, however, a certain hierarchy is observed; the king's eight hundred wives were divided into first-class, second-class and third-class wives. Only Farandoul and Mandibul were admitted to the table of the fifty fist-class wives; the rest of the marines shared the meal of the second-class wives. The sentries were not forgotten; a few ladies, slightly excited, took them some small dishes and bottles of light and sparkling coconut wine. Only the interpreter refused to take part in the breakfast, nourishing himself entirely on vi-sions of various tortures. At each dish—which is to say, in remembering one by one each of the tortures customary in Siam—he released a somber groan.

Later that morning, a loud noise under the colonnade drew the mariners to the windows. The king had just arrived, shielded by the famous seven-story pa-rasol, the insignia of royalty. The mandarins following him only had three-story parasols. Behind the court, between two columns of Amazon, came a long procession of talapoins and bonzes. The king was about to sit down on a chair prepared for his sacred person; mandarin and bonzes were squatting around him.

"One might think that a ceremony were about to begin," said Farandoul.

The interpreter, dragged to the window, only needed a single glance to recognize what ceremony it was.

"The bonzes of the great pagoda of Wat-Chan!" he cried. "They're going to judge us. O Buddha, save me!"

Indeed, everything seemed to be organized for a solemn hearing. Farandoul and his sailors had furnished Siam with a fine *cause célèbre*; the gravity of the audience, the solemn and indignant attitude of the bonzes and everything else indicated that the trial in question was unlikely to terminate with the acquittal of the accused.

The trial began immediately, in conformity with all the regulations of Siamese justice. Firstly, the accused were summoned to surrender themselves to the tribunal, but when they refused it was decided that their presence at the windows was sufficient for the arguments to begin.

The interpreter had to be carried to a window and held in place by four strong sailors in order to have the strength to listen without fainting to the minister of the police's speech for the prosecution. Farandoul had to administer several doses of courage to him in the form of digs in the ribs to persuade him to raise his voice before the august tribunal. As a last resort, the application of a saber to his kidneys fortified him sufficiently. He began speaking, and explained to the bonzes that the mariners had only come to the palace with the intention of putting their courage and strength at the service of His Majesty the King of Siam, in particular to offer to undertake a search for the missing white elephant. Finally, he added by way of conclusion that the mariners profoundly regretted having mistakenly entered the sacred apartments, but did not consider themselves to be criminals on account of that inadvertence.

A thunderous reply from the mandarin of the police literally knocked the interpreter over. Nao-Ching elaborated the accusation, demonstrated the horror of the crime committed against the religious law, and once again summoned the mariners to deliver themselves to justice.

When Farandoul disdained to reply to this invitation, the chief bonze got to his feet and declared that the marines and the interpreter were convicted of a serious crime. After a short deliberation by the bonzes and the ministers, the assembly condemned the guilty "to have their heads cut off by the sword for the atrocious, unprecedented and ever-execrable crime of having penetrated into the sacred apartments of the first wife of the first class, Lang-lo-chang."

The judges' verdict, translated by the interpreter, was very badly received by the mariners; they released a cry of anger and brandished their sabers and revolvers.

"Come and collect them then—our heads!" cried Tournesol. "Come and see if you can!"

"Bah!" said Mandibul. "Let's calm down. What can they do to us, since they can't arrest us? We're all right here; we'll stay."

"Bravo! Sultans forever!"

"Silence!" shouted Farandoul. "It's not finished—our judges are resuming the session."

Indeed, the bonzes had resumed their severe expressions to listen to a second speech from the mandarin of the police, Nao-Ching. The interpreter, a little calmer since his condemnation to death, resumed his function. Nao-Ching's discourse was a second speech for the prosecution, couched in almost identical terms.

The bonzes deliberated once again, and the president of the tribunal eventually condemned the mariners "to have their heads cut off by the sword for the atrocious, unprecedented and ever-execrable crime of having penetrated into the sacred apartments of the second wife of the first class, Kailaa".

"What, again?" murmured Mandibul. "That's a bit strong."

"Wait, wait!" said the interpreter.

The mandarin Nao-Ching took the floor again, making a third speech for the prosecution, and the bonzes, after a third deliberation as long as the first two, condemned the mariners "to have their heads cut off by the sword for the atrocious, unprecedented and ever-execrable crime of having penetrated into the sacred apartments of the third wife of the first class, Mith-ta."

"What, yet again?" cried Mandibul. "How cruel these Asiatics are!"

In two hours, the mariners were further condemned to have their heads cut off for having penetrated into the apartments of the fourth, fifth, sixth and seventh wives of the first class. The last time, Mandibul left the window to find out from the sacred wives what time the next meal would be served. "Condemned to have my head cut off seven times!" he murmured. "I think I'll need to keep my strength up..." And while he savored the delights of a light lunch with the king's wives, the judges, remaining in session, condemned him and the others to be subjected to decapitation by the sword five more times.

On the 13th condemnation to the punishment of the sword the impatient Tournesol caused a scandal by interrupting the court from the window. "I'm getting bored with your decapitation by the sword," he shouted. "Try to find something more elaborate—we're worth better than that!"

The session continuing, the tribunal condemned him personally for gravely offending His Majesty to the torture of "serious impalement, preceded by 300 strokes of a baton on the soles of his feet". When the interpreter had explained this, Tournesol became very proud of this flattering distinction.

The audience was suspended from noon to 3 p.m. so that the judges might eat and sleep, and then reopened with the same solemnity.

Between 3 and 8 p.m., the mariners were condemned to be beheaded 18 times—which, together with the 13 condemnations of the morning, added up to 31 condemnations to decapitation, plus a particular condemnation for Tournesol.

The sailors, condemned to lose their heads 31 times, were dining with the king's wives when the judges closed the session. They did not bother to get up; only Farandoul and Mandibul ran to the windows to bid the tribunal farewell and wish it a good night.

The evening passed very agreeably in the sacred apartments; the king's 800 wives had resumed their little routines, some taking light meals of sweetmeats and preserves, others performing bayadere dances to the strains of pianos and harps. Farandoul and Mandibul were the object of delicate attentions from the entire clan of first-class wives; services were performed for them, they were offered refreshments and immense feathery fans were agitated above their heads.

Mandibul delighted all the sacred wives by organizing a gigantic game of blind man's bluff, which lasted until midnight. The beardless slaves made themselves as inconspicuous as possible in order not to irritate their terrible guests. Farandoul was tranquil; the barricades established at the doors made any invasion of the Siamese impossible—a needless precaution, in any case, since the solemn prescriptions of the religion forbade entry into the sacred apartments on pain of death.

The following morning, at the same time as the previous day, the bonzes of the great pagoda arrived, along with the ministers and the royal parasol, which was charged with representing the monarch and presiding in his place.

Before the commencement, the mandarin of the police recalled the 31 condemnations of death pronounced the day before and asked among the guards for volunteers to go and apprehend the condemned men in the sacred apartments—warning them forthrightly that they too would have to be decapitated on their return, in obedience to religious law. There was no hesitation on the part of the guards; they did not even consult one another. With one accord, the entire regiment remained mute in the face of the proposition.

The mandarin Nao-Ching began his 32nd speech for the prosecution. The bonzes deliberated and pronounced a thirty-second condemnation for the crime of having penetrated into the sacred apartments of the 32nd queen.

We have no intention of giving a full-length account of this celebrated trial; that would take too long. Readers desirous of following the debates step-by-step can consult the *Gazette of Bangkok* , the official organ of the Siamese government, in the library. They will find the proceedings of the session recorded there one by one, along with the speeches of the mandarin of the police and the pleas of the Siamese interpreter, the sole defender of the accused.

The debates lasted 24 full days without any interruption. From the second day onwards the King of Siam was represented by his parasol, but the mariners glimpsed him many times, hidden in the galleries facing the sacred apartments, attempting to enter into communication by means of signs with one or other of his 800 wives. Farandoul was alert; he had strictly forbidden any sort of communication with the monarch, in order to incline him to gentler ideas. The unfortunate husband was profoundly bored in his solitude. It was all getting on top of him; his white elephant had been stolen, his people were restless and, to put a cap on his misfortune, his 800 wives had been sequestered by cruel enemies!

On the evening of the 24th day, after the last speech for the prosecution and the last condemnation, the exhausted mandarin of the police made a summary of the debates. The persons named Farandoul and Mandibul, their 17 mariners and the Siamese interpreter, having merited death 800 times, had been condemned to be decapitated by the sword 800 times; in addition, the mariner Tournesol, for gravely offending the majesty of the judges, would, preliminary to the execution of the other sentences, receive 300 strokes of the baton and be subjected to the punishment of serious impalement.

The mandarin concluded by calling for volunteers, as he had done at the commencement of every hearing, to extract the condemned from the sacred apartments. Needless to say, apart from one young guard driven to suicide by the grievous cruelty of a lover, none presented themselves.

As the tribunal was about to close its session, Farandoul began to speak.

"Thank you, 800 times over, honorable bonzes! I don't want to waste your time, but I ought, before allowing you to depart, to submit one small observation to you. We have been condemned to be decapitated 800 times, plus a few trivia for one of us—that's all well and good. But the execution of your sentences will encounter a few difficulties. Firstly, you cannot come to apprehend us physically, under pain of undergoing the same punishments, and secondly, we have no intention of surrendering. We shall therefore take up residence in the sacred apartments, organizing our life there as comfortably as possible. We shall have no lack of distractions. In the meantime, your white elephant, which we sought to recover, will have time to disappear forever, and your monarch will be more inconvenienced than us. That's all I have to say."

II.

Farandoul was right. The Siamese monarch, wandering like a soul in torment, had been seeking a way out of the difficulty for 24 days. The situation was not promising; he understood perfectly well that, rather than expose themselves to having their heads cut off even once, the mariners would prefer to spend their entire lives in the sacred apartments. And what about his 800 wives? O sadness! And his white elephant, which might be gone forever?

All these thoughts troubled the monarch, all the more so because the political horizon was visibly darkening. The loss of the white elephant had upset the people, and now an extraordinary trial had overexcited minds in the capital. It was known in the palace that strange rumors were circulating in the city; under the pressure of public opinion, an intense ministerial crisis had now broken out. All the ministers were under suspicion, save for the minister of the police—who, by virtue of his energetic attitude in the course of the debates, had become the idol of the populace.

After a week's reflection, the king, could only see one way to crush the hydra of anarchy and re-establish the tranquility of his nation. He had to negotiate with the audacious mariners who had invaded his palace; he had to offer them mercy and launch them in pursuit of the sacred elephant. In that fashion, he would recover his 800 wives and his white elephant. Order would be restored to the capital.

The proposal, put before the council of ministers, gave rise to the stormiest discussions; the mandarin Nao-Ching, in particular, was hostile to any conciliation, but the majority prevailed and negotiations were opened.

Things proceeded rapidly, quickly concluding in an agreement. The most difficult thing was to have the Siamese interpreter included in the amnesty. The king refused; finally defeated, he demanded by way of compensation that Tournesol, let off his 800 condemnations to decapitation, should at least submit to simple impalement for the satisfaction of the tribunal. Finally, Tournesol too was granted mercy. Solemn letters of full and complete amnesty, duly sealed, were sent to Farandoul. The latter then came down, followed by a few mariners, to make the final arrangements with the king regarding the search for the white elephant.

The king took Farandoul to the deserted temple of the white elephant, explained to him the circumstances in which the theft must have been committed, and gave him a life-sized photograph of the animal to assist in the conformation of its identity.

The sum of the reward was, of course, maintained. Farandoul promised the king to bring the white elephant back, dead or alive, and staked his reputation on it. To cover his initial expenses he received a small advance on the reward.

It was now necessary to organize the departure. The sailors bade farewell, almost regretfully, to the 800 sacred wives; a few of them carried away photographs signed in the Siamese language as souvenirs. As for Tournesol, who was full of fury against Siam, it required all Farandoul's diplomacy to persuade him to leave the sacred apartments, where he wanted to remain alone.

That was not the end of it, though. A new storm was gathering over the palace. The mandarin of the police having whipped up popular passion by clandestine means, a considerable commotion had broken out in the city. The palace was already surrounded by a tumultuous mob loudly demanding the sacking of the ministers and the execution of the court's sentences.

The regiment of Amazons, so faithful hitherto, sided with the mob. Its colonel, in violent harangues, spoke of solving the ministerial crisis by hanging the ministers if the white elephant was not returned immediately.

The situation was serious. The palace gates, defended by timid slaves, could easily be forced. Farandoul, brought up to date with the situation, asked the king for full authority over the defense. To begin with, he sent Mandibul to load the two cannons at the main gate, and distributed his mariners at vulnerable points. This would gain him a few hours, of which it was necessary to take full advantage. But what should he do? Farandoul quickly came up with an idea; he gathered four sailors, visited the palace's store-houses and outbuildings, and discovered what he needed in a summer-house under repair. The slaves having been sent away, Farandoul and his sailors, shielded from all indiscreet gazes, shut themselves up with the king in the royal stables to undertake a mysterious enterprise.

At the main gate, Mandibul was on watch with a lighted match. The rest of the mariners were stationed at the minor gates, fortified and barricaded, with an arsenal of loaded rifles at their disposal. Outside, the mob howled without daring to approach too close to the rifles gleaming in the crenellations.

What were Farandoul and his four sailors doing in the royal stables in the meantime? Were they preparing a mine, hollowing out a tunnel for an escape? No—they were simply doing some painting, before the monarch's eyes.

Pots of white lead were distributed on the ground; armed with gigantic brushes, they were struggling to cover a large elephant with paint while it ate sugar-lumps from the king's hand. Their work was progressing; already the elephant was three-quarters transformed into a sacred elephant. Only the head remained; that was the most difficult part. Farandoul took charge of it personally, and while the legs were being finished off, he distempered the cranium and trunk of the intelligent animal with infinite artistry and an attention to shading that would have made a miniaturist jealous.

Finally, the work of art, completed by a few brightening touches, seemed worthy of being submitted to the admiration of the Siamese in the temple and the residence of the disappeared white elephant. In consequence, they made a surreptitious exit from the stables, and conducted it to the temple without being spotted. The monarch, fully satisfied, declared that the illusion was complete at ten paces and that, were it not for a rather strong odor of paint, any Siamese who had not been forewarned would take the falsely-tinted elephant for the true white elephant. To remedy the odor of paint, Farandoul had a large quantity of incense burned in cassolettes distributed in front of the elephant.

Everything was ready; the slaves, informed of the miraculous return of the white elephant, came running and delivered themselves to raptures of adoration. The news soon reached the gates; when the king came to the main gate in person to harangue the Amazon regiment and inform them of the elephant's return, the Amazons threw themselves to their knees with signs of the most earnest repentance.

The revolt was appeased. A long queue of people, controlled by the Amazons, came in the most orderly fashion to present its respects to the sacred elephant, returned by courtesy of a miracle of the Buddha.

Farandoul and his mariners, armed and equipped, were preparing to leave the palace, having received the congratulations and encouragements of the king. Definitively abandoning the sacred apartments, they met up with the Amazon regiment under the porticoes. This time, the entire regiment welcomed them with the greatest possible enthusiasm; public opinion attributed to them the honor of having recovered the white elephant. In spite of their modest protestations, the Amazons wanted to carry them in triumph, and whether they liked it or not, they had to make a triple circuit around the elephant's temple on the shoulders of the joyous Amazons.

A long procession of the faithful was filing through the interior, its members prostrating themselves before the immobile elephant in the midst of incense-fumes. Just as Farandoul and his sailors were passing in front of the temple door for the third time, carried by the delirious Amazons, two individuals came rapidly down the steps and threw themselves into the midst of the procession. They were the minister of the police Nao-Ching and the colonel of the Amazons. The colonel and the minister pronounced a few curt words; all of a sudden, the clamors of joy turned into cries of horror, and the mariners found themselves choked beneath a heap of assailants. Before they knew what was happening, they were stripped of their weapons, their arms and legs were secured with solid ropes or shackled, and they were gagged.

Fatality! Caught up in the Amazons' fit of enthusiasm, our friends had quit the palace and delivered themselves into the grip of their enemies. What had happened? What circumstance had changed the joy of the Siamese to furious anger? Nothing that could have been foreseen. The Siamese might easily had gone several weeks or months without discovering the fraud, but the tenebrous Nao-Ching, the mandarin of the police, had not been content to honor the sacred elephant with a few distant genuflections. In his capacity as a high-ranking individual, he had climbed over the balustrade intended to keep the common people at a respectful distance and, quietly approaching the incarnation of the Buddha, had drawn a suspicious finger over its rump. Horror! The finger had come back covered in white lead! Nao-Ching, summoning the colonel of the Amazons, had then made her pass her hand over the elephant's flank. The colonel had leapt backwards; her five fingers had left distinct marks on the sacred flank....

Everything was discovered; the respects of the faithful were being addressed to an imitation white elephant. At this news, an immense clamor had burst forth in the temple and...you know the rest.

Thrown into a corner under the guard of a platoon of Amazons, Farandoul, Mandibul and the mariners contemplated their situation despairingly. Tournesol, especially, infinitely regretted leaving the sacred apartments. The adventure had turned decidedly sour; would not the sentences passed by Siamese justice be executed at its next session? As the populace invaded the place, threatening to put an end to the uncertainty of the condemned men, the colonel of the Amazons ran in and ordered that they be transported to the monumental barracks established between the third and fourth walls of the palace.

The unfortunates, loaded on to a few elephants, soon arrived at the barracks and were rudely deposited in the Amazons' guardroom, which was completely empty that day. Farandoul, whose eyes were the only part of his body at liberty, searched among his companions in captivity for Mandibul, but in vain; Mandibul was not there. The colonel, reserving the privilege of interrogating him for herself, had placed him in a separate room, whose key she had kept.

Night fell during this interval. A contingent of Amazon guards remained in the barracks, while the others went out to guard the palace, which was still plunged into the most complete disarray.

The colonel, remaining in the barracks, paced feverishly back and forth in her office; a terrible preoccupation had laid siege to her thoughts, evident in her furious gestures. About 10 p.m., she appeared to reach a decision and abruptly went out with a lantern and a bunch of keys. Where was she going? And why was she darting suspicious glances in all directions?

The silence reigning in the barracks was only troubled by the rhythmic march of the sentry outside and sonorous snoring emerging from the large room in which Mandibul had been locked. It was to this room that the colonel directed her steps. She was presumably about to begin our friend's interrogation. She opened the door abruptly. Mandibul, with his arms and legs bound and forcefully gagged, was asleep on the floor.

The colonel studied him for a few minutes; then, suddenly bending down, she deposited a kiss on his serene forehead! The snoring suddenly ceased. Mandibul opened his eyes. His gag preventing him from uttering any cry of astonishment, he made no sound, but seemed evidently disconcerted.

The colonel thought she could read a bitter reproach in Mandibul's eyes. She drew her sword and freed him from his gag.

"Oof!" said Mandibul.

The colonel set the lantern down and sat down on the floor beside Mandibul. All her pride had disappeared, along with her military bearing. Beneath the colonel's uniform, a woman's heart was beating at a hectic pace. Haven't you already guessed? In their first conversation under the great gateway of the palace, Mandibul had made a deep impression on the colonel. Finding him in unfortunate circumstances, under the threat of 800 condemnations to death, she wanted to sweeten the bitterness of his final hours.

The conversation began in Siamese, of which Mandibul did not understand a word. He replied in French, which was equally incomprehensible to her. What was she saying? What did he reply? It is supposable that she made warm declarations, but we cannot swear to it, having been, like Mandibul, brought up in ignorance of the Siamese language. He replied in French that the cords securing his arms were causing him too much pain for him to give all the attention to her speech that it deserved, and that perhaps he would understand better with his hands free. The colonel understood to some degree, the mind of a woman being so finely-tuned. She hesitated briefly; then as her heartbeat accelerated further, she did what our friend desired. Mandibul had recovered the use of his arms. The first use that he made of his relative liberty was to seize the colonel's arms.

Presumably, he was about to thank her by kissing both her hands—at least, the colonel closed her eyes. The ever-gallant Mandibul, always the French *chevalier*, did not entirely neglect the duty required of him, but, having brushed the warrior woman's velvety epidermis with his lips, he held both hands in a solid grip and rapidly tied them together with the cords detached from his own wrists.

It was the colonel's turn to seem disconcerted. Mandibul left her stunned with amazement and took her sword to cut the bonds securing his legs. He was free!

A quarter of an hour later, an Amazon colonel carrying a lantern and a bunch of keys emerged from the room on tiptoe. This colonel was Mandibul. The real colonel was inside, carefully trussed up, and Mandibul, dressed in her uniform, went in search of his friends. Fortunately, he had seen them locked up in the guard-room and knew where to find them.

The most difficult thing was to discover the key to their prison in the bunch; finally, Mandibul put his hand on it and got into the room where his friends were lying, victims of cruel anguish. An immense astonishment was appeared in the prisoners' eyes on seeing Mandibul transformed into am Amazon. The latter lost no time in rapidly cutting their bonds.

Poor Tournesol was the last. Mandibul took pleasure in tormenting him: "My poor Tournesol, prepare to submit to your punishment—we were only able to obtain facilities for our escape on condition that we left you for the satisfaction of the judges."

When Tournesol and the interpreter were freed with the rest it became a matter of getting out of the barracks. Mandibul had a plan. He had just observed the store-room of the quartermaster in change of dressing the Amazon regiment; he took his friends there and told them to imitate him by dressing in Siamese uniforms.

While the mariners were getting dressed, Mandibul and his bunch of keys continued their search. In the colonel's room, our friend had the good fortune to find all the company's weapons. He came back down with revolvers and cartridges, and found everyone ready. "Now let's make ourselves scarce!" he said.

"Just a moment," said Farandoul. "We need elephants, to protect us from pursuits."

"The great park is nearby. We'll have the choice of the garrison's 300 elephants."

"Let's go!"

They got out of the barracks without difficulty. The sentinel, recognizing the colonel's lantern and uniform, presented arms to the mariners, who made themselves as inconspicuous as possible.

The elephants' great park was to the left; the little troop presented itself boldly before the drowsy unit that was guarding it, captured the sentry and made the others out down their weapons.

Six elephants were soon chosen from among the finest. The mariners were about to install themselves in their palanquins when Farandoul stopped them. "At daybreak," he said, "our enemies will launch themselves in our pursuit on the elephants we leave here. The roads are unfamiliar to us; they'll catch us up. We mustn't risk having the entire Siamese army on our back tomorrow."

"But what can we do?"

"There's one way. Elephants have their vices too! It's those vices that will give us our security."

"What vices?"

"Drunkenness! A keen appetite for strong liquor! That vice is encountered in all superior creatures, as in man: monkeys, elephants…it's sad, but what can one say? It's the way it is. Elephants are good, honest and, above all, hard-working, but they love to be rewarded for their labors with a few little sweeteners. By promising elephants a few pints of cognac or fermented coconut, one obtains a greater sum of work by accelerating their march."

"Well?"

"Well, somewhere in the park there must be a stock of fermented coconut milk; we must find it, and our enemies won't be able to pursue us tomorrow."

The officer from the guard-unit, interrogated, pointed to the alcoholic liquor store. The door was soon forced and the delighted Farandoul discovered large vats full of alcoholic beverages.

"Quickly! A bucketful of that liquor to each elephant! We'll keep a few bottles back for our own."

The sailors, understanding that their salvation depended on it, hastened to carry out Farandoul's orders. A chain was organized as if for a fire, and buckets full of liquid were carried to the elephants. The latter, delighted with the windfall, demonstrated their respect for their benefactors by accepting the buckets politely with their trunks and emptying them internally with shudders of sensuous pleasure. In similar circumstances of a gratuitous distribution of strong liquor, many men would have rushed the distributors *en masse*, and would have been sure to spill a large proportion of the liquid, but the elephants—serious and very reasonable creatures even in their minor bouts of debauchery—did not act in this way. The distribution was carried out in the most orderly fashion; none of them tried to drink out of turn. It was merely the case that the neighbors of those which sipped a little too lengthily begged them, by means of a few amicable taps of the trunk, to accelerate their ingurgitation.

Soon, each of the 300 or 310 elephants had swallowed its three bucketfuls of liquid. A few of them, with family responsibilities, had even had five or six; as prudent fathers, they had not wanted to permit their children more than two measures, and had awarded the surplus to themselves.

Another bucketful per head was distributed; already many of the elephants were sleeping blissfully, dead drunk, or surrendering themselves to 1000 eccentricities; the last bucketful finished the job. The entire camp lost its head. Order disappeared, gravity evaporated, and even the old ones suddenly felt an impulse to frolic madly running through their heads.

The mariners could now leave without fear; the elephants, abominably drunk, would require two or three days to sleep off the fermented coconut milk.

The six elephants that Farandoul had reserved, a trifle lit up by the alcoholic fumes, watched the scene enviously. To give them an incentive, Farandoul distributed a quarter of a bucketful to each of them, and gave the signal to depart.

The agile seamen scaled the high rumps of their mounts and installed themselves, three to each animal—one on the neck to serve as a mahout or driver, and two in the palanquin. Farandoul, Mandibul and the interpreter took the lead, and entire troop departed north-westwards.

Sitting on his elephant, Farandoul studied a map of the Siamese peninsula by the light of a lantern. His intention was to head straight for Ayutthaya, the ancient capital of the kingdom of Siam, now in ruins, to go up the great river Me-Nam, the "mother of waters," as far as Bank-Ta, where they could cross a ford in order to head for Burma.

A few words overheard by the interpreter in a conversation between the mandarin of the police and the Amazon colonel, and reported to Farandoul, had made him decide to take that direction.

"The white elephant, if my agents' reports are not mistaken," the mandarin had said, "must have been sold by the thieves to the Emperor of Burma. It has reportedly been seen in one of the pagodas of Amarapura."

Amarapura , a city situated on the Irrawaddy, the great Burmese river, 250 leagues from Bangkok, was therefore the objective of our friends' journey. It was a matter of arriving there incognito, searching the temples, discovering the elephant and taking possession of it in order to return it to its rightful owner. The thing was simple, if not easy.

Needless to say, our friends were not pursued at all by the Siamese army. The mandarin of the police, however, had taken a great pleasure in busying himself during the night with the preparations for the execution. The executioners were ready, and from daybreak onwards the stake destined for Tournesol's impalement was surrounded by an excited crowd. When the condemned men did not appear at the hour prescribed by the Amazon colonel, the mandarin had only to make a short journey to the barracks, where he arrived just in time to liberate the colonel, who was prey to a violent attack of nerves.

Escaped! The guilty parties had escaped! The general immediately had the drums beaten to call the troops to arms, and the army had raced to the elephant park. What a spectacle! The entire park was plunged into a state of indescribable intoxication.

It took three days to bring the elephants to their senses, and after three days, pursuit was futile because the condemned men undoubtedly had a start of more than 100 leagues.

The colonel paid the price, and was stripped of her rank. Soon, however, on receiving the news that the condemned men had arrived in Burma and were searching all the pagodas in search of the white elephant, a change of opinion was brought about, and calmer minds invested all their hopes in the brave mariners they had wanted to decapitate 800 times over. Only the mandarin of the police had departed in their wake with a few men, on elephants of his own.

Our friends, traveling at top speed, only required 12 days to cover the distance between Bangkok and for Burmese towns of the Irrawaddy. The journey was certainly not without its difficulties, but they were long accustomed to overcoming all obstacles and never turning back. The temples of Amarapura were all visited, without result; there was no trace of the white elephant there.

At Ava, they had better luck. A few indications of the passage of the sacred animal were gathered there; finally, absolutely reliable information convinced Farandoul that the elephant was to be found at the great pagoda of Pagam.

The order for departure was immediately given. They came in sight of their goal. Farandoul and four mariners went into Pagam as scouts while the rest of the company remained in the jungle. As soon as they entered the town, they noticed an extraordinary excitement, an inexpressible desolation similar in every respect to that into which Bangkok had been plunged on their arrival. It was necessary to discover its cause; a European trader encountered by chance gave Farandoul the solution to the mystery: the white elephant, bought by the Emperor of Burma a few days previously from Siamese pirates, for four millions, and solemnly placed in the great pagoda of Pagam, had just disappeared, doubtless re-stolen by those same Siamese.

Farandoul and the European trader headed for the pagoda where the theft had been committed to try to find some clue. The bonzes and the Burmese mandarins consented to let them visit the pagoda and gather all the information they desired. After two hours of scrupulous investigation, Farandoul left the temple without having discovered anything. The theft of the elephant had been effected, as in Bangkok, with prodigious skill; the priests and slaves charged with guarding it had slept inexplicably deeply that night; no one had seen or heard anything!

It was only after a week of searching in the vicinity of Pagam and journeys along the Irrawaddy that our friends discovered any evidence of the passage of the white elephant. In the jungle, 15 leagues to the north of the town, Farandoul picked up a blue pearl similar in all respects to those the King of Siam had shown him in the temple treasure. That pearl must have been detached from one of the strings ornamenting the sacred animal's neck.

There was no possible doubt; the thieves and their captive were heading for India; they must have crossed the Thalawaddy and taken the road to Manipur, the nearest Hindu town. Farandoul and his mariners urged their elephants to the gallop.

The Siamese interpreter was still with them; enticed by the hope of receiving a share of the promised reward, he had volunteered to continue his functions, claiming to have learned the majority of Asiatic languages at the great College of the Talapoins of the Wat-Chan Pagoda in Bangkok.

The mariners reached Manipur in two days and, not discovering any clue there, continued their journey at top speed. At Jaintiapur there was the same absence of information. It was necessary to go into the wild Langau mountains, foothills of the great Himalayan chain, and head up the Brahmaputra as far as the first ford.

Were the elephant-thieves heading for Tibet, to sell their captive to the High Lama, or had they veered westwards towards the great Hindu cities of India? The Siamese interpreter, still seeing information relentlessly, could not obtain any. It was necessary to take one direction or the other at random.

An encounter with a band of pilgrims on their way to Kifir, one of the holy cities of India, in the independent states, decided the issue.

At Kifir, great religious solemnities were being advertised; there was to be a procession of the chariot of the Chattiram pagoda, a rival of those of Djaggernat,[85] and people were hastening there from all over India, attracted by the hope

---

[85] I have retained Robida's spelling here rather than substituting the more familiar Jagganath (an avatar of Krishna). The reference is to the "chariot" used in the Ratha Yatra ceremony at the Jagganath temple in Puri. The myth that fanatical devotees lay down in the chariot's path to allow it to pass over them originated in a famous 14th century fake travelogue recounting the imaginary journey to the East of "Sir John Mandeville," which originated in France and survived in even more copies than the model it was intended to parody, Marco Polo's account of his travels. The anecdote was revived by 19th century Christian missionaries for use as slanderous propaganda, when it gave rise to the English term

of being numbered among the fortunate mortals over whose backs the stone wheels of the chariot would pass—a prompt and infallible means, as everyone knows, of obtaining a first-class place in the paradise of Indra.

Farandoul did not hesitate. "It's in Kifir," he said, "that we'll find our elephant! *En route* for Kifir!"

Another 400 leagues to cover and half of India to cross. The journey through the English possessions was not without danger for Farandoul and his men; the conquest of Australia they had effected was still remembered by the English bimanes. As soon as he arrived in English territory, therefore, Farandoul posed as a photographic artist traveling with his assistants. His disguise was nearly pierced several times over, however, by inopportune encounters with officers who had served against him in the two sieges of Melbourne.

The caravan followed the bank of the Ganges, the sacred river of the Hindus; it went through the great cities of Patna, Benares and Allahabad and, quitting the English possessions, entered into Bundelkund.[86]

Farandoul no longer had any doubt regarding the presence of the white elephant in Kifir. In the last week of their journey, the rumor had spread out into all the Hindu districts that Kifir the holy had been favored by the arrival in the temple of a sacred elephant, a direct emanation of the Great Buddha.

III.

First of all, let us say right away that it would be no use searching for Kifir on the most complete map of India, even those of the English general staff; no city of that name exists. Important reasons and motives of the highest gravity have forced us not to reveal the true name of the city in which such terrible event unfolded. The city is well-known—too well-known; if we wrote it here, the name would set fire to our pen and blood would run there; the blades and stakes of executioners would do their work, and 40 women—the majority of them charming—would go to the pyre!

You will understand our reserve; we do not want any executions on our conscience. However, as history has its rights, the name of the city has been deposited in a sealed envelope with a notary, whose name we shall also not disclose, in order not to expose him to the danger of receiving a visit from a few

---

"juggernaut" and became a popular item of modern legend. The name given to the fictional pagoda, Chattiram, is a generic term meaning "pilgrim's rest."

[86] I have retained Robida's spelling rather than substitute the modern Bundelkhand; in Verne's *L'Ile mystérieuse*, Captain Nemo reveals that he is really Prince Dakkar of Bundelkund, and that is why he hates the British so much.

thugs. This envelope will not be opened until 50 years hence, when all risk will have disappeared.

The festivals of Kifir had attracted an enormous crowd of fanatics, camped randomly in the suburbs and along the river, on an esplanade overlooked by the splendid palaces of the old rajah Nana-Sirkar. The faithful of the higher castes were resident in the city, with numerous bayaderes and countless fakirs, attracted by the Great Pagoda of Chattiram's reputation for holiness. Among these people, the most remarkable included a strange troop of fakirs—brought, it was rumored, from the far side of India on six elephants by a rich Siamese aristocrat.

These fakirs, drawn from all the Hindu castes, had made a vow not to pronounce a single word of their maternal tongue, and had made up a sort of private language which they only employed in rare circumstances; no Hindu word ever escaped their lips; they were so far plunged into nothingness, in obedience to the prescriptions of Brahma, that they had forgotten that language completely.

Only the venerated chief of these fakirs, an old man with a long white beard, still pronounced a few Hindu words, but that was only a phrase in honor of Brahma, Indra, Sura and Vishnu, repeated as a prayer.

These fakirs, whose holiness was admired by all Kifir, were—as you will already have guessed—none other than Farandoul and his mariners. The interpreter played the role of the rich Siamese aristocrat. Rajah Nana-Sirkar had forbidden Europeans to come into Kifir during the festivals, on pain of death. Besides, it was understood that a European caught in the midst of that fanatical population would have been instantly torn into pieces, without any need for the rajah's solders to do it.

Farandoul and his mariners were, however, admirably begrimed and costumed. Farandoul, the venerable chief of the troop, dressed in costume of rags and coiffed by a huge turban, wore around his neck a circlet of iron surcharged with all manner of objects: bullets, feathers and fragments of marble collected in all the temples of India. Over the rags covering his Herculean torso, Mandibul, transformed into a *sapwallah*,[87] or snake-charmer, had a little basket full of cobras, whose bites were deadly, slung over his shoulder.

Since their arrival, it had been necessary for them to devote a few hours, in the bungalow in which they were lodged, to the pious crowd of Hindus attracted by the reputation for holiness that the interpreter had created for them.

---

[87] As with some of Robida's other borrowing from contemporary travelogues, this one never made it into common parlance and was rarely sighted after its first use; he obtained it from Louis Rousselet's *L'Inde des rajas* (1875), his principal source for this part of the narrative. Rousselet was primarily a photographer, and it is presumably in his honor that Farandoul adopts that guise for part of his journey.

The mariners, gathered in the central courtyard, all assumed the poses of fakirs sunk in the contemplation of nothingness, some with their arms in the air, others crouching without appearing to on the adapted heels of their footwear. It was tiring, but indispensable.

Tournesol and the Breton Trabadec, heads down with their feet in the air, were backed up against the wall and gazed at the audience with expressions of the utmost seriousness, without moving a single facial muscle. The Siamese aristocrat, interrogated by the crowd, skillfully put about the rumor that these two fakirs had been living in that uncomfortable position and sleeping head down for more than 30 years without interruption. Only the rumor of the festivals of Kifir had made them decide to use their legs for walking, and they had still covered nearly half the route head-down, resuming that pose in their rooms in order to sleep.

The emaciated Escoubico, thanks to the loquacity of the Siamese, became an anchorite who only ate like other men for one month every ten years; this time, in order to make the journey, he had accorded himself two months of nourishment.

Only the Englishman Kirkson, a burly and rotund eater of beefsteaks, did not look the part, transformed into a vegetarian fakir who had lived since infancy buried up to the shoulders in a field near Calcutta, nourishing himself solely on grass growing within arm's reach. Like the others, of course, he had only quit his hole in order to witness the festivals of Kifir.

Mandibul the sapwallah was obliged, by the light or torches, to bring out the cobras sleeping in his basket. He had no need, like other snake-charmers, of a bowl of milk to awaken the dangerous reptiles; without any hesitation, he introduced his hand into the basket and abruptly drew out three superb serpents, which he waved above his head. The circle increased its diameter very quickly, no one caring to get too close to the reptiles that the sapwallah handled with such incredible audacity, without any of his colleagues' precautions.

A troop of bayaderes, also longed in the bungalow, mingled with the crowd; their musicians—flute-players and drummers—accompanied Mandibul's exercises with their music, alternately monotonous and furious.

In the end, Mandibul, in an excess of verve, threw his serpents into the air, caught them, wrapped them around his neck, made them descend into his clothing and exit through the sleeves, the jerky movements of the reptiles betraying their fury. The breathless crowd retreated further, but, with a rapid gesture, Mandibul replaced them in the basket and resumed his initial position and his air of detachment from earthly things. Needless to say, the terrible cobras were mere imitations given to Mandibul as a souvenir by one of the inhabitants of the sacred apartments.

Farandoul, the old white-bearded fakir, had not budged. As all gazes strayed towards him, he thought that the moment had come to make his entrance in his turn.

"The world being dead," he said, "Brahma and Vishnu wished to re-create it. The Devas and the Danavas transported Mount Mandara into the middle of the Ocean on the back of the queen of turtles; then, with the aid of the serpent of Vishnu, they began the churning of the sea. Soon, the waters of the ocean changed into milk, and then butter. Finally, from that butter was born the Moon, which flew into the firmament like an air-bubble, followed by the cow Surabhi, the fountain of milk, the horse and the elephant of Indra, Dhanwantari, and Sura, the goddess of wine!"[88]

Farandoul fell silent; that was all he knew of the Hindu language—a fragment of theological discourse that the interpreter had made him learn by heart, and which the faithful greeted with solemn respect.

Meanwhile, the bayaderes came together in a corner of the courtyard and set their scarves flying; the drums and flutes resumed their concert at a rapid tempo, and the crowd parted to leave the field free for the dancers. Seen thus, whirling by the light of torches lit by hurried servants, the dancers seemed to belong more to the world of dreams and fantastic apparitions than to any actual world. Soon, however, the movement slowed, the dance became slower, and the audience was able more easily to admire the marvelous costumes and charming features of the bayaderes.

The false sapwallah Mandibul almost lost his impassivity in his excited contemplation of the leader of the troop, a tall and superb woman with dark eyes, surmounted by stars in their brows. Standing and leaning slightly backwards in the middle of the circle of bayaderes, she made her scarf fly above her head in a sculptural pose; large rings hung down from her ears, gold circlets encased her neck above a little corsage of scarlet, and other circlets wound around her arms from the shoulder to the wrist. Mandibul, electrified, took up his serpents again and launched himself into the group of bayaderes to pose in the midst of them as he had once seen done in Paris in ballets. His entrance was well-received; the dance resumed, swift and staccato, around Mandibul, brandishing his frightful serpents above his head.

The day following this well-spent soirée was the first of the festivals of Kifir. The fake fakirs and the Siamese aristocrat had spent the night in a large, tightly-closed room, sheltered from indiscreet gazes. Their plan was made; first they had to study the surrounds of the temple of Chattiram, in which the white elephant was exposed to the veneration of the faithful, then wait for nightfall and steal it somehow.

Our friends had no need of a guide to find their way about Kifir. An immense crowd filled the streets, going to the temple to watch the first ceremonies and the procession of the chariot of Chattiram. At the sight of the fakirs, the crowd parted respectfully. A procession formed behind them; it was assumed that the holy anchorites would crown their austere existence with a supreme aus-

---

[88] This Vedic creation myth is borrowed from the epic poem *Mahabharata*.

terity, by having themselves devotedly crushed by the wheels of the sacred chariot.

To all the questions of the curious our friends disdained to reply; the Siamese aristocrat, taking the lead enthroned on an elephant, reminded the Hindus that the honorable fakirs had made a vow of eternal silence.

The great temple of Chattiram soon came into view over the rooftops, sparkling in the sunlight: a colossal pyramid populated with an entire world of statues of gods, demons, elephants and sacred animals. The crowd around the temple was so compact that it required more than three hours of effort to reach and cross the threshold, not without jostling and bruises-which the fakirs endured patiently. A few muttered exclamations of *ventre de phoque* and *bagasse* escaped Mandibul and Tournesol, southerners not over-blessed with patience, astonishing those who heard them, but no hint of suspicion slipped into the minds of the Hindus.

The white elephant was there! Through the clouds of incense, Farandoul caught sight of it among the gods and eight-armed goddesses. Farandoul had studied the large photograph given to him by the King of Siam carefully enough to recognize the sacred animal at the first glance. It was definitely the same one: its enormous curved tusks, with a fracture at the tip of the one on the left, made it sufficiently recognizable—but how could it be removed in the midst of this immense population. How could they even get close to it?

Farandoul decided to spend that first day in the temple and to try to hide himself there when night fell. Armed with an invincible patience, the mariners silently established themselves, like good fakirs, as close as possible to the elephant, without paying any heed to the crowd.

Until midday all went well; the interpreter had gone to find out how many priests were attached to the temple and to try to insinuate himself into their confidence. He came back just as the great procession was getting under way. The crowd was pressing around our friends, more compact than ever, surrounding the fakirs with evidences of the utmost veneration. As he made his way through the crowd towards them, its clamor informed the interpreter of the reason for this increase in fervor.

Farandoul and his friends were positioned at the entrance to the temple, at the exact point where the fatal chariot would emerge; this circumstance had confirmed in the eyes of the Hindus the rumor that the fakirs had come with the intention of being crushed by the enormous mass, so they had quickly been surrounded by all the most fanatical individuals in Kifir—by men who really had decided to force the gates of paradise in that uncommon fashion, and by others who were merely desirous of providing themselves with the edifying spectacle of these heroic immolations.

The interpreter scarcely had time to reach the mariners to warn them what the crowd expected of them. Farandoul was on the alert; he had already noticed a face that was not unknown to him holding forth in the midst of the fanatics and frequently pointing at the fake fakirs. It was that of one of the bayaderes' musicians from the bungalow. Farandoul had already begun to wonder, the previous day, where the Devil he had seen him before, without being able to remember.

At that moment, a great clamor within the temple advertised the fact that the procession had begun. Behind the colonnades, an enormous pyramid carved with 1000 sculptures and mounted on colossal wheels began to move forward. It was the chariot of Chattiram, which had already passed over the bodies of a few privileged Hindus. It was advancing quite rapidly, drawn by 1000 men harnessed to it by ropes.

In the narrow passage where the mariners were stationed, a dreadful crush was in prospect. Many people were likely to be choked in the crowd or precipitated involuntarily under the wheels of the chariot. Farandoul whispered a few words to the interpreter and told him to warn all the false fakirs individually of the danger, without exciting the suspicions of the Hindus.

He was just in time. The clamor increased further; the men hitched to the ropes were entering the passage. All eyes were upon the fake fakirs; the moment had come for them to fulfill their vow—and five or six frantic devotees slipped into the midst of them in order to pass beneath the terrible wheels in such good company.

"Back! Back!" ordered Farandoul, by means of gestures—but that was easier to say than to do. A living wall of fanatics cut off any possible retreat. The chariot slid to which in a few paces of Farandoul, with a horrible noise; he had to make a decision rapidly.

The crowd, seeing the fakirs retreat, was already howling angrily and shoving them towards the chariot. Farandoul made up his mind; making a sign to his friends, he threw himself on to one of the wheels, set his foot on a projection, grabbed one of the goddess Kali's arms, and climbed on top of the chariot. Mandibul and all the mariners did likewise. Leaping up above head height, they scaled the chariot and installed themselves triumphantly astride stone elephants or on the shoulders of gods.

There was a terrible commotion in the crowd; some saw the fakirs' action as an impulse of religious mania, but the majority were crying sacrilege and making frightful threats against the profaners of the sacred chariot.

The chariot was still moving forwards, following the esplanade in the direction of the palace of the rajah Nana-Sirkar. Farandoul had anticipated that; the interpreter had told him that the chariot of Chattiram would pay a call on the old rajah, and he was hoping to take advantage of the brouhaha occasioned by its arrival at the palace to jump down from the chariot and slip away unobtrusively.

It would be futile to attempt to describe Nana-Sirkar's palace; these magical palaces cannot be described. A dazzled painter might make a sketch, but the impotent pen can only note the principal beauties: sparkling façades sculpted by light, aerial colonnades, balconies surcharged with sculptures, miraculous windows, roofs bristling with 1000 spires and sunlit bell-turrets. At the entrance to the palace of Kifir, in front of a wall crowned with fantastically-carved crenellations, a highly-ornamented gate was standing wide open to give passage to the chariot.

Farandoul, looking over the entire crowd, took in a strange and grandiose scene at a single glance. In the great courtyard of the palace, the rajah's guards were lined up immediately in front of the central colonnade, where the dignitaries of the court were standing. Right at the back, behind a balustrade, the white head of Nana-Sirkar was visible; he was immobile on a divan, in the midst of his 40 wives.

The chariot, passing rapidly in front of the troops, stopped immediately in front of the balustrade, 20 meters from the rajah. All eyes were staring in astonishment at the fake fakirs, who had not found any opportunity to escape.

Having entered with the crowd behind the chariot, the interpreter was able to slide up to them. "Beware!" he said. "The adventure caused a fuss; people are vociferating against the profaners of the chariot—it's necessary to get out."

Indeed, shouts could be heard behind the guards; fanatics could be seen hoisting themselves up on to their shoulders and shaking their fists at the poor fakirs. Of all these fanatics, the bayaderes' musician seemed to be the most enthusiastic.

Farandoul darted a rapid glance around him; two ranks of guards had moved forward quietly to range themselves behind the mariners. The retreat was cut off; it was necessary to keep his composure and maintain his role impassively.

Meanwhile, a young man with a handsome face, who had been standing beside the rajah, came forward to the balustrade to interrogate the crowd of fanatics. His officers had brought him the bayaderes' musician, who was still gesticulating. To Farandoul's great astonishment, a long conversation began between the highly-placed individual and the humble musician, almost on an equal footing. The musician certainly began with marks of apparent humility, but their heads gradually moved closer and the conversation continued in low voices.

"The bayaderes' musician!" murmured Mandibul. "Damn! Damn! *Ventre de phoque!*"

Farandoul was struck by a sudden thought. "Mandibul! You've been chatting with the bayaderes—a fatal imprudence! You're not impassive enough to be a fakir. Be ready for anything—we've been discovered."

"The highly-placed person who is talking to the musician," the interpreter whispered, is the jaghirdar Rundjet, the first minister of old Nana-Sirkar, whom you see over there in the midst of his wives."

"Doesn't he ever move?"

"The rajah hasn't been out of his palace for a long time. He's more than 90 years old; his longevity surprises everyone in Kifir, but you'll understand that his 40 wives have a serious interest in conserving his health. For them it's a matter of avoiding *suttee*—which is to say, of being burned with him on the day of his funeral.

"The custom of burning widows is conserved in Kifir?"

"Of course! It's still maintained in the English possessions; it's even stronger here. In Kifir, no widow of high rank neglects the custom—least of all the rajah's wives, required by their high position to set an example. Besides, for them, the sacrifice would not be a matter of choice but of compulsion!"

"I wouldn't like to be in their shoes—the rajah's very old."

"Bah! With care…personally, I think the custom is excellent for husbands!"

"Pay attention!" said Farandoul. "Jaghirdar Rundjet is coming over to us. Take care—he doesn't look pleased. Try to explain our situation as fakirs deprived of speech by a vow…"

After his conversation with the musician, Jaghirdar Rundjet had gone to confer with the rajah and his wives; now he was advancing towards the fake fakirs with a severe expression and furrowed brows.

The circle of guards had closed in around them. Like it or not, it was necessary to confront the jaghirdar. Standing behind the balustrade, a few paces away from Farandoul, he stared at the false fakirs, one after another, without saying a word. Then he signaled to his officers to close ranks even more tightly.

"This is going badly," murmured Mandibul. "O perfidious bayadere!"

The jaghirdar finally started speaking, in English: "You obviously know, Europeans, about the prohibition issued by the rajah of Kifir, since you have adopted disguises to introduce yourselves into the holy city on the days of the solemn ceremonies of Chattiram. You knew, therefore, what you would be risking if you were discovered."

"Powerful Jaghirdar," said the interpreter, humbly, "these men are not Europeans; they are holy anchorites from my country, fakirs who have come to Kifir for religious motives."

"Silence! You are an accomplice of these men and will share their fate. You are in the hands of a powerful rajah whom you have provoked by insolently presenting yourselves in Kifir. For that crime alone, you already merit death, but that is not all. You have pushed audacity to the point of profaning our temples by your presence, to the point of laying your impure hands upon the sacred chariot of Chattiram, to the point of setting foot on the venerated statues of Shiva, Vishnu, Hanuman and Kali. All that can only be paid for by terrible tortures! Nana-Sirkar, the rajah of Kifir, condemns you to die in long torment, Here your sentence, therefore: the rajah Nana-Sirkar has ordered that you be taken to the great pagoda of Chattiram, and there, on the peristyle that overlooks Kifir, within the sight of all the faithful that you have insulted by your profanations, you will be flayed alive with skilled slowness, in such a fashion that your torture will last until the end of the festivals—which is to say, or three days. Have you anything to say in your defense?"

"Not to you, most amiable Jaghirdar, but to the rajah himself," replied Farandoul, who had not taken his eyes off the old rajah, still motionless on his cushions, during the whole of Rundjet's speech. And before the jaghirdar could stop him, Farandoul leapt over the balustrade with a single bound—which testified to the skill of monkeys as professors—and landed on his feet ten paces behind Rundjet. In another three strides he was in front of the rajah, in the midst of Nana-Sirkar's wives, who were appalled by his audacity.

In spite of their screams and the blows distributed by their fans and parasols, the audacious Farandoul put his hand on the rajah's shoulder, without the latter deigning to move his head or furrow his white eyebrows. Very strange! Impassive in the majesty of his long white beard, old Nana-Sirkar had not budged; his plume of diamonds had not even quivered; his swords and daggers, enriched with fine pearls, had not been drawn from their scabbards.

The audacious Farandoul, careless of his royal majesty, dared to put his hand on that august beard and tug it disrespectfully! Not a muscle twitched in the rajah's face; his bright eyes did not flinch.

Finally, the terrible Farandoul, not content with these assaults on the dignity of their lord and master, set his elbow on the rajah's head and leaned over his breast.

The rajah's wives wrung their hands; their secret was discovered!

Nana-Sirkar, whose longevity was admired by the whole of Kifir, was a stuffed rajah! Nana-Sirkar had been dead for 12 years. For 12 years the kingdom of Kifir had been ruled by an embalmed rajah. For 12 years, nobody had noticed it. It had required the keen eyes of Farandoul to discover the fraud; since his arrival in front of the balustrade he had been struck by the immobility of the old rajah. He had observed; he had discovered the truth.

How can the alarm of the rajah's wives and their terror before the menacing Farandoul be described?

"The rajah of Kifir had cruel intentions!" shouted Farandoul, in a strident voice.

"Silence!" murmured Jaghirdar Rundjet, squeezing his hand. "Don't ruin us—you won't be flayed, I promise!"

"I'm relying on it," Farandoul replied. "Do you know that you're in peril, at this moment, of burning with these ladies on a pyre!"

"Shut up, in the name of Brahma! Let's make a pact. "I'll save you—don't ruin us!"

"First have my friends brought forward. Send the chariot of Chattiram away, and let's talk quietly."

The jaghirdar obeyed. He went to the balustrade and gestured benevolently to the false fakirs. The astonished Brahmins stared at the jaghirdar; the latter declared that the rajah Nana-Sirkar had now recognized the sanctity of the fakirs had had taken them under his protection. The priests did not ask any more questions, and signaled to the procession to get under way again. As for the fanatics who permitted themselves to murmur, the soldiers showered blows on them from above with pike-shafts, rapidly dispersing them. The musician who was the author of the tumult had disappeared without waiting for this distribution.

Order having been reestablished, the jaghirdar graciously invited Mandibul and his sailors to climb over the balustrade in order to present their compliments to the rajah.

The mariners had only caught glimpses of the scene that had just taken place, the rajah's wives having striven to use their fans and parasols to conceal it from the eyes of the high dignitaries of the court standing some distance away. Farandoul brought his friends up to date succinctly; condemned by the cruel rajah Nana-Sirkar to be flayed in a delicate fashion lasting three days, his discovery had saved their lives. Instead of finding themselves in cruel peril, they were now the ones holding a terrible revelation, suspended like the sword of Damocles, over their enemies' heads.

Nana-Sirkar's 40 wives were truly charming, further enhancing their striking beauty with the refinements of Hindu coquetry. Rings and precious gems ornamented their nostrils and foreheads, the surrounds of their eyes were gilded or silvered, and bracelets adorned their arms and legs.

Mandibul, standing contemplatively in front of poor Nana-Sirkar, lost all gravity within the group carefully formed by the 40 widows. "Stuffed!" he murmured. "Stuffed! How imaginative these Far-Eastern wives are!"

"Shh! Shh!" muttered the jaghirdar. "Remember that everyone's lives—yours and those of the charming widows of Nana-Sirkar...."

"You're right. It's a serious matter. These ladies would be condemned to climb on to the pyre if anyone noticed, and we would be...the matter is, indeed, serious. But how long has the throne of Kifir been occupied by such an extraordinary rajah?"

"I'll tell you everything. It happened 12 years ago. Nana-Sirkar, who was already very old then—but was not yet past it—wanted to marry 20 young and charming wives to add new luster to that of 20 other wives who were already shining in his harem like a sparkling river of diamonds, or an immense constellation of stars in the firmament! That made 40 pearls in the rajah's jewel-box, 40 roses, 40..."

"Yes, yes, fine! You're an admirer of the shine of pearls and the perfume of roses—I'm beginning to understand."

"So, on the very night of his marriage, Nana-Sirkar experienced a fearful fit of anger on seeing me, Jaghirdar Rundjet de Ghapol, his first minister, depositing a respectful kiss on the hand of one of his new wives. Nana-Sirkar started, went pale, roared, seized his sword, and...fell down stone dead, choked by that thoughtless anger. The rajah's 40 wives came running, in floods of tears. They were widows; it would be necessary, in the full flower of their youth, to follow their august spouse's funeral procession and mount the pyre as *suttees*. A cruel prospect! An evil ceremony!

"A flash of genius passed through my mind; no one in the court except for me and the august widows knew about the fatal event. I decided to save them and had the body transported to an isolated chamber. The 40 widows immediately shut themselves away, and the celebration continued without the rajah, who was believed to be in his harem.

"The next day and the days thereafter, the rajah did not show himself at all for, during that time, I had him embalmed by skillful artists whom, fearful of indiscretion, I took care to have decapitated when their work was done. When he was presentable, I dressed him myself in his most sumptuous garments and summoned the august widows. They were rapt with admiration—the rajah was perfect!

"An ingenious mechanism made the head move from time to time and the eyes roll; at ten paces, the illusion was perfect. In a *durbar*, or general assembly, the rajah was presented to the court, at a respectful distance and surrounded by his wives, busy plying long feathery fans around him. I read the high dignitaries a letter from the rajah announcing his intention of relieving his old age by transferring the burdens of his office to me. The rajah made signs of acquiescence from time to time, by means of little stimuli administered to my mechanism. The high dignitaries fell over themselves to offer signs of approval and the durbar as concluded without any suspicion."

"And since then," asked Farandoul, "no one has seen anything?"

"No, the necessary precautions being so well taken, I continue to govern on behalf of old rajah Nana-Sirkar, whose longevity so admired throughout India; I show him to the people once or twice a year on important occasions, and that suffices. The rest of the time, the terrible rajah is shut up in a secret cupboard, to which I have the only key, and we remain tranquil."

"Accept the expression of our total admiration, ingenious jaghirdar, you deserve it! You've saved the lives of 40 charming ladies! You deserve a medal."

"You're too kind!"

"No, no, I'm just, I'm happy, doubly happy, to have seen through it; it permits me to admire at close range the 40 pearls in Nana-Sirkar's jewel-box, the blooming roses of the garden of Kifir, and it has saved the lives of my friends and myself—for three days of being flayed, no matter how delicately, would leave very little hope! Tell me—why did the diabolical rajah of Kifir have such cruel intentions in our regard?"

"That's another matter. You came here to steal our white elephant—the former elephant of the King of Siam—didn't you?"

"Yes, but how do you know that?"

"Did you see me talking to the bayaderes' musician? He's the one who told me—he's the one who revealed the secret of your disguises. He knows all your plans; he knows that you intend to steal the elephant to take it back to the King of Siam, and he's sworn to prevent that."

"But who is this musician? What interest does he have in the matter?"

"The musician is a fake—he's the leader of the Siamese pirates who sold me the white elephant! Having received the four millions, the price of the sale, he loyally undertook to warn us about the peril our purchase was running."

Farandoul, deep in thought, soon emerged again. "Let's wind this up," he said. "We're all in great danger here. My friends and I are risking being flayed alive, you're running the risk of a decapitation, more rapid but no less disagreeable, and Nana-Sirkar's widows will have to be sacrificed if the fraud is discovered. We're keeping one another alive; you're saving us from torture and we're sparing you from the blade and the pyre by keeping quiet. Quid pro quo! But I'm not stupid enough to find an equal balance between our 18 more-or-less unprepossessing masculine faces and the rajah's 40 seductive widows..."

"An academy of roses in bloom," said Mandibul, with a smile for the ladies.

"No, the precious existence of a single one of these charming widows is worth all of ours. In consequence, as there are 40 whose lives were are saving, we cannot be content with 18 reprieves. We require something else..."

"What do you mean?" cried the anxious jaghirdar. "What do you want? Spit it out—you're frightening me. Some of Nana-Sirkar's widows, perhaps—or a few millions? I must warn you that the State coffers have almost run dry...a rajah who has 40 wives can't help having a lot of expenses..."

"Don't worry—all I want is the King of Siam's white elephant."

"But it's ours—we've paid for it. The Brahmins of the Chattiram pagoda won't want to part with it."

"I'm only taking the white elephant to return it to its rightful owner—that should silence all the hesitations of a man as scrupulous as you. Come on, I'm only asking you to let us steal it. In return, I promise you eternal silence regarding the causes of the longevity of the Rajah Nana-Sirjkar and the freedom to enjoy it. We'll be content to brush the hands of a few of the unburned widows of Kifir with our lips. Is that agreed?"

"Yes, it's agreed," said the jaghirdar. "You can have your white elephant—that's a loss of four millions for me."

"Bah! The rajah will decree some new tax—you'll get them back. This evening, then, at nightfall, you'll take us to the pagoda of Chattiram, you'll help us to evade the surveillance of the Brahmins, and we'll go our separate ways s good friends."

During the final part of this scene, the curtains closing off the colonnade had completely isolated the members of the court from the group formed by our friends and the rajah's widows. Nana-Sirkar, august and impassive, had been taken to the back of the room and seated on his throne. When everything had been settled between the mariners and the jaghirdar, the latter asked them for a few minutes to greet, along with his master, the ambassadors of the Maharajahs of Baroda, Udaipur and Mysore and the English *chargé d'affaires*, the only European admitted to Kifir. As soon as this tedious ceremony was over, he would be entirely at their disposal to discuss the means of stealing the white elephant with the least possible risk.

Farandoul made a few objections. "What?" he said "You have the imprudence to receive the English ambassador? But he'll see through the fraud!"

"Fear not—for 12 years he's had interviews with old Nana-Sirkar every three months; he holds long discussions with him on thorny questions. Nana-Sirkar utters his replies by way of his faithful minister Rundjet; he discusses alliances, concludes treaties, and the English ambassador has never noticed anything odd."

"You've set my mind at rest. You understand that, now that I've had the honor of making your acquaintance and that of the rajah's charming widows, I wouldn't want anything bad to happen to you."

"Don't worry."

In fact, everything went well. The fake fakirs, hidden in the shadows of the curtains, were able to observe the session. The high dignitaries came in first, taking up positions in two groups 20 meters from Nana-Sirkar's throne, and the ambassadors were introduced. Magnificently dressed, streaming with precious stones, the Maharajahs' ambassadors stopped at a respectful distance from Nana-Sirkar's throne. The red coat of the British *chargé d'affaires* soon joined them. Each ambassador, after bowing to the impassive rajah, took a scroll of paper from his pocket and read a long and pompous speech. On the steps of the rajah's throne, his 40 wives, skillfully disposed to cast a shadow over his person, agitated fans of peacock feathers with gilded shafts two meters long.

"Not bad, not bad," murmured Mandibul. "I think the rajah of Kifir is destined to astonish the world for a long time yet by his obstinacy in remaining on this Earth."

When the speeches were concluded, Jaghirdar Rundjet seemed to consult briefly with the august whitebeard, and then descended the steps of the throne to reply to the ambassadors.

Half an hour later, the assembly broke up, with countless genuflections before the rajah. The flood of great lords flowed through the porticoes, and the august widows went back into their apartments with the jaghirdar and our friends.

"That's that for another three months!" murmured Rundjet, stowing the stuffed rajah into the secret cupboard. "Now, let's get back to the white elephant—so you're going to steal it tonight!"

"This very night," said Farandoul, "without delay—for we can't let ourselves be forestalled by others. Perhaps you don't know that the white elephant you bought had been previously purchased by the Emperor of Burma, and restolen from the Burmese one night, probably by the seller, the Siamese pirate-chief."

"I understand! It's 4 p.m.—we can't do anything before nightfall. Let's wait patiently, and..." The jaghirdar broke off, cocking his ear towards a noise that had just burst out in the palace. "What's that?" he said. "There's shouting in the palace...running..."

He was about to go out to investigate when an officer, anticipating his summons, entered the room precipitately.

"Jaghirdar!" said the breathless officer. "A terrible occurrence has just disturbed the festival! The pagoda of Chittaram...."

"Oh!" said Farandoul, abruptly getting to his feet, having understood the last few words.

"The white elephant?" said the jaghirdar.

"The white elephant has been stolen!"

"Run!" cried the jaghirdar. "Gather all the troops; send cavalry units in every direction; search all the mountain gorges; comb all the roads—it's necessary that the thieves be subjected to an exemplary punishment. Go!"

"Stolen again!" cried Farandoul. "This fake musician, this pirate, is a very clever man! Seeing that the machination that should have ended in our being flayed had been aborted, he suspected that we'd go to Chittaram this very night, and he's forestalled us. He's definitely a very clever man. It's a pleasure to do battle with him. He's triumphed for the moment, but be patient—we'll catch up. We must leave you, jaghirdar, and launch ourselves on his track. I've promised His Majesty the King of Siam to bring back his elephant; I'll throw in the thief for free, I swear it! It's the two of us, false musician—you against me, pirate! One thing bothers me, though—where the Devil have I seen his face before?"

"Wait for the initial reports from my street patrols," the jaghirdar said. "That way, you'll set out on the right track. Besides, you can't leave the palace before nightfall."

The initial reports were not long delayed. Soon, it was established beyond a doubt that the thieves had taken a north-easterly direction. Their passage had been signaled in a little village on the road to Lucknow, but on departure from there, their trail had been lost in the dense jungle.

"I suspected as much!" exclaimed Farandoul. "They're heading straight for the Himalayas; they're going to China. Well, that's where we'll catch up with them. Let's go get our elephants and shed our fakirs' rags. *En route!*"

The jaghirdar and Nana-Sirkar's widows got up to bid farewell to the mariners. Farandoul and Mandibul were showered with testimonies of friendship; attempts were made to retain them with offers of good positions in the court or the army; then, on their polite but firm refusals, they were made to swear again on Brahma, Vishnu and Shiva that they would never reveal to the world the causes of the rajah of Kifir's longevity.

All the mariners swore. All of them have kept their oaths, for even today, at X***, the rajah's 40 widows are alive in complete tranquility. Old Nana-Sirkar, who will soon be a centenarian, has not changed; every three months the jaghirdar takes him out of the secret cupboard and shows him to the court.

IV.

To follow a trail through dense jungle is not an easy thing to do. The thieves of the white elephant, launching headlong into that tiger-infested wilderness, knew that they would be impossible to find. In any case, Farandoul was not entertaining any hope of catching the up in the jungle. All that he asked was not to miss the slightest clue, and not to go astray in the mountain roads. The enormous chain of the Himalayas, looming up like a defensive wall between India and China, offers few openings to pass from one of these countries to the other. They had to make sure to take the same pass as the elephant-thieves, so as to come down into the same province behind them.

When they reached the initial ranges of the Himalayas, the mariners' elephants could do no more. In addition to fatigue, the route presented many dangers. It had been necessary to endure the assault of a pack of famished tigers, and the poor elephants had not come through it without incurring serious wounds. The pirates, moving straight ahead, had gained an advantage of three days over the mariners; it was only with a great deal of difficulty that Farandoul extracted a few items of information from a few savages, denizens of the ancient crags that were their ancestral home.

The white elephant, led by a troop of men on horseback, had taken the pass of Bala-tchats, which led into Tibet. Our mariners could not dream of going into the mountains with their elephants, so they quickly decided to abandon them and proceed on foot.

What a march! The pirates, knowing that they were pursued, had thrown themselves into chaos of rocks and precipices through which the narrow pass wound. The mariners, always well-received, overtook them, and found at the exit from the pass that they had lost the track.

Farandoul was in no doubt that the pirates would try to sell their white elephant, either to the High Lama in his palace at Lhasa, the capital of Tibet, or at one of the fabulously rich Lamaseries on the large island on Yamdrok Tso, the "vast turquoise lake." Abandoning direct pursuit, therefore, impracticable in the mountains, he descended into Tibet to take up a position on the bank of the Tsangpo, the Tibetan name of the Brahmaputra, where the roads to the lake and the city forked. He was dealing with a strong opponent, though. The pirates had sent scouts in advance; seeing their enemies in a good position to seize them as they went past, they renounced all hope of selling the elephant to the Dalai Lama and undertook a forced march into China proper.

The mariners camped on the river bank studied the little-known country. They found a custom institutionalized there that astonished them greatly. This was the occasion on which that discovery took place:

Not far from their encampment stood a large village with which they existed on good terms. One day, a brilliant cavalcade came out of the village and headed for the sailors' camp. At its head was a superb young woman riding beside an old chief whose hair was as white as the summit of Gauri Sankar, the highest peak in the country. Farandoul and Mandibul greeted them with exquisite politeness, and asked them what they wanted. They had a great deal of trouble understanding; the Siamese interpreter knew very little of the language. Finally, they caught on.

The old chief had come on behalf of his daughter to ask for the hands in marriage of Farandoul, Mandibul, the 15 seamen and the Siamese interpreter himself!

"What, all of us? Just for her?"

The old chief made an affirmative nod of the head; then, seeing the foreigners' astonishment, he told them that—by contrast with that of the Turks, in which the men possess an indefinite number of wives—the women of Tibet could have several husbands, and that, in consequence, his daughter, taken with the fine appearance of the foreigners, wanted to marry all of them.

Farandoul told the old chief that the request was exceedingly flattering, but that he did not think he ought to accept the proposal. He offered his apologies on everyone's behalf to the young lady, who frowned and seemed very annoyed.

Without saying a word, the old chief and his troop left the camp. Trabadec ran after them and promised, in low Breton—which, by virtue of its affinities with Sanskrit, the Tibetans understood—to return the following year to offer his hand and his heart.

"Alone?" the young woman asked.

Trabadec understood her well enough; the Tibetan brunette, humiliated, turned her back on him. Another lost opportunity for poor Trabadec!

Several days after that original marriage proposal, Farandoul, having seen no sign of the pirates, began to fear that they had changed their plans. Mandibul and four men sent forth as scouts combed all the roads for a week without discovering any trace of them. On their return, Farandoul did not hesitate; he broke camp and headed directly into the Katzi to go into the Chinese provinces by the Mimiats, between the chains of Baigau-Kharat and the mountains of Khangai.

There, again, terrible difficulties cropped up. By virtue of the absolute lack of forage, the horses bought in Tibet all perished and, after a month of fatigue, having withstood several attacks by bands of Sipan[89]—redoubtable Tibetan bandits—the mariners arrived on foot in the Chinese province of Szechuan, or the Four Valleys.

It was a matter of making progress as rapidly as possible, for the interpreter, in his conversations with the Chinese encountered en route, told him that the white elephant had passed that way a fortnight before, bound for Chengdu, the capital of the province.

What should they do? In that distant corner of the immensity called China, the horse was unknown; the Chinese could scarcely remember having once seen a few mandarins mounted on the little horses of the South—and yet it was necessary to forge ahead and make up the ground made by the elephant. To go forward on foot was impracticable; they risked losing the track entirely.

Fortunately, as our friends were searching for some means of transport, Farandoul noticed a strange vehicle advancing along a sufficiently well-maintained road. It was a wheelbarrow, and a wheelbarrow with a sail![90] The imaginative Chinese mind had come up with this means of locomotion. It was more than bizarre, it was baroque—but it worked.

The wheelbarrow moves on a single centrally-placed wheel; the traveler on one side of it and places his luggage on the other to form a counterweight. A little mast at the front supports a large sail, which inflates as the breeze blows and triples the speed; as an initial condition, however, it requires a breeze. Fortunately for the wheelbarrows, the breeze blows almost constantly on the high plateau where there are no horses, sometimes too violently.

The wheelbarrow that our friends were admiring carried a young upper-class Chinese girl, gracefully seated, with her fan in her hand and her legs

---

[89] Sipan is actually the name of a region, but the larger region of which it is a part, Koko Nor, was represented as notorious bandit country in the few 19th century accounts that exist of Tibet, including one by the British traveler Thomas Hungerford Holdich.

[90] Robida's illustrations make it clear that he really does mean wheelbarrows with sails, not vehicles styled like rickshaws; the driver is positioned at the rear of the vehicle, pushing it along.

stretched out on the board. The driver, carried away by the wind, was running breathlessly. As with couriers in India or Japan, families of sail-barrow coachmen have developed extraordinary lung capacity; they can run for six hours without stopping for a second and resume, after a short rest, for a further six hours.

Farandoul hired the services of 25 sail-barrows at a fee of 40 centimes a day, without haggling. On the promise of a big tip at the end of their service, the brave Chinamen promised devotion and rapidity. Each of the mariners installed himself in his own in the proper manner, with an equivalent weight of baggage on the other side and loaded weapons within arm's reach in case of trouble. The seven supplementary wheelbarrows followed as reserves. A nice breeze picked up immediately, and the drivers hoisted the sails, to the great joy of the mariners, who had not been under sail for a long time. Hurrah! The wind filled the sails and the 25 wheelbarrows set off with the rapidity of arrows.

Farandoul and Mandibul went side-by-side at the head of the convoy, studying the landscape with their telescopes in hand and discussing to the route to follow. Until dusk they sailed with the wind behind them at the same velocity. The next day was just as good, but on the third day the wind had changed direction; it was necessary to veer north-north-east and tack, as at sea, for part of the day.

Navigating on land in sail-barrows was not unpleasant; there were more jolts than on a liquid surface, but one ought to be spared—so, at least, our mariners thought—the awful surprises of true navigation. They averaged 25 leagues a day. The mariners, familiar with the use of sails, lent considerable aid to the maneuvering. Not an inch of canvas was wasted; they flew rather than marched, and once the vehicle was in full flow, the driver often found a means to sit down for a few moments on the shafts.

The journey continued for a week, sometimes with the wind behind and sometimes tacking. They arrived thus within sight of Chengdu; the interpreter asked about the road ahead in an inn before entering the city. It was as well for our friends that he did, because he learned that the mandarin of the city, doubtless alerted by the thieves of the white elephant, was not well-disposed to the travelers; his intention was to let them enter the city and then retain the under some pretext or other.

As for the elephant, it had continued on its way. Where had it gone? Had it taken the northern route to Peking, passing through the provinces of Kansu, or Salutary Fear, and Shansi, the Western Mountains? Had it descended southwards to reach Canton via Yunan, or Cloudy South, and Kwangsi, the Extended West? Or, finally, had it headed for Nanking through the central provinces? A problem! A precaution taken by the mandarin of Chengdu furnished the solution. On circling round the city in search of some indication, our friends saw that all the roads were open save the one to Nanking, which a platoon of Chinese soldiers had the ridiculous pretension of guarding. That was the one it was necessary to follow.

The Chinese guards took up their arms and waved their shields in an intimidating manner as the mariners approached; the latter continued to advance. The anxious guards sounded gongs with no greater success. Then, judging the defense sufficient, the officer sounded the retreat, and the road was open.

Within three days the mariners reached the Yangtze-Kiang, the famous Blue River—the Chinese Mississippi, which describes a course through the Celestial Empire of 4,200 kilometers. The wind, blowing as a strong breeze, lifted up the sail-barrows; a few hours after sighting the river, the wind became a squall and the barrows literally took off without the aid of the drivers, who were dragged along involuntarily.

They could have hauled in the sails and waited for the storm to end, but Farandoul wanted to take advantage of the strong wind in order to gain a dozen leagues. Soon, the thunder and the rain joined in the party. From their dwellings, the inhabitants of riverside villages watched with alarm as 25 wheelbarrows passed like lightning along the storm-swept road.

It was even worse when they arrived on a bare plateau where no obstacle arrested the furious gusts of the tempest. In spite of the mariners' skill, there was a collision between three wheelbarrows. The sails split; one wheel was broken. A fourth wheelbarrow, trying to change course in order to avoid a further collision, presented its flank to the squall and was instantly thrown into the river, running 60 feet below the road. They stopped to help the accident victims. It was poor Tournesol who took the forced bath; it was only with great difficulty that he and his driver regained the bank. As for the wheelbarrow and its luggage, the river had swallowed them

Apart from this minor accident the journey was smooth; they had covered 35 leagues and reached the province of Kweichow—a poetic name which means Distinguished District. To avoid the possibility of dangerous accidents in the dark they made an early stop at an inn in the vicinity of Chungking. The white elephant, concealed by its thieves by a coat of red paint, had stayed in exactly the same place ten days before. They were on the right road!

The tempest had ended when they got under way the next day, but a brisk breeze promised further rapid navigation. The region being rather populous, Farandoul decided to avoid all the cities and large towns they encountered. It was a wise precaution, for a certain agitation was noticeable in the countryside; in the villages, people gathered around the travelers without manifesting much astonishment, which seemed to indicate that the arrival of Europeans had been anticipated. Two days from Chungking, bad news awaited our friends.

Doubtless won over by the pirates, the governor of the province and the powerful Mandarin of the Fifth Cardinal Point of China, the center—also known as the general of the central provinces—had mobilized militias to bar the route of "the barbarians," the word *barbarians* evidently referring to our friends.

Proclamations pinned up even in the smallest villages described, with a great wealth of detail, the bearded men of the Occident, their costumes and their weapons. In spite of the flagrant hostility of the locals, however, they were able to advance for a further week without coming up against any real obstacles. They encountered several bands of militiamen, acting under the orders of a few aged officers recalled to military service, but these brave soldiers pretended not to recognize "the barbarians" in order not to have to oppose their passage.

The wheelbarrow-drivers, on the promise of a large supplementary payment, consented to continue their service until horses were found for the entire troop. There was a moment of hesitation, however, in Sukiu, the first town in the province of Hupeh, when they learned that the Chinese army was occupying a narrow pass two league further on, between the Blue River and the Tapaling Mountains.

Mandibul set off with four men on a scouting expedition to assess the gravity of the situation.

The militias of three provinces, regiments of the line and a regiment of tiger warriors from the Imperial Guard, under the orders of the Mandarin of the Fifth Cardinal Point—a former general well-known for his exploits in the Taiping War[91]—were prepared to meet the barbarian attack courageously. Their position had been well-chosen; in order to penetrate into the central provinces it would be necessary to make a long tour through the mountains and the terrible Gobi Desert, or pass over their bodies.[92]

The arrival of the barbarians had been signaled; the Chinese advance positions, having been judged too exposed, had been pulled back toward the main body of the army. The militias on the wings occupied a series of arid small hills; the depths of the gorge and the road itself were guarded by the line-regiment and the tiger warriors.

Sukiu had been abandoned by its population. Our friends found the gates open, only guarded by old pairs of boots suspended from the fortifications. Farandoul explained the custom to his men; in China, whenever a mandarin fled the town entrusted to his care, the population, if it were content with his administration, gave him a new pair of boots and took away his old ones in order to hang them above the main gate in solemn testimony.

Our friends took advantage of the solitude of the town to prepare themselves for their confrontation with the Chinese army by means of a good meal and a nice siesta. The wheelbarrow drivers not wanting to take the risk, the mar-

---

[91] The Taiping rebellion broke out in 1850, when Hung Siu-tsuen's forces captured Nanking and Shanghai and attacked Peking. It was eventually put down in 1855.

[92] To reach the Gobi Desert from Hupeh would require a very long detour indeed—at least 1000 miles—but here, as elsewhere, Robida's physical geography is a trifle inexact.

iners got them drunk, promised them yet another marvelous wage-supplement and finally, to calm their fears, tried to make them proof against bullets and arrows by means of armor-plating, formed by four large shields attached in front, in rear and to the sides. When everything was ready, taking advantage of a fit of bravery on the part of the drivers, they climbed on to the wheelbarrows, hoisted the sails and set off rapidly under the impulsion of a brisk breeze.

Two kilometers from Sukiu, an infernal noise struck the mariners' ears; it was the Chinese army getting ready for the anticipate attack.

It took more than a quarter of an hour to come within sight of the enemy. On the higher ground, the Chinese militiamen were beating their shields in rage and brandishing their terrible swords. Gongs and drums were resonating like thunder. In the advance positions, the roaring tiger warriors and the heroes of the line were waving images of flamboyant dragons, mounting a terrifying fantasia. Fortunately, the wheelbarrow drivers could scarcely see any of this from behind their armor plating, or their courage might perhaps have failed. The breeze blew; they went forward like lightning; the mariners readied their weapons, hatchets and revolvers.

"Charge!" cried Farandoul, when they were 100 meters from the enemy.

The soldiers of the line, armed with wheel-lock muskets, had been exciting the wicks of their fuses for half an hour—now the moment had come. "Fire!" cried the officers.

The wheels grated, and finally turned; the wicks came down and—bang! bang! bang!—the detonations burst forth…but the wheelbarrows had already passed by and the mariners were engaging with the guard's tiger warriors.

The Mandarin of the Fifth Cardinal Point was there, urging the tigers to carnage. What a mêlée! Launched forwards with violence, the sail-barrows had ploughed through the fist ranks and were cutting through the regiment at various points. Our friends, standing up on the wheelbarrows, were belabored by the hatchets, sabers, pickaxes and six-pointed spears of the brave tigers. They had only to follow the furrows that Farandoul and Mandibul were tracing through the Chinese ranks. Mandibul's driver, seized by curved picks, fell into the power of the tigers, but Tournesol was able to gather him up and throw him on to his own barrow, almost unhurt.

The Mandarin of the Fifth Cardinal Point, seeing that things were going badly for the tiger warriors, sounded a rallying-cry and hastened to support of the heroes of the line with fusillades from the flank and the rear. To plant the props in the ground, load, prime and support the arquebuses, to light the wicks, excite them and make the wheels turn was, for the heroes of the line, the affair of a moment—which lasted seven minutes!

"Fire! Fire!" cried the mandarin, waving his swords.

Too late! The wheelbarrows were out of range; only one stray bullet struck the rearmost driver on the shield protecting his back.

The passage was forced! The rearguard of the Chinese army continued to wave its shields and beat its gongs; the heroes of the line sent a few more volleys along the road and the tiger warriors licked their wounds. The Mandarin of the Fifth Cardinal Point, considering that he was, after all, still master of the battlefield, hastened to send a triumphant dispatch to Peking.

V.

The news of the extermination of the barbarians by the Mandarin of the Fifth Cardinal Point having spread throughout China, our friends' journey was untroubled by any further incidents. They calmly descended the course of the Blue River on the track of the white elephant—which was quite easy to follow, for the pirates, like everyone else, believed that the mariners, exterminated by the tiger warriors, could not trouble them now. The region possessed horses, but as the sail-barrows had proved themselves, they decided to continue their route in that kind of vehicle for as long as the wind did not turn around. They gained ground on the elephant thieves, who were no more than five days ahead of the brave mariners—another five days of fatigue, and the objective would be attained!

"Where are they going?" Farandoul wondered. "To the great temples of Nanking, no doubt, to sell the bonzes the elephant of which they have already heard so much. We must try to catch them up beforehand."

After a journey of 55 days, still traveling in the sail-barrows, our friends arrived within a few league of Nanking, only a few hours behind the pirates. At the last moment, however, when they only needed one final effort to reach their goal, the wind abruptly veered south-south-west. In less than a quarter of an hour the wheelbarrow-drivers' accounts were settled and all of our friends, provided with good horses, were able to continue on their way.

Dusk fell. The cavalcade, launched at top speed, ate up the road; the feverish ardor that animated the mariners was communicated to the horses by persuasive spur-thrusts. This breathless ride had been going on for two hours when Farandoul gave voice to a loud cry. Less than 500 meters ahead, a confused mass of men and horses was distinguishable in the first rays of moonlight. The troop appeared to have halted on the bank of the river.

Farandoul signaled to his friends to halt, concealed them in a fold in the terrain and set forth on foot to investigate, only taking the Siamese interpreter with him.

Their absence was brief. The company was indeed that of the pirates. Hidden in the tall grass, they had been able to get close enough to the bandits to overhear their conversations.

Our friends tried in vain to pierce the darkness, in order to pick out among the horses and the tents the elephant for which they had been search for so long. They circled around the clump of trees sheltering the pirates, but in vain. The white elephant was not there.

The conversation of two lanky individuals informed them of the reason for this absence. The bandits had already concluded a deal; the elephant had just been purchased by the bonzes of a great pagoda on the opposite bank of the Blue River, and a junk from the bonzery had come with great ceremony to fetch the sacred animal, while the leader of the pirates eagerly set his hands on the price of the sale. In fact, Farandoul and the interpreter could still see the junk's large sails a quarter of a league away on the river. Without losing a minute, they returned to the place where the mariners were waiting for them.

Farandoul's plan was simple. They had to get to the river without being seen, take possession of a few boats, and follow the junk. In the vicinity of Nanking the Blue River is no less than seven or eight kilometers wide. On the two banks, where towns and villages are closely clustered, there are also numerous rich bonzeries. It was for one of these bonzeries, on the right bank, that the junk with the white elephant was bound. They had to find out which one as soon as possible, in order to carry off the sacred animal that very night, without leaving the pirates time to repeat the trick they had pulled off in Kifir.

Three large boats discovered in a little bay accommodated all the mariners. They set off in the direction taken by the junk and soon had the joy of catching sight of it. It was already three-quarters of the way across; they had to make haste.

A superb pagoda flanked by a high 15-story tower rose up on the right bank; that was the objective of the voyage. Suddenly, the mariners saw signals exchanged between the junk and the pagoda. The entire bank appeared to be in joyful celebration; rockets burst in the air, and hundreds of lanterns were bobbing in the distance.

The exhausted mariners finally came ashore not far from the pagoda, just in time to see the white elephant make a processional tour of the buildings, to the sound of music that was as unharmonious and sacred as possible. After pausing at every corner of the bonzery, the elephant was led to the great tower, still with the same ceremony, and carefully locked in.

Then the crowd dispersed and the bonzery gradually fell silent.

The mariners, hidden on a little hill overlooking the bonzery, had not missed a single detail of the scene.

At about 2 a.m., when all the lights had gone out and the darkness seemed to Farandoul to be sufficiently profound, the mariners emerged from their hiding-place one by one and crept with infinite precaution to the wall of the pagoda.

There was a ditch to cross and a high defensive wall to scale; that was soon done. As soon as they had descended into the sacred enclosure the mariners opened a gate to prepare their retreat.

An observer placed at a window in the tower would then have been able to see two long black serpents slithering through the long grass, one to the right and one to the left. The one to the left was Farandoul and his men, creeping towards the tower—but what was the serpent to the right? The men composing it suddenly came to an abrupt halt; they had noticed Farandoul and his sailors.

The latter, tranquilized by the silence of the pagoda, had not seen anything. Having arrived near the door, hidden from all eyes by the shadow of the tower, they came to their feet with a single movement. They had a long piece of wood with them—a beam picked up in the ditch. They lifted it together, holding it like a battering-ram, ready to launch themselves at the door that the bonzes had locked. Breaking down the door would, it is true, wake up the monastery, but once in possession of the elephant, the mariners reckoned on making a quick getaway.

At the sight of these preparations, the men of the second serpent quickly moved backwards and hid themselves in one of the pagoda's outbuildings.

It was a solemn moment.

"One...two...three!" said Farandoul. One the word *three*, the beam, swung by 36 arms, struck the door violently. A terrible crack was heard, and the broken door groaned on its hinges.

"One...two...three!"

The beam returned with frightful force, almost staving in one of the panels and tearing away a hinge. A loud rumor was audible in the convent; lanterns were on the move. It was necessary to get the job done quickly.

"Come on!" said Farandoul. "One last strike! One...two...three!"

This time, it seemed as if the shock of an earthquake had just broken the ground. A crack reminiscent of the shearing of a mountain resounded, accompanied by whistling sounds. The entire tower, with its balconies, its bulging roofs, its dragon-formed gutters, its colonettes and its 15 stories, came down on the backs of its invaders and the sacred elephant!

A gigantic heap of debris now covers the ground in the place where the superb tower stood. The bonzes, having recovered from their initial terror, howl lamentations in front of the ruins of what had been glory of their pagoda. The crowd becomes denser; soldiers who have come running try in vain to bring a little order to the chaos.

But how has such a monumental tower been able to crumble under the blows of a wooden beam maneuvered by only 20 men? What is the reason for this inexplicable collapse?

Alas, our unfortunate friends, arriving in the dark, had not been able to reconnoiter the monument they were attacking, or they would have employed another means than brutal effraction to get to the elephant. The 15-story monument, now scattered on the ground as shapeless debris, was none other than the famous Porcelain Tower, the glory of the Canton region, the marvel of China![93]

That alone suffices to explain the fury of the Chinese. What a dreadful event, a monumental sacrilege! The Porcelain Tower smashed by barbarians! Lying in little pieces like a million broken plates!

Alas, the authors of this act of involuntary vandalism, our poor friends, are doubtless dead, crushed beneath the wreckage. The white elephant must also have perished!

The Chinese work with a feverish ardor to clear the rubble in order to recover the corpses and to take revenge upon them for the damage.

It was only after 18 hours of continuous effort that the 700 or 800 workers obtained their first result. The body of a mariner and the end of the beam that had served to commit the crime appeared beneath the debris. The mandarin in the blue hat directing the search had the body transported to a shed, where physicians perceived that the man was merely unconscious, with bruises of no great consequence covering his body.

"Put him in chains," said the mandarin.

---

[93] The actual Porcelain Tower of Nanking, built in the 15th century and occasionally nominated as one of the wonders of the modern world, had been badly damaged in the Taiping Rebellion and was subsequently destroyed in 1856. It was only nine stories high, so this imaginary substitute seems to be an even finer edifice.

Another 16 hours sufficed to finish the work and collect the inert bodies of all our friends. The seamen, the interpreter, Mandibul and Farandoul were brought in succession to the floor of the shed, where doctors in spectacles awaited them. They were all alive! Their unconsciousness was only caused by lack of air and bruises.

When they opened their eyes, it was to see that they were bound by heavy chains and guarded by fearsome-looking tiger warriors.

Meanwhile, the Chinese were still digging in vain, trying to find the body of the white elephant....

"What about...the white elephant?" Mandibul murmured, in a feeble voice.

"I saw it," Farandoul replied. "It should be safe. Our beam, as it broke through the door, struck it from the rear and launched it into the opposite wall. The tower crumbled...perhaps the elephant went through the wall...before the fall. Perhaps it has saved itself!"

Indeed, the Chinese were beginning to despair of recovering the sacred animal. Farandoul's inductions were correct. The white elephant, launched by a violent blow from the beam, had gone through the wall like a bullet a mere second before the collapse, while the tower was swaying before falling. Bewildered and furious. it had been about to run straight ahead when the men of the second troop, who were none other than the pirates, abruptly surged forth, seized it as it passed, and fled with it before the arrival of the bonzes.

Meanwhile, the mandarin with the blue hat, Tsi-tsang, after 40 hours of labor, had established the complete disappearance of the white elephant. He gave the order to transport the authors of the crime, under escort, to the prison in Nanking.

Farandoul and the mariners were beginning to recover from their long period of unconsciousness; they were suffering greatly from the many bruises they had sustained, but, in the terrible situation into which they had been thrown, such petty troubles were of no account. The Siamese interpreter had a smattering of the learned language, and had repeated to them several conversations between the mandarin and his officers, which did not bode well.

The officers had been inclined towards an immediate execution on the scene of the crime, but the mandarin had announced the intention to proceed by due legal process—first to exact payment for the damage, if that were possible, and then to regulate the affair with great ceremony.

It is not in terms of the comforts they provide that the prisons of any country in the world usually excel, so you will not be surprised to learn that, on their arrival in Nanking prison, our friends found themselves very badly lodged, very disagreeably treated and so ridiculously nourished that their brains were soon working overtime on plans for escape. They had, however, been given the honor of a special building at the back of a courtyard, and the no-less-great honor of a guard of tiger warriors, not to mention other attentions ordered by the mandarin Tsi-tsang, to wit: six kilos of iron on the feet of each man and a first-class cangue—which is to say, an enormous piece of wood provided with a hole for the head—on his shoulders. The mandarin, judging these precautions sufficient, left them at relative liberty; they could walk in the courtyard with their irons, or sleep sitting up with their cangues propped up on a few stones, as they pleased.

It was only after a week of this charmless existence that our friends were brought before the terrible mandarin in the blue hat. Their case, already dark, had taken on an even blacker hue during that week, politics having become mixed up in it. Tsi-Tsang's enemies at the court in Peking had profited from the disaster of the Porcelain Tower to accuse the mandarin of administrative weakness, and to put the blame on the incompetence of his police—so Tsi-Tsang had decided to exact a dreadful vengeance for the crime in order to silence his detractors, by means of one of those striking tortures that surprise and captivate the imagination.

In spite of a thorough search, the white elephant had not been found; the accused had therefore to answer for "the dreadful demolition of the Porcelain Tower, ornament of the flourishing province of Kiangsu, and the theft by breaking and entering of a sacred animal from a thrice-holy pagoda"—crimes not previously envisaged by the laws of the Celestial Empire.

The mandarin Tsi-Tsang was assisted in his solemn audience by four other mandarins, with yellow and red hats, four officers, and four learned men fulfilling the office of clerks of the court. A guard of tiger warriors kept the populace as far away as possible from the noble judges.

Interrogated in Chinese, none of the mariners was, of course, able to reply. Farandoul, observing the hostile disposition of the tribunal, forbade the Siamese interpreter to say anything. Although the work of the judges was abridged thereby, that did not prevent the trial from lasting two weeks—to the great annoyance of Farandoul, for whom the days spent at the hearing were time lost, because no opportunity to attempt an escape could arise in the middle of a courtroom besieged by a crowd and guarded by 300 men.

Finally, the accused not having wished to answer any questions and having said nothing regarding their situation or the circumstances that had brought them to China, the mandarin broached the question of damages and asked them whether, by combining all their resources, they might be able to pay the sum of 165 millions, the approximate cost of the damage—promising, if the material damage were repaired, only to put them to death with relative gentleness.

In the face of the obstinate silence of the accused, it only remained for the tribunal to pass sentence. After six hours of consultation with the most intelligent executioners, summoned to a solemn conference from all the provinces of the empire, the tribunal came back into session in the midst of the breathless murmurs of the audience.

The interpreter, half dead with fright, cocked a desolate ear to listen to the sentence read out in a severe tone by the mandarin Tsi-Tsang. After a considerable number of "givens" and "considerings," the guilty parties were condemned to be subjected, over three days, to the terrible *torture of the 98,000 pieces.*

A shudder went through the crowd. The torture of the 98,000 pieces, formerly reserved for the crime of treason, had not been applied for 800 years. Before the session closed, therefore, the auditorium requested a stay of a week, in order to have the time to inform friends and relatives in other provinces of the solemnity that was in preparation.

Our poor friends, now certain of their fate, were immediately taken back to prison. As they had passed from the rank of remand prisoners to that of condemned prisoners, certain formalities had to be carried out on their arrival. Their chains and cangues were taken off in order that they could be refitted with the cangues of the condemned, which were more than twice as heavy. The two leaders, Farandoul and Mandibul, became the objects of special attention; they were not fitted with the cangues of the condemned but were introduced, in chains, into barrels pierced, like the cangues, with holes for their heads. In such a barrel— a considerable aggravation of the punishment—one could only sustain oneself on one's knees or squatting on one's heels. Farandoul and Mandibul pulled horrible faces when they found themselves thus treated; how could anyone maintain the faintest hope of escape with that infernal barrel on his shoulders? The mandarin Tsi-Tsang could sleep easy on his two pillows, without any fear that his prey might escape!

The first visit that our friends received after their reintroduction to the prison was that of the executioner—the conference prize-winner!—who had re-discovered, by dint of research in libraries, the exact tradition of the curious torture of the 98,000 pieces. He came politely to pay his respects to the unfortunates who would furnish him the occasion to consolidate his artistic reputation. To begin with, his advances well ill-received by the mariners, but Mandibul, having been informed of his quality and being curious to know beforehand exactly what the famous torture comprised, asked the interpreter to interrogate the brave executioner.

In truth, the torture of the 98,000 pieces was nothing vulgar. The instrument, remarkably ingenious, was far in advance of the saber, the rope or simple, sempiternal and routine decapitation. Firstly, he set in motion the mechanism—a neat device, operable by the hand of a child. One had only to turn a wheel and, all the cogs being set in motion, the machine would cut a criminal into 98,000 little flakes within the space of six hours.

In response to Mandibul's objections, the executioner took the plans of his machine out of his pocket and entered into a long series of explanations. The Siamese interpreter had fainted in his cangue; the executioner complaisantly flung a few drops of water in his face to revive him. Before leaving, he informed our friends that their status as prisoners condemned to death entitled them to certain privileges, including additional food and a few pipes of opium.

"Well," said Mandibul, after the executioner's departure, "did you understand? In a week, we'll be divided into 98,000 little slices. It's hopeless!"

"You're right," Farandoul replied. "It's hopeless. Well, let's smoke to stupefy ourselves. We have a right to opium, I want opium, and all of you want it…"

"My word, no—I don't have the heart for a pipe…"

"I tell you that you all want opium, and a great deal of it. Recall the executioner—he's a fine fellow!"

The executioner was not far away. A tiger warrior ran after him and brought him back.

"Executioner," said Farandoul, via the interpreter, "you're an intelligent man; we're flattered to be passing through the hands of an artist, instead of falling into those of some vulgar flayer. We have the right to smoke a few pipes, did you say? As I don't want to ask anything of anyone else, would you be so kind as to obtain opium and pipes for us? I have a few gold coins hidden in my belt; take them and bring us opium—as much as possible, for there are 18 of us, all smokers."

"Rely on me!" replied the executioner, flattered by this confidence. "I'll come back with everything necessary in a quarter of an hour."

"Why do you want so much opium?" asked Mandibul.

"To smoke, of course! We shall all smoke for five minutes—then, when the executioner has gone, we shall declare that opium is a drug good only for the Chinese, and...silence! Here's the executioner."

The worthy man came in with a fine collection of pipes and a large packet of opium, purchased with Farandoul's savings. He distributed the pipes to the condemned men himself, and stuffed them with grains of opium. "Just try not to break the pipes," he said, via the interpreter. "I'll keep them to remember you by!"

"Thank you," Farandoul replied. "In recompense for your good deed, I'd just like to give you a little advice about your machine. It's perfect; I can only see one small improvement. If I were you, I'd have it driven by steam...."

"I've already thought about that, vaguely," the executioner replied, "but in China, you know, people don't like innovators. I'd make enemies. I'll think about it, though, and I shan't despair of being able to bring your idea to fruition some day. I have to leave you, though—must get on! I'll come back in a week; you have enough opium to smoke until then."

The executioner had scarcely departed when the 18 condemned men took the first drags on their pipes; on a signal from Farandoul they stopped after five minutes, with grimaces of disgust. The tiger warriors looked at them and darted glances at the provision of opium that Mandibul had appeared to put prudently aside.

"Pooh, what a drug!" cried Farandoul, after making faces for five minutes.

The 18 condemned men threw away their pipes.

"If you don't want it...?" said the leader of the tigers, coming forward.

"You can take the opium if you want it," Farandoul replied, "but on one condition—you let us have a breather outside our barrels."

"Provided that you get back into them when the officer makes his rounds."

In consequence of this agreement, Farandoul and Mandibul were released from their barrels, and the tiger warriors, leaping upon the opium, lost themselves delightedly in clouds of aromatic smoke.

The mariners had understood Farandoul's plan. Mute and motionless, they prayed for the happy moment to arrive when the surly guards, lost in divine ecstasy, would only be paying scant attention to things of this world.

Lying at the back of the room, the half-closed eyes of the tiger warriors followed the spirals of smoke that were beginning to take on, for them, the vague forms of pretty women with friendly smiles and imperceptible feet. The leader of the tigers, deeply intoxicated, forgot everything, including the imminent arrival of the nocturnal round and the strokes of bamboo that would be his reward if he were caught in that state of somnolent bliss.

Farandoul did not forget; taking advantage of the increasing obscurity, he had slipped behind the smokers with infinite precaution. What was he doing there? From time to time, the Chinamen moved their heads and put their hands to their long plaited hair, as if something were troubling them.

Suddenly, Farandoul leapt to his feet and, in spite of his chains, seized some of the tiger warriors' swords. The mariners were already running forward, in spite of the weight of their cangues.

The tiger warriors, stunned at first, made an effort to shake off the opium fumes; they got to their feet, but could only mill around in inextricable confusion. Farandoul had taken his precautions; he had had attached them all to one another by tying their long pigtails together, and could now laugh at their efforts.

"Quickly, quickly!" he cried, strangling the leader of the tigers' leader somewhat, to make him hand them over more rapidly. "The keys to the cangues!"

The tiger protested hotly. The interpreter understood his explanation that the keys to the cangues were in the possession of the officer who would make the round.

"Shall we wait for the round?" Farandoul asked the sailors.

"No, no! They're a bit heavy, but let's get out of here anyway."

The mariners ran outside after having gagged the tigers. During the journey between the hearing and the prison, Farandoul had studied the locality. Without hesitation, he steered his troop towards the wall of the enclosure overlooking the bank of the Blue River. As they reached the wall, they hurled themselves upon a sentry. Without giving him time to cry out, Tournesol and Escoubico seized him between their cangues, squeezed him a little, and let him fall, three-quarters strangled.

The way was open. They had to scale the wall with 20-kilo cangues on their shoulders;[94] they succeeded regardless, and as soon as they were on the other side, they gained open country, in order to put as much distance as possible between the ingenious machine of the 98,000 thin slices and the unfortunates charged with its inauguration.

"Oof! Oof!" repeated Mandibul, as he ran. "How good it is to be free. How good it is to walk about intact instead of feeling oneself being subdivided into little flakes. Oof! Oof! When the Devil will we be able to get out of this infernal China?"

"When we've retrieved the white elephant!" replied Farandoul.

When dawn broke, at about 4 a.m., our friends were forced to seek refuge somewhere to hide from all eyes. No forest was discernible on the horizon. Farandoul was beginning to get direly anxious when a bed of reeds bordering a long stretch of the river caught his eye.

---

[94] Presumably, we have to assume that the "tigers" did have the keys to Farandoul's and Mandibul's chains, as the intrepid duo no longer seem to be burdened by them, although Farandoul was still impeded by his when he grabbed the swords. It is not clear whether or not the barrels needed keys in order to be removed, but if they did, the tigers obviously had them in their possession.

"There's no time to hesitate," he said. "It's in there that we must hide until dusk. It's wet, but it's better than prison."

VI.

Our friends established themselves in the middle of the reed-bed, well-hidden but knee-deep in water. To occupy their leisure, they tried to break the hinges of their cangues, but without result.

As the hours seemed long while they were enduring their forced bath, it was with envious eyes that they contemplate the Tankaderes,[95] the pretty Chinese boatwomen who were passing by on the river, singing, or preparing food 200 meters from their hiding-place. Save for a few imprudent frogs, they had nothing to calm the pangs in their stomachs, already debilitated by the prison food.

Towards dusk, the boats and the boatwomen became rarer. Our friends, quivering with impatience, were only waiting for the right moment to get under way again. Night fell; they were about to depart. Suddenly, a large junk passing along the edge of the reed-bed sent them hurrying back into their hiding-place. Farandoul started. In the prow of the junk, a man with a lantern in his hand was leaning over the river.

Like Farandoul, Mandibul had made a forward movement. "It's him! It's him!" he said, in a stifled voice.

"Yes," replied Farandoul. "It's him—the bayaderes' musician, the stealer of the white elephant. Enough! We've got him! The elephant must be aboard. He'll go down the river and head for the sea. We must try to find a boat and follow the junk. Forward—and don't make any noise."

The pirates' junk had regained the open water and was sailing 200 meters from the bank. The mariners made themselves as inconspicuous as possible and followed it at a gymnastic pace, in spite of their cangues.

After two hours, the course of the junk and its followers entered a busier region. The riverbank sparkled in the distance with thousands of lights; there was a town there—an immense accumulation of dangers for our friends: the danger of being captured; the danger of losing the junk.

The town was Siposi, the pleasure resort where the businessmen of Nanking came to relax from their affairs in the tea-houses or on the flower-boats. Visible ahead, garlanded with lanterns, were several of these floating cafés, where

---

[95] I can find no evidence that this term has the meaning that Robida attaches to it, but *Tankadere* was the name of a ship featured in Verne's *Le Tour du monde en 80 jours*.

one could always be sure of finding exquisite cuisine and music, private cabins and charming little Chinese women with almond-shaped eyes.

The junk had already passed the town and disappeared into the darkness in the distance. As yet, the mariners had only found one wretched boat with no oars.

"No more hesitation!" cried Farandoul. "Let's float downstream in this wreck, board the first boat we come too, and steal it!"

Huddled together in the bottom of the boat, the mariners set themselves adrift. Soon, the high poop of a white and blue boat anchored by a little island appeared some distance away. Lanterns were swaying cheerfully from its masts and yard-arms; the sounds of hectic music, escaping from all its portholes, clearing indicated that they were dealing with some sprightly flower-boat.[96]

"Are we boarding her?" Mandibul asked. "We'll have difficulty…"

"Too bad!" retorted Farandoul. "Let's go." And the boat ran violently into the stern of the flower-boat. No one on board paid any attention. The marines scaled the high sides of the vessel silently and leapt on to the deck.

The music stopped abruptly, and a terrible scream went up in the boat at the sight of these unknown men wearing the cangues of criminals. Four ravishing Chinese women who were dancing in the middle of a circle of pleasure-seekers let themselves fall on to the knees of their admirers. The mariners brandished the swords stolen from the tiger warriors in such a bellicose fashion that any inclination to defense vanished of its own accord. The little Chinese women emerging frantically from all parts of the boat released screams of desperation, but none of the men present sought the honor of dying for them.

While Farandoul held the population of the boat in respect, Mandibul and a few men ran to the foredeck, to the mast terminated by oriflammes and gilded depictions of birds. A few minutes sufficed for them to hoist the large multicolored sail, and the boat, under the influence of the breeze, was son swaying, ready to set off along the river.

"Cut the anchor-rope!" cried Farandoul. "Well done, lads!"

At the sight of these preparations, the Chinamen leapt overboard like a flock of sheep and swam to the little island, save for the infirm and feminine elements of the crew, who remained aboard.

"We've no time to lose—we'll drop you off further on," Farandoul told them. "In the meantime, stay calm."

The handful of Chinamen still aboard and the 25 pretty women forming the ornamentation of the flower-boat were gathered together in the stern, guarded by two men.

---

[96] The word I have translated, literally, as "sprightly," is *pimpant*, whose metaphorical meaning—as is obvious from its English transliteration—enhances the obvious suggestion that the vessel is a floating brothel.

They were nearing Siposi. The mariners headed into the middle of the river in order to avoid the lights of other flower-boats as much as was possible; they were, however, hailed several times by groups of party-goers desirous of supping in good company. Only one of these bands succeeded in accosting the boat: four Chinamen, bearing gifts of flowers and roasted suckling-pigs for the ladies climbed up the port-side ladder, singing and hooting with laughter, but their joyful mood vanished when they were suddenly grabbed by men charged with the familiar cangues of those condemned to death.

Mandibul was already searching the crew's cabins for some instrument capable of breaking the hinges of the cangues to free the sailors. It was difficult to find one, but finally, after hours of effort, the mariners were released from the apparatus that weighed upon their shoulders and could breathe easily. How light they felt, and how ready they were now to challenge all the regiments of tiger warriors!

The young Chinese women, a little less frightened, looked at these brave matelots with astonishment; for their part, the latter were not so absorbed by maneuvering the vessel not to risk winking at their elegant captives from time to time. These flowers of the Celestial Empire were clad in long tight-fitting dresses in the most vivid colors, with low necklines in the form of flowers, gently retained by scarves. All their anxiety was a matter of not knowing where they were going; the strangest rumors were already circulating around the flower-boat. Some thought they had simply fallen into the hands of Formosan bandits and were expecting to be taken as beautiful decorations to the pirates' lair, while others, more romantically inclined, thought they were being kidnapped on behalf of some monarch of distant Europe. While waiting, to get well in with their ravishers, they competed for everyone's attention, as much for the simplest sea-man as for the worthy Mandibul.

Hunger was beginning to make itself felt aboard. Farandoul had the trem-bling Chinamen removed to the deepest hold and decided that the crew ought to prepare a restorative supper. In consequence, the boast's cook, discovered un-derneath his oven, was summoned to serve the most exquisite dishes he had with the least possible delay. The young Chinese women had already set the table with an accumulation of little pots, and ivory chopsticks fulfilled the role of spoons and forks. The first course, composed of preserves, was rushed through with disdainful smiles; then came other preserves in castor oil—which, with common accord, were thrown overboard.

"The main course, immediately!" commanded Farandoul, looking at the cook with such a terrible expression that he almost tipped an entire plate of sticky and scented sauce, in which a few small squid were swimming, over Mandibul's back. The cook quickly came back with two whole roasted dogs in the middle of an immense plate of apples cooked in oil.

"Bah!" said Mandibul, philosophically. "I've always been a dog-lover; let's tuck into those."

Finally, the swallows' nests arrived, awaited impatiently, then a soup of earthworms and more pots of preserves.

"Oof!" said Mandibul, getting up from the table. "We won't get fat here; what a diabolical cuisine! *Ventre de phoque*, it seems to me that I could eat an apothecary's stock!"

Farandoul had already gone back up to the deck to inspect the river. The Sun was rising brightly; Nanking and Siposi were far away. As the breeze was strong, they ought to be arriving soon at the junction with the Imperial Canal from Peking, a dangerous place for our friends because of the considerable number of junks circulating on the canal between the northern provinces and the Blue River.

Soon the river became busier; barges, junks, customs boats, smugglers' boats and flower-boats were furrowing the 12-kilometer width of the beautiful Blue River. As they approached the Imperial Canal the mariners, disguised to varying degrees as fantasy Chinamen, dressed the boat's three decks with flags and hung lanterns everywhere: on the yardarms of the large sail, the projections of the top deck, the windows and the fantastically-sculpted stairways. Banners ornamented with diabolical animals floated from the rigging, and at the very top of the mast, gilded balloons floated about a golden dragon with its red mouth vastly agape, inflated by the breeze.

Envious glances were darted at the joyous boat from all the barges they en-countered, but no one dared accost it, doubtless thinking that it had been hired by some mandarin. The poor Chinamen in the depths of the hold reflected sadly as they heard their compatriots' jests.

Farandoul had recognized the triangular sail of the pirates' junk in the dis-tance, more than two leagues ahead, and made every effort not to lose sight of it. That was not easy; the slow-paced flower-boat was not made for rapid sailing. It was not allowed to get too far ahead, though, and when dusk came the junk was still visible.

"We're nearing the coast," Farandoul said. "Our thieves will head out to sea, without a doubt, but in which direction will they steer? Their junk is a fast vessel; who knows how our flower-boat will fare at sea?"

"What about our Chinese passengers?" asked Mandibul. "Are we setting them ashore?"

"Impossible. We can't lose an hour without risking letting the junk escape. Let's take them with us! It'll be a nice little pleasure-trip for them."

The two junks, separated from one another by a mere four kilometers, reached the mouth of the Blue River the following morning, after having passed through the town of Chingkiang in the middle of the night. At the first shock of the waves the flower-boat's beautiful captives had a fit of anxiety, but the ever-persuasive Farandoul calmed them down, merely promising them a simple sea excursion.

Mandibul, having discovered a Chinese spyglass aboard, shook his head as he watched the pirates' junk disappearing in the distance.

"Yes, yes," said Farandoul. "I see it clearly; they're heading for Japan. So much the better! We haven't been condemned to death over there."

As the weather was fine, no one had any further desire to complain.

"A funny voyage!" Mandibul never ceased to murmur during the 30 days that their pursuit of the pirates lasted. "A funny crew! I'm not complaining, though, and if it weren't for the awful cuisine, I could sail like this for a long time!"

The crew of the pirates' junk had quickly perceived the obstinate pursuit of which it was the object, so it tried to lose itself in the middle of the labyrinthine Ryukyu islands, but the attempt was vain; the flower-boat always found it again and followed it at a distance of a few leagues. Changing tactics then, it made straight for the Japanese coast, seeking an opportunity to disembark its passengers without being seen. It was only after a fortnight's journey along the coast that the junk was able to lose itself, by courtesy of an exceedingly stormy night.

The battered flower-boat had a great deal of trouble staying at sea; it required all the skill of its crew to avoid running dangerously aground on the reefs. In the morning, Farandoul anxiously scanned the horizon, but the pirates' junk had disappeared. For three days he visited the smallest inlets of the coast. There was no sign of any shipwreck, so the white elephant's junk could not have perished. Soon, he became certain that the pirates must have disembarked in the estates of the Prince of Miko,[97] one of the most powerful feudal daimios of the Japanese Empire, a near-independent prince very hostile to Europeans.

---

[97] In Japan a *miko* is a female attendant at a Shinto shrine, the word originally referring to a kind of magician roughly analogous to a Greek pythoness, but there does not seem to be any significance in Robida's use of the term as the name of a fictitious province.

Farandoul did not hesitate. He steered for Yokohama, a city open to Europeans in the estates of the Mikado, landed his flower-boat there and bid farewell to his ex-captives with a rapidity that offended them somewhat—but time was pressing. After two hours devoted to purchases in the city, he took passage with all his men on a fishing-boat, which disembarked them secretly the following night in the estates of the Prince of Miko.

It is appropriate here to give a brief sketch of this Prince of Miko, known in Europe only for his eternal difficulties with the Mikado.

The prince, named Si-Kamito-Kaido, was then a rather mature young man of 35 or 36, ruddy-faced, irascible by nature, as turbulent as all the great daimios of the empire, and a little more so than some. His ancestors had lived independently, contenting themselves with sending an occasional tribute to the Tycoon[98] or the Mikado, the spiritual emperor—or, rather, his palace administrator. Lord Kaido asked no more than that he be allowed follow the example of his forebears and isolate himself as much as possible from the suzerain authority, but times had changed, alas; the Mikado had seized the scepter with a firm hand again, had triumphed over the resistance of the Tycoon, and had reduced the majority of great vassals of the crown to the status of simple prefects!

Already Kaido, Prince of Miko, successor to a long line of powerful overlords, had felt the weight of the Mikado's large hand. His rights as a reigning prince had been subject to more than one obstruction and the day was perhaps not far off when he would have to resolve himself to living with a mere shadow of authority over his patrimonial lands.

Kaido was determined to delay that day as long as possible and to defend his prerogatives step by step, with the collaboration of the two- and three-sword nobles of the province. His ministers strongly encouraged him in this firm policy. Unfortunately, he had already been living for some time under the influence of a sort of fatal ill-luck; all his enterprises failed, with a constancy and obstinacy calculated to give rise to reflection. By dint of seeing the best-laid schemes regularly come unstuck, the anxious Kaido had tried consulting his friends, ministers and finally, in despair, the most renowned bonzes and astrologers. The stars, interrogated by these learned men in silence and solitude, had replied; one day, the bonzes and the astrologers, somewhat intimidated by their mission, had come in a group to inform Prince Kaido of the results of their research.

Alas, the oracles were unanimous. The reign of Prince Kaido would remain constantly ill-fated, until—and here the astrologers hesitated—Prince Kaido was deceived by his wife. In that case, everything would change for the Prince; he

---

[98] Before its adoption into English to refer to a plutocrat, "Tycoon" was the title by which the Shogun—the Mikado's worldlier counterpart—was represented to foreigners.

would enjoy every success; his reign would become perfectly happy and would attain the highest degree of prosperity.

The irony of fate was that Prince Kaido was not married!

Prince Kaido, a heroic man, interrupted the bonzes and astrologers then and declared that, renouncing his bachelorhood, he would take a wife forthwith, in order to give the oracle the possibility of fulfillment. There was nothing that he was not willing to suffer for the happiness of his people! Since the gods demanded it, he would sacrifice himself for the salvation of his province; within a month, he must be married and deceived! The ministers, immediately convened, had approved wholeheartedly of the prince's determination. At the end of the day, one had to be able to endure the blows of destiny.

After three weeks of diplomacy, great news was announced in the province; the powerful Lord Kaido was to marry the beautiful Yamida, daughter of a great lord in Osaka.

The brilliant Kaido, as jealous as a tiger, awaited with feverish impatience the moment when he could be deceived by a legitimate wife. The oracle had been precise; one single error would suffice. Kaido asked no more than that, and had not concealed from his ministers his firm intention to have the head of the guilty party cut off immediately afterwards.

It was in a bay 15 leagues to the south of the city of Miko that Farandoul, Mandibul, the 15 seamen and the Siamese interpreter were disembarked covertly on a moonless night. Our friends, aware of the powerful Kaido's pronounced antipathy towards Europeans, had taken their precautions; in Yokohama they had furnished themselves with 18 Japanese officers' costumes, complete with helmets, armor, coats of mail, fans and swords.

Their first concern, on disembarking, was to throw their useless European costumes into the sea and put on their Japanese armor. It was a fine sight; they all looked marvelous in their black breastplates, armbands and checkered thigh-guards. Bizarre sealed helmets concealed their grimacing faces and bristling moustaches; through their belts were passed the three swords of first-class gentlemen. Only Farandoul, in his capacity as leader, had granted himself four.

After four hours devoted to rest, our heroes set off for Miko, with the hope of arriving that same day. Our friends walked boldly through the cheerful countryside, showered by the polite greetings of the good villagers, who took them for noblemen out for a stroll. About 11 a.m., Farandoul's keen eyes spotted a numerous procession in the distance, advancing along the highway.

A few yacounines were at the head, mounted on little brown horses with long manes, of a race particular to the country. Then came a long file of norimons, or palanquins, richly-decorated in bright and variegated colors, each one carried by two strong men.

In the first of these norimons the dazzled Farandoul made out the most charming of apparitions: a young Japanese woman of 18, with profound black eyes, shaved eyebrows replaced by black marks, painted cheeks and pink lips, displaying a double row of gilded teeth.

Farandoul—dazzled, as we have said—had moved into the middle of the road in order to see better. Suddenly, the entire convoy stopped; the yacounines dismounted, and the leader of the procession, after a long series of bows, advanced towards Farandoul as if to make a speech. Because of his absolute ignorance of the Japanese language, Farandoul had no idea what that might mean; he looked around for the Siamese interpreter but, not seeing him, recalled that he had sent him on ahead to gather information about the white elephant.

Farandoul, thwarted, could only reply to the bows. The young Japanese woman having got down from her norimon, however, he got himself out of trouble with more solemn and hurried bows. There was a further speech from the leader of the procession and—an unexpected conclusion—at the end of the speech the amiable man put the hand of the young Japanese woman into Farandoul's.

The hand was charming. Farandoul deposited a kiss upon it, which permitted him not to reply in Japanese. When he raised his head again, he saw that the procession was getting under way again. The young woman had not withdrawn her hand. Farandoul had to walk alongside her, without knowing where she was taking him.

Where were they going? And what did it all mean? The young Japanese woman was so pretty that Farandoul, entirely caught up by the alternate play of the lovely child's eyelids and fan, would have gone to the ends of the Earth in that manner without demanding an explanation.

They did not go as far as that; after a few minutes, they arrived in front of a superb temple backing on to the side of a mountain and hidden beneath its forest. The procession as obviously expected at the temple, for the bonzes were there; under the triumphal gate and at the back, at the foot of a large statue of Buddha, a numerous and brilliant crowd was visible.

How amiable these great Japanese lords are, the worthy Mandibul said to himself. *We've scarcely arrived, and already we're being treated like old friends!*

The procession had advanced as far as the great Buddha of gilded bronze. The young Japanese woman, having arrived there, sat down gracefully on a mat and, in response to an invitation from the leader of the procession, Farandoul did likewise. He heard a murmur of European voices then; not far from him, an Englishman in a brightly-colored uniform was chatting with a French officer—two diplomats, presumably.

When a richly-clad Japanese man arrived with a superb tray charged with a sort of teapot, Farandoul thought that refreshments were about to be distributed to the assembly. The man gave the teapot to the pretty Japanese woman, who made a flirtatious gesture to Farandoul.

We're going to drink saki, the national beverage, our hero thought.

The saki-bowl had two mouthpieces; the pretty Japanese took one and offered the other to Farandoul—and applying his lips to it, he drank the saki at the same time as her.

The entire assembly gave voice to a joyful cheer, which Farandoul's companions instinctively echoed behind their visors.

"What! Is that it?" murmured the French ambassador.

What's that? our hero thought, suddenly pricking up his ears.

"Yes," replied the diplomat, "the ceremony isn't long. Prince Kaido isn't unhandsome, so why hasn't he taken off his helmet? I don't know that custom—getting married in a helmet. It's original. Anyway, the famous Prince Kaido is finally married...."

Kaido...the Prince of Miko? What are they saying? Farandoul asked himself.

"Young Yamida is charming, you know," the diplomat went on. "I wouldn't have minded being in Prince Kaido's place and drinking the saki from the spousal bowl with her! Come on, everyone's getting up—the ceremony's over, they're married."

The audience was, indeed, getting up. The anxious Farandoul remained seated, as if lost in contemplation of the young Japanese woman. In reality, he was flabbergasted. What a catastrophe! Everything was now clear to him. He had run into the procession of the Prince of Miko's bride-to-be, on its way to the temple for the marriage-celebration; because of his four swords he had been mistaken for the prince, and, without being aware of it, he had married the intended wife of the fierce Kaido!

A terrible adventure! What should he do? It was impossible now to undo what had been done; the ceremony was complete! What would be the consequence of that fatal error?

At that moment, the interpreter whose absence had caused so much trouble reappeared, making his way through the crowd of Japanese lords. He was able to get as far as Farandoul, in spite of the astonishment of the assembly, and whisper a few words to him.

"What have you done? Marrying the prince's fiancée! I arrived too late to warn you. We must flee immediately, or we're lost...there's still time. There was a daimios' plot. On the road we were following I met the procession of the real prince arriving for the nuptial ceremony, but, before my very eyes, the daimios lying in ambush threw themselves on the escort, scattered them and made off with the prince, bound as a prisoner. Without that coincidence, you'd have been taken already. We have to go quickly, as you can see!"

Farandoul shut his eyes in order to bring his thoughts into better focus. He had just glimpsed another and more promising outcome of the adventure.

A gentle squeeze of his hand from his anxious bride made up his mind. "Flee?" he said to the interpreter. "Impossible! Don't you see that at the merest sign from the father-in-law, the swords of the 500 Japanese surrounding us would be glinting in the sunlight. There's another means to get us out of this affair; Prince Kaido has disappeared, they've mistaken me for him; they've married his bride to me—well, I'll maintain my role. I'll remain Prince Miko, fortunate spouse of the beautiful Yamida. Start talking—tell the assembly that a conspiracy of partisans of the Mikado has been discovered, and that the prince begs all his friends to return to Miko immediately, to organize the resistance."

The interpreter hesitated, alarmed by Farandoul's boldness; a forceful gesture from our friend gave him courage. Addressing himself to the astonished Japanese, he warned them in exaggerated terms of the discovery of a conspiracy against the life of the Prince of Miko and announced the intention of the false prince to fight the rebels energetically.

There was but one cry from all the Japanese nobles; swords gleamed, to the great alarm of the ladies, and the entire audience swore to fight to the death for the rights of the prince and the liberty of the province of Miko.

The ladies were already being ushered to their norimons by hurried servants. All the men—fathers, brothers, husbands or relatives—arranged themselves to either side, swords in hand. Farandoul brought up the rear, with the slightly fearful Yamida; he gallantly placed her in her norimon, showed her his four swords to reassure her as to the dangers of the road, and made a sign to the porters to get under way.

On an order from the interpreter, men of the escort had brought horses for the false prince and his friends. Farandoul leapt into the saddle; Mandibul and his mariners immediately did likewise and came to arrange themselves around Farandoul, swords in hand.

This must be why Prince Kaido came to his wedding armed to the teeth and helmeted, thought the daimios, as they rode off. *In spite of the dangers of the*

*situation, the gallant prince did not want his marriage to Yamida to be delayed
for a single minute, but he took his precautions. The three-sword warriors surrounding him seem to be solid men, and it wouldn't be a good idea to attack
them.*

While Farandoul, having become Prince of Miko, galloped with his wife
Yamida along the road to Miko, the true Prince Kaido, thrown bound and
gagged into a sealed norimon, was being carried by the conspirators at a forced
march towards Fatzouma, the province's second city, where the standard of revolt had been raised that same morning.

Poor Kaido was very depressed. His enemies obviously did not want to allow him time to deflect his destiny! If he had not been abducted until after the
marriage, he would still have had hope. The oracle might very well have been
fulfilled during his captivity, but the conspirators had not even left him that
chance!

Let us return to our friends. Night had fallen when the procession presented itself at the gates of Miko. They ran to the palace; there, five or six imposing individuals wanted to talk to the prince.

"Who are these men?" Farandoul asked, in a whisper.

"The prince's ministers," replied the interpreter.

"Damn! They mustn't get close to me. Stop them—tell them that I accept
their resignation. They were unable to foresee the troubles, so they're handing in
their portfolios! Go on—talk! Be severe! Sack all the officials and sent all the
palace staff packing! I'll clear the house!"

While Farandoul, having received the blessing of his father-in-law, went to
his apartments—somewhat at hazard—with the young Yamida, the crowd of
palace officials discussed the Prince's severity towards his ministers. It was even
worse when they saw all of Kaido's own household staff leaving the palace,
leaving their duties to 16 warriors, armored and helmeted as for combat.

The interpreter had followed Farandoul.

"Take all possible defensive measures," the latter said to him. "Summon
all the militias and nobility of the province for tomorrow; we need to be ready to
repel any attack!"

Blushing with confusion, Yamida, the young bride of Kaido, Prince of Miko—or, rather, our friend Farandoul—had gone to sit down on a pile of sky-blue
silk cushions. Her languid eyes remained fixed on the floor-mats or hidden behind her feebly-agitated fan. Farandoul, sitting beside her, said nothing more,
absolutely dazzled by the smiles and graceful gestures of the young woman
whom unexpected events had just precipitated into his life with the charming
title of wife.

What an eventful day! And how far away from his thoughts was the King
of Siam's elephant!

Meanwhile, the pensive Yamida darted a covert glance at the silent Farandoul. She must be astonished by his prolonged silence; he had to talk to her—but how? Farandoul cursed his ignorance of the Japanese language.

The interpreter was still there; Farandoul spoke to him in a whisper.

"Powerful Princess, Pearl of the Empire!" cried the interpreter, after three deep bows. "The prince, your husband, has sworn by the dragon Tatsumaki not to speak a word of Japanese before having subjugated the rebels as completely as he has been subjugated himself by your eyes—and yet, he would like to tell you that his heart, like the volcano Fujiyama, burns with an inextinguishable fire. His oath forbids him to speak to you in Japanese, but he may do so in a foreign language. Do you know French, Princess?"

Yamida shook her head, desolately.

"English?"

"No better."

"In that case," the Siamese went on, "it will be necessary for him to speak through an interpreter until further notice. I beg you, gracious Princess, to be indulgent of my feeble voice, which can only repeat to you coldly what the prince has said to you with much more heart and passion. Now, the prince would like to know whether his face has the good fortune to please you?"

"How can I tell?" sighed Yamida. "The prince keeps his visor lowered."

"Did you never see the prince before the ceremony?"

"You know full well," Yamida replied, naively, "that I have always lived in seclusion in my father's house in Osaka; I have only seen the portrait of the prince that he sent when he asked for my hand.

Hurrah! thought Farandoul. *She doesn't know the prince; I can take m helmet off when we're together. Oof! I'll be able to breathe!* And he got up to say a few words to the interpreter.

"Gracious Princess," the latter continued, "the prince has something to confess to you; the portrait did not much resemble him."

Yamida uttered a little exclamation of annoyance, which changed its expression into one of surprise; Farandoul had just taken off his helmet.

"Ah!" cried Yamida. "No resemblance at all! The prince is better than his portrait! But why is his hair cut like a foreigner's?"

"That, Princess, is for political reasons! The mysteries of diplomacy. You understand the difficulties of the situation; the prince is seeking to gain the confidence of the foreign diplomats by means of a few concessions."

VII.

The city of Miko had an uneasy awakening the following day. News had arrived during the night; the rebels had proclaimed a new prince in Fatzouma, the city having fallen into their power, and also boasted, with extreme impudence, of having taken Prince Kaido prisoner. Already, numerous partisans had boldly set out on campaign along the road to Miko.

The situation was deteriorating. What reassured the inhabitants of Miko was that the prince, who was said to have fallen into the hands of the rebels, was among them organizing the defense. Thanks to the interpreter, a proclamation by the false Kaido had been pinned up. The militia was urgently mobilized, in order to cooperate with the troops in the defense of the city. The old general Faxiba, commander of the regular troops, called to the palace with his officers, had received written instructions from the prince.

The prince was known to be a man of iron; General Faxiba found him even more energetic than usual. He gave him three hours to assemble the militia, intending to lead them against the enemy immediately.

General Faxiba, galvanized, left at top speed for the esplanade where the troops were gathered. In a speech of classic conciseness, he communicated the energy of Prince Kaido to the hearts of his colonels; three colonels swore to disembowel themselves if the enemy was not defeated before sundown. As midday sounded, all the troops were under arms and ready to depart. They were only waiting for the prince.

At the appointed hour, tearing himself away from the lamentations of poor Yamida, who was mortally grieved to see him going into danger the day after their marriage, the prince left the palace at the head of his platoon of fearsome three-sword warriors.

The interpreter had needed some persuasion to put his armor on, but he knew that he would be more necessary than ever, in order to carry orders, so he had consented to do so with a sigh.

Farandoul, placing himself at the head of his troops, made a gesture; commands and signals burst forth, and the entire army moved off as one on the road to Fatzouma. The prince and his three-sword warriors galloped ahead, followed at a rapid pace by the breathless regiments. Old General Faxiba, a prudent man, had sent out a few light companies that morning to scout the route. After a three-hour march, the archers of this advance guard found themselves at grips with the foremost rebel troops.

Farandoul-Kaido gave his men an hour to breathe. The rebels were arriving rapidly and deploying in the plain; when he saw that they were considerably hampered in their movements, our hero suddenly gave the signal to attack. His troops launched themselves furiously upon the enemy. After the first volleys of arrows and gunfire from platoons armed with flintlock rifles, they surged forward, swords in hand. The three-sword warriors of the prince' guard, having dismounted, wielded their two-handed swords with a skill that attracted general admiration; in the blink of an eye, the rebels on which they had hurled themselves had scattered into the plain.

The affair worked out well for the false Prince Kaido. A charge by Farandoul, at the head of one of General Faxiba's reserve companies, completed the rout of the rebels, who were all driven back and dispersed. The burgers of Miko, proud of their prowess, took a large quantity of prisoners. Only the rebel general staff took flight in good order and disappeared into the mountains.

The army, drunk with joy, took the road back to the city with its trophies and its prisoners; it made a triumphant entrance that evening. The false prince had to pass beneath an improvised triumphal arch, submit to speeches of which he did not understand a word, and to respond to congratulations through the medium of the interpreter. At the great gate of the palace, illuminated by thousands of lanterns, Yamida was waiting for Farandoul impatiently; as soon as he appeared, she threw her lantern aside and fell into his arms.

That same evening, there was a conference between Farandoul, Mandibul and the interpreter. It was a matter of deciding on a plan of action. The rebels had been beaten; it was now up to diplomacy to complete the work of Bellona. The only diplomat available to Farandoul was the Siamese interpreter, but he could not send him to Fatzouma, his presence being indispensable. It was agreed that they would send guarantees of safe conduct to the rebel leaders the following day, in order to open negotiations in Miko itself.

As the march and the battle had worn everyone out, the palace was soon plunged into a profound silence.

In the middle of the night, at the very hour when the most dazzling dreams were fluttering over the pillows of our profoundly sleeping friends, a dust-covered man, breathless and furious, presented himself at the city gate, thrust the sentinels violently aside, introduced himself to the bewildered duty-officer, gathered a few guards, and marched to the palace. The men on guard there nearly fell over backwards on seeing him; they made a sign and all the doors were opened.

This man, surrounded by soldiers, headed unhesitatingly for Farandoul's apartments. Our friends the three-sword warriors, full of confidence, were asleep in the antechambers. They were bound and gagged within two minutes.

Then the mysterious man, followed by his hired assassins, exploded into to Farandoul's bedroom like a bomb.

As you have doubtless guessed, this furious man was Prince Kaido himself: the true one, the one and only, avid for vengeance.

Farandoul had beaten the rebels too soundly; the latter, despairing of their enterprise, had set the prince free in order to obtain his forgiveness and, on releasing him, had acquainted him with all his simultaneous misfortunes—which is to say, the appearance of a false prince, the marriage of the false prince to the beautiful Yamida, and the appropriation of the palace of Miko by the usurper of the throne and the true prince's fiancée.

A sad awakening for our friends! A general collapse of all their dreams! They were all there, laid out on the floor, the mariners on one side and Farandoul on the other. Not far away, Kaido was pacing back and forth in a gallery overlooking the still-illuminated city, giving orders in a thunderous voice to officers standing in front of him. The entire palace was in an uproar; the staff-officers, hastily summoned, were arguing, accusing one another of lacking perspicacity and furiously disemboweling themselves in the course of the debates.

Old General Faxiba, furious at having been deceived like all the rest, had disemboweled himself in front of his troops, and his example had been followed by several ministers.

At dawn, the fatal moment appeared to have arrived for our friends; a unit of fierce soldiers came to stand before them, swords drawn. On the command of an officer, the cords retaining our friends' legs were cut and our friends, urged to get up by blows with the flat of a sword, filed out of the gallery. Instead of being taken down to the courtyard for the supreme ceremony, as they expected, they were taken into an immense room, which Farandoul recognized as the throne room. A dozen officers sitting on a podium were waiting for them. It was a court martial charged with their summary judgment.

In front of the judges were the exhibits in evidence—which is to say, the throne of Miko, on which Farandoul had sat for 36 hours, the arms and armor of the three-sword warriors, and, finally, Yamida herself, the prince's fiancée, espoused by the usurper.

Farandoul and the princess exchanged a desolate glance. O joy! Farandoul did not read any reproach in Yamida's eyes; on the contrary, a tear was running down that charming cheek—which consoled our hero in advance for all that might follow.

When the terrible Kaido arrived, the judges immediately set to work. There was only a brief interrogation, to which the accused disdained to respond for lack of having understood the questions; then Kaido, adopting the office of public prospector, simply showed off the exhibits. That eloquent indictment was sufficient for the judges. The deliberation commenced, while Prince Kaido manifested a feverish impatience. It was soon concluded; the president rapidly scribbled his verdict, the judges signed it, and it was read out to the condemned men.

By the frightful grimace the Siamese interpreter made on hearing the sentence, the mariners understood that the court martial had been severe.

"Come on," said Mandibul. "Tell us—what is it? Hanging? Beheading? Disemboweling? Damn! This is worse than China."

"Alas," aid the interpreter.

"Don't leave us in suspense. Tell us, right away."

"We've been sentenced to be thrown into boiling fat and cooked until we're dead."

"Boiling fat—how horrid!" cried Mandibul, forcefully. "I'm appealing!"

The judges' only response was to scribble a few lines that the president read out. It was a small postscript, added on the recommendation of Prince Kaido, which fixed the execution for the same day.

Yamida, who had fainted, had been taken back to her apartment. The mariners, furious at the severity of the sentence, made free with their recriminations. They heaped reproaches upon Prince Kaido. After all, had they not battled his enemies, the rebels, the day before and was it not to their bravery that the prince owed his liberty? Tournesol, especially, was beside himself; to perish in a frying pan seemed to him to be the ultimate ignominy. Perhaps, in his capacity as a native of Marseille, he would have preferred oil!

The surly Kaido, still grinding his teeth, gave orders for the funereal preparations. Soldiers were already dragging the condemned men to the palace gate, where the executioners were putting the final touches to the apparatus of their infernal work, when Prince Kaido suddenly started. An idea had just crossed his mind. He gave the order to take the condemned men back to the hall of judgment and ran to his general staff.

The officers immediately mounted up and disappeared in all directions. The astonished crowd wondered what had occasioned the prince's change of mind. The astonishment was even greater when they saw the officers coming back, accompanied by aged bonzes and antique savants bowed down by study. Kaido waited for them, and immediately closeted himself with them.

What did it mean? It was quite simple. A scruple had occurred to Kaido. You will recall he prediction of the bonzes and the savants regarding the good fortune that the heavens would bestow upon the prince as soon as he was deceived by his wife. Had that prediction been fulfilled? Could the prince consider himself well and truly deceived? This was a potentially controversial issue; the prince had been deceived, that was certain, but casuists might raise objections.

Indeed, as soon as the assembly of the bonzes and scholars had been apprised of recent events, it declared with one voice that the prediction could not be considered as fulfilled. The beautiful Yamida had only been the prince's fiancée; that was not sufficient for the oracle. The prince had no right to claim to have been deceived; everything must be done again.

Poor Kaido, absolutely desolate, plunged into somber reflection. What should he do? What course should he take?

An old bonze permitted himself to offer an item of advice which renewed hope in Kaido's heart. After all, the condemned Farandoul had not been executed; all was not lost.

Kaido was about to race to the room serving as the mariners' prison, but he paused for reflection, then ran to Yamida's apartment, brought her before the bonzes and had a spousal saki-bowl brought to the palace chapel.

When the saki appeared, he presented himself to the surprised Yamida; when she hesitated, he whispered a few words to her that made up her mind. The charming Yamida, still very tearful, lifted the saki to her lips. This time, Kaido and Yamida were married.

"And now that destiny is satisfied, may the province of Miko be fortunate!"

Calm, proud and resolute, Prince Kaido headed for the room in which the prisoners were awaiting the march to the scaffold. He went straight to Farandoul, drew his sword and cut his bonds. "All is forgiven!" he said. "You're a man after my own heart. I'll make you my prime minister!"

The astonished Farandoul looked at the prince uncomprehendingly. "What did the prince say?" he asked the interpreter.

"The prince forgives you and appoints you as his minister," stammered the interpreter. "Implore him for mercy on our behalf; it wouldn't be just to make us perish in the boiling fat."

Kaido had understood, and his orders had already been given. The same officers that had condemned our friends to such terrible torments hurried to cut the cords binding their wrists. The president of the tribunal, a susceptible man, considered himself offended by this unforeseen outcome, and demonstrated his ill-humor by brutally disemboweling himself with the sword of his fathers.

"No more boiling fat?" asked Tournesol.

"A free and complete pardon," replied the prince, shaking hands with the sympathetic Mandibul, "and even friendship."

The brave men who had fought under Farandoul's orders the day before were delighted to learn that their young leader would not, after all, be subjected to the terrible torture of boiling fat on the day after his wondrous triumph over the rebels. Only a few courtiers, who had displayed particular hostility to our hero since the return of the true prince, judged that their dignity required them to disembowel themselves proudly by way of protest. Apart from these slight signs of dissent, the joy of the daimios and soldiers was shared by the whole population.

Without losing any time, Kaido had given orders to his former ministers to gather together so that they could be introduced to Farandoul. In the presence of all of them, and in spite of the grimaces of some, he confirmed Farandoul's new titles and made him commander of the regular army, replacing General Faxiba, who had disemboweled himself that morning.

Complimented and pampered by everyone, Farandoul ought to have felt joy in his heart. Condemned to death in the morning, prime minister in the evening; the difference was great, not to mention the salary: 80,000 sacks of rice, the first quarter of which had just been paid in kind. But there was a shadow over the scene; Yamida was lost to him. His marriage, invalid in consequence of the error regarding his identity, had been annulled by the bonzes, and Yamida was now the wife of Prince Kaido!

There was also another man whose mind, in spite of his apparent gaiety, was preoccupied with somewhat disagreeable thoughts; this was Prince Kaido, who was still thinking about the annoying oracle and ardently desirous of seeing the prediction fulfilled, in order that he might be tranquil thereafter.

It was with a veritable chagrin that Prince Kaido learned, the following morning, that his new commander-in-chief, Fa-ran-doul, had set out in the middle of the night for Fatzouma, with the aim of dispersing the last bands of rebels still campaigning in the environs of that city. The prince did not hesitate, and dispatched one of his officers in a carriage to beg Farandoul not to risk a life that was vital to the good fortune of the province of Miko in this needless fashion.

A funny country! thought Mandibul, who had no suspicion of the prince's hidden motives. *Yesterday, he wanted to fry us in a pan like simple potatoes, and today he watches over us with maternal solicitude. Strange! But I like this better.*

The mere announcement of the arrival of the general had, of course, sufficed to make the final rebels revert to their allegiance. The province of Miko was entirely pacified. On his return, Farandoul was received with the greatest honor. The prince increased his salary, conferred a few new titles on him, and promoted all his mariners by several ranks in the Japanese hierarchy.

Farandoul and his men were about to return to their lodgings, after having received the prince's thanks, when the latter stopped them.

"Wait, General Fa-ran-doul; I want to give you a confidential mission. Do you know the Temple of the 33,333 spirits in Tocoto?"

"No," said the astonished Farandoul.

"Then you don't know that, in addition to the statues of the 33,333 spirits and the innumerable ones of the auxiliary gods, the Kwamon, the Bosatz and the Dsizoo, the chapels of Raiden, god of thunder, and the dragon Tatsumaki, that famous temple now offers to the venerations of the faithful an emanation of Buddha himself: a sacred elephant of the most dazzling whiteness!"

"The white elephant!" cried the interpreter.

What is he getting at? Farandoul wondered.

"This is the mission with which I'm entrusting you: my wife Yamida and her 50 maids of honor are going on a pilgrimage to the Temple of the 33,333 spirits. I want you to escort them."

Farandoul and the interpreter exchanged glances; Mandibul seemed extraordinarily surprised.

What an unexpected stroke of luck! thought Farandoul. *Yamida and the white elephant!*

"Yes," the prince continued, with an enigmatic smile. "I'm counting on you." And Kaido went off at top speed, while Farandoul, still stunned by this double stroke of luck, went to get the princess's orders.

After the terrible events that had occurred, Farandoul had many things to say to Yamida; the latter, for her part, seemed to have a few things to confide to him—but as the interpreter was not there, they had to content themselves with the eloquent, but slightly obscure, language of the eyes.

A mere hour sufficed to prepare for the departure.

The 50 maids of honor followed the princess in their finest dresses, all as young and charming as her. Fifty open and brilliantly decorated norimons came forward. The ladies arranged themselves gracefully in the palanquins. In response to a signal from Farandoul, the porters lifted up their delicate burdens and departed at a rhythmic pace.

What a delightful excursion through the charming countryside of Miko! They crossed several rivers by wading or swimming. The sight of the 50 gaudily-painted palanquins floating like enchanted boats over the smooth surfaces of the rivers in the wake of their porters, swimming like fish, was perfectly charming.

They arrived at dusk at a way-station, a pleasant little village in which they were to spend the night. A large tea-house accommodated the entire caravan. Everything was ready there for the evening meal and the night's rest. The 50 maids of honor supped by the joyous light of lanterns in the tea-house garden; Yamida ate her meal on an upper terrace, and did not neglect to invite Farandoul to share it with her.

The terrace occupied by Yamida and Farandoul was delightfully garlanded with flowers and branches. Immense colored windows illuminated them with yellow, red and blue light; at the rear, 12 large vases, veritable monuments, were arranged in front of the balustrades, standing out on a deck bathed with blue light by courtesy of the full Moon.

After a Franco-Japanese conversation in which both of them were heard without being understood, Farandoul and Yamida came to rest their elbows on the balustrade in order to contemplate the beauty of the marvelous location.

Whether or not it was an illusion, it seemed to Farandoul that the large vase on which he was leaning trembled when he spoke to Yamida in a passionate tone. Our friend paid no heed to it, however; he took Yamida's charming hand in his own.

"Oh, Yamida, Yamida!" he said, in an emotional voice.

"Oh Fa-ran-doul!" the young woman replied, having learned his name and seemingly taking pleasure in pronouncing its three syllables.

Farandoul deposited an ardent kiss one the hand that had been surrendered to him.

"Oh, Fa-ran-doul!" repeated Yamida.

A frightful noise cut their conversation short. The 12 huge vases had just shattered noisily on the floor of the terrace. Twelve men stood up amid the debris and threw themselves on Farandoul, knocking him down before he could draw a single one of his three swords and burying him beneath their mass.

"Deceived! I am deceived!" cried the triumphant Prince Kaido. "The oracle is satisfied! Finally, my reign can be fortunate!"

The fearful Yamida had thrown herself at his feet.

"Get up, Madame," said the prince, "and deign to accept my arm as far as your norimon. Be calm, Japan is watching us!"

The route so joyfully undertaken by day, capering around the princess's norimon, Farandoul retraced that same night in a sadder situation. Locked up in a narrow and unpadded norimon, he was able to count all the bumps in the road and all the jolts to which the brutal porters, launched at a running pace, submitted his ambulant prison.

As soon as he arrived at the palace of Miko, Farandoul was extracted from his box, somewhat the worse for wear, and locked in a narrow, dark dungeon in which sad reflections came once more to assail him. What cruel blows of destiny! What sudden changes of fortune! Bah! All hope was not lost. Mandibul and the mariners were free; they would be able to get him out of here.

Kaido came back exceedingly cheerful, ready to experience the good life at last. His first concern as soon as he had taken off his boots was to summon the council of ministers and the great functionaries of the crown.

These noble persons came running, slightly surprised by such an urgent summons, wondering whether some new revolt had broken out in the province. The prince's sprightly attitude reassured them as soon as they came into the council chamber.

"Noble daimios!" cried the prince, as soon as they were all assembled, "a cruel burden of anxiety has been lifted from your prince. The principality of Miko can henceforth be happy; nothing is any longer opposed to its felicity!"

"Nothing!" cried the ministers, overcome with emotion.

"Absolutely nothing! The oracle is fulfilled! The condition imposed by destiny has been met; the prince has sacrificed himself for the welfare of his people!"

"And the guilty party?" asked the Minister of Justice and Executions, "in a severe tone."

"The guilty party is awaiting sentence—but here are the bonzes and the savants I summoned; we shall see whether they too are satisfied."

The old doctors of astrology and the learned bonzes were coming into the room. The prince received them with the greatest respect and explained the situation to them in an emotional voice.

"Praise be to Buddha!" they cried, after having heard him. "The principality of Miko is saved; its prince has been deceived by his wife!"

VIII.

In the afternoon of that memorable day, which was marked by great rejoicing among the population, informed of Prince Kaido's sacrifice, Farandoul was extracted from his cell and taken, dragging his chains, before a tribunal composed of the most powerful lords of the principality.

The procedure did not take long. Kaido exposed the facts and the tribunal decided, with one voice, on the death penalty. The discussion of the kind of torture to inflict on the guilty party lasted much longer. The assembly wanted something solemn and worthy of both the offended prince and the high status of the convicted felon.

As the conference threatened to go on indefinitely, a minister had an idea. "But we're exerting ourselves needlessly to find an imposing means of death. Has not the guilty Fa-ran-doul already been sentenced to the torture of boiling fat? We have only to revert to that idea—we won't find a better one."

"Bravo!" cried all the daimios. "It's perfect; all that remains is to write up the sentence."

"Stop!" shouted Kaido, all of a sudden. "Not boiling fat; I forbid it. It shall not be said that, under my reign, a man to whom Japan owes so much—for, let's not forget, it is to him that our fatherland owes its good fortune—should perish in such an ignominious fashion! Pooh! Boiling fat! No, it's by the sword that he ought to perish, as a true knight and a courageous warrior! With a firm hand he shall slit his belly, with two crosswise incisions—*flick flick!*—and that's that.

The galvanized judges did not hesitate any longer. The sentence written by a scribe was proudly signed by each of them and read out to the unfortunate Farandoul. As he had not had the time, in so few days, to learn the sweet and beautiful Japanese tongue, our friend did not understand much of the sentence and would have remained in uncertainty for a long time if the obliging Kaido had not explained to him, by means of pantomime and repeated *flick flicks*, of the dolorous operation he would be called upon to perform on himself.

The judges and the prince, famished after the long session, were reunited at a banquet. The prince, being in a good mood, invited the condemned man and was insistent on having him at his right hand all evening.

Farandoul, rather badly nourished in his prison, did not refuse this favor and outdid the most enthusiastic saki-drinkers on the council of ministers. There is no company so good that it cannot end, through; at about 11 p.m., the unfortunate condemned man had to return to his cell. Scarcely had he gone back in than he suddenly remembered that he had forgotten to ask the prince what date had been fixed for his execution. It was too late to repair the omission, and he had to remain in uncertainty.

There was no news of anyone on the following day. No one but the jailer visited the condemned man. The day seemed long to Farandoul. The following morning, however, the Minister of Justice and Executions had the cell opened and came in to read Farandoul a thick wad of papers.

A mere judiciary formality, our friend thought, unable to understand a single word—but the Minister of Justice, seeing his distracted air, began speaking in more-or-less intelligible French.

"What luck!" cried Farandoul. "You speak French—you can inform me. When will the little ceremony of the sword take place?"

"But that's what I'm here to tell you—it's this evening."

"This evening! Already! I thought I'd have more time."

"If it's inconvenient for you, perhaps we can postpone it for a few days...you can say that you're indisposed. But that would be annoying, because the populace has been alerted. The...event has to take place in great solemnity, on a private esplanade at the Gate of Nippon. The posters have gone up...."

"The posters, you say?"

"Yes, to advertise your passing to the population, for you'll be led processionally to the esplanade."

Good, thought Farandoul. *If there are posters, if everyone knows about it, Mandibul knows about it; he must have everything in hand to get me out of the situation—let's not change his plans!* "Well," he continued, aloud, "since the posters have gone up, I don't want to spoil the ceremony. I accept your time— until this evening, then, and thank you for your kindness."

That day passed more rapidly than the previous one. As dusk fell, Farandoul was taken out of his cell and led into the central courtyard of the palace. A crowd of officials was waiting to salute him. At their head, the Minister of Justice and Executions greeted Farandoul and handed him a red lacquer box one and a half meters long, covered with charming designs.

"What's this?" asked Farandoul, astonished.

"Open it!" replied the Minister of Justice.

Farandoul undid a few silk ribbons, lifted the lid and stopped, amazed. The box contained a superb sword with a tempered and damascened blade and a splendid, diamond-enriched hilt.

"This is…the instrument?" our hero asked.

"This is the fatal instrument. Prince Kaido begs you to accept it in memory of him and to make good use of it—you know, two incisions crosswise, *flick! flick!* It's the best method."

"I'll do my best," Farandoul replied, modestly. "I'd like to be relieved of these uncomfortable chains, though."

"I would not grant that favor to a vulgar criminal, but to you I can refuse nothing—your chains will be removed!"

The entire population of Miko, overexcited by so many emotions in the previous week, filled the streets that the procession was to follow. The women wept openly for the young hero marching to execution; the men, more serious, bowed to the condemned man as he passed by. All eyes were fixed on the sword destined to play such a great role in the final ceremony.

Farandoul was all eyes and ears; at every street corner he expected to see Mandibul and the matelots hurl themselves on the procession, and prepared himself to make valiant use of the sword of honor provided by the prince—but nothing happened. He did not see anyone or hear any signal—and the fatal esplanade as getting closer.

A vast quantity of lanterns was visible some distance away, around a brilliantly-illuminated central point. That must be the place reserved for the drama. As if to remove the final doubt, the Minister of Justice turned round just then and pointed out the illuminations with a graceful gesture. "There it is," he said. "We've arrived!"

They had, indeed, arrived. And Mandibul had not put in an appearance!

Uh oh! thought Farandoul. *Things are going awry.*

A superb podium had been prepared, raised two meters above the ground, flanked by multicolored masts and garnished with numerous lanterns of every color. Fifteen warriors, all armed with naked swords, stood on the podium's wide stairway. The Minister of Justice seemed surprised by their presence; while the other troops formed a circle around the scaffold and restrained the crowd, the minister approached these warriors and asked them whether the prince had sent them.

"It was the prince!" replied a voice that made Farandoul shiver, for it strangely resembled that of the Siamese interpreter. He attempted to peer beneath the helmets of the somber warriors, and finally recognized beneath one of them the steadfast eyes of Mandibul. "Ah!" he said, as he went up on to the podium, looking for the least well-guarded side. "The prince's sword will do its work!"

A significant clicking of swords informed him that Mandibul and his men were ready.

Farandoul stopped.

"The crosswise incision!" the Minister of Justice and Executions called out to him. "*Flick! Fli...!*"

He did not finish. An abrupt shove from Mandibul had just precipitated him to the base of the podium—and the mysterious warriors, releasing loud *hurrahs*, threw themselves on the circle of real soldiers on guard around the scaffold. Farandoul had taken the lead; his sword of honor flashed like lighting and sent the yacounines' weapons flying into the distance. The circle had broken; a few brave men were still fighting, but a few lunges from the mariners quickly made them see reason.

Farandoul was saved, for the moment, but it was necessary to flee as quickly as possible, for the guards from the Gate of Nippon, seeing the disorder, were already running forward, brandishing rifles and spears.

"Charge!" cried Mandibul. "Let's get out of here now!"

Alert as tigers, the mariners set off along a tranquil street, to the great alarm of a few male and female residents. Behind them, the running soldiers of the guard-unit were further reinforced with every passing minute.

"*Bagasse!*" cried Tournesol, turning the corner of the street. "It's a dead end!"

Fatality! Our friends were crowded together at the rear of the dead end by the number of their pursuers. The mariners had already turned to face the enemy.

"No, No!" cried Farandoul. "Break through the houses. You know full well that in Japan, the walls are made of cardboard and the partitions of paper—we can get through! Heads down, let's go!" And with a single sweep of his sword he made a hole in a wall through which they all rushed, heads down.

The tenants of the house, terrified by this sudden invasion of furious warriors, leapt out of the windows or fainted in corners.

"Charge!" cried Farandoul, hurling himself through the partition-walls, cleaving the most resistant with his sword and passing from one house to the next with as much ease as a circus rider jumping through paper-covered hoops. Mandibul, the interpreter and the 15 sailors ran behind him, their swords cutting large openings in the partitions and gashes in the intermediate walls. What damage they did! A great deal of repair-work would, alas, have to be undertaken by the landlords of the immovable properties they went through!

These offences against property made Farandoul's heart bleed, but he had a legal defense in this instance: the lives of 18 men were in danger! And what breaches of privacy! Sometimes they threw themselves through a shredded wall into the mist of a family meal; the dishes were knocked over, the facing partition wall was caved in, and they fell into a bedroom; sometimes, as they cut through walls with all the discretion of a cannonball, they wound up in a boudoir or a dressing-room, just in time to witness a lady having a little lie-down!

The most touching episode of this race through the houses of an entire quarter occurred when our friends had just passed like lightning through the kitchens of a large restaurant; after having gone through two empty rooms, they through themselves upon a cardboard partition, slashed it with sweeping sword-thrusts and fell into a private booth occupied by a lady of the highest society, at whose feet a handsome Japanese youth was murmuring sweet nothings. When Farandoul appeared with a naked sword, the lady thought it was her husband, released a terrible scream, and fainted. The 18 fierce and helmeted warriors filed past the terrified pair. The compassionate Mandibul, bringing up the rear, paused to throw a few drops of water into the lady's face, and did not rejoin his friends until he had seen her come round.

The Japanese soldiers launched in pursuit of the mariners had stopped in bewilderment before the initial breach; then, with forceful apologies for the people they were disturbing, they too had plunged into the houses—but instead of forging straight ahead like the fugitives, they had lost a good deal of time in hesitations and precautions. After a quarter of an hour, they had lost the track, and the Japanese gave up the pursuit.

Having traversed an entire quarter of the city in this time our friends had reached a street leading out into open country and had set off across the fields. After three hours of forced marching, without encountering anyone, they were finally able to rest without anxiety in the middle of a thick forest, whose uneven ground was cut through by ravines in which it was easy to hide. In consequence, after a little supper supplied by the restaurant where they had thrown such a fright into the two lovers, the brave mariners threw themselves down on beds of dry leaves and went to sleep.

"Well," said Mandibul, as he stretched his arms and legs on waking up the following morning, "what do we do now? This is still a country that seems to me to be unhealthy for us."

"We'll stay here for a few days more," Farandoul replied. "We won't have time to get bored, for we now have two projects to bring to a successful conclusion: the removal of the white elephant from the Temple of the 33,333 Spirits, and the removal of the charming Yamida from the palace of that frightful Kai-do!"

"Very well—but how shall we get out of Japan afterwards? A princess and a white elephant will be no small encumbrance."

"Yes, that's the real difficulty. No boat and no money to charter one! Hang on, though—what about our flower-boat? We left it rather abruptly…suppose we were to go to find it in Yokohama and propose to take those ladies back to China? We could head for Siam first, with the elephant…"

428

"Good idea! It's a matter of three days to travel to Yokohama and return to the little port where we disembarked."

"Well, my dear Mandibul, take six men with you, return to the flower-boat, be persuasive—steal it, if necessary—and come back as quickly as possible! During that time, we'll make plans for our two enterprises."

The mariners knew the way. Scarcely six leagues separated them from the coast; they soon covered that distance, without any unfortunate encounters, and recovered the boat that had brought them. Everything went well. The flower-boat's occupants were getting bored in Yokohama and eagerly welcomed the idea of returning to China under the direction of the skillful mariner who had taken them away from their Blue River.

Three days later, our friends were at the rendezvous. Farandoul had spent his time well; he had been to reconnoiter the Temple of the 33,333 Spirits, fortunately situated not far from the sea, and had ventured, well-disguised and in the company of the interpreter, into the city of Miko, to the very walls of Kaido's palace.

The interpreter had been able to gather a few items of information. Princess Yamida went out every evening in a norimon, without an escort, to take the air in the immense gardens of the palace. It would be easy to get into the gardens and carry off the norimon and the princess.

Farandoul fixed the execution of his two projects for the same evening. He took personal responsibility for the more delicate of the two missions, the abduction of Yamida, and entrusted the theft of the white elephant to Mandibul, supported by ten sailors. The two groups separated immediately, in order to reach the fields of their operations as dusk fell.

Mandibul and his ten men had to climb the mountain that bore the Temple of the 33,333 Spirits at its summit; when the night was far enough advanced, they had to make a hole in the surrounding wall, break down a few doors, and make a quick departure with the elephant.

Farandoul and the interpreter, followed by five sailors, would head for the city of Miko; by the first rays of moonlight, they would climb over a breach in the wall of the park and make their way from thicket to thicket in the direction of the palace.

What luck! In front of the door of the princess's apartments was the norimon that Farandoul had observed the day before, carrying Yamida in the city. The four porters were sitting on the steps of the palace, awaiting orders.

Eventually, when a nocturnal calm had descended upon the park and the palace, Yamida appeared on the first floor and leaned thoughtfully on the elegant balcony, supported on her elbows. Farandoul's heart beat faster. Of whom could she be thinking, if not the valiant foreigner who had violated the throne of Prince Kaido for her sake and almost become the sovereign of the province?

After a few minutes of reverie on her balcony, Yamida said a few words to the norimon-porters who were waiting for her and went back into her apartment.

She was undoubtedly about to descend. The porters had stood up and had brought the norimon closer to the staircase.

A woman, wrapped up against the cold, appeared on the steps and slipped into the norimon. The robust porters lifted up their gracious burden and departed at a rhythmic pace in the direction of a little lake, a fantastic mirror in which the bizarrely-trimmed trees were reflected in the moonlight, their branches curled like florid arabesques.

Farandoul and the mariners followed behind, on tiptoe. After circling the lake several times, the porters were about to head back to the palace again when seven men, all heavily armed, threw themselves upon them and put swords to their throats.

"Not a word, not a sound, or you're dead!" the interpreter murmured to them in a muffled tone. "Follow us, with the princess!"

"But…" one of the porters tried to say.

Two sharp squeals from the norimon interrupted him. Farandoul ran to the norimon to reassure Yamida, but an exclamation from the interpreter stopped him dead.

"Look out! A night patrol is coming!"

Indeed, scarcely 50 meters away, 20 soldiers were coming at a run, each with a lantern in one hand and a pike in the other.

"Straight ahead!" cried Farandoul, gesturing to the porters to run. "To the breach!" And he remained as a rearguard himself, with Tournesol.

The patrol gained ground, but the mariners succeeded in getting the norimon through the breach; then half the troop continued on its way while the other half remained in the breach to prevent the Japanese patrol passing through.

The position was good, the mariners taking advantage of it to lash out for a good half hour. Eventually, despairing of getting over the wall, the officer in command of the patrol sent someone to the palace to obtain reinforcements. Farandoul and his mariners leapt to the ground and set off at top speed to catch up with the norimon.

The route was long; the porters were exhausted, but the Japanese were running 50 meters behind the little troop and it was vital that they should not catch up. They covered a few leagues thus, which seemed mortally long to everyone. Farandoul never quit the rear-guard, in order to cover the retreat with his best blades.

Finally, they drew near to the place of rendezvous, the little fishing-port where the flower-boat was and to which Mandibul, if he had succeeded, would have brought the white elephant.

Cheers raised from close by made Farandoul shiver. It was Mandibul—who, seeing his friends hard pressed by the Japanese, was running towards them with a few men.

"Well?" Farandoul shouted to him, increasing his speed.

"Complete success!" Mandibul replied. "The white elephant is ours! The pirates are thwarted! I was afraid of arriving after them, like the other times."

"Bravo! The King of Siam's millions are in the bag!"

"Look!" Mandibul continued, pointing to the flag-decorated masts of the flower-boat, visible some distance away amid the rocks. "Our men are putting the elephant aboard; you have the princess. We can cut the mooring-ropes immediately and set out to sea!"

Meanwhile, the mariners, having completed the rather awkward embarkation of the white elephant, were running to confront the numerous Japanese launched in pursuit of Yamida's abductors.

The norimon, having reached the rocks, had been deposited on the strand by the worn-out porters. A boat had been fetched in order return them to the flower-boat, anchored a few meters from the shore. Farandoul hurled himself towards the norimon, opened the side-door, and released a terrible cry.

The Japanese woman whose abduction had just cost him so much trouble was not Yamida! It was the governess of the maids of honor—an eminently respectable lady—that Farandoul had carried off.

A frightful catastrophe! What should he do? What could he do? And what about the Japanese, who would hurl themselves upon the mariners in two minutes?

"Let's get aboard anyway!" cried Farandoul, leaving the poor governess semiconscious in her norimon. "Let's save the white elephant, at least!"

All the mariners gathered on the beach were about to leap into the boat to head for the flower-boat when a loud *hurrah* resounded aboard the latter vessel. Twenty horrible figures had just emerged from the hold and were throwing themselves upon the mooring-cable, hatchets in hand.

The young Chinese women, terrified, had taken refuge at the stern. The white elephant, solidly installed by the mariners, wedged on the deck, also released desolate squeals. It had just recognized its persecutors, the pirates who had already sold and stolen it so many times.

Farandoul understood everything. Once again, the white elephant had escaped him; a complete triumph had turned into an irreparable disaster!

The flower-boat, caught by the tide, drew away from the shore, and the pirates hoisted the large sail with howls of triumph. Farandoul recognized the man standing on the top deck as the man glimpsed in Nanking on the Blue River, the fake bayaderes' musician from Kifir.

"I'm going to collect the king of Siam's millions!" the pirate shouted, insolently. "Goodbye, and thanks for bringing us the elephant yourselves!"

Farandoul darted a rapid glance behind him. His men had already come to grips with the Prince of Miko's soldiers.

"Retreat! Retreat!" he cried, pointing to the little boat grounded on the shore.

They all piled into it pell-mell and shoved it away from the shore. They were just in time, for the flood of Miko's soldiers as about to overwhelm, them—but the situation was not good; the little boat seemed liable to founder at any moment beneath its load.

Farandoul and Mandibul leapt upon the oars. "Too many enemies on land!" Farandoul shouted. "Let's try to reach the open sea and catch up with the flower-boat!"

Mandibul shook his head. "We can follow them," he said, "but catching up with them will be difficult. See how the breeze is getting up, making them fly over the waves!"

Indeed, the distance between the feeble rowing-boat and the flower-boat was increasing by the minute. Within an hour, it would have disappeared, carrying with it any hope of ever winning the reward promised by His Majesty the King of Siam.

"It doesn't matter—keep following! Besides, what else can we do? Don't we have to get away from the Japanese, who are looking for a boat at this very minute in order to chase us? Fortunately, all the fishermen from the port are at sea...but now I think of it, if we can get hold of one of the fishing-boats that's plying the coast out there, two or three leagues away, we might have a chance of getting our elephant back. That's it! Row hard; all is not lost! We'll catch up!"

"Oh, the brigands!" murmured Mandibul, tearing out a few hairs. "Who could have suspected that, while we were going to so much trouble to steal the elephant from the Temple of the 33,333 Spirits, those villainous pirates were waiting for us, hidden on the flower-boat, ready to snatch it from under our very noses!"

IX.

The crew of a large Japanese fishing-boat could not have been more surprised when they saw a troop of wild-eyed three-sword warriors climb aboard. The owner thought at first that they were conspirators in flight and got ready to ask them for a good price to transport them no matter where, but when he understood, from the interpreter's discourse, that it was a matter of running after a gang of pirates, he pulled a face.

Farandoul, standing sadly in the stern of the fishing-boat, darted one last glance towards the land of Japan, which he might never see again, and among the bushes of which he had left a shred of his heart—a heart so often and so cruelly rent! It was over! Yamida would have to remain Princess of Miko, and Kaido triumphant! Destiny had intended it thus; the charming Yamida must remain a mere apparition in his life.

432

Soon, night fell; the coasts of Japan disappeared and the flower-boat vanished into the darkness. Fortunately, its signal-lights shone all through the night, and maintained our friends on its track.

At daybreak they saw it again; it had resumed the course it had followed in coming from China and was heading southwards in order to reach the Yellow Sea, either by the Bango channel or the Van Diemen strait, between the southern point of Japan and the Ryukyu Islands.

Unfortunately, squalls were frequent in these parts, and in the afternoon of that day the strong morning breeze turned into a veritable tempest.

The flower-boat, dancing over the waves and presenting a large surface to the wind, would have considerable difficulty maintaining itself. The pursuing mariners anxiously followed the maneuvers of their imperiled enemies; if they foundered, they would take the poor terribly-shaken white-elephant with them.

Eventually, the expected denouement arrived; the two vessels, almost within sight of one another, were carried on to the coast of Korea and wrecked.

Farandoul and his men succeeded in swimming ashore and set off in search of the debris of the flower-boat. What had become of the white elephant in that lamentable disaster? They marched for hours without discovering any wreck; they scoured all the ramifications of the coast and all the clefts in the rocks without finding anything. And yet they had seen the vessel adrift, dismasted by the storm!

After a great deal of fatigue, they finally caught sight of the poor flower-boat, almost intact, lying on the sand at the far end of a small bay. It was surrounded by a multitude of Koreans, who were busy ardently taking it apart. The mariners soon arrived into their midst, to their great amazement. A rich lord, the owner of this part of the coast, was there, sharing out the Chinese women between the distinguished folk of the region, who were delighted with the windfall. The flower-boat and its cargo belonged to him, according to the law governing shipwrecks. The Chinese women seemed content with this conclusion to their peregrinations; as soon as they saw Farandoul, their benefactor, they ran to thank him.

"What about the white elephant?" asked the latter, cutting their demonstrations short. "Did any harm come to it when you ran aground?"

"No, the impact wasn't that bad—we got stuck in the sand. It rolled on to the ground, breaking the sides of the boat. The pirates jumped down and ran after it, leaving us behind. Oh, the brigands! Not the slightest delicacy! Brutal creatures! Do you know…?"

"There's no time. Which way did they go, and when?"

"That way, in the middle of the night."

"Twelve hours start! We'll catch them up. Forwards!"

Our friends got under way and were soon following the elephant's tracks across the plain. Where were they, and where were they headed? No one had any idea. At dusk they arrived at a Korean village called Tsin-Tsou. The elephant had been seen there that morning, but it was no longer white, the pirates having had time to paint it grey.

On the following day they passed through the mountains and arrived on the coast of the Yellow Sea; the thieves were following the coast, heading towards China, doubtless to make contact with some Korean pirate junk on which they would be able to obtain passage.

The interpreter's questions about a white elephant had, however, attracted the attention of the Korean authorities. The Koreans also set out to capture the pirates and the white or grey elephant. The coasts were being watched; the pirates had undoubtedly noticed that, for they made numerous detours in order to put all the searchers off the track.

It was in this manner that the pirates, with the elephant, and Farandoul, with his mariners, arrived at the Chinese border after crossing the Pepisehan and Tsi-jouan mountains and the province of Chingking, a hilly country that the Chinese called the province of 1000 mountains. The Great Wall of China displayed its towers and its interminable crenellated line over the slopes of hills, in the depths of ravines and the cloud-shrouded summits of rocks.

"Ugh!" said Mandibul, on seeing it. "China: the 98,000 pieces! We're condemned to death here."

"Bah! We're getting used to condemnations now."

Our friends then committed the extreme imprudence, with regard to the extent of their police record in China, of once more setting foot in the Celestial Empire. They entered the country one evening and stopped off at an inn in order to converse with the local inhabitants.

The hostelry was mediocre; it had nothing to serve them but friend leeches from the nearby lakes. As they were in the process of searching the kitchens, unsuspectingly, in the hope of discovering some food of a less Chinese nature, a whirlwind of tiger warriors suddenly fell upon them and succeeded in knocking them down and tying them up inextricably.

They were prisoners, and, to put the cap on their misfortune, they had been recognized. A mandarin in a blue hat arrived to examine them with a scroll of paper in his hand, and established their exact resemblance to the description sent from Nanking of the barbarians who had broken the Porcelain Tower. The mandarin rubbed his hands and gave the order to take them to the small town of Koufau six leagues away.

As soon as they arrived in Koufau, the mandarin consulted his wife, a somewhat mature woman but one capable of wise counsel, with regard to a matter that was worrying him. Ought he to have the sentence of the judges in Nanking carried out immediately, or send the guilty parties to Peking to flatter the Son of Heaven?

A nice torture is a pleasant thing to contemplate, but advancement takes precedence, so the mandarin's wife inclined towards sending them to Peking. The people of Koufau would have to settle for a little exhibition.

In consequence, the leader Farandoul was locked in a narrow iron cage suspended from a hook at the town gate, four meters above the ground. His accomplices, each one lodged in a barrel hermetically sealed and nailed shut, with only his head outside, were arranged in two rows to either side of the gate to await their departure for Peking.

The mandarin's idea was a runaway success. The entire population, save for invalids, considered it a duty to come to contemplate the horrible criminals. Children of both sexes amused themselves greatly throughout the day by playing jokes on the unfortunate marines exposed as talking severed heads; the girls tickled the poor mariners' noses with their fans; the boys pulled their hair or made their defenseless noses breathe in powdered tobacco. Fits of sneezing followed which plunged the entire society into intense joy. Poor Tournesol, irascible by nature, became the butt of the nastiest jokes. He could only reply, alas, with explosions of Marseillaise curses, which posed little danger to his persecutors.

One wearies of everything, even the purest pleasures. At dusk the condemned men were left alone with their reflections and a sentry from the regiment of tiger warriors. The poor man had a six-hour tour of duty. He sought a few distractions to while away the time, and amused himself by exercising his skill at throwing stones, aiming at the heads of the most distant mariners.

Farandoul had not remained idle. Overheated by the Sun all day, frozen by the cold of the night, he had employed all his strength—multiplied tenfold by fury—in silently demolishing the bottom of his cage. His hands were bloody, but the cage was already half-broken.

At about 10 p.m., when the town was completely silent and the guard-unit of tigers established 50 meters away on the rampart seemed to be asleep, he resolved to finish the job with one final effort. He waited for the moment when the marching Chinese sentry would pass underneath the cage; when he saw him coming he broke through it with a formidable kick and remained suspended by his arms from the upper bars.

The heavy wooden board fell on top of the sentry with a dull thud and laid him on the ground, unconscious. Farandoul immediately let himself fall to earth and made a grab for the sentry's weapons, in order to defend himself should the need arise. The soldier had two swords, a dagger, a wheel-lock musket and a shield. Farandoul took them all and put on his uniform.

The event made little noise; there was no movement in the guard-post. Slightly reassured, Farandoul ran to his friends, who were following his movements anxiously.

"Alas," said Mandibul, "Chinese coopers do their work well. It'll need tools and time to extract us!"

Farandoul examined the barrels and frowned. The barrels were very nearly proof against a hatchet; the lids had been nailed shut with the greatest care. The matter was serious.

Suddenly, Farandoul slapped his forehead. He had an idea!

"From the height of my cage," he said, "I saw a little river which seemed to me to flow eastwards along the Great Wall. I'll roll your barrels to it and put them in the water. After that, we'll see."

"Forward!" exclaimed Mandibul. "But start with the others; I'm an officer—I'll stay until last."

Farandoul had to roll 17 barrels more than 150 meters away from the town. When he had got them all to the bank he launched them gently into the stream; the rapid current soon bore them away.

"Oof!" said Mandibul, when he felt himself bobbing on the waves. "That feels better already."

The 17 barrels floating in convoy made a rather bizarre spectacle. The poor prisoners stuffed in up to the shoulders could do nothing to assist their progress; sometimes they went astray and threatened to get caught in the reeds or spin round without moving forward. It was hardly a common-or-garden escape. Fortunately, at a particular moment, all the barrels were stopped by the guide-rope of a ferry. Farandoul cut it, doubled it up and used it to tie all the barrels together like a chaplet. When he had united them all, he leapt into the ferry-boat, attached them to the stern, and continued downstream, rowing vigorously with both oars, followed by his chaplet.

At dawn, after three hours of navigation, Farandoul judged it prudent to disembark. He landed, with all his barrels, on a wooded islet and carefully hid his men and his boat.

"Well," said Mandibul, "what do we do now?"

"You'll see," replied Farandoul. "We must get you out of your barrels, mustn't we? Now, as I have no tools and no time to spare, only one means remains. I'll light a fire with the Chinese sentry's powder; I'll put you on the fire, and when the planks of your barrels are sufficiently charred and disjointed, I'll roll you into the water to put you out. It will be easy to demolish the barrels thereafter."

The operation went smoothly; in two hours it was complete. The joyful sailors stretched their numbed arms and legs sensuously. Farandoul was very tired; he alone had been working rather than floating idly downriver in a barrel; nevertheless, he got to his feet and gave the signal to depart.

The Great Wall stood out on the horizon. They arrived without incident at the foot of the gigantic structure, but it was necessary to find a means of getting over it, because they could not go through the gates, which were always guarded. By night, the mariners discovered a sufficiently degraded section, which permitted them to attempt to scale it. After a few violent efforts, they succeeded in hoisting themselves up to the crest of the wall.

The descent was even more difficult than the ascent; they went along it for leagues without being able to find a less elevated spot. From time to time, they came to stout towers built at intervals along the wall. In moving around one of these keeps, Farandoul was surprised to hear a murmur of voices emerging from a loophole.

The interpreter had scarcely cocked an ear to a voice that reached him when he let out a stifled exclamation and nearly fell over.

"What is it?" demanded Farandoul, holding him up.

"It's them!" he murmured. "The pirates!"

"Ah!" exclaimed Farandoul. "Chance brings us together again! I knew that we'd catch up with them. But what are they doing in this tower? What are they saying?"

"Hang on! They're arguing…they're…"

"What?"

"Heavens! The elephant! The elephant!"

"Well?"

"They're going to eat it!"

"Eat it! Eat our white elephant, damn it! But we're here. Translate their words for us…"

They were, indeed, arguing inside the tower. Voices elevated in pitch by anger resonated clearly beneath the immense vault.

This is what the interpreter heard:

"Well, Nao, I tell you that only one course remains to us and we must hasten to take it. They've been on our track for a long time now; it's been two months since our shipwreck in Korea, and we've always been on the point of been captured and massacred by the mariners or by the Chinese! Now famine's taken a hand; it's a week since we hid in this tower to escape our enemies, and…"

"They won't find us; the breach we discovered in order to get in has been carefully masked…"

"That's not the point. The breach is sealed, but the famine's in here! We're dying of hunger. Well, let's eat the elephant!"

"Eat the elephant! So you're renouncing the reward?"

"Bah! With people on the lookout for us everywhere, as they are now, it'll be impossible for us to get through the Chinese provinces with it. The elephant is both useless and injurious, so we'd do better to eat it. Isn't that so, comrades? Do you agree?"

"Yes, yes. He's right—let's eat the elephant!"

Farandoul heard no more. He slid through the window-slit on to a staircase that led down into the depths of the keep. It was a wooden staircase supported by iron crampons, whose broken steps offered little security. It did not matter; they could make use of it, and, with great care, they could descend all the way to the bottom. The staircase ended on the first floor of the tower, the half-ruined floor of which was littered with large stones and huge beams. In the middle, a large opening allowed the base and ground floor of the tower to be seen, along with the 20 pirates seated around a dying fire. The emaciated rump of the poor white elephant was distinguishable in a corner.

The pirates, in the heat of their discussion, had heard nothing. Mandibul, sword in hand, was about to jump down into their midst when Farandoul stopped him. "Don't move! The position is excellent; we can crush them from here—there's no lack of projectiles—but the elephant might be killed in the combat. Let's negotiate first."

"Yes!" cried one of the pirates. "Let's eat the elephant!"

"Don't eat anything!" cried the interpreter, in a voice that he tried to render mighty. "You're trapped. If you move, we'll crush you like dogs!"

The pirates rose to their feet tumultuously and grabbed their weapons. A gunshot rang out; the bullet passed within two inches of Mandibul's head. The latter, furious, launched an enormous beam through the aperture.

"Surrender," the interpreter went on, "or you're all dead men!"

The sight of the stones and beams suspended over their heads made the pirates think again; they threw down their weapons and flattened themselves against the walls.

"Pass us your weapons!" said the interpreter. "That's the first condition. Your lives will be spared. Give us the elephant, and you'll be set free."

They consulted one another. The leader of the pirates, convinced of the impossibility of defense, bowed his head and silently surrendered the weapons. When all the swords, daggers and rifles had passed from the pirates' hands into those of the mariners, the latter jumped down to the ground floor of the tower.

"Finally!" cried Farandoul. "I was quite sure of catching up with you, but you've done us a great deal of harm!"

One of the mariners revived the fire; the light of the flames suddenly illuminated the face of the pirates' leader, who was standing in front of Farandoul looking confused.

"Aha!" cried Farandoul. "You're the man from the Blue River and the bayaderes' musician—but that's not all. I finally recognize you. You're Nao-Ching, the mandarin of the police of Siam!"

"It's not possible!" cried Mandibul.

The pirate bowed his head. "I admit everything," Nao-Ching said. "My salary was so rarely paid, and life is so expensive! I have 34 wives to feed, gentlemen—don't ruin the father of a family! I'm entirely guilty, I confess. It's me who stole His Majesty the King of Siam's elephant, me who sold it to the Emperor of Burma, then to the Rajah of Kifir, then to the Chinese bonzes, then to the Prince of Miko! But I repent, gentlemen. Remorse had taken hold of me and I was taking it back to Siam...."

To collect the 60 million reward! I understand your plan!"

"I'm the father of a family!"

"That's all right! Go get yourself hanged wherever you wish; we have the elephant that has led us such a merry dance, and we'll hold on to it. That's all we need, and we shan't let go of it!"

A loud exclamation, released by the mariners and the pirates simultaneously, made him turn round abruptly. The white elephant, which the mariners had believed to the securely imprisoned, had just passed abruptly through the wall and was fleeing into the countryside.

439

This is what had happened. When the mariners had revealed themselves, a few of the pirates had run to the breach in the wall to reopen it and get into the open. Once peace was made, though, they had abandoned their work. The white elephant, an intelligent animal, seeing an exit almost open, had launched itself at the wall and had abruptly broken through. Now it was galloping at liberty, far from the thieves and far from those who had gone to so much trouble to recover it.

"This time, it's the final catastrophe!" cried Mandibul, letting himself collapse on a stone. "It's over. We'll never get our hands on it."

"Get after it!" retorted Farandoul. "No weakness! We must have it, even if we have to comb the depths of the Gobi Desert for it!"

X.

The King of Siam's white elephant, which had already seen many countries and had caused our friends so much trouble, was destined to force them to cover many more kilometers, by rather disagreeable roads, sometimes in the endless sands of the Gobi Desert, sometimes in the stony ravines of the Mongolian mountains.

They often had nothing to eat, save for a few meager mountain plants or a few bears even thinner than they were. The dangers were numerous, though fewer than the gastronomic miseries of every sort; to Mandibul's great astonishment, the marines raised no objection to any condemnation to death, either in Manchuria or Mongolia.

The elephant, often perceived but never captured, led them, after many detours, as far as the land of the Khalkhas on the Siberian border. As you can see, the elephant was getting further and further away from its native land and its gilded palace in Siam, where an entire legion of priests and slaves, attentive to its desires, had once provided it with so easy a life.

Every time the hunters were able to catch a glimpse of the animal, rendered mistrustful by misfortune, they observed a visible diminution of its former plumpness. The elephant was growing thinner with every week that passed, in consequence of so much moral and physical suffering.

To put the cap on their misfortune, a terrible war as devastating these countries. Tartar hordes were ravaging the Russian frontier and threatening Irkutsk. The elephant, closely followed by the mariners, passed into Siberia and went northwards toward the mouth of Lake Baikal.

The cold suddenly descended with a truly Siberian intensity. There was snow and ice everywhere; it was in the remoteness of regions prey to polar horrors that our friends, almost at the point of despair, finally succeeded in encircling the elephant.

Cornered by the lake and numbed by the snow, the elephant could not avoid the mariners' lassos; after a long resistance, it had to yield to the weight of numbers.

The white elephant had been captured! Everything was forgotten—perils, sufferings, privations—in the joy of triumph.

The mariners found temporary shelter in a ruined and uninhabited isba.[99] Another traveler was also resting there. He was a tall fellow dressed as a Russian officer, with a big moustache and a long beard. The fatigue of a long journey had hollowed out his features, shredded his overcoat and afflicted his furs with premature baldness. The man's name was Michel Strogoff; he was fleeing from the Tartar hordes and trying to reach Irkutsk, which was under threat from them.

The mariners shared the little bear-meat they had left with Michel Strogoff, fraternally. Strogoff was the first civilized person they had encountered in Asia, so they welcomed him as if he were a long-lost friend.

As they had to go at the first light of what was passed for the Sun in this dismal land, everyone took full advantage of that first night of tranquility after so many alarms, and slept soundly. What fine slumber! The man charged with keeping watch over the safety of the troop could not resist, and slept like the rest, dreaming about the King of Siam's millions.

Towards morning, however, a slight noise woke Farandoul up with a start. He rolled over a few sleepers and reached the door just as the elephant, mounted by a sort of shadow, made off into the fog.

Farandoul's yell woke everyone up.

"Who's stolen our elephant? The Russian's not here, damn it! It's him!"

The mariners exploded into wild imprecations. Fate was definitely dead set against them. The Breton Trabadec put forward the suggestion that the astonishing animal must be the Devil in person, and some of the others echoed his opinion.

"Quick!" cried Farandoul, loading the only firearm the entire troop possessed. "Fire to light the wick of my arquebus!"

The antique Chinese musket required 12 minutes to be put into a state of readiness, however; by the time Farandoul, blowing on the wick, launched forth in search of the elephant, the unfortunate animal, spurred on by the thief, was already far away.

"Let's go!" cried Mandibul. "Strogoff's going to Irkutsk. He has to follow the shore of Lake Baikal. We can take that direction in all security!"

The mariners hastily picked up their weapons and a few remaining provisions. On making one last inspection of the isba to see whether they had forgotten anything, Mandibul found a piece of paper in the place that Strogoff had occupied, containing these simple words:

---

[99] A Russian log cabin

I requisition this white elephant
IN THE SERVICE OF THE TSAR.
Michel Strogoff, Imperial courier.

Fortunately for the mariners, the elephant's tracks were easy to follow. The animal's heavy legs sank to a depth of two feet into the snow. As its progress was considerably hindered by that layer of snow, Farandoul did not despair of catching up with it.

They followed the small pits left by the beast until nightfall without catching a glimpse of it on the horizon. One subject of dread had begun to assail the mariners. Instead of going around Lake Baikal to reach Irkutsk by land, Strogoff had headed straight on to the lake, as if to cross it. Lake Baikal was frozen—but was the ice strong enough to support the animal's weight? What anxiety! The infamous Strogoff might perhaps launch himself on to excessively thin ice with the poor elephant, and sink it under 300 meters of icy water!

It was fated, however, that our marines should not be spared any anxiety. A new disquiet was added to those that were already torturing them. A pack of wolves had, like them, set off on the track of the white elephant. Alongside the footprints of the elephant, the tracks of numerous paws were perceptible.

"This time, if we catch it, it will be lucky," murmured Mandibul. "If not, it'll be drowned or eaten!"

"Forward! Forward!" retorted Farandoul.

That vertiginous course lasted several more hours. At midnight, at the moment when they caught sight of the white cliffs of Lake Baikal in the distance, a frightful howling became audible.

"It's the wolves' tally-ho!" murmured Mandibul, in a breathless voice. "They're in the process of devouring our 60 millions."

Ten minutes of running brought them to the goal of their efforts. On the shore of Lake Baikal a white mass stood out, cornered in the rocks. It was the white elephant, still mounted by Michel Strogoff. But why were they maintaining that frightful immobility in the face of the wolves' assault? Not a movement, not a gesture, to repel the increasingly emboldened wolves! The elephant was standing up, backed up against a rock-face, tusks forward. Michel Strogoff was in the palanquin, leaning out with his arms extended.

"Frozen stiff!" cried Farandoul. "We've arrived too late!"

The wolves paused before the frozen group suddenly turned round; intact and furious enemies were about to fall upon them in a body. Within five minutes, the battlefield was clear; a dozen wolves remained in the arena; the rest were in flight, limping.

Farandoul precipitated himself towards the poor white elephant.

Its body was cold; its stiff and icy trunk hung down towards the ground like a dead branch. Farandoul, on shaking it to see whether a single spark of vitality remained within it, had the pain of seeing a large fragment of the trunk remain in his hand. As for Michel Strogoff, it required the greatest possible care to get him down from the palanquin without breaking him too.

"It's over!" said Mandibul. "Our 60 millions haven't been drowned in the lake or devoured by wolves, they've been frozen—which comes down to the same thing, so far as we're concerned."

All hope was lost. It was inevitable now—and the prospect of returning to Siam to take the fatal news to His Majesty was not the most cheerful one imaginable.

"We'll camp here," Farandoul said. "We'll leave at daybreak."

In order not to suffer the same fate as the unfortunate elephant, the mariners had to light large fires. There was no lack of wood; enormous fir-trees felled by storm-winds were lying in the snow. Soon, they had a fire fueled by an entire forest to warm them up.

Only Mandibul and Farandoul stayed on watch, depressed by the ruination of their hopes. Suddenly, Mandibul, who was sitting at the feet of the frozen elephant, felt a drop of some liquid fall upon his forehead. He raised his hand to it mechanically. It was blood! Mandibul raised his head. The blood was coming from the broken trunk of the poor elephant.

Farandoul leapt to his feet.

"It's bleeding! So it can't be completely frozen! Quickly! The fire! The fire! If we have to burn the entire region, we have to warm it up...!"

These enormous masses have such a power of vitality that death cannot do its work at a stroke. The elephant was alive—feebly, it is true, but it was alive. The reawakened mariners set to work; while some heaped mountains of wood on the flames, others warmed up blankets and took turns to rub the elephant.

After an hour of energetic massage, they perceived that the circulation of its blood was re-established in a normal fashion. In the meantime, the elephant began to recover consciousness; hoarse sighs escaped from its throat and shivers passed over its skin.

"Tea!" cried Farandoul. "Hot tea!"

Seaman Kirkson made haste; as an Englishman, the was very appreciative of hot water, and had not neglected to lay in a plentiful stock of green tea during his passage through China; he had saved this provision of tea from every shipwreck, and he had even conserved it in the barrel in which he had been placed in Kou-Fau. A huge Mongol cooking-pot was put on the fire, with a large quantity of green tea. When the liquid had reached boiling-point, the dazed elephant was forced to drink it.

A visible improvement resulted from this ingurgitation. The elephant moved its head and seemed to be disturbed by the disappearance of its trunk. After a second pot of tea, the poor animal found the strength to lie down on the ground; it was covered with all the troop's blankets, with a few large stones on top.

"If it starts breathing," Farandoul said, "there's hope."

The reader should not think, however, that all the mariners' concerns were for the elephant, while Michel Strogoff lay there, abandoned to his fate. No! Like the elephant, Strogoff had been brought to the fireside and rubbed with equal energy. For some time this had been fruitless, but finally, after two hours of effort, and slightly roasted by the fire, Strogoff recovered consciousness. He had had his share of the two pots of tea offered to his victim; by virtue of the strength of his constitution, that had been sufficient to put him on his feet again.

O joy! The elephant drew breath. They threw several fir-trees on the fire and added a few more blocks of stone to its blankets to avoid any possibility of it getting cold again.

In the morning, the reawakened elephant began to cough. It was given more warm water, which it drank without having to be persuaded, turning a grateful eye to Farandoul.

"If we save him, he won't leave us again," murmured our hero, "for he's finally understood that we are his friends."

Strogoff, as tough as a Siberian, had not suffered unduly; he did not cough and did not feel ill at all, but he had perceived with horror that his temporary freezing had made him somewhat brittle. The sight of the broken trunk gave him pause for reflection. Setting his pride to one side, he asked if he could have a word with Farandoul.

At first, our friend treated him coldly, but his heart soon softened and he sought some means to soothe his enemy's distress. The remedy for the fragility of which Strogoff complained was soon found; four mariners went into the forest to search for solid and flexible pieces of wood with which to circle the courier like a simple barrel. This work took all morning. Finally, Michel Strogoff, solidly engirdled, thought he was in a fit state to continue on his way without running the risk of breaking at the slightest knock. He bid farewell to his benefactors and disappeared on the road to Irkutsk without daring to turn to look at his victim, the elephant.

The great enterprise for which Farandoul and his mariners had already run so many dangers had, therefore, almost come to nothing as a result of their fatal encounter with Michel Strogoff, courier of the tsar. How strange! Yet again, it was one of Jules Verne's heroes who had got in our Farandoul's way. Once again, a Jules Verne hero, by an evil machination fortunately undone by Providence, had almost nullified all our friend's future projects!

The poor elephant's head-cold was so bad that it was bordering on pneumonia. Mandibul, who had some slight knowledge of botany, went off in search of certain plants that might serve to make a tisane. He came back with a huge armful of herbs, which they set about infusing. The tisane, given to the poor elephant in buckets, along with fumigations of lichen, made it much better; the cold yielded to the energetic medication, the fever disappeared and its respiration became normal again.

After a fortnight, the elephant finally began to convalesce; only its trunk still caused it to suffer, and in that respect its suffering was more moral the physical, for the stump had scarred over. It was the memory of the absent trunk and the idea that it would be crippled for life that was grieving the noble animal.

One morning, after breaking camp, they left the ill-fated environs of Lake Baikal to plunge back into the deserts of Mongolia. Compared with their preceding journeys, the voyage had become a simple pleasure-trip; they advanced in easy stages so as not to tire the convalescent out, taking the time to choose good camp-sites for the night, and they did not set off again until they were well-rested and well-provided with provisions by courtesy of hunting.

After many days of traveling, they finally saw the sea! Farandoul had steered his company towards Unggi, the northernmost point of Korea on the Sea of Japan. His intention was to charter a small ship of some sort to sail to Bangkok. It was not without difficulty that he succeeded in making contact with a large Korean junk capable of carrying the precious elephant without subjecting it to too much discomfort.

The poor elephant had shown signs of distress on seeing the sea again; it remembered its peregrinations with the pirates and long weeks of sea-sickness. Full of confidence in its new friends, however, it played its part bravely and embarked without objection.

It was a beautiful day when the junk arrived in port at Bangkok. The white elephant, very lively since it had been returned to the tropical Sun, was hardly coughing at all any longer. As soon as they entered the harbor it recognized the land of its birth and greeted the domes of the pagodas with hoarse cries of joy.

An immense crowd was waiting for the junk on the shore. The quays, boats, roofs and trees were all garnished with breathless Siamese. The Amazon regiment, summoned in all haste, formed a line on the quay where they were to disembark, with the brilliantly-adorned colonel at the head.[100] When the junk touched the stones of the quay, an immense cheer went up. Farandoul leapt to the shore to supervise the disembarkment of the idol.

In the first rank of the group of officials that advanced to greet our friends, Farandoul recognized the now-familiar face of the author of all the poor elephant's ills: the man who had stolen it in Bangkok and marched it from city to city across the whole of Asia—Nao-Ching, the mandarin of the police. He came forward, smiling, to congratulate the mariners.

"This is a bit strong!" murmured Mandibul. "Here you are again!"

"Did we not make peace, out there in China?" replied Nao-Ching. "After leaving you I came back to inform His Majesty of your imminent arrival with the elephant, recovered from its thieves, and I resumed my duties as mandarin of the police, which I had left during my absence to my vice-mandarin and secretary.

"Very good!" said Farandoul. "I have no doubt that, under your direction, the police are doing an admirable job in Bangkok. But tell me—you can admit it now that it's all over—was it really your intention to bring the elephant back to Bangkok?"

"Of course! Since it was me who gave His Majesty the idea of offering the 60 million reward. I had even taken the precaution, knowing that the State coffers were not always full, of having the sum set aside; that will ensure that you have only to present yourselves to my dear colleague, the mandarin of finances, to receive your reward. In consideration of the service that I have rendered you by my foresight, I hope that you will reserve me a small 5% commission?"

---

[100] Obviously, her rank—stripped when he allowed the mariners to escape—had been restored to her in the interim.

The colonel of the Amazons, advancing towards Farandoul with her hand extended, interrupted the claims of the mandarin of the police. Her fine and honest military figure made Farandoul think better of the Siamese race. He turned his back on the impudent mandarin and presented his compliments to the colonel. The interpreter, companion of all our friends' perils, came forward to offer his services.

The brave Mandibul had no need of an interpreter; he grasped the significance of the bitter reproach in the warrior woman's eyes perfectly—an entirely personal reproach, for she chatted with Farandoul in the most amicable tone. Mandibul was about to slip away when the colonel, leaving Farandoul, seized him unceremoniously by the arm.

"What?" asked Mandibul's astonished eyes.

The colonel put her hand on her sword in a significant manner.

"A duel!" cried Mandibul, taking two steps back. "Let's see—what if I were to apologize?"

"I would not accept it!" replied the colonel's eyes.

Damn! Damn! thought Mandibul. *Play for time!* And he made a movement of his head indicating the elephant, as if to ask the colonel's permission to complete his mission before being called to the dueling-field. The colonel understood and bowed.

Soon, an immense procession formed on the quay and followed the idol on its triumphant journey to the palace. There is no need to describe the pomp with which the sparkling procession was greeted at the king's palace; ministers, mandarins of every rank, dignitaries of every caste—everyone was there.

To describe the joy of His Siamese Majesty would also be futile; it was, in any case, tempered by a great anguish. His Majesty, after the first embraces, perceived that the sacred elephant, the emanation of the divine Buddha, had lost its august trunk!

The poor white elephant was overcome by the emotion of this return to its home; one could see that in its eyes. The king, warned about the delicacy of its health, ordered that it be taken to its temple.

It only remained for our friends to pay a visit to the mandarin of finances. When they took their leave of the His Majesty, a few roses falling at their feet from the windows of the palace made them raise their heads. The king's wives were there, behind the blinds! The roses were souvenirs addressed to the men formerly condemned to be decapitated 800 times over by the sword.

The next day was a solemn occasion. They collected the reward of 60 millions in local and European currency from the mandarin of finances.

"Finally!" cried Mandibul. "Quickly—to the port! Let's embark right away."

"Why are we in so much of a hurry?" asked Farandoul. "What's up?"

"What's up is that I have a duel on my hands, and I'm running away! The colonel of the Amazons has called me out!"

"The colonel! Let's go, then! To the junk, my lads, and off to Calcutta! There we can find steamboats bound for every country in the world. Where do you want to go, lads, now that you're millionaires?"

"Paris! Paris!" replied the new nabobs, unanimously.

"So be it! Let's head for Europe!"

PART FIVE: EUROPE

HIS EXCELLENCY THE GOVERNOR OF THE NORTH POLE

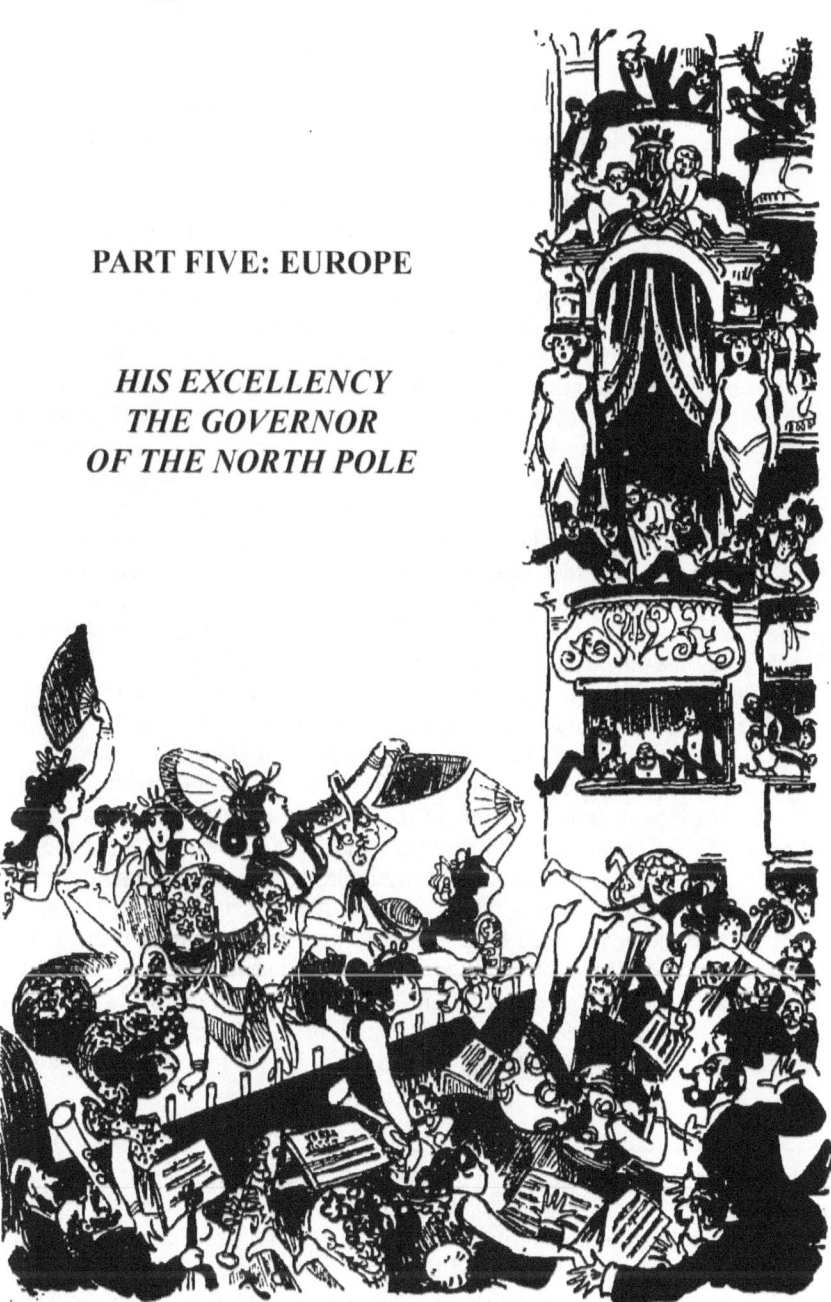

I.

You will recall that in October 18**, the attention of Paris was strongly gripped—separately, it is true—by two events, one purely scientific and the other entirely mundane.

The first event was the announcement of a huge German expedition to the North Pole, departing upon mysterious projects that were not without political implications.

As for the second preoccupation of Parisian society, it was to do with the assiduous presence in a box at the Opera, facing the stage, of a noble foreigner, always accompanied by four mariners bronzed by the tropic Sun. From the first evening on, this noble foreigner had attracted all the gazes in the auditorium and commanded all the pairs of opera-glasses; scandalously, the members of the audience had turned their backs on the singers and neglected the music in order to focus on him! The female spectators, leaning out of their boxes, did not miss a single one of his movements and followed his every eye-blink, breathless and oppressed, to such a point that several husbands were annoyed; more than one divorce case dated from that memorable evening. The famous Persian of the old Opera had found a successor![101] A profound mystery surrounded the foreigner; no one knew his name or his social position; all that was known was that his friend the mariners had arrived from India heaped with millions.

Soon, all Paris, excited by the mystery, was speaking of nothing else but the noble stranger; as soon as he appeared in his box, followed by his four friends, a shiver ran through the auditorium and over the stage.

One of the glories of the Opera, the baritone ***, recently returned to the scene of his triumphs, turning round at the sound of his entrance during a performance of *Don Juan*, uttered a frightful croak; the unfortunate artist did not finish his performance, but went back to his dressing-room to commit suicide and begin preparations for his funeral. People threw themselves at his feet in vain; all that could be obtained from him was a promise not to have recourse to a violent death. He left the Opera, went home and shut himself away for three days. Thick smoke emerging day and night from all the chimneys of his house intrigued everyone; the celebrated artist was pitilessly burning all his papers, love-letters, souvenirs, portraits and locks of hair. By the morning of the fourth

---

[101] The mysterious individual who became known as "the Persian of the Opera" during the Second Empire, eventually vanishing from public view in 1868, is said to have been a political refugee by the name of Mohammed Ismael; his literary inspiration extended far beyond this brief parody, the character being borrowed more-or-less entire by Gaston Leroux in *Le Fantôme de l'Opéra* (available in a Black Coat Press edition).

day, everything having been consumed, the great artist renounced the world, distributed all his wealth to the poor and went into a monastery.

That was not the only incident caused at the Opera by the troubling presence of this mysterious individual. One evening, during a performance of *Yedda*,[102] a lavish Japanese ballet that was greatly appreciated by the mariners, the entire *corps de ballet* seemed more excited than usual. A general distribution of bracelets adorned with precious stones had been made during the first entr'acte and this gesture of anonymous munificence had been attributed to the foreigner. No ballet had ever been danced by nimbler artistes; it was no longer even a ballet, but a whirlwind. In the finale, the fan-dance in the palace, the principal dancers, overextending themselves, went over the edge of the stage and fell into the orchestra-pit. There was a moment of terrible anxiety. The entire audience rose tremulously to its feet; the fops in the orchestra stalls, jumping over the rails, launched themselves to the assistance of the imperiled dancers. Thanks to an unusual stroke of luck, there was no serious accident to regret; a few first violins and petty flutes, badly bruised, were carried out in a faint to the pharmacy, but the ballerinas were intact, merely ornamented here and there with a few interesting pale blue marks. As for the foreigner and his mariners, they were literally writhing on the velvet cushions of their box.

This is a good opportunity to offer a description of this mysterious melomaniac, which our readers might already have recognized; his photograph once appeared in all the Parisian shop-windows and his portrait, published by all the illustrated periodicals, remains in everyone's memory.

This tall and strongly-built stranger was no longer young; his hair was a specimen of the wig-maker's art and to compensate for the irreparable ravages of the years his beard had to soak up a bottle of rejuvenating dye every day. A pair of gold-rimmed spectacles sat upon his unusually flat nose. His costume was always the same, in intimate circumstances, on the boulevard and at the Café Anglais as well as at the Opera. He was constantly dressed in a blue ankle-length ulster, coiffed by a scarlet fez and gloved in an irreproachable manner.

Who was this exotic aristocrat?

The society periodicals had been reduced to guesswork on that score. Their newshounds could find no means of getting past the wall surrounding his private life. The staff of the town house in which the unknown lived knew nothing; they could have been put to torture without any information being extracted from them.

Only one reporter succeeded in getting into the house; he had a long interview with the strange individual without any more result, for, without allowing himself to pronounce a single word, the unknown seized a case of champagne,

---

[102] *Yedda*, by Philippe Gille, Arnold Mortier and L. Mérante, with music by Olivier Métra, was premièred at the Opera in 1879, while *Saturnin Farandoul* was being serialized.

set a bottle in front of the reporter, uncorked another and savored it languorous-ly. After the first bottle, as the reporter tried to say something, the unknown un-corked two more and obliged the journalist to follow his example by ingurgitat-ing the generous liquid. When the reporter came to, he was lying in an open-topped landau between the four mariners and the unknown; they deposited him, utterly bewildered, in a corner of the famous box at the Opera. The more silent and melancholy the unknown seemed, the noisier the four sailors became; that evening they had particular difficulty preventing themselves from accompanying the singers in the grand arias. The reporter returned to his paper two days later with only one item of information: one of the mariners was named Tournesol.

The foreign nobleman and the marines threw gold through every window, even those of boudoirs—for it must be admitted that the frequented the wings of small theaters, the Bal Mabille and private dining-rooms as assiduously as the Opera. For a long time, the foreign nobleman had had his entrée to the Opera's foyer; he was often seen there, always grave an melancholy, spending hours in the middle of a triple circle of charming girls with ruffled skirts, soft calves and lips full of smiles.

In the anxious clubs the danger was not unappreciated; the entire Opera seemed vanquished; even the dancer's mothers and aunts were dreaming about the foreign nobleman. Riding in the woods in the morning, on the boulevard in the open-topped landau with his friends in the afternoon, in evening at the Cir-que, the Français, Mabille or the Opera, the magnificent stranger was every-where. At Trouville, a few months before, he had been the king of the beach; having arrived in joyous company, he had revolutionized his hotel with his whims and bowled over the elegant population of that charming resort with his Asiatic pomp.

His servants brought carpets and cushions on to the sand, along with hookahs and pipes, bottles of liqueurs and telescopes; at midday, the foreigner appeared, followed by his inseparable mariners. All five of them, often accompanied by graceful women, installed themselves on their cushions in the midst of the beach-huts and deck-chairs and spent the afternoon as tranquilly as could be imagined, shaded from the Sun by docile servants, savoring choice liqueurs in golden goblets, or losing themselves, telescopes in hand, in the contemplation of the female bathers.

In Paris, several celebrities of the demi-monde who claimed to have been honored by his favors, were literally besieged by reporters, who hoped to acquire by that means a few hints regarding the brilliant and mysterious character who was the subject of so much preoccupation. It must be supposed that the foreign nobleman had always been decidedly uncommunicative, for these ladies knew no more of his life than other mortals; always silent, no one had ever seen him involve himself in a conversation other than by means of grunts, variously modulated according to his humor.

A complete mystery!

The other event—the polar expedition—certainly preoccupied the great city less than the noble foreigner of the Opera. It was only on the rebound that the attention of Paris had been called to that subject; communications between institutes had made that question the topic of the day in scientific societies and journals, and polemics had been exchanged with newspapers from beyond the Rhine.

The determinant cause of the German expedition to the North Pole was the discovery made in the waters of Novaya Zemlya by the *Dorothea*, out of Hamburg, of a tribe of seals speaking Latin. There was no denying this strange discovery; two members of the tribe—two young seals—had been brought back by the *Dorothea* and solemnly presented at the scientific congress of Berlin, convened in extraordinary session. The most incredulous scientists had been forced to yield to the evidence; the seals, very different from vulgar seals that say *Papa* and *Mama*, distinctly pronounced *Pater* and *Mater*. The most learned professors from the universities of Dresden, Jena, Heidelberg, Munich and so on, were summoned to the congress to take part in the appointment of a grand scientific commission charged with an in-depth examination of every aspect of the question of the Latin seals.

The commission set to work without abandoning the grounds of the Academy, specially fitted out for the occasion and provided with large dormitories for night sessions. This innovation permitted members of the commission to work almost without interruption day and night. They discussed, ate, studied, replied, slept and woke up only to recommence. It was, in reality, a single four month session filled with Herculean labors, at the end of which the scientific commission published six volumes of reports enriched with maps, diagrams and tables, and two volumes of conclusions, which could be summarized thus:

(1) The seals speak Latin.

(2) They must have learned it.

(3) That seems to prove the existence, in the polar regions, of a nation descended from some ancient Roman colony, separated from the world for centuries, the sole survivor of the ancient metropolis, whose language it has retained.

(4) It is up to the German people, the successor of the Republic, to rediscover that colony.

German Academia, profoundly excited by these conclusions, was soon covered with subscription lists for the dispatch of a national expedition to the North Pole. Money flowed into the coffers of the scientific commission; in only a few months, the expedition was fully organized, provided with fresh and salted food-supplies, high-quality coal, splendid instruments and eminent scientists. There was no more to do than depart for the Latin colony.

At the same time as the German expedition's ship left the port of Hamburg, carrying all the prayers of German Academia, an English ship left Dover, charged by jealous Albion with an analogous mission. At the end of October, it was learned in London and Berlin that both expeditions were on the ice-sheets of the Arctic Circle.

Let us return to Paris and unveil, in a few lines, the mystery that still enve-lops, for the majority of our contemporaries, the identity of the noble foreigner of the Opera. This unknown nabob, this magnificent aristocrat wearing a veil of anonymity, was none other than Farandoul's foster-father, the monkey from the island in Pomotou whom our hero had placed as a day-resident in the Jardin des Plantes when he returned from Oceania after his attempt to organize a bimane and quadrumane nation in Australia.

Thus, the aged monkey, having reached the end of his career, after an en-tire life of honorability and calm respectability, had launched himself whole-heartedly into the whirlwind of Parisian pleasures. As philosophers have already remarked, when a quinquagenarian goes off the rails, he very quickly exceeds all limits and his antics surpass by a considerable distance the follies of the stor-miest adolescents. Let us say immediately, however, that the brave monkey had been drawn into high society rather than throwing himself into it. He had been led astray from his social duties and modest habits by four of our old friends—four of Farandoul's mariners, who had come to Paris to spend their share of the 60 millions of the King of Siam's white elephant.

These millions, which had cost them so much effort and for which they had nearly been subjected to so many and such horrible tortures—decapitations by the sword, slicing into 98,000 pieces, boiling fat, simple or serious impalement, etc., etc.—the mariners had set about spending recklessly.

On arriving in Paris, Tournesol, their leader, remembering the good rela-tionship he had previously established in Australia with Farandoul's foster-father, had run to the Jardin des Plantes to embrace the old monkey. He had found him in good health, content with his lot and held in such esteem by the administration that he was entrusted with serving as mentor to the young mon-keys on days when they were let out.

How had that honest monkey been seduced away from the path of virtue by the mariners? Why had he weakened? We still do not know. At any rate, hav-ing gone out the day after Tournesol's visit with the young monkeys ordinarily confided to his care, Farandoul's foster-father did not come back at 4 p.m., as usual, nor at 5, 6, 8, or even 10 p.m.

At midnight, the staff of the Jardin des Plantes, at the height of their anxie-ty, had seen two omnibuses escorted by mounted policeman arrive at their gates. It was the young monkeys that were being returned. They had been found at the Folies-Bergères, where they had caused an enormous scandal, and they had been brought back drunk, exhausted and ashamed. As for Farandoul's foster-father, he had disappeared and no one at the Jardin des Plantes ever saw him again.

Accommodated by Tournesol in the town house in which the mariners had set up home, dressed in sumptuous garments thanks to their munificence, he had begun to astonish Paris and the seaside resorts on the coast of Normandy with his grandiose manners and mysterious appearance.

Where was Farandoul while his foster-father was surrendering himself to these excesses? Our hero was a long way from Paris at the time. While returning from Siam, after the fortunate outcome of the affairs of the white elephant's 60 millions, he had stopped off in Constantinople at the invitation of High Highness the Sultan, to involve himself in the great project of the reconstitution of the Ottoman Empire.

While our friends scattered right and left to enjoy their millions, or hero, under the name of Farandoul Pasha, astonished the European powers by the loftiness of his views on the Eastern question. At a congress spontaneously gathered in Constantinople, the representatives of the old diplomacy debated with Farandoul Pasha the terms of definitive settlement of that sempiternal question.

Russia had, you will recall, repurchased—at the cost of enormous sacrifices—the greater part of its Turkish bonds, and was talking about nothing less than forcing Turkey to file for bankruptcy. Russia's plan had been very quickly brought to light; it consisted, first of all, of obtaining, by judiciary means, the seizure of the Sublime Porte[103] and returning the keys of the Dardanelles to the official receivers, and then—which greatly interested the boyars holding the bonds—of sharing out the residents of the royal harems, seized as movable property, in proportion to the bonds.

---

[103] The *Sublime Porte* was the "open court" of the Sultan, in which all of the Ottoman Empire's diplomatic affairs were conducted. Like its closed counterpart, the High Porte, the institution was known to Westerners by a title that hybridized French and English terminology.

England had other ideas on the subject of the famous keys of the Dardanelles, and it seemed rather difficult to reach an agreement, but Farandoul Pasha was there, debating toe-to-toe and battling victoriously with both the voracious northern bear and the insatiable Britannic leopard.

Poor Turkey had finally glimpsed the light at the end of the tunnel—continental Europe breathed again and five per cent Turks climbed to 99.95—when these hopes suddenly evaporated; an unknown but powerful motive had led Farandoul Pasha abruptly to hand in his resignation and quit Constantinople for an unknown destination!

Bad news had arrived. Farandoul had received a blow-by-blow account of the scandalous existence led in Paris by his foster-father and an entire series of misfortunes, accidents or annoyances that had afflicted his friends in the exercise of their new profession as millionaires.

Were these men made for the unpoetic existence that envelops us in our cities? No, in truth. Even with their millions, they immediately felt out of place, hemmed in by the thousand borders of our narrow civilization.

Seaman Kirkson, having left for London with three millions in his pocket, had, like Tournesol in Paris, launched himself into the high life. On arrival, he had founded a club, the Rolling Stone Club—an original institution that possessed no headquarters, nor even a domicile, since it had been initially established with seven founder members in a large, carefully-refitted omnibus, which rolled by day and night around the streets of London. Kirkson, accustomed to a nomadic existence, could no longer resign himself enter any house, great restaurants aside.

His idea had been a success; within a few days, the Rolling Stone Club had comprised four omnibuses and 30 members. They were still on the move; every three or four hours they stopped, as the opportunity presented itself, at an aristocratic restaurant, and they had a meal of some sort—breakfast, lunch or dinner. On leaving the restaurant, they furnished the vehicles with a reasonable quantity of bottles of champagne, Kirkson's favorite tipple, and enlivened the intervals between meals with repeated libations.

The Rolling Stone Club's four omnibuses had, of course, often run into trouble with some policeman or other, but how could one get annoyed with such fine fellows? "Put him out!" said Kirkson, and, according to his expression, the policeman and his claims were "put out" by floods of champagne.

One day, Kirkson wearied of this existence; finding the Rolling Stone Club too fastidious, he got his colleagues abominably drunk and abandoned them on the public highway He had had another idea; the improvement of the equine species—an eminently national task—claimed him and what remained of his three millions. In consequence, Kirkson bought a job lot of 30 horses and hired a considerable number of jockeys and grooms.

For a fortnight, under the pretext of training them, he raced his string over the countryside between London and Windsor, galloping through the fields, scaling the heights, jumping hedges, walls, fallen trees and almost anything else he could jump over, occasionally leaving behind a broken-legged horse or a crippled jockey. After two weeks of this exercise, Kirkson judged his stable sufficiently trained and gave the signal to return to London. It was the eve of the Derby, but Kirkson, detesting flat-racing, wanted to show his compatriots how much interest would be generated by courses with well-designed obstacles. He therefore took his string to the Strand and suddenly launched the entire troop through the tightly-knit ranks of carriages and omnibuses.

Clearing omnibuses, leaping over cabs and unseating the coachmen, entering shops through one widow and exiting through another—that was what Kirkson meant by obstacle courses. Setting the prime example himself, he had selected the gates of St. Paul's Cathedral as a finishing-post. He arrived there well ahead, followed several minutes behind by only five of his horses. The others remained scattered along the route, with various things broken to various degrees.

The joyous Kirkson was about to take his men to a public house to water them with spirits, when he was astonished to see the hand of a breathless policeman descend on his collar. There were damages. Kirkson, seeming greatly offended, declared that he had every intention of paying them. In response to this statement, the policemen bowed. Alas, the improvement of the equine species cost Kirkson dear; the residue of the three millions was insufficient to pay for the indemnities claimed for that single race and Kirkson, declared insolvent, was thrown into a debtors' prison.

He was not alone in his misfortune. Our friend Escoubico, a Spaniard by birth, had also harvested his share of annoyances, similarly in the cause of sport. There was of course, no question with Escoubico of improving the equine species; the races he preferred with those of bulls. Cut off from that sort of pleasure since he had quit Spain, as soon as he became a millionaire he had rushed back to his fatherland to catch up with it. Scarcely having disembarked, he had raced to Grenada, the town of his birth, with the intention of hiring that city's arenas at any price, extortionate if necessary. He got them cheaper than that.

Numerous ferocious bulls were purchased and brought to Grenada at great expense, the most renowned toreadors were engaged, with their teams of toreros, by theatrical agents to whom the ostentatious Escoubico had given only one instruction: get the best, at an extortionate price, if necessary.

Thus provided with bulls and toreros, the Grenada bull-ring commenced a long series of magnificent fights, but almost in private. Escoubico wanted the fights for himself alone, and for the ladies. Enthroned in a huge box previously reserved for the authorities, he gleefully contemplated the prowess of his toreadors and, during the intermissions, let his eyes wander over the steps covered with charming senoras and senoritas.

Escoubico was happy. One day, unfortunately, these pleasures were disturbed by a storm. Escoubico quarreled with the celebrated torero Cuchares, the *prima spada* of Andalusia!

What had happened? A bouquet, thrown by a dark-eyed Grenadine to Cuchares, was, it is said, seized in flight by Escoubico, who was stupid enough to claim it for himself. The toreadors, furious at the insult to their leader, went on strike the following day. Escoubico's only response was to declare that he would dispense with them henceforth and fight the bulls himself.

That was too much. All the toreadors in Spain declared that their honor had been besmirched and swore revenge. Escoubico, besieged in his private bull-ring, was nearly transpierced by numerous Toledo *navajas* simultaneously deployed against him. It was necessarily to flee—regretfully, of course, but it *was* necessary.

Pursued by starlight, Escoubico finally found a refuge. His persecutors, navajas in hand, scoured the entire city, Alhambra and all, but they could not discover his retreat. Eacoubico had hidden in the Grenada museum, in the armor of Boabdil, the last Moorish king.

Thanks to the connivance of the daughter of the keeper, who, touched by his fate, brought him nourishment in his armor, he was able to avoid all searches—but it was impossible for him to quit that uncomfortable shelter; the toreadors were on the lookout, and whether he liked it or not, he would have to live in it for an indefinite period.

The Breton sailor Trabadec was the only one of our friends who was not in Europe. He wanted to remain on Asian territory, not to live there as a nabob in the bosom of luxury and the sweetest idleness, but rather to pursue a secret objective. As soon as he became a capitalist, he went to open a finance house in Burma.

Trabadec was, therefore, a banker—or rather a money-lender—in Amarapura. Travel furnishes a young mind with a great deal of useless information; while passing through Amarapura in pursuit of the white elephant, Trabadec had learned a strange fact: in Burma, mortgage loans are unknown; only pawnbroking is customary; when a client borrows a sum of money, he gives his creditor a pledge of one or two of his wives.

Trabadec, an honest Breton, had his idea; his millions would permit him to oblige a few upper-class Burmese. In accordance with custom, he accepted feminine guarantees, carefully chosen from among those his debitors were able to offer.

His banking house soon acquired a colossal reputation; the ladies given as security were treated with an exquisite delicacy; instead of serving the creditor they had numerous eager servants at their disposal. It was rumored in high places that the Trabadec Bank and our friend were on the point of being commissioned to negotiate a large national loan in Paris on the usual Burmese conditions—which is to say, with a certain number of royal wives as security—which could not have failed to revolutionize the Bourse. One fine morning, however, the Burmese found the bank closed. Trabadec had put the key under the door and fled with the pledges!

The injured Burmese made a great fuss; the affair made so much noise that the authorities had to intervene. The Burmese cavalry, launched in pursuit of the bankrupt, caught up with him at the frontier and brought him back to Amarapura in chains.

Trabadec's recklessness had put him in a bad position; his trial was about to begin and threatened to end badly for him if Farandoul, informed of his plight, could not find a way to get him out of Burmese custody by skill or by force.

As you can see, our friends' opulence had only served to get them into serious trouble; the other sailors, each granted three millions in the division of the reward received for the salvation of the white elephant, were all in more-or-less similar situations, some in prison for debt, others on the brink of ruination, a few on the run for different reasons. Even our brave Mandibul had got himself into an awkward situation. Having remained in Constantinople with Farandoul, he had launched into a tenebrous intrigue of a harem nature, and suddenly became impossible to find.

Farandoul, gripped by the most powerful affections, had not hesitated. He had abandoned Turkey to its destiny in order to race to the aid of his unfortunate friends.

First he had to find the vanished Mandibul, which was no small matter; finally, thanks to his energy and promptness, Farandoul had the pleasure of arriving just in time to pay off four scoundrels charged with throwing a tightly-stitched strong canvas sack, in which Mandibul and two ravishing odalisques were struggling, into the Bosphorus.

One saved!

On the same night, Farandoul, Mandibul and the two odalisques took passage on a French mailboat. The two odalisques disembarked at Smyrna, their native region; Farandoul and Mandibul continued as far as Naples, where they took it upon themselves to settle the difficulty of Seaman Bassol, retained in a hotel for the sum of eight francs, Bassol had lived life to the full; nothing remained of his three millions but memories and that small debt.

From Naples the sailor and his saviors had set sail for Cartagena in Spanish territory. Escoubico had summoned them; he was beginning to get bored inside Boabdil's armor and was very happy to see them arrive at the museum. Escoubico's escape only required one day; while the toreadors persisted in blockading the Alhambra, the mariners took a railway train and set off for Madrid.

Tournesol, his three friends and Farandoul's foster-father were very surprised to see Farandoul arrive one morning in their town house in the Avenue de Friedland. Needless to say, Tournesol was expecting the bailiffs; the association's millions had run out a week before, and the sumptuous house was besieged by creditors.

The mariners had set up a number of buckets of water to greet the bearers of IOUs, and when the stern-faced Farandoul fell into the midst these preparations he almost received a cold shower.

At the sight of his foster-father dressed as an eccentric dandy, Farandoul frowned. Tournesol hung his head in embarrassment, and within a minute, became aware of the villainous aspect of his conduct. We shall pass over the recriminatory scene that followed in silence. Farandoul, bitter at first, eventually calmed down and forgave them.

By that evening, everyone was reconciled; Farandoul's foster-father had renounced the Opera, the foyer and intimate suppers forever. He had burned an extensive collection of photographs and swept away the numerous souvenirs that cluttered up every corner of the house, along with empty champagne-bottles.

Farandoul assembled the creditors and paid a few 100,000 francs to liquidate the situation. Mandibul had already left for London to obtain the prodigious Kirkson's release from the debtors' prison and to collect three or four other mariners scattered around London and Le Havre.

They did not forget poor Trabadec; for a small fee, the Siamese mandarin Nao-Ching had been commissioned to get him out of Burma by diplomatic means and send him back to France.

All went well. It was to be expected that within a matter of weeks, all the former sailors of the *Belle Léocadie* would be reunited again. Farandoul was already making grand plans. Understanding that everyday life could not be sufficient for men of that stripe, and that, for reasons of health, they required action, perils and great enterprises replete with excitement, he was firmly resolved to extract them from any danger of idleness to launch them once more on the high life of adventures!

What had they not yet done, that they still might do? Formerly, when they had departed on their expeditions to America, their Oceanian journeys or their infernal white elephant hunt in Asia, they had been short of money and deprived of means of action. This time, however, Farandoul and Mandibul, still millionaires more than ten times over, were able to organize some magnificent expedition.

Farandoul had already traced the plan of this magnificent expedition in his mind. Where would he lead his brave friends the mariners this time? What dangerous countries would they go off to confront? To what point of the globe would they take their energy and their courage?

Where? Quite simply, to the NORTH POLE!

The North Pole was about to cease to be unknown; that irritating geographical mystery was about to be brought into the light; Farandoul had sworn that he would reach it, through the redoubtable sheets of polar ice.

The announcement of Farandoul's expedition to the North Pole ran across the continent like a gunpowder train. Paris quivered; foreign correspondents telegraphed their newspapers. The news produced great emotion in German Academia, which trembled at the thought of our hero overtaking the Berlin Scientific Congress expedition in the search for the country of origin of the Latin-speaking seals in the polar regions.

There was also a stir in London, for Farandoul received a letter just as he was beginning the work of organization. It read:

North Pole Co. Ltd., London
Lord Farandoul is hereby
FORMALLY PROHIBITED
from pursuing his expedition to the Pole.
(illegible signature)
Governor of the North Pole.

Farandoul smiled disdainfully, threw the letter in the waste paper basket, and resumed his preparations without giving this fantastic governor any further thought. Thanks to his millions, generously spent, the project proceeded rapidly. The temporary workshops specially constructed for the expedition on the Esplanade des Invalides were busy day and night.

The courtyard of the Tuileries, hired by Farandoul, had been put at the disposal of his men; it was above those celebrated ruins, you will remember, that in the exposition of 1878, the tethered balloon of Giffard and Tissandier[104] accomplished its fine series of ascensions, taking hundreds of aspiring aeronauts 500 meters up into the sky. Soon, the imposing rump of an aerostat was seen rising above the blackened walls, by comparison with which the enormous balloon of yesteryear would have lost much of its majesty. Beneath this mastodon, in the workshops carefully screened from all gazes, Farandoul's mariners were super-

---

[104] Henri Giffard (1825-1882) was the first French aeronaut to attempt to make balloons dirigible by attaching steam engines to them, thus tacitly providing the inspiration for all of Farandoul's aeronautical adventures. Giffard never contrived to make dirigible airships practicable, but he was a regular exhibitor at technological expositions. His "tethered balloon" offering excursions in the air to members of the crowds at such exhibitions made its debut in London in 1869 before appearing in Paris in 1878, when it was given an enthusiastic write-up, illustrated by numerous photographs, by Giffard's fellow aeronaut Albert Tissandier; Tissandier's photographs are nowadays available on the internet.

vising the fabrication of all sorts of new engines, which completely overturned the ideas of a few scientists admitted to the enclosure.

Farandoul, evidently, was far from making his expedition to the pole a purely maritime affair. Abandoning all received ideas, disdaining the routes mapped out by his forebears, Farandoul intended to reach the pole in a balloon—not, it is true, in a simple balloon with a modestly-sized gondola, an aerial vessel too fragile to confront the perils of polar regions, but in a solid balloon with a gondola-sloop invented for the occasion by our hero's fertile mind.

The future belongs to gondola-sloop balloons. Let us indicate, by means of a short description, the advantages of this mode of locomotion. The balloon itself only differs from familiar balloons in its proportions and a few minor details, but the gondola is quite simply a ship: an authentic ship, lightly but solidly constructed, covered with iron plates; a fully-equipped ship ready to take to sea at the shortest notice. The hull in connected to the netting of the balloon by long circular cords passed through the rings of the netting. When the captain of the gondola-sloop balloon wants to take to sea he merely has to give the mechanics the signal to descend; the easily-controllable balloon tacks downwards and stops when the gondola touches the waves. Then, by a very simple maneuver, the netting is detached and the balloon separates, perhaps to be towed behind or even deflated, until the moment when necessity requires it to resume its aerial course again.

The Farandoul balloon floating over Paris undertook practice maneuvers every day, watched with ardent curiosity by the Parisians. Thousands of optical instruments were aimed at it in the hope of spotting the commander of the expedition—or, if not him, Lieutenant Mandibul, who was almost as popular—on the gondola's deck. The roof of the Théâtre-Français had been transformed into a little observatory; all day long one saw nothing but telescopes and binoculars of every dimension aimed at the balloon by feminine hands.

Eventually, Farandoul fund himself assailed every day by hundreds of unwelcome visitors; some of them proposed organizing pleasure-trips to the Pole using his balloon, others asked to go with him. An eminent tragedienne found a way to get into his study and beg him in the most enthusiastic terms, practically in verse, to enroll her in his crew.

"I renounce art—all the arts," she said, by way of conclusion. "I want to be an explorer; I want to contemplate the somber and icy pole face-to-face!"

"Impossible, Madame, absolutely impossible—we have just enough places aboard for our men; with everything that is indispensable for such a voyage, the available space is strictly calculated. Our gondola-sloop could not even accommodate an extra child!"

"What does that matter? I'll lodge in the balloon if necessary!"

"Insistence is useless, Madame. I could never forgive myself for exposing such an illustrious tragedienne—the Rachel of our era—to perils without number!"
The illustrious tragedienne threw herself at his feet, but Farandoul was inflexible. She had a glimmer of hope, though, because she noticed an unknown man at the back of Farandoul's office who sank into an armchair to conceal the tears that her desperate performance wrung from him. It was our hero's foster-father, who could not hide his emotion; the eminent tragedienne, mistaking him for Mandibul, implored his help. Stifled grunts replied; the tragedienne took them for a refusal and departed in a fury, declaring that she would depart with the expedition in spite of everything and everyone!
Finally, everything was ready; Farandoul was able to fix a date for depar-ture, impatiently awaited by the mariners. Everything was embarked—equipment, fuel, provisions, stocks of polar clothing, scientific instruments, weapons, etc., etc.
Trabadec, released from the Burmese prison, had arrived, still ashamed of his financial misadventures; he had not renounced his credits on that account, and expected to recover his money or his pledges some day, through the intermediation of Siamese mandarins.

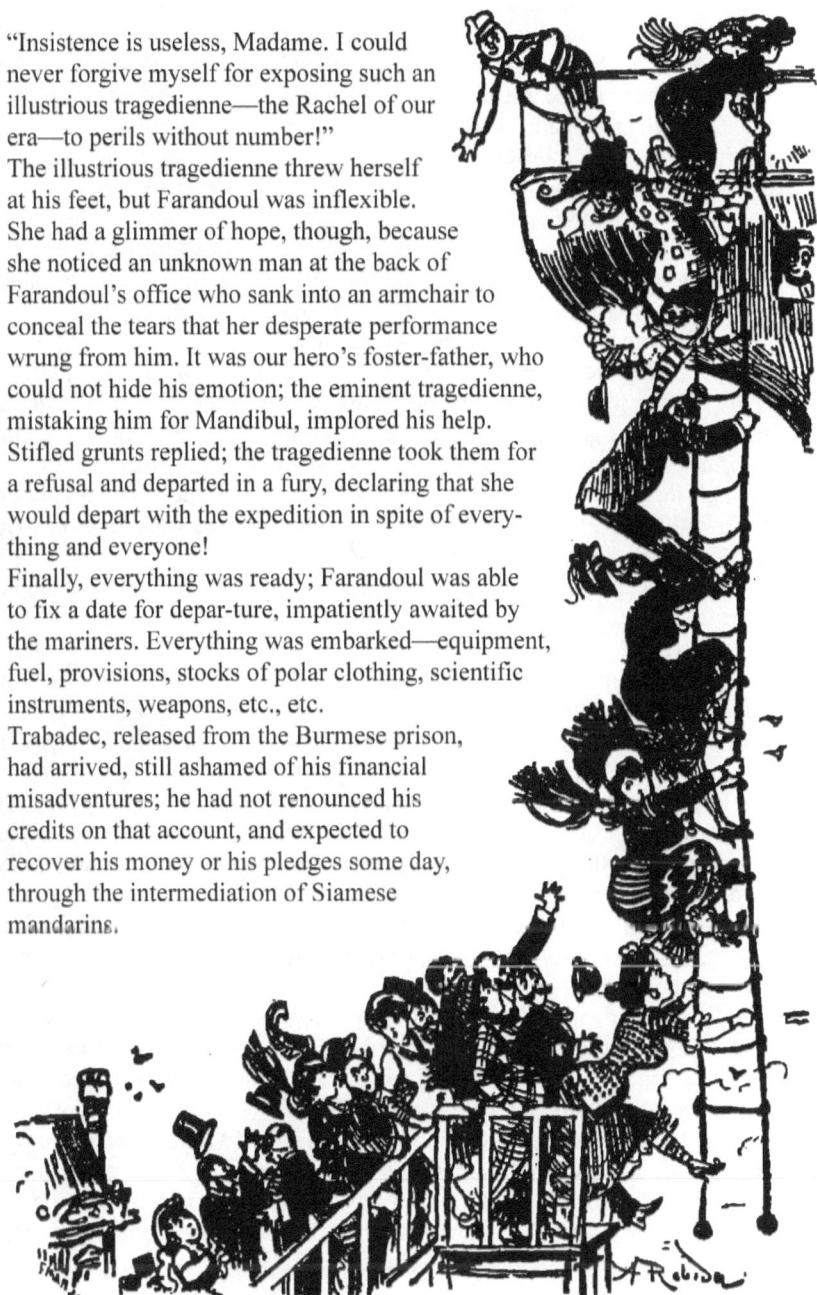

Farandoul, after long hesitation, had decided to take his foster-father on his great expedition. He had searched in vain for a respectable bourgeois family with which to lodge him as a paying guest in the vicinity of the capital, but had not found one that offered sufficient reliable guarantees. As for placing him at the Jardin des Plantes again, there was no hope of that; the administration was still smarting from the after-effects of his escapade with the young monkeys. There was only one remaining option—that of taking him to the Pole.

Paris was only informed 24 hours in advance that the moment had come for Farandoul's balloon to leave. This brief interval sufficed for the authorities to take the measures necessary to prevent disorder among the crowds assembled around the Tuileries, in the Champs-Elysées and all the points from which people were able to watch the balloon's maneuvers.

Before giving the solemn order to cast off, Farandoul made a final inspection of the balloon to make sure that everything was in order and that no intruder had sneaked into the gondola. All was well; everything was in place—weapons, food supplies, instruments, emergency escape-balloons, magnetic buoys, etc. etc.—and all the men were at their posts. Mandibul was at the helm and our hero's foster-father, appointed chief able seaman, climbed into the balloon's rigging to monitor the aerial maneuvers.

Farandoul leapt on to his quarter-deck and put his telephonic mouthpiece to his lips.

"Cast off!"

Powerful engines in the courtyard of the Carrousel cut through the four enormous cables retaining the aerostat promptly and precisely. The latter, as if breathed in by the firmament, rose into the atmosphere with a single bound, to an altitude of 1800 meters.

An immense cheer released by two million human throats went up from the crowds accumulated at all points, from the Tuileries to the Arc de Triomphe, from Montmartre to the Buttes-Chaumont and Vincennes. The expedition to the North Pole was under way!

In less than three minutes, the balloon had left the Carrousel and gained the upper layers of the atmosphere; it disappeared northwards and floated five or six leagues over the fields of the Ile de France.

All of a sudden, the two million observers shuddered; the balloon, launched unhesitatingly toward the North, had just come about and was returning to Paris at top speed! What had happened? Had it suffered some mechanical breakdown? What did this sudden return signify?

The balloon returned at full steam; the residents of Montmartre saw it pass over their heads and descend vertically over Paris. A unanimous cry of terror sprang from every throat—the balloon was going to crash into the ground and pulverize the houses beneath! The new Opera was under threat; that monument, so dearly bought, was about to be destroyed...

But no, the balloon descended rapidly to the height of the Apollo on top of the Opera, stopped momentarily, and went up again as rapidly as it had come down into the upper layers of the atmosphere, to disappear conclusively into the blue.

This is what had happened:

The balloon had just reached the first clouds when an incident occurred on board. Farandoul, desirous of saluting Paris with a few salvoes of aerial artillery, had charged the two on-board cannons with powder when a human form suddenly emerged from one of the barrels, to the profound stupefaction of the gunners. Who was this intruder? Farandoul only needed a single glance to recognize the illustrious artiste who had begged him to take her to the pole. She had sworn to depart in spite of every obstacle, and she had kept her word!

"O North Pole, I shall know thee!" she cried, as she exited from her cannon. "Here I stand, an explorer! I shall give my name to the islands and continents I shall discover; I shall study the splendors of the aurora borealis; I shall hunt polar bears; I...."

The irritated Farandoul interrupted her. "Stop there!" he cried. "You shall go no further! What! You have the audacity to introduce yourself by climbing into, perhaps breaking into, my gondola! I am the master of my ship—do you realize that I could put you in irons for the entire duration of the voyage? But you're a woman, and in consideration of that precious quality, I shall content myself with abandoning you on the first available bell-tower. We're returning to Paris—prepare yourself!"

And Farandoul telephoned an order to the engineers; the balloon turned round and set a course for the capital. At a word from his adoptive son, our friend the old monkey had offered his arm to the eminent tragedienne. He had his orders; as they passed over Paris, he was to deposit her on some elevated monument.

We have already said that the balloon passed over Montmartre and paused for half a minute above the new Opera. That brief stop was sufficient; the eminent tragedienne, in a fit of anger, bit her knuckles in rage when she felt herself suddenly seized and lifted up by the monkey. Terrified, she closed her eyes. The monkey leapt over the rails and swung through the air with her, on the end of a rope.

Thirty seconds, 30 centuries!

The swinging stopped; she opened her eyes. Horror! The monkey was in the process of sitting her, piggy-back fashion, on the shoulders of a statue. The eminent tragedienne shuddered and clung on desperately to the monkey's arm. She had recognized the statue; it was the great Apollo that stands, lyre in hand, at the most elevated summit of the new Opera.

The monkey detached himself gently, deposited a kiss on each of the tragedienne's hands, and let himself be carried aloft by the balloon.

Two minutes later, the Farandoul balloon disappeared into the sky and the Opera's firemen were preparing to effect the difficult rescue of the imprudent disciple of Melpomene.

The gondola-sloop balloon, moving full steam ahead and favored by the atmospheric currents, took less than seven days to reach the first the polar ice-floes, at about 78 degrees latitude. All was going well aboard. Before setting out over the ice-sheet, Farandoul thought it necessary to conduct a serious trial of the navigability of the gondola-sloop. In consequence, the maneuvers commenced and the gondola-sloop descended gently to sea-level. The balloon, detached from the gondola, was put in tow, in such a fashion as not to inhibit the progress of the sloop.

For two days, the gondola-sloop sailed northwards, towing the balloon behind; they made less rapid progress by this means than by air, but all went well. On the evening of the second day they reached the ice-sheet, the enormous, almost-uncrossable barrier of ice, which loomed up menacingly between the navigators and the Pole.

It was here, above all, that the aid of the balloon was indispensable; only the balloon would permit the gondola-sloop to cross that frightful rampart of icebergs and arrive at the *Open Sea*.[105]

Farandoul, quite satisfied with the performance of the sloop, allowed himself and his men 12 hours sleep before commencing the rather tedious maneuvers necessary for the resumption of aerial navigation. The sloop was moored for the night, with its balloon still tethered astern, in a little bay formed in the ice-sheet by an accumulation of gigantic icebergs.

The next day, at dawn, they would take off into the sky.

The weather being calm and the cold so intense that no disintegration of the icebergs was to be feared, Farandoul, Mandibul and the entire crew slept in absolute tranquility. Even the men on watch, not seeing any danger, allowed themselves to go to sleep—a culpable weakness on the part of some, mistaken security on the part of the others.

At dawn, when the men on watch opened their eyes, they let out a terrible cry. The balloon, solidly attached the previous evening to the stern of the sloop, had disappeared! Farandoul and Mandibul, who had come running at the first sound, raced to the rear to ascertain the cause of this deplorable accident. Was it a weakness of the cables, or an omission of precautions?

---

[105] The Open Sea (*mer libre* in French) is a significant feature of the polar landscape in Verne's *Les Aventures du Capiaine Hatteras* (1866), in which Verne scrupulously lists all the observations by mid-19th century explorers supporting the notion that the Arctic ice-sheet was a ring rather than a solid disk.

One mere glance sufficed to disabuse them; there had been no accident. It had not happened as a result of some fortuitous rupture—a crime had been committed. The cables had been cut!

But no one had seen or heard anything! And they were in the middle of the ice, 200 leagues from any habitable terrain!

Who could they suspect? What wretch could they accuse of this abominable crime, which reduced all their savant schemes to nothing and would stop the expedition at the first hurdle? A placard nailed to the rail provided a revelation. In large letters, it bore the following lines:

SECOND WARNING
The order is given to everyone to renounce any expedition to the pole.
Any contravention will be severely punished.
(illegible signature)
Governor of the North Pole

Farandoul roared. "So it's serious! Well, Monsieur Governor of the North Pole, it's you and me. We can't go by balloon, but we have our sloop, and we'll cross the Open Sea in her once we've got her over the entire ice-sheet!"

No one, in the course of that fatal night, had heard or seen anything, save for Trabadec, on watch between midnight and 3 a.m., who claimed that, on emerging from a fit of somnolence, he had seen the shadow of a ship among the icebergs. He had taken the shadow for the well-known phantom ship and had contented himself with making a few signs of the cross before going back to sleep.

"There's no doubt remaining," Farandoul murmured in Mandibul's ear. "Our expedition has an enemy, and a serious one. Who this Governor of the North Pole might be and what interest he might have in preventing us from arriving at our goal, I don't know—but we'll certainly find out!"

"We're going on, then?" said Mandibul.

"Undoubtedly! Straight ahead, in spite of everything. Our gondola-sloop handles he sea admirably; we'll get to the pole in her!"

"What about the ice-sheet?"

"We'll find a pass! Many mariners have gone through these ice-fields to the environs of the Open Sea; we shall do likewise. Forwards!"

The gondola-sloop lost no time in seeking to discover what had become of the lost balloon. It set off on a detailed exploration of the cracks in the ice-sheet, searching among its countless ramifications for the desired passage. They were, moreover, sailing in a region crossed by the warm waters of the Gulf Stream in their immense journey from the Gulf of Mexico to the North Pole, and there was nowhere in the ice-fields where they might search for a breach with any greater chance of success.

What had become of the phantom ship glimpsed by Trabadec? Our Breton, on watch from the topsail, affirmed that he had seen it again, and that it was by heading in the direction it had taken that they would find the desired passage.

Farandoul had no more doubt; the expedition's mysterious enemy was also forging ahead in the direction of the Pole.

III.

For three weeks the gondola-sloop sailed through the ice-field on the way to the Pole. Apart from the collapse of some monumental icebergs that almost sank them in a difficult passage—a collapse attributed to malevolence—no further incident occurred.

The cold was intense. Although ameliorated by the Gulf Stream, whose final branch they were still following, the temperature nevertheless reached 40 degrees Centigrade below zero. Before going any further, Farandoul permitted his crew to go hunting for polar bear furs with which to make garments—a luxury much appreciated in these regions.

These hunts did not even involve any prolonged delay. The white bears were literally swarming on the ice-floes, in the midst of numerous families of seals and walruses, which seemed to be there for no other reason than to provide the thick layers of fat with which the skins of the bears were padded. Unfortunately, bullets had very little effect on the gigantic bears; when they chanced to penetrate the skin they were lost in the fat, without seriously inconveniencing the individuals that had received them. The bears scratched themselves slightly, but that was all.

The mariners did not persist in making use of firearms; they equipped themselves with more terrible devices brought by Farandoul in anticipation of what might happen. We are talking about chloroform-filled bombs, of which our hero had already made such good use during the war of the Disunited States of Nicaragua, and which he had considerably improved since then.

Armed with these hand-grenades, the hunters left the gondola-sloop and leapt from one ice-floe to another in pursuit of polar bears. At the sight of these audacious enemies, unfamiliar to them, and furious at being disturbed, the ferocious bears advanced, growling, with their claws extended.

Mandibul was in the forefront of the hunt; threatened by a bear of the largest size, and on the point of being reached by the animal's terrible paws, he contented himself with extending his arm towards it and, when it was beneath the bear's muzzle, pressing a switch. The chloroform, suddenly released, did its work and the bear fell backwards with a frightful howl. Its comrades came to avenge it, but the mariners copied Mandibul's stratagem and brought their chloroform Orsini bombs into play.[106] Within five minutes, 17 unconscious bears were laid out on the ice; there was nothing more to do than harvest the pelts. The hatchets and knives were ready, but, as they were about to begin their work, the mariners hesitated.

"*Sapristi!*" murmured Mandibul. "There they are, put to sleep by our chloroform. We can't kill them now—that would be murder!"

"What if we were only to steal their fur coats?" suggested Trabadec.

"And when they wake up in a few days, how are they supposed to get by at 40 degrees below zero?"

"Bah! They'll get used to it—skin them anyway!"

"What about their fat?" cried Tournesol. "We need their fat too, for heating. We can't steal their fur coats and their layers of fat and leave them absolutely naked—that would be cruel. We have to kill them."

The sentence was pronounced; the bears perished painlessly in their sleep, and the mariners went back to the gondola-sloop with furs and a good provision of fat.

In three days, 60 bears succumbed, first chloroformed and then massacred. Each man had a fur overcoat, bedcovers and a change of clothes proof against arbitrary falls in temperature.

The seals, walruses and other animals had disappeared, alarmed by the carnage. Only white bears, stupid brutes, continued to show themselves among the floes. They had already become more ferocious and difficult to approach; now that seals and walruses, their usual nourishment, were in short supply, they wandered hungrily over the ice around the ship, with their noses in the air, as if fascinated by the culinary emanations coming from the launch, where the melting of the fat was proceeding apace.

When the well-provisioned gondola-sloop resumed its journey, there was a momentary disturbance among the bears. The food-stuffs were leaving! With a single moment the gigantic animals precipitated themselves towards an enormous block of ice closer to the vessel. Beneath their weight, the iceberg cracked, split and sank beneath the waves. When the eddies of foam produced by this fall had dissipated, the mariners suddenly caught sight of an enormous ice-floe loaded with 30 menacing bears, advancing upon the ship only a short distance away.

"Damn!" cried Farandoul. "We're being attacked in our turn! All hands on deck! Get the chloroform! The chloroform!"

---

[106] Félix Orsini and three other Italians attempted to assassinate Napoléon III on January 14, 1858, employing the crude and absurdly inefficient tactic of throwing hand-held bombs at his carriage. He failed, and was executed in consequence, but the method became strangely fashionable, especially in popular fiction, where the image of the "bomb-throwing anarchist" was elevated to the status of a cliché.

The sailors came running, but in the tumult occasioned by that sudden attack a few of them put their chloroform Orsini bombs too close to their comrades' face—clumsiness that knocked five men out for 48 hours. The crew of the sloop, thus reduced, found itself in an awkward situation; the 30 famished bears were beginning to climb off their ice-floe on to the deck, threatening to overwhelm the mariners, in spite of their valor, by sheer force of numbers—all the more so because, in these conditions, the bombs were becoming difficult to handle, each carrier risking chloroforming himself along with the target bear.

Tournesol, half-anaesthetized by a comrade's chloroform, slumped down on the launch's fire-extinguisher. Before closing his eyes completely, he still had enough presence of mind to point the pump out to Mandibul.

"That's it!" cried Mandibul and Farandoul, simultaneously. "The pump! Quickly, man the pump!"

"Fight bears with that?" murmured a few mariners, uncomprehendingly. "Anyway, the water's frozen!"

"The water in the engine isn't frozen—quite the opposite! We'll fight them with boiling water. Stand aside!"

They had understood. With a turn of the hand, the pump, connected up to the engine, received a flood of boiling water from its reservoirs. Farandoul rapidly pulled on two pairs of thick fur gloves and seized the nozzle with a firm hand. Standing on the rail, he let the bears draw closer to him.

"Pump!" he cried, when they were well within range.

The hopeful bears were already opening their terrible jaws and lifting their paws to grab the sides of the gondola-sloop. Suddenly, a jet of boiling water descended upon their bodies with a frightful sizzling noise and great gouts of vapor. The nearest ones fell backwards beneath that unexpected shower and their roaring changed into a lamentable whimpering.

"Pump!" ordered Farandoul. "Pump hard! It's working!"

The pitiless jet of boiling water whistled down upon the mass of bears, toppling the ferocious attackers of the sloop on to one another. The ice-floe that bore them began to melt and threatened to shatter; finally, in the midst of the vapor cloud, the variously injured bears were seen to throw themselves into the water and dive in order to avoid the scalding blast of boiling water. A few remained on the battlefield, too well-cooked to have enough strength left to jump into the sea.

The launch was disengaged; Farandoul ceased fire. "Saved!" he cried. "We shan't be eaten this time!" And the crew, all danger alleviated, were able to devote themselves entirely to steering the ship. The men put to sleep by the chloroform were laid in their hammocks to enjoy their three or four days of enforced rest; the others accepted the additional work incumbent upon them with resignation, content to have escaped so cheaply the annoyance of wintering inside a polar bear. The fire-extinguisher remained on the bridge, ready for use in case of unfortunate encounters.

No notable event occurred in the course of the week following the attack of the polar bears; the explorers carefully studied the movements of any bears that were seen prowling around the ice, but they had no occasion to make use of the boiling water. On the eighth day, however, the man stationed in the bow signaled an ice-floe floating in the fog only a short distance away, on which several shapeless shadows were moving that might be bears.

The floe slowly drifted into a narrow channel, in which its edges were forced to brush the ironclad flanks of the gondola as it moved forward. The bears that it carried had seen or scented the vessel, for they trotted across the ice releasing raucous cries and waving their paws frantically.

"They're not as numerous as the others," murmured Farandoul, counting them. "Five, six, seven, and a few cubs. That's nothing—but prepare the boiling water anyway."

Within an eye-blink the pump was ready to function, and Farandoul waited for the bears. "Will they pass by without attacking?" he went on. "If they pass by, I won't spray them."

He was still speaking when the ice-floe touched the port side of the gondola. All the bears immediately stood up and raced forward to scale the side; a jet of boiling water fell upon them; they disappeared in a cloud of vapor...

Screams burst out on the ice-floe, accompanied by curses in English and German.

"Stop!" cried Farandoul, throwing away the nozzle of the pump. "They're not bears—they're talking!"

All the mariners had run forward at the same time, and two lifeboats had been lowered into the water in order to catch up with the ice-floe, which was drawing away with the scalded false bears.

There were, in fact, no bears on the floe; the eight unfortunates that had been taken for ferocious beasts were human shipwreck-victims! The thick furs in which they were covered from top to toe had assisted the error; at two paces, in the fog, an animal-tamer would have made the same mistake. The astonished mariners recognized the smaller ones, which Farandoul had mistaken for bear-cubs, as seals, securely linked to them by chains.

The scalded unfortunates being not wanting to be separated from their seals in order to climb into the lifeboats, they seized them in their arms and did not let go of them until they had set foot on the gondola's deck.

Farandoul, full of remorse on account of his mistake, greeted them with apologies and told them how sorry he was to have deluged them with boiling water.

"On the contrary!" sighed one of the unfortunates, with a slight German accent. "Without your hot water we'd probably be dead; we were already three-quarters frozen in spite of our furs, and on seeing your vessel we scarcely had the strength to stand up on our ice-floe. Your delightful boiling water has reanimated us. Yes, I'm scalded, but reanimated, reanimated, reanimated! On my own account, thank you! I'd much rather be cooked than frozen—my friends too, I think..." Turning towards his companions in misfortune, the German continued: "Isn't it so, gentlemen and dear colleagues, that I'm right to approve of the boiling water? Frozen or cooked—which is your preference?"

"Cooked!"

"Cooked!"

"Cooked! Cooked!"

"You see—it's unanimous! Thank you, sir, a thousand thanks, in the name of German Academia, in the name of England, and in the name of science! Thank you also for my seals, which you have also saved!"

This astonishing adventure brought eight additional passengers into the gondola-boat, not to mention the four seals. Before asking these half-frozen and half-cooked individuals any for any details of their misfortunes, Farandoul let them restore their strength with a good meal, after which they were put to bed, well wrapped-up, in the bunks in the infirmary. The four seals also lay down in the infirmary, the shipwreck-victims having refused to be separated from them.

"Strange!" murmured Farandoul., as he left them. "Not a single mariner among the shipwreck victims—nothing but scientists! We'll find out tomorrow what they were doing on the ice-sheet."

The scientists slept for a long time. For 48 hours there was no movement in the infirmary. Farandoul and Mandibul anxiously established themselves by their bedsides, waiting impatiently for the unfortunates to wake up. Finally, one scientist opened an eye. As if it were a signal, within a minute, all eight scientists were stirring, groaning, rolling over and, finally, looking at one another with profound astonishment.

One of them slapped his forehead; he remembered. The others did likewise, and, like him, murmured: "The hot water! Frozen, then cooked, then saved...."

"What about the seals!" they suddenly cried, leaping out of their bunks.

"Calm down," said Mandibul. "They're here. Look—they're still sleeping in their bunks."

"Mein Gott!" cried one of the scientists. "What events! What events! You see before you, gentlemen, members of two scientific expeditions to the North Pole, one German and one English, abandoned in the ice by the ships that brought them, lost in the midst of bears and—but for you—inevitably frozen. Permit Hermann Knapp, president of the Commission of Polar Research and Exploration appointed by the Scientific Congress of Berlin to introduce his colleagues: Ulric von Koplipmann of the University of Bonn; Otto Rabus, chancellor of the Academy of Jena. The two gentleman accompanying us are colleagues from an English expedition to the north pole, also gone astray and encountered by us in an igloo on an ice-berg. [107]

"And the seals?" asked Mandibul.

"Oh, that's true; I forgot to introduce them. This is Brutus, this is Coriolanus, this is Cassius and this is Numa Pompilius!"

The four seals thus identified uttered inarticulate grunts beneath their bedclothes, but did not budge.

Farandoul and Mandibul looked at one another in astonishment.

"Ah, I see," Hermann Knapp went on. Those names astonish you, you don't understand. Know, then, that these animals are not simple and vulgar seals; they are Latin seals—the celebrated Latin seals discovered in the polar

---

[107] The reader might be wondering what happened to the other three, given that eight full-sized individuals were still present a few paragraphs ago; there is, alas, no explanation of the discrepancy. Robida seems simply to have decided that three of them were surplus to the requirements of the narrative and erased them from the story.

ice! Have you not heard mention of the expedition organized to hasten to the discovery of a Roman colony indubitably existing in the polar regions?"

"Indeed, I remember!" exclaimed Farandoul, suppressing a smile. "They're the Latin-speaking seals reported to the Scientific Congress of Berlin."

"Yes, two of them are: Brutus and Cassius; the other two were captured by us 50 leagues further north—and if any doubt had remained in our minds, that doubt would have been dispelled after a single instant of conversation with them!"

"What conversation?" Mandibul put in. "I once saw a seal that could almost say *papa* and *mama*, but that was all."

"That was a vulgar seal. Ours say *pater* and *mater*."

"*Fichtre!*"

"Yes, and what's more, the other two—the ones we captured—pronounce even more Latin words quite distinctly. How can we doubt after that? They're still a little unwell today, but as soon as they feel better, you can judge for yourselves. If it were not for the incomprehensible misfortunes that have overtaken our expedition, we would be heading for the pole—which is doubtless inhabited by the remnant of a Roman colony. And who can appreciate the immense consequences of such a discovery for science, for…?"

The two English scientists, buried in their furs, had not spoken a word; nor had they manifested any opinion whatsoever by means of signs. Mandibul, bursting out laughing, turned to them and asked them whether they too were traveling the seas in pursuit of Latin seals.

A slight smile behind their spectacles was the sole response of the English scientists.

Doctor Hermann Knapp became furious. "English jealousy!" he cried. "They are pretending to disdain our seals and trying to steal our discovery! What were they doing behind us on the ice-sheet? We were following our seals, and they were following us, with the intention of arriving at our goal at the same time. Disdain our seals—our admirable Latin seals! You shall see them and hear them, Captain; they're still suffering, but I cannot let them spend another minute under the burden of this disdain. A cordial—a cordial, quickly!"

Farandoul made a sign. A bowl of strongly-spiced hot wine was brought from the stores and given to Dr. Hermann Knapp. The seals, woken up again in spite of their groans, each drank a measure of the liquid and soon seemed reinvigorated. It was then just a matter of making them talk; for half an hour, Hermann Knapp lavished quasi-maternal care upon them, rubbing them and tapping them on the head with solicitude to stimulate the activity of their brains, while the other German scientists pronounced an uninterrupted sequence of *paters* and *maters* to get them going.

Finally, one of the seals spoke, initially in an unintelligible fashion, but then more and more distinctly, and its three companions, fully awakened, joined in:

"*Pater, Mater! Pater, Mater! Pater, Mater!*"

"Bah!" said Mandibul. "Is that all? Some circus performer must have taught them!"

"Wait a while before pronouncing judgment," Hermann Knapp said, solemnly. "That's not all!"

"*Polus, polus!*" said one of the seals.

"*Pater, mater. Navis, navis,*" said another.

"*Us, us…lus, lus…tus, tus….*"

"*Servus, servus! Infelix!*"

"*Polus, polus!*"[108]

"Well, do you still doubt?" cried Hermann Knapp triumphantly. "Is that Latin or isn't it?"

Farandoul and Mandibul stared at the knowledgeable seals with astonishment as they continued to pour out a series of *us, us…*, confused fragments of evidently Latin words. What did it mean?

---

[108] Most of these Latin words support the theory that Farandoul is about to produce reasonably well. *Infelix* means "unlucky," *navis* means "ship" and although the literal meaning of *servus* is "servant," the word was also used as a greeting, after the fashion of "your humble servant," thus being an approximate equivalent of "hello." On the other hand, *us/lus/tus* is merely a set of suffixes. Robida was probably working on the assumption that many of his readers would construe *polus* as "pole," but it actually means "colt" and is most familiar to the Classically-educated as a nickname attributed by Plato to a character in one of his dialogues, a pupil of the philosopher Gorgias.

"I've got it!" cried Farandoul, slapping his forehead. "By means of the voices of these seals, unfortunates stranded in the polar seas on some frozen rock—perhaps some Eskimo tribe—are calling for help. Lacking a bottle in which to entrust a document to the sea, as shipwreck-victims normally do, they have ingeniously domesticated seals, and by dint of patience have taught them to repeat, after a fashion, a few words indicating their sad situation! It's very vague, but it's better than nothing. Perhaps we'll find them!"

The German scientists were white with fury. This simple explanation left them beside themselves. As they were about to launch into an extraordinarily scientific discussion, Farandoul took his leave of them and left them at grips with the English scientists. For a long time, the German scientists could be heard arguing animatedly, combating the Englishmen's objections.

In the end, the Englishmen escaped and climbed up on deck, but the obstinate Knapp followed them. Fortunately for them, he lost them in the fog and latched on to Farandoul's foster-father, who was smoking his pipe while striding back and forth to keep himself warm. Thinking that he was still dealing with a colleague, Hermann Knapp continued to develop his argument, refuting all objections one by one and reducing Farandoul's hypothesis to dust.

The honest foster-father, astonished at first, replied without understanding with approving nods of the head. Hermann Knapp spoke for a long time—so long that, in order to escape him, the poor monkey had to resort to extreme measures; a his persecutor passed in front of a hatchway, he grabbed him by the legs and threw him head-first down to the lower deck.

Farandoul conferred with Mandibul. Both of them were of the same mind; somewhere, on a rock in the polar region, unfortunates were appealing for help; doubtless they had employed Latin in order that they might be understood by the officials of any nation whatsoever. It was necessary to head for any land or rock signaled by the lookout; perhaps they would arrive in time to save them.

Land was scarce in these parts; however, the maps indicated a long coastline glimpsed by the mariners of the most recent polar expeditions a few 100 leagues to the north-west. This nameless coast had not been explored; it was necessary to reach it and see whether unfortunate navigators might be there, lamenting the horrors of an eternal winter.

A few extracts from the ship's log, kept by Mandibul, will acquaint us with the incidents of this research, which led the expedition somewhat astray from its principal goal, but which humanity demanded.

SHIP'S LOG

April 8. Weather lousy. Snow. Fog. 43 degrees below zero.

April 9. Weather lousy. Minus 44 degrees. Fog. Snow. The German scientists are sulking. Since our discussion, they haven't appeared on deck. They're well, though, for they eat a lot. The English scientists are cross with them; we've been obliged to separate them. Dr. Hermann Knapp complains a great deal about the older one, who is apparently driving him mad, since he has manhandled him over some point of science on which they're not in agreement. The old English scientist has a stronger grip that I'd have thought; he got hold of Hermann Knapp and threw him through a hatchway into the middle of the table in the chart-room. Mount surveillance on the English scientist when he goes on deck.

April 10. Weather lousy. Minus 46 degrees. Snow. Fog. One of Dr. Knapp's seals has escaped through a porthole, Chloroformed a bear that had jumped from an iceberg on to the deck.

April 11. Weather lousy. Minus 44 degrees. Fog. Snow. Numerous icebergs. Mountains of ice 300 meters high, but no vanilla.

April 12. Weather lousy. Minus 43 degrees. Fog. Snow. Land spotted in the east thanks to a clear spell. Impossible to approach; completely encircled by ice.

April 13. Weather lousy. Minus 42 degrees. Fog. Snow. Dreadful event: my dear Farandoul's brave foster-father, that honest and charming monkey, so gentle, so kind, so devoted—that friend, in sum—has disappeared! Lost in the eternal snows! Probably frozen by now, or fallen beneath the claws of a bear! Farandoul is inconsolable, but he had not lost hope and I supervising the searches. This is how misfortune occurred. This morning, a fissure in the ice-sheet having allowed us to get close enough to the coast to attempt a landing, I departed with six men and our friend the unfortunate monkey for whom we are in mourning. Disembarkation was effected comfortably, exploration began well. We found no trace of the shipwreck-victims whose existence has been revealed to us by the Latin seals. Unfortunately, we separated in the rocks and when after three hours of fatigue and peril, we reassembled in order to return to the gondola-sloop, the brave monkey was missing.

April 14. Weather lousy. Minus 43 degrees. Snow. Fog. Continuation of searches. Alas, alas, will it be necessary to despair of ever seeing again the good and honest face of our lost friend? Not the slightest trace! No clue! Tomorrow, great expedition. Farandoul and eight men departing with three days' rations. This is our last hope.

April 15. Weather lousy. Minus 42 degrees. Fog. Snow. Great news. The expedition has come back. Farandoul has just told me about the adventure. They had covered four leagues in a northerly direction without discovering anything when, all of a sudden, a slight trail of smoke on the horizon announced the presence of human beings. Ten minutes of running brought our men to the smoke; it was an Eskimo village: a group of five or six reindeer-hide huts covered with snow. The entire population was standing in front of the largest hut, which had to be that of the chief. There were 50 individuals, so hunched up in their bear-skins that one might have taken them for ambulant fur hats rather than human beings.[109]

Our men seemed to have interrupted the preparations for a ceremony. Standing in front of an old Eskimo—probably the chief—with a stout staff in his hand, a couple of individuals were humbly bowing down. Tournesol, who was

---

[109] In the course of this paragraph and the next the text jumps from reproducing the record of Mandibul's log to the author's customary narrative voice; this might be carelessness on the author's part, but it seems more probable that some text is missing. The dates also become confused, as the events described in the subsequent passage take longer than the interval specified by the log entries. As this botched transition occurs on the penultimate page of an instalment, what might have happened is that the text overran and had to be brutally cut, removing the text that operated the transition between the two narrative modes. On the other hand, this instalment is one of very few occasions on which the text ended up two or three lines short of the bottom of the final page, so the relevant omission might have been accidental.

once a whaler, recognized it as a marriage—the marriage of the chief's daughter, to be precise. The staff of espousal was already raised over the backs of the bride and groom.

"Come on!" murmured Farandoul, going forward. "He can give them his blessing later; first, let's try to obtain some information from the old Eskimo."

At the noise of the intruders' arrival, the two future spouses turned round. Farandoul and his men released a cry of joyful astonishment. The fiancé of the young Eskimo woman was none other than our hero's foster father.

Everything was soon explained. The brave monkey had got lost in the fog, had walked until nightfall and, gripped by the cold, had begun to despair when the Eskimo village suddenly presented itself to his eyes. He had been cordially received, offered hospitality and nourishment. The next day and the day after that he had gone fishing with his new friends; he had shown himself to be skilful, each time bringing back a veritable abundance of cod, and had deposited it at the feet of the chief's daughter, a flirtatious Eskimo girl with a rather flat nose. This, in the eyes of the father, had qualified as a proposal. He had made a long speech to the brave monkey, explaining the duties of the head of a family, had wiped away a tear and had concluded with a "put it there, son-in-law!" in Eskimo—to which the old monkey had only responded with a few grunts.

Farandoul had arrived just in time; the paternal staff had not yet fallen on the shoulders of the bride and groom; the monkey was not married.

The explanation given by Farandoul to the Eskimos—who wanted to hang on to their new comrade—was long and stormy. There were tears from the tribe's feminine contingent. Finally, a few gifts settled the affair; Farandoul gave a dowry to the young woman—a good hatchet and a pair of boots—which would help her considerably in finding another husband.

After an agreeable evening spent in the hut and a good night, the whole troop returned in triumph to the gondola-sloop, bringing back the lost friend.

IV.

On the evening of May 25, the gondola-sloop reached the Open Sea. The ice-field had been crossed; there was no longer any obstacle between the gondola-sloop and the objective of its voyage, the North Pole.

No one else had ever got so far—and yet, a man placed as a lookout on the mast affirmed that he had seen the topmost yardarms of a ship disappearing over the horizon.

The thermometer, which had fallen during the previous week to minutes 48 degrees, had risen appreciably. The further forward they went, the more the climate seemed to ameliorate; it was already no lower than minus 41 degrees. The mariners explained this phenomenon by the proximity of the waters of the Gulf

Stream, conserving the last residue of their warmth after their long journey from the Gulf of Mexico.

The gondola-sloop, proceeding full steam ahead, had been sailing the calm waters of the Open Sea for more than a week when, on the morning of the ninth day, a cry of "Land ho!" suddenly rang out. In the distance, to the north, a coast appeared: a mere dot crowned by a plume of smoke.

The news caused great excitement aboard. The English and German scientists, who had not come out of their cabins for a fortnight, ran on to the deck, telescopes in hand. The coast that had been glimpsed became visibly larger; its entire configuration was soon clearly distinguishable, recognizable as an island surrounded by reefs.

Farandoul calculated their position with particular care. All of a sudden he stood up triumphantly. "The North Pole!" he cried. "That island is the Island of the Pole!"[110]

All the mariners threw their bearskin bonnets in the air and voiced loud hurrahs.

"But it's a fully active volcano!" cried the German scientists.

"It's a fireship," Mandibul replied. "Let's be careful of getting too hot, having been too cold!"

The entire island did, indeed, resemble a vast fireship. An immense circle of flames surrounded a central plateau, dominated by a volcanic peak smoking like Vesuvius.

"We'll be there in a few hours!" Farandoul went on. "We're traveling at full steam, and our speed is further increased by a particular phenomenon: our gondola-sloop, almost entirely plated with iron, is subject to the attraction of the Pole and is literally flying towards the island."

A heart-warming scene was taking place in the bow. The German scientists, Knapp, Rabus and Koplipmann had been to fetch their seals and were holding them in their arms showing them the Island of the Pole.

"*Polus! Polus! Polus!*" the seals repeated. "*Pater! Mater!*"

Suddenly, an exclamation from Hermann Knapp attracted Farandoul's attention. One of the seals had just pronounced the word *Caesar* quite distinctly.

"Caesar! You heard! No more doubt! No more doubt!" repeated Knapp, almost fainting with joy. "He said Caesar!"

The sea was becoming appreciably worse, however. Farandoul no longer lowered his telescope; rocks barely covered by the waves and ferociously jagged jutting reefs seemed to be mounting guard around the Island of the Pole, forbidding any approach.

---

[110] Initially, this description reproduces the description of the polar island featured in Verne's *Les Aventures du Capitaine Hatteras*.

The gondola-sloop, increasingly attracted by the Pole's magnetic current, became more difficult to control; it required all of Farandoul's attention and all the crew's skill to pass between the redoubtable breakers.

Eventually, at about six kilometers from the coast, the girdle of frightfully-battered reefs that protected it seemed to the mariners to be virtually impassable. Farandoul decided not to risk the gondola-sloop therein, and set about searching for a mooring between two rocks in order to take shelter. The place was soon found and the sloop, skillfully maneuvered into a sort of tranquil inlet in the centre of an archipelago of large rocks, came safely to a stop.

"Well?" said Herman Knapp. "Aren't we going to the Pole, then?"

"Yes, and more quickly than you imagine—but not with our gondola-sloop, which we'd risk breaking on the reefs.

Hermann Knapp stepped back. "Not by swimming, undoubtedly! I can't swim..."

Farandoul's only response was to show him some bizarre items of apparatus that the mariners were in the process of getting ready. "These are lifebuoys of a particular sort. Look—at the center of each buoy is a perfectly watertight iron barrel, provided with a conical lid with a crystal porthole. Thanks to the magnetized iron, as soon as they're put into the water, they'll move straight toward the Pole, merely by the force of attraction."

"But how will we get back to the gondola-sloop?"

"That's been anticipated. In the largest of the magnetic buoys we'll take a little steam engine; coming back, it will tow us. Let's go! Are you coming?"

Four men had to remain behind to guard the gondola-sloop. The rest of the crew and the English and German scientists embarked in the magnetic buoys. Each man, well-provided with weapons and munitions, got into his iron barrel; the conical lids were sealed and they prepared to cast off. The buoys were taken one by one to the opening of the inlet and detached from their mooring-ropes. It was a curious sight; as soon as they were free, the buoys turned in the direction of the Pole and cut through the waves with a prodigious speed in the direction of the island.

The buoys carrying Farandoul and Mandibul were dancing at the head of the procession on the crests of the waves. They required no more than a quarter of an hour to cross the six kilometers separating the line of reefs from the rocks of the island.

A hundred meters from the shore, Farandoul fired a rifle-shot into the air, a conventional signal in case of an alert ordering weapons to be made ready. Hardly had the detonation sounded when a series of gunshots rang out and a hail of bullets struck the iron barrels of the electric buoys.

The North Pole was inhabited!

Drawn by the Pole's magnetic current, the iron buoys slammed into the rocks two minutes later. The mariners were hastening to get out of their carapaces, in order to defend themselves against the inhospitable inhabitants of the Pole, when a ragged and emaciated human figure appeared, leaping from rock to rock. At the same time, more rifle-shots rang out—but the bullets flattened themselves against a huge rock, behind which our friends were sheltering.

The unknown man, waving his long arms, flew through the hail of bullets. Finally, without having been hit, he fell into the midst of the stupefied mariners.

"Here you are at last!" he cried, in French. "Saved! Thank God!"

French was spoken at the North Pole; the German scientists went white.

"First, and most important," the man went on, "be on your guard against surprise attacks. The Governor…"

"What Governor?" demanded the German scientists.

"The Governor of the North Pole! He's up there, lying in ambush with his men. Don't move from here, where you're sheltered. These rocks that are protecting us from the bullets are easy to defend, and I know a sort of cave from which we can defy any attack."

The semi-naked man who was speaking to them did not seem to be suffering from cold and the mariners were panting under their furs.

"Oof!" exclaimed Mandibul, suddenly. "I can't stand it any longer. What a funny temperature to find at the North Pole! I don't think I'm mistaken, but it seems to me that I'm too hot!" He took off some of his bearskins. All the mariners did likewise, looking at one another in surprise. They were still too hot.

Mandibul ran to his buoy and came back with a thermometer that he had prudently brought along. His face was painted with extreme astonishment. "Thirty-five degrees above zero!" he cried. "At the North Pole!!!"

The man from the North Pole drew the mariners toward the cave and resumed speaking: "I'll explain everything!" he said. "First, though, tell me—was it my seals that put you on the track?"

"Ah!" murmured Farandoul. "You're the shipwreck-victim!"

"The seals!" cried the three German scientists, breathlessly. "The Latin seals?"

"Yes, my seals!" replied the shipwreck-victim.

"Your own seals, seals that speak Latin, which say *pater, mater* and *polus* in Latin! The Scientific Congress of Berlin, after having examined them, concluded that there must exist, in the polar ice, the remnant of some Roman colony..."

"The Roman colony is me!"

Hermann Knapp, Otto Rabus and Uric Koplipmann stood up straight, furiously. "You! your seals! Come on! *Pater, mater, polus*...and *Caesar*. One of them pronounced that great name a little while ago..."

"César, that's me!" the shipwreck-victim went on. "César Picolot, ex-professor of philosophy at the College of Le Havre, involuntary voyager and unwilling inhabitant of the Island of the Pole. For eight years I've vegetated among these rocks, the butt of ill-treatment by the Governor's pirates."

"Eight years!"

"Yes, Messieurs, eight long years I've been miserably wandering these shores, waiting for help that didn't come! What could I hope for, anyway? The civilized world is entirely ignorant as to the existence of the Island of the Pole, and I had no means of making my unfortunate fate known. I've always heard talk of castaways who found means to make their positions known by introducing documents into bottles, which they then confided to the waves, but I lacked the necessary bottle. It was only after three years, after much thought, that an idea occurred to me. I had often seen, in my youth, seals in circuses that had been taught to pronounce *papa* and *mama* more or less distinctly, so I decided to use the faculty of elocution that seals possess to attempt to send my news to the world. There is no lack of seals; in spring and autumn thousands of the animals cover the shores of the Island of the Pole. I appointed myself their educator. What patience! What precautions! What cares! Incessantly in their midst, sharing their frolics on land, and even in the waves, I carried their infants my arms, attempting to teach them to talk. Hard work! For every pupil who pronounced a few words, hundreds produced nothing but baroque and incomprehensible sounds! Alas, I had not the resource of setting extra homework to force the recalcitrants to work. It took me three years of patience to obtain a few results. After three years of relentless effort, I had two dozen pupils producing *Polus* quite distinctly..."

"But why the Devil did you teach them Latin?" asked Mandibul, in surprise.

"Why? What about the pirates, my persecutors? If my seals had spoken French, those wretches would have understood that I was trying to communicate with the outside world by this bizarre means. Because I employed Latin, they didn't suspect anything. They laughed at me because I taught seals to say *pater* and *mater*, and left me alone. And I have succeeded, since these interesting animals have put you on the track of the unfortunate César Picolot!"

Hermann Knapp, Otto Rabus and Ulric Koplipmann were flabbergasted. There was no longer any shadow of a doubt; the Roman colony did not exist. The great name of César, pronounced by the seals, was that of the poor castaway.

"Finally, your troubles are over," said Farandoul. "Console yourself; we shall take responsibility for your repatriation. But tell me—to wind up here, beyond the ice-field, you must have been part of an expedition to the Pole. Your ship must have gone down—can you tell us where and how?"

"An expedition to the Pole? Never! I'm no sailor, much less a polar explorer. I've always had a horror of sea voyages."

"How did you end up here, then?"

"Alas, I only ever made one sea-crossing, and that was fatal for me—the crossing from Le Havre to Trouville."

"From Le Havre to Trouville!"

"Yes, Messieurs. Alas, it was love that doomed me. Eight years ago, a café concert-party gave performances in Le Havre. One evening, a pupil to whom I was explaining the philosophy of Descartes, Fichte, Kant and Hegel by means of strict individual tuition, dragged me to a theater consecrated to the joyous muse. How beautiful they were, Messieurs, the lovely singers of that company—how beautiful they were! The next day, when the temple opened, I was there, drinking beer with my pupil. We had a mountain of bouquets; at every piece, serious or light, to every singer, a bouquet! That lasted a week, during which I spent three-quarters of my savings on flowers. In our capacity as theater-lovers we were admitted to rehearsals, but I never got any further. My course in philosophy at the Lycée du Havre suffered considerably, of course, from my going astray. During this interval, it seemed to me that my pupil was more greatly favored than me; I glimpsed an exchange of significant gestures between him and a robust chanteuse. What would you have done if you were me?"

"Hmm!" said Mandibul, scratching his ear.

"Indignantly, I took him back to his family and informed his father of his debauchery. He never came back; I had got rid of my rival. Alas, the company left Le Havre, bound for Trouville. In spite of my horror of maritime voyages, I embarked with them. What a voyage, and what a terrible adventure en route! Interrogate your memories, Messieurs; did you ever hear, eight years ago, of the inexplicable disappearance of a café concert-party between Le Havre and Trouville? The event must have made the news...."

"Indeed," said Mandibul. "I vaguely remember it."

"Yes, Messieurs, we departed from Le Havre but never arrived in Trouville. My memories are confused, because, laid low by sea-sickness from the moment we left the jetty, I was lying down in a corner on a bundle of rope. *En route*, the steamboat was accosted by a yacht whose occupants claimed to have been sent to meet the company by admirers in Trouville. They transferred the pretty travelers, and the yacht was about to draw away with them when, in the midst of my suffering, I realized what was happening. In spite of the sailors' shouts I jumped overboard, and, thanks to some ropes, I reached the yacht. Once on board, the sea-sickness took hold of me again and prevented me from noticing the singularity of the situation. Strangely enough, they had only taken the feminine component of the party; the men had remained aboard the Le Havre boat! I didn't notice anything. Without being seen, I slipped into one of the yacht's cabins and lay down to try to soothe the sea-sickness. I stayed there for two days, rather surprised by the duration of the voyage. We did not arrive at Trouville.

"Finally, getting impatient, I decided to go up on deck, where my appearance surprised everyone. They did not know I was there. In order to relieve the tedium of the long journey, the ladies were making music in the main cabin with the captain. I interrogated the latter to find out what time we would arrive. He gave me an evasive answer, attributing the delay to currents. I decided to be patient. The ladies were there; I chatted with them about philosophy and music. A week later we still hadn't arrived. This seemed to me to be a little strong and I made observations to the captain, who explained to me with a desolate expression that he ship's chart had been lost and that, in consequence, the impossibility of determining the exact position of Trouville required a long search. The wretch!

"A month passed: no Trouville! The ladies were beginning to be astonished by the length of the voyage. Finally the horror of our situation became clear to us one day, at the sight of the first floes of the ice-field. There were polar bears on the floating ice; there could no longer be any question of Trouville. The captain set aside his mask and told us our true destination: the North Pole! The Governor of the North Pole needed a café concert party to delight his polar evenings and distract his men, so he had requisitioned the company that I idolized! By way of response to my indignant observations, the captain contented himself with laughter and proposed to disembark me on the first convenient ice-floe. The ladies, thinking of the furs that they would harvest in these desolate regions, were soon reconciled to their part in the situation. The comic singer intoned: *I keep polar bears in the ice-field...*

"Finally, after long weeks of navigation through the ice-field, in a pass known only to the captain, we arrived here, at the Island of the Pole. That captain was the Governor of the North Pole himself!"

"I understand the abduction of the concert party," Mandibul observed, "but why did they bring you here?"

"Why? Simply because I had stumbled on part of his secret; he was forced to imprison me to keep me from revealing it. And that's why I was obliged to have recourse to the seals to call for help...but I haven't finished. On our arrival at the Pole, the climate was very different from the one we are enjoying at present; instead of 35 degrees above zero, we had 45 or 50 degrees below. In spite of our furs we were three-quarters frozen. It's the Governor of the Pole, a remarkable man in spite of everything, who has transformed the climate. This island is volcanic; wells of naphtha emerge everywhere in the form of geysers around a great central rock. The governor set light to them; the island went up in flames like a huge punch-bowl. The climate rapidly became milder; under the influence of that warmth, a near-tropical flora has developed."

"But what is the purpose of this polar installation?" Farandoul asked.

"You shall see! When you've seen more of the Island of the Pole, you'll recognize its commercial importance. Oh, the mysteries of the Gulf Stream! The great current of the Gulf Stream ends here and brings us all the shipwrecks in the Atlantic: the hulls of ships, boxes of merchandise, etc. A great part of the riches swallowed up by the waves is washed up on our shores. For example, only recently, following a big storm, the waves threw up a Spanish galleon lost in the 16th century while returning from Mexico loaded with gold! Do you understand now? After an initial voyage, the Governor, instead of giving science the advantage of his discoveries, set up the North Pole Co. Ltd., shares not traded on the London Stock Exchange. In partnership with powerful bankers, he has installed himself here, along with a company of criminal types, to supervise the exploitation under the title of the Governor of the North Pole."

"I understand everything now," said Farandoul. "That's why the Governor has made several attempts to block our expedition to the Pole, and why we came under rifle-fire!"

"Of course!" said César Picolot, bitterly. "He intends to keep the fruitful North Pole for himself; he doesn't want anyone to disturb the delightful life he leads in the midst of this verdant paradise, embellished by the presence of ladies kidnapped from all over. The wretched Governor loves music; all his unfortunate captives have been lyrical stars in Europe or America; thus, we have Rosita, from La Scala in Milan; Fanny Meyer, the principal singer of the Vienna Opera; two artistes from San Francisco; Carlotta Fabri; Princess Kriskapoulioff, etc., etc.—all eminent artistes whose incomprehensible disappearance the world must be mourning.

"All these wretched pirates' evenings are consecrated to music, singing and the piano...yes, we even have pianists, prize-winners from the Conservatoire! All genres are represented: religious music, serious music and comic opera. Do you like music? Personally, I once loved café concerts in Le Havre, but having thought long and hard about it since, I've reverted to saner ideas, and I abhor it! Consult history, and you'll see that all great criminals had a passion for music. Papavoine played the harp, Lacenaire the piano, Dumollard felt his eyes fill with tears at the sound of the Barbary organ.[111] Was it the music that pushed them

---

[111] Papavoine was the name of a child-murderer guillotined in Paris in 1823, whose case was primarily notable because the advocate defending him entered one of the earliest pleas of not guilty by reason of insanity. There is no evidence that he played the harp, but he did have an earlier namesake who composed music for that instrument. Pierre-François Lacenaire's lasting fame was ensured by the publication in 1836 of his sensational *Mémoires*, which he might even have written, although fake memoirs of famous criminals were a successful popular genre at the time. Martin Dumollard was guillotined in 1861 after a series of sensational press stories alleged that he was a serial killer who had murdered numerous servant girls over an eight year period in the vicinity of Lyons, but it

into crime, or did they find it convenient for stifling the voice of remorse? I don't know, but the fact alone ought to suffice to reproach the art on behalf of all honest men."

"I agree with you," said Mandibul, "but let's get back to the Governor."

"I was coming back to that. The pirates' houses, and those of their victims, are in the center of the island, in a fortified location. All the resources of luxury have been imported here; the artistes are prisoners, but lack for nothing: comfortable apartments, sumptuous cuisine—a little too much fish, perhaps. Every evening, they gather in the great hall and he concert begins. Poor captives, they have no means of avoiding the pirate's orders; the program is fixed and must be performed. The piano tinkles, the major instruments burst forth, then the light instruments and the chorus...horror! I hear it all in the cabin that I've build for myself in a hole in the rock—for my presence on the island is barely tolerated and I have no right to vegetate along with them. But all that is about to end! Three days ago, the Governor came back in his infernal little ship from a voyage to Europe, bring a cargo of new music and two singers that he kidnapped by means of a false engagement in America. I saw the pirates immediately begin various preparations for defense and I understood that liberators were on their way. You know everything now; the Governor and his pirates, who number about 30, are 100 meters away, hidden in the rocks..."

"But who is this Governor. You haven't said."

"Alas, an eight year sojourn hasn't told me any more than I've told you. Mystery—mystery everywhere! Not one of the captives, perhaps not one of the pirates, has any inkling of that infernal man's name."

"I can tell you!" exclaimed one of the English scientists, who had not said a word until then—and who, moreover, had not said much aboard the gondola-sloop. "This man, the Governor of the North Pole, is Captain Hatteras!"

Farandoul released a cry of amazement. "Captain Hatteras! The intrepid explorer of the polar regions—the man for whom Jules Verne has made a reputation as a navigator and a gentleman?"

"The very same."

Another of Jules Verne's heroes! At the North Pole, so remote from the rest of the world, Farandoul is bumping into yet another of these fatal individuals. Farandoul sets off to discover the Pole, after 1000 frightful dangers he succeeds in finding this mysterious rock...fatality! The North Pole is inhabited. And by whom? By one of Jules Verne's heroes, by Captain Hatteras!

"*Ventre de phoque!*" cried Mandibul. "But are you sure that this Governor is Captain Hatteras. How do you know that, Monsieur?"

---

is doubtful that modern standards of evidence would have allowed him to be convicted even of the single murder with which he was charged..

The English scientist came forward into the circle of sailors. "Because he is my husband. Because I am his legitimate spouse, cruelly abandoned!"[112] And the false scientist took off her spectacles, lifted up her wig, and appeared to all their astonished eyes with the face of a pretty English blonde of 27 or 28.

"Oh!" said Mandibul.

The second Englishman advanced into the circle in his turn.

"I'll wager that this is Madame Hatteras' famous chambermaid!" cried Tournesol.

"You'd lose!" replied the Englishman, and introduced himself: "I'm James Codgett,[113] solicitor of 7 Chancery Lane, open every day from one till five, circumstances permitting, acting for Mrs. Hatteras in divorce proceedings brought before the court by the aforementioned lady against the honorable Captain John Hatteras, her husband. It is necessary for us to establish the debauchery of the said Captain Hatteras, in order to obtain the divorce on the grounds of outrageous behavior, and I'm counting on you, gentlemen, to sign witness-statements."

V.

"This is an astonishing turn of events," murmured Farandoul. "We could scarcely have expected to encounter all this at the North Pole!"

"Alas," said Mandibul, sadly, "there are only two married people on this rock of the Pole, and they're getting divorced! What a lesson for all us bachelors!"

"So you knew of the existence of the Island of the Pole?" Farandoul went on.

"I only had my suspicions; that's why Mr. Codgett and I joined the English expedition to the North Pole. Now, we're going to unmask the odious swine!"

"Pardon me," said Mandibul, "but that's our business. The pirates are close at hand, rifles in hand, and we have to drive them back to their lair."

---

[112] From this point on, Robida's story diverges quite sharply from that related in *Les Aventures du Capitaine Hatteras*, in which the noble but obsessive Hatteras had no wife, and ended up going harmlessly mad after recklessly climbing up to the volcanic crater in order to plant the English flag on the actual North Pole. The reader will observe that the volcanic peak has mysteriously disappeared from Robida's island, henceforth being conspicuous by its absence.

[113] Robida (or his amanuensis) initially spells this name "Codjett" but subsequently reverts to the more plausible version, which I have preferred by way of unification.

"No—you're my witnesses. If they kill you, I shan't have your signatures. Let me go find them and negotiate."

"That's a good idea," said Farandoul. "Before attacking, we might as well try to come to some arrangement. If Hatteras consents to set his captives free, we won't interfere with the possession of his island."

On Farandoul's orders, a white flag was raised to request a truce. The pirates replied to the signal with a similar flag and the false English scientist, having readjusted her wig and put on her spectacles, set off towards the position occupied by Hatteras, followed by the solicitor James Codgett.

His Excellency the Governor of the North Pole, John Hatteras himself, came to meet them. The mariners, watching his movements from afar, saw him interrogate the negotiators brutally. James Codgett replied. Suddenly, Hatteras abruptly changed his attitude; the fake Englishman had just removed her wig and rendered herself recognizable.

"A matrimonial showdown!" murmured Mandibul. "To come all the way to the Pole to see that!"

Hatteras and the negotiators had disappeared behind the rocks; they did not see the rest of the scene. Sentries with loaded rifles kept watch on both sides.

The conference lasted a long time; the negotiators did not reappear until three hours later.

"What result?" Farandoul shouted to them, as soon as they were within range.

James Codgett made the reply. "Captain Hatteras asks for 12 hours to reflect before making a decision. Tomorrow morning, at daybreak, we'll have his response. The confrontation was stormy. At first, Mrs. Hatteras heaped scalding reproaches upon him, and I saw that things were about to get out of hand, so I intervened and proposed a short break. It was the right thing to do, I think. The

Governor of the North Pole, moved by our arrival, seems to me to be ready to start on the road of repentance; it's necessary not to treat him roughly."

"Did you see the...?" Mandibul asked, curiously.

"The Governor was opposed to it, but I insisted on fulfilling my duty, and I have established the perfect verity of the assertions made by Monsieur César Picolot, the unfortunate voyager to Trouville. I shall write my deposition, and tomorrow, when you have seen for yourselves, I will ask you to add your signatures to it."

"Well," said Farandoul, "the delay granted to Hatteras seems to me to be an imprudence, but it's done now; we'll hold our respective positions until tomorrow. The temperature is delightful; we'll be perfectly all right in our cave, refreshed by the sea breeze—but two men must mount guard to prevent any surprise. Now, let's attack our provisions"!"

Night fell without bringing darkness; the great naphtha fires, launching columns of flame 20 meters into the air, lit up the sky for six kilometers around. By the light of this false Sun, they supped cheerfully in the cave, and then got ready to go to bed down on the bearskins brought from the gondola-sloop.

Only the solicitor and the two sentries stayed awake; everyone else went to sleep. James Codgett prepared his legal documents for use the following day. As for poor César Picolot, having borrowed a pen and ink from the solicitor in order to write the first chapter of his memoirs, entitled *Eight Years of Captivity at the North Pole*, the long-delayed joy of rescue had disturbed his inspiration and he had set off, armed with a sailor's carbine, in the hope of getting to the singers from Le Havre, to inform them that their troubles were over.

The temperature was truly delightful; at midnight, Mandibul, waking up briefly, observed that it was 31 degrees above zero, and only went to sleep again after having inscribed that extraordinary figure in his notebook.

At 6 a.m., four rifle-shots fired some distance away woke everyone up. Farandoul leapt up from his bearskins and bumped into Mandibul in the darkness.

"What?" he cried. "What's this? What profound darkness! The naptha fires...."

"Extinguished ten minutes ago," replied the sailor on guard.

"Oh! That doesn't bode anything good. The Governor must be planning some surprise—those fires have burned without interruption for eight years. Light a lantern, quickly—the Sun won't rise until quarter past noon, so we still have six hours of night before us."[114]

---

[114] Robida seems to have no inkling of the actual pattern of daylight and darkness in the polar regions. It is now late spring in the northern hemisphere, so the sun ought to be perpetually above the horizon, at least in part, and ought to remain so for almost the entire duration of the subsequent adventure—far from the situation that the narrative describes.

At the same moment, a further dozen rifle-shots rang out and a number of shadows appeared, running through the rocks."

The sailors pounced on their carbines. One of the shadows perceived the movement. "Don't fire!" it cried. "It's me and them!" It was the voice of César Picolot.

A man and seven women, exhausted and breathless, leapt into the middle of the camp and let themselves fall on to the bearskins.

"Safe! They're safe!" cried César Picolot, collecting himself. "Safe for the moment, at least, for…"

"Come on, what's happening, and why have the naphtha fires gone out?" Farandoul demanded, sharply.

"Thanks be to God, here they are, safe!" replied César, entirely in the grip of his joy. "Here they are, Messieurs, the unfortunates of the Trouville ferry, the eminent lyric artistes of the Le Havre café concerts, Mesdames Angelo, Stanislas, Léa d'Arcis (sur Aube), Bichart, Antonia, Judith and Henriette d'Ingouville, whom all lovers of art are undoubtedly mourning, even today, along the entire coast of Normandy. I arrived in time…"

"What's happening?" Farandoul repeated. "Tell us!"

"Simply this: Governor Hatteras is evacuating the Island of the Pole, along with his pirates, Instead of settling matters, the arrival of Madame Hatteras has ruined everything. Hatteras only asked for time yesterday to prepare his flight. One group of pirates has been loading bales and provisions on to his yacht, while the others, under the direction of the Governor himself, were working on a clandestine task…."

"The naphtha wells?" cried Farandoul.

"You've guessed it! The pirates are diverting the wells. Five or six hours of work were sufficient; the wells of naphtha now empty into the sea and the Island of the Pole has become the domain of darkness again."

"And of cold! This artificial temperature, maintained by the naphtha fires, will soon decrease, and the frightful cold will return!"

"By now," César went on, "the Governor and his pirates will be embarked. At the moment when the naphtha fires went out, I succeeded, by courtesy of the darkness, in stealing a few of their victims. The others were already aboard; it was then that the pirates fired several rifle-shots at me…."

César interrupted himself abruptly. Four magnetic buoys landed on the shore and four mariners emerged from them, armed to the teeth. They were the men left to guard the gondola-sloop; alarmed by the pirates' rifle fire they had set out to sea to come to their friends' rescue.

"*Mille tonnerres!*" cried Farandoul. "The gondola-sloop is no longer guarded, and if Hatteras…"

A dazzling light suddenly lit up at sea, near the line of breakers, and a frightful explosion rent the air.

"The gondola-sloop!" cried all the mariners, tearing their hair.

It was the gondola-sloop that had exploded! By the light of the explosion, everyone could see the masts of another vessel—Hatteras's yacht—some distance away, moving off under full steam.

What a catastrophe! No more ship and no more resources! With the naphtha wells diverted, the cold would return. The infernal Hatteras, seeing his secret discovered, permitting the Island of the Pole to fall into the hands of the bold mariners, had annihilated everything, including food-supplies and accommodation. He had put out the island's fires, which were the only things rendering a sojourn practicable, and, to rob his victims of any other means of return, he had blown up the ship that had brought them as he left.

The most desperate of all of them was the unfortunate César Picolot. All hope of his ever seeing Le Havre again seemed lost, alas! The terrible cold of the Pole would seize its prey; the air was freshening already and the gentle breeze of a little while ago had transformed into a bitter wind that was forcing all of them to blow on their fingers.

"Uh oh!" said Mandibul, on consulting his thermometer.

"Well?" asked Farandoul. "It's getting lower, isn't it?"

"*Fichtre!*" replied Mandibul. "Thirty degrees lower, to be exact. It's no more than three degrees above zero."

"That's very quick! Have we enough bearskins for everyone? Yes? Very good! Let's make sure we don't freeze. We need to keep clear heads if we're to get out of this; the main thing is not to catch chilblains in our imagination. Now, let's head for Hatteras's houses and install ourselves there so that we can combat the cold."

The entire troop, guided by César Picolot, set off in the direction of Hatteras Houe, guided by the flickering light of a lantern. The sense of smell alone would have been sufficient to get them there; as they advanced further, a frightful odor of burning spread through the atmosphere, and revealed only too clearly, alas, the destruction wrought by the Governor.

The unfortunate lyrical artistes, so cruelly tried, were shivering beneath their bearskins. As for Mrs. Hatteras, she heaped the weight of her fury upon her unfortunate solicitor, whom she accused of having lost everything by granting the Governor a delay.

The entire troop, bumping into rocks, rolling among pebbles and slipping on slopes, finally arrived at the pirates' living quarters. Farandoul made a rapid inspection, lantern in hand. Alas, all as ruin and desolation! The pirates had taken everything they could possible carry and thrown everything that would burn into the naphtha fires. Only the walls remained. Hatteras had not had time to knock them down; he had contented himself with removing the roofs, doors and windows. All the provisions had, of course, disappeared.

"Cold and famine!" moaned the lyrical artistes.

"No," said Farandoul, "only the cold is to be feared; the sea will furnish us with our nourishment. Calm down, Mesdames. We'll eat seals and walruses, and drink whale-oil! Let's see—how many degrees on the thermometer?"

Mandibul moved the lantern closer to the thermometer in his belt. "Eight degrees below zero! The North Pole's cooling down quickly!"

"Come on!" Farandoul went on. "To work, lads—we need a domicile, and quickly, or we'll be frozen within two hours!"

The least damaged corner of Hatteras's house was selected as a shelter and the mariners set about making it a little more comfortable, almost groping their way. With a little wood that had escaped destruction, they improvised a roof of sorts and stopped up the window-openings. Every quarter of an hour, Mandibul consulted his watch. First he found 13 degrees below zero, then 17, then 28, then 31, 33, and finally 41!

When the Sun appeared, at 12:15 a.m., the thermometer had fallen another seven or eight degrees. The unfortunate castaways were almost frozen in spite of the fire they had maintained, with great difficulty, with few pieces of wood collected from here and there.

What desolation appeared to them in daylight! All the vegetation that the heat maintained by the naphtha fires had nursed had been wiped out by the cold of that terrible night; the tall grass, the lianas and the nascent coconut trees were stiff with frost; everything was dead.

"Quickly!" Farandoul ordered. "Let's take advantage of the few hours of daylight to cut wood and brushwood, and heap it up in our lodgings!"

Everyone, including Mrs. Hatteras and the lyrical artistes, set to work, knife or hatchet in hand. Unfortunately, the vegetation had not had the time to become very sturdy; there were more leaves than wood. In three hours, it had all been harvested. The island soon presented nothing but a denuded plateau in the midst of a rocky chaos.

As night fell, they went back into the uncomfortable cabin to warm themselves up with a good flame.

"What about a meal? We haven't eaten yet," observed the ladies.

"We'll provide one now," replied our hero. "Light the fire; we're going seal-hunting."

"No need! No need!" cried César Picolot. "I'll go call some of my pupils, and bring them here. It's a betrayal, but, at the end of the day, he who doesn't desire to go hungry desires the means…let's see: how many seals make a meal? There are 30 of us; two should suffice, it seems to me. Right—I'll get two fat and healthy pupils. I'll bring them here immediately."

"What about vegetables?" asked one of the German scientists.

"Leguminous plants are not abundant, alas; I can only offer you a salad of frozen leaves."

The two pupils of César Picolot, ex-professor of the Lycée du Havre, might have been remarkable in terms of their intelligence and moral qualities, but they left much to be desired from a purely gastronomic point of view. They were fat, but tough. They were roasted on a spit and carved up very swiftly with swords. Nothing was wasted; the ladies complained a great deal, but had to admit, in the final analysis, that the oily nourishment was filling.

Two men were given responsibility for maintaining the fire with brushwood and the rest of the company went to sleep rolled up in bearskins. Mandibul woke up in the middle of the night, his legs numb with cold. He ran to his thermometer, hanging from the wall. In spite of the infernal fire maintained within the room, it marked 23 degrees below zero.

"Damn! Damn!" he said, going back to sleep.

At 8 a.m., César Picolot went outside briefly and woke everyone up by returning with two more of his pupils.

"It's breakfast," he said. "I've catered for all tastes by bringing you one fat one and one thin one."

While everyone was busy with César Picolot's pupils, Farandoul and Mandibul went out to see how much combustible material remained. The stock was considerably depleted, and it was obvious that it would all be consumed in two days.

"No fire during the day!" Farandoul said, when he went back in. "We can only have one by night; that will make our fuel-supply last longer. That way, we'll have enough for four days. It's necessary, therefore, that within four times twenty-four hours we have to find a way of leaving this inhospitable island."

"Well, what about the buoys that brought us?"

"Impossible—they're magnetic, they'll never be able to get away from the pole."

"What can we do, then?"

"Build a raft, if we can find the materials. We've no other chance of salvation. We'll go to investigate. During that interval, make sure you don't let yourselves freeze—replace the fire with gymnastics."

Farandoul and Mandibul made a tour of the island, but, in spite of all their research, only discovered a few items of wreckage, a few fragments of masts with which they could hardly construct a raft big enough to accommodate everyone. No matter; if necessary, the demolished electric buoys could furnish a few further materials, as could the fabric of Hatteras House and a piano that Hatteras had left behind.

On retuning, our two friends found the entire crew in the process of warming themselves with obligatory gymnastics. Kirkson was carrying two ladies with his arms outstretched; the solicitor Codgett was teaching César Picolot to box; everyone was moving about as much as possible, under the exacting instructions of Tournesol, who was not giving anyone time to rest.

After having eaten two more of César Picolot's pupils, they set to work. Even the ladies worked actively on the construction of the life-raft. Farandoul had ordered that, not for lack of gallantry, but because they could only live in the terrible atmosphere of the North Pole in a condition of energetic activity, without a moment's rest.

Carrying planks of shoulders, moving yardarms and fragments of masts and plying hatchets was healthy, but tiring. That evening, when the raft was far enough advanced, it was necessary to return to gymnastics while awaiting the fire.

In spite of the 50 degrees of frost that the Pole enjoyed, the sea, continually agitated and warmed by the great current of the Gulf Stream, kept it almost free of ice. They could leave; Farandoul's plan was to abandon themselves to the current and descend with it in the direction of less desolate regions, where there might be a chance of encountering some whaling-ship.

By the first light of dawn the following day—which is to say, about noon—the raft was taken to the shore. It was very small; they would be very cramped, but would have to be content. The steam-buoy was, however, usable. Farandoul was counting on it to tow the raft outside the island's girdle of reefs, and to assist their progress for as long as the small amount of coal saved from the destruction of the gondola-sloop lasted. They also took—with great difficulty, since they had to drag them away from the Island of the Pole—a few iron buoys. They were a hindrance at first, but might subsequently be able, once the action of the pole was no longer sensible, to render important services to the castaways.

Everyone worked courageously to hasten the moment of departure; an almost-sealed shelter was established on top of the raft's planking with the roof of Hatteras House, and César Picolot brought 30 of his pupils, which were attached to the front of the raft, with a beam on which they could rest from time to time. At 2 p.m., everything was ready. They had one more hour of daylight; it was necessary to take advantage of it to get out of the reefs.

Immediately before embarkation, Farandoul and a few men returned to Hatteras House; the others were surprised to see them come back with two barrels that they did not recognize. It was a precious find: two barrels of rum from Hatteras's stores, which Farandoul had discovered in a hidey-hole. Everyone clapped; several empty barrels, found in the same store-room, served to consolidate the raft.

The steam-buoy was heated up; everything was ready.

"All aboard!" cried Farandoul.

After an effortful hour, the fragile raft finally succeeded in getting through the redoubtable line of reefs, and the steam-buoy was able to draw them at top speed on the waters of the Gulf Stream. A large tot of rum was poured for the whole crew by way of rejoicing, and there was talk of sacrificing two of César Picolot's pupils for the evening meal.

They had departed! That fatal isle, that frightful North Pole that might have been the tomb of so many brave men, thanks to the treason of Captain Hatteras, had already disappeared over the horizon. But all was not settled. Could they battle the ice-field and the polar cold with such feeble means, with a raft so cramped and a shelter of such problematic solidarity? The first night was terrible; no one could sleep, and Farandoul had to order the initiation of a general boxing tournament to avoid an imminent congelation of the unfortunate navigators.

The only bearable post was aboard the steam-buoy, huddled against the boiler; there one was one frozen on one side and roasted on the other. Each of the raft's passengers occupied that post in turns. Unfortunately the cold intensified in the morning, and great misfortune seemed imminent. Gymnastics and boxing no longer had much effect, and in any case, everyone was injured as a result of the day's exercises. Almost every nose seemed to be damaged, either by boxing or by frost.

There was not a moment to lose. Farandoul had a barrel of rum emptied into one of the iron buoys brought as a precaution, and set fire to the liquid—with some difficulty, for the flames of the matches froze as soon as it was exposed to the air. Finally, the rum caught alight.

What joy! They came back to life; the blood began to circulate. The most badly-injured, liberally sprinkled, rapidly defrosted without deterioration. Only James Codgett, Mrs. Hatteras's solicitor, nearly lost the most beautiful ornament of his face—an aquiline nose that was, quite rightly, his pride and joy—but a generous ladleful of flaming punch saved the unfortunate organ. James Codgett had the joy of feeling reborn—slightly burned but alive.

The joy of our poor castaways did not last long. The punch had preserved them from an immediate congelation, but while they savored it externally and internally, another danger just as terrible was threatening them: gigantic icebergs, which the mariners had not noticed, were advancing towards the raft.

In the midst of that profound darkness, the flames of the punch suddenly illuminated the horrible jagged masses of ice-mountains to port and starboard: enormous blocks whose summits, bristling with 1000 peaks like fantastic steeples, were lost in the intense blackness of the sky.

These icebergs, stirred by the big waves, loomed over the feeble raft with all the majesty of their cliffs. They hardly had time to glimpse them; at the very moment when they appeared in the firelight of the punch, there was a frightful shock. The raft, impacted by icy points, came apart instantaneously. The crudely-constructed cabin was thrown into the air along with all those it sheltered; the spars wet flying, and the punch was extinguished by a deluge of icy water.

The majestic icebergs passed rapidly over the scene of the disaster, and everything was silent again....

After a minute, however, a sonorous "Ahoy! Ahoy!" revealed that not everyone had perished. It was Tournesol, who had surfaced and was trying to pierce the darkness to discover some remnant of the shipwreck. Other repeated "Ahoys!" replied, close at hand; half a dozen men clinging to a spar had heard him and made a space for him on their piece of wood.

Then Mandibul appeared, towing Mrs. Hatteras in an empty barrel, César Picolot astride another hogshead, the excellent chanteuse Léa d'Arcis on the piano, Escoubico and Kirkson on a plank, then James Codgett and the rest of the sailors astride the mast of the raft.

What about Farandoul? Had he disappeared under the iceberg? Just as the matelots were anxiously coming to that conclusion, Farandoul reappeared. He had climbed on to the steam-buoy at the moment of the shipwreck; the shock had thrown the cabin of the raft on to the buoy, and it had fallen on top of him, along with the German scientists and the lyrical artistes from Le Havre. The poor individuals had grabbed hold of the buoy and succeeded in maintaining themselves above the surface.

No one was dead! But were they much better off! Could any glimmer of hope remain for these unfortunates, lost in the sea five or six leagues from the North Pole?

Suddenly, Tournesol released an exclamation and raised his arms in the air, abandoning his piece of wreckage.

"There's a foothold here!" he cried.

Farandoul immediately shone his lantern in that direction. Strangely enough, the last barrel full of rum had also surfaced beside Tournesol. Almost immediately, the rest of the mariners stood up. The water hardly came up to their ankles. How could that be? Had they set foot on some unknown land? Were they in the shallows? The icebergs had just passed over it, though....

Farandoul grabbed a sounding-line and immediately felt resistance; the lead came back dragging a herring with it!

"A shoal of herrings!" he cried. "Saved! We're saved! It's the huge shoal of herring that descends at this time of year towards the coast of Holland..."[115]

A splendid aurora borealis suddenly sprang up at that exact moment, illuminating the horizon for our friends. The entire sky was on fire; long trails of light lit up the sea as far as the eye could see.

Farandoul put out his unnecessary lantern and leapt along the shoal of herring to carry out a rapid reconnaissance. It was indeed the great shoal of herring awaited with impatience by the fishermen of Europe; there were millions of millions heaped up one atop another over a breadth of 500 meters and double that length. In the middle of the shoal, their mass was scarcely covered by a centimeter of water; it was necessary to reach that spot and establish themselves there.

The living ground shifted under their feet and they sank into it slightly, but with care they could stand on it. In the middle, as Farandoul had hoped, the aggregation was tighter and the denser mass of herrings offered more resistance. Our hero planted a section of mast and beckoned to his friends. After a few minutes of indecision the ladies took the risk; they abandoned the buoy and walked toward the center of the shoal, holding hands. They suffered a few falls, but finally arrived.

The mariners lost no time. Numerous pieces of wreckage were floating here and there over the shoal; Mandibul had them gathered up and brought to the center. It also became urgent to put out the fire in the steam-buoy in order to save fuel and not to disturb the herrings too much. Before doing that, Farandoul gave the order to heat a little rum to warm up the ladies after their glacial bath.

"And now, to work!" cried Farandoul.

In two hours, the mariners succeeded in establishing a more solid floor of sorts on the mobile shoal of herrings. Fragments of mast supported on empty casks formed an immense frame, cut across by lighter cross-pieces. Over this

---

[115] Curiously enough, although the etymology of the two words is quite different, the French *banc* and the English *shoal* have exactly the same double meaning, capable of referring either to a large aggregation of fish or to a sandbank, thus providing the pun on which this flamboyantly absurd narrative move is founded.

504

frame they extended all the sail-canvas that they were able to join together, and replaced the cabin shattered by the encounter with the iceberg as best they could. When all that was done, everyone admitted that the installation, exceedingly precious as it was, was better than the poor storm-tossed raft. Apart from a slight pitching movement and a kind of formication underfoot, they could almost believe that they were on an island.

The mariners rubbed their hands, as much to congratulate themselves as to relieve numbness.

Only César Picolot was visibly anxious; he roamed around the shoal of herrings, vainly calling out to his seals—his pupils—which had disappeared during the shipwreck. Only two responded to his call; despairing of his cause he brought them to the center of the shoal and tied them to the mast.

"No more than two seals now!" he said, sadly, to Mandibul. "It's enough for one meal, and then what? What shall we do for food?"

"O distraught philosopher," Mandibul replied, "What about our shoal? We'll eat our shoal, of course!" Turning to Mrs. Hatteras, he added: "Pardon Madame—do you like fresh herring? Until further notice, our master cook will be serving it for every meal."

VI.

A strange and new situation for navigators! Lost at sea, carried by a shoal of herrings! Only Mandibul was overjoyed. "I've sailed in every sort of vessel in the world," he said, "tried them all, from simple fishing-boats to great transatlantic liners, from Venetian gondolas to Malaysian proas—but this is the first time that a shoal of herrings has had the honor of transporting me!"

"Let's see about establishing a little order on board," said Farandoul. "We have 18 mariners, three German scientists, Madame Hatteras and her solicitor, César Picolot and the seven lyrical artistes—that makes 31 people, plus two seals. Our entire resources comprise a cask of rum—that's all that we've saved, isn't it?"

"Pardon!" cried Mandibul. "I've saved something else…"

"What's that?"

"I've save 4,558,664.69 francs in drafts on the banks of the principal coastal cities of England, Norway and Russia. Still a good sum, with which we'll be swimming in abundance as soon as we arrive in one or other of those countries."

"Yes, it's just a matter of getting there."

Tournesol had understood. "Will we have enough herrings for the journey?" he asked. "I think that, even if I tighten my belt a little, I'll need at least 18 herrings a day, and there are 31 of us…"

"Don't worry, and eat 36," Mandibul replied. "I've already thought about that—we have no need to fear famine. Follow my calculation: our shoal is about 1000 meters long by 500 wide and ten deep, a total of 500 cubic meters of densely-packed herrings. I estimate 1800 herrings per cubic meter, which makes nine billion herrings. I divide by 30 and I obtain approximately 300 million herrings to eat per person. You see that we can sail on quite contentedly. What grieves me is the monotony of the menu—herring and yet more herring."

"I'd like to be clear," Tournesol went on. "At 30 a day, how long would 300 million herrings last?"

"Damn! I certainly hope that we'll encounter a whaler or a port before then-your 300 million herrings at 30 a day would last 27,937 years and 95 days!"

"Yes, but what about leap years? And isn't it necessary to conserve enough to carry us?"

"You're forgetting births, scatterbrain that you are! We'll have newborns a-plenty; within a fortnight we'll have six times as many herrings as today and we'll be able to stroll on a shoal that's a league and a half longer!"

Tournesol slapped his forehead. "That's true—I was forgetting births! I won't worry any longer, then, and I'll make every effort to get fat. I'll ask the master cook whether he can smoke part of the shoal…"

During this discussion, Farandoul was busy with the installation of passengers in the cabin in the center of the shoal. The cabin formed a shelter as uncomfortable as could possibly be imagined; the wind got in everywhere, nothing held firm, nothing closed; the roof, walls and everything else were made of bits and pieces. It was necessary to consolidate the miserable dwelling as quickly as possible if they did not want to perish inevitably from the cold.

A floor was constituted first, to avoid contact with the herrings. This floor, of course, bore little resemblance to a Hungarian point parquet[116] and there was no question of waxing it; it was a simple raft formed of planks and crosspieces tied together with rope. A square opening was reserved in the center for building a fire. It was cruel for the poor herrings, but, at the end of the day, they could not do without a fire, nor could they contemplate putting fire on the planks.

One of the iron buoys was installed in the center of the opening and a nice coal fire was lit in it with the last of the fuel-supplies from the steam-buoy. As an economy measure, the cabin fire was also used for cooking; the master cook installed himself there and commenced his duties by grilling 300 herrings for a meal, the need for which was felt without anyone, in view of the profound darkness, knowing whether to call it breakfast or supper.

The master cook was, personally, quite satisfied with his installation. Never, aboard the ships on which he had served, or even on land during expeditions

---

[116] Hungarian point is a kind of embroidery stitch resulting in a zigzag pattern similar to the pattern employed in some parquet floors.

in Asia or America, had he been able to practice his art with the same convenience. He had only to bend down beside his oven to grab the herrings that were always within reach, for the gaps were filled as soon as they were made. The 300 herrings making up the meal having been snatched from the bosom of their family and thrown on the grill, the shoal closed ranks slightly, and their absence did not appear to bother the others at all. Besides, they had other things to worry about; the iron buoy serving as an oven got hot very quickly, which caused the water and the herrings that got too close to crackle and sputter. That was the sole inconvenience of the installation, and it was only serious for the herrings. As a humanitarian measure, it was decided that the herrings for meals should always be chosen from among the scorched.

That first meal on board, very copious and washed down with a nice drop of burning rum, cheered up the castaways. The fatigues of the emotionally-trying day were forgotten and everyone, after the meal, set to work under instructions from Farandoul and Mandibul to complete the task of installation. The disjointed partition walls were consolidated, boards were nailed over the breaches, and tarred canvas, stretched over everything, completed the interception of any passage of glacial air from outside.

It was just in time, for Mandibul's thermometer marked 46 degrees below zero outside. The temperature inside the cabin was more tolerable; it was only 31 below next to the fire.

Farandoul's first concern was to establish regulations for the maintenance of order within. It was decided that the ladies would always occupy places nearest to the buoy-oven and that the men, divided into shifts, would take turns to occupy the rest of the places in the front row. This having been decided, they settled down to spend a pleasant and tranquil evening, a satisfaction well and legitimately earned by Herculean labors.

Only Mrs. Hatteras seemed prey to melancholy.

"What's up?" Mandibul said to her, confidentially. "Are you missing your bandit husband?"

"It's not that," replied poor Mrs. Hatteras. "I only regret having been the cause of your misfortunes. But there's something else. James Codgett, my solicitor, has just informed me that he'll be forced to raise his fee to a higher level. He warned me, when he quoted his initial figure, that the expenses of the voyage would be charged to me and that I would have to provide him with a comfortable first-class cabin. The shoal of herrings on which we're traveling appears to him to constitute accommodation of the lowest category and he's claiming an indemnity of 2000 pounds sterling by virtue of that fact."

"Without prejudice to any subsidiary claims for colds and illnesses that might ensue," said James Codgett, indiscreetly joining in the conversation. "You understand, Madam, that the disturbances occasioned by the case of Hatteras spouse versus Captain Hatteras have been much more serious than the normal course of cases pursued in the courts of London. And to tell the truth, you wouldn't find many solicitors or distinguished advocates who would consent, as I have, to travel in all the peculiar vessels that you have caused me to frequent for some time. Permit me to enumerate: first the ice-floe; then we were lost in the ice-field…"

"A matter settled at 1000 pounds sterling!" Mrs. Hatteras observed, quietly.

"Then the gondola-sloop, hardly comfortable, not being equipped to carry passengers…"

"Settled at 500 pounds!"

"Pardon!" cried Mandibul. "That's much too dear. The gondola-sloop was a scientific curiosity; many people would have offered fabulous sums for the simple honor of taking a trip aboard her! Therefore, acting in the interests of Madame Hatteras, I claim a substantial discount…"

"Impossible! I'd lose by it! Don't you know that people like us, solicitors, have considerable office expenses…but I'll go on. After the gondola-sloop, you made me travel in a magnetic buoy!"

"Another 500 pounds!" murmured Mrs. Hatteras.

"What!" cried Mandibul, furiously. "Five hundred pounds! We'll take it to court! The magnetic buoy is a new scientific invention and the honor of trying a form of transport absolutely unknown to the rest of the world was certainly sufficient compensation for any inconvenience that a simple landlubber used to his creature comforts could experience thereby!"

"I should have been warned; I would not have accepted the case under those conditions...but I shall go on. After the buoy came the raft. I've got you there—you can't pass your raft off as a scientific curiosity; everything about it was old and worn-out! Throughout history castaways have used nothing else...hence, navigation devoid of interest. Very well—and the comfort of your raft, aren't you going to brag about that? You see that, in charging the raft at a 1000 pounds sterling, I'm being very reasonable. But after the raft, here I am, traveling on a shoal of herrings! This time, it surpasses everything that one can imagine, and no solicitor has ever been treated so unceremoniously. I have been made to go back and forth, drowned and frozen, nourished in the most bizarre fashion, and when I exercise my right to compensation, it is disputed, quibbled...no, I repeat, never has any solicitor been treated thus! We have reached the point at which I shall not dare admit to the shoal of herrings on our return to London, and at which, from now on, I must ask Mrs. Hatteras to keep silent regarding our sojourn on the backs of these nine billon herrings...."

"That," Mandibul put in, interrupting him, "is rank ingratitude! Here are brave fish that you were very glad to run into, in order to be gathered up, and which, not content to carry you over the waves almost without rolling, will also nourish you with their flesh during the voyage—and you're black-hearted enough to refuse to render them due thanks for your return to your fatherland! Come on! The heart of a solicitor can't be as hard as all that!"

"That's something for later discussion; in the meantime. I think that, in view of the strangeness of this means of transport, I have every right to a further indemnity, which I shall fix at 2000 pounds sterling."

"Monsieur!" cried Mandibul. "I've always heard it said that men of law have no soul, and this confirms me in that dolorous opinion! I pity you, Monsieur! But we shall go to court and we shall see whether, rather than owing you such formidable honoraria, it isn't you who will remain indebted to Madame Hatteras for the delightful and picturesque voyage that the case of Hatteras versus Hatteras has allowed you to take at that lady's expense!"

"What about my practice! What has become of that in the course of my peregrinations? Do you think that my other cases are not in jeopardy in my absence, in the hands of my principal clerk—an intelligent young man, but who possesses neither my enlightenment nor my experience? At the outset, we were only supposed to undertake a short northward journey, and it was only by degrees that I allowed myself to be dragged all the way to the Pole...not to mention, alas, the mortal anxiety into which my long absence must have plunged Mrs. Codgett—who will be the object of a further claim that I cannot fix as yet, but which I shall formulate thus in my invoice: *indemnity for familial anxieties and annoyances anticipated on return by virtue of the irascible character of the honorable Mrs. Codgett, at...*the relevant fee."

"But this is ruination!" murmured Mrs. Hatteras. "A fatal lawsuit! My family fortune will be exhausted by it. Shall I at least be successful!"

"Assuredly, Madame, the divorce will be granted by the high court on the deposition of these gentlemen—and I shall take advantage of our present tranquility to draft a statement regarding our visit to Captain Hatteras and collect the signatures of witnesses to the delinquency of the aforesaid captain."

The worthy solicitor, taking a sheet of headed notepaper and a writing-case from his pocket, sat down beside the oven to draw up the document. His pen flew over the paper, and a few moments later he communicated the following to his client:

To the Gentlemen of the Divorce Court, Chancery Lane, London.

The undersigned James Codgett, solicitor, acting for Mrs. Hatteras, petitioner, in the claim for divorce against Captain John Hatteras, defendant, declares that, having departed for the glacial sea with that lady in order conclusively and dutifully to establish, in an ocular fashion and without possibility of error, the extra-conjugal delinquency of the aforesaid Captain John Hatteras, defendant, the abovenamed and undersigned solicitor has eventually been able, after fatigues and perils without number, for which he reserves the right to fix and charge rightful fees, to witness personally the misdeeds of which the defendant is accused.

The scene of the defendant's delinquencies being, unfortunately, too distant for the High Court to be able to transport itself there by commission, the undersigned solicitor has been obliged to limit himself to collecting the irrefutable attestations of the honorable mariners and travelers who observed them as he did—attestations that will be found further on. It is in an island unknown to the Office of the Admiralty and situated at the Pole of the northern hemisphere that the undersigned solicitor, accompanied by the petitioner, has been able to recover the proofs necessary to the granting of the divorce. The honorable defender was there, reigning as lord and master over a very mixed population, formed partly of men fully worthy of the title of pirates and partly of unfortunate lyrical artistes kidnapped by the honorable defender and sequestered by him.

The undersigned solicitor declares that the matrimonial rights of Mrs. Hatteras have been totally violated by the defender and concludes by asking the High Court to grant a divorce in favor of the petitioner.

James Codgett,

Solicitor

presently at sea, in the vicinity of the Island of the Pole.

Certified and signed by us, mariners forming part of the French expedition to the North Pole:

Mandibul had been reading over Mrs. Hatteras's shoulder; he seized the pen from the solicitor's hands and was the first to sign, along with Farandoul. Then he read the statement aloud to the mariners and collected their signatures. Our hero's foster-father, not knowing how to sign his name, marked the headed paper with a fine cross. The German scientists then attested the perfect verity of the observations and passed the pen to César Picolot, who added a simple line, eloquent in its conciseness:

> *Certified by us, unfortunate victims of Captain Hatteras.*
> *Artistes of the Alcazar du Havre.*

"Thank you," said Mrs. Hatteras, simply, as she took back the piece of paper.

The solicitor James Codgett was about to put the important attestations in his pocket when Mandibul stopped him. "One moment!" he said. "This document is of capital importance; it's necessary to make certain of its conservation. Does anyone have a bottle?"

"A bottle of what?" asked Trabadec. "I've got one that I picked up on the shore of the Island of the Pole, but it still has a little cognac in it."

"Drink it and give it to me."

Trabadec handed over the bottle. Mandibul folded the piece of headed paper neatly, put it into the bottle, replaced the stopper and, warming up what remained of the wax in the flames of the oven, rendered the seal absolutely impermeable. "Now," he said, "I'll answer for it. We might be shipwrecked, but the document will be found and will still reach its destination."

With this delicate business thus concluded, they all resumed blowing on their fingers—for, in spite of the fire still being maintained in the oven, the cold was making itself keenly felt. After consulting the thermometer outside, Farandoul found that it was minus 48 degrees.

"What time is it?" he asked Mandibul.

"Nine o'clock," the latter replied, "but I don't know whether it's 9 a.m. or 9 p.m."

"It's evening—we still have another 15 hours of darkness."

"Damn, that's a long time! Come on, we must try to sleep. Two men had better stay on watch to maintain the fire."

"Not without a great deal of difficulty," said the master cook. "We have enough fuel for an hour—after that, we'll have to blow on our fingers."

"What about the herrings? Fire or death! We have the choice…and the choice is made, I think. In the face of that absolute necessity, we must resolve to burn the herrings! Save the little carbon and wood we have left for unforeseen circumstances, then, and keep the fire going with armful of herrings. They're quite fat, and will burn admirably!"

"Alas," said Mandibul, "here's a shoal of herrings that can consider itself unlucky for having run into us."

The cook, banishing all scruples, carried out Farandoul's orders and the first herrings crackled on the fire. The unfortunate castaways, rolled up in their bearskins and huddled into a compact mass, slept under the guard of two vestals charged with maintaining the fire.

Were their dreams rose-tinted? We cannot affirm it. In spite of the confidence affected by their leaders, everyone sensed that the situation of proprietors of a shoal of herrings left something to be desired in respect of security.

At about 4 a.m., the navigators were woken up by sharp itching sensations and violent fits of coughing. The itching was caused by chilblains and the coughing by the thick smoke that filled the cabin. They were half frozen and three-quarters asphyxiated!

After rubbing their hands, the unfortunate shipwreck-victims suddenly understood the danger. "Smoked! We'll be smoked by that herring-fire!" they cried, in chorus.

"No," said Tournesol, gallantly, "we'll only turn red."

The exclamations grew louder. The fire, continually fed by armfuls of herrings, gave out a moderate heat, but was, by way of compensation, belching out swirling clouds of reddish-brown smoke and emitting a frightful odor of grilled fish. The female castaways looked at one another by lantern-light. Within a few hours their faces and hands had taken on quite a marked russet tint.

"He's right!" they exclaimed. "We'll be as brown as kippers!"

"We won't dare show our faces in public!"

"Why did they have to come looking for us at the North Pole? After all, life was bearable there!"

"It's César Picolot's fault!"

César Picolot went pale. "O feminine ingratitude!" he cried. "I'm as brown as you are and I'm not complaining. When we disembark, you can say that it's the tropical Sun, or pass yourself off as Africans!"

"Let's wait for daylight," said Farandoul. "We'll de-smoke ourselves in the open air and replace the fire with vigorous exercise."

And they all tried to go back to sleep, after having begged the men on guard to moderate the combustion of herrings. Even so, after a few hours they could stand it no longer, and at 7 a.m., they decided to take a stroll outside in spite of the profound darkness.

"Minus 44 degrees," Mandibul observed. "That's quite bearable."

"Let's go!" cried Farandoul, taking the lead with lantern in hand. "At the double!"

Just then, a splendid aurora borealis suddenly lit up the sky. An intense light appeared on the horizon, grew a little, then soundlessly launched an immense spray of radiance, like ten bouquets of fireworks bursting at the same time, which persisted in their intensity. They could see as plainly as in broad daylight. In the distance, icebergs were bobbing on the sea: great sparkling masses like mountains of diamonds, more densely packed than ever. It was the edge of the great ice-field, the frightful polar ring of ice. They had got over it coming—would they have as much luck crossing it on the return journey?

The mariners were anxious. There was the danger. How would the shoal of herrings get past that obstacle?

"As long as they don't go underneath it!" murmured Mandibul.

The solicitor James Codgett jumped up and down. "And you protested against the indemnity of 2000 pounds that I claimed for sailing on your shoal of herrings! I'm raising it to 4000!"

"Don't worry," said Farandoul. "We shan't go under the ice-sheet—that's not the herrings' habit. Our shoal will go through some pass like the one we discovered on the way in."

And the entire company, well wrapped-up in their furs, set off at a jog on the backs of the herrings. They were glad to have impermeable boots, for the water came up to their ankles in places. The herrings disconcerted by this little excursion, had dived slightly under the weight of the castaways.

They covered two or three kilometers at a run without encountering anything else on the shoal but the two seals brought by Picolot. They were at the front, neck-deep in herrings. César Picolot had difficulty recognizing them, they had stuffed themselves with so much food. As he approached, they paused in levying their tribute from the unfortunate shoal and repeated a few joyful *paters* and *maters*.

"Bravo!" said Mandibul, caressing them with his eyes. "That will provide us with a nice roast when we're tired of fresh herring."

The rear of the shoal was less tranquil than the front, for more than 100 meters of the extremity they felt numerous somersaults beneath their feet and, in confusion, observed a sort of jostling. It soon stopped, though, and the ground resumed its solidity. The poor herrings of the rear-guard had numerous enemies behind them, large troops of hammerhead sharks were tormenting the shoal and devouring its members by the thousand; porpoises and cod were doing similar damage—but in the swirl of pirates that were rushing upon it in this manner, three or four whales[117] were most conspicuous of all in their voracity.

Farandoul and Mandibul went forward as far as possible to assess the situation, and were chagrined to see the harm done by the enormous cetaceans; every

---

[117] The term I have translated as "whale" here is *baleine*. Subsequently, the text introduces a distinction between *cachalots* [sperm whales]—a term I have retained, since it is also used in English—and other whales, implying that *baleine* ought thereafter to be construed in its narrower sense, meaning filter-feeding baleen whales. Robida still has such whales attacking the herrings, but this is far from being the worst of his offences against actual natural history.

time the whales launched themselves at the shoal they swallowed nearly a cubic meter of herrings.

"Damn!" murmured Farandoul. "That might become dangerous. We'll have to keep an eye on it."

Following his orders, the entire troop—which could not stop, under the threat of perishing of cold—headed back to the cabin, still at a jog, and came back at the same pace with an empty barrel. The barrel was set down some 30 meters from the extremity of the shoal, to serve as a reference-point, so as to gauge the extent of the ravages caused by the herrings' exceedingly numerous enemies.

When the aurora borealis suddenly died out, they went back to the cabin in darkness. It was time for breakfast; 200 herrings were only waiting for the castaways before perishing on the grill.

The master cook was smiling; Mandibul saw at the first glance that he was pleased with himself. "You!" he cried. "You're a rogue—you've got a surprise for us! Let's see, I'll wager that it's a matter of some leg of marine veal..."

The master pulled a disdainful face, which meant *better than that!*—and handed his superior a little piece of slightly greasy paper.

"A menu!" Mandibul exclaimed. "What a fine fellow you are, and what a pity you weren't the chef aboard the raft of the *Medusa*!"

The curious castaways gathered around Mandibul, who studied the menu, written and spelled in a very liberal fashion. Finally, he read:

Herring soup.
Smoked herring in cachalot oil.
Herring-egg omelet with marine algae.
Grilled herring.
Herring roes fried in oil, spiced with gunpowder.
Puréed herring.
Small pots of herring-milk cream.
Roe sorbet.
Beverages: Melted snow. Herring-spawn toddy.

"Splendid!" cried the entire company. "Let's go! To the table!"

It was a manner of speaking, for the table did not exist; everyone sat on the floor and breakfast got under way. The herring soup was found to be delicious, although a little too well-supplied with bones. The herring-egg omelets enjoyed the same success, but what excited the enthusiasm of the diners most was the arrival of the little pots of herring-milk cream. Two loaves of sugar, forgotten by Hatteras, had permitted the chef to make that cream into something intermediate between nectar and ambrosia; it was fine, delicate and fondant.

"Quite simply marvelous," said Mandibul, summarizing the general opinion. "We must make that herring cream known to the blasé palaces of rich

515

land-dwellers! On our return, we shall introduce it to the Faubourg Saint-Germain and the West End of London!"

There was only one shadow over the scene and one slightly discontented diner. That was Mrs. Hatteras, who nearly choked on a stray bone in the sorbet. Had it not been for Mandibul, who hastened to her assistance, the poor lady might perhaps have perished. The master cook, desolate at the accident, attributed the overlooking of the bone to the negligence one of his assistants and heaped reproaches upon the unfortunate, whom he threatened to deprive of toddy. Mrs. Hatteras, feeling somewhat better, went to some trouble to obtain mercy for him. The master cook felt that his reputation had been compromised and remained severe, but finally forgave him.

Dawn broke as they were finishing the toddies. It was ten minutes to noon; a pale Sun appeared, like an immense dim lantern hanging in the sky, and shone wanly for three hours, after which the dim lantern went out, giving way to the Moon, a timid night-light still half-hidden behind a veil of fog.

"Shall we have a nice siesta?" proposed one of the German scientists, weighed down by the plentiful breakfast.

"Certainly not!" cried Farandoul. "It's necessary to stimulate the circulation of the blood and breathe the pure air. Off we go, at the double!"

Farandoul was right. It was necessary not to allow the castaways to become numb through inaction; it was necessary to remain active and indulge in violent movement without respite. The female castaways, suppressing a few sighs, got up and followed the mariners; they resumed jogging around the floating and living island. At the front, Picolot's seals were sleeping with the blissful smiles of satisfied gastronomes. In the rear, the porpoises, hammerheads, cod, cachalots and other whales were continuing their assaults, tormenting the unfortunate herrings. The distance between the barrel and the edge had diminished considerably.

"Wait a minute, though!" murmured Farandoul. "The herrings are our friends; we mustn't allow them to be devoured like this! We have to defend them!"

"But how?"

"Any way we can, damn it! We have rifles and hatchets…unfortunately, we only have one chloroform bomb—we must try to use it cleverly."

"That's right!" howled Tournesol. "Fight! Let's not allow our herrings to be eaten…by anyone but us!"

They resumed jogging to return to the cabin. They came straight back out again, returning to the rear of the shoal with two iron buoys. As they arrived there, the reference-point barrel had just been reached by the enemy; a cachalot greedier than the rest, seeing this significant prey, disdained the herrings and swallowed it whole. As it seemed somewhat indisposed after this violent effort, Tournesol took advantage of its condition to attack it with hatchet-blows; the frightened cachalot made a violent effort and spat the barrel out, intact, before disappearing beneath the waves.

Farandoul and Mandibul had the buoys carried as far as possible and jumped inside them in order to do battle with the herrings' enemies. Ropes retained in the mariners' hands prevented them from drifting away. Cachalots and other whales were soon within their range and blood ran freely; attacked with spear-thrusts to the body, the cetaceans responded with violent blows of their flukes and charges from the depths beneath the buoys. In that crowded environment, though, mixed up with the laggards of the shoal, battalions of porpoises and hammerheads, the cetaceans could not easily maneuver their terrible flukes. At each attack, Farandoul and Mandibul withdrew their whole bodies into the interior and, as the buoys were solidly built, got away with severe jolts.

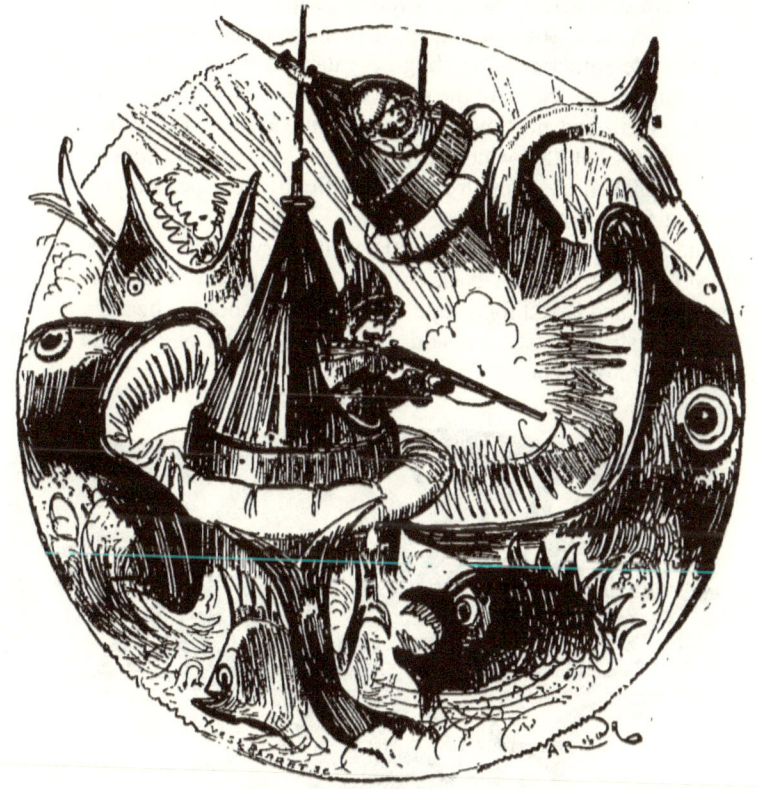

Meanwhile, the unoccupied men were making sturdy lassos with the ropes and, not being able to fight the fish in the liquid element, lassoed them from a distance after the fashion of gauchos; when they succeeded in catching one, they dragged it on to the shoal by the strength of their arms and killed it swiftly, in spite of the formidable sideswipes launched by the cetaceans' flukes.

The cachalots, smaller than the other whales, suffered most and lost two or three of their number, mortally wounded; few others, injured to some degree, fell behind in order to recover. The other whales came out of it better, though; spear-thrusts in their thick layers of fat had little effect. On seeing that, Farandoul abandoned his spear and seized the last chloroform bomb. In order not to get in his way, Mandibul climbed back on to the shoal.

Farandoul waited for the whales to attack; just as the largest of the cetaceans came forward with its mouth open to swallow the buoy, Farandoul, pressing the trigger, swiftly threw the bomb into the gaping maw and signaled to the mariners on the shoal to haul on the retaining rope—a maneuver that they executed immediately.

The enormous whale, having swallowed the chloroform bomb, remained still momentarily, as if stupefied; then, shaken by an interior commotion, it performed a terrible somersault, sending up cataracts of sea-water with its fluke, and, leaping upwards, fell on to the shoal of herrings with frightful violence.

The mariners had no time to retreat. A breach was made in the densely-packed herrings—but the whale, after that terrible effort, suddenly stopped, seemed to be shaken by a few tremors, and finally became completely motionless on the surface of the waves.

Farandoul, emerging from the buoy, slid forward as far as possible and jumped up on the cetacean's back. After a few minutes' study, he planted his spear in its flesh and asked for a rope with which to moor the beast.

"It was a strong dose," he said. "It's dead. That's one enemy less and a good provision of oil to boot."

VII.

Two hours sufficed for the skillful mariners to extract a few barrels of oil from the chloroformed whale without much difficulty. Tournesol declared it excellent. It was a fine windfall for our friends; they would be able to use the oil to fry herrings for meals and it would also make a good provision of light for the interminable polar nights.

As they finished filling the barrels a thick fog suddenly formed, covering the wan polar Sun with a somber veil. Within a few minutes, everything vanished: the sky, the assailants of the herring shoal, and the shoal itself; they could see no further than 25 centimeters. Farandoul, taken by surprise, could not find his lantern to re-light it. The scattered mariners only managed to gather around their superior officers after numerous stumbles and falls; fortunately, the female castaway had not strayed far from the main group. Only the solicitor Codgett lost his way and fell into the open mouth of the chloroformed whale.

While trying to get out of that gulf, Codgett was in so much of a hurry that the jaw snapped shut of its own accord and he remained a prisoner. He was gripped by a terrible fear; he thought he had been swallowed by a living whale and collapsed, almost unconscious, on the cetacean's baleens.

Meanwhile, Farandoul took a roll-call and established his disappearance. Tournesol recalled that he had been beside him before the fog came down, but had not heard him since. Codgett was lost! Perhaps he had walked toward the rear of the shoal and fallen into the midst of the cachalots!

Farandoul told everyone to shout loudly.

"Ahoy! Ahoy! Cod...gett! Cod...gett!"

"Ahoy, you old porpoise!"

"Over here, you freshwater shark! Ahoy!"

Everyone cocked an anxious ear, but no sound came in reply. Inside his whale, however, Codgett could hear perfectly. He had come round, surprised not to be dead yet; having no understanding of the situation, he judged it prudent not to move, in order not to give the whale the idea of finishing its work. He made himself very small, and refrained from replying to the calls of the mariners.

In the end, Farandoul concluded that the solicitor had gone back to the cabin and thought of doing likewise—but as they had turned to all points of the compass in order to hail Codgett, they had lost the way, and when the time came to leave they could no longer determine the direction of the cabin in the fog. Which way should they go? Forwards, backwards, right or left? No one could tell. They set off at hazard, holding hands. After ten minutes, Farandoul, who was in the lead, put his foot in the water and realized that he had reached the shore of the floating island, one of the flanks of the shoal.

They moved backwards and took another direction at hazard. The sound of jaws and seething water indicated with no possibility of error that they had returned to their point of departure, to the place attacked by the cachalots.

They made an about-turn and walked straight ahead. Another quarter-hour of marching through the fog, and the sea again! They were lost again. If it had not been for Mandibul, who had extremely sensitive olfactory nerves, the marches and counter-marches might have gone on for a long time, but he suddenly scented a very distinct emanation of grilled herring. Taking charge of the troop, he marched straight towards the source of the emanation, and after ten minutes, bumped his head on the cabin door. The master cook was there, tending the fire.

"Come on!" cried Farandoul. "Light another lantern, and let's get back out there!"

The castaways made a few observations, and claimed to be exhausted.

"It doesn't matter! It's necessary to keep moving anyway. In this terrible cold, inaction would be fatal. We'll go in search of the unfortunate Codgett and our barrels of oil. When we come back, I promise the men a nice swig of rum and the women as many herrings as they want. Forward!"

The fog was still as thick and the lantern, at three paces, was a mere red stain. This time, however, they did not go astray; after a quarter of an hour's march, they ran into the chloroformed whale again.

The four barrels full of whale-oil were there. It only remained to find the unfortunate Codgett.

The unfortunate Codgett was still in his whale, where he as awaiting developments, fainting and coming round by turns. More *ahoys* were shouted nearby without his daring to reply. People were already accusing the innocent cachalots of having eaten him between two mouthfuls of herring when Mandibul, on going around the whale, picked up a fur bonnet, which everyone recognized as having belonged to the solicitor.

Damn! Mandibul said to himself. *If our whale weren't chloroformed, I'd suspect it of having sequestered Codgett.* Mechanically, he introduced the butt of his rifle into the monster's mouth to lift it up slightly. "Uh oh!" he said, taking a step back. "What's that?"

Farandoul handed him the lantern. Mandibul slid it cautiously into the open mouth. "A boot!" he cried. "Our unfortunate companion has been swallowed! The whale wasn't entirely dead!"

Handing the lantern back to the seamen, Mandibul seized the boot and tugged violently. A muffled groan emerged from the gulf; the boot came out with a confused mass attached.

"Alive! He's still alive!"

Everyone pressed forward, and the haggard solicitor Codgett, his hair bristling on one side and stuck down on the other, was set on his feet, with considerable difficulty. When he had been thoroughly rubbed, cleaned and shaken, they were forced to conclude that he had sustained no damage. A loud discussion followed. Codgett claimed that he had been well and truly swallowed, and left no delay in laying claim to a further indemnity.

In the end, Mandibul got annoyed.

"You claim to have been eaten by a living whale? Very well, I agree with you; by virtue of that fact you claim an indemnity of 1000 pounds from Madame Hatteras. Perfect! I agree with you again! But for your part, you must agree that I have extracted you from the bosom of that whale, and you'll agree with me that in claiming a salvage fee of an equal sum of 1000 pounds, I'm not asking too much! You're worth more than that!"

James Codgett made a face and did not say another word.

"Let's see to our oil now," Mandibul went on.

They had brought two or three saucepans and a few smaller receptacles. Farandoul had them filled with oil, fitted them with wicks improvised with spare clothes and disposed these lamps at intervals on the edge of the shoal.

"Now our shoal of herrings is illuminated, at least we won't get lost again. Now, back to the cabin!"

Leaving this unusual illumination behind them, the entire troop went back to the cabin, rolling the barrels of oil. The promised grog awaited them; after that had been ingurgitated, Farandoul busied himself making an enormous signal-light, which was hoisted on to a little mast on top of the cabin.

Night came, and with it more intense cold. Mandibul, consulting the thermometer, found it to be minus 48 degrees!

"A little more fire!" ordered Farandoul.

Further armfuls of herrings were thrown on the fire. The flames sprang up, along with swirls of brown smoke. The castaways of the fair sex gave voice to further exclamations of protest.

"There's no middle way," Mandibul told them. "It's freeze or be smoked!"

"Or get back to the gymnastics," Farandoul put in.

"Let's burn everything here that will burn!" cried one of the ladies. "There's the piano, which is no use to us…"

"I beg your pardon, but the piano serves us as a buffet; it's in its flanks that we've arranged what green stuff we were able to bring away from the Pole. Those salads, carefully, managed, will enable us to avoid scurvy!"

"Well, put the salads somewhere else—in an iron buoy, for instance—and burn the piano."

"Wretched child!" cried Mandibul. "That piano whose combustion you're demanding won't furnish us with more than five minutes of fire; it's a ridiculous piece of furniture from which we can't extract anything…but in the present circumstances, it's precious to us as a buffet. Then again, in the case of a further shipwreck, remember that its case, being perfectly watertight, would become a lifeboat for one person."

The piano was saved once more; the ladies resigned themselves to being smoked in silence until dinner-time. The meal, less whimsical than the breakfast, was primarily characterized by its abundant solidity. Enormous whale-meat steaks formed its main course, and herrings were only invoked as hors-d'oeuvres and dessert.

"Minus 49!" cried Mandibul, on leaving the table. "Quickly! Don't get numb, my lads—extreme gymnastics!" And, matching example to speech, he engaged in a skillful bout of boxing with the solicitor Codgett.

Everyone understood the absolute necessity of these violent exercises; it resulted in a general mêlée in which slaps and shoves were liberally distributed and joyfully received. The circulation of the blood was soon reestablished; the numbness disappeared. Then the pushes and punches were accepted less philosophically; a few grimaces and little squeals accompanied their reception. A momentary respite was granted; numerous bruises were observed and, on the person of the solicitor Codgett, a black eye, which he claimed to owe to the solicitude of Mrs. Hatteras.

The gymnastics and the boxing having become tiresome for the moment, it was necessary to find something else.

"Dancing," suggested one of the female castaways.

"Adopted!" replied Farandoul. "But we have no orchestra and you know very well that the piano is empty."

The master cook leapt upon an iron buoy, and his assistants precipitated themselves on two saucepans. The orchestra was found. It immediately launched into a portentous piece with a magisterial beat, in which César Picolot—who had an ear for music—claimed to recognize one of the most remarkable of Beethoven's symphonies.

"Isn't that the Pastoral Symphony that you're playing?" he asked the leader of the orchestra.

The master cook, nonplussed, looked at his pupils, who shook their heads in embarrassment. The poor devils were playing the Pastoral Symphony without knowing it!

"We won't play reveries or ballads to the Moon," César Picolot went on. "It's not what the situation calls for. We need uplifting music—something catchy...."

"A polka!" roared Mandibul.

"A jig!" shouted Kirkson.

"Sainte-Anne-d'Auray!"[118] howled Trabadec. "If only I had some bagpipes!"

The galvanized musicians struck up the opening bars of "I've got good tobacco in my snuffbox" on their saucepans.

The dancers stopped.

"That's not it!" cried Mandibul.

"We know what to do!" the three German scientists suddenly exclaimed, emerging from the crowd. "Give us the instruments!" And, taking possession of the saucepans and the iron buoy, the scientists produced a vibrant melody. "This is Richard Wagner!" they cried.

Mandibul had paused; a vague memory was coming back to him. He seemed to have heard it before somewhere. Suddenly, he slapped his forehead. These fragments of the Richard Wagner's *Ring* were very similar to certain pieces by the quadrumane maestro Coco, had once played in the Opera *mixte* in Melbourne. Thus were confirmed the rumors that had circulated, according to which Richard Wagner had cruelly imprisoned the unfortunate monkey maestro in a cave at Bayreuth in order to force him to compose the music for his operas.

Horror! But there was no time for sentiment; it was necessary to devote himself to movement. Mandibul issued a gracious invitation to Mrs. Hatteras, and the two of them launched into the first steps of an idiosyncratic dance. The seamen followed his example. The cabin soon became too small and the dancers, braving the rigors of the polar cold, spilled outside.

Just then the herring shoal was brightly illuminated by a splendid aurora borealis. No opera-house chandelier or ballroom candelabra could ever have rivaled that magnificent and entirely gratuitous lighting. Mandibul, who had once regularly frequented the salons of the president of the Republic of Haiti, de-

---

[118] The association of the Breton Sainte-Anne-d'Auray with dancing arose because the departure of Medieval pilgrimages from her principal seat of worship were allegedly celebrated with quasi-Bacchanalian partying.

clared that the splendors of most the brilliant diplomatic receptions were being absolutely eclipsed, in his mind, by the dazzle of that ball of the herring shoal.

After the waltzes came the polka, and the polkas were succeeded by jigs.

"An intoxicating night!" murmured Mrs. Hatteras. "A magical ball! Ah! The pure calm of this delightful evening is even soothing the memory of my misfortunes…"

She was still talking when she found herself suddenly sitting on the ground, with Mandibul lying in front of her. The music had stopped. Most of the dancers were lying on their backs with their legs in the air, trying to figure out why they had fallen over.

Farandoul was the first to get to his feet.

"An earthquake!" cried one of the German scientists, a very eminent geologist.

"No," retorted Farandoul, "a herring-quake! Be careful—watch out for aftershocks!"

The ground shook; a sequence of violent movements agitated the shoal to port and starboard, fore and aft. The people who had stood up had a great deal of difficulty remaining upright. A few crevasses were opening in the shoal and a huge wave was breaking almost on top of the poor castaways.

"Into the cabin!" Farandoul ordered.

The ball was over. The unfortunate dancers, ankle-deep in water, had a great deal of difficulty maintaining their equilibrium. The shocks soon diminished in intensity, though, and then came to a complete stop. The castaways dried themselves and shivered in front of the fire.

"What does it mean?" asked Mrs. Hatteras.

"It's definitely an earthquake," the geologist insisted. "Our shoal must have felt the repercussion of some Plutonian cataclysm…."

"Go on, then!" exclaimed Mandibul. "Are you going to tell us there's been a volcanic eruption next? A volcano on our shoal—that would be very convenient to warm us up! Unfortunately, it's something more serious…"

"What? What is it?"

"Our shoal is getting angry. After having supported our weight without a murmur as we came aboard, then our comings and goings, then the tax imposed by our appetite, our herrings are finally getting angry, and our ball has tipped them over the edge. Our jigs and polkas on their backs have annoyed them, and they're letting us know it! What's need now is gentleness and tranquility, to persuade them to endure patiently the overly numerous irritations we have caused them, for if we persevere in our agitation, the shoal will enter into all-out rebellion and—who knows?—the greatest misfortunes…"

"Oh, a revolution!" said the sailors, waving their swords "The herrings are trying to scare us…"

"That's not the point! What we have to worry about is the dislocation of the shoal—battalions of herrings dispersing to the right and the left while we go straight down into the icy water…"

The solicitor Codgett turned abruptly to Mrs. Hatteras. "Do you hear, Madam!" he cried. "There are the pleasures of the case of Hatteras versus Hatteras! And you quibble about just compensation!"

"Calm down, solicitor—we're not there yet," Mandibul went on. "The herrings seem to have quietened down; harmony will be restored between them and us! Treat them with politeness, respect and diplomacy and I'll answer for everything!"

"Save for meal-times," put in one of the mariners, in a mild voice.

"At meal-times, of course, the considerations are suspended and we shall stifle the plaints of our victims in the frying-pan—but, by way of compensation, we shall fight between meals in defense of the shoal against the voracious cachalots. And now, it's 9 p.m.; let's forget our sufferings in sleep!"

The most complete calm soon reigned in the cabin and on the shoal. Until morning, no tremor disturbed the castaways' slumber. At 7 a.m., Mandibul, full of joy, sounded the reveille by banging a saucepan loudly on an iron buoy.

The master cook resumed his duties and served an agreeable breakfast of herring-milk coffee. Fortunately for the castaways, the cold had diminished considerably; the thermometer marked no more than 41 degrees Centigrade below zero. When Farandoul proposed a walk in the open air, no one even dreamed of protesting; they all picked up their weapons, sealed themselves as hermetically as possible in their furs and made ready to follow him.

Outside, dawn had not yet broken, but a superb moonlight illuminated the shoal and made the distant jagged masses of numerous icebergs glitter.

"Softly, softly!" repeated Mandibul.

"And death to the cachalots!" replied the castaways. "Let's defend our shoal!"

The rear of the shoal of herrings could not by any means pass for a domain of tranquility. The cachalots, porpoises and hammerheads, more numerous than ever, were still engaged in attacking the poor herrings. The shoal had lost seven or eight meters to the predations of these cruel enemies during the night. The inroads had been frightful, almost reaching the bowls of oil set to light the shoal.

The sailors were equipped with planks, which they placed as close as possible to the extreme edge of the shoal, and reached out from these moving plants with hatchets or harpoons in hand to meet the cachalots. One corner, singled out for attack by hammerheads, became the combat position of the seamen under Tournesol's command.

The battle began: violent assaults on the part of the cachalots, prodigious kill and agility on the part of the mariners. The affair soon became more hectic, and the poor herrings enjoyed a moment of respite. Two cachalots, killed by harpoon-thrusts, were solidly moored and served, so to speak, as a forward bastion. Standing on their backs, the mariners greeted the boldest or most reckless of the cachalots with the points of harpoons, while Farandoul and Mandibul, mounted on iron buoys on the flanks, launched themselves at intervals into the midst of the assailants.

At the places attacked by porpoises and hammerheads, the castaways were also performing prodigies of valor. Mrs. Hatteras, in particular, distinguished herself by her courage and skill; in the first hour of the battle, three porpoises, a little overstuffed with herring and hindered in their movements by corpulence, ended their careers beneath her valiant hand, and six hammerheads only avoided certain death by taking cowardly flight.

In three hours, the herring shoal lost no more than a further meter and a half from the 30-meter rear, which amounted to only 45 cubic meters, or 81,000 herrings—not counting the remaining side-edges, assailed by the small fry of sharks, tuna, cod and other less significant enemies.

Everything was, therefore, going well. Just as the mariners, taking advantage of a moment of respite in the attack, were congratulating one another on their fine defense of the shoal, however, a violent shock similar to those of the night suddenly knocked them over and threw the entire company into an indescribable confusion. That first shock was followed by a series of irregular movements and intermittent shocks, during which the shoal seemed to be threatened by imminent disintegration.

When the first moment of surprise had passed, the mariners got to their feet again and looked for the cause of these unexpected phenomena. Farandoul and Mandibul understood very quickly. At the other end of the shoal, to the right and the left, immense icebergs were extending their jagged summits out of the water—and the shoal, instead of avoiding them and swimming through the more tranquil channel ahead of them seemed, on the contrary, to be launching themselves directly at their sides.

"*Sacrebleu!*" cried Farandoul.

"*Ventre de phoque!*" roared Mandibul.

"What? What?" demanded the anxious female castaways, while the mariners calmly awaited their leaders' orders.

"What! The herrings are definitely in revolt. They're showing dire ingratitude towards us, who have been fighting all morning in their defense. Look! Our herring shoal is scraping the icebergs in the hope of throwing water over our cabin and us!"

James Codgett whimpered inarticulately.

"Don't worry!" Farandoul went on. "We'll stay all the same. We'll fight to the end, and we'll triumph!"

"Are we far from the coast of Holland?" asked Codgett, feebly.

"I suppose we must have covered 50 or 60 leagues since our departure from the Pole, but I can't tell exactly where we are or where we're headed, all our instruments being at the bottom of the sea. Now, back to the cabin, and let's see what happens with regard to the icebergs."

And the whole company, holding hands for fear of accidents, headed toward the center of the shoal, abandoning the rear to the attacks of the cachalots. The tremors continued and they were spilled on to the moving floor more than once. Farandoul, Mandibul and four men headed for the icebergs, leaving the rest of the company in the cabin, with instructions to avoid overly violent movements.

The shoal was still scraping. Farandoul and Mandibul, getting forward with considerable difficulty, saw the herrings precipitating themselves at the icy masses with a mad range, after the fashion of a furious bull hurling itself at a picador's horse. The situation was grave. At each shock to the head, the shoal splintered; entire fragments sliced away by the ice dispersed in meager groups immediately tracked by hammerheads, or formed small separate shoals, offshoots of the flagship shoal.

The assaulted icebergs also broke sometimes under the impact and crumbled on to the shoal, which creased under the weight and was split by long crevasses. In the midst of the whirlwinds of foam, mingled with herrings, which every impact sent up, two unfortunate creatures were in danger: César Picolot's two seal pupils. Atoning for the immense greed they had indulged since their arrival on the shoal, it was impossible for them to move and quit the post, dangerous now, that they had taken up. The space separating the icebergs was diminishing rapidly, and the poor seals, half-dead with terror, were no longer thinking of stuffing themselves with herrings.

There was no way out of the situation; behind them the shoal was already breaking up. The fatal moment would soon arrive. Suddenly, the impact of a monumental iceberg sent them flying through the air and they disappeared before the mariners' grieving eyes.

"There's the danger," said Farandoul, "and there's no means of combating it effectively. We have to be patient and hope that the shoal will calm down. While we wait, let's return to the cabin and strengthen it as much as possible."

The cabin had suffered somewhat from the successive shocks that had shaken it. The mariners were already busy with indispensable repairs. Farandoul's first concern was to consolidate the fragile floor on which it rested. He had all the barrels saved from disaster slid underneath, and also the empty piano. The planks were spaced out slightly to cover a larger area and solidly joined together with carefully-pinned spars. This operating visibly soothed the shoal, for it appeared to be scraping the icebergs more gently.

The great crisis seemed to have passed. Nevertheless, as a prudent measure, Farandoul had a large fragment of mast laid down horizontally in front of the cabin, in order to ward off, as far as was possible, the danger of running unexpectedly aground.

Everyone was more tranquil; all immediate danger seemed to have been dispelled and they were able to think about preparations for dinner. Night had fallen—a night deprived of all illumination, for the Moon was veiled by thick cloud and no aurora borealis illuminated the depths of the sky.

The herrings provided the entire meal, with a lichen salad in pure cachalot-oil, but no one complained; combat and the ground-quakes had given everyone a raging appetite.

After the meal, they had no need to go back to gymnastics, in view of the relative mildness of the temperature—minus 42 degrees—and spent the evening peacefully in the luxury of general conversation. The German scientists, who had saved their pipes from all the successive shipwrecks, sought a means of replacing the absent tobacco; after numerous trials they succeeded in fabricating a pseudo-tobacco from the fur of their bearskins mixed with small herring-bones. The female castaways complained a little about the clouds of nauseating smoke emitted by the pipes, but they soon got used to it.

When Tournesol had intoned a few old drinking-songs, César Picolot begged the castaway artistes to cheer the company up with a few of the brighter items in their repertoire. Madame Léa (d'Arcis-sur-Aube), a fine singer, obtained a great success with an item from *La Favorite*,[119] and Madame Bichard declaimed a verse narrative improvised by César Picolot, who improvised its stanzas as she went along:

> *It was far far, away in the polar snows,*
> *On a barren and mobile herring shoal,*
> *Enemies everywhere snapping their jaws,*
> *Sharks on the lookout, taking their toll,*[120]
> *That poor castaways....*

By the 175th stanza, everyone was asleep; the courageous artiste followed suit, and Picolot, ensconced in his bearskin, began the 176th:

> *The unfortunate herrings, too anxious to run,*
> *To the foggy bank where...shivered....the frying-pan...*

He did not finish, but slumped forward and falling asleep. His rhythmic snoring seemed to conserve the Alexandrine form for some time, but in the end the lyre was extinguished and Picolot, after a few snores of 13 or 14 feet without a cesura, snored in prose like any common mortal.

The company's unanimously calm and pure sleep lasted several hours. All of a sudden, Farandoul woke up, the sound of something scraping on the wall of the cabin having attracted his attention. He listened. The scraping continued. Mandibul and a few other men also awoke.

"What's that?" asked Farandoul. "Has someone gone out?"

"No, we're all here...it's a stranger!"

"A stranger! Is there someone else on our herring shoal?"

A formidable thump on the wall provided conclusive evidence that there really was someone outside. Everyone was sitting up.

"Who goes there?" demanded Farandoul, picking up a lantern.

---

[119] The opera *La Favorite* (1840) had music by Gaetano Donizetti and a libretto by Alphonse Royer and Gustave Vaez.

[120] As usual, I have made a small sacrifice of accuracy in order to conserve the rhyme-scheme and approximate the scansion of Robida's original.

The only response was another violent blow. The stranger certainly had only the vaguest idea of politeness. With a lantern in one hand and a hatchet in the other, Mandibul went to the door to greet the visitor, followed by several armed men.

Mandibul had no sooner pushed the door ajar and stick out the hand holding the lantern than a sudden impact ripped the door from its hinges and knocked it flat. At the same time, a white form precipitated itself into the cabin on to the group of mariners.

The stranger was a gigantic white bear. It was poor Tournesol which received its first embrace; in response to the vigorous hatchet-blows landed on its thick skull by the mariner, furious at being disturbed, the white bear grabbed Tournesol between its paws and crushed him to its body.

Fortunately, Mandibul had seized a Turkish khanjar made of Damascus steel, which he always carried with him in memory of certain odalisques with whom he had almost perished, stitched in a sack. With a firm hand, he sought out a plum spot in the bear's back and plunged it in all the way to the hilt. The bear immediately opened its arms and released Tournesol in order to turn on Mandibul—but four mariners seized it by the paws from behind, tipped it backwards and finished it off with knife-thrusts.

"Where is the security of our shoal of herrings?" cried James Codgett. "Where, now that it's inhabited by polar bears? Oh, the case of Hatteras versus Hatteras…"

"What are you complaining for?" riposted Mandibul. "Don't you understand what chance has sent us? Just as we were beginning to get tired of eating nothing but herrings and more herrings, Providence, which never abandons us, sends us something else. That white bear will be delicious, spit-roasted…"

"I'm not saying anything different. Perhaps I'll find it delicious tomorrow—but that doesn't alter the fact that it would also have been very well able to find me delicious today. Henceforth, I shan't dare to go walking on the shoal…"

"Bah! That bear must have fallen from one of the icebergs that our shoal grazed; we probably won't have the same luck twice."

The mariners were of the same mind as Mandibul. They went out, led by Farandoul, to see whether the bear might have a comrade prowling in the vicinity. They soon came back empty-handed; no bear had had turned up.

The shoal of herrings, doubtless tormented by the coming and goings provoked by the unexpected visit of the white bear, started scraping the icebergs again. The rest of the night was disturbed by various shocks and prolonged tremors.

At 7 a.m., the Moon slid out of the veil of cloud that had obscured it until then, and its rays illuminated the shoal sufficiently to allow the castaways to leave the cabin. Farandoul immediately took advantage of the opportunity to make a general tour of inspection.

As soon as he stepped away from the cabin, he noticed numerous moving crevasses streaking the shoal in every direction. In certain places, he sank to his knees amid less densely-packed herrings. Further away, the shoal had caved in over a rather large area and the bottom of the hole was full of sea-water fed into it by several steams running through the crevasses. The herring shoal   a floating and living island—now possessed a lake 20 meters wide and rivers. At the front, where the greatest threat was, the disaster had taken on the greatest proportions. The shoal had lost more than 150 meters during the night, and the disintegration was continuing. The crevasses were growing wider; from time to time a fragment of the shoal, complexly detached, separated from the bulk of the troop and vanished behind the icebergs.

The pensive Farandoul headed for the rear, followed by the mariners, marching with infinite precaution. The shoal had also lost much of its width; the sides, incessantly scraped by the icebergs, were gradually rumbling. Instead of the 500 meters of width with which it had started out, the shoal could now count little more than 350.

At the rear, things were not changing as rapidly; thanks to the reference-points established by the mariners, the calculation was easy. The shoal had only lost 7,50 meters to the teeth of the cachalots and other voracious enemies.

"If we can't do anything against these icebergs," said Farandoul, "we can do a great deal against the cachalots! Let's fight to ensure that our shoal lasts as long as possible!"

VIII.

We have no intention of following our friends' monotonous voyage on the herring shoal day by day, for fear of falling into details devoid of interest. We say *monotonous*, because the first few days, which we have described at length, were followed by a very considerable number of almost identical days. The most complete monotony was the essential characteristic of that long journey, which lasted no less than 28 days and four hours.

Monotony in occupations. Every morning, before dawn, a tour of inspection, reparation to the cabin for breakfast; then, combat at the rear from sunrise to sunset, and even during the evening when the Moon was full.

Monotony in nourishment. Always herring and cachalot, and more herring and cachalot! The master cook was very ingenious, and found new culinary combinations every day, but it was still only herring and cachalot.

Monotony in recreations. Gymnastics having been abandoned to avoid annoying the shoal, they were reduced to innocent games and soirées exclusively devoted to literature and dancing. When they were very tired—and only then—Farandoul permitted César Picolot to give public performances of the produce of his lyre; usually, the audience would depart for the land of dreams around the 12th or 15th stanza.

To occupy the long evenings, the solicitor James Codgett offered to give a series of lectures on the civil and criminal codes of procedure, but his idea was welcomed with such scant enthusiasm that he took offence and retreated into his bearskin, promising to demanded compensation for the injury to his self-respect from Mrs. Hatteras.

César Picolot, however, desirous of finding an outlet for lucubrations of great literature, has a stroke of genius. He decided to found a literary periodical on the slightly-reduced model of the *Revue des Deux Mondes*. After having meditated for eight days and nights as to what title to give this compilation, he decided on:

THE RED HERRING

A MARITIME AND LITERARY GAZETTE

Published daily on Farandoul Shoal,

A great shoal of herrings in the process of voyaging from the North Pole to the coast of Holland

Editor-in-chief: César Picolot - Editorial secretary: James Codgett

The *Red Herring* having not set caution aside, politics was forbidden; it therefore limited itself to giving, every morning, a summary of the previous day's events, augmented by the reflections and suppositions of the editor-in-chief, on the front page, and a few words on the events of the night—if any—in the stop press. The rest of the paper was devoted to philosophy and literature.

Let us not forget to say that the *Red Herring* appeared on headed notepaper at a shilling a sheet. César Picolot did not recoil at any luxury, and yet the paper, absolutely devoid of subscribers, brought him no reward. The print-run comprised one single and unique manuscript copy, which Picolot attached personally to the cabin door every morning at 8 a.m. The headed paper, it is true, cost him nothing but a literary sacrifice. Picolot had stolen the first sheets from the solicitor Codgett; then, when the latter complained, he had bought the rest of the supply by admitting the solicitor to the editorial staff in the capacity of secretary and by consenting to publish as a serial *Considerations on Roman and Britannic Law* by James Codgett, solicitor, 7 Chancery Lane, open from one till five, circumstances permitting.

The most remarkable item in the first issue of the *Red Herring* was a sonnet entitled:

THE ICEBERG

by Madame L. d'A (s.A.)

It commenced thus:

Enormous block, bristling with spires of frost.

The iceberg, etc. etc.

And terminated:
...and your heart, Madame,
Is sharper and colder than the berg!

After the sonnet came an article on the education of seals and a few brief philosophical pensées signed "Descartes junior."

It is by means of a few extracts from the *Red Herring* that we shall continue our narrative of our friends' voyage on the great shoal of herrings; disdaining trivial facts, we shall choose only the most remarkable and the most touching episodes of that dramatic journey.

It is the issues of May 27 and 28, July 5, 7 and 8 and September 11 that will furnish us with the necessary materials of our work of condensation. Readers desirous of following all the ups and downs of the drama may consult the very full report of Lieutenant Mandibul and the complete collection of the *Red Herring* in the archives of the Société de la Géographie, or peruse Monsieur César Picolot's own account in the *Revue des Deux Mondes*.

We begin:

May 27

ANOTHER HERRING-QUAKE

Last night, as a result of unknown irritations, the herring shoal reverted, with an indomitable fury, to scrape against all the icebergs that we incessantly run across in the course of our journey to more fortunate climes. The first shock was felt at 11:35 p.m.; it lasted three minutes 27 seconds, during which the cabin never stopped creaking violently.

After an interval of ten minutes, the tremors resumed, even more violently, until morning.

At the moment when these lines are being written, the appreciable damage consists of a series of profound cracks in the port-side wall of our cabin, a collapse of the forward external planking and, most importantly, injuries and contusions of varying degrees of seriousness sustained by the following persons:

Madame Bichart, dramatic artiste, a bruise on the left shoulder.

Monsieur Trabadec, mariner, a bloody nose caused by the fall of a piece of the ceiling.

Monsieur James Codgett, editorial secretary of the Red Herring, *numerous bruises and general curvature.*

Madame Hatteras, gentlewoman, contusions.

May 28

THE DISASTER

As our readers know, the central part of the shoal has been more resistant than the rest to the formidable shocks that have continued without interruption since yesterday.

The forepart has suffered particularly, as in previous catastrophes. At first light, Commodore Farandoul organized a relief operation to the threatened locales; our editor-in-chief, admitted to the number of volunteers for that expedition, displayed throughout the entire day a courage and activity that excited the admiration of all the witnesses to his heroism.

Thanks to the measurements taken, it was possible to estimate at 39 meters the portion of the shoal that has crumbled under the repeated impacts with the icebergs. Commodore Farandoul attempted by all possible means to oppose and halt the disintegration of the shoal; standing with a few men at the extreme forward point, skillfully directing the maneuver, he succeeded, with the aid of a long wooden beam, in pushing back the icebergs with which the shoal had made contact, but that was accomplished at the price of superhuman fatigue and running immense dangers.

Thanks to his efforts, the shoal did not lose more than six meters in the first half of the day, but in the afternoon, even huger icebergs having appeared, the maneuvering of the beam no longer had sufficient effect and the disaster assume colossal proportions.

The exhausted expedition was forced to beat a retreat to the cabin in order not to risk disappearing into the ocean depths with the crumbling fragments of the shoal.

The day's losses are estimated at 150 meters.

CACHALOT AND COD
A Drinking-Song

The refrains of alternating currents will suffice to give an idea of this new production of the muse of César Picolot, who still sings with much success in the elegant cabarets of Norway:

FIRST COUPLET

Let us now with Eskimo liqueur
Snap our fingers at Death, that boor

....

....

With pleasure and souls consigned to God
Let us drink the liver oil of cod!

SECOND COUPLET
To have a pale complexion not,
Let us drink the oil of the cachalot!

July 5

OFFICIAL SURVEY: WIDTH 121 METERS; LENGTH 380

Combat continues at the rear of our shoal and on a part of the starboard flank.

We have only had a week of calm following the extermination of the cacha-lots on June 26, in the glorious battle in which our editor-in-chief, Monsieur César Picolot, literally covered himself with laurels. For a week our shoal had only sustained the less dangerous assaults of porpoises and hammerheads, but yesterday morning the lookouts signaled a tribe of cachalots to the south, which seemed to be waiting for the shoal to pass.

As soon as the herrings were within range, the cachalots joined in the assault and commenced a carnage so frightful that the pen refuses to describe it—but the defense, briefly disconcerted by the number and boldness of the assailants, was soon reorganized under the skillful direction of Commodore Farandoul, supported by the heroism of our editor-in-chief.

Nightfall did not bring an end to the combat. Commodore Farandoul ordered that a row of tubs full of lighted oil should be disposed in front of the attack, and the valiant defenders of the shoal were able, by the light of those flames, to halt the destruction initiated by the cachalots.

July 6

THE BATTLE

Two terrible days of combat have not extinguished the ardor of the assailants, nor the courage of the mariners. The battle is still going on. The cachalots have suffered enormous losses, but their tribe receives reinforcements incessantly. Forty meters of herrings have succumbed.

536

July 7

Commodore Farandoul has found a more effective means than hand-to-hand combat to repel the attacks of the cachalots. As in the ancient sieges of the Middle Ages, we are now employing boiling oil. Our editor-in-chief proposed Greek fire, but, in view of the impossibility of assembling the necessary ingredients, was forced to withdraw the suggestion.

In a furnace established on the battlefield, four mariners boil oil extracted from the bodies of cachalots killed in the preceding days. In Commodore Farandoul's breach, Lieutenant Mandibul and Seamen Tournesol and Escoubico receive the pans of boiling oil passed on by a chain formed by the rest of the mariners; they fix them to the ends of long poles fabricated for that purpose. When the cachalots launch themselves forward with mouths agape, with a movement as rapid as lightning, they tip the contents of each pan into the threatening maws. The scalded cachalots release horrible screams and hurl themselves abruptly backwards, unfortunately ceding their places to other attackers no less avid.

September 11

After an interruption of five days, the Red Herring is back. We beg the indulgence of our readers for the irregularity with which their favorite newspaper has appeared for some little while. Grave events taking place five days ago are our excuse. The inhabitants of the herring shoal had other preoccupations than literature; it was necessary to fight, and fight incessantly!

Five days ago the official survey gave a length of 125 meters and a width of 58 meters. Today, when a momentary respite in the attack permitted Lieutenant Mandibul to measure the extent of our losses, he fond that we no longer have any but a much reduced territory to carry us: 62 meters of herrings by 35!

Sine our departure from the Pole, our domain has lost 19/20th of its initial extent; whales, cachalots and porpoises have devoured what the icebergs have spared. The terrain no longer has the solidity it once had. The herrings are no longer as densely crowded as they once were. The cabin, too heavy for them now, would sink were it not for the barrels that sustain it somewhat.

Fortunately, we have now arrived in more temperate regions; it only freezes at night now; during the day it is five or six degrees above zero.

AN ALARM

Yesterday evening, when everyone, exhausted by five days and five nights of battle, was preparing to repair depleted strength with a hearty meal, a sudden alarm upset all the gastronomic hopes founded on the well-known skill of the master cook. A magnificent repast of fried herrings was ready on the stove-buoy, set up in the middle of the cabin, when it was suddenly observed through the opening contrived in the floor that the herring shoal seemed to be prey to disor-

derly movements. The master-cook, frying-pan in hand, leaned over the opening to examine the phenomenon more closely; at the same time, the shoal opened up and an enormous wide-open maw appeared, swallowing the stove, still lit, along with its flue.

The whale—for it was a whale—fixed its round eye momentarily on the inhabitants of the cabin, who could not have been more surprised; then, doubtless discomfited by the heat of the oven, released a formidable bellow and vanished as it had come.

The mariners, recovering from their astonishment, ran forward, harpoons in hand, to recover their stove, but it was too late! It was past midnight by the time a second stove had been installed and everyone could finally proceed with a restorative meal.

That September 11 issue is the last. The *Red Herring* did not appear the next day, nor in the days following, nor ever again. It had come to the end of its life! The unfortunate shoal of herrings had also terminated its career. The fishermen who had been impatiently waiting for it on the coasts of Holland would never see it arrive; it had perished *en route*, in its entirety.

The supreme catastrophe arrived during the night of September 11 and 12, 24 hours after the whale's invasion of our friends' home. We shall take up the pen that slipped from the hand of César Picolot and relate the events of that terrible night succinctly.

Having no instruments at all, Farandoul had been obliged to allow himself to be steered at hazard by the shoal of herrings. It went southwards; that was the main thing. The herrings had progressed without deviating overmuch from their habitual route to the latitude of Novaya Zemlya, but there, doubtless disturbed by their unaccustomed load, they had gone into the Kara Sea instead of proceeding along the north-west coast of Novaya Zemlya to reach North Cape and the coast of Swedish Lapland.

Thick fogs had prevented the mariners from distinguishing the coasts of Novaya Zemlya at the moment when the herrings had gone into the strait of Kara between Novaya Zemlya and Vaigach Island. The herring shoal, returned to the glacial ocean, could have regained its proper route by steering westwards, but, doubtless increasingly distressed by the attacks of cachalots and the actions of its passengers, it had continued to head southwards in the direction of the White Sea, a blind gulf into which no shoal of herrings had ever ventured before.

On the night of September 11 and 12, the mariners were sleeping profoundly in the cabin. The day had been hard; they had been fighting without a minute's respite all day long, but at nightfall it had been necessary to let the cachalots continue their work of destruction. The worried Farandoul held a whispered discussion with Lieutenant Mandibul regarding the impending eventualities.

Suddenly, as he was explaining a new method of consolidating the shoal to Mandibul, a formidable shock was produced fore and aft, and the cabin, violently struck by a hard impact, collapsed on the sleepers.

Everything was overturned—the floor, the roof and the walls—and the mass of debris, lifted up by an enormous wave, was thrown once again upon the obstacle. Five seconds had sufficed; the catastrophe was complete. The cabin, so warm and comfortable a little while before, had literally melted into the sea.

How had it happened? Quite simply because the shoal of herrings, tormented, harassed and finally driven mad, heading directly south without the slightest precaution, had run into a lighthouse erected in the open sea on a mass of rock 20 kilometers from Cape Kanin. Thus, a lighthouse, a savior torch for so many ships, had been the ruin of the unfortunate herring shoal—and that was because the torch was unlit; the lighthouse had gone out.

Our friends had not perished—at least, not yet. Clinging to the debris of the cabin, they were searching in vain for the backs of the faithful herrings beneath their feet. The ladies, awakened with a start, were screaming lamentably.

In the profound obscurity, Farandoul strove to recognize the obstacle that the shoal had struck; gripped by a second wave, he was carried once again to a great height and, in spite of cruel injuries, searched for some uneven surface to which he might cling. To his profound astonishment, his hand encountered an iron ring. Farandoul seized it powerfully and remained suspended there when the wave fell back. He was able to hang on with one hand and unwind a long piece of rope that he had around his waist, in order to throw it to the castaways.

Tournesol had an inspiration. Farandoul's foster-father was swimming nearby, moving from wave to wave to assist castaways in peril, gathering up items of wreckage here and there and bringing them back to the main group. Tournesol made a sign to him, threw a bundle of ropes over his shoulder and pointed in the direction from which Farandoul's voice was calling.

In two bounds the brave monkey was at Farandoul's side, ropes were attached and thrown to the shipwreck-victims, and then the monkey climbed on to our hero's shoulders. Suddenly, he disappeared upwards—but the monkey's joyful cry told Farandoul that he had made a fortunate discovery. At the same moment, a rope brushed his face; he grabbed it and swiftly lifted himself up. About three meters above the ring he felt himself grasped by a solid fist, and disappeared into an opening.

"A window!" he shouted. And while the monkey threw his rope into the abyss to draw up another victim, Farandoul departed on a groping voyage of discovery. The window gave access to a narrow and winding stairway. Our hero understood.

"A lighthouse! We're in a lighthouse!"

Climbing briskly, at the risk of bumping his head on the turnings, he soon arrived on the upper floor of the lighthouse, in a room in which a smoky lamp was burning. Sonorous snores emerging from two camp-beds informed him that the room was inhabited. Without bothering with the sleepers, he took the lamp, picked up a bundle of ropes and lifebelts that were lying in a corner and threw himself toward he ladder leading to the balcony.

A general cry coming from below told him that the lamp had been seen.

"Ahoy, lads! Catch the ropes!"

Farandoul's foster-father had already brought up a number of mariners through the lower window; their boots cold already be heard on the staircase. Tournesol, swimming around the lighthouse, organized the rescue down below; he had attached the ladies to two or three barrels and a few spars of debris that had survived the wreck and was working to hoist the up to the window. Three men on the balcony and three at the inferior window sufficed to maneuver the ropes. Tournesol kept the others at sea to assist the departures. Madame Léa d'Arcis, supported by a lifebelt, was the first to be lifted up, and was hoisted up to the balcony without suffering any damage.

The brave mariners redoubled their efforts. Three ladies found refuge on a cask containing dregs of rum; the German scientists were sitting astride another, bobbing on the waves. The mariners swam out to them and brought them to the lighthouse. The solicitor Codgett, scared half to death on the staves of a third cask, was also solidly attached to a mooring-rope thrown from the balcony.

Tournesol darted one final glance around him. Cachalots in search of the shoal were arriving, propelled by their powerful fins.

"Hoist away!" he shouted.

César Picolot and several ladies were already swaying in the air. The last victims of the wreck were rapidly lifted up. Just in time! The cachalots had perceived these marvelous items of prey and were launching their attack—but they were too late. Tournesol and the mariners were climbing up by the strength of their wrists; the other castaways were already too high. Just one of the scientists was seized by a cachalot nimbler than the rest, but he was able to free himself by wriggling violently and escaped, leaving a boot between the monster's teeth.

After a few minutes as long as centuries, the shipwreck-victims reached the balcony. Everyone was safe. The cachalots having gone all the way round the lighthouse, the castaways were able to defy their voracity.

"Fire, quickly!" cried Farandoul, when all the victims had arrived safe and sound. "Let's signal for help!"

They could only warm themselves in shifts; the room, being very narrow, could not accommodate more than seven or eight people at a time. The rest of the castaways had to stand on the staircase awaiting their turn.

IX.

While the stove was being lit, Farandoul threw himself on to the stairway in order to take a roll-call of the shipwreck-victims. Having arrived at the final turning he suddenly went pale. "Mandibul!" he shouted.

The final landing was empty.

The astounded mariners looked at one another. Mandibul was not in the lighthouse. No one had seen him since the impact. He had disappeared, along with Mrs. Hatteras!

Farandoul had already thrown the lifebelts and casks back into the sea. He shouted, but no cry replied. The Moon, which emerged at that moment from its veil of mist, allowed a considerable range of vision, but the mariners, leaning over the drop, could not see anything in the water but the shadows of cachalots chasing the debris of the shipwreck.

"Nothing!" murmured Farandoul, tearing his hair. "Nothing!"

Tournesol had saved his carbine. Fortunately, it was loaded. Farandoul took it and fired it, in the hope that the detonation would reach Mandibul's ears, if he were still alive.

Two minutes went by after the gunshot. No voice replied—but a flash of light suddenly appeared on the horizon and a distant detonation replied to Farandoul's rifle-shot.

"He's alive!" Farandoul cried. "He's alive!"

A second detonation rang out, then a third and a fourth, at regular intervals. Two or three more rifle-shots resounded, but the sounds were growing more distant and eventually nothing more was heard.

"A shipwreck-victim clinging to a piece of wreckage couldn't contrive that fusillade," Farandoul said. "Mandibul must be on a fragment of our herring shoal. There's still hope!"

Tournesol searched every corner of the lighthouse, guided by the less bewildered of the two Russian keepers. One of the German scientists, who spoke Russian, served as an interpreter. The Russian gave stammering explanations. As it seemed to Farandoul that the explanation was turning into an altercation, he judged it necessary to intervene.

Tournesol lashed out at the keeper with his fists and accused him of being the cause of the poor herring shoal's wreck; indeed, the lighthouse had gone out for lack of oil, the keeper and his comrade having drunk the remainder of the supply! Farandoul knew that this happened quite frequently in lighthouses on the coasts of Russia, so, without wasting time in recriminations, he posed several important questions to the keeper. The answers were far from satisfactory. They were in the open sea, five leagues off Cape Kanin, in the administrative district of Archangel. The keepers were only re-provisioned once a month, and a fortnight wood pass before the arrival of the supply boat. That was serious. The food would run out; although there was enough for two, there was not enough for 30!

The crew, and Tournesol in particular, were crushed. The herring-shoal was open to a good deal of criticism as a vessel, but it had had the immense advantage of furnishing its passengers with healthy and—more importantly—abundant nourishment.

The lack of food was not the only disadvantage of the Russian lighthouse; as a dwelling it presented an inconvenience to which they paid little attention at first, when they emerged from the icy water, but which was no less grave. It lacked space. It was very cramped in the upper room; no less than three quarters of the castaways had to establish themselves on the dark and damp spiral staircase, lodged very uncomfortably.

The solicitor Codgett was in despair, by virtue of the loss of Mrs. Hatteras, who had disappeared with Mandibul in the catastrophe. With her went any hope of being compensated for the numerous annoyances endured by the honorable man of law since he had imprudently taken on the difficult case of Hatteras versus Hatteras. When he learned that he might have to stay in the lighthouse for another fortnight, lying on a staircase and very feebly nourished, his desperation knew no bounds.

Without waiting for orders from their leader, the mariners had already taken measures to add the produce of fishing-lines to the lighthouse's meager resources. Standing on the balcony or leaning out of the windows they had thrown numerous lines into the sea and were awaiting the good will of the fish.

Farandoul, having discovered an old map of the White Sea in the keepers' room, studied the position of the lighthouse. Five leagues of sea, as we have said, separated it from the coast. The nearest town was three or four leagues further to the south; it was called Krasnow and counted no more than 5000 inhabitants. But how could they get a call for help that far? How could they make contact with the land?

When he learned that a civilized town was at such a relatively close distance, the solicitor Codgett's spirits revived and he asked to speak in order to make a proposition.

"There's a means," he said. "A five-league swim isn't drinking the sea. It's necessary that one of us should undertake it for the sake of common salvation. Great dangers give birth to great devotions. I therefore propose..."

"Bravo!" cried Picolot. "It's magnificent that you should do that!"

"Yes, my friends—rather than vegetate for a fortnight in this cruel situation, I much prefer that one of these gentlemen should set out for Krasnow and come back with a boat. I have spoken!"

The mariners shook their heads. To cover five leagues, swimming in an icy sea, did not appear to them to be an easy or agreeable task. On reflection, however, a few strong swimmers were about to volunteer, when Farandoul told them that he and his brave foster-father would undertake the dangerous mission themselves. Experienced in all kinds of bodily exercise, both endowed with a prodigious muscular elasticity, they were better equipped than anyone else to succeed in that difficult navigation. The mariners, long accustomed to seeing Farandoul reserve delicate or dangerous enterprises for himself, bowed to their leader's will.

Codgett rubbed his hands and lavished warm congratulations on himself. "A man of law is perhaps good for something, you see," he said. "It's me who'll save you."

Farandoul and the old monkey had already begun their preparations to depart at first light—which is to say, at about 9 a.m. You will remember that the wreck of the herring shoal had take place in the middle of the night; the installation of the victims had taken several hours, and daylight would not be long delayed.

Having left the North Pole in May, at the end of winter, our friends had arrived on the Russian coast in the middle of September, just as another winter was beginning. While they were sailing through the polar ice-sheet the summer had come and gone. The White Sea, ice-free for a few months, would soon form a thick sheet of ice over its waves. For swimmers like Farandoul and his foster-father the danger was not the distance to be covered but the coldness of the water.

When wan sunlight added a yellow tint to the thick banks of fog on the horizon, however, Farandoul and his foster-father intended to leave. All the provisions they had were a little Russian pancake, a few herrings and a small flask of rum discovered at the bottom of one of the casks saved from the final shipwreck. Each of them fixed a lifebelt around his waist and, after giving a few last instructions to the mariners and exchanging a last few emotional handshakes, they went down to the sea. Scarcely had they lowered themselves on to the crests of the waves than a breaker carried them away in its swirl of foam, to the sound of a last hurrah.

We'll get to the coast at about 1 p.m. and we'll be in Krasnow about 3, at sunset, Farandoul said to himself.

So as not to get behind schedule, the two swimmers cut through the waves rapidly. After two hours of swimming, the mist having dissipated somewhat, Farandoul glimpsed the coast in the distance. He swallowed a shot of rum and lay on his back in order to be towed by the monkey. After a quarter of an hour's rest he turned round, had the monkey ingurgitate some rum, and made him play the plank in his turn.

At 1 p.m., less a few minutes, the two exhausted swimmers finally reached land. Before setting out for Krasnow they were obliged to take a full half-hour's rest. Farandoul lit an immense fire, as much to get warm as to inform the lighthouse that they had arrived in good condition.

"Now, forward!" cried Farandoul, when he was dry and rested.

The monkey got to his feet unhurriedly, put on his fur overcoat, put up his hood and set off at a brisk pace. There was no actual road to take them to Krasnow; it was necessary to follow the coast, taking the best short cuts to avoid the curves of the shoreline.

It was pitch dark when our two friends reached the first houses. Everything was closed; snow filled the streets and there was not a pedestrian in sight. It was necessary to find the authorities, in order to organize a rescue mission as quickly as possible.

Unfortunately, as they tried to find their way around the town, the two travelers became separated and lost sight of one another in the fog. Farandoul had gone into a tavern in the hope of obtaining some information from the drinkers assembled around bottles of vodka, and when he went back into the street he could not see any sign of the old monkey.

There was no response to his call. He was about to launch forth on a search at hazard when he spotted a sentry-box adjoining a gate and a few men from a guard unit. He went into the post immediately and took the chance of speaking in French to the officer.

The officer leapt out of his chair at Farandoul's first words. "Shipwreck-victims! Entirely at your service, Monsieur!"

Farandoul, starting with the most urgent matter, asked him whether anyone had seen a gentleman in a fur overcoat. The sentry, interrogated, had seen no one. The officer gave Farandoul a sergeant and four men to guide him around the town and take him to the local commandant as soon as the lost traveler had been found.

Then commenced an interminable promenade around the streets of Krasnow. Following the sergeant, Farandoul explored all its quarters without being able to rediscover his companion. The poor monkey seemed to have vanished into thin air. No one had seen him; he had disappeared without leaving any trace.

Farandoul made a tour of all the guard-posts. Lieutenant Rastatoff sent him to Police-Captain Papoff, who had him taken to Commandant Tschlstopoff, who sent him to wake up General Borogodoloff, all without result.

The lieutenant was very polite, the captain less so, the commandant not at all, and as for General Borogodoloff, doubtless furious at being woken up, he had Farandoul arrested by his Cossacks, under the pretext that he had no passport. Our hero had swiftly related the story of his shipwreck, but the general was inflexible on the matter of the passport. When Farandoul mentioned his lost companion, the general furrowed his brow suspiciously.

In the meantime, a breathless messenger arrived carrying a folded piece of paper. The general read it, then folded his arms and looked at Farandoul fixedly. "I was sure of it!" he cried. "Your friend has no passport either, and refuses to answer any questions…"

"Has he been found?"

"Yes, he's been found; his number is up! He's been recognized, in spite of his disguise. He's a nihilist leader to whose presence I've been altered by the government!"

"Him, a nihilist! General, just one word, and…"

"I'm going to visit the guard-posts. Nihilists interned here are dangerous. On my return, Monsieur, we'll settle your account." And the general hurried off, leaving Farandoul locked in, after having instructed the four policemen stationed in the antechamber to exercise the utmost vigilance.

Farandoul was about to search for some means of escape when a door hidden by a curtain suddenly opened. A young woman appeared, putting her finger to her lips.

"Silence!" she said, in French. "I'm General Borogodoloff's niece. I heard everything, and I'll save you in spite of my uncle. I'm a nihilist, like you!"

Farandoul, petrified, could not take his eyes of this charming apparition. The general's niece, Olga Borogodoloff, was 20 years old; she was tall, as white as the snow of her native land and as blonde as the harvests on its plains.

Olga had seized the piece of paper brought be the messenger. "Oh, the poor man!" she said. "Your companion, the nihilist leader, is to be sent to Siberia within the hour! How reckless it was to come here without taking more precautions, without a passport…."

"Mademoiselle!" exclaimed Farandoul. "Just one word would suffice…."

"Silence, imprudent fool! All is not lost. Our brothers must have been alerted. We shall free him. Follow me, and don't make a sound!"

An Olga, after having bolted the door of the general's room from the inside, took Farandoul into a little corridor leading to a little courtyard ringed by stables. Olga went into one of these stables, woke up a muzjik buried in the straw and ordered him to harness a sleigh immediately.

Ten minutes later, Farandoul and Olga, wrapped in furs, were flying over the snow across the plain. The muzjik was urging his horses, sometimes with caresses and sometimes with curses, to catch up with the exile's convoy as quickly as possible.

Farandoul was burning with impatience and anxiety. He was desperate to save his foster-father from the frightful danger he was in. After his turbulent existence, the poor old monkey must not end his career in unjust exile in Siberia.

The sleigh flew; several versts were soon devoured. Eventually, they saw the Cossacks halted on the bank of the river Pushkaya, ready to cross the river one by one, at any price.

"Halt!" commanded Olga, leaning out of the sleigh.

Recognizing their general's niece, the Cossacks took Farandoul, wrapped in his furs, for the general himself and opened their ranks. Farandoul was invisible in his cloak, but his eyes were free; with an inexpressible joy he recognized the brave monkey, the foster-father of his infancy, alive but tied to the rump of a horse.

Noiselessly, our hero opened his knife beneath his cloak—and before the Cossacks could stop him, he cut the bonds retaining the monkey with a rapid sweep. The latter uttered a cry of joy and leapt into the sleigh.

Olga's muzjik was intelligent; he slackened the reins and launched his horses on to the ice of the river. The Cossacks, already recovered from their surprise, galloped after them, not daring to shoot for fear of hitting Olga. The fugitives had reached the middle of the river when the ice suddenly cracked beneath the furious gallop of the horses. They stopped instantaneously; a seething gulf opened up in front of them. Behind them, the Cossacks were racing forward, only a few meters separating them from their prey, when the ice cracked again…

X.

Our friends felt the ice oscillate beneath their sleigh, then move off smoothly. The Cossacks' charge had brought about a premature break-up of the river, and the sleigh, borne by an ice-floe, was sailing towards the glacial sea, whose groaning could be heard a few leagues away!

"Lost!" cried Olga, while the Cossacks disappeared in the distance. "We're lost!"

"Not at all," replied Farandoul. "I'm a sailor; leave the direction of the ice-floe to me!"

Far from trying to run aground on the bank of the Pushkaya, Farandoul contrived to remain in mid-stream; in this way they reached the river's mouth at mid-day. Farandoul offered to set the charming Olga ashore, but she refused. Her uncle, the general, would never forgive her for having liberated the nihilist leader, whose capture would have won him promotion. It was better not to return to Krasnow.

Without admitting it to himself, Farandoul felt a strange sentiment of joy in his heart at the thought that he would not be separated from Olga just yet. He offered to take her to the Kanin lighthouse, where numerous friends were waiting for him.

"All nihilists?" asked the beautiful Russian.

Farandoul made a vague and mysterious gesture with his head, not yet daring to confess that the famous nihilist leader for whose deliverance she had risked everything was a simple monkey.

The intention expressed by Farandoul to go back to the Kanin lighthouse on his ice-floe was not at all excessive. Our hero had scanned the coast with his mariner's eye and had seen that the wind and the current were heading in the exact direction of the lighthouse. In ten minutes, the flow was transformed into a passable vessel. The sleigh's tiller became an improvised mast and Farandoul's and the muzjik's cloaks furnished a sail, which the south-east wind soon inflated.

The sea was calm and the fog had almost entirely dissipated. The ice-floe danced on the waves, but the horses experienced a little sea-sickness. Farandoul, who had a plan, was very attentive to them.

After an hour of plain sailing, Olga spotted the lighthouse to the north-west.

"If the breeze keeps up, we'll be there in less than three-quarters of an hour," said our hero.

Farandoul was not mistaken. Two minutes before the end of the third quarter-hour, the skillfully-steered ice-floe arrived within a few cables of the Kanin lighthouse. The mariners had caught sight of it long before and had followed its course with an easily understandable anxiety. Tournesol had prepared pulleys and ropes; when the floe was securely moored, Farandoul had a barrel sent down, in which Olga took her place, and which was lifted up in a matter of seconds.

Then the horses were hoisted up, one by one, and deposited on the balcony of the lighthouse, utterly bewildered by their voyage. Never, since the lighthouse had been built, had horses found themselves in that situation. After the horses, Farandoul had the sleigh lifted, then Olga's coachman; then he scaled the wall with his foster-father, abandoning the ice-floe to the mercy of the waves.

"Well," he said to the mariners who surrounded him, "we're re-provisioned; I've brought you food! These three horses will last a few days while we wait for an opportunity to leave the lighthouse."

Olga manifested some surprise at the sight of these false nihilists. Farandoul was about to tell her everything and had called his foster-father in order to introduce him to the young woman in his true capacity, when a lookout on the balcony cried: "Sail ahoy!"

Farandoul, postponing the explanation until later, ran to the balcony and saw a vessel sailing northwards scarcely half a league away. "Signals, quickly!"

Olga's muzjik swiftly brought a carbine and cartridges. Farandoul fired off all the cartridges one by one, and finally succeeded in attracting the ship's attention. The vessel tacked back and was soon within range of the lighthouse; the captain and crew seemed most intrigued by the sight of so many people in the lighthouse, especially by the presence of three horses on the balcony.

The captain sent a launch, which initially collected half a dozen females; it was necessary to make six trips to move everyone. After two hours of comings and goings, no one remained on the lighthouse any longer but the two Russian keepers and the three horses perched sadly on the balcony.

The ship was a Russian brig out of Archangel. The captain offered to take Farandoul to Krasnow, but agreed, on a promise of rich remuneration, to put himself entirely at Farandoul's disposal. Our friend had not a sou immediately available, Mandibul having all their funds—which is to say, some four millions in bonds—about his person. He merely promised the captain a few of a million if they could find the unfortunate Mandibul—and with that, the captain handed over his loudhailer, the badge of his authority.

In all probability, the fragment of the herring shoal carrying the unfortunate Mandibul, having turned back at the moment of the impact with the lighthouse, would have resumed the herrings' usual route and headed for North Cape in order to go around the Lofoten islands and along the Norwegian coast. In consequence, Farandoul stoked by the brig's furnaces and launched her in that direction at full steam.

Now that they are safe aboard a good ship, let us leave Farandoul and his companions and return to Mandibul, our unfortunate friend in peril.

When he felt the cabin on the herring shoal collapse on top of him, Mandibul hand held on automatically to the first piece of wreckage that came to hand. That was one of the iron buoys. Mandibul, scarcely getting damp, rapidly tucked himself inside it and looked around.

All was confusion: herrings, planks, castaways and items of furniture were whirling on the waves in a lamentable saraband. The first distinct object he perceived was feminine hair floating on a wave; Mandibul had the good fortune to grab hold of it and draw the unconscious Mrs. Hatteras from the bosom of the ocean.

What should he do? There was not enough room for two in the buoy. Supporting the unfortunate female traveler in his extended arms, Mandibul searched for a second piece of wreckage for her. A second buoy presented itself. Mandibul had a world of difficulty in getting Mrs. Hatteras, who was still unconscious, into it. Finally, he succeeded. A wave larger than the rest caught up both buoys, which were attached to one another, and threw them on to something almost solid.

Mandibul thought that they had reached land, but when he looked at it more closely he perceived that the ground was composed of herrings. The herrings, continuing on their way, had already carried him away from the scene of the catastrophe. Mandibul, pricking his ears, could hardly hear a few shouting voices in the distance.

Mandibul shivered. Were his companions safe, like him, or would they perish desperately in the waves?

Mrs. Hatteras came to. Mandibul hurriedly lavished cares upon her. Suddenly, a rifle-shot rang out. Mandibul understood that it was a signal and sought a means to respond to it. Good luck had placed him in the munitions buoy; he had three carbines and plenty of cartridges. He was therefore able, in his turn, to let his friends know that he was safe for the moment.

After a long and terrible night, dawn finally came and Mandibul was able to see his situation clearly.

It was, in truth, not the best imaginable. The two buoys, slightly damaged by the collapse of the cabin, were resting amid the last remnant of the unfortunate herring shoal, on a minuscule shoal of dubious solidity scarcely ten meters long by six wide. Alas, this was all of the great floating island that so many successive disasters had spared.

The downcast Mrs. Hatteras looked sadly at the waves that were coming as far as the buoys to break, imparting a strong pitching motion to the shoal.

In order to reassure her, Mandibul summoned up all his strength of mind and affected the greatest tranquility. "Alone at last!" he said. "Alone with the Ocean! I can, therefore, without fear of the ear of your indiscreet solicitor, paint the sentiments of my soul for you and tell you...."

A violent impact interrupted him.

"A cachalot!" cried Mrs. Hatteras.

Damnation! It was another of the frightful cachalots that had been fattening themselves for months at the herrings' expense. The wretched cetacean was back on the track of the last remnant of the shoal; it was chasing its quarry without any pity for he unfortunate survivors of the carnage.

Two days passed without bringing any change in the situation. The cachalot was still following the shoal, and Mandibul passed the time by stabbing at it occasionally with a harpoon. The shoal gradually diminished, each attack by the cachalot costing a few herrings.

There was a battle in the sea and a battle in the sky: clouds against clouds, east wind against north wind, waves against waves! In that unleashed tumult of the elements, the poor herring shoal found a chance to lose its enemy; the cachalot, doubtless frightened, abandoned its pursuit.

Through two hours of daylight, 14 hours of darkness, and then another ten hours of daylight, the tempest did not relent. By the glare of lightning-flashes, the glow of the aurora borealis and the tremulous gleam of moonlight, the herring shoal still appeared, with only Mandibul's energetic head and the charming but slightly unkempt face of Mrs. Hatteras protruding from its two iron buoys.

Mandibul blessed the tempest, for it had permitted him to hear sweet confessions from his companion's lips. Amid all the thunderbolts, their two hearts had reached an understanding!

The tempest finally came to its conclusion, though, and so did the tranquility of our two friends. The ill-fated shoal of herrings, dicing with disaster until the end, had just run into the middle of an innumerable shoal of cod. Fatality!

The cod, which had not eaten for two days, seemed delighted with the windfall and hurled themselves into an attack in numbers that that bewildered the valiant Mandibul. Our friend struck out at the mass with thrusts of his harpoon, but the shoal was still surrounded and regularly put to the sword.

It was the beginning of the end. They could resist one cachalot, but how could they resist these irresistible enemies?

"We're lost!" cried Mrs. Hatteras.

"Not yet!" replied Mandibul. Seizing his carbine, he attacked the cod with rifle fire.

The herring shoal diminished rapidly. At dusk Mandibul observed a diminution of two meters in its length. The width had diminished proportionately and the buoys were sinking deeper and deeper.

The meal continued all night. At daybreak, scarcely a meter of herrings remained around the buoys. Mandibul resumed his fusillade to make them last as long as possible. Mrs. Hatters fainted and slid into the interior of her buoy.

Suddenly, Mrs. Hatteras's head emerged from the buoy again.

"Didn't you hear it?" she cried.

"What's that?"

"A cannon shot!"

Mandibul started. Indeed, it did seem to him that he had heard something like the last echoes of a cannon shot in the distance. Mandibul's fusillade must have been heard, and that cannon short was doubtless a reply. Mandibul picked up his rifle again and fired into the air.

Then Mandibul released a joyful hurrah. As the buoys were balanced momentarily on the crest of a wave, there was just time to perceive a merchant ship at least half a league away steaming straight toward them at top speed.

A quarter of an hour later the distance had diminished considerably. On the deck and in the rigging of the ship the two castaways could make out a company of mariners waving their caps.

Another ten minutes went by. The ship had dropped a launch into the sea. Suddenly, Mandibul released an exclamation and almost fainted in his buoy.

"Well?" cried Mrs. Hatteras, breathlessly.

"It's Farandoul!" exclaimed Mandibul.

It was, indeed, Farandoul himself who was in change of the launch. The savior ship was the Russian brig encountered by our friend in the waters of the Kanin lighthouse. Farandoul had made no mistake in his calculations; within a few days, in spite of the tempest, he had caught up with his friend, carried off by the last remnant of the herring shoal.

A quarter of an hour later the buoys, towed by the launch, came alongside the ship. Mandibul and Mrs. Hatteras threw themselves into the arms of Farandoul and the entire crew. We can avow that no one pressed the two castaways more ardently to his heart than the worthy solicitor Codgett; along with Mrs. Hatteras, he recovered the hope of some day seeing his invoice paid.

The sailors, charge with hoisting the buoys on board, were greatly astonished. The unfortunate herrings, the last survivors of so many disasters, did not want to abandon the buoys, and had themselves hoisted up with them, thus providing an example of fidelity worthy of figuring in a new edition of *Morality in Action.*

Mrs. Hatteras tore herself away from Codgett's greetings and ran to the buoys. Picking up a herring, she held it out to Mandibul, saying softly: "Promise me that you'll have it stuffed by a natural scientist; I want to keep a souvenir of these recent days of emotion!"

Mandibul still had the company's treasure. He took out a wad of bills to the value of a million and gave it to the Russian captain as a salvage fee. The good captain, delighted with his lucrative campaign, asked which port he should head for.

"Europe!" was everyone's vote—but Farandoul intervened. He had reflected a great deal, and had privately formed a firm resolution to shield his friends from a civilization that was too advanced. Could any veritable tranquility be found in Europe, that land of sterile agitations, that feverish part of the world in which what people called life was nothing but ridiculous torments or artificial pleasures? No, no, no! After such an agitated existence, Farandoul wanted to give his friends a taste of the pure and limpid happiness of a peaceful life in the bosom of solitude.

In spite of the clamors, therefore, he set a course for the Atlantic Ocean instead of setting sail for Europe.

No one except Mandibul knew where they were going. The journey was very long.

One day, the German scientist perceived a region of tropical vegetation of which Farandoul refused to tell them the name. Instead of landing, our hero contented himself with sending Mandibul ashore to re-provision the ship.

Twenty-four hours later, Mandibul having been conscientious, the ship put out to sea again, still heading southwards.

A few weeks later they sighted land again; in heavy seas they doubled a cape in which the scientists believed that they recognized Cape Horn, and they found themselves confronted by limitless ocean again. It was the Pacific!

You have doubtless already guessed that Farandoul's ship was heading for the little island in Pomotou, the corner of the globe where he had spent his happy childhood. There was the safe and tranquil port in which our hero expected, after so many shocks, to spend some peaceful days with his friends.

After Cape Horn, the brave monkey spent his days on the mast, telescope in hand. One day, he manifested signs of anxiety; he was seen repeatedly rubbing the lenses of his spy-glass and scanning the horizon tenaciously. Suddenly, the telescope slipped from his hands; he cried out and slid down to the deck. At the same moment, the lookout signaled land ahead.

It was Pomotou!

The ship dropped anchor a quarter of a league from the land. On the shore a lively animation was visible; large numbers of individuals were coming and going around the huts of a large village.

A cry of "Man overboard!" was heard. That was the foster-father, who, unable to restrain himself, had just jumped into the water and was swimming to the shore.

He was soon seen, and caused a considerable stir among the group of natives. The excitement on the beach was further increased when he arrived; the village seemed to be in revolution!

After a few minutes, a boat cast off and moved in the direction of the ship. When it came alongside, the German scientists fell over backwards with astonishment. It was manned exclusively by monkeys!

Meanwhile, these monkeys had rapidly climbed the sides of the ship and leapt on to the bridge. The German scientists broke their pipes in the excess of their surprise; the monkeys had precipitated themselves into Farandoul's arms. O emotion! The monkeys were our hero's five foster-brothers, found on the shore by their father.

The process of disembarkation began immediately. The sailors bid farewell to the Russian captain. Hatteras's ex-captives did not want to hear any more talk of returning to Europe and proposed to found a colony in Pomotou. When he learned of their decision, César Picolot requested naturalization from Farandoul's foster-brothers, and obtained it on Farandoul's recommendation.

Mrs. Hatteras, putting her hand in Mandibul's, declared that she considered herself to be divorced and expressed her intention of granting the wishes of her companion in misfortune as soon as they could be given legal status by the Pomotouan authorities.

As for the beautiful nihilist Olga Borogodoloff, she leaned on Farandoul's arm with enough abandon for there to be no need to ask her whether she wanted to return to Europe.

No longer daring, after such a long absence, to confront the reproaches of Mrs. Codgett, the solicitor Codgett asked for, and obtained, a hut on the island. Only the German scientists asked to be repatriated, in order to give an account of their polar mission to the Scientific Congress of Berlin.

We shall pass over all the details of the establishment of our friends in the monkeys' village. Farandoul, elected Governor General of the mixed nation, took the reins of government in hand, to the great satisfaction of bimanes and quadrumanes alike. Olga soon became Madame Farandoul and Mrs. Hatteras assumed the sweet title of Madame Mandibul. The singers found good matches among the former crew of *La Belle Léocadie*. Trabadec, Codgett and Picolot took quadrumane spouses, and the rest of the crew, desirous of not remaining bachelors, sent Tournesol to Lima on a mission to bring back a job lot of assorted spouses. The mixed Pomotouan nation was founded.

What more is there to say? Happiness has no story value. The historian, having arrived at the conclusion of his task, can only break his pen, while dreaming enviously of the fate of the happy inhabitants of that Fortunate Isle in Pomotou. [121]

THE END

---

[121] The reference an *île fortuné* [Fortunate Isle] is a deliberate reference to the paradisal Fortunate Islands or Isles of the Blessed of Greek and Celtic mythology.

APPENDIX:
ROBIDA'S CHAPTER SYNOPSES

PART ONE: OCEANIA - THE MONKEY KING

I. How Saturnin Farandoul, aged four months and seven days, embarked upon a career of adventure. His adoptive family take him for an incompetent monkey.

II. In which we are introduced to *La Belle Léocadie*. The Bora-Bora Company for the Skimming of the Sunda Islands. The boar filled with grape-shot.

III. Siege and blockade. The heroic conduct of the tortoises of the Mysterious Island. A terrible stew!

IV. Captain Nemo's divers. Lieutenant Mandibul is swallowed by an oyster. Love in a diving-suit.

V. How poor Mysora ended up in the aquarium of Valentin Croknuff, an aged but very ardent man of science. Saturnin Farandoul declares war on England.

VI. The Conquest of Australia. Telegrams and Correspondence in the Melbourne Herald. The great Melbourne Aquarium will not capitulate!

VII. The assault on the Great Aquarium. The horrible wickedness of the bimane Croknuff! The world devoid of happiness; Mysora is no more.

VIII. The organization of the Farandoulian Empire. Biographies of the principal bimane and quadrumane leaders. In which the great ideas of Saturnin I regarding the regeneration of the world in general, and old Europe in particular, are revealed to the reader.

IX. The Perfidious Schemes of Perfidious Albion. Lady Arabella Cardigan, a bimane spy, seduces quadrumane Colonel Makako. How empires perish!!!

X. How the bimane generals imprisoned by the English regained their liberty. Bora-Bora's treasure. The lamentable fate of *La Belle Léocadie*.

PART TWO: THE TWO AMERICAS - AROUND THE WORLD IN MORE THAN 80 DAYS

I. A Great Rattlesnake Hunt. Farandoul's heart beats again! A fine reception from the Mormons.

II. Farandoul's 17 Wives. The hour of tranquility has not come. Attached to the war-pole!

III. Rising Moon. A warning to the young as to the terrible consequences that can arise from declarations tattooed on a lady's breast. What a bear!

IV. A duel of gigantic locomotives. The Farandoulist Crisis. Horatius Bixby's three hairs.

V. Three hundred and fifty-eight women surrounded on a hill! The strange and terrible adventures as a result of which these Parisian, Spanish, Japanese, Turkish and Chinese ladies came to be lost in the Patagonian pampas!

VI. How the Fogg caravan went from gauchos to Patagonians. All Patagonia under arms! Refuge with the beavers. Foundation of a lakeside city.

VII. Beavertown attacked! The deplorable conduct of 350 ladies. Treason upon treason. Clarification of the mysterious fate of Passepartout. To the last drop of Nicaraguan blood!

VIII. The Railway War. The new siege warfare. Concentrated vervain gas bombs, chloroform shells and smallpox canisters. Pneumatic aspirators. Submarine warfare!

IX. In the air! The appearance of new blue moons at Cayman City. An escape in the clouds; the fugitives' last pigeon. The heroic devotion of Barbara Twinklish.

X. Aerial operations. Flying mines. A great battle at 800 meters. The deplorable end of Sir Phileas Fogg.

PART THREE: ACROSS AFRICA - THE FOUR QUEENS

I. The Saucepan Boat. The Niam-Niams manifest the intention of eating Farandoul boiled. Emotion in the scientific world. A triumphant arrival among the Makalolos.

II. Giraffe-riders and ostrich-borne sharpshooters. The wisdom of 500 queens. Preparations for a solemn feast. How, after becoming weary of the nation, Farandoul abducted the reigning queens and their reserves.

III. All-out Pursuit. Minor adventures hunting and fishing. The sail-equipped hippopotamus. A long discussion with an impaled rhinoceros. A letter from Mandibul.

IV. Continuation of the flight. Kidnapped by gorillas. The powerful effect of morality on simple nature.

V. Continuation of the flight! Adventures of six gods of the Sacred Isles. Their escapes and successive transformations. Six very unhappy gods.

VI. Encounters and complications. An army of locusts. A fatal night in the ruins of Thebes. Farandoul, mummified, travels in the luggage of the Klaknavor clan.

VII. Vengeance! Seven Simon Stylites. Miss Flora MacKlaknavor is compromised! Tranquility is not of this world. Scarcely arrived in Cairo, our friends are carried off by an unknown comet!

VIII. A voyage through interplanetary space, on a very small and scarcely fertile star. How the inhabitants of the minaret saved themselves by fishing for satellites. Hector Servadac!

IX. A terrible landing on the planet Saturn! The strangeness of Saturnian nature. Seven female species. Servadac and his friends, treated as curious animals, are put in cages in the zoological gardens.

X. Another cataclysm! Return to Earth. How the four queens, remaining on Saturn, married powerful monarchs and became the founders of a new race.

istence, found himself launched into the whirlwind of worldly pleasure. Farandoul the savior.

II. Preparations for departure to the North Pole. The balloon with the gondola-sloop. Cast off. A passenger on board! Repeated advertisements of the Governor of the North Pole.

III. The ice-sheet. Combat by boiling water. Bears and scientists. The seals of the ice-sheet speak Latin. The engagement of Farandoul's foster-father to a young Eskimo.

IV. The mystery clarified. Terrible adventures of a professor of philosophy and a singing café troupe traveling from Le Havre to Trouville. Concerts at the North Pole. Mrs. Hatteras.

V. Horrible treason of Governor Hatteras. Abandoned at the Pole. The fire extinguished, the flame frozen. Departure and shipwreck. Run aground on a providential shoal of herrings.

VI. The misfortunes of a shoal of herrings. Provisions for 27,397 years, including leap years. A point of procedure. The unfounded claims of the solicitor Codgett. The brilliant defense of the shoal of herrings.

VII. Codgett swallowed. An evening's dancing. A herring-quake. How the shoal of herrings entered into all-out rebellion and went to scratch itself on the icebergs.

VIII. Some extracts from *The Red Herring*. Disasters and poetry. The lighthouse reef. Impact and disintegration.

IX. Thirty castaways in a lighthouse! Lack of food and comforts. Farandoul's foster father arrested as a nihilist. Olga Borogdoloff's horses.

X. The lighthouse re-provisioned. The last herrings. How, after many trials, our heroes finally found tranquility in the heart of the Pomotou Archipelago. A Fortunate Isle.